turn page for checkout

P9-CLG-719

THE JULIANTHES

(The Weathered Isles)

Pireth
Vanguard

of
Corona

MIRIANIC

OCEAN

Pireth
Dancard

Pireth
Tulme
Tinson

Macomber

The Broken Coast

N

FINNEY CO. PUBLIC LIBRARY

502563

F SALV
Salvatore, R. A., 1959-
Mortalis /

DATE DUE

AUG 7 2000	AUG 2 4 2002
SEP 5 2000	JAN 1 3 2003
OCT 2 7 2000	
1 1 2000	
DEC 1 1 2000	
FEB 2 2 2001	
JUL 3 0 2001	
MAR 2 5 2002	
MAY 2 1 2002	
JUN 2 0 2002	
JUL 3 2002	
SEP 2 1 2002	
JUN 1 9 2002	

DEMCO INC 38-2931

MORTALIS

FINNEY CO. PUBLIC LIBRARY
605 EAST WALNUT
GARDEN CITY, KS 67846

Also by R. A. Salvatore

THE ICEWIND DALE TRILOGY
The Crystal Shard
Streams of Silver
The Halfling's Gem

THE DARK ELF TRILOGY
Homeland
Exile
Sojourn

THE DARK ELF BOOKS
The Legacy
Starless Night
Siege of Darkness
Passage to Dawn
The Silent Blade
The Spine of the World

THE CLERIC QUINTET
Canticle
In Sylvan Shadows
Night Masks
The Fallen Fortress
The Chaos Curse

THE SPEARWIELDER'S TALES
The Woods Out Back
The Dragon's Dagger
Dragonslayer's Return

THE CRIMSON SHADOW
The Sword of Bedwyr
Luthien's Gamble
The Dragon King

*Tarzan: The Epic Adventures**

*The Demon Awakens**
*The Demon Spirit**
*The Demon Apostle**

*Echos of the Fourth Magic**
*The Witch's Daughter**
*Bastion of Darkness**

Published by Ballantine Books

MORTALIS

THE BALLANTINE PUBLISHING GROUP • NEW YORK

A Del Rey® Book
Published by The Ballantine Publishing Group

Copyright © 2000 by R. A. Salvatore

All rights reserved under International and Pan-American Copyright Conventions.
Published in the United States by The Ballantine Publishing Group, a division of
Random House, Inc., New York, and simultaneously in Canada by Random House of
Canada Limited, Toronto.

Del Rey is a registered trademark and the Del Rey colophon is a trademark of Random
House, Inc.

www.randomhouse.com/delrey/

A record of the Library of Congress Cataloging in Publication Data is available upon
request from the publisher.

ISBN 0-345-43039-5

Endpaper maps by Laura Maestro

Manufactured in the United States of America

First Edition: July 2000

10 9 8 7 6 5 4 3 2 1

This is Gary's book.
There is no other.

CONTENTS

PROLOGUE

Jilseponie—Pony—sat on the crenellated roof of the one squat tower of St. Precious Abbey in the great city of Palmaris, looking out over the snow-covered rooftops, her gaze drifting inevitably to the dark flowing waters of the Masur Delaval. A bitterly cold wind nipped at her, but Pony, deep in memories, hardly noticed the sting. All the region, the northwestern expanses of the kingdom of Honce-the-Bear, had experienced an early snow only a week before, winter coming on in full force, though the year had not seen the end of the tenth month.

By all estimations, the war against the demon Bestesbulzibar and its goblin, giant, and powrie minions had gone unexpectedly well, had been completed with minimal loss of human life and without a single major city burned to the ground. Now with winter, though, the aftereffects of that war were beginning to show, most notably the food shortages in villages whose supplies had been diverted to towns that had harbored the King's soldiers. Rumors had come to Palmaris of uprisings in some of those villages against King Danube and against the Abellican Church, whose leader had surely acted in the interests of the demon. Other rumors spoke of several mysterious deaths along the coast of the Mantis Arm and of a group of fanatics threatening to break away from the Abellican Church while rejecting outright the notion of any church dedicated to Avelyn Desbris.

So the war had ended here in Palmaris, but it seemed to the grieving Pony as if the turmoil had only begun.

Or was it merely a continuing thing? she wondered. Was such travesty and turmoil, such unrest, merely a reflection of the human condition, an unending procession of one battle after another, of one cause of bitterness replacing another? The notion stung Pony deeply, for if that were the case, then what had they really accomplished? What had been bought by their sacrifice?

Why had Elbryan, her beloved husband, died?

Pony gave a helpless sigh at the futility of it all. She thought back to her early days, up in the wild Timberlands, in Dundalis, when she and Elbryan had grown up together, carefree. She remembered running down the wooded trails beside the boy, running particularly among the white caribou moss in the pine-filled valley north of their village. She remembered climbing the northern slope beside him one chilly night, looking up at the sky to see Corona's Halo, the beautiful multicolored ring that encircled the world, the source, she had later come to learn, of the blessed magical gemstones that served as the power and focus of faith of the Abellican Church.

The next dawn, Pony and Elbryan had witnessed the return of their fathers and the other hunters. How clearly Pony now remembered that, running, full of excitement, full of anticipation, full of—

Horror. For suspended from a shoulder pole had hung a most curious and ugly little creature: a goblin. Never could Pony or Elbryan have foreseen that slain little brute as a harbinger of such doom. But soon after, the goblins had attacked in force, burning Dundalis to the ground, slaughtering everyone except Pony and Elbryan, the two of them somehow managing separately to elude the monsters, each not knowing that the other had survived.

And afterward Pony had wound up here, in Palmaris, bereft of memory and identity, adopted by Graevis and Pettibwa Chilichunk, patrons of the bustling tavern Fellowship Way.

Pony looked out across the quiet city now, in the direction where that establishment had stood. What wild turns fate had placed in her path: married to the favored nephew of the city's Baron Bildeborough; the wedding annulled forthwith and Pony indentured in the King's army; her ascension to the elite Coastpoint Guard and her appointment to Pireth Tulme; the coming of the powries and the fall of that fortress. It had all taken years, but to Pony now it seemed as if it had happened overnight. She could again feel the chill deep in her bones as she had escaped doomed Pireth Tulme, floating in the cold waters of the Gulf of Corona. Perhaps it was fate, perhaps mere chance, that had pulled her from those waters in the vicinity of Avelyn Desbris, the "mad friar" from St.-Mere-Abelle who was being hunted by the Church for the death of a master and the theft of many of the sacred magical gemstones. Avelyn had taken Pony back to Dundalis, and there she had been reunited with Elbryan, who had returned to the region after being trained as a ranger by the mysterious Touel'alfar.

What a dark road the three had walked from there: to Aida and the demon dactyl; back across the kingdom to St.-Mere-Abelle, where Pony's adoptive parents had been imprisoned and had died; and then back again—a road that should have lightened, despite the grief, but that had only darkened more as the evil that was Bestesbulzibar, the dactyl demon, infected Father Abbot Markwart with a singular desire to do battle with Elbryan and Pony.

And so he had, in that same mansion where Pony had spent her wedding night with Connor Bildeborough, the mansion of horrors where Elbryan and Pony had waged the final fight against Markwart, and had won, though at the price of Elbryan's life.

Now Pony wasn't sure what they had won and what it had been worth. She recognized the almost circular nature of her long journey; but instead of drawing comfort from that, she felt restless and trapped.

"It is far too cold for you to be up here, I fear," came a gentle voice behind her, the voice of Brother Braumin Herde, the leader of the band of monks who had followed Master Jojonah away from the Church, believing as they did in Avelyn's goodness, one of the monks who had come to join Elbryan and Pony in their efforts against Markwart.

She turned to regard the handsome man. He was older than Pony by several years—in his early thirties—with black, woolly hair just starting to gray and a dark complexion made even more so by the fact that no matter how often he shaved his face, it was always shadowed by black hair.

"It is too unimportant for me to care," she answered quietly. Pony looked back over the city as he walked up to lean on the wall beside her.

"Thinking of Elbryan?" he asked.

Pony smiled briefly, believing the answer to be obvious.

"Many are saddened," Brother Braumin began—the same hollow words Pony had been hearing from so many for the last three months. She appreciated their efforts—of course she did!—but, in truth, she wished they would all leave her to her thoughts in private.

"The passage of time will heal . . ." Brother Braumin started to say, but when Pony fixed him with a skeptical glance, he let his words die away.

"Your pain is to be expected," he tried again a moment later. "You must take solace and faith in God and in the good that came of your actions."

Now Pony glared sternly at him, and the gentle monk retreated a step.

"Good?" she asked.

Braumin held up his hands as if he did not understand.

"They are fighting again, aren't they?" Pony asked, looking back over the snowy city. "Or should I say that they are fighting *still*?"

"They?"

"The leaders of your Church," Pony clarified, "and King Danube and his advisers. Fighting again, fighting always. It changes not at all."

"If the Church is in turmoil, that is understandable, you must admit," Braumin returned firmly. "We have lost our Father Abbot."

"You lost him long before I killed him," Pony interjected.

"True enough," the monk admitted. "But still it came as a shock to so many who supported Dalebert Markwart to learn the truth: to learn that Bestesbulzibar—curse his name, the ultimate darkness—had so infiltrated our ranks as to pervert the Father Abbot himself."

"And now he is gone and you are better off," Pony remarked.

Brother Braumin didn't immediately respond, and Pony understood that she wasn't being fair to him. He was a friend, after all, who had done nothing but try to help her and Elbryan, and her sarcasm was certainly wounding him. She looked at him directly and started to say something but bit it back immediately. So be it, she decided, for she could not find generosity in her heart. Not yet.

"We are better off by far," Braumin decided, turning the sarcasm back. "And better off we would be by far if Jilseponie would reconsider the offer."

Pony was shaking her head before he completed the all-too-predictable request. Reconsider the offer. Always that. They wanted her to become the mother abbess of the Abellican Church, though nothing of the sort had ever been heard of in the long history of the patriarchal Order. Brother Francis, Markwart's staunchest follower, had suggested it, even while holding the dying Markwart in his arms, the demon burned from the Father Abbot's body by the faith and strength of Pony and Elbryan. Francis had seen the truth during that terrible battle, and the truth of his terrible master. Pony had killed the demon that Markwart had become, and now several very influential monks were hinting that they wanted Pony to replace him.

Some of them were, at least. Pony didn't delude herself into thinking that such a break with tradition as appointing a woman to head the Church—and a woman who had just killed the previous leader!—would be without its vehement opponents. The battles would be endless, and, to Pony's way of thinking, perfectly pointless.

If that wasn't complicated enough, another offer had come to her, one from King Danube himself, offering to name her Baroness of Palmaris, though she obviously had no qualifications for the position either, other than her newfound heroic reputation. Pony wasn't blind to the reality of it: in the aftermath of the war both Church and Crown were jockeying for power. Whichever side could claim Jilseponie, companion of Elbryan the Nightbird, as friend, could claim to have promoted her to a position of power, would gain much in the battle for the hearts and loyalty of the common folk of Palmaris and the surrounding region.

Pony began to laugh quietly as she looked away from Brother Braumin, out over the snow-blanketed city. She loved the snow, especially when it fell deep from blustery skies, draping walls of white over the sides of buildings. Far from a hardship such weather seemed to Pony. Rather, she considered it a reprieve, an excuse to sit quietly by a blazing fire, accountable to no one and without responsibility. Also, because of the unexpectedly early storm, King Danube had been forced to delay his return to Ursal. If the weather did not cooperate, the king might have to wait out the winter in Palmaris, which took some of the pressure off Pony to either accept or reject his offer of the barony.

Though the weather had cooperated, Pony felt little reprieve. Once she had called this city home. But now, with so much pain associated with the place—the ruins of Fellowship Way, the loss of her adoptive family and her beloved Elbryan—no longer could she see any goodness here or recall any warm memories.

"If he retains the barony, Duke Kalas will battle St. Precious in every policy," Brother Braumin remarked, drawing Pony from her thoughts. But only temporarily, for the mere mention of the forceful Duke, the temporary Baron of Palmaris, inevitably led her to consider the man's residence, the very house in which her marriage to Connor Bildeborough had swiftly descended into chaos, the house wherein Markwart had taken Elbryan from her forever.

"How will we win those battles without heroic Jilseponie leading us?" Braumin dared ask. He draped his arm about Pony's shoulders, and that brought, at last, a genuine smile to the woman's beautiful face. "Or perhaps Jilseponie could take the King's offer instead. . . ."

"Am I to be a figurehead, then?" she asked. "For you or for the Crown? A symbol that will allow Braumin and his friends to attain that which they desire?"

"Never that!" the monk replied, feigning horror; for it was obvious that he understood Pony was teasing him.

"I told Bradwarden and Roger Lockless that I would join them up in Dundalis," Pony remarked; and, indeed, as she said it, she was thinking that traveling back to her first home might not be such a bad thing. Elbryan was buried up there, where it was . . . cleaner. Yes, that was a good word to describe it, Pony decided. Cleaner. More removed from the dirt of humankind's endless bickering. Of course, she, too, was trapped here, and likely for the entire winter, for the road north was not an easy one this season.

She glanced over to see a disappointed Brother Braumin. She honestly liked the man and his eager cohorts, idealists all, who believed they would repair the Abellican Church, put it back on a righteous course by following the teachings of Avelyn. That last thought made Pony smile again: laughing inside but holding her mirth there because she did not want to seem to mock this man. Braumin and his friends hadn't even known Avelyn—not the real Avelyn, not the man known as the mad friar. Braumin had joined the Abellican Order the year before Avelyn, God's Year 815. Both Master Francis and Brother Marlboro Viscenti, Braumin's closest friend, had come in with Avelyn's class in the fall of God's Year 816. But Avelyn and three others had been separated from the rest of their class as they had begun their all-important preparations for the journey to the Isle of Pimaninicuit. The only recollection Braumin, Viscenti, or Francis even had of Avelyn was on the day when the four chosen monks had sailed out of All Saints Bay, bound for the island where they would collect the sacred gemstones. Braumin had never seen Avelyn after he had run off from St.-Mere-Abelle, after he had become the mad friar, with his barroom brawling and his too-frequent drinking—and wouldn't the canonization process of rowdy Avelyn Desbris be colorful indeed!

"Too cold up here," Brother Braumin said again, tightening his grip on Pony's shoulders, pulling her closer that she might share his warmth. "Pray come inside and sit by a fire. There is too much sickness spreading in the aftermath of war, and darker would the world be if Jilseponie took ill."

Pony didn't resist as he led her toward the tower door. Yes, she did like Brother Braumin and his cohorts, the group of monks who had risked everything to try to find the truth of the world after the turmoil stirred up by the defection of Avelyn Desbris and his theft of so many magical gem-stones. It went deeper than liking, she recognized, watching the true con-cern on his gentle and youthful face, feeling the strong and eager spring in his energetic step. She envied him, because he was full of youth, much more so than she, though he was the older.

But Brother Braumin, Pony realized within her darkened perception, was possessed of something she could no longer claim.

Hope.

"Brennilee! Ye've not fed the chickens, ye silly lass!" Merry Cowsenfed called out the front door of her small house. "Oh, Brennilee, where've ye got yerself to, girl?" She shook her head and grumbled. Truly Brennilee, her youngest child, was the most troublesome seven-year-old Merry had ever heard of, always running across the rocky cliffs and the dunes below, sometimes daring the brutal tidewaters of Falidean Bay—which could bring twenty feet of water rushing across the muddy ground in a matter of a few running strides—in her endless quest for adventure and enjoyment.

And always, always, did Brennilee forget her chores before she went on her wild runs. Every morning, Merry Cowsenfed heard those chickens com-plaining, and every morning, the woman had to go to her door and call out.

"I'm here, Mum," came a quiet voice behind her, a voice Merry hardly recognized as that of her spirited daughter.

"Ye missed yer breakfast," Merry replied, turning, "and so've the chickens."

"I'll feed 'em," Brennilee said quietly, too quietly. Merry Cowsenfed quickly closed the distance to her unexpectedly fragile-looking daughter and brought her palm up against Brennilee's forehead, feeling for fever.

"Are ye all right, girl?" she asked, and then her eyes widened, for Bren-nilee was warm to the touch.

"I'm not feelin' good, Mum," the girl admitted.

"Come on, then. I'll get ye to bed and get ye some soup to warm ye," the woman said, taking Brennilee by the wrist.

"But the chickens . . ."

"The chickens'll get theirs after ye're warm in yer bed," Merry

Cowsenfed started to say, turning back with a wide, warm smile for her daughter.

Her smile evaporated when she saw on the little girl's arm a rosy spot encircled by a white ring.

Merry Cowsenfed composed herself quickly for her daughter's sake, and brought the arm up for closer inspection. "Did ye hurt yerself, then?" she asked the girl, and there was no mistaking the hopeful tone of her question.

"No," Brennilee replied, and she moved her face closer, too, to see what was so interesting to her mother.

Merry studied the rosy spot for just a moment. "Ye go to bed now," she instructed. "Ye pull only the one sheet over ye, so that ye're not overheatin' with the little fever ye got."

"Am I going to get sicker?" Brennilee asked innocently.

Merry painted a smile on her face. "No, ye'll be fine, me girl," she lied, and she knew indeed how great a lie it was! "Now get ye to bed and I'll be bringing ye yer soup."

Brennilee smiled. As soon as she was out of the room, Merry Cowsenfed collapsed into a great sobbing ball of fear.

She'd have to get the Falidean town healer to come quickly and see the girl. She reminded herself repeatedly that she'd need a wiser person than she to confirm her suspicion, that it might be something altogether different: a spider bite or a bruise from one of the sharp rocks that Brennilee was forever scrambling across. It was too soon for such terror, Merry Cowsenfed told herself repeatedly.

Ring around the rosy.

It was an old song in Falidean town, as in most of the towns of Honce-the-Bear.

It was a song about the plague.

PART ONE

▼

TRANSITION

Was the victory worth the cost?

It pains me even to speak those words aloud, and, in truth, the question seems to reflect a selfishness, an attitude disrespectful to the memory of all those who gave their lives battling the darkness that had come to Corona. If I wish Elbryan back alive—and Avelyn and so many others—am I diminishing their sacrifice? I was there with Elbryan, joined in spirit, bonded to stand united against the demon dactyl that had come to reside in the corporeal form of Father Abbot Markwart. I watched and felt Elbryan's spirit diminish and dissipate into nothingness even as I witnessed the breaking of the blackness, the destruction of Bestesbulzibar.

And I felt, too, Elbryan's willingness to make the sacrifice, his desire to see the battle through to the only acceptable conclusion, even though that victory, he knew, would take his life. He was a ranger, trained by the Touel'alfar, a servant and protector of mankind, and those tenets demanded of him responsibility and the greatest altruism.

And so he died contented, in the knowledge that he had lifted the blackness from the Church and the land.

All our lives together, since I had returned to Dundalis and found Elbryan, had been one of willing sacrifice, of risk taking. How many battles did we fight, even though we might have avoided them? We walked to the heart of the dactyl, to Mount Aida in the Barbacan, though we truly believed that to be a hopeless road, though we fully expected that all of us would die, and likely in vain, in our attempt to battle an evil that seemed so very far beyond us. And yet we went. Willingly. With hope, and with the understanding that we had to do this thing, whatever the cost, for the betterment of the world.

It came full circle that day in Chasewind Manor, when finally, finally, we caught, not the physical manifestation of Bestesbulzibar, but rather the demon's spirit, the very essence of evil. We won the day, shattering that evil.

But was the victory worth the cost?

I look back on the last few years of my life, and I cannot discount that question. I remember all the good people, all the great people, who passed from this world in the course of the journey that led me to this point, and, at times, it seems to me to be a great and worthless waste.

I know that I dishonor Elbryan and likely anger his ghost with these emotions, but they are very real.

We battled, we fought, we gave of ourselves all that we could and more. Most of all, though, it seems to me as if we've spent the bulk of time burying our dead. Even that cost, I had hoped, would prove worthwhile in those few shining moments after I awakened from my battle with the demon spirit, in the proclamations of Brother Francis, of Brother Braumin, and of the King himself that Elbryan had not died in vain, that the world, because of our actions, would be a better place. I dared to hope that my love's sacrifice, that our sacrifice, would be enough, would turn the tide of humankind and better the world for all.

Is Honce-the-Bear better off for the fall of Markwart?

With sudden response, the answer seems obvious; in that shining moment of clarity and hope, the answer seemed obvious.

That moment, I fear, has passed. In the fog of confusion, in the shifting and shoving for personal gain, in the politics of court and Church, that moment of glory, of sadness, and of hope has diminished into bickering.

Like Elbryan's spirit, it becomes something less than substantial and drifts away on unseen winds.

And I am left alone in Palmaris, watching the world descend into chaos. Demon inspired? Perhaps, or perhaps—and this is my greatest fear—this confusion is merely the nature of humankind, as eternal as the human spirit, an unending cycle of pain and sacrifice, a series of brilliant, twinkling hopes that fade as surely as do the stars at dawn. Did I, and Elbryan, bring the world through its darkness, or did we merely guide it safely through one long night, with another sure to follow?

That is my fear and my belief. When I sit and remember all those who gave their lives so that we could walk this road to its end, I fear that we have merely returned to the beginning of that same path.

In light of that understanding, I say with conviction that the victory was not worth the cost.

—JILSEPONIE WYNDON

CHAPTER

❖ 1 ❖

The Show of Strength

The mud sucked at his boots as he walked along the narrow, smoky corridor, a procession of armored soldiers in step behind him. The conditions were not to his liking—he didn't want his "prisoners" growing obstinate, after all.

Around a bend in the tunnel the light increased and the air cleared, and before Duke Targon Bree Kalas loomed a wider and higher chamber, its one entrance securely barred. Kalas motioned to a soldier behind him, and the man hustled forward, fumbling with keys and hastily unlocking the cell door. Other soldiers tried to slip by, to enter the cell protectively before their leader, but Kalas slapped them back and strode in.

A score of dwarvish faces turned his way, the normally ruddy-complexioned powries seeming a bit paler after months imprisoned underground.

Kalas studied those faces carefully, noting the narrowing of eyes, a reflection, he knew, of seething hatred. It wasn't that the powries hated him particularly, but rather that they merely hated any human.

Again, almost as one, the dwarves turned away from him, back to their conversations and myriad games they had invented to pass the tedious hours.

One of the soldiers began calling them to attention, but Duke Kalas cut him short and waved him and the others back. Then he stood by the door, calmly, patiently letting them come to him.

"Yach, it's to wait all the damned day if we isn't to spake with it," one powrie said at last. The creature removed its red beret—a cap shining bright with the blood of its victims—and scratched its itchy, lice-filled hair, then replaced the cap and hopped up, striding to stand before the Duke.

"Ye comin' down to see our partyin'?" the dwarf asked.

Kalas didn't blink, staring at the powrie sternly. This dwarf, the leader, was always the sarcastic one, and he always seemed to need a reminder that he had been captured while waging war on the kingdom, that he and his wretched little fellows were alive only by the grace of Duke Kalas.

13

"Well?" the dwarf, Dalump Keedump by name, went on obstinately.

"I told you that I would require your services at the turn of the season," Duke Kalas stated quietly.

"And we're to be knowin' that the season's turned?" Keedump asked sarcastically. He turned to his fellows. "Are ye thinkin' the sun to be ridin' lower in the sky these days?" he asked with a wicked little laugh.

"Would you like to see the sun again?" Duke Kalas asked him in all seriousness.

Dalump Keedump eyed him long and hard. "Ye think ye're to break us, then?" the dwarf asked. "We spent more time in a barrelboat, tighter and dirtier than this, ye fool."

Kalas let a long moment slip past, staring at the dwarf, not daring to blink. Then he nodded slightly and turned, leaving the cell, pulling its door closed behind him as he returned to the muddy corridor with his soldiers. "Very well, then," he said. "Perhaps I will return in a few days—the first face you will see, I assure you. Perhaps after you have murdered some of your companions for food, you will better hear my propositions." And he walked away, as did his men, having every intention of carrying through with his threat.

He had gone several steps before Dalump called out to him. "Ye came all the way down here. Ye might as well be tellin' us what ye gots in mind."

Kalas smiled and moved back to the cell door. Now the other dwarves, suddenly interested in the conversation, crowded behind Dalump.

"Extra rations and more comfortable bedding," the Duke teased.

"Yach, but ye said we'd be walkin' free!" Dalump Keedump protested. "Or sailin' free, on a boat back to our homes."

"In time, my little friend, in time," Kalas replied. "I am in need of an enemy, that I might show the rabble the strength of the Allhearts and thus bring them the security they desperately need. Assist me in this, and the arrangements will be made for your release soon enough."

Another of the dwarves, his face a mask of frustration, rushed forward, shouldering past Dalump. "And if we doesn't?" he asked angrily.

Duke Kalas' fine sword was out in the blink of a powrie eye, its point snapping against the obstinate fellow's throat, pressing firmly. "If you do not, then so be it," Kalas said calmly, turning to eye Dalump directly as he spoke. "From our first meeting, I have been clear in my intentions and honest in our dealings. Choose your course, Dalump Keedump, and accept the consequences."

The powrie leader glared at his upstart second.

"Fairly caught," Duke Kalas reminded, rather poignantly, considering that his sword was still out and the statement was true enough. Dalump and his group had been fairly caught on the field of battle, as they had attacked this city. Duke Kalas was bound by no codes or rules in dealing with the powries. He could execute them openly and horribly in Palmaris' largest square, or he could let them starve to death down here in the dungeons beneath Chasewind Manor, forgotten by all.

Dalump shifted his gaze back and forth between Kalas and the upstart powrie, his expression hinting that he wanted to choke them both—wanted to choke anybody or anything—just to relieve the mounting frustration accompanying this wretched situation. "Tell me yer stinkin' plan," he reluctantly agreed.

Duke Kalas nodded and smiled again.

Duke Kalas walked onto the rear balcony of Chasewind Manor early in the morning a few days later. The air was heavy with fog and drizzle, a perfectly miserable day, but one to Kalas' liking. It had turned warmer again, though they still had more than a month before the winter solstice. The remnants of the previous blizzard, winter's first blast, were fast melting, and the reports Kalas had received the day before indicated that grass was showing again on the windblown western fields.

That fact, plus the gathering storm clouds in the west threatening a second storm, had prompted the Duke's action, and now, with the poor visibility, he could not have asked for a better morning. He heard the door open behind him, and he turned to see King Danube Brock Ursal step out to join him.

He was a few years older than his dear friend Kalas, and rounder in the middle, but his hair remained thick and black, and his beard, a new addition, showed no signs of graying.

"I hope to sail within the week," Danube remarked. Kalas was not surprised, since Bretherford, Duke of the Mirianic and commander of the King's navy, had indicated as much to him the previous evening.

"You will have favorable weather all the way back to Ursal," Duke Kalas assured his beloved king, though he feared the decision to travel. If winter weather came on again with the fleet still in the northern waters of the Masur Delaval, the result could be catastrophic.

"So Bretherford believes," said Danube. "In truth, I am more concerned about the situation I leave behind."

Kalas looked at him, his expression wounded.

"Brother Braumin seems formidable and, to the common man, likable," Danube elaborated. "And if the woman Jilseponie stands by him—along with Markwart's former lackey Francis—then their appeal to the folk of Palmaris will be considerable. I remind you that Brother Francis endeared himself to the people in the last days of Markwart, when he served the city as bishop."

Kalas could find little to dispute, for he and Danube had discussed the situation at length many times since the fall of Markwart and the hero, Elbryan, in this very house.

"Jilseponie has formally refused your offer, then?" Kalas asked.

"I will speak with her one last time," King Danube replied, "but I doubt that she will comply. Old Je'howith has spent much time in St. Precious, and has indicated to me that the woman is truly broken and without ambition."

The mere mention of Je'howith, the abbot of Ursal's St. Honce and a close adviser to Danube, made Kalas narrow his eyes suspiciously. It was no secret among the court that Je'howith hated Jilseponie above all others. He had been Markwart's man, and she and her dead lover had killed Markwart, had turned his secure little church world upside down. Je'howith had pushed King Danube to raise the woman to the position of baroness. With Pony in secular circles, answerable to the King, her influence on the Church would come from *outside*, far less dangerous, to Je'howith's thinking, than from *inside*.

"Abbot Je'howith favors the appointment of Jilseponie as baroness," Danube pointedly reminded Kalas.

"Abbot Je'howith would more favor her execution," Kalas replied.

Danube gave a laugh at the irony. At one point, both Pony and Elbryan, imprisoned in St. Precious, had been slated for execution by Father Abbot Markwart.

Their conversation was interrupted by a tumult in the grand house behind them.

"Reports of a powrie force outside the western wall," Duke Kalas explained with a wry grin.

"You play a dangerous game," the King returned, then he nodded, for he did not disagree with the necessity of the ruse. "I will not go to the wall," he decided, though he and Kalas had previously spoken of his attendance. "Thus will suspicions of any conspiracy be lessened."

Duke Kalas paused, staring thoughtfully for a moment, then nodded in agreement.

The King's other close adviser—but one who was unaware of Kalas' strategem, a lady of the court named Constance Pemblebury—came through the balcony doors, her face flushed. "Bloody cap powries," she said breathlessly. "There are reports that they are attacking the western gate!"

Kalas put on an alarmed expression. "I'll rouse the Allhearts," he said, and he rushed from the balcony.

Constance moved beside the King, who draped an arm casually about her and kissed her cheek. "Fear not, dear Constance," he said. "Duke Kalas and his charges will more than meet the attack."

Constance nodded and seemed to calm a bit. She knew the proud Allheart Brigade well, had seen their splendor on the field many times. Besides, how could she be afraid, up here on the balcony of the magnificent Chasewind Manor, in the arms of the man she adored?

*   *   *

She woke to the sounds of shouting, lifted her head from her pillow just as a brown-robed monk ran by her small room, crying, "Powries! Powries at the western gate!"

Pony's eyes popped open and she scrambled out of her bed. Not much could rouse her from her grieving lethargy, but the cry "Powries," those wretched and tough murderous dwarves, made her blood boil with rage. She was dressed and out the door in moments, rushing along the dim corridors of St. Precious, finally finding brothers Braumin Herde, Francis, Anders Castinagis, and Marlboro Viscenti gathered together in the nave of the abbey's large chapel—the same chapel wherein Pony had married Connor Bildeborough all those years ago.

"Are they in the city?" she asked.

"We know not," said Francis, seeming calm indeed.

Pony spent a long moment studying him. Once she had considered Francis a hated enemy, had watched Elbryan beat him senseless in the bowels of St.-Mere-Abelle, but what a change had come over the man since the revelations and subsequent fall of Father Abbot Markwart! Pony still held no love for him, but she had come to trust him somewhat.

"They are out beyond the west wall, so say the reports," Brother Braumin put in. "Whether they have breached the city—"

"Or even whether or not those reports are accurate," Brother Viscenti, a nervous little man with fast-thinning light brown hair and far too many twitches, quickly added. When Braumin looked at him hard, he continued. "The people remain nervous. Are such frantic reports to be believed out of hand?"

"True enough," said Braumin. "But, still, we must assume that the report is accurate."

Another group of monks hustled in then, the lead brother waving a bag in front of him.

Pony understood without even asking. They had brought gemstones— mostly hematite, likely, that any wounds might be magically tended.

"Out to the wall we go," Brother Braumin said to her as the others started away. "Will you join us?"

Pony thought on it for just a moment. She wanted nothing to do with any battles, in truth, but neither could she ignore the responsibility laid before her. If there were powries outside Palmaris' western gate, then likely there would be fighting, and any fighting against powries would mean wounded men. No one in all Corona could wield the gemstones as powerfully as Pony. Was there a wound she could not heal?

One, at least, she reminded herself, the one in her own heart.

She followed Brother Braumin out to the city's western wall.

*   *   *

From an alley, Duke Kalas watched the bustle upon the western wall. "There!" one man cried, and the city guardsmen nearly fell over themselves trying to bring their bows to bear, letting fly a volley of arrows into the mist that likely hit nothing but grass.

They were frightened, Kalas recognized, scared nearly witless. The folk of Palmaris had been involved in more fighting than those of any other major city in Honce-the-Bear during the war, and their city guard had done themselves proud. But they had had their fill of it, Kalas knew, and no one who had ever battled powries wanted another fight with the rugged dwarves.

Unless, of course, they had made a previous agreement with the dwarves concerning how that battle would go.

More cries arose and more arrows flew out from the wall. Then a large group near the center of the crowd cried out and scrambled away, many leaping the ten feet from the parapet back to the ground.

A moment later came a thunderous report as something heavy slammed into the wall.

Kalas smiled; his gunners had spent the better part of the previous day lining up that catapult shot perfectly so that it would hit the wall but do no real damage.

In response, another volley of arrows went out from the wall into the mist, and then a series of howls, shouts, and the gravelly voices of the rugged powries came back at them.

Duke Kalas slipped back into the shadows as another group—Abellican monks and the woman Jilseponie—rushed to join those soldiers and commoners at the wall. The Duke observed their arrival with mixed feelings. He was glad that the monks had come, and especially thrilled that beautiful Jilseponie would witness this moment of his glory. But he was also trepidatious. Might Jilseponie take up a gemstone and lay low the powries?

With that disturbing thought in mind, Kalas rushed back to the other end of the alley and waved his arm, the signal to the trumpeters, then ran to his large pony, the lead To-gai-ru pinto in the line of fifty armored Allheart knights.

From nearly every rooftop in the area, it seemed, the trumpets blared, the rousing battle chorus of the mighty Allheart Brigade. All heads along the wall turned at the sound and at the ensuing thunder of pounding hooves.

"Throw wide the gates!" came a commanding cry. The city guardsmen rushed to pull wide the western gates, opening the path.

Out they went, bursting through the gate and onto the field, their silvery armor gleaming despite the dim light of the drizzly day. With practiced precision, they brought their powerful ponies into a wedge formation, Duke Kalas at the point.

The trumpet song continued a few moments longer, and then, as suddenly as it began, it ended. All on the wall hushed and gawked at the spectacle of the legendary Allheart Brigade. Even Pony, who had seen so much, could not miss the majesty of the moment, the King's finest soldiers in their bright plate mail. Could any force in all the kingdom, in all the world, stand against them?

At that moment, to Pony, who had felled giants with strokes of magical lightning, who had witnessed Avelyn blasting away the top of a mountain with an amethyst, it didn't seem so.

In a powerful swift motion, Duke Kalas brought his sword from its scabbard and raised it high into the air.

All was silent, the brief moment of calm before the battle.

From somewhere out in the mist, a powrie cursed.

The charge was on—the blare of trumpets, the thunder of horses, the clash of steel, and the cries of battle.

From the wall, Pony and the others couldn't see much, just ghostly forms rushing to and fro in the fog. But then one group of powries burst out of the mist, charging for the wall. Before the archers could level their bows, before Pony could even take the offered graphite stone from Brother Braumin, Duke Kalas and a group of knights charged out behind the dwarves, trampling and slashing, disposing of them in mere seconds, then whirling their superb To-gai-ru ponies and thundering back across the field.

Some of those on the wall uttered a few prayers, but most remained hushed in disbelief, for never had they seen a band of tough powries so completely and easily overwhelmed.

Out in the mist, the sounds of battle began to recede, the powries obviously in flight, the Duke and his men giving chase.

The hundreds on or near Palmaris' western wall broke out into cheers for the Duke, the new Baron of Palmaris.

"Pray they are not being baited," Brother Francis remarked, an obvious fear given the ease of the rout.

Pony, standing quietly next to him, staring hard at the opaque veil that had kept so much from her eyes, didn't fear that possibility. She simply had a sense that it was not so, that Kalas and his Allheart knights had not gone off into great danger.

Something about the whole battle hadn't seemed . . . right.

She thought about taking up a hematite then, and spirit-walking across the field, through the veil of mist to watch the Duke's moves more closely. But she dismissed the notion with a shake of her head.

"What is it?" the observant Brother Braumin asked.

"Nothing at all," Pony replied, running her hand through her damp mop of thick blond hair. She continued to stare out at the mist, continued to listen to the cries of battle and dying powries, continued to feel that something here was not quite right. "Nothing at all."

*   *   *

From a copse across the field, another set of eyes curiously watched the spectacle of battle. Bedraggled, wet, and miserable with a scraggly beard, his monk's robes long ago tattered by inner demons, Marcalo De'Unnero could not understand how a substantial powrie force—and he figured any force that would go so boldly against Palmaris had to be substantial—had arrived on the field so suddenly without his noticing the approach. He had been here for several days, seeking food and shelter, trying to stay alive and stay sane. He had watched every movement of the few farmers who had dared to come back out from within the walls of their city, to sit buttoned down in their modest homes for the winter. He had spent long hours studying the graceful movements of the skittish animals.

Mostly De'Unnero had watched the animals, his primary prey. He could sense their moods now, could see the world as they did, and he had noted no unusual smell of fear in the air that any approaching army, especially one dragging machines as large as catapults, would likely provoke.

So where had the powries come from?

De'Unnero made his way back into the copse and through the trees, at last sighting the catapult—just a single war engine—and its crew, its human crew, in a small lea amid the trees. The gunners, as far as he had discerned, had lobbed but a single shot and appeared in no hurry to load and fire another.

"Clever Duke Kalas," De'Unnero, the former brother justice, remarked, figuring out the ruse and the purpose behind it.

He hushed immediately, hearing the snap of a twig not so far away. Close enough for him to smell the blood.

"Yach, damned swordsman," he heard a powrie grumble, then he spotted the bloody cap dwarf, trudging along a path.

Then De'Unnero spotted the gash on the dwarf's shoulder, a bright line of blood crystal clear to him despite the fog. Yes, he saw it and smelled it, the sweet fragrance filling his nostrils, permeating his senses.

He felt the first convulsions of change an instant later, growled quietly against the sudden, sharp pains in his fingers and toes, and then in his jaw—the transformation of the jaw always hurt the most.

De'Unnero's shoulders lurched forward suddenly as his spine twisted. He fell to all fours, but that was a more comfortable position anyway, as his hips rotated.

Now he was a cat, a great orange, black-striped tiger.

"Damned," the approaching powrie cursed. "Said 'e wouldn't hit me so hard!"

The last words vanished in the powrie's throat as the dwarf came on guard, sensing suddenly that he was not alone. He started to turn back, but swung in a terrified rush as the brush rustled and the great cat leaped over him, bearing him to the ground with frightening speed and ease. The dwarf flailed wildly and tried to call out, but the cat paws were quicker and stronger, hooking leathery skin and forcing the powrie's arms away. The powerful jaws clamped onto his throat.

A moment later, De'Unnero began his morning meal.

His keen senses soon discerned the sounds of others approaching—horsemen and cursing dwarves—so he bit into the dead powrie's shoulder and dragged the meal away.

"Ye kilt them to death in battle!" Dalump Keedump accused, spitting with every word, waggling his stubby finger at Duke Kalas, who sat tall astride his brown-and-white To-gai-ru pony, seeming unconcerned.

"I told you that several might die," Kalas replied.

"Too many!" grumbled another dwarf, the same one who had challenged Kalas in the dungeons of Chasewind Manor those days before. "Ye're a lyin' bastard dog."

A single urging kick sent the Duke's well-trained pony into a leap that brought him right by the powrie; and with a single fluid motion, Kalas, as fine a warrior as Honce-the-Bear had to offer, brought his shining sword out and swiped down, lopping off the powrie's head.

"You think this a game?" the Duke cried at Dalump, at all the remaining powries. "Shall we cut you all down here and now and make our victory complete?"

Dalump Keedump, hardly frightened by the death of several of his kinfolk—in fact, a bit relieved that Kalas had finally disposed of the loudmouth—hooked his stubby thumbs under the edges of his sleeveless tunic and tilted his head, staring hard at the Duke. "I'm thinkin' that our blood just bought us a boat fer home," he said.

Duke Kalas calmed, stared long at the dwarf, and then nodded his head. "In the spring," he agreed, "as soon as the weather permits. And you will be treated well until then, with warm blankets and extra food."

"Keep yer blankets and get us some human women for warmin'," Dalump pressed.

Kalas nearly gave the command to slaughter the rest of the powries then and there. He'd keep his word to let this group go free, back to their distant homeland, and he would make sure that they fared better in the dungeons over the winter, with more supplies. But if he ever saw a grubby powrie hand anywhere near a human woman, even a lowly peasant whore, he'd surely cut it off and then take the powrie's head, as well.

"Drag them back in chains tonight," he instructed one of his knights, "as quietly as possible. Tell any city guards that the captured dwarves will be interrogated and summarily executed, then put them back in their cell."

Kalas spun his pony and started away, his closest commanders hurrying to get their mounts at his side. The Duke stopped, and turned back.

"Count the dead and the living and scour the field," he instructed. "Every powrie is to be accounted for."

"Ye think we'd stay in yer miserable land any longer than we're havin' to?" Dalump Keedump asked, but Kalas simply ignored him.

His triumphant return into the city awaited.

They came out of the mist more gloriously than they had entered, the Duke and his men, and the grime and blood of battle only made their armor seem all the more brilliant.

Duke Kalas drew out his bloodstained sword and lifted it high into the air. "Honor in battle, victory to the King!" he cried, the motto of the mighty Allheart Brigade. Nearly every person on or near the western wall was cheering wildly, and most were crying.

Duke Kalas soaked it all in, reveling in the glory of the moment, in the triumph that would strengthen his, and thus, King Danube's, grasp upon this fragile frontier city. He swept his gaze along the wall, taking in the relieved and appreciative expressions but then lingering on one figure who was neither crying nor cheering.

Still, Kalas was thrilled to see that beautiful and dangerous Jilseponie had witnessed his glorious moment.

❖ 2 ❖

Distant Voices

"We must stand united on this," the always excitable Brother Viscenti loudly insisted to Abbot Je'howith. "Would you prefer that King Danube insinuated himself into affairs of the Church?"

The way Brother Viscenti changed his inflection at the end of that question altered it from rhetorical to skeptical, even to sarcastic, a point not lost on brothers Francis and Braumin Herde, who were holding their own conversation a short distance away. All the important monks who were in Palmaris had gathered this morning in preparation for their final meeting with King Danube before his departure from the city. Braumin Herde and his trusted companions, Holan Dellman, Castinagis, and Viscenti, were there, along with Francis of St.-Mere-Abelle, Abbot Je'howith of St. Honce in Ursal, and a contingent of lower-ranking monks, the only remaining leaders of the home abbey of St. Precious, led by Brother Talumus, a young but eager man who had been instrumental in the momentous events of the previous months. All the Abellican Church owed a great debt to brave Brother Talumus, in the estimation of many, Braumin Herde included.

"You think of the King as an enemy," Abbot Je'howith replied at length to Brother Viscenti. "That is a mistake, and possibly a very dangerous one."

"Nay," Brother Braumin remarked, coming over to intervene. Brother Viscenti would often lose his good sense in the throes of his agitation, and any ill-considered retorts at that time would not bode well. Abbot Je'howith, who had lived for so many years in Ursal, who had helped tutor young Danube Brock Ursal upon the man's premature ascent to the throne, held the base of his power in the secular rulers of Honce-the-Bear. "Not as an enemy," Braumin Herde continued, pointedly moving in front of Brother Viscenti, cutting him off from Je'howith. "But King Danube's agenda is not our own. His is based in the worldly, while ours must ascend to the spiritual."

"Pretty words," Je'howith said with more than a little sarcasm.

"But true enough," Master Francis was swift to respond, moving quickly to Braumin's side.

Je'howith glared at the man; there was no love between them. Francis had been Markwart's right hand. Markwart had even prematurely promoted him to master, and then to interim bishop of Palmaris, and then to the coveted position of abbot of St. Precious, though Francis had immediately resigned when Markwart died, after the revelations that the demon dactyl had been guiding the Father Abbot. But Je'howith, too, had been firmly in Markwart's court, and that court could have remained strong even after the Father Abbot's demise. Indeed, if Francis and Je'howith had stood unified then—with Elbryan the Nightbird dead in the other room and Jilseponie unconscious—both the abbots might have taken up the reins of power right where Markwart had left off, assuring Je'howith the position of Father Abbot. He would have groomed young Francis to take his place after his death, and he was not a young man. But, for some reason that Je'howith could not understand, Francis would not play the political game.

Indeed Francis, citing Markwart's last words and drawing liberal inference from them, had called upon the Church to appoint Jilseponie Wyndon as mother abbess!

"King Danube would take us in a direction that best suited him," the Abellican Church's youngest master went on.

"And in these times of despair, when so many have died in the fighting, when food is short in so many reaches, and illness is rampant across the land, when so many are unsure in both their secular and spiritual concerns, would not a joining of Church and Crown be seen as a reassurance that they, the common folk, have not been abandoned?" Abbot Je'howith recited with a dramatic flourish. "Would not the show of a bond between beloved King Danube and the new leaders of the Church bring confidence and hope to the despairing kingdom?"

"And there will be such a bond," Brother Braumin replied, "a partnership, but we will not be subjugated to the King of Honce-the-Bear. While our immediate goals of alleviating the ravages of war seem similar, our long-term aspirations remain very different."

"Not so different," Je'howith insisted.

Brother Braumin slowly shook his head, making it clear to Je'howith and all who were watching—and that included every monk in the room, by this time—that he was not going to surrender this crucial point.

Everyone in the room understood that if King Danube tried to insinuate himself into the Abellican Church now, it would be very difficult, given the lack of experienced and charismatic leadership, for the Church to hold him at bay.

"Father Abbot Markwart attempted such a joining," Master Francis reminded them, referring to the fairly recent appointment of Marcalo

De'Unnero as bishop of Palmaris, a title that conveyed the power of both Church leadership and secular control over the city. The city had been without a baron since beloved Rochefort Bildeborough had been murdered on the road to Ursal—and the subsequent evidence had implicated De'Unnero and his preferred use of the tiger's paw gemstone as the killer—and Markwart had tried to take advantage of the emergency.

But that action had only prompted Danube to come north, with his army and his entourage, to protect his power base within the city.

"A complete disaster," Francis went on. "And so it will be again if the King asserts his power and influence where they do not belong."

Brother Braumin looked over at Francis and nodded solemnly. The two were not friends—far from it!—despite Francis' apparent transformation since Markwart's death, but Braumin did appreciate his support at this crucial time. All the Church could crumble around them, Braumin understood, if they did not act and choose wisely in the coming months.

Braumin looked back at Je'howith and saw clearly that the man could become a difficult enemy. Je'howith had spent decades securing his comforts and his power, and both owed more to King Danube than to the Abellican Order.

Braumin stared at Je'howith solemnly, then slightly nodded his head, indicating a quiet corner of the room where they might negotiate this disagreement less publicly.

She had a difficult time climbing out of bed that morning, as on almost every morning. By Braumin Herde's estimation, the events of this day would be more critical than any powrie attack that ended short of the vicious dwarves conquering the whole of the kingdom. But to weary Jilseponie, it was just another in an endless, and futile, stream of meetings. Always they talked and organized, shifting the balances of power, but Pony had come to believe that in the overall scheme of things, in the history and the future of humanity and the world, all their little games would have very little impact.

So many people viewed everything as momentous and important, but was it really?

That question had haunted Pony since the death of Elbryan, had followed her every step, had stilled her tongue during those meetings when she knew the consensus was in error. In the end, what did it matter?

Even the war with the demon dactyl. They had gone to Aida and destroyed its physical manifestation, but that seemingly important and heroic deed, in which Avelyn and Tuntun the elf had given their lives, had only led to more misery. Father Abbot Markwart, who was fearful of his power base, was on the road to declaring Avelyn a heretic and had sent out brothers to murder him. In Markwart's desperate search to find the new keepers of the stolen

FINNEY CO. PUBLIC LIBRARY
605 EAST WALNUT
GARDEN CITY, KS 67846

gemstones—Elbryan and Pony—he had gone after Pony's adoptive family, killing her stepbrother, Grady, on the road, and imprisoning Graevis and Pettibwa in his dungeons, where they had died horribly.

That had only spurred more conflict that Pony had hoped would end it all. And so it had—for Markwart and Elbryan—but they were hardly cold in the ground before the bickering had begun anew, before new problems, grave problems according to Brother Braumin, had reared up to threaten the supposed fruits of all their sacrifices.

As she considered it all, Pony put her hand to her belly, to her womb, which the demon Markwart had so violated, taking her child from her, stilling the heartbeat that had found such rhythm with her own.

Now they were fighting again, and in her time of grieving, Pony could not bring herself to believe that it would ever end. Without that optimism, that flicker of hope, how could she leap out of bed with excitement to attend to another of the so-called important meetings?

She did manage to rise, wash, and dress, though, for the sake of brothers Braumin, Dellman, Castinagis, and Viscenti, who had stood strong beside her and Elbryan in their time of need, who had refused to turn against them despite their own imprisonment and the threat of torturous deaths at the hands of Markwart. She had to do it for Brother Romeo Mullahy, who had leaped from the blessed plateau at the Barbacan to his death rather than surrender to Markwart. She had to do it for Avelyn, for the Church he had envisioned—even though she was certain it would never come to fruition.

Her responsibilities enabled her to put one foot in front of the other along the corridors of St. Precious.

When she turned the last corner into the hallway that ran in front of the meeting room, she came upon another whose stride, markedly different from her own, was full of eagerness and strength.

"Greetings, Jilseponie," Duke Kalas said, edging to walk close to her side. "I would have thought that you would have been inside with the brothers long before this, preparing for the King's visit."

"I have spoken with Brother Braumin many times," Pony casually replied, her reference to Braumin only—and not the higher-ranking monks, particularly Abbot Je'howith—speaking volumes about her stance on the present issues.

Kalas remained quiet; the only sound in the corridor was the soft padding of Pony's light shoes and the hard clacking of Kalas' military boots.

Before they reached the door, the Duke strode ahead of her and then turned back so that she had to look at him. "A difficult fight on yesterday's morn," he said.

Pony chuckled at his abrupt subject change. "Not so, I would think," she replied, "since so few were wounded."

"A testament to the power of the Allheart Brigade," the proud Kalas quickly added. "The powries were many and were eager for battle, but our precision formations and practiced coordination cut their ranks asunder and sent them running."

Pony nodded despite her nagging suspicions. She had no hard proof, after all, to dispute the Duke's words.

Kalas moved in front of her and forced her to stop abruptly. "I was pleased to see you on the wall when I rode back into Palmaris," he said, staring at her intently. "It is good that you should witness such a spectacle as the Allheart Brigade in these troubled times, that you might gain confidence that we, you and I, are fighting the same enemies."

It took all of Pony's considerable composure not to laugh in the man's face. He was making a play for her—oh, not for the present—for he, like everyone else, understood that she, less than four months widowed, was still grieving for Elbryan. No, Kalas was being far more subtle and polite. He was sowing seeds—she saw it so clearly. In truth, such occasions had become quite common. She was able to easily put aside her vanity and harbor no illusions that her beauty and charm were winning the hearts of the visiting nobles of Danube's court. She knew she was a beautiful woman, but so were many of those who had followed the King and his court to Palmaris, courtesans well versed in the arts of seduction. Pony understood the truth behind Kalas' words. She was an important figure now, with more potential for power within Church or State than any other woman in the kingdom, including Delenia, the abbess of St. Gwendolyn, the highest-ranking woman in the Abellican Church. Pony had been tentatively offered the highest position in the Order by several of the monks in Palmaris and certainly would have been given, at least, the Abbey of St. Precious as her own with a mere word. And she had been offered Palmaris by Danube, to serve him as its baroness.

If Pony was at all interested in this game of political intrigue, she could, in a matter of days, step into the thick of the highest levels of power.

Duke Kalas, a political animal if ever Pony had seen one, understood that, of course, and so he thought his charms well placed. Except that, to Pony, those charms themselves were the most lacking.

"If injured upon the field, I would have insisted on Jilseponie for my healer," the Duke went on; and it was obvious that he thought he was paying her the highest compliment.

Again, Pony had to work hard not to laugh. She understood Duke Kalas very clearly. The man could have nearly any woman in the kingdom; he could snap his fingers or run them through his thick black mop of curly hair and bat those pretty dark eyelashes of his and have the ladies of Ursal's court fainting on the floor. Pony knew that, and didn't deny that the man was physically handsome, beautiful even.

But how that image faded next to her Elbryan! Kalas was like a magnificently painted landscape of majestic mountains, an image of beauty, but

Elbryan's beauty went far deeper. Elbryan had been those mountains—with the crisp, fresh air, the sounds, the sights, the smells, the exhilarating and *real* experience. Kalas was mere swagger, but Elbryan had been the substance; and this man, for all of his pride and puff, seemed a pale figure beside the ghost of Nightbird.

She recognized that she wasn't keeping enough of her true feelings off her face when Duke Kalas stiffened and moved aside suddenly, clearing his throat.

Pony turned her head away from him, chewing her bottom lip, hoping that she had not done too much damage to Brother Braumin's cause, and hoping that she would not burst out into mocking laughter.

"The King was delayed," came a voice behind them, and they turned to see Lady Constance Pemblebury moving fast to catch up to them. The woman repeated her message, eyeing Pony directly as she spoke. Neither Pony nor Kalas missed Constance's point: King Danube had been delayed because of her.

Pony rolled her eyes, fighting the feeling of mocking helplessness in the face of such abject stupidity. Constance—who, by all rumors, had been seducing King Danube for years—saw the attractive Pony, ten years her junior, as a threat and wanted to openly lay her claim to Danube.

How could Pony explain it to her? Could she grab the woman by the shoulders and shake her until her teeth rattled?

"He bids that we wait for him before entering the audience chamber," Constance went on, shifting her gaze to Duke Kalas. "Of course, you may go," she said dismissively to Pony, who chuckled, shook her head, and turned back for the door, acutely aware that Duke Kalas' eyes were following her every step.

She had rebuffed the man, perhaps had even embarrassed and insulted him, but likely, she knew, he would take that as a challenge and would come after her all the more blatantly in the days ahead.

A man like Kalas always had something to prove.

"It was only a year ago since the last College of Abbots was convened," Brother Braumin said to Abbot Je'howith when the two were alone at the side of the large audience hall. "How much the world has changed since then!"

Je'howith eyed the younger monk with suspicion. That last College of Abbots had been a disaster, of course, considering all that had occurred since then. Markwart had declared Master Jojonah a heretic and had used the King's own soldiers—for some reason that even Je'howith had not understood and still did not understand—to have the doomed heretic dragged through the streets of St.-Mere-Abelle village and then burned at the stake. At that same College, Markwart had issued a formal declaration of Brother Avelyn as a heretic; and now, it seemed as if the Church might begin the process of canonizing the man!

Braumin read Je'howith's expression correctly, and he gave a helpless chuckle to alleviate the tension. "We have learned much since then," he said. "Hopefully, the Abellican Church can begin to mend the wounds it has opened."

"By canonizing Avelyn Desbris?" Je'howith asked skeptically.

Braumin held up his hands. "In time, perhaps that process will find enough support to begin," he said noncommittally, not wanting to start that fight now. "But before we begin to discuss any such action, before we even begin to determine who was correct—Father Abbot Markwart or Master Jojonah and Brother Avelyn—we must, by the King's own command, put our present house in order."

Je'howith's skeptical glare returned tenfold. "You have long ago decided which of them chose the proper course," he said accusingly.

"And it is a case I intend to make against you, and strongly, should you decide, after all that we have seen, to side with Markwart," Brother Braumin admitted. "But, again, we have not the time, nor the folly, to begin such a battle at this hour."

Je'howith backed off. "Agreed," he said.

"And we must quickly convene a College of Abbots to elect a new Father Abbot," Brother Braumin went on, "and to secure the position of abbot of St. Precious."

"Why, Brother Braumin, you are not yet even a master. As an immaculate, you would likely be invited to a College of Abbots, though you would have no voice there. And yet you speak as if you personally intend to call one."

"Master Francis will nominate me as abbot of St. Precious before King Danube this very day," Braumin announced. "Brother Talumus and all from St. Precious will second that nomination." He paused and looked at the old monk directly. "And Jilseponie, who has refused the post, will act as third."

"Children leading children!" Je'howith retorted, raising his voice in ire. Braumin knew that the man's anger was born of frustration, for, in truth, the old abbot would have little leverage in preventing the ascension of Brother Braumin. "And," he sputtered, "that woman! Jilseponie! She is not of the Order! She will have no say in any of this!"

"She is of the Order, my friend," Brother Braumin calmly replied. "Can you doubt her prowess with the gemstones, a clear sign that she is in God's favor? Can you deny Father Abbot Markwart's last words?"

"He was delirious," Je'howith insisted. "He was near death. And, besides, he did not nominate Jilseponie—that was foolish Brother Francis' doing."

"It was the greatest moment of clarity our Father Abbot experienced since long before the last College of Abbots," Braumin Herde replied. "Since before he sent Brother Justice to hunt and kill Brother Avelyn. Since before he abducted the poor Chilichunk family and let them rot in the dungeons of St.-Mere-Abelle. You know that my words are true and that they will ring powerfully to the other abbots and masters, many of whom had come to question Markwart long before the most recent revelations. Master Francis followed Markwart along that dark road, and he has returned to the light to tell the truth of it."

Je'howith spent a long while digesting Braumin's argument, seeking some flaw. "I will not oppose your ascension to the position of abbot," he conceded.

Braumin's smile was cut short as Je'howith pointed a long, thin finger at him. "But only if Bishop De'Unnero does not return."

"He is discredited by his own actions even if he does," Braumin argued. "We know that he stood with Markwart in the final battle."

"We know little of his role," Je'howith countered.

"He is implicated in the murder of Baron Bildeborough."

"Hardly," Je'howith scoffed. "He is implicated only in the eyes of those who so hated Markwart that they saw his treachery in every event. There has been no formal connection to the murder of the Baron, other than the fact that Bishop De'Unnero is known to be proficient with the tiger's paw gemstone. Hardly damning evidence."

"Then why has he run off?" asked Braumin.

"I will support your nomination if he does not return with some plausible reason why he should reassume the leadership of the abbey, as Father Abbot Markwart had determined," Je'howith said resolutely. Brother Braumin, after a moment, nodded his concession.

From Je'howith's posture, though, Braumin soon came to realize that there would be a price for that support. "What do you want?" the young monk asked bluntly.

"Two things," Je'howith replied. "First, we will treat the memory of Father Abbot Markwart gently."

Braumin's expression was one of sheer incredulity, fast transforming into disgust.

"He was a great man," Je'howith insisted.

"Who culminated his life's work with murder," Braumin retorted quietly, not wanting to draw anyone else into this particular phase of the discussion.

Je'howith shook his head. "You cannot understand," he replied. "I'll not argue concerning the final actions of Dalebert Markwart, but you cannot judge the whole of his life on an errant turn—"

"A wrong choice," Braumin interjected.

Je'howith nodded, apparently conceding the point—but only for now, Braumin understood.

"By either definition, an errant turn in his life's work," Je'howith said. "And we would be in grave error to judge all he accomplished based on the failings of his last days."

It was more than just "his last days," Braumin knew, and the whole manner in which Je'howith was framing the discussion left a sour taste in the idealistic young monk's mouth. "A man might lose sainthood over a single indiscretion," he reminded him.

"I am not asking you to beatify Dalebert Markwart," Je'howith replied.

"Then what?"

"Let us honor his memory as we have his predecessors'," Je'howith explained, "as we have for every father abbot, save the few who led the Church far astray."

"As did Markwart."

Je'howith shook his head. "He was a man thrust into a difficult situation, a position complicated by war and by the actions of those two men you so dearly cherish. You may argue that he chose wrongly, but his reign as father abbot was not one marked by controversy and terror. Indeed, under the guidance of Father Abbot Dalebert Markwart, the Church attained great heights of power. Had there ever been such a cache of gemstones granted in the most recent stone showers?"

"Avelyn's work," Braumin dryly put in; but Je'howith hardly seemed to notice, so caught up was he in his mounting tirade.

"Under his leadership, we achieved the position of bishop of Palmaris. Though that did not end well, the mere fact that King Danube allowed such a maneuver speaks volumes for the Father Abbot's diplomacy and influence."

Braumin started to shake his head, but merely sighed instead. He did not want to allow any mercy into the discussions of the wretch Markwart; he wanted the Father Abbot condemned throughout history as the downfallen sinner that he had become. But there were practical considerations here. Je'howith might well prove an unconquerable obstacle to any tributes, canonization or otherwise, that Braumin and his companions tried to formalize for Avelyn or Jojonah. Braumin held no love for Je'howith—he considered the man a kindred spirit to Markwart—but he understood that Je'howith stood at a crossroads now, that the man could either become a dangerous enemy or, if Braumin managed to handle him properly, an inconsequential onlooker.

"And you should consider the emotions of the populace," Je'howith went on. "They are nervous and hardly certain of whether good or evil triumphed in Chasewind Manor that fateful day."

"Markwart had fallen long before that battle," Braumin Herde stated flatly.

Je'howith nodded, his grin wry. "Perhaps, and perhaps the common folk will believe that. But do understand, my young friend, that Markwart was no enemy to the people of Palmaris."

"De'Unnero . . ." Braumin Herde started to argue.

"Was not Bishop Francis," Je'howith replied. "Yes, they hated De'Unnero, and they curse his name still, though I believe the man was misunderstood."

Braumin Herde nearly choked.

"But they were not so badly disposed toward Francis."

"Who speaks ill of Markwart," Braumin put in.

"Not so," Jo'howith replied, "not publicly. No, Brother Braumin, the folk of Palmaris are nervous. They know the outcome of the battle at Chasewind Manor, but they do not know what that means. They hear the edicts of King Danube, proclaiming victory for all the folk, but they take in those words but tentatively, recognizing the truth of the rivalry between the two great men, Danube and Father Abbot Markwart."

Braumin Herde shook his head as if to dismiss the notion, but Je'howith stared at him hard and paused there, allowing him time to let the words sink in. The old abbot had a significant point here, Braumin had to admit. When Pony had tried to assassinate Markwart the first time—and had, by all appearances, succeeded—there had been open weeping in the streets of Palmaris. Markwart had done well in his last days to win over the folk, had come to the city under flags of honor, with glorious trumpets blaring. He had reconciled, through Francis, with the merchants by compensating them for De'Unnero's confiscation of their magical gemstones. He had taken on King Danube privately; the peasants knew little of that skirmish. Perhaps old Je'howith was indeed speaking wisely, the young monk had to concede. Perhaps treating Markwart's memory with a bit of mercy would serve them all well in the coming days.

"What is your second demand?" Braumin asked.

Je'howith paused, a telling hesitation to perceptive Braumin. "There is a vacancy within the Church, obviously," the old man began solemnly.

Braumin nodded for him to continue. Of course he knew what Je'howith might be hinting at, but he wasn't about to make this any easier on the old wretch.

"Master Engress is dead," Je'howith went on, "and while Father Abbot Markwart might have desired to see young Master Francis as his heir, it is obvious that such a thing cannot come to pass now. Never would so young and inexperienced a man be accepted as father abbot. Many do not even truly accept him as a master."

"He would have been eligible for the title this coming spring," Braumin replied. "His tenth year."

"And you?" Je'howith asked, his tone offering to Braumin a trade-off of support. "A year ahead of Francis and not yet even a master. Have you enough years, Brother Braumin, to be elected as an abbot of an abbey as prominent and important as St. Precious?"

Braumin knew that Je'howith's words of opposition against him and Francis would sound reasonable to any gathering of abbots and masters. If

Je'howith was to claim that Markwart, delusional and ill, erred in promoting Francis prematurely, then how might Braumin and Francis, both attempting to discredit Markwart on just those grounds, make the opposite case? Despite that, Braumin remained steadfast and would not follow Je'howith to that which he apparently desired. "No," he said simply. "You are asking me to support you in a bid for the title of father abbot, but that I cannot do."

Je'howith's eyes narrowed and his lips became very thin.

"Even Master Francis will not back you," Braumin said bluntly. "And as he was deeply connected to the Father Abbot, as were you, his abandonment of your cause will ring loudly in the ears of the other electors."

Braumin did not blink, matching the angry man's stare. "It will not be you, Abbot Je'howith," he said. "Never were you prepared for such a position, and your allegiance to the King in a time such as this—when the lines between Church and Crown have been so blurred, when the people have so turned against your former ally, Markwart—is not a desirable trait."

For a long while, Je'howith seemed to Braumin to be composing a retort, perhaps even a tirade, but then there came a call that King Danube was in the building, and the news seemed to calm the old abbot dramatically. Braumin understood the change, for Je'howith had been put under great pressure by King Danube to put the Abellican house in order, a demand the King would not debate.

"Who then?" Je'howith asked sharply. "The woman?"

Braumin shrugged and wound up shaking his head. "If Jilseponie would accept the nomination . . ."

Je'howith began resolutely shaking his head.

"As your Father Abbot desired, by the interpretation of Master Francis," Braumin pointedly added. "Then I, and Francis and many others, would back her with all our hearts."

"I am not so sure that Brother Francis' heart remains strong on this issue," Je'howith said slyly.

"We could rally enough support without him," Braumin insisted; though in truth, he didn't believe his declaration. He knew that Francis was indeed leaning against Pony's nomination now, and that without Francis—or even with him—selling the idea of a mother abbess at all, let alone someone not even formally affiliated with the Church, would be no easy task!

"And you would tear the Abellican Church apart," Je'howith insisted.

"And better our Church of Avelyn might be for that!" Braumin snapped back. "But no, fear not, for Jilseponie has declined the offer. She will not be the next leader of the Abellican Church."

"Who then?" Je'howith asked. "Does young Braumin reach so high?"

Indeed, Braumin had been considering that very thing, though while his closest friends, Castinagis and Viscenti, had thought it a wonderful notion, even Brother Francis had hesitated. Francis had been very blunt with

Braumin, telling him that he was too young and far too inexperienced to be accepted by the other leaders, and far too naive to handle the realities of the politics that would accompany such a position.

If Je'howith had given him any hint of softening, though, Braumin might have continued to consider the try.

"You are not nearly ready," Je'howith said, and Braumin recognized that the man was speaking sincerely. "Perhaps if you backed me and I was elected, I would consider taking you as my protégé."

"No," Braumin returned without hesitation. "It will not be you, Abbot Je'howith."

Je'howith started to say something, but paused and sighed. "There is Abbot Olin of St. Bondabruce in Entel."

Braumin bristled visibly, shaking his head.

"He will be a strong candidate," Je'howith replied.

"His ways are more attuned to those of Behren than those of Honce-the-Bear," Braumin pointed out; and it was true enough, and everyone in the Church knew it. Entel was Honce-the-Bear's southernmost major city, on the coast in the northern foothills of the Belt-and-Buckle, a mountain range that separated the kingdom from Behren. Entel's sister city was, in fact, Jacintha, Behren's seat of power, located on the coast in the southern foothills of that same range, a short boat ride from Entel.

"Even so, if we, who have witnessed the drama of the last weeks, do not present a unified front, Abbot Olin will likely win the day," Je'howith replied.

"But you—as I—do not think him a wise choice."

Je'howith shrugged.

"There are many masters of St.-Mere-Abelle qualified in experience and in temperament," Braumin suggested. He saw that Je'howith was obviously not enamored of the idea. "Fio Bou-raiy and Machuso."

"Bou-raiy is not ready, and is too angry; and Machuso spends his days, every day, with peasants," Je'howith said. "Better another—Agronguerre of St. Belfour, perhaps."

Braumin had no answer; he hardly knew the abbot of that northernmost Honce-the-Bear abbey, St. Belfour in the wilds of the kingdom's Vanguard region.

"Yes, Abbot Agronguerre would be a fine choice," Je'howith said.

Braumin started to ask why, but he stopped short, recalling an image from the previous year's College of Abbots, the only time he had ever seen Abbot Agronguerre of St. Belfour. The man had been sitting right beside Je'howith, chatting easily, as if the two were old friends.

Only then did Brother Braumin appreciate that Je'howith had led him to this point purposefully. Je'howith hadn't held serious thoughts of becoming the next father abbot. Of course not, for his ties to the King were too great and many of the other abbots, involved in continual power struggles with regional dukes or barons, would outright oppose his ascent.

"There are other masters at St.-Mere-Abelle—" Braumin started.

"Who will not even attempt to gain the post if Brother Braumin and his friends, the very monks who witnessed the demise of Markwart, were to throw in their votes for an abbot of a different abbey," Je'howith interrupted.

Brother Braumin chuckled at the absurdity of it all and admitted to himself that Francis had been correct in assessing that he, Braumin, was not yet ready for the politics of the position of father abbot.

"Go and ask Master Francis, if you wish," Je'howith offered, "or any of your other friends who might know of Abbot Agronguerre. His reputation for fairness and gentility is without reproach. True, he is not a forceful man, not a firebrand, as was the younger Markwart, but perhaps the Church is in more need of stability now, of healing."

Braumin nodded as Je'howith played it out, as he came to understand the man's interest in Agronguerre. For Agronguerre would undoubtedly support Je'howith, would protect the abbot of St. Honce's interests in the coming years. Agronguerre was abbot of St. Belfour, after all, in wild Vanguard, which was ruled by Prince Midalis, Danube Brock Ursal's younger brother; and Braumin knew enough of that situation to recall that it was a tight bond in the northland, a friendly camaraderie between Church and Crown.

"He is a good man of sterling reputation," Je'howith insisted, "and he is not a young man, not much younger than myself. Understand that I am asking you for our mutual benefit. Even without your backing, or that of Brother Francis, I could throw the College into turmoil by announcing my intent to try for the office. Perhaps I would not command the votes to win, but surely I could persuade many away from you—or whomever it is that you choose to back—enough so that either Abbot Olin or the Abbot Agronguerre would gain the position in any case."

"Then why do you speak to me of it?" Braumin asked.

"Because I fear that Olin will take the post, and will try to strengthen the ties between the Abellican Church and the pagan yatol priests of Behren," Je'howith replied.

And Olin would not look so kindly on Je'howith and his close ties to the King of Honce-the-Bear, Braumin thought.

"So allow the memory of Father Abbot Markwart its peace," Je'howith said, "as it should have, given the man's decades of honorable service to the Church."

Braumin's lack of retort was all the confirmation Je'howith seemed to need.

"And support me as I support Agronguerre," the old abbot went on.

"And when he dies, if you have proven yourself in the position of abbot of St. Precious—an appointment I will support—and if I am still alive, then I give you my word now that I will back your own ascent to that highest level, Brother Braumin."

"I will learn what I can of Abbot Agronguerre," Brother Braumin agreed, "and if he is all you say, then I agree to your choice." He nodded and bowed slightly, then turned to go and join his friends.

"One thing you should know as well, Brother Braumin," Je'howith remarked, turning the younger monk back around. "At last year's College of Abbots, Abbot Agronguerre did not agree with Father Abbot Markwart's damning decree against Master Jojonah. He even expressed his concerns to me that we might be too quick to condemn Brother Avelyn, given that we did not know the extent of the man's actions in league with, or against, the demon dactyl."

Braumin nodded again and began to consider that the meeting with Je'howith had gone much better than he could have ever hoped possible.

Pony saw the final exchange between Braumin and Je'howith, the latter surely no friend of hers! She had heard nothing of their discourse, though, and so she watched Brother Braumin closely as he turned and started away, noting the apparently satisfied spring in his stride, a gait that only increased when he spotted Pony and headed straight for her.

"Jousting with the enemy?" she asked.

"Trying to smooth the trail," Braumin replied. "For surely it is filled with deep ruts since Jilseponie will not heed our call."

Pony laughed at the man's unrelenting pressure. They simply could not hold any conversation without Brother Braumin pushing at her to ally formally and openly with the Church, with the new Abellican Church that he and his companions had determined to bring into being. "If you believe that the road would become smoother and easier if I accepted your invitation to bid to become mother abbess, then you are a fool, Brother Braumin," she replied.

"You have the deathbed blessing of a father abbot."

"A fallen father abbot," Pony reminded, "a man I brought to that deathbed."

"One who found a moment of clarity and repentance in his last moments of life," Braumin came back. "And that moment will be honored within a Church that espouses penitence."

Pony chuckled again at the brother's unrelenting idealism. Could he not see the fallacy of his own prediction, that the College of Abbots would become so enmeshed in attempts at personal gain that Markwart's last statement, and Francis' interpretation of it, would be viewed with skepticism or even dismissed outright?

But they had already been through this argument a dozen times at least, and Pony had no heart for it again. Nor the time, for a moment later, Duke Bretherford entered the room and announced the arrival of King Danube Brock Ursal.

Danube swept into the room, Constance and Kalas flanking him and a line of Allheart knights in shining armor behind them.

"My time is limited, for the tides will soon be favorable," he said, motioning at the large oval table set for the gathering. As one, the monks and the nobles—and Pony, who still wasn't sure exactly how she fit in or where she was supposed to sit—headed for their seats, then waited patiently and deferentially as King Danube took his own.

"Grace us with the blessing," the King bade Abbot Je'howith, a slight against Braumin, Talumus, and particularly Francis that was not lost on Pony.

Je'howith gladly complied, calling for God's blessings in these troubled times, for His guidance that His Church might put itself into proper order to erase the errors of the past year.

Pony listened carefully and marveled at how well the old man avoided specific judgments in his prayer, at how he gave no indication of who it was he thought had made those vague mistakes. Yes, Je'howith was a crafty one, she reminded herself. She—and, to her thinking, Braumin and the others would do well to follow her lead—didn't trust him in the least.

"What are your plans?" King Danube asked immediately after the prayer was ended. He looked to Braumin as he spoke, but his bluntness had obviously caught the monk by surprise, and Braumin quickly turned to Francis for support.

"We will convene a College of Abbots as soon as it can be arranged, obviously," Abbot Je'howith interjected, "perhaps in St. Precious rather than St.-Mere-Abelle. Yes, that might prove wise in these troubled times."

The other monks around the table didn't seem to agree at all. "The College is always held at St.-Mere-Abelle," Brother Viscenti pointed out rather sharply.

"But, perhaps—" Je'howith started.

"We have not discussed the location," Brother Braumin put in, "and now is not the time to announce any such change as you propose."

Brother Viscenti started to respond again, as did Brother Francis, while Brother Talumus and some of his St. Precious entourage began talking excitedly about the possibilities of such an honor. But then suddenly King Danube slammed his fist on the table and leaped up from his seat.

"I have warned you!" he began. "All of you, to put your house in order. Can you not see the fear on the faces of the people you pretend to serve? Can you not understand that your foolish bickering will rip this kingdom apart, spiritually at least? Well, I shall have none of it!"

"Brother Braumin and I have come to agreement concerning the next father abbot," announced Je'howith, obviously uncomfortable at the startling outburst and likely regretting his suggestion of a change of location for the College.

King Danube settled back into his seat, staring at Braumin for confirmation, as were many surprised Abellican monks.

"We have come to . . . an understanding," Braumin began. "My choice, and Father Abbot Markwart's—repentant Father Abbot Markwart's—choice to lead our Church sits beside me," he explained, patting Pony's shoulder. "But, alas, Jilseponie will not heed our call at this time, and so Abbot Je'howith and I have found some common ground."

"And will the rest of us be enlightened concerning that ground?" a scowling Master Francis put in.

"Of course," Brother Braumin replied. "We made no decisions—such are not ours to make—but merely discussed the matter and tried to find some agreement, a proposal shaped between us that I might bring to my colleagues and Abbot Je'howith to his."

Francis nodded, indicating that Braumin should go on.

"We must speak privately about this," Braumin answered and turned to the King. "But the College of Abbots will succeed in its task of appointment, and of the correct appointment for the times. I assure you, your Majesty."

"As we have come to agree on the new abbot of St. Precious," Je'howith added, surprising everyone. "Master Francis, with great generosity and foresight, has abdicated the post, and plans to nominate . . ." He paused and motioned to Francis.

"I had th-thought that Brother Braumin," Francis stuttered, obviously caught off his guard. "Once he has been formally proclaimed as master . . ."

"Yes," they heard Brother Talumus say with enthusiasm.

"Immaculate Brother Braumin will become interim abbot of St. Precious within the week," Abbot Je'howith insisted, "and we will formalize that appointment as soon as we have heard any assenting or dissenting arguments."

King Danube looked at Braumin, and the monk shrugged. "If asked to serve, I would not refuse," he said.

Danube nodded, apparently satisfied with that. He paused then and put his chin in his hand, his gaze drifting off to nowhere in particular. All the rest of the people around the table likewise quieted in deference to the King, and Pony understood then that Danube was in control here and that the brothers of the Abellican Church would do well to disturb him not at all. The less King Danube needed to turn his gaze toward the Church, the better the Church would survive.

Danube remained apparently distant for a long while—Pony got the distinct feeling that the man was testing the patience of those around him, waiting to see if anyone would dare to speak. Finally, he sat up straight and stared at Pony.

"And is your decision—or shall I call it your compromise?—Brother Braumin, that it will be a man or a woman who heads the Abellican Church?" Danube asked.

Pony, embarrassed as she was, didn't turn away but met Danube's stare.

"Unless Abbess Delenia of St. Gwendolyn makes a bid for the position of mother abbess, it will be a man," Braumin answered.

"And Abbess Delenia would have no chance of assuming leadership of the Church, even should she so desire it," a bristling Abbot Je'howith was quick to add.

The man's tone made Pony glance his way, trying unsuccessfully to determine whether he was upset because of the mere suggestion that a woman might head the Church or because King Danube had asked the question of Brother Braumin instead of him.

"So you have refused the offer, then," Danube said to her as she turned back to him. "The Abellican Church hands you one of the most powerful positions in all the world, and you turn it down?"

"Brother Braumin and others offered to *sponsor* me as a candidate for mother abbess," Pony corrected, "but many others within the Church would have rejected such a proposal. It is a fight I choose not to wage, and the leadership of the Church is a position I do not feel that I have earned."

"Well said," said Je'howith, but Danube cut him short with an upraised hand.

"You underestimate your charisma, Jilseponie," the King went on, "and your accomplishments and potential accomplishments. I doubt not at all that the Abellican Church would fare well under your guidance."

Pony nodded her thanks for the somewhat surprising compliment.

"But perhaps Je'howith's and the others' loss might become my gain," the King went on. "Since you have chosen to reject the offer of the Church, I ask again if I might somehow persuade you to accept the barony of Palmaris."

Pony looked down and sighed. Everybody wanted her in his court. She understood the attention—she was a hero among the common folk now, and those common folk had been doing more than a little grumbling about the King, and especially about the Church, of late—but she could not believe how much faith these leaders were willing to place in her. "What would I know of ruling a city, my King?"

Danube burst out into laughter—too much so, it seemed to Pony and to several others who, she noticed, were glancing nervously around, particularly Duke Kalas and Constance Pemblebury, who were both scowling.

And when she thought about it, Pony wasn't surprised. Kalas, after all, had hinted at some amorous feelings for her, and Constance was the King's favorite. Had Danube's exaggerated laughter just put Pony into the middle of some intrigue with those two?

She sighed and looked away, back at Brother Braumin, who was staring at her nervously.

Pony gave in and started laughing as well.

"So you agree that your statement was absurd?" Danube was quick to ask. "What would Jilseponie know of leadership indeed!"

"No, your Majesty," Pony replied. "I laugh because I cannot believe . . ." She stopped and just shook her head helplessly. "I am not suited to be baroness, or for any other rank you wish to bestow upon me," she said, "as I am not suited to be mother abbess of a Church whose policies and intricacies I hardly understand."

"Nonsense," Danube declared, but Pony was shaking her head even as he barked out the word. "Nobility runs in your blood," the King went on, "if not in your lineage, and your ascent to the court of Honce-the-Bear would prove most beneficial."

Still she shook her head.

The King stared at her long and hard then, another uncomfortable moment, and then he gave a helpless sigh. "I see that I shall not convince you—no, Jilseponie Wyndon, you are one of extraordinary character and determination."

"Stubborn," Brother Braumin dared to interject, breaking the tension.

Again the King laughed. "But in a manner suited to heroes," he said. "A pity that you'll not change your mind, and truly a loss for both of us, eh, Abbot Je'howith?"

"Indeed," the old abbot said unconvincingly.

Pony continued to alternate her gaze between the King and his two secular advisers, and neither of them stopped staring at her for one moment.

"Palmaris will be in firm and fine control," the King went on, addressing the whole of the gathering again. "Duke Kalas will stay on as ruler, for as long as he feels necessary. Also, because of the continuing hostilities outside of Palmaris' wall with the powries, goblins, and even reports of giant bands roaming the region, he will keep half the Allheart knights. That should suffice to allow the folk of Palmaris some peace of mind."

Pony glanced at Francis and Braumin and the other young monks, their distress showing her that they understood well the meaning of the King's decision. Danube didn't fear any goblins or powries or giants, for Palmaris' garrison had proven itself time and again in the war against them. No, when the King spoke of potential enemies, he was subtly referring to those enemies Duke Kalas might face from within, particularly from St. Precious. The Allheart knights would make Chasewind Manor a veritable fortress and would strengthen Duke Kalas' influence tremendously.

At first, Pony, too, was more than a little distressed by the news. Privately, at least, she found herself siding with Brother Braumin; she did believe in the man and his cause. That admission nearly made her speak up then, announcing that she had changed her mind and that she would accept an offer to join the Church, not for the position of mother abbess but as an adviser to Brother Braumin in his new position of abbot of St. Precious. Almost—but even as she considered the action, Pony thought of Elbryan and her lost child, thought of the futility of it all, the waste of effort to battle enemies that seemed to her, at that moment, eternal.

She kept silent; indeed, she turned inward through the rest of the meeting. No further surprises came forth, from either Danube or the monks, and their business was quickly concluded. Pony did note the glare that Constance Pemblebury bestowed on her as they were leaving the audience hall, a scowl that deepened tenfold when King Danube took Pony's hand and kissed it, expressing his gratitude yet again for her actions and her sacrifice and proclaiming that Honce-the-Bear was a better place by far because of Jilseponie and Elbryan, Avelyn Desbris and the centaur, Bradwarden, Roger Lockless, and—to Pony's and everyone else's absolute surprise—because of the quiet working of the Touel'alfar.

And then Danube and that moment of gratitude were abruptly gone; the King, Constance Pemblebury, and Duke Bretherford rode forth to the docks and the waiting ships. The reality of the still-gloomy day settled over St. Precious.

A temporary moment of truce, Pony thought as she considered the King's last words to her. A brief shining moment, unlasting in the gloom. Like all such moments.

Pony was on the roof of St. Precious's highest tower again later that day. The spectacle over at the dock section—with the tall ships unfurling their sails, the crowds cheering, the trumpets blaring—did not hold her attention for long. Rather, she found herself looking north, beyond the city's great wall, beyond the farmhouses and the rolling hills. Looking in her mind's eye to Dundalis and her past—and perhaps, she thought seriously, her future.

❖ 3 ❖

Joined by War

T he icy rain drummed heavily against the bare trees, blowing in sheets through the forest, soaking Prince Midalis and his army. They had hoped for snow, a great blizzard as so often blasted Vanguard, a storm gathering strength over the Gulf of Corona, drawing up the water and then dumping snow thigh deep throughout the region. But it was just rain this time: icy rain, and miserable to be sure, but nothing that would drive the goblin horde from their entrenched positions around the large, solitary stone structure, St. Belfour, on the small, bare hill amid the trees.

The cowls of their cloaks pulled as low as they could go, the young Prince and his closest adviser and confidant, Liam O'Blythe, the Earl of Tir-Mattias, made their cautious way to the rocky ridgeline that afforded them a view of the abbey and of the monstrous army firmly encamped about it.

"There's two thousand o' the skizzes if there's a dozen," Liam remarked, surveying the scene before them. He was a thin fellow, all gangly arms and legs, freckle faced with red hair and gray eyes, as was common among the Vanguardsmen. "They got us five to one, even countin' that them monks'll come out and give a hand."

"A bolt of lightning would be better welcome," Midalis replied with just a hint of the Vanguard brogue creeping into his Ursal court–trained diction. His crystal blue eyes peeked out from under the edge of the hood, sparkling brightly despite the dullness of the day. When he stood in a room with native Vanguardsmen, it was obvious that Midalis was not from the region. He was of medium height and build, but with a darker complexion and dark brown hair. Anyone who saw Midalis standing beside the older Danube would guess that they were brothers.

"If they got any o' the magic left to 'em," said Liam, and he pulled off his soaked hood and shook his unruly mop of red hair, running his hand through it to get it out of his eyes. "They ain't tossed a bolt or a burst o' fire out at the goblins in a fortnight."

"They've got it left," Midalis answered with confidence. "But they know that if they use their magic, they'll just bring the goblins on in full against them. The goblins understand how much the monks have got to throw, and if those in the abbey grow weary from using their magic, they will find a difficult task in holding back the horde."

Liam nodded, but his expression remained doubting and grim. "Well, they better have a bolt or two for throwin' when we go against the horde, or we'll be chased off or cut down."

Prince Midalis did not doubt the man's observations. Vanguard was having a much harder time in the aftermath of the war than the rest of Honce-the-Bear, because in Vanguard, the war wasn't over. The minions of the demon dactyl had hit the region hard, both along the rocky coast and with a force marching across the land. South and west of the Gulf of Corona, the lands were cultivated, and much more heavily populated; and there, the King's army had been able to push the hordes away. But here, where the land was much wilder, where forests predominated over farmland and the population of humans was measured in hundreds instead of tens of thousands, the powries and goblins had not so readily retreated. Always, Vanguard had been the roughest region of Honce-the-Bear, its forests full of huge brown bears and hunting cats, its northern border continually crossed by the warlike barbarian tribesmen of Alpinador. The folk of Vanguard had known goblins and powries as more than fireside tales to scare children long before the demon dactyl had awakened to remind the more civilized regions that such monsters did exist.

And though they were certainly outnumbered by their monstrous enemies in the region, the people of Vanguard knew how to fight such foes.

Still, this was a battle that Midalis did not want; this particular army of goblins was too large and too skilled, and the ground around St. Belfour of Tir-Mattias was too rugged for the Prince's troops to fully utilize their greatest advantage: horses. Thus, Midalis had hoped the dark clouds they had seen gathering over the gulf would bring a killer blizzard, a storm that would weaken the goblins' resolve to continue their siege.

"The weather won't be holdin' so warm much longer," Liam remarked.

Midalis shook his head, his expression grim. "The monks haven't got much longer," he explained. "The goblins have held them in there for near to two months now, and with all the folk who came running before the horde, they've not the food to hold on." He paused there and stood staring long and hard at the windswept rain slashing against the abbey's stone walls and at the dozens and dozens of sputtering, smoking campfires of the goblin army encircling the place.

"Ye're to go to him, ain't ye?" Liam asked.

Midalis turned to regard him. "I see no choice," he answered. "Abbot Agronguerre came to me last night, in my dreams, begging for our help. They've a day more of food, and then they'll be going hungry. We cannot wait any longer."

Liam's expression showed that he was less than enthusiastic about the prospects.

"I'm no more happy about the possibilities than you," Midalis said to him. "In another time, we'd be fighting the barbarian savages, and now I am asking them for help."

"Help for the Abellican Church," Liam reminded him, which only made the prospects darker still.

"Aye, there's no friendship between the barbarians of Alpinador and the Church," Midalis agreed; for indeed, the Church had made many forays into the wild northern kingdom, usually with disastrous results, particularly one not so distant memory of slaughter in a small town called Fuldebarrow. "But I've got to try, for the abbot and his brethren."

"And I'll try with ye, me Prince," Liam said with a nod. "And all yer men'll fight beside the demon hisself, if Prince Midalis' naming him an ally!"

Midalis put his hand on Liam's elbow, grateful, as always, for the unyielding loyalty of his hardy men and women. The folk of Vanguard had survived all the trials, the killer storms, and now the invasion, by standing united behind their beloved Prince Midalis, younger brother of King Danube Brock Ursal. And Midalis' loyalty was no less heartfelt and intense. As Danube's brother, he could have ruled whatever duchy he chose. He could have taken the Mantis Arm and its prosperous trade, or the Yorkey region between Ursal and Entel, with its gentle climate and rolling farmlands. He could have even been named Duke of Ursal, as was usual for a lone sibling prince, ruling the mighty city beside his brother in the luxury of Ursal's bountiful court.

But Vanguard had held Midalis' heart ever since his childhood, when his father had sailed with him into the Coastpoint Guard fortress of Pireth Vanguard on a trip to hunt the huge northern elk. Something about the nature of the place—untamed, seemingly unconquerable—had touched a spiritual chord within young Midalis, had shown him an alternative to the bustle and the dirt of the cities. His brother had been leery about letting Midalis come up to this wild land—would the nearly autonomous people accept him? Or might he meet with an "accident" on a hunting trip?

Those fears had been dispelled the moment Midalis had stepped off the boat onto the low dock of Pireth Vanguard, when a host of folk from all the neighboring communities had arrived to set out a huge feast of venison and fowl, with pipers playing tunes both melancholy and joyous all through the day, and all the young ladies of Vanguard taking turns dancing with their new Prince.

Truly, Midalis had found his home, and so when the minions of the demon dactyl had arrived in force, Midalis had not only called out the militia and sent a message to his brother for aid but he had personally led the Vanguard forces. Never could it be said of Prince Midalis that he sat on a horse in safety at the back of the battlefield, commanding his troops into action.

Thus, when the barbarian Andacanavar had come to Midalis' camp that night a week before and Midalis had agreed to meet with him, other Vanguard men and women, traditional enemies of the barbarians, had deferred to the judgment of their heroic Prince without complaint.

Still, it was with great trepidation that Midalis and Liam made their quiet way over the forested hills to the field where Andacanavar and his fellows had set up camp. Might the huge barbarian have baited him, feigning friendship so that he could decapitate the Vanguard forces?

Midalis swallowed that distrust and forced himself to focus instead on poor Abbot Agronguerre and the other forty monks of St. Belfour and the three hundred commoners holed up within the abbey's walls.

At the edge of the field, the pair were met by a trio of huge muscled men, the shortest of whom stood nearly half a foot taller than the nearly six-foot Midalis. Huge spears in hand, the barbarians walked right up before the horses of the visitors, one going to each horse and grabbing the reins just below the beasts' mouths, pulling down forcefully.

"Which is Midalis?" the third of the group, standing back a couple of steps, asked.

The Prince reached up and pulled back his hood, shaking the wetness from his straight brown hair. "I am the Prince of Honce-the-Bear," he said, noting that all three of the barbarians narrowed their eyes at the proclamation.

"Your leader bade me to come to him," Midalis went on, "under a banner of alliance."

The barbarian in the back nodded his head quickly to the side, indicating that the pair should dismount; then, while his two companions walked the horses away, he motioned Midalis and Liam to follow him.

"They should be unsaddled and brushed down," Prince Midalis remarked.

The barbarian turned back on him skeptically.

"They're not knowin' much about horses," Liam whispered to his companion. "The folk of Alpinador ain't much for ridin'."

"But we have eaten more than a few," their huge escort promptly added. He looked at Liam and snickered, for Liam's voice, like his frame, was quite delicate.

Midalis and Liam exchanged skeptical glances; this wasn't going to be easy.

They were led to a large tent in the middle of the encampment. Both noticed that few eyes were upon them throughout the march, and when their escort pulled aside the flap, they understood why.

More than three hundred barbarian warriors—all tall and most with long flaxen hair, some with braids, others with ornamental jewelry tied in—filled the tent, hoisting great foaming mugs and making such a general ruckus that Midalis was amazed that he and Liam hadn't heard them a mile away or that the goblins outside St. Belfour hadn't taken note and sent scouts to investigate.

Or maybe they had, Midalis realized, when he looked to the side and saw a row of goblin heads staked out like macabre party decorations.

"Tunno bren-de prin!" their escort cried above the tumult in his native tongue, a rolling, bouncing language that the Vanguardsmen jokingly referred to as "bedongadongadonga."

Almost immediately, the hall quieted, all eyes turning toward the two smaller men at the entrance. The Prince heard Liam swallow hard, and he shared that nervous sentiment completely. Though it was late fall, and cold, most of the barbarians were wearing sleeveless tunics, revealing their huge, muscled arms, as thick around as Midalis' thigh.

The barbarian ranks slowly parted then as an older man, his face weathered by more than fifty winters, scooped up an extra pair of goblets and started to walk slowly across the tent. He was huge, his muscles taut despite his age; and though there were others his size or even larger, and though most of the men in the hall weren't half his age, from his balanced gait and stern visage, from the obvious respect he commanded from everyone in the hall, Midalis understood that this man Andacanavar could best any two of the others, perhaps any three, in battle.

Without a word, without a blink, he strode toward the pair of visitors, but stopped some dozen paces away. He lifted his own flagon and drained it in one huge swallow, then took the other two, one in each hand, and came forward slowly, the rustling of his deerskin breeches the only sound in the hall—other than the heavy breathing of both Midalis and Liam.

Right before the pair, Andacanavar stopped again and slowly brought his arms out wide and high above his head.

And then he closed his eyes and howled, turning it to a roar, primal and feral and as frightening a sound as either of the Vanguardsmen had ever heard.

And all the others took it up with vigor, a deafening communal roar that shook the tent walls and sent shivers coursing down the spines of the two visitors.

Continuing to roar, Andacanavar now opened his eyes and winked to the two, a signal that Midalis did not miss. Up went the Prince's arms, and he, too, loosed a tremendous bellow; and Liam, after an incredulous glance, did likewise, though his sounded more like a squeak. That only seemed to spur the barbarians on to greater heights, their shouts reaching a thunderous crescendo.

Andacanavar dropped his arms suddenly, foam flying everywhere, and all cut short their howls—except for Midalis and Liam, who didn't understand the game and kept howling a few embarrassing moments longer. Both met the powerful gaze of Andacanavar, and the three stared at one another a few moments longer, before the imposing barbarian came forward and thrust the mugs into their hands, then reached back and called for another drink.

Liam started to bring the mead-filled mug to his lips, but Midalis, catching on, held him.

Then Andacanavar had a mug of his own, presenting it to the pair. "Ah, but we have a bunch of goblins to kill, now don't we?" the barbarian ranger asked.

Midalis took a chance. He raised his mug above his head—even splashing some mead on Andacanavar, though the man hardly seemed to notice—and shouted, "To the death of the goblins!"

Andacanavar slapped his mug against Midalis' and held it there, both men eyeing Liam, who quickly smacked his mug up there, too, while all the gathering took up the toast, "To the death of the goblins!"

Andacanavar drained his mug, as did Liam, for none in Honce-the-Bear could outdrink a born-and-bred Vanguardsman, and Midalis got his close enough to empty to call for more.

"Drink hearty, my friends," said Andacanavar.

"But not too much so," Midalis replied. "We've important business."

Andacanavar nodded. "But my men are wishing to see the truth of you both," he explained. "When you have taken enough of the mead, you will wag your tongues honestly, and let us see if we have a bond that can be forged."

Midalis considered the words and glanced to his friend, and then both held their flagons out as younger barbarians, barely more than boys, rushed about with bulging waterskins, refilling each mug in turn.

"This is Bruinhelde, who leads Tol Hengor," Andacanavar explained, holding his arm back and sweeping forward another imposing, stern-faced man, his blond hair tied with feathers and ornaments, his jaw square and strong. It occurred to Midalis that if he ever punched that jaw, he'd do more damage to his hand than to Bruinhelde's face. His eyes were the typical Alpinadoran blue, burning with inner fires.

"Your closest neighbors, they are," Andacanavar continued. "Far past the time for you two to meet as friends, I say."

From the expression on Bruinhelde's face, Midalis wasn't sure that the man agreed with the ranger's assessment. But the powerful barbarian leader did nod slightly and did present his flagon to Midalis for a clap of mugs. Liam started to add his, but Bruinhelde wilted him with a glare.

"Have we?" Midalis asked bluntly.

Bruinhelde looked at him curiously, then turned to Andacanavar.

"Met as friends," Midalis clarified. "For so many years, our two peoples have had little contact, and rarely has that contact been on friendly terms."

"And you place the blame for this on my people?" Bruinhelde, obviously an easily agitated fellow, roared in reply; and all the Alpinadoran warriors bristled, and poor Liam seemed as if he would simply melt away.

But Midalis kept his eyes firmly on the imposing Bruinhelde. "Blame?" he asked with a chuckle. "I would not presume to blame anyone—likely, there is enough of that to go around, and each of the disastrous meetings would have to be judged on its own circumstance. But, no," he continued as Bruinhelde's look softened somewhat, "I seek not to place blame, nor to take blame upon my own shoulders, but rather to accept that which has happened and hope to learn from it, that it never happens again. Good Bruinhelde, if the invasion by the minions of the demon dactyl brings a new understanding and alliance to our peoples, then there is a bright edge to the dark cloud. Far too long have we skirmished, to the detriment of both our peoples. Let this night of Hengorot"—Bruinhelde and the others were obviously caught off guard that Midalis knew their name for the mead hall celebration—"forge a new bond between us, one for benefit and common good." As he finished, he held his mug aloft.

A long and uncomfortable moment slipped past, with Bruinhelde glancing once at Andacanavar, then fixing his stare on Midalis. Another moment slipped by, the mead hall perfectly silent, every man holding his breath waiting for Bruinhelde's answer.

He clapped his flagon hard against Midalis'. "We could not have picked a better common foe than the smelly goblins!" He roared, and so, too, did every man in the hall, a thunderous battle cry, full of excitement, full of rage. The sheer enthusiasm and volume of that barbarian war cry weakened Liam's knees, and when Prince Midalis looked at his companion he knew that Liam was thinking the same thing as he: they were glad that the Alpinadorans were on their side!

Though he had to go to rally his troops for the morning's battle, Prince Midalis did not leave the mead hall early that night. Nor was he able to escape until after Bruinhelde had poured a dozen flagons of drink down his throat.

"I'm not sure we're better with 'em as friends or enemies," Liam remarked as the two made their way through the forest, each man as groggy and drunk as his companion. "Oh, but me head's to hurt tomorrow, before any goblin even clunks me with its club."

"They'll all awaken with sore heads and tongues of cloth," Midalis agreed. "Likely, it will only make them more fierce."

The mere thought sent a shudder along Liam's spine.

Midalis stopped then and stood with a curious expression upon his face.

"What's it about, then?" Liam asked.

Midalis held his hand up, motioning for the man to wait. A sensation had washed over him, much like the night before, a silent, spiritual cry for help. Abbot Agronguerre, he knew, using the hematite gemstone to reach out to him. It was a subtle call, nothing distinct, an imparting of emotion, of need, and nothing more. Midalis concentrated with all his willpower, trying to reciprocate the call, hoping that Agronguerre, who was floating spiritually about him, would sense his reply. "In the morning," he said aloud, for he was unsure of how the gemstone magic worked, unsure of whether the abbot could physically hear him in his spiritual form. "We will come on against the goblins in the morning."

"As we already said," a confused Liam answered, and again, Midalis held up his hand for the man to wait. But the sensation passed, the connection broke, and the Prince could only hope that his friend in the abbey had heard.

"It was Agronguerre," he explained to Liam. "He came to me again."

Liam held up his hands, seeming unnerved. "The magic again?" he asked, and Midalis nodded. "What're ye thinkin' our new barbarian friends'll think o' them monks and their magic?" he asked, for it was common knowledge among the Vanguardsmen that, while the monks considered the magical gemstones the gifts of God, the Alpinadorans mistrusted the powers completely, even spoke of the monkish magic as the work of Fennerloki, the god of their pantheon representing the powers of evil.

"We start the fightin' and the monks loose a fireball from their stone walls, and then Bruinhelde and his boys turn against us and pull St. Belfour down around Agronguerre," Liam reasoned.

Midalis blew a sigh as he considered the words, but then shook his head. "The ranger, Andacanavar, knows of the magic," he explained. "And so Andacanavar will warn Bruinhelde and the others. They know that we march against goblins besieging the abbey, and yet they join with us anyway."

"Andacanavar," Liam echoed with obvious respect.

The Prince did not sleep at all the rest of that night. He had seen battle many times in the last months, but always against smaller groups of monsters and always upon a field of his own choosing. This time, he had a large portion of his total army with him, more than three hundred men, and all of the monks in Vanguard were bottled up in St. Belfour. If the goblins won this day, the results for the region would be devastating—it was possible that those remaining men and women here would have to retreat to Pireth Vanguard, perhaps even board the few ships there and sail south across the gulf, surrendering the region altogether.

With the dawn, all weariness left the Prince, and the surge of excitement he found in organizing his soldiers erased his sore head from the night before.

"None to be seen," Liam O'Blythe reported a short while later. "Not a barbarian in the area, by what our scouts're sayin'. Not even their campground."

Midalis stared out into the forest. "Are they sure?"

"Can't find them," Liam confirmed sourly. "Might be that they changed their minds and went away."

"Or that they're preparing an attack from a concealed position," Midalis said hopefully.

"And are we to wait?"

Midalis spent a long while considering that. Should he wait for Andacanavar and Bruinhelde? Or should he trust them, and begin the attack now, before the sun had climbed into the sky, as he and Andacanavar had discussed? He recalled Abbot Agronguerre's spiritual plea and knew that those within the abbey were going hungry this day. He and his men had to go against the goblins soon or lose the abbey, but with so much at stake . . .

"We go," he said firmly.

"We'll be outmatched if Andacanavar—"

"We go," Midalis said again. He flattened the parchment map of the region, which lay on the small table in his tent. Midalis had trained in tactics with the Allheart Brigade during his days in Ursal, had learned to recognize his strengths and his enemies' weaknesses. He knew that his men could outfight goblins two to one—more than that if they could bring their horses into play. But the numbers today were far less favorable than that.

Midalis studied the map, focusing on the clear area around the abbey and on the rocky, forested hills to its west. At the least, he and his men had to get some supplies into the abbey.

The Prince nodded his head, settling on a plan. He called together all of his commanders, and within the hour, the Vanguard army was on the move.

"He heard yer call, did he?" the nervous young Brother Haney asked Agronguerre, joining the old abbot in St. Belfour's bell tower, which afforded them a view of the area. The rain had stopped, the stars fading away as the eastern horizon began to lighten with the coming dawn, but the air had turned much colder, leaving an icy glaze on the grass and trees.

Abbot Agronguerre stared out past the goblin campfires. He understood the depth of the disaster here; they were out of food, already with growling bellies, and they needed Midalis to come on in force. But Agronguerre knew well the limits of the Prince's army and knew that, even if Midalis attacked with every available soldier, the odds were against them. Even worse, Agronguerre couldn't honestly answer Brother Haney, for he simply did not know.

"We must pray," he replied, and he turned to regard the young man, barely into his twenties.

Brother Haney shook his head. "They must," he insisted. "If they do not—"

"If they do not, then we shall find our way out of St. Belfour with the fall of night," Agronguerre replied.

Brother Haney nodded, obviously taking some strength from the determination in Agronguerre's voice.

But they both knew the truth of their desperate situation, both knew that this time, it seemed, the goblins had won.

"They're keeping it quiet, then," Liam O'Blythe remarked to Prince Midalis shortly before the dawn. They sat on their horses on the wooded trail behind St. Belfour, all the forest about them deathly silent. The scouts had just returned, though, with news that the goblins were beneath the shady boughs, in great numbers.

Midalis looked back over his line of riders, each horse sporting bulging saddlebags. They had to get to the abbey wall, at least, and heave the supplies in to the monks and common folk trapped within. And so they would, Midalis understood, but he knew, too, that getting back away from the abbey would prove no easy task.

"How long are ye planning to stay and fight?" Liam asked him, apparently reading his thoughts.

"We rush the northeastern corner," Midalis explained, pointing in that direction. St. Belfour was situated with its northern wall near a wooded hillock. That hillock, unfortunately, was thick with goblins, but Midalis believed that he and his riders could get past them to reach the abbey. The other three sides of the rectangular stone structure faced open fields, thirty yards of cleared ground in every direction. Beyond those fields loomed more thick woodlands—thick with brush and trees and goblins. While the fields offered Midalis and his men the best advantage, using their horses to trample enemies and within easy magical support from the monks, he understood that they'd have a difficult time if a retreat became necessary, scrambling their ranks back into the thick brush helter-skelter, with goblins coming at them from every angle, separating them and pulling them down. The Vanguardsmen had survived the war by picking their battlefields carefully; this was one the Prince did not see as promising.

But they had to go, had to get the supplies to their starving kinsmen.

"The fight will come to us quickly, I believe," Midalis remarked, "pursuit following our line and goblins rushing from the brush on all sides."

"How many might them monks be killin'?"

Midalis shrugged; he knew not the extent of Abbot Agronguerre's magical resources, though he understood that they would not be significant for long. "If we can get to the wall and away without a fight, then that is our best course," the Prince said. Several men around him, grim-faced warriors thirsty for goblin blood, groaned. "Let winter break the siege—if the monks are supplied they might hold out until the first deep snows," Midalis explained.

"Too many goblins," Liam agreed, speaking to the others.

"Ah, but they'll be on us afore we get near to the wall," one man in the ranks behind remarked, and Midalis noted that there was indeed a hopeful tone to his voice. In truth, the Prince could not argue the assessment.

"Then we fight them as hard as we can, and for as long as we can," he replied. "Our valor and the magic thrown from the abbey walls may scatter them quickly to the forest, where we can hunt the smaller bands down one by one and eliminate them."

He spoke with conviction, but the seasoned men of his fighting force understood the truth of the situation, and so did Midalis. The goblins would indeed come at them, and hard, and the ugly little creatures wouldn't be quick to retreat. Midalis and his men had one other gambit: The Prince had sent his archers around to the south with orders to hold their shots until the situation turned grim, then to concentrate their fire on the weakest section of the goblin line, hoping to give the riders a breakout route.

It was a plan of retreat and of loss, of salvage and surely not of victory.

"Comes the dawn," Liam remarked, looking to the east, where the red curve of the sun was just beginning to peek above the horizon.

Midalis shared a grim look and a strong handshake with his dear friend, and he led on, slowly down the trail at first, but gaining speed with each loping stride.

In the bell tower of St. Belfour, Abbot Agronguerre breathed a profound sigh of relief when he heard the cries, "Riders to the south," and turned to see the dark shapes moving along the path toward the back corner of the abbey.

"Catchers to the rear corner!" the old abbot cried to Brother Haney, and then he hustled, huffing and puffing, toward the front wall, for he knew that Midalis and his brave men would soon need his assistance.

He heard the cries and shrieks echoing through the forested hillock, heard his own men crying out, predictably, "Goblins!"

Abbot Agronguerre resisted the urge to rush toward the back wall and offer magical support there. Prince Midalis and his riders would simply have to outrun the pursuit!

Agronguerre was inside then, scrambling down the spiral stairs. He met Brother Haney on the lower landing, then they ran through the tunnel that brought them to the parapet along the front wall. Several monks were already there, as they had been ordered, holding gemstones—the few graphite stones within St. Belfour—and peering out, pointing to the thick forest beyond. Agronguerre joined their ranks and produced his own

stones, serpentine and ruby, while Brother Haney did likewise, taking the most potent graphite stone of all the abbey's inventory from his pouch.

Cheers arose inside the abbey courtyard behind them as Midalis and his men swooped past the rear corner, slowing only enough to toss saddlebags up to eager hands.

"Eyes ahead!" Brother Haney scolded another of the front wall contingent, as the errant monk turned to view the scene. "Keep watch on the forest, to the true enemy we know will come forth."

"Goblin!" another monk at the wall yelled, pointing to the thicket across the field and to the right. The young brother lifted his hand and gemstone, as if preparing to loose a stroke of lightning, but Abbot Agronguerre quickly brought his hand to the younger man's arm, bringing it down.

"Let them swoop out in full," the abbot explained, understanding the limitations of their magic and knowing that they had to make use of the stones for emotional as much as physical effect. "When the goblins charge out in force, and before the battle is joined, we hit them quickly and hard. Let us see if they have the stomach for the fight."

The lead riders came around the southeastern corner then, across the front of the abbey, with Prince Midalis and Liam O'Blythe leading the charge.

The Prince slowed enough to share a salute with Abbot Agronguerre and a smile.

And then the goblins came on—a hundred goblins, a thousand goblins—swarming from every shadow.

In a matter of a few seconds, Midalis understood the dire trouble. Goblins rushed from the south and west, ringing the field in deep ranks; and more goblins came behind them, charging down the hillock, blocking the trail and throwing spears at the trailing riders of the Prince's line.

Then came the barrage, *boom, boom, boom!,* of lightning strokes flashing out from the abbey's walls, dropping lines of goblins, and then another flash from Abbot Agronguerre, a line of fire spurting forth from his serpentine-shielded hand, to immolate the largest goblin as it barked orders to its ugly kin. Shrouded in fire, the creature's commands became high-pitched squeals and it ran wildly, flapping its arms. The abbot wasted no time, shifting the flow of flames to engulf the next creature in line.

But for all the sudden shock—the fast-flashing, brutal, and thundering retort—very few goblins went down and stayed down. After the initial moment of terror, in which half the goblin force turned as if to flee, the creatures came to understand the truth—that a dozen well-placed archers could have done as much damage—and quickly tightened their ring.

Another report thundered out from the abbey walls as Midalis pulled his ranks into a tighter defensive formation, *boom, boom, boom!* as Agronguerre sent forth another line of flame, but again to minimal real damage.

And even Midalis noticed that those lightning bolts didn't thunder quite as loudly.

The call came up that the last of his line, with goblins on their tails, had delivered their saddlebags, and the Prince and his men formed a tight wedge and charged into the closing goblin ranks. And from the abbey walls came another volley, this one of arrows and quarrels, and the goblins scattered before the charging horses.

And those goblins behind, trying to catch up, got hit from behind, as Midalis' archers slipped over the back of the hillock, replacing the charging monsters.

"Break to the back!" came the cry, and the Prince swung the wedge around—swords slashing, spears stabbing, hooves trampling—thinking to flee back along the trail.

Or did they even have to flee? Prince Midalis wondered, for if they could destroy the goblin pursuit, opening the way back around the hillock, they could make a stand on the field, slaughtering many; and as long as they didn't allow the goblins to flank them they could retreat if necessary.

Midalis brought his men back around the southeastern corner. Many of the goblins in pursuit, having a wall of horses suddenly turned back against them, skidded to a stop and whirled to retreat.

Right into a wall of arrows.

Cheers rent the air from Midalis' men, the monks with their magic and bows joining in from the abbey walls. The goblin ranks along the eastern wall of St. Belfour quickly thinned.

And for a moment, just a moment, the Prince and his men thought the day was theirs.

A scream from atop the hill showed them the truth: another goblin force had swung around the back of the hill, pressing the archers. Now those men came running down, stumbling and sliding, some crashing headlong into trees or tearing through brush. Before Midalis could react, the crucial high ground was lost. Now he and his horsemen worked furiously to scatter those goblins who remained by the side of the abbey, so that the archers could join them.

More thunderous reports issued from in front, and those were followed by a host of screams and fierce goblin war cries. When Midalis glanced back over his shoulder at the abbey's wall, he was dismayed, for many, many spears and arrows arced over the front wall or flew away into the air, a tremendous barrage.

The Prince turned his force yet again, spearheading the wedge, putting the infantry archers in the second line with a wall of horsemen behind, to fend off the goblins regrouping atop the northern hillock. They could not slip into the forest from this area, for too many enemies had come to the hillock, so around to the front of the abbey they went, hoping for some break in the goblin line.

And when they came around that corner, when they saw all the field before them thick with goblin masses, when they saw a hundred spears and arrows flying against the abbey walls for every one the monks could throw down, the Prince knew the grim truth. He thought of charging the abbey door, of calling for it to open that he and his men could seek refuge within.

But who, then, would break the siege? And would they even hold out through the morning from inside those stone walls?

"Fight on, for all our lives!" he cried. "For the lives of those in St. Belfour and for the memory of those who this morn will fall!"

The magic coming from the abbey showed weaker now, one lightning bolt hitting a goblin squarely in the chest and not even dropping the creature. That fact did not go unnoticed among the enemies, and the goblins, no ragtag band, howled and pressed even farther.

Midalis and his front riders plunged into the goblin line, swords slashing, spears piercing goblin chests. But the goblins swarmed around them in a rush as strong as the tide, filling every channel, every opening. One man was pulled down from his mount, a host of ugly creatures falling over him, slashing and stabbing; another had his horse slashed out from under him and died before he even hit the ground.

The archers in the second rank kept firing their bows, most behind at the pursuit from the hillock; but within moments, they, too, found themselves hard-pressed, with many using their bows as clubs, smashing goblin heads.

On the field, Prince Midalis knew it; on the wall, Abbot Agronguerre, his magical energy expended, knew it. St. Belfour was doomed. The Prince of Honce-the-Bear was doomed. The Vanguard army would soon be shattered and the region would know only blackness.

Another mountain of shadow flowed through the forest, another legion of goblins, the Prince assumed, and he could only wonder in blank amazement at how many had come to destroy his homeland.

Out of the trees came the forms, screaming and howling, a primal, feral cry that sent shivers through the spines of all who heard it, that froze the battle for a long, horrifying moment.

Wearing browns and greens that rendered them practically invisible, the barbarian horde swarmed onto the field. The front line came on fast but stopped almost as one, pivoting, then launching heavy stones from the ends of swinging chains into the closest goblin ranks, opening holes, knocking monsters back into their wicked kin.

Again came that unified war cry, drowning all other sounds, bringing shivers to the goblins and hope to Midalis and his valiant men. And through the ranks of the hammer throwers stormed Andacanavar, his mighty claymore cleaving down goblins three at a swing. Like a gigantic wedge, the hardy Alpinadoran barbarians of Tol Hengor drove on.

"Fight on!" Midalis cried, but this time, hope replaced resignation. Now for the first time, the goblins seemed unnerved. The Prince seized the moment to pull his cavalry back together, to begin the determined march that would get his vulnerable archers to the abbey's front gate.

He signaled to Agronguerre on the wall, and took hope that the wise old man would understand his intent and begin calling to his monks to secure the portal.

With sheer determination, Midalis got there, the horsemen shielding the running archers from monstrous goblin spears, the monks pulling wide the doors and battling those few goblins nearby until the archers could get inside.

The battle threatened to disintegrate into chaos again, except that the barbarians, the great warriors of the north, followed Andacanavar with fanatical bravery, keeping fast their lines of defense as the mighty ranger plowed on. Midalis and his horsemen would have been overwhelmed right there at the wall, goblins coming at them from every angle, but then the ranger broke through, his elven-forged claymore cutting a goblin in half at the waist right as the Prince raised his own sword to strike at the creature.

Before Midalis could begin to thank Andacanavar, he stabbed his sword into the ground before him and gave a howl, lifting his arms above his head and putting his fingertips together, his arms mirroring the barbarians' wedge formation. Then Andacanavar slid the fingers of his right hand down to his left elbow, and the right line of the formation followed the command, turning with practiced efficiency, so that Andacanavar was now the trailing man on the new right flank, and Bruinhelde, the man who had taken the rear position on the initial left flank, was now the spearhead.

Prince Midalis understood the beautiful maneuver, the brilliant pivot, and knew the role that his men must now play. He swung away from the mighty ranger, charging his horse along his ranks, then, when he reached the midpoint, breaking out onto the field, his men flowing behind him, left flank and right.

And by then, the rescued archers had gained the abbey's parapets and their bows began to sing anew, leading the Prince's charge.

From the wall of St. Belfour, Abbot Agronguerre watched with tears welling in his gentle eyes. He had been in Vanguard for three decades and knew well its history—knew of the massacre at Fuldebarrow, where his Church had tried to establish a monastery. He knew of the many skirmishes between the men of Honce-the-Bear and the hardy Alpinadorans, knew the prejudice that lingered on both sides of the border.

But now, apparently, both the men and women of Honce-the-Bear and of Alpinador had found a common enemy too great to be ignored; and if this enemy, these minions of the demon dactyl, could bring these peoples together—could get the Alpinadoran barbarians to fight for the sake of St. Belfour of the Abellican Church!—then perhaps the light had begun to shine through the darkness.

The old abbot could hardly believe it, and the emotions of the moment lent him new strength. He took the graphite from Brother Haney, lifted his hand, and let fly the most powerful lightning stroke of the morning, a searing blast that blew aside a score of goblin spearthrowers, the monsters dying with their weapons still in hand.

"Ring the bells!" the invigorated old abbot cried, and he let fly another thunderous bolt. "To arms! To arms!"

The tide had turned, the appearance of the powerful Alpinadorans lending strength and courage to the besieged men of Honce-the-Bear and shattering the previous discipline of the goblin attackers. As many monsters turned and fled as remained to do battle, and those that did remain caught arrows from above or lightning from the abbot, or they were trampled down by horses and barbarians alike.

Within a matter of minutes, the only goblins that remained alive on the field were on the ground and squirming in agony. Some begged for mercy, but they would find none, neither from Midalis and his men nor from the fierce barbarians.

The day was won, the siege broken, the goblin army scattered and running, and Prince Midalis trotted his mount across the field to meet with Andacanavar and Bruinhelde, each with their respective forces lining up behind them.

"A great debt we owe you this day," the Prince graciously offered.

Andacanavar looked to Bruinhelde, but the stoic chieftain did not reply to the Prince in kind, nor did he offer any hint of where his heart might be. He did glance up at the abbey wall, though, his face stern and set, and Midalis followed that gaze to the reciprocal look of Abbot Agronguerre.

The abbey doors had opened again, and monks were fast exiting, many carrying bandages, some with soul stones in hand. Their line bent to the right, Midalis noted with distress, toward the wounded warriors of Vanguard, and not at all to the left, where lay the wounded Alpinadorans.

The day was not yet won.

CHAPTER

❖ 4 ❖

Harsh Reality

Winter had found the mountain passes west of Honce-the-Bear, with snow falling deep about the elven valley of Andur'-Blough Inninness, strong winds piling it up into towering drifts. That hardly proved a hindrance to Belli'mar Juraviel, though, the nimble elf skipping across the white blanket, leaving barely a trace of his passing. For the Touel'alfar of Corona did not battle the moods of nature, as did the humans. Rather, they adapted their ways to fit the seasons outside their protected valley, and they reveled in each season in turn: a dance of rebirth each spring, of excitement and play in the lazy summer heat, of harvest and preparation in the autumn, and of respite in the winter. To the Touel'alfar, the harshest winter blizzard was a time of snow sculpting and snow-throwing games, or a time to huddle by the fire.

Prepared, always prepared.

This blizzard had been just that type, with stinging, blowing snow; and though it had abated greatly, the snow was still falling when Juraviel left the cloudy cover of the sheltered elven valley.

But, despite the storm, he had to get out, to be alone with his frustrations. Again Lady Dasslerond had refused his request to parent the young child of Elbryan and Jilseponie, the babe the lady had taken from Pony on the field outside Palmaris, when Markwart had overwhelmed the woman and left her near death. In the ensuing months, Lady Dasslerond had kept Juraviel very busy, had sent him running errand after errand; and while he had suspected that she was purposefully keeping him away from the babe, he could not be certain.

Until that very morning, when he had asked her directly, and she had refused him directly.

So Juraviel had run out of the valley, up onto the slopes, to be alone with his thoughts and his anger, to let the quiet snow calm his frustration.

He skittered up one drift, using the piled snow as a ladder to get him to the tip of a rocky overhang, and there, in the wind, he sat for a long, long while, remembering Elbryan and Pony, remembering Tuntun, his dear elven friend who had given her life in the assault on Mount Aida and the demon dactyl.

Gradually, like the storm, his angry energy flowed out, and he was sitting quite comfortably when he saw another form rise out of the low clouds of Andur'Blough Inninness. He looked on curiously for a few moments, thinking that another of the Touel'alfar had decided to come out to enjoy the storm or to see if it had completely abated yet or perhaps to check on Juraviel's well-being. But when the new-come elf turned his way, stared at him from under the cowl of the low-pulled hood, Belli'mar Juraviel recognized those eyes and that face and was surprised—indeed, stunned—to discover that Lady Dasslerond herself had come out to find him.

He started to move down to her, but she motioned for him to stay and scampered up the snowbank at least as easily as he had, taking a seat on the stone beside him.

"You were correct in your guess," she informed him. "Tien-Bryselle returned this morning with information concerning Tempest and Hawkwing."

Juraviel breathed a sigh of sincere relief. Tempest and Hawkwing had been the weapons of Elbryan. The elven sword Tempest had been forged for the ranger's uncle Mather and won by Elbryan in honest duel with the dead man's spirit; and Hawkwing had been crafted by Juraviel's own father specifically for Elbryan the Nightbird. Both weapons had been lost when Elbryan had been captured by Father Abbot Markwart. Juraviel, convinced that they were in St. Precious in Palmaris, had tried to find them.

But then had come the confrontation between Elbryan and Markwart in Chasewind Manor, a battle that the elf could not ignore, and Juraviel had run out of time. Thus had Dasslerond sent another to find the weapons, following a report that they had gone with Elbryan back to Dundalis, his final resting place.

"Bradwarden confirmed their location," she explained, "and took Tien-Bryselle to them."

"He is a fine friend," Juraviel remarked.

Lady Dasslerond nodded. "A fine friend who came through the trials of the demon dactyl, and who came through the responsibilities of calling himself elf-friend."

Juraviel narrowed his eyes, easily catching the not-so-flattering reference to both Elbryan and Jilseponie. Lady Dasslerond had not been pleased to learn that Elbryan had taught Jilseponie the elven sword dance, *bi'nelle dasada,* nor had she been happy with many of Jilseponie's choices during the final days of conflict with Father Abbot Markwart.

"But we are glad to know that the weapons are safe," she quickly added—for his benefit, Juraviel knew, "guarded by the spirits of two rangers. Perhaps they will belong to *yel'delen* one day."

Yel'delen, Juraviel echoed in his mind, so poignantly reminded that Lady

Dasslerond had not even yet named the baby; for in the elvish tongue, *yel'delen* meant simply "the child."

"Jilseponie did not fight the return of the weapons," Juraviel dared to remark.

"She is in Palmaris still, and likely knew nothing of their return to the north," she answered, "nor that we went to find them."

Juraviel looked at her curiously, hardly agreeing with her first claim. If Tempest and Hawkwing left Palmaris with Elbryan's caisson, then they did so on the instructions of Jilseponie. "But she would not have fought the interment of the elven weapons even if she had known," Juraviel insisted, "nor would she argue if we decided to take them back."

Dasslerond shrugged, apparently not prepared to argue the point.

"You underestimate her," Juraviel went on boldly, "as you have from the very first."

"I judged her by her own actions," the lady of Caer'alfar replied firmly. She shook her head and chuckled. "You cloud your memories with friendship, yet you know that your friend will be cold in the ground centuries before your time has passed."

"Am I not to befriend those of like heart?"

"The humans have their place," Dasslerond said somewhat coldly. "To elevate them beyond that is a dangerous mistake, Belli'mar Juraviel. You know that well."

Juraviel looked away, feeling the tears beginning to rim his golden eyes. "And is that why?" he asked, and then he blinked away the tears completely, replacing them with resolve, and looked at her squarely. "Is that why you deny me the child?"

Dasslerond didn't blink, nor did she shrink back an inch. "This child is different," she said. "He will carry the weapons of Nightbird and Mather, the Touel'alfar weapons of a true ranger."

"And a glorious day it will be," Juraviel put in.

"Indeed," she agreed, "even more so than you understand. The child will become the purest of rangers, trained from birth to our ways. He will hold no allegiance to the humans, will be human in appearance only."

Juraviel considered the words and her determined tone very carefully for a long moment. "But is not the true power of the ranger the joining of the best that is human and elven?" he asked, thinking that his beloved Lady Dasslerond might be missing a very important point here.

"So it has been," she replied, "but always I have understood that it is the joining of the elven way with the human physical form and the impatience that is human. This child will have physical strength beyond that of even its father, a strength fostered by the trials we shall place upon him and the health that is Andur'Blough Inninness. And we will foster, as well, the understanding of mortality, the short life which he can expect, and thus, the sense of immediacy and impatience so crucial for warriors of action."

Juraviel looked at her, not quite understanding her reasoning behind this talk—words he almost regarded as nonsense. Understanding the source, though, the lady of Caer'alfar, the leader of his people, Juraviel looked past the words to the hopes and the fears. She had taken the child and had flatly refused to return him to his mother, even now that the darkness of Markwart and Bestesbulzibar had passed. Indeed, it seemed to Juraviel that Lady Dasslerond had *claimed* the child for Andur'Blough Inninness.

And then he understood those hopes of his lady even more clearly. This child, perhaps, so true of bloodline, so strong of limb and of thought, would have the power to heal Andur'Blough Inninness. This child of the ranger might aid Lady Dasslerond in her defense against the spreading rot, the stain the demon dactyl had placed upon the elven valley.

"He will be strong and swift, as was Elbryan," Juraviel remarked, as much to measure the response as to speak the truth.

"More akin to his mother," Lady Dasslerond replied.

Juraviel cocked an eyebrow in surprise that she would offer such a compliment to Jilseponie.

"Jilseponie is strong and swift with the sword, strong in *bi'nelle dasada*, as was her teacher," Dasslerond explained. "And though she was not as strong in the dance as Nightbird, she was the more complete of the parents, powerfully versed in the gemstone magic, as well. The complete human warrior. This child will be all that his mother was and is and more—for he will have the guidance of the Touel'alfar throughout his journey."

Belli'mar Juraviel nodded, though he feared that Lady Dasslerond might be reaching a bit high here in her expectations. The child was but a few months old, after all, and though his bloodlines seemed as pure as those of any human—and Juraviel, who had loved both Elbryan and Pony, understood that more clearly than did Lady Dasslerond!—that was no guarantee of anything positive. Furthermore, Juraviel, apparently unlike Lady Dasslerond, appreciated that bringing up the infant in Andur'Blough Inninness was an experiment, an unknown.

"Jilseponie made mistakes that we cannot tolerate," Lady Dasslerond stated flatly, a sudden and stern reminder to Juraviel of her feelings toward the woman, "as Elbryan, our beloved Nightbird, erred in teaching her *bi'nelle dasada*. And do not doubt that we will continue to watch her from afar."

Juraviel nodded. On that point, at least, he and his lady were in agreement. If Pony started sharing the elven sword dance, became an instructor in the finer points of *bi'nella dasada*, then the Touel'alfar would have to stop her. To Juraviel, that would have meant taking her into their homeland and keeping her there; but he held no illusions that Lady Dasslerond, whose responsibility concerned the very existence of the Touel'alfar, would be so merciful.

"Yet that was Nightbird's error," he replied, "and not Jilseponie's."

"Not yet."

Again, Juraviel nodded, taking well her point. He wasn't sure that he even agreed with his own last statement—that Elbryan's tutoring of Pony was a mistake at all. Juraviel had watched them fighting together, each sword complementing the other to the level of perfection, a weaving of form and of weapons so beautiful that it had brought tears of joy to the elf's eyes.

How could such a work of art be a mistake?

"You trust her," Lady Dasslerond stated.

Juraviel didn't disagree.

"You love her as you love Touel'alfar," she went on.

Juraviel looked at her but said nothing.

"You would have us forgive her and return to her the child."

Juraviel swallowed hard. "She would have made a fine ranger, had she been trained in Andur'Blough Inninness," he dared to remark.

"Indeed," she was quick to reply, "but she was not. Never forget that, my friend. She was not.

"I'll not deny, diminish, or refute your feelings for the woman," Lady Dasslerond went on. "Indeed, your faith in her gives me hope that Night-bird's error will not lead to disaster. However, Jilseponie's role was in bearing the son of Elbryan. Understand that and accept it. He is ours now. Our tool, our weapon. He is our repayment for the sacrifice that we made to help the humans in their struggle with Bestesbulzibar, and our way to minimize the lasting effect of that sacrifice."

Juraviel wanted to argue that the war against the demon dactyl was for the sake of elves as well as the humans, but he held his words.

"And thus, and because of your honest feelings, understand that you are to have no contact with the child," she went on, and Juraviel's heart sank. "He is not Nightbird—we will name him appropriately when he has shown to us the truth of his soul. But Belli'mar Juraviel will learn that truth in time, through the work of others more suited to the task."

Juraviel was not happy at all with the news, but neither was he surprised. Through all these months, he had been complaining, and often, about the lack of interaction with the child, by him or by any other Touel'alfar, and complaining that what interaction there was came more often in the form of testing, and hardly ever the simple act of sharing a touch or a smile. That had bothered Juraviel profoundly, and he had spoken rather sharply to Lady Dasslerond about his fears.

And his words had not been met with sympathy.

So he was not surprised now, not at all.

"You know of the other?" Lady Dasslerond asked him.

"Brynn Dharielle," Juraviel replied, naming the other human currently under Touel'alfar tutelage, a young orphaned girl from To-gai, the western reach of the kingdom of Behren, the land of the greatest human horsemen in all the world.

"You will enjoy her," Lady Dasslerond assured him, "for she is possessed of more spirit than her little frame can contain, a creature of impulse and fire much akin to young Elbryan Wyndon."

Juraviel nodded. He had heard as much concerning Brynn Dharielle. He hadn't yet met the novice ranger, for though Brynn had been in the care of the Touel'alfar for almost a year, and though Andur'Blough Inninness was not a large place, Juraviel's business had been elsewhere—his eyes, his heart, in the paths of Elbryan and Pony, his concern in the fate of the demon dactyl and Markwart and the turn of the human world. Those in the valley who knew of Brynn Dharielle had spoken highly of her talents and her spirit. Dare the Touel'alfar believe they had another Nightbird in training?

"I give you her charge," Lady Dasslerond went on. "You will see to her as you saw to Nightbird."

"But do you not believe that I failed with Nightbird?" Juraviel dared to ask. "For did he not fail in his vow as ranger, in teaching *bi'nelle dasada*?"

Lady Dasslerond laughed aloud—for all of her anger at Elbryan and his sharing of the elven sword dance with Pony, she knew, as all the elves knew, that he had not failed. Not at all. Nightbird had gone to Aida and battled Bestesbulzibar; and when the demon had found a new and more insidious and more dangerous host, Nightbird had given everything to win the day, for the humans and for all the goodly races, Touel'alfar included, of the world.

"You will learn from your mistakes then," Lady Dasslerond replied. "You will do even better with this one."

Now it was Juraviel's turn to chuckle helplessly. Could his lady even begin to appreciate the standard to which she had just set Brynn Dharielle? Would his lady ever see past her immediate anger to the truth that was Elbryan the Nightbird, and the truth that remained in the heart of Jilseponie?

Or was he wrong? he had to wonder and to fear. Was he too blinded by friendship and love to accept the failings of his human companions?

Belli'mar Juraviel blew a long, long sigh.

CHAPTER

❖ 5 ❖

Diplomacy

Constance Pemblebury watched the docks of Palmaris recede into the morning fog. She was glad to be away from the city, away from dead Markwart and his all-too-complicated Church, away from a populace so on the edge of hysteria and desperation, and, most of all, away from Jilseponie. Even thinking of the woman made her wince. Jilseponie. The heroic Pony, the savior of the north, who defeated the demon dactyl in Aida and in the corporeal vessel of Markwart. Jilseponie, who could become abbess of St. Precious with but a word and could cultivate that into something much greater, perhaps even become mother abbess of the entire Abellican Church. Jilseponie, the woman to whom King Danube had offered the city of Palmaris. Baroness, governess. What other title might she choose? What other title might King Danube bestow upon her?

Jilseponie hadn't been at the dock when the *River Palace*, the royal barge, and its fifteen escort warships had left the city. She hadn't shown herself to the royal entourage at all since the final meeting in St. Precious.

Constance was glad of that.

In truth, Constance admired the woman—her fire, her efforts—and she could not deny the value of Jilseponie's actions in the war and in the even more dangerous aftermath of the war. In truth, Constance recognized that, had the situation been different, she and Jilseponie might have become the best of friends. But that was a private truth Constance would not admit to anyone but herself.

For the situation *was* different; Constance had not missed the looks King Danube had bestowed on Jilseponie.

Beautiful and heroic Jilseponie. A woman who had, in the eyes of the majority of the kingdom, raised herself above her commoner birth to a position of nobility. Nobility of deed and not blood.

And how King Danube had stared at her, fawned over her with a sparkle in his tired eyes that Constance had not seen in years. He would make no move toward Jilseponie yet—not with her husband, Elbryan, barely cold in

64

the ground. But Constance didn't doubt the length of Danube's memory or the magnetism of his charms. Not at all.

When she looked at Jilseponie, then, was she seeing the next Vivian? The next queen of Honce-the-Bear?

The thought made her clench her jaw and chew her lower lip. Yes, she admired the woman, even liked the woman, and, yes, Constance had understood for some time now that while she might share Danube's bed, he would not take her as his wife. But, still, to have the door—through which she understood she could never walk—so obviously closed before her, offended her. She was in her mid-thirties now, a decade older than Jilseponie, and she was starting to show her age, with wrinkles about her eyes— eyes losing the luster of youth—and a body that was just beginning to lose the war against gravity. Measured against Jilseponie's smooth skin and sparkling blue eyes, her strong muscles and the spring in her youthful stride, Constance understood that she would lose.

Thus she had taken Danube the previous night, and the night before that, seducing him shamelessly, even coaxing him with drink so that he would not ignore her obvious advances. Thus she would take him again this night on the ship, and every night all the way to Ursal, and every night after that.

Until she became great with his child.

Constance hated her actions, her deception, for Danube believed that she was taking the herbs—as per the arrangement with every courtesan— that would prevent pregnancy. She hated more the thought of serving Queen Jilseponie. How many years had she worked by Danube's side, easing him through crises, serving as his best adviser? How many years had she stood by him against all his enemies, and quietly reinforced his better qualities to his allies? To Constance's thinking, she had been serving as queen ever since Vivian had died, in every capacity except that of the King's constant bed partner and the mother of his children.

Now she meant to remedy that situation. He wouldn't marry her, likely, but he would sire her children; and in the absence of another wife, he might grant one of them the status of heir to the throne. Yes, she could get that concession from him. His other bastard children—and there were two at least—were grown now and had never been trained for the crown, had never been as sons to Danube; and he held little love for his lone sibling, his brother, Midalis, a man he had not seen in years. Constance believed with all her heart that he would come to love their child and would train the child, boy or girl, as he had not trained the others and could not train Midalis, to serve as heir to the throne of Honce-the-Bear.

Constance recognized the unlikelihood that she would ever be queen, but she realized that she would be more than pleased with the title of queen mother.

Still, she wished it could be different, wished that she could inspire an honest love in Danube. She had hoped that the situation in Palmaris, the greatest crisis in Danube's reign, would provide opportunity for her to raise her station through deed; and indeed, by Danube's own accounting, she had performed admirably over the weeks of trial. But how her efforts paled against those of Jilseponie! As her fading beauty paled beside that woman's luster!

"It is, perhaps, time to relax," came the voice of Abbot Je'howith behind her, startling her. When she glanced at him and followed his gaze to the taffrail, she understood the source of his comment, for she was unintentionally clutching the railing so tightly that all blood had gone from her knuckles.

"The trials are behind us," Constance agreed, letting go of the rail and self-consciously hiding her hands within the folds of her thick woolen cloak.

"Most, perhaps," said old Je'howith, his expression pensive. "For the Crown and court, at least, though I fear that I've many trials ahead of me." The old man walked up beside Constance, gripping the rail and staring out, as she had been, at the receding shapes of Palmaris' dock.

Constance eyed him curiously; never had she and Je'howith been on good terms, though neither had they been openly hostile toward each other, as was the case between the elderly abbot and Duke Kalas.

"They are so young and idealistic," the abbot continued, and he glanced over at Constance. "The young Abellican brothers, I mean, who take the downfall of Father Abbot Markwart as a signal that it is their time to step to the forefront of the Abellican Church. They believe they have seen the truth; though the truth, you and I both understand in our wisdom of experience, is never as simple as that. They will overreach, and pity the Church if we older abbots and masters cannot tame the fire of youth."

Constance's expression turned even more curious and skeptical; she wondered why old Je'howith was confiding in her, and she trusted him not at all. Was he, perhaps, using her ear to get his seemingly sincere feelings whispered to King Danube? Was he seeking an unspoken alliance with the King by using the mouth of an unwitting third party? Though, of course, Constance Pemblebury was hardly that!

"The young brothers now leading St. Precious are nearly my own age," she reminded Je'howith; and it was true that Braumin, Marlboro Viscenti, and Francis were all near their thirtieth birthdays.

"But how many of their years have been spent within the sheltered confines of an outland abbey?" Je'howith asked. "The other houses of the Abellican Church are not as St. Honce, you see. Even great St.-Mere-Abelle, with its seven hundred brothers, is a secluded place, a place of few viewpoints and little understanding of anything that is not Abellican. We of St. Honce have the advantage of the city of Ursal about us, and of the wisdom of the King and his noble court."

Constance's expression betrayed her skepticism, particularly given the recent battles between Church and Crown. If Je'howith meant to call her on that point, though, he did not do so immediately and lost the opportunity as another voice piped in.

"Farewell, Palmaris," King Danube said with a chuckle, "and good luck to you, my friend Duke Kalas! For your task, I know, is the most wretched by far!" He walked up to Constance and Je'howith, his smile wide and sincere, for it was no secret among them that King Danube was glad indeed to be sailing for home.

"My King," said Je'howith, dipping a bow.

"Ah, so you remember?" Danube replied slyly. Behind the old abbot, Constance smiled widely, barely suppressing a laugh.

"Never did I forget," the abbot insisted seriously.

Danube looked at him doubtfully.

"Can you doubt the influence of the Father Abbot?" Je'howith asked, and Constance did not miss the fact that a bit of the cocksureness seemed to dissipate from King Danube's serene face.

"Will the new father abbot prove so influential, I wonder?" Danube retorted, his voice thick with implication. He narrowed his eyes as he spoke, and Constance understood him to be signaling the influential abbot of St. Honce in no uncertain terms that he had tolerated about all that he would from the troublesome Abellican Church.

"A gentler man, whomever it might prove to be," Abbot Je'howith replied calmly. "And fear not for Duke Kalas, my King. The Duke of Wester-Honce, the Baron of Palmaris, will find the brothers of St. Precious accommodating."

"Somehow I doubt that," said Danube.

"At the least, they will come to understand that they are not enemies but allies in the war to reclaim the souls of Palmaris," Je'howith went on.

"For Church or for Crown?" Constance asked.

Je'howith glanced back at her, and, surprisingly, he appeared wounded by her attitude. What was he about? she wondered. Did he seek alliance with her, and, if so, to what advantage for her?

"I must go and see about my duties, my King," Je'howith quickly said. "I must begin the letters to summon the College of Abbots." He bowed again and, with no objections forthcoming, hustled away.

Danube watched him go, shaking his head. "Never am I quite certain where that one stands," he remarked to Constance, moving close beside her at the taffrail, "for Church or for Crown."

"For Je'howith, more likely," said Constance. "And with his mentor, Markwart, dead, and the Church turned hostile to his old ways, that path, it would seem, now lies with the Crown."

Danube stared at her, nodding, admiring. "You always see things so clearly," he complimented, and he draped his arm about her shoulder. "Ah, my Constance, whatever would I do without you?"

The woman nudged closer, liking the support from the strong man. She knew the rules, knew that by those rules she was not fit to be queen. She trusted that Danube cared for her deeply, though, and while it was friendship more than love, she could be satisfied with that.

Almost satisfied, she reminded herself, and soon after, she led the King to his stateroom belowdeck.

Prince Midalis watched the hefty Abbot Agronguerre come bounding out of the gates, huffing and puffing and wiping the sweat from his brow with a dirty kerchief. The man shook his head repeatedly, muttering prayers. He brought his right hand up before his face, then swept it down to the left and back up, then down to the right and out, the sign of the evergreen, an old, though now seldom used, Church gesture.

Glancing around at the carnage on the field, the Prince understood. Many goblins were down, most dead and some squirming and crying. And many men had fallen as well, the Prince's brave soldiers, most to Midalis' right, and some of the Alpinadoran barbarians, over on the field to the left. Those monks who had come out before the Abbot, had gone to the right almost exclusively, moving to tend their own countrymen.

Abbot Agronguerre surveyed the situation briefly, then looked at Midalis, who caught his attention with a quick wave of his hand. The abbot nodded and rushed over.

"We have allies," Prince Midalis remarked gravely, "wounded allies."

"And will they accept our soul stones?" the abbot asked in all seriousness. "Or will they see our magic as some demonic power to be avoided?"

"Do you believe—" the Prince started incredulously.

Agronguerre stopped him with a shrug. "I do not know," he admitted, "nor do the younger brothers, which is why they instinctively went to the aid of the Vanguardsmen."

"Bring some, and quickly," the Prince instructed, then he turned his mount and started at a swift trot to the left toward the barbarian line. The bulk of the Alpinadorans were on the edge of the field now, and many had gone into the shadows beneath the boughs in pursuit of the fleeing goblins. Several others had been left behind on the open field, wounded.

"Where is Andacanavar?" the Prince called out, then, trying to remember his bedongadongadonga, he translated. "*Tiuk nee* Andacanavar?"

A couple of whistles were relayed along the line, and the giant ranger appeared from the brush, mighty Bruinhelde at his side. The pair spotted Midalis at once and strode over quickly.

"Our debt to you this day is great," Midalis said, sliding down from his horse and landing right into a respectful bow. "We would have been lost."

"Such debts do not exist between friends," Andacanavar replied, and Midalis did not miss the fact that the man glanced to the side, and somewhat unsurely, at Bruinhelde as he spoke.

"We did not know if you would come," Midalis admitted.

"Did we not share drink in the mead hall?" Bruinhelde asked, as if that alone should explain everything and should have given Midalis confidence that the barbarians would indeed appear.

The Prince, taking the cue, nodded and bowed again. "I feared that perhaps you were delayed by yet another goblin force," he answered, "or that our agreement on this morning's tactics had not been clear."

Bruinhelde laughed. "No agreement," he started to say, somewhat sharply.

"We could not have hoped to sort through coherent plans," Andacanavar cut in; and Midalis understood and appreciated the fact that the ranger was trying to keep things calm between the leaders. "We know little of your fighting tactics, as you know little of ours. Better that we watch you take the field, then find where we best fit in."

Midalis looked around the field, taking note of the scores of goblin dead, and he smiled and nodded.

He noted, too, that Abbot Agronguerre and several brothers were fast approaching, the abbot looking somewhat tentative.

"You have wounded," the Prince said to Bruinhelde. "My friends are skilled in the healing arts."

Bruinhelde, his expression unyielding, glanced over at Andacanavar; and the ranger moved past Midalis, sweeping the Prince and Bruinhelde into his wake, heading quickly for the nearest fallen Alpinadorans.

"Bandages alone," the worldly ranger said quietly to Abbot Agronguerre. The two men stared at each other for a long moment, and then the abbot nodded. Agronguerre turned and motioned to his brethren, assigning each a fallen Alpinadoran, and then moved for the most grievously wounded man, who already had a couple of Alpinadoran women working hard to stem the flow of his lifeblood.

Andacanavar, Midalis, and Bruinhelde met him there, the Prince bending low beside the abbot.

"They are leery of magic," he whispered to his monk friend. "Better that we use conventional dressings."

"So said the large one," Abbot Agronguerre replied, indicating Andacanavar. He ended his sentence with a grunt as he pulled tight the bandage crossing the man's chest, shoulder to rib cage, trying hard to stop the crimson flow. "For the others, perhaps, but this one will not live the hour without the use of the soul stone, and may not live even if I employ one."

Both Vanguardsmen looked up then to see Andacanavar and Bruinhelde looking down at them, the ranger seeming somewhat unsure but Bruinhelde with a determined stare upon his face.

"The bandage will not stem the blood," Abbot Agronguerre remarked calmly, and he reached into his belt pouch and produced the gray soul stone, the hematite, and held it up for the two Alpinadorans to see. "But I have magic that—"

"No!" Bruinhelde interrupted firmly.

"He will die without—"

"No," the barbarian leader said again, and his look grew ever more dangerous—so much so that Midalis grabbed Agronguerre by the wrist and gently pushed his hand down. The abbot looked to his Prince, dumfounded, and Midalis merely shook his head slowly.

"He will die," Agronguerre insisted to Midalis.

"Warriors die," was all that Bruinhelde replied; and he walked away, but not before bringing over two of his other warriors and issuing instructions to them in the Alpinadoran tongue.

Midalis understood enough of the words to know that Bruinhelde would not bend on this matter, for he told his two warriors to stop Agronguerre, by whatever means, if the monk tried to use the devil magic on their fallen comrade. The Prince fixed Agronguerre with a solid look then, and, though it pained Midalis as much as it pained Agronguerre to let a man die in this manner, he shook his head again slowly and deliberately.

The abbot pulled away, glanced once at the two imposing barbarian guards, then pocketed the gemstone and went back to work with conventional means upon the fallen warrior.

The man was dead within a few minutes.

Abbot Agronguerre wiped his bloody hands, then rubbed them across his cheek, brushing away his tears, unintentionally leaving light bloody smears on his face. He rose in a huff and stormed away, to the next brother in line working upon a wounded Alpinadoran, and then the next. Midalis and Andacanavar, and the sentries, followed him all the way.

Without a word to his unwelcome entourage and growling with every step, Abbot Agronguerre stalked across the field back toward the fallen Vanguardsmen, pulling out his soul stone as he went, showing it, as an act of defiance, to the Alpinadoran guards.

The barbarian warriors bristled, and Prince Midalis worried that his friend's anger might be starting even more trouble this dark morning; but Andacanavar dismissed the two others with a wave of his hand, then motioned for Midalis to wait with him.

"The monk errs," the ranger remarked quietly.

"It does not set well with Abbot Agronguerre to watch a man die," Prince Midalis replied, a harsh edge to his voice, "especially when he believes that he might have saved that man's life."

"At the expense of his soul?" Andacanavar asked in all seriousness.

Midalis blinked and backed off a step, surprised by the stark question. He studied the ranger for a long while, trying to get a measure of the man. "Do you truly believe that?" he asked.

Andacanavar shrugged his huge shoulders, his expression vague. "I have lived for many years," he began. "I have seen much that I would not

have believed possible. Monsters, magic, and, yes, the demon dactyl. I have learned of several religions, your Abellican one included, and I know well the premise of the Abellican Church that the gemstones are the gifts of their god."

"But your people do not view them that way," Midalis reasoned.

Andacanavar chuckled, showing the Prince that his words were a bit of an understatement. "My people do not believe in magic," he said. "Those practices that transcend the bonds of the elements—the magic of Abellicans and of elves, of demons and of yatol priests—are all the same to us, all wrought in the mystical world of illusion and deceit."

"And how does worldly Andacanavar view the use of such gemstones?" Prince Midalis dared to ask.

"I was raised outside of Alpinador," the man answered. "I understand the differences between the various forms of magic."

"And yet you let the man die," the Prince remarked, his words an accusation though his tone surely was not.

"Had your Abbot Agronguerre tried to use the soul stone upon fallen Temorstaad, Bruinhelde and his warriors would have stopped him, and violently, do not doubt," the ranger explained. "They are a simple folk, a people of honor and resolute principles. They do not fear death, but they do fear the realm of the mystical. To them, it was a choice of Temorstaad's body against the price of his soul, and to them, that is not so difficult a choice."

Prince Midalis shook his head and sighed, showing that he was not impressed.

"Understand that this alliance is a tentative one yet," Andacanavar warned him. "Your fears that Bruinhelde and his people would not come to the field this day were justified—for, indeed, had the majority of his warriors been given the choice, they would have turned north for their homes, trying to beat the onset of the winter winds. But Bruinhelde is a wise leader, a man looking past the immediate comforts and to the future welfare of his people. He desires this alliance, though he'll hardly admit it openly. Yet if you or your Abellican companions try to force your ways upon us, if you insist upon foisting the realm of the mystical upon Bruinhelde's warriors— even if you believe you are doing so for the good of those warriors—then know that the goblins will become the least of your troubles."

"It pained me to watch a man die," Midalis replied, "a man who could have been saved."

Andacanavar nodded, not disagreeing.

"And it pained Abbot Agronguerre," Midalis went on. "He is a good and gentle man, who battles suffering."

"But does he fear suffering?"

Midalis shook his head.

"And does he fear death?"

Midalis snorted incredulously. "If he does, then his title of abbot of the Abellican Church is misplaced, I would say."

"Neither Bruinhelde nor any of his warriors fear death," Andacanavar explained, "as long as they die honorably, in battle."

Prince Midalis considered the words for a long while, even glanced back over his shoulder to the fallen Temorstaad. The Alpinadoran women were working on him now, taking his valuables and wrapping him in a shroud. Midalis wasn't thrilled with Andacanavar's explanation or the reality of the situation, but he knew that he had to accept it. This alliance with the Alpinadoran barbarians wasn't going to be easy, he recognized. Their customs and those of the Vanguardsmen were too disparate. Midalis' gaze drifted about the field to the slaughtered, hacked goblins, to those Alpinadoran women walking among the goblin bodies, mercilessly slashing any that moved, even sticking knives into a few that did not move, just to be sure. A shudder coursed down the Prince's spine. Not an easy alliance but a necessary one, he realized. He certainly didn't want Bruinhelde and his bunch as enemies!

"And you brought your womenfolk along for battle," Andacanavar remarked, noting that many women were also among Midalis' ranks. "Never would Bruinhelde accept women as warriors. Their tasks are to comfort the warriors, to tend the wounded, and to kill the fallen enemies."

Prince Midalis couldn't hide the grin finding its way onto his face. "And does Andacanavar believe this as well?" he asked slyly, for, while the ranger had made another good point concerning the differences between the two peoples, he had pointedly spoken for Bruinhelde and not for Andacanavar.

"I was raised among the Touel'alfar, and had more than one of the diminutive creatures—females and males alike—put me to the ground," the ranger replied, and he returned the smile. "I speak for Bruinhelde and his followers because I understand them. Whether I agree with them or not, whether you agree with them or not, is not important, because they are as they are, and you'll not change that. Nor will your Abellican companions, and woe to them if they try."

Midalis nodded, and was glad for these few moments alone with the insightful ranger. He knew well the story of Fuldebarrow, where an Abellican church, established to convert Alpinadorans to the faith, had been burned to the ground and all of the missionary brothers slaughtered.

"It might be that I can get them to look past your faults—and that you can get your friends to look past theirs—long enough for the two sides to see the common ground instead of the differences," Andacanavar said. Then he patted Midalis on the shoulder and headed back for the Alpinadoran lines.

Midalis watched him for a moment, further digesting the words—wise words, he understood. Then he turned to find Abbot Agronguerre hard at work over one of the fallen archers, and he went to speak with the man, to smooth the hard feelings from the morning's disagreements, to remind the abbot that he and his brethren would still be besieged within the abbey— and that Midalis and his followers would be trapped in there as well, if they had been lucky this morning—had not Bruinhelde and his proud warriors come to their aid.

Yes, it would be a difficult alliance, but the ranger's observations gave Prince Midalis hope that Vanguard and Alpinador might use this time of war to begin a lasting understanding.

"Common ground," he whispered, reminding himself.

"I trust that your day was enjoyable," Abbot Je'howith remarked to Constance Pemblebury when he found the woman again standing alone at the taffrail, gazing wistfully at the waters of the great Masur Delaval.

Constance turned a sour look upon him, not appreciating his off-color attempt at humor.

"So do tell me," the abbot pressed, "did King Danube remember your name?"

Constance stared at him hard.

"In his moments of passion, I mean," the surprising old abbot continued. "Did he call out 'Constance'?"

"Or 'Jilseponie'?" the woman finished sarcastically and bluntly, wanting Je'howith to understand in no uncertain terms that he was not catching her by surprise.

"Ah, yes, Jilseponie," Je'howith said, rolling his eyes and sighing in a mock gesture of swooning. "Heroine of the north. Would any title do justice to her actions? Baroness? Duchess? Abbess?"

Constance gave him a skeptical look and stared back out at the waters.

"Mother abbess?" the old man continued. "Or queen, perhaps? Yes, there would be a title befitting that one!"

Je'howith's wrinkled face erupted in a wide grin when Constance snapped a glare over him. "Have I hit a nerve?" he asked.

Constance didn't blink.

"You saw the way King Danube looked at her," Je'howith continued. "You know as well as I that Jilseponie could find her way to his bed, and to the throne beside his own in Ursal, if she pursued such a course."

"She would not even accept the barony of Palmaris," Constance reminded him, but her words sounded feeble even in her own ears.

Now it was Je'howith's turn to stare skeptically.

"She grieves for the loss of Nightbird, a wound that may never heal," Constance said.

"Not completely, perhaps," Je'howith agreed, "but enough so that she will move on with her life. Where will she choose to go? I wonder. There is no road she cannot walk. To the Wilderlands, to St.-Mere-Abelle, to Ursal.

Who in all the world would refuse Jilseponie?"

Constance looked back at the water, and she felt Je'howith's gaze studying her, measuring her.

"I know what you desire," the old abbot said.

"Do you speak your words to wound me?" Constance asked.

"Am I your enemy or perhaps your ally?"

Constance started to laugh. She knew the truth, all of it, and understood that old Je'howith was taking great amusement from this posturing because he figured that he could win in any event. If Danube married Constance, or at least sired her children and put them in line for the throne, then Je'howith would be there, ever attentive. That did not make him an ally, though, Constance realized, for Je'howith's greatest concern was to keep Jilseponie out of his Church, away from the coveted position of mother abbess; and what better manner for doing that than to have her marry the King?

"Jilseponie intrigued Danube," she admitted, "as her beauty and strength have intrigued every man who has gazed upon her, I would guess." She turned and fixed the old abbot with a cold and determined stare.

"Beautiful indeed," Je'howith remarked.

"But she is a long way from Ursal, do not doubt," Constance went on, "a long way, down a road more perilous than you can imagine."

Old Je'howith returned her stare for a long moment, then nodded and bowed slightly, and walked away.

Constance watched him go, replaying his words, trying to find his intent. Obviously, the wretch did not want her to fall under Jilseponie's charm and ally with the woman. Je'howith was trying to sow the seeds of enmity against Jilseponie, and she had readily fallen into his plan.

That bothered Constance Pemblebury profoundly as she stood there at the taffrail, staring at the dark water. She had liked Jilseponie when first she had learned of the woman's adventures, had admired her and had cheered her in her efforts against Markwart's foul Church. In Constance's eyes, Jilseponie had been an ally—unwitting, perhaps, but an ally nonetheless— of the Crown, of her beloved King Danube. But now things had changed. Nightbird was dead, and Danube was smitten. Jilseponie had gone from ally to rival. Constance didn't like that fact, but neither could she deny it. Whatever her feelings for Jilseponie Wyndon, the woman had become a danger to her plans for herself and, more important, for her children.

Constance didn't like herself very much at that moment, wasn't proud of the thoughts she was harboring.

But neither could she dismiss them.

CHAPTER

❖ 6 ❖

Season's Turn

Abbot Braumin walked through the great gates of Chasewind Manor humbly, his brown hood pulled low to protect him from the light rain, his arms crossed over his chest, hands buried in the folds of his sleeves. He didn't glance up at the imposing row of Allheart knights lining both sides of the walk, with their exquisite armor, so polished that it gleamed even on this gray day, and their huge poleaxes angled out before them.

He understood the meaning of it all, that Duke Targon Bree Kalas had offered to meet him on the Duke's terms and in the presence of his power. The battle between the two was just beginning, for the city hadn't really settled down after the fall of Markwart until after King Danube had departed. Then winter weather had minimized the duties of both Church and Crown. Now, the King was back in Ursal and most of the brethren from St.-Mere-Abelle had returned, or soon would, to that distant abbey. For the first time in more than a year—indeed, for the first time since the coming of the demon dactyl and its monstrous minions—the common folk of Palmaris were settling back into their normal routines.

He was let in immediately, but then he spent more than an hour in the antechamber of Kalas' office, waiting, waiting while it was reported to him several times that Kalas was attending to more pressing matters.

Abbot Braumin recited his prayers quietly, praying mostly for the patience he would need to get through these trying times. He wished again that Jilseponie had agreed to accompany him—Kalas would never have kept her waiting!—but she would hear none of it, claiming that her days of meetings and political intrigue had reached their end.

Finally, the attendant came out and called for the abbot to follow him. Braumin noted immediately upon entering Kalas' office that several other men stood about—bureaucrats, mostly—shuffling papers and talking in whispered, urgent tones as if their business were of the utmost importance.

Duke Kalas, Baron of Palmaris, sat at his desk, hunched over a parchment, quill in hand.

"Abbot Braumin Herde of St. Precious," the attendant announced.

Kalas didn't even look up. "It has come to my attention that you have put out a call for craftsmen, masons, and carpenters," he remarked.

"I have," Braumin agreed.

"To what end?"

"To whatever end I desire, I suppose," the abbot replied—and that brought Kalas' eyes up, and halted every other conversation in the room.

Kalas stared hard at him for a long and uncomfortable moment. "Indeed," he said at length, "and might those desires entail the expansion of St. Precious Abbey, as I have been told?"

"Perhaps."

"Then save time," Kalas said sternly, "both for yourself and for the craftsmen. There will be no such expansion."

Now it was Braumin's turn to put on a steely expression. "The land about the abbey is Church owned."

"And no structures may be built within the city walls, Church or otherwise, without the express consent of its baron," Kalas reminded him. He looked to one of the bureaucrats at the side of the room, and the mousy man rushed over, presenting Abbot Braumin with a parchment, signed and sealed by Baron Rochefort Bildeborough and by Abbot Dobrinion Calislas, that seemed to back up Kalas' claims.

"This refers to structures built by 'common men,'" Braumin noted, pointing out the phrasing.

Kalas shrugged, not disagreeing.

"This text was written to prevent the influx of Behrenese," Braumin reasoned, "to prevent every open space within the city walls from becoming even more crowded. Common men, which includes neither the Church nor the nobility."

"That is one way to interpret it," Kalas replied. "But not the way I choose."

Abbot Braumin tossed the parchment to the desk. "You obscure meanings and pervert intentions, then," he said. "This parchment is irrelevant to any construction upon St. Precious Abbey, upon lands owned by the Abellican Church."

"No, my good Abbot," Kalas said, rising up ominously and matching the monk's unblinking stare with one of equal determination. "It is perfectly relevant. It is the written law, endorsed by your own beloved former abbot, which I can use to arrest any who work upon your abbey, the written law I can use to confiscate tools and materials."

"You risk angering the populace."

"As do you, good Abbot," Kalas snapped back. "You offer work to craftsmen who already have much work to do in the aftermath of the war.

They do not need your work at this time, Abbot Braumin, but they do need their tools. Who will they come to hate? I wonder. The lawful baron, acting according to law, or the presumptuous new abbot of St. Precious?"

Braumin started to answer, but stuttered repeatedly, having no appropriate reply. He understood the bluff—Kalas would be starting a battle for the hearts of the Palmaris citizenry that could go either way. But was Braumin ready to join such a battle? He knew the fights he would soon face within his own Church; would he be able to withstand those inevitable challenges if the people of Palmaris turned against him?

A smile found its way onto Braumin's face, an admission that, for the time being at least, Kalas had outmaneuvered him. He chuckled and nodded, then turned and walked briskly from the room and out of the mansion, this time leaving his hood back despite the rain. The Allheart knights remained in position along the walk to the gates, and the nearest soldier moved over and pulled them wide for the abbot's exit.

"Your workers did an excellent job in repairing them," he remarked loudly, noting the gates, "after Jilseponie so easily threw them aside, I mean, as she threw aside your brethren who tried to stand before her."

He heard the bristling behind him as he walked out and took some comfort, at least, in that minor victory.

He smelled it, so thick in the air that he could almost taste the sweet liquid on his feline tongue. The young girl had hurt her arm, scratching it on a branch, and now she was coming his way, calling for her mother, holding the arm up, the line of red, sweet red, visible to the weretiger.

De'Unnero turned away and closed his eyes, telling himself that he could not do this thing, that he could not leap out and tear her throat. He had killed only once throughout the harsh winter, an old lecherous drunk who had not been missed by the folk of the town of Penthistle.

The scent caught up to him, and the tiger's head shifted back toward the approaching girl.

She would be missed, De'Unnero reminded himself, trying to make a logical argument to go along with his moral judgment. These people, who had taken him in during the early days of winter, after he had devoured the powrie and run away from the fields west of Palmaris, had accepted him with open arms, glad to pass an Abellican brother from house to house. He had offered to work for his food, but never had the folk of Penthistle given him any truly difficult jobs, and always had they given him all that he could eat, and more.

Thus, De'Unnero had run off into the forest whenever the tiger urges had called to him, too great to be withstood. He had feasted many times on deer, even on squirrel and rabbit, but he had killed a person only that one time.

But now the winter had passed. Now it was spring and with the turn of the season, the folk were again active outside their homes. De'Unnero had come out in search of conventional prey, hopefully a deer, but he had found this child instead, far from her home. As soon as he had spotted her, he had managed to turn away, thinking to run far, far into the forest, but then she had cut her arm, then that too-sweet scent had drifted to his nostrils.

Hardly even aware of it, he gave a low growl. The girl tensed.

De'Unnero tried to turn away, but now he could smell her fear, mingling with that sweet, sweet blood. He started forward; the girl heard the rustle and broke into a run.

One leap and he would have her. One great spring would put him over her, would flatten her to the ground at his feet, would lay bare that beautiful little neck.

One leap . . .

The weretiger held his place, conscience battling instinct.

The girl screamed for her mother and continued to run.

De'Unnero turned away, padding into the darker thicket. The hunger was gone now, for the girl, even for a deer, and so the creature settled down and willed himself through the change, bones popping, torso and limbs crackling and twisting.

It hurt—how it hurt!—but the monk pressed on, forcing out the tiger, fighting the pain and the killing instinct resolutely until a profound blackness overtook him.

He awoke sometime later, shivering and naked on the damp ground, the cold night wind blowing chill against his flesh. He got his bearings quickly and found his brown robes, then donned them and headed for Penthistle.

As chance would have it, the first person he encountered within the small cluster of farmhouses was the same little girl he had seen out in the forest, her arm now wrapped in a bandage.

"Ah, but there ye are," said her mother, a handsome woman of about forty winters. "We were needin' ye, Brother Simple. Me girl here lost her fight with a tree!"

De'Unnero took the girl's hand and gently lifted her arm up for inspection. "You cleaned the wound well?" he asked.

The woman nodded.

The monk lowered the girl's arm, let go, and patted her on the head. "You did well," he told the mother.

The monk headed for the house now serving as his home. He stopped just a few steps away, though, and glanced back at the little girl. He could have killed her, and, oh, so easily. And how he had wanted to! How he had wanted to feast upon her tender flesh.

And yet, he had not. The significance of that hit De'Unnero at that moment, as he came to understand the triumph he had found that day. Fear had forced him out of Palmaris after the fight in Chasewind Manor, after he had been thrown out the window by Nightbird.

It was not fear of Nightbird or of the King or of the reprisals from the victorious enemies of Markwart, the monk realized. No, it was fear of himself, of this demanding inner urge. Once he had been among the most celebrated masters of St.-Mere-Abelle, the close adviser of the Father Abbot, the abbot of St. Precious, and then the Bishop of Palmaris. Once he had been the instructor of the brothers justice and had been touted as the greatest warrior ever to walk through the gates of St.-Mere-Abelle, the epitome of the fighting tradition of the Abellican Order. In those days, Marcalo De'Unnero had relied heavily on the use of a single gemstone, the tiger's paw; for with it, he could transform a limb, or perhaps two, into those of a great cat, a weapon as great as any sword. During Markwart's rise to unspeakable power, the Father Abbot had shown De'Unnero an even stronger level of the stone's transformational magic, and with that increase of intensity, the young master had been able to transform himself totally into the great cat, an unprecedented accomplishment.

But then something unexpected had happened. De'Unnero had lost the gemstone, or rather it seemed to him as if he had merged with the gemstone, so that now he could transform himself into a tiger without it—and often against his will.

That was really why he had run away from Palmaris. He was afraid of himself, of the murderous creature he had become.

It had been a wretched existence for the man who had once achieved such a level of power, despite the hospitality of the folk of Penthistle. Marcalo De'Unnero had feared that he would be forever doomed to travel through the borderlands of civilization, running from town to town whenever the killing urge overpowered him. He pictured himself in the not too distant future, fleeing across a field, a host of hunters from half the kingdom in close pursuit.

But now . . .

The ultimate temptation had been right before him—the smell of fear and blood, the easy, tender kill—and he had battled that temptation, had overcome it. Was it possible that De'Unnero had gained control over this disease?

If he could control it, then he could return to Palmaris, to his Church.

De'Unnero pushed the absurd notion away. He had murdered Baron Bildeborough, after all, and his escorts. He had wounded Elbryan, which had sent the man, weakened, into battle with Markwart, the wound that, as much as the Father Abbot's efforts, had truly killed the man. If he went back to Palmaris, what trial might await him?

"What trial indeed?" De'Unnero asked aloud, and when he considered it, his lips curled up into the first real smile he had known in more than half a year. There was no evidence implicating him in Bildeborough's murder, nothing more than the speculation of his enemies. And how could he be held accountable for anything that had happened at Chasewind Manor?

Was he not merely performing his duty of protecting his Father Abbot? Were not Elbryan and Jilseponie, at that time, considered criminals by both Church and Crown?

"What's that, Father?" the girl's mother asked, not really catching his words.

De'Unnero shook himself out of his thoughts. "Nothing," he replied. "I was only thinking that perhaps it was time for me to return to my abbey."

"Ah, but we'd miss ye," the woman remarked.

De'Unnero merely nodded, hardly hearing her, too lost in the intriguing possibilities his victory over the weretiger urge had presented to him this day.

"The *Saudi Jacintha* will take me," Brother Dellman reported to Abbot Braumin, the younger monk entering the abbot's office at St. Precious to find Braumin talking excitedly with Brother Viscenti. "Captain Al'u'met plans to sail within the week, and he was excited to be of service, so he said."

"And you discussed the price?" the new abbot asked.

"Captain Al'u'met assured me that the price has been paid in full by the new brothers of St. Precious, that our actions against the evil that was Markwart and our defense of the Behrenese of the docks more than suffice."

"A wonderful man," Brother Viscenti remarked.

"You understand your duties?" Braumin asked.

Dellman nodded. "I am to observe first, to try to get a feeling for the intentions of Abbot Agronguerre," he replied, "and then, on my instinct and judgment, I may inform the man that you and others plan to nominate him at the College of Abbots that will be convened in Calember."

"You are a messenger first, bringing word of the College and of the events in Palmaris," said Braumin.

"Likely, he has already heard," Viscenti put in, shaking his head. "Who in all the world could not have heard?"

Abbot Braumin smiled and let the point go to his excitable friend, though in truth he doubted that anyone in Vanguard had heard of the events in Palmaris in any more detail other than the unexpected death of Father Abbot Markwart. The Abellican Church would have been the only real messenger to that distant place; and even if St.-Mere-Abelle had sent a courier, no one there truly fathomed the implications of the events, and certainly no one there would have been so bold as to take sides in the budding philosophical war. But that was just what Braumin had instructed the wise and trustworthy Brother Holan Dellman to do: to take the side of the victors, to show that the good had won out over the cancerous evil.

"Treat Markwart's memory gently," Braumin urged Dellman yet again,

"but foster no doubts concerning the fall of the Father Abbot—the fall from grace before the fall from life."

Dellman nodded, then turned as Brother Talumus entered the room.

"Go and accept the passage from Al'u'met," Braumin instructed Dellman. "Extend to him our profound thanks, and then prepare your thoughts and your belongings. Go with the blessings of Avelyn."

That last line, spoken so casually, raised Talumus' eyebrow.

As soon as Dellman had exited, Braumin motioned to Viscenti, and the man quickly closed the door.

Talumus glanced around, seeming suspicious.

"St. Precious is not nearly as strong as it will have to be, if we are to withstand the continuing assault by Duke Kalas," Braumin remarked to Talumus. Indeed, many times over the course of the winter, Kalas and Braumin had argued over policy, over minor issues, mostly, but ones that perceptive Braumin understood might well grow in importance now that winter had relinquished its grasp and the folk were out and about the city.

"Jilseponie is leaving," the younger monk reasoned.

"Very good, Talumus," Braumin congratulated, and he raised a finger into the air. "Keep vigilant, and pay attention to every clue."

"She said she would leave when the roads were clear," Talumus explained. "Many times has she met with Belster O'Comely these last days, and I have heard that it is his intent, with prodding from Jilseponie, to return to the northland."

"She will indeed take her leave of us, though truly it pains my heart to let her go," Braumin confirmed. "What an ally she has been to the Church, a force to counter any potential intrusions on our sovereignty by the aggressive Kalas. But she has her own path to follow, a road darkened by grief and anger, and I cannot turn her from that path, whatever our needs.

"To that end," he continued, "we must bolster the strength of St. Precious." As he spoke, the abbot turned his gaze over Brother Viscenti.

"A promotion," Brother Talumus reasoned.

"From this day forth, Marlboro Viscenti will be known as a master of St. Precious," said Braumin, and the nervous little Viscenti puffed out his chest. "Master Francis, who departs this very day for St.-Mere-Abelle, will see that the promotion is approved at every level; and even if some wish to argue the point, which I cannot fathom, I am certainly within my rights as abbot of St. Precious to make the promotion unilaterally."

Talumus nodded and offered a smile, somewhat strained but more genuine than not, to Viscenti. Then he looked to Braumin, his expression turning curious. "Why tell me now, and why behind a closed door?" he asked.

Braumin chuckled and walked around his desk, sitting on its edge right before the other monk, removing the physical barrier between them as he hoped to remove any possibility of insincere posturing. "The risks you took and your actions in the last days of Markwart speak highly of you," he began. "Had you more experience, there is no doubt that Talumus, and not Braumin, would have become the abbot of St. Precious, a nomination that I would have strongly supported. In the absence of that possibility, it has occurred to me that Talumus, too, should soon find his way to the rank of master. Yet, in that, too, you've not enough years in the Order for such a promotion to be approved without strong opposition—and, in all honesty, it is not a battle I choose to fight now."

"I have never asked—" Talumus began to protest, but Abbot Braumin stopped him with an upraised hand.

"Indeed, I will support your nomination to the rank of master as soon as it is feasible," he explained. "As soon as you have enough time—and I do not mean the typical ten years as the minimum. But that is a matter for another day: a day, I fear, that will be long in coming if St. Precious is to withstand the intrusions of Baron Kalas. We need more power and more security, supporters of my—of our—cause, in line to take the helm in the event of unforeseen tragedy."

His words obviously hit a strong chord within Brother Talumus, who had recently witnessed the murder of his beloved Abbot Dobrinion Calislas. The man stiffened and straightened, his eyes unblinking.

"Thus, there must be others, like Master Viscenti, who will ascend above you within the Order at St. Precious," Braumin explained. "I will need voices to support me at the College of Abbots, as well as against Duke Kalas. I wanted to tell you this personally, and privately, out of respect for your service and loyalty."

He stopped, tilting his head and waiting for a reply, and Brother Talumus spent a long while digesting the information. "You honor me," he said at length, and he seemed genuinely content. "More so than I deserve, I fear. I was not enamored of Jilseponie and Elbryan. I feared . . ."

"As we all feared, and yet you certainly took the right course of action," Braumin interjected, and Viscenti seconded the remark.

"Very well," Talumus replied. "I understand now the implications of the battle within Chasewind Manor. My path is obvious to me, a shining road paved with all the glories of the true Abellican Church. My voice will not ring out with the commands of a master at this time, but it will be no less loud in support of Abbot Braumin Herde of St. Precious and of Master Viscenti."

The three men exchanged sincere smiles of mutual appreciation, all of them relieved that their team was forging strong bonds now for the fights—against Kalas and against those within the Abellican Church who feared any change despite the momentous events—they believed they would soon find.

*   *   *

Francis had thought that the road ahead would be an easy one. He started with his stride long and full of conviction. But as he considered the reality he now faced, Francis began to recognize that this journey might prove as troublesome and dangerous, to the Church at least, as the one that had brought him to Palmaris in the first place. For he was walking a delicate line, he came to understand, stepping between the future Church he envisioned and the past one he had served. He believed in Braumin's cause, in the cause of Master Jojonah, burned at the stake for his convictions, and in the cause of Avelyn Desbris, who had flown in the face of Markwart's Abellican Church and had, subsequently, destroyed the physical form of the awakened demon.

Yes, Master Francis had come to accept the truth of many of the explanations that Braumin and the others were according the actions of Jojonah and of Avelyn, and he had come to recognize that Jilseponie and Elbryan were indeed heroes to both Church and Crown. But Markwart's last words haunted the man: *Beware that in your quest for humanism you do not steal the mystery of spiritualism.*

There was a threat to all mankind in sharing the mysteries of the gemstone magic with the common folk—not of war or of uncontrolled power, but a threat of secularizing the spiritual, of stealing the mysteries of life and the glory of God. What good would the Church do the world, Francis wondered, if, in its quest to become more compassionate, it took from the populace the one true inspiration of faith, the promise of eternal life? Soul stones or not, everybody would one day die, and how much darker that moment would be, to the one whose life had come to its end and to those loved ones left behind, if there was no faith in life eternal. Men who entered the Abellican Order trained for years before entering St.-Mere-Abelle or any of the other abbeys, and then they trained for many more years before learning the secrets of the gemstones. The Abellican monks understood the reality of the gemstones, the orbiting rings and the stone showers, but they could place that reality within the cocoon of their greater faith as inspired by the years of study. But what of the common man, the man not privy to the days, weeks, months, years of meditation? Might that man come to see the soul stones, the very fabric of the Abellican religion, as a *natural* occurrence, no more mysterious than the fires he kindled for warmth or the catapults the King's army used to batter the castles of enemies?

Francis didn't know, and he feared that it would take a wiser man than he to comprehend the implications of Markwart's final warning.

What he did know, however, was the reality of the situation in St.-Mere-Abelle; and even beyond his private doubts about how far Braumin and his friends should be allowed to open the Church, the young master understood that they would find more enemies than allies at the prime abbey. Thus was Francis, so close an ally to the demon that Markwart had become, walking a delicate line. If he strayed too far against Markwart, he would, in effect, be implicating himself, thus diminishing his own voice. And yet, he could hardly support the dead Father Abbot. He knew now that Markwart had been very wrong; and even aside from that truth that was in his heart, Francis knew that the Church would be inviting disaster if it continued to follow Markwart's path, that the populace would turn against it, and that Braumin and his followers would successfully establish the church of Avelyn Desbris.

It was all too troubling for the young master, the former bishop of Palmaris, the former lackey of Markwart—positions all, he feared, far beyond his abilities and experience.

Now the road to St.-Mere-Abelle lay before him, the road to the past and the future, the road to the wounded masters—such as gentle Machuso, no doubt—who would need reassuring, and to the more volatile and confident masters—the names Bou-raiy and Glendenhook stood out most prominently in his thinking—who would resist change and would likely resist demeaning the memory of Father Abbot Markwart, a man whom they had gladly served.

Yes, Bou-raiy, Francis told himself; and an image of the man, holding a burning branch in one hand and cheering as the pyre around the heretic Jojonah caught flame, rattled him.

He heard the door open behind him and turned to see Abbot Braumin entering.

"So you have not yet departed," said the abbot. "I had hoped to see you before you began your journey."

Francis nodded, though he hardly saw any point to Braumin's seeing him off. The two did not see things eye to eye, as Braumin painted the world, it seemed to Francis, too much in black and white. Though Braumin had not been pleased when Francis had retracted his support of Jilseponie for mother abbess, they had come to an understanding.

"Did you find any time alone with Abbot Je'howith before he departed?" Braumin asked.

Francis chuckled. "Do you fear that I did?"

"Fear?"

Francis chuckled again. "I did speak to him, and he told me, I expect, exactly what he told you that morning before the final meeting with King Danube," said Francis. "Abbot Agronguerre seems a fine choice, a man possessed of a healing soul. Exactly what is needed within the Church, I would say."

"So you support his nomination?"

"I would like to learn a bit more about Agronguerre, but from what I already know, yes," answered Francis.

"And was that all Abbot Je'howith expressed to you?" asked Braumin.

Francis looked at the man hard, tried to get a feeling for the trouble about which his words were hinting. "The memory of Markwart," he stated more than asked.

Braumin nodded slightly, his expression grim.

"Believe me, brother, I am more confused by that issue than are you," Francis assured Braumin.

"But you know the evil that Markwart had become?" Braumin pressed.

"I know the mistake the man made," Francis pointedly answered.

"You step backward," Braumin accused.

Francis thought about that for a moment, and almost agreed. "Sideways," he corrected. "There was error in Father Abbot Markwart's reasoning, to be sure, but there was also a ring of truth that Abbot Braumin would do well to hear."

Francis saw the man's face get very tight.

"We have been through this before," Francis remarked, holding up his hands as a peace gesture. "We are not of so different beliefs that you should fear me, Abbot Braumin. I go to St.-Mere-Abelle to speak the truth of the events in Palmaris."

"Which truths?" the skeptical Braumin demanded.

Francis chuckled yet again. "You—we—are both too young for such cynicism," he said. "The painful events in Palmaris brought resolution, though at a price too high for any of us to be satisfied. Markwart was wrong—he admitted as much to me before he died—and so I threw my support behind Braumin Herde and Jilseponie."

"But not enough to nominate her, as you said you would," Braumin reminded him.

"Not enough to destroy that which is left of the most stable institution in all the kingdom," Francis corrected. "We will find our common way, I believe, but by small steps and not ground-shattering leaps. The people are confused and frightened, and it is our duty to comfort them, not to provide more confusion." He fixed Braumin with a determined stare. "I am not your enemy," he declared. "And neither need be the memory of Father Abbot Dalebert Markwart."

Braumin asked, "What of Jojonah? What of Avelyn?"

"Resurrect those memories in the light of our recent revelations," Francis answered without hesitation, "bring them up beside Elbryan the Nightbird as victors over the darkness. Yes, I intend to work to those very ends, my brother. Master Jojonah forgave me, though he knew he was a doomed man—no small feat! And I will see him properly interred in consecrated ground, his good name fully restored."

"And Avelyn?" the abbot prompted.

"Avelyn must be investigated . . . honestly," Francis replied. "I will second the nomination to beatify Brother Avelyn, should you begin the canonization process at the College of Abbots. I will second it with all my heart and with my voice strong and full of conviction. But that does not mean that I believe him to be a saint. It means only that I believe him worthy of the investigation that might lead us to that end. Let us see what the man truly espoused and accomplished. Let us decide rationally if Avelyn truly saw a better course for the Church or a path that would lead to our destruction."

"Do you mean to balance his canonization on a matter of philosophy?" Abbot Braumin asked, shaking his head, his eyes wide.

"Not his sainthood, no," answered Francis, "but rather, his belief. I may be willing to vote for his sainthood without necessarily believing that his methods would be the appropriate course for the Church. It is his intent that will determine the decision of the canon inquisitors. But neither will my support for his canonization be wholly based upon the man's intentions for the Abellican Church, if he even had any such intentions."

He paused and watched as Abbot Braumin digested the words, the man finally coming to nod his head in agreement.

"Travel your road carefully and wisely, brother," Braumin said. "I expect that you will find fewer brothers of like heart than those opposed."

"The Church changes slowly," Francis agreed, and Braumin took his leave.

Master Francis Dellacourt, thirty years old and feeling as if he had the weight of the world on his shoulders, left St. Precious soon after, an escort of nearly a score of monks, brothers who had come to Palmaris in the procession that had brought Father Abbot Markwart to this fated city, beside him.

"What is left for us here?" Pony asked in all seriousness, curling her lips into an obviously manipulating pout. She was in Tomnoddy's, a bustling tavern that reminded her, somewhat painfully, of Fellowship Way in its best days.

"What isn't?" Belster O'Comely responded, smiling as he asked the question and without any sharpness in his tone. He was glad to see Pony excited about something again—about anything—even if that happened to be a decision that the portly innkeeper did not necessarily agree with. Also, Belster was happy that Pony had come to him, begging him to go north. They had been through a fair amount of arguing in the last days of the struggle, when Pony had laid bare Belster's prejudice against the dark-skinned Behrenese. "We've got our friends, after all, bonds made fast in the turmoil."

"Prym O'Brien's going north," Pony reminded him.

"He's been saying that every fair day since last summer," Belster replied. "Doubt that he'll ever do it."

"It is time to go home, Belster," Pony said seriously. "I know that, and so I'll be leaving in two days. I hope that you will share my road to Caer Tinella and to Dundalis, for there I will need you, I fear."

"To do what, girl?" Belster asked.

"To rebuild," said Pony without the slightest hesitation. "To put up a new Howling Sheila on the very spot of the previous, on the stone foundation that had once served as the base for Elbryan's home."

"Probably a house there already," Belster mumbled, reaching for his foaming drink and draining half the mug.

"Tomas assured me that the place would be mine, should I ever return," Pony said. "I mean to hold him to that promise, even if it means tearing down his own house in the process!"

"Bringing some of them gemstones with you, are you?" Belster snipped, and he wanted to take back the words as soon as he spoke them, seeing the cloud suddenly cross Pony's fair face.

"I will raise the tavern," the woman said quietly, "the Howling Sheila, or perhaps I shall call it Fellowship Way in honor of the Chilichunks. More enjoyable will the task be if Belster O'Comely walks the road with me, but even if you do not, I leave in two days."

"You mean to run a tavern?" Belster asked skeptically. "After all that you have seen and done? You're not thinking that to be a bit of a boring task, girl?"

"I mean to run a tavern," Pony replied sincerely. "I mean to sit with Roger on a hillock at sunset and hear the piping of Bradwarden as it drifts through the forest. I mean to tend the grove. . . ." Her voice trailed off, and Belster turned a sympathetic gaze on her.

"Are you sure that you're not just running away?" he asked her bluntly. "Haven't you tasks left unfinished right here?" Even as he spoke the question—a question that he knew Pony would not answer—Belster considered her last statement more carefully and found the insight that convinced him of her convictions. Pony had chosen not to go north with Elbryan's caisson, had chosen not to be present when the ranger was lowered into the cold ground. How could he refuse her request now? Pony and Elbryan had saved his life, and the lives of all his friends, during the days of the dactyl and in the troubled times immediately following the demon's fall. Pony and Elbryan had stood beside Belster and all the others, at great personal peril; and the innkeeper had no doubt at all that if the demon had captured him and put him in the very pits of blackness, Pony and Elbryan would have come for him, would have given their very lives to save him.

"Two days?" he asked. "Have you talked to Dainsey?"

"Dainsey is staying," Pony replied, referring to the woman who had served the Chilichunks at Fellowship Way before Markwart had taken them hostage, and then had served as Belster's companion in the tavern when he had reopened it at Pony's request. "She has become sweet on a particular young man, and never would I take her from that."

"The poor girl's deserving some happiness," Belster agreed, for Dainsey Aucomb had indeed lived a trying life. The innkeeper gave a belly laugh and emptied his mug, then wiped the foam from his lips and glanced at Pony—to find her staring at him hard.

"Two days?" he asked again.

Pony's stern look melted into a smile. "Meet me at the front doors of St. Precious," she instructed. "And don't you be late! I want an early start and a long day's ride."

"Well, bring a horse for me, then," Belster said with a resigned sigh. "If I'm to go back to that wilderness, I'm planning to spend all my funds beforehand." He finished and turned to the barkeep, motioning for the man to refill his mug.

Pony kissed him on the cheek and rushed out of Tomnoddy's, heading straight for St. Precious and a meeting with Abbot Braumin that she knew would pain her friend profoundly.

She found him in his office, the same office that had served for Abbot Dobrinion Calislas, and for Bishop Francis. Brother Anders Castinagis, arguably the most fiery of the followers of Jojonah, was there with Braumin, and Pony heard his agitated voice long before she entered through the room's open door.

"Come in, come in!" Braumin said to her, motioning to a chair at the left-hand side of his desk. Castinagis was standing, Pony noted, his big hands planted on the front of the desk, his eyes locked on the new abbot of St. Precious. "We were just discussing Master Francis' departure," Braumin explained. "He set out this day for St.-Mere-Abelle, to bring the word to our brethren and to confirm the appointment of Brother Viscenti to the rank of master."

That last statement caught Pony by surprise, and her blue eyes widened. "So soon?" she asked. When her words brought a somewhat crestfallen look to Braumin, she quickly added, "Well, never was there a man more deserving."

"So I believe," said Braumin. "And Brother Viscenti will soon enough pass the minimum time required by our Order, so there should be no serious complaints."

"Unless the messenger presents the nomination in an unfavorable manner," Brother Castinagis remarked, and then Pony understood the reason for their apparent argument.

"You do not trust Master Francis?" she asked the towering man.

"Should I?" Castinagis replied.

"Yes," she answered simply, and the brevity of her pointed response put Castinagis on his heels.

"As I was just saying," Abbot Braumin added. "Brother Castinagis wished to accompany Master Francis, but I have been trying to explain to him that we who follow Avelyn's beliefs are more vulnerable here in Palmaris than perhaps anywhere else in the world. With Brother Dellman leaving for Vanguard and with Master Francis gone, we of expressed con-

viction number only five, including us three and Brothers Talumus and Viscenti. We must rally the flock of St. Precious behind us," he went on,
aiming his words now at Castinagis and not Pony, "first and foremost, if we
are to hold ground with Duke Kalas."

"You are soon to be four," Pony interrupted, drawing the attention
of both men. "Belster O'Comely has agreed to accompany me," she
explained. "I leave for Caer Tinella in two days."

Abbot Braumin seemed to sink back into his chair, and Brother Castinagis just stood there, shaking his head. The news was not completely unexpected, but Braumin had hoped to keep Pony in Palmaris at least through
the first half of summer.

"And how long will you remain in Caer Tinella?" the abbot asked.

"A few days, no more," Pony replied. "I hope to be in Dundalis before
summer proper, that I might establish my home fully before the onset of
next winter."

My home. The words echoed as a bell of finality in the head of Abbot
Braumin. "Be not so quick to tie yourself to the place," he advised.

"You may find your road turning back to Palmaris," Brother Castinagis
added. "This is the center of the world at this time, for the future of the
Church, at least." He continued, gaining volume and momentum with each
passing word. "How might the memory of Master Jojonah, and that of
Brother Avelyn—" Abbot Braumin stopped him by clearing his throat
loudly. When Castinagis turned to regard the man, the abbot nodded
toward the door, and Castinagis took that as his cue to leave.

"He is an excitable fellow," Braumin said to Pony as soon as the brother
had departed.

"And he overestimates our importance, I fear," she replied.

"Does he?"

Pony just smiled.

"Or is it, perhaps, that you, in your grief, have come to underestimate
everything else in all the world?" Abbot Braumin asked.

"Perhaps I have come to see the truth of the material world," Pony was
quick to answer, "the truth of the folly and of false hopes. Are you then to
promise me eternal life?"

Braumin stared at her hard, his expression a cross between anger
and pity.

"If I accept your Church's definition of eternal life, then I say again that
Brother Castinagis overestimates our importance," Pony declared, "because
no matter what we do here, we will all die. True?"

The abbot continued to stare, to chuckle helplessly, and, in the end, to
merely shake his head. Yes, Pony had lost her way, had given up, he knew;
and he understood, as well, that there was nothing he could do to persuade
her differently, to show her the error of her despair.

Pony came around the desk, then, and hugged the abbot. "You are my friend, Braumin Herde," she declared, "a true friend to me and to Elbryan, a kin in heart and soul. You stood with us in the darkest hour, and better is all the world for your efforts."

Braumin pushed her back to arm's length. "If you truly believed that—" he started to argue, but Pony put her finger over his lips.

"The road to Caer Tinella and the Timberlands will be well traveled over the next seasons," she said. "I promised you that I would attend the opening of the chapel of Avelyn in Caer Tinella, should that come to pass. Send word and I will be there."

"But that will be years hence," the abbot protested.

"And we are both young, my friend," Pony said. She bent low and hugged Braumin again, then kissed him on the cheek and walked out of his office.

When he heard the door close behind her, Abbot Braumin felt as if his heart would break. Suddenly he felt very alone and very afraid. He had allowed his hopes to soar, despite his pain, after the battle at Chasewind Manor. Francis had declared that he would nominate Pony as mother abbess, and Braumin had dared to hope that this woman, his hero, would stand tall at the front of his straying Church and, through sheer determination and willpower, put them back on the proper course. Even after it became obvious that Pony would not so ascend within the Church, Braumin had thought his position solid, and the ascension of the followers of Jojonah and Avelyn certain.

But then Francis had withdrawn his support for Pony, and—despite the man's continuing opposition to Abbot Je'howith—Braumin wondered now how much trust he could put in Francis.

And now Pony was leaving, and though he still had Castinagis and Viscenti supporting him, and though he understood that Brother Talumus and several other minor-ranking monks of St. Precious had given themselves to his cause, Braumin remained afraid. Because now he was in charge of it all. His would be the primary voice battling stubborn Duke Kalas; he would be the one answering any questions that came to St. Precious from St.-Mere-Abelle; he would be the one fronting the cause of Master Jojonah at the College of Abbots. And that cause, he knew, would not be an easy one to sell to many of the Abellican leaders, including many of the masters whom Braumin had served at St.-Mere-Abelle less than a year ago.

Only then, with the sound of that closing door, did Abbot Braumin come to realize the truth of it all: he had depended upon Pony to protect him and bolster him, to fight the battle for Avelyn and Jojonah from the lead position.

He was very afraid.

On a drizzly spring morning two days later, the small wagon bearing Pony and Belster O'Comely rolled through Palmaris' northern gate, bouncing along the road that would take them to Caer Tinella. Many heads turned to regard them as they crossed the city and then the rolling farmlands just north of Palmaris, and the departure of this most notable woman sparked many whispered conversations.

In a copse of trees on a hill just beyond those farmlands, Marcalo De'Unnero, too, noted their passing. From the farmers, he had heard that Pony meant to leave Palmaris, and now he was very glad to see that the rumors were true. De'Unnero didn't want to face Jilseponie now, for he believed that any such encounter would end in violence, a battle that would prove disastrous for him, whether he won or lost.

He waited for more than an hour after the wagon had rolled out of sight, considering his course. Many times during that hour, the former bishop reminded himself that he *had* controlled his inner beast, despite the ultimate temptation. He had defeated the demon within, and thus was ready to take his rightful place back in the Abellican Order.

Though what that place might now be, the man could not be sure.

Marcalo De'Unnero had never marked the days of his life with fear or lack of confidence, and would not do so now. He jumped up from his mossy seat and trotted down the face of the hill onto the road, turning south for Palmaris. The same heads that had regarded Jilseponie's departure turned to mark his approach, but they seemed not to care.

And why should they? De'Unnero asked himself. He hardly resembled the man they remembered as their bishop, the man who had fled Palmaris months before. He was leaner now, a thick beard upon his face, his black curly hair hanging several inches longer, bouncing at the base of his neck. Indeed, the guards at the open north gate hardly seemed to pay him any notice at all and didn't even ask his name.

He felt even more invisible as he moved unrecognized along the busy streets of the city, and he found that he did not enjoy that anonymity. Rationally, he knew it to be a good thing—he had not left the folk of Palmaris on good terms, after all!—but still he did not like it, did not like blending into a crowd of people he recognized as his inferiors.

Soon enough, he came to the front door of St. Precious Abbey, and he paused there, staring at the structure with his emotions churning. The farmers had told him the name of the new abbot, and that alone made him want to spit at the place. Braumin Herde? When De'Unnero had fled the city, the man wasn't even formally a master! And though De'Unnero knew that Markwart had once meant to promote Herde, it was only for political reasons, to quiet the other side, and certainly not the result of anything Braumin Herde had ever accomplished in his mediocre existence.

De'Unnero stood there, outside the door, for a long time, playing through his emotions and his anger, throwing the negativity aside with conscious reminders that he would have to find a way to fit into the new order of his Abellican brotherhood.

"May I help you, brother?" came a question from a monk approaching De'Unnero from the side, a monk whom the former bishop did recognize.

De'Unnero pulled back his hood and turned a hard stare on the man.

"Brother?" the oblivious monk asked again.

"Do you not recognize me, Brother Dissin?" De'Unnero asked rather sharply.

The younger man glanced up, scrutinizing the speaker, and then his eyes widened.

"B-bishop De'Unnero," he stammered. "But I—I—had thought—"

De'Unnero waved at him to stop his blabbering. "Lead me in," he instructed. "Announce me to the new abbot of St. Precious."

"May I help you, brother?" came a question from a monk approaching De'Unnero from the side, a monk whom the former bishop did recognize.

De'Unnero pulled back his hood and turned a hard stare on the man.

"Brother?" the oblivious monk asked again.

"Do you not recognize me, Brother Dissin?" De'Unnero asked rather sharply.

The younger man glanced up, scrutinizing the speaker, and then his eyes widened.

"B-bishop De'Unnero," he stammered. "But I—I—had thought—"

De'Unnero waved at him to stop his blabbering. "Lead me in," he instructed. "Announce me to the new abbot of St. Precious."

bouncing along the road that would take them to Caer Tinella. Many heads turned to regard them as they crossed the city and then the rolling farmlands just north of Palmaris, and the departure of this most notable woman sparked many whispered conversations.

In a copse of trees on a hill just beyond those farmlands, Marcalo De'Unnero, too, noted their passing. From the farmers, he had heard that Pony meant to leave Palmaris, and now he was very glad to see that the rumors were true. De'Unnero didn't want to face Jilseponie now, for he believed that any such encounter would end in violence, a battle that would prove disastrous for him, whether he won or lost.

He waited for more than an hour after the wagon had rolled out of sight, considering his course. Many times during that hour, the former bishop reminded himself that he *had* controlled his inner beast, despite the ultimate temptation. He had defeated the demon within, and thus was ready to take his rightful place back in the Abellican Order.

Though what that place might now be, the man could not be sure.

Marcalo De'Unnero had never marked the days of his life with fear or lack of confidence, and would not do so now. He jumped up from his mossy seat and trotted down the face of the hill onto the road, turning south for Palmaris. The same heads that had regarded Jilseponie's departure turned to mark his approach, but they seemed not to care.

And why should they? De'Unnero asked himself. He hardly resembled the man they remembered as their bishop, the man who had fled Palmaris months before. He was leaner now, a thick beard upon his face, his black curly hair hanging several inches longer, bouncing at the base of his neck. Indeed, the guards at the open north gate hardly seemed to pay him any notice at all and didn't even ask his name.

He felt even more invisible as he moved unrecognized along the busy streets of the city, and he found that he did not enjoy that anonymity. Rationally, he knew it to be a good thing—he had not left the folk of Palmaris on good terms, after all!—but still he did not like it, did not like blending into a crowd of people he recognized as his inferiors.

Soon enough, he came to the front door of St. Precious Abbey, and he paused there, staring at the structure with his emotions churning. The farmers had told him the name of the new abbot, and that alone made him want to spit at the place. Braumin Herde? When De'Unnero had fled the city, the man wasn't even formally a master! And though De'Unnero knew that Markwart had once meant to promote Herde, it was only for political reasons, to quiet the other side, and certainly not the result of anything Braumin Herde had ever accomplished in his mediocre existence.

De'Unnero stood there, outside the door, for a long time, playing through his emotions and his anger, throwing the negativity aside with conscious reminders that he would have to find a way to fit into the new order of his Abellican brotherhood.

confront the most basic questions of my existence, of any existence: the meaning of my life itself and of what may come after this life. I am choosing a course of faith and of hope, and not with any illusions that those necessary ingredients for contentment and joy will be waiting for me in Dundalis. Far from it—for I understand that those questions may be beyond me. And if that is the case, then how can I even begin to fathom the answers?

But this is a battle I cannot avoid or delay. I must come to terms with these basic questions of humanity, of who we are and why we are and where we're going, if I ever hope to solidify the ground beneath my feet. I have come to the point in my life where I must learn the truth or be destroyed by the doubts.

Brother—Abbot—Braumin wants me to stand beside him now and fight the legacy of Markwart. King Danube wants me to stand with him now in restoring order to a kingdom shattered by war and the corruption of its very soul. They see my refusal as cowardice, I am sure; but in truth, it is mere pragmatism. I cannot fight their battles until my own personal turmoil is settled, until I am grounded in a place of solid conviction—until I am convinced that we go, not in endlessly overlapping circles of false progress, but in the direction of justice and truth, that we evolve and not just revolve. That we, in the end, pursue paradise.

And so I go to Dundalis, to Elbryan's grave site, in the hope that there I will find the truth, in the hope that the place where I learned the truth about living will also teach me the truth about dying.

—JILSEPONIE WYNDON

❖ 7 ❖

Brynn Dharielle

She edged closer, closer, and the biggest challenge to her, it seemed, was trying hard not to giggle. For though this was considered one of the prime tests of her training, to Brynn Dharielle it was just a game, and an easy one! She blew a strand of her long black hair—hair so dark that it seemed to show all the colors of the rainbow within its depths—from in front of her equally dark eyes and chewed her lip, again to prevent the giggle.

She saw the white-tailed deer, and it saw her, and it believed her no enemy. As long as she made no sudden movements, no sudden sounds . . .

As long as she continued the quiet humming, the song of grazing that she had learned as a very little child, before she had ever come to the land of the Touel'alfar . . .

The young girl crouched lower, slowly and deliberately placing one foot ahead and twisting it gently into the moist grass, shifting her weight forward, slowly, slowly.

Another step. The deer seemed frozen in place now, staring at her intently, and so the girl likewise stopped all movement, even keeping her jaw set, though she continued to hum that coaxing, calming song. The moment of tension passed, and Brynn began to lift her hand, opening it palm up to reveal the sweet, crushed pulossa cane.

The deer caught the scent, its ears popping straight up, its nose twitching.

Brynn Dharielle took a slow deep breath, holding her patience, though she wanted to run right up to the beautiful animal. She continued to move delicately and unthreateningly, her hand out. And then, almost anticlimactically, she was there, beside the deer, letting it lap the pulossa cane from her hand while she lovingly stroked its sleek, strong neck and rubbed it behind the ears.

She knew that she was being watched, monitored, and measured, but she didn't care at that moment. All that mattered was the deer, this beautiful creature, this new friend she had just made.

What a wonderful spring day in the most wonderful place in all the world.

Over in the thicket not so far to the side, Belli'mar Juraviel put his head in his hands and groaned. Did this spirited young lady do anything by the rules? Ever?

But Juraviel was chuckling, too—and not out of helpless anger, not even out of frustration—but out of sheer surrender. Brynn Dharielle had charmed him, he had to admit. Never had the elf encountered a human female quite like her. She seemed possessed of two spirits: the warrior intensity of the To-gai-ru—the fierce nomadic riders of the steppe region of western Behren—combined with a level of playfulness and impertinence beyond anything Juraviel had ever seen, even in an elf! Her given name was Dharielle Tsochuk, but Lady Dasslerond had quickly added the name Brynn, in honor of the ancient elven heroine credited with aiding in the creation of Andur'Blough Inninness by relinquishing her life and soul to the spirit of a tree that became the heart of the enchanted valley. In the tongue of the Touel'alfar, *brynn* meant "butterfly," and ironically, there was an elven word very similar to *dharielle* which meant a bee stinger. So Brynn Dharielle could be translated into "butterfly with a bee stinger," and how appropriate a description Juraviel thought that to be for this little one!

"You were supposed to be hunting the deer, not befriending it," Juraviel scolded, walking up to Brynn and her newfound pet—and the creature seemed quite relaxed, licking the last remnants of the pulossa cane from the girl's hand.

"You instructed me to touch the deer," the kneeling Brynn Dharielle replied, looking up at Juraviel, her smile gleaming brightly against her brown skin.

She was indeed a paradox, Juraviel recognized, both physically and emotionally. Her eyes were so bright, yet her irises so black. Her skin, typical of the To-gai-ru, was much darker than that of the people of Honce-the-Bear, and certainly darker than the smooth and delicate golden-hued skin of the Touel'alfar; and yet on Brynn Dharielle it seemed as if possessed of an inner glow. Inside she was the gentle huntress, the friend of deer and rabbit, and yet she was also a savage warrior, able to turn on primal instincts for survival when the elves brought her out for training in *bi'nelle dasada*.

So complex and yet so simple, and so possessed of the finer qualities of both human and elf. This one would do well, Juraviel knew, and he was glad that Lady Dasslerond had given him this task.

"The point of the lesson was for you to move up to the deer unnoticed," Juraviel tried to explain. "The silent hunter."

"Is it not better to befriend your enemies or your prey?" Brynn asked innocently. "An easy kill," she said, looking into the deer's huge eyes.

Juraviel doubted that claim, doubted if he could ever get Brynn to actually kill a deer unless—or perhaps even if—she was starving.

"That is not the way we intended the lesson," Juraviel tried to explain.

"And did you not tell me that I should develop my own style?" Brynn asked without hesitation. Surely Juraviel wanted to drop his head into his hands yet again. The deer turned and started to wander away, and Brynn slapped it on the rump to get it moving more quickly. "Am I to be the imitation of every other ranger, then?" the girl asked, wiping her hands and standing up—and she was almost as tall as Juraviel. "Am I to be Andacanavar the strong, cleaving goblins with my great sword, or Nightbird, perhaps—the great Nightbird who went to Mount Aida to wage battle against the greatest enemy of all?" Her voice trailed away and she looked down.

For a cloud had crossed over Juraviel's fair face.

"I am sorry," Brynn offered.

Juraviel held up his hand, then lifted his face and managed a smile. "No," he said. "No need for any apology; and no, you are not to be an imitation of any other ranger. In the case of the two you just named, though, I assure you that some imitation would not be a bad thing."

"Mostly of Nightbird, right?" Brynn asked. "Tell me about him again."

"There is so much to tell," Juraviel replied.

"And we have all the day!" Brynn said happily. "You thought it would take me all day to pat the deer and yet it is still not midmorning and I have passed the test."

Juraviel wanted to dispute that, but he found, against the girl's disarming smile, that he could not. He suspected that Brynn had asked him about Elbryan the Nightbird only to heal any wounds she might have caused by her mentioning the dead ranger, but when he saw the joy and eagerness on her face and that dazzling and innocent—and yet he knew not so innocent!—smile, he could not resist.

And so he led her to a mossy bank, sat her down, and told her of Elbryan, the lost boy who had watched his town of Dundalis sacked by goblins; of Elbryan, the impetuous youngster, headstrong and prideful, who had so frustrated Tuntun of the Touel'alfar. And he told her of Nightbird, the man Elbryan had become, as mighty a ranger as Andur'Blough Inninness had ever produced; of Nightbird, who had gone to Aida to battle the demon dactyl and who had traveled back to the civilized lands to continue the battle against the demon's eternal spirit. With tears filling his eyes, Belli'mar Juraviel told her of Nightbird, who had given his life to save the world.

Juraviel closed his eyes and described how Nightbird's caisson was pulled by the centaur and then by Symphony, the most wondrous horse in all the world, through the streets of the great city of Palmaris, through the farmlands, and to the north to the town that had been his home.

When he finished, Juraviel opened his eyes, to find Brynn standing right before him, her expression full of sympathy and sadness. "Thank you," she said and she gave her elven mentor a hug.

Juraviel led the girl away, along the spring-blossoming slopes and wooded thickets of the elven valley of Andur'Blough Inninness, back toward the heart of the enclave, the deepest part of the forest, sprinkled with tree houses and low, unobtrusive cottages. This was Caer'alfar, *the home of the people,* a place of song and of dance, of poetry and philosophy, and the spouting of wisdom gained in centuries of living. This was the very heart of the Touel'alfar, now as it had been for millennia, a place that many of the elven folk had believed eternal. But in the day of the dactyl, Lady Dasslerond had gone out to save Juraviel and some human refugees he had gathered together. The demon dactyl had come upon them and would have destroyed them all, but Dasslerond had used her potent magic, a powerful emerald gemstone, to transport herself, Juraviel, the humans, and, unintentionally, Bestesbulzibar, back to the elven valley; and there, before he ran away in defeat, Bestesbulzibar had left his lingering scar, a rot that infested the very ground and was slowly spreading.

On their way to Caer'alfar, Juraviel and Brynn passed that region of disease, and though a couple of years had passed the infection had not spread very far at all, only to a single tree, and that tree was still alive, though not blooming as vibrantly as in years past. To a human, the disease would not have seemed such a threat, but to the elves, who measured time so differently—who viewed the passing of a year as a human might view a month—it seemed as if Bestesbulzibar had begun a fire.

Juraviel winced at the sight, as he always did, for he could clearly see the illness within the tree, and he knew that it had come about because of his own choices. Perhaps he should have left the human refugees and continued on his quest for Aida with Nightbird and Jilseponie and Brother Avelyn. Lady Dasslerond had only gone out to face Bestesbulzibar, after all, because one of her own, one of *the people*, was out there. If Juraviel had been true to the tenets that guided the Touel'alfar, then the refugees would have been slain; but to the elven way of thinking, a few human lives were not worth the price of the rot within Andur'Blough Inninness. To the true elven way of thinking, the rot was too high a price to pay, even to save all the humans in the world.

More than a few of Juraviel's brethren had reminded him of that fact these last months, this springtime bloom of illness. None had openly accused him, of course, but their songs reflected a melancholy, a wistfulness for what had been and what could never be again; and every reference shot a dart of pain into Belli'mar Juraviel's heart.

His bright spot now was Brynn Dharielle, the butterfly with a bee stinger, the spirited lass who reminded Juraviel of why he had come to love Nightbird and Pony, even Avelyn and Roger Lockless. To Juraviel, Brynn embodied the best qualities of humanity, and he did not doubt that she would become one of the finest rangers, that her reputation would rise high among the ranks that included Terranen Dinoniel, half elf; Elbryan and Mather Wyndon; mighty Andacanavar of Alpinador; and the legendary heroes, Bimriel the wise and A'juge, who led Brother Allabarnet of the Abellican Church throughout the Wilderlands, seeding the inhospitable forest with bountiful fruit trees.

Brynn Dharielle, who had such trials ahead of her when she returned to her enslaved people of To-gai-ru, would take her rightful place, Juraviel believed, and he was thrilled that Lady Dasslerond had placed the girl in his care.

Except . . .

"When will I get to see him again?" Brynn asked innocently, and Juraviel knew of whom she was speaking.

He shrugged and wanted to let it go at that. But the girl, true to her spirit, persisted. "Tell me, please," she said, rushing about Juraviel and intercepting him, forcing him to look at her directly. "The child—have you even named him yet?—when will I see him again? I would love to hold him and rock him to sleep, as my own mother used to do."

Juraviel had no answer for her—none that she would want to hear, at least. Lady Dasslerond had made it quite clear to him that neither he nor Brynn was to have any contact at all with the child of Nightbird and Jilseponie. As great as that pain was for Juraviel, he knew that it was stronger for young Brynn. She wanted to see another human being; what could be more instinctual? Juraviel understood his own longing whenever he ventured out of Andur'Blough Inninness for too long. Humans needed the company of humans as much as the Touel'alfar needed others of their own kind. True, almost every one of the other rangers had gone through training without human contact, Nightbird included. But in this rare case, the elves had taken two humans in at the same time, and that knowledge of proximity, of possibility, made the girl's heart long all the more for human companionship.

Even more than that, Brynn repeatedly told Juraviel that she could help care for the child, and promised with all her heart that she would do a good job; and Juraviel understood the truth of her claim even better than she. Both Brynn and the child would greatly benefit, he knew.

"If I pass your test the way you intended?" Brynn asked, her smile ever hopeful. "If I sneak up on the deer and slap it hard on the rump instead of letting it know me as a friend?"

Belli'mar Juraviel took a long, deep breath, changing his focus from the girl's beaming face to the image of rot within the valley, the disease that had come from the actions of Touel'alfar who bent the rules—even as Juraviel had done by transforming duty to friendship with *n'Touel'alfar*; by Dasslerond in bringing both Juraviel and the humans back to the valley, thus opening the way for Bestesbulzibar; by Nightbird for teaching Pony *bi'nelle dasada*, the most secretive elven fighting technique. So many of their guiding principles had been temporarily abandoned, and Juraviel had to admit the truth: had the true elven tenets been followed, though the human world might be a darker place, Andur'Blough Inninness would remain healthy and the threat that valuable elven secrets would soon be in the hands of humans would be nonexistent. He pictured the rot and reminded himself of all of that, and so his words came out more sternly than poor Brynn could ever have expected.

"The child is not your concern," he declared flatly. "I doubt that the babe even remains within Caer'alfar, and if he does, then Brynn Dharielle would do well to stay far away from him, on pain of great punishment."

"But I—"

"No buts," Juraviel interrupted. "This is not a matter for discussion. You are in training here—you would do well to remind yourself of that. And to remind yourself of the plight of your people, of the death of your parents. Find your heart, Brynn Dharielle, and your focus, for all our sakes."

The girl appeared confused, which Juraviel understood, given his sudden mood shift and the barrage of overwhelming responsibilities he had just placed upon her. She stared at him for a few moments, blinking her eyes, then wiping her sleeve across one. Then she turned and sprinted away.

Juraviel nodded. He had done his proper duty to the Touel'alfar.

He was still looking down the path she had run when he saw another figure step into view, moving his way.

"The memory still pains her," Lady Dasslerond remarked, glancing back at the trail where Brynn had disappeared. "Thus it still inspires her. That is a good thing."

Juraviel nodded, but he was staring at Dasslerond and not at the trail, wondering how much of his last conversation the lady had heard and wondering how much she had been paying attention to him and Brynn, in more quiet ways, over the last days. Juraviel understood that his position with Dasslerond was somewhat tentative these days. When he thought about it—again, forcing himself to stay fully within the Touel'alfar view of the world and tenets of behavior—he really couldn't blame her.

He told her, then, of Brynn Dharielle's remarkable achievement that morning with the deer. Not even Andacanavar had been so close to a deer at this young age; and, in this test at least, Andacanavar of Alpinador had previously held the benchmark. "Her fighting progresses," Juraviel finished, "but her understanding of the natural world is truly amazing—more akin to the Touel'alfar than to the humans." He knew as soon as he finished, as soon as he heard the words and then saw Lady Dasslerond's scowl, that his choice of phrasing hadn't been particularly diplomatic.

"She is *human*," Lady Dasslerond was quick to remind him, "*n'Touel'-alfar*. Never forget that."

Belli'mar Juraviel lowered his gaze submissively.

"But she is also To-gai-ru," the lady went on. "And as such, she is a horsewoman, first and foremost. Her people are as close to the land as any humans in all the world, even more so than the Alpinadorans. Before we took her to Caer'alfar, before her clan was overrun by fanatical Behrenese soldiers, her parents murdered, and her village burned to the ground, she was already an accomplished rider, though she had not yet seen her ninth winter. If her legs were longer and stronger, as they will become, our Brynn could outride the finest Allheart knights."

An image of the budding ranger upon Symphony flashed in Juraviel's mind, but he let it go quickly, too pained to imagine anyone but Nightbird atop the magnificent stallion. He closed his eyes and saw again Symphony pulling the caisson bearing Nightbird's body to the north.

"What will her years with us do to diminish that riding ability?" Lady Dasslerond asked.

Juraviel looked into his lady's eyes, at first wondering if she was being sarcastic, but then understanding the sincerity of her question. What indeed? The Touel'alfar could ride horses, and ride them well, but their riding style—often using their wings for balance—was not adaptable to humans. Also, the Touel'alfar preferred to use their legs and their wings rather than ride, for they could travel great distances, and swiftly, on their own. Given that, there were no fine riding horses in Andur'Blough Innin-ness, certainly none "broken" in the manner that any human would be able to ride.

"We cannot take that away from her," Lady Dasslerond went on. "Above all else, Brynn will need to perfect her riding skills to the very highest level if she is to return to her people with any manner of stature."

It was true enough, Juraviel knew. The To-gai-ru valued their pinto ponies above their children and measured themselves mostly based on how well they could ride one of those tough and strong beasts. Any To-gai-ru aspiring to a position of leadership would have to outride his or her competitors.

"Many of her lessons must soon center around riding," Lady Dasslerond explained. "Perhaps you and she can find a way to adapt the To-gai-ru riding style with *bi'nelle dasada*."

"We can catch a horse this day," Juraviel replied, and he chuckled, imagining Brynn Dharielle walking right up to one of the wild horses in Andur'Blough Inninness and coaxing it back to Caer'alfar. "And begin the training process, on horse first and then with Brynn."

Lady Dasslerond was shaking her head before he finished. "There are no horses in Andur'Blough Inninness suitable for the girl," she explained.

"This will be her greatest challenge, her chance to bring our gifts to her to their pinnacle, and as such, we must give her the proper tools."

Juraviel narrowed his gaze, hardly believing what his lady was saying. "You wish me to go to To-gai?" he asked doubtfully.

"That is not possible," Lady Dasslerond was quick to answer. "No, my eyes look in a different direction, to call in the favor of a friend."

"Bradwarden," Juraviel stated, finally catching on, but then his expression turned to one of doubt. "Are you thinking that Brynn Dharielle should ride Symphony?"

Lady Dasslerond rocked back at the notion, apparently caught off guard but also apparently intrigued.

"She could not begin to handle that one," Juraviel said. The thought of anyone other than Elbryan or Jilseponie riding Symphony didn't sit well with the elf. "She is not nearly large enough to control the horse," he went on. "Her legs would not reach around Symphony's considerable girth, and never would Symphony even feel the press of her skinny limbs."

"Tuntun rode him," Lady Dasslerond reminded him; for indeed, Tuntun had ridden Symphony all the way to the Barbacan in pursuit of Avelyn's party. "She was no larger than Brynn."

"But she was stronger," said Juraviel, "with muscles honed by years and years of training."

"You do not wish to see Symphony given to Brynn," Lady Dasslerond noted slyly.

"I do not believe that Symphony can be *given* to anyone," Juraviel answered. "By Nightbird's own description to me—supported by Bradwarden—Symphony chose him as much as he chose the horse."

"And if Symphony accepted her?"

Juraviel didn't reply, just stood there staring at the lady.

"You do not believe her worthy of Nightbird's mount," Dasslerond went on, easily gaining the upper hand now, "as Tuntun did not believe Nightbird worthy of Mather's sword."

"Nightbird taught her differently."

"As Brynn will teach you," Lady Dasslerond said. "Go out this week, Belli'mar Juraviel. Find Bradwarden, the centaur, and discover his feelings on this matter. You will enjoy the visit with your old friend, I believe, and with Roger Lockless, who is rumored to be in Dundalis with the centaur."

Juraviel didn't begin to disagree.

"Return with a horse for Brynn Dharielle," the lady instructed. "Remember that she will carry on the responsibilities of a ranger, as did Nightbird, and that her road will be no less fraught with danger. And remember, Belli'mar Juraviel, that much of the power Brynn Dharielle will find will come as a result of her horsemanship.

"Choose well," she continued, her tone friendly but stern. "When you are with Bradwarden you will learn if that horse is to be Symphony, and if you see the way clear, do not let your personal jealousies defeat our cause."

Juraviel straightened, recognizing clearly that he had just been put in his place, in no uncertain terms. Lady Dasslerond was placing her trust in him; she could have sent any of the others to Bradwarden with instructions to retrieve Symphony. No, this was a test, Juraviel understood, a way for the lady to measure whether or not he intended to repeat the same errors he had made with Elbryan and Jilseponie. At that moment, Belli'mar Juraviel realized that he would return with mighty Symphony, if the centaur and the horse would agree to it.

"There is one other matter for you to investigate while you are in the lands of the humans," the lady added. "Our scouts have reported that the gemstones Jilseponie used were never recovered after the battle in Chasewind Manor."

"The Touel'alfar have never been concerned with the magical gemstones," Juraviel replied, "except for the emerald given to you. They are the domain of the humans, by your own words."

"And I mean them for a human," Lady Dasslerond interrupted. "Have we not discussed this? The child will be all that his father was and all that his mother once was. We will teach him the sword and the magic."

Juraviel thought back to that fateful day. Brother Francis had been the first one into the room, he remembered; but if Francis had found the stones, he would have turned them over to the Church immediately and so they would not still be missing. But there was another in the area of the battle, according to the version of the tale Juraviel had heard, another human with a reputation for light fingers. He looked at Dasslerond, and she nodded and walked away. She had a pretty good idea that he could locate the missing gemstones, Juraviel knew.

Yes, Juraviel had a good idea who had the stones.

Eager to see his old friends again, the elf was out of Andur'Blough Inninness that very night.

CHAPTER

❖ 8 ❖

Diplomacy

A bbot Agronguerre held his breath as his guests at St. Belfour—Prince Midalis and the two barbarians Andacanavar and Bruinhelde—entered the study. The abbot had purposely removed the room's normally comfortable chairs, replacing them with five straight, hard-backed seats arranged in a circle with no apparent "head" position. Brother Haney would be the fifth in attendance, seated away from Agronguerre—again purposefully, for the abbot wanted his guests to feel as if this was a meeting of comrades and friends and not a drawing of lines between Vanguard and Alpinador, between Church and barbarian.

He watched the expressions of the two Alpinadorans carefully, nodding his agreement when Prince Midalis quickly took the seat to Brother Haney's right, thus leaving the chairs on either side of the abbot for their guests. Bruinhelde seemed to bristle a bit, but Andacanavar calmed him with a pat on the shoulder, motioning for him to take the seat to Agronguerre's left, while the ranger slid easily into the seat to the abbot's right.

That scene fit in well with what Midalis had told him about the Alpinadoran leaders, Agronguerre realized. The Prince had indicated that the ranger Andacanavar was by far the more worldly and friendly of the pair; and that Bruinhelde, though obviously an ally, was more set in the ways of his northern people and far more suspicious of the Vanguardsmen, and particularly of the Church, whose precepts were not in any way in accord with the Alpinadoran perception of God—or, in their case, of the gods, for their pantheon of deities was quite extensive.

When the pair were seated, and after a moment of uncomfortable silence, Prince Midalis began to speak, but Agronguerre, as the host, interrupted him immediately.

"A glorious victory on the field this morning," the abbot said, nodding in turn to each of his guests, "though we grieve for your losses, as we grieve for our own."

"Temorstaad died bravely," the stern Bruinhelde answered, his voice halting and accented, revealing his lack of command of the language. "I hope I may die as well."

Agronguerre widened his eyes at that for just a moment, until he realized that Bruinhelde wasn't calling for his own death, but was merely indicating that he hoped he would die as honorably as had Temorstaad.

"We do not grieve for those killed in battle as you might," Andacanavar tried to explain.

"We, too, pray that we might die honorably," Midalis put in.

"Though we surely pray that more of our enemies will find such a fate," Abbot Agronguerre dared to chime in, somewhat lightheartedly. He thought he had just committed his first blunder of the meeting when Bruinhelde fixed him with a confused stare, but then the barbarian leader chuckled and nodded.

With the tension alleviated, for the moment at least, Agronguerre bade Andacanavar and Midalis to lead them to the purpose for the meeting, a discussion concerning their continued alliance in the effort to rid the region of the minions of the demon dactyl. It went well for some time, rolling along, with plans for future tactics interspersed with reminders of the victory that day on the field, and even a remark from Bruinhelde that he thought Midalis and his riders had performed bravely and honorably.

It didn't slip past Agronguerre, though, that the barbarian seemed reluctant to offer any thanks or praise for the efforts of the monks; and that, the wise abbot feared, would be the true test of the depth of this unlikely alliance.

"With strength of sword and strength of magic, we will sweep the land of the goblins," the excited Brother Haney remarked at one point. The room fell silent, and Agronguerre could sense Bruinhelde tightening at his side. He turned slowly and deliberately to face the proud Alpinadoran, held up his hand to ward off attempts by both Andacanavar and Midalis to try to deflect the conversation back to more common ground.

"You mistrust my Church and our use of the gemstone magic," he said bluntly to Bruinhelde. Before the barbarian could respond, he added, "As we, who do not know of or understand the ways of the folk of Alpinador, mistrust many of your traditions and beliefs. That is ignorance, on both our parts, and it is something, I fear, that neither of us will be able to overcome at a meeting or in any short amount of time."

Bruinhelde's expression became more curious than angry, and he looked past Agronguerre to Andacanavar, who immediately translated the abbot's words and sentiments into the Alpinadoran language.

"Given that, we both must put our suspicions and even our anger aside," the abbot went on. "You need not trust our techniques, as we do not trust yours, but trust only that our goal is the same as your own: to rid the region of goblins and powries and giants. Take faith, my ally, that our magic and our ways will not be turned against you, that we are your allies in this and that we truly value that alliance."

He paused and let Andacanavar translate again, just to make sure that there would be no misunderstanding between them on this most crucial point, and he took some hope as Bruinhelde nodded, his stern expression beginning to brighten.

"I know that I overstepped my bounds as an ally when I tried to use the gemstone magic on your fallen companion," the abbot said. "And I do not agree with your decision to refuse such treatment for Temorstaad." Brother Haney gasped at the admission, Prince Midalis widened his eyes in surprise that Agronguerre would even bring up such a difficult subject, and Bruinhelde surely tightened once again at the mention.

The abbot, though, pressed ahead. "But I respect your decision and assure you that neither I nor any of my brethren will make such an intrusion against your ways as that again," he said. The ranger beside him was quick to translate. "However, Bruinhelde, my ally, should you see a different course as time goes along, as we each become more used to the other's ways, I, and all of my brethren, would accept any change of mind on your part. If you come to believe that the gemstone magic is a valuable tool for healing the wounded, as it is a tool for battling our common enemies, then I will work tirelessly to alleviate the suffering of Alpinadorans, as I try now to do for the men of Vanguard, the men who claim allegiance to my Church."

"And you expect that we, too, will make such a claim of allegiance?" Andacanavar interjected before Bruinhelde could.

"I do not," the abbot answered sincerely. "I expect, and have seen, that your people will battle for the sake of my own, as my own will battle for the sake of yours. I ask no concessions, no abandonment of ways or traditions, no premise that the Abellican Church is superior and correct."

"Abbot!" Brother Haney blurted, but Agronguerre merely laughed.

"Of course, I view the Abellican Church as the true way to paradise, and hope that everyone in all the world will come to see the same light of truth as I," Agronguerre admitted, his tone lighthearted and not in the least intimidating. "But that, I fear, is a personal decision, a choice that must come from within, and not through any pressure applied by brothers. Missionaries should spread their views with tolerance of difference, my friend."

"And they should listen as often as they speak," the ranger replied.

"Indeed," agreed Agronguerre. "And even more than that, I assure you that in this common cause, the brothers of St. Belfour are not missionaries. Certainly not! We believe that the joining of our forces against the common enemy will be to the betterment of both Vanguardsmen and Alpinadorans. This is not about who serves the correct God."

Andacanavar looked past the abbot to Bruinhelde, and Agronguerre, too, turned to regard the pivotal leader.

"You will use no magic to tend my wounded," Bruinhelde said determinedly, "not even if one is near death, as was Temorstaad. And take care that none of your magical attacks falls over my brethren!" he warned.

"But you do not wish us to stop throwing lightning and fire at the goblins," Abbot Agronguerre reasoned.

"Gilnegist clokclok gilnegist beyaggen inder fleequelt bene duGodder," Bruinhelde replied, settling back in his chair and crossing his huge arms over his chest, his expression contented.

Agronguerre immediately turned back to the smiling Andacanavar.

" 'Demon battling demon brings joy to the godly man,' " the ranger translated.

Brother Haney seemed as if he would jump up and shout out against the obvious insult, but the abbot of St. Belfour gave a great belly laugh and turned back to Bruinhelde. "Exactly!" he said with obvious irony. "Exactly!" He laughed some more, and Bruinhelde joined in and then the others, somewhat more tentatively, and it ended when Abbot Agronguerre, in all seriousness, extended his hand to the barbarian leader. Bruinhelde stared at the man and the gesture for a moment, then clasped Agronguerre's wrist firmly.

And so the alliance was sealed, with a mutual understanding of common benefit if not friendship. The rest of the meeting went beautifully, mostly rallying cheers designed to bring up the level of excitement for the battles that lay ahead and the shared confidence that, joined as one, the humans would drive out the minions of evil Bestesbulzibar.

Prince Midalis lingered behind when Brother Haney led the two Alpinadorans back to the gate of St. Belfour. "I had feared that you would hold to your anger from the events on the field concerning Temorstaad," he admitted to Agronguerre as soon as they were alone. "To press your opinion on that matter would have proven disastrous."

"It took me a long while to purge my heart of that anger," Agronguerre admitted, "but I recognize the greater good and understand that all of your work in bringing the barbarians to our cause has been nothing short of miraculous, my friend. I would not destroy those efforts for the sake of my own pride. And I know, too, that with or without the gemstone magic, Temorstaad will not be the only man to die in this campaign."

"True enough," Midalis solemnly agreed. "But now, at least, we can look forward to the war with true hope." He paused and gave Agronguerre a sly look. "And when it is finished, perhaps you can begin the task of converting Bruinhelde and his brethren."

That brought laughter from both, which increased when Agronguerre, in all seriousness, replied, "Perhaps I would rather try to sway Bestesbulzibar and his minions."

*   *   *

If the specter of death itself had walked into his office, Abbot Braumin Herde's expression would have been no less incredulous and no less horrified.

De'Unnero came swaggering in, walking with confidence—with a smile, even—right up to the new abbot's desk. He bent low, placing his hands upon the lacquered wood, staring down at Braumin Herde. His eyes sparkled with the same intensity Braumin remembered from their days together at St.-Mere-Abelle, the fire that always had the younger monks on edge whenever Master De'Unnero was around, the same fire that had made the dangerous man a legend among the younger brothers.

"You seem surprised to see me," De'Unnero said innocently.

Abbot Braumin couldn't even begin to respond, had no words to convey the astonishment and trepidation churning within him.

"You believed me dead?" De'Unnero asked, as if the thought were absurd.

"The fight at Chasewind Manor . . ." Abbot Braumin began, but he just ended up shaking his head. He was still sitting, wasn't even sure if his legs would support him if he tried to stand. And all the while, the monk was well aware that Marcalo De'Unnero, perhaps the most dangerous monk to ever walk out of St.-Mere-Abelle, could reach across the desk and kill him quickly and easily.

"I was there," De'Unnero confirmed. "I tried to defend Father Abbot Markwart, as was my solemn duty."

"Markwart is dead and buried," Braumin said, growing a bit more confident as he considered the events and the fact that De'Unnero was without allies within Palmaris. "Buried and discredited."

If De'Unnero was surprised, he hid it well.

"Elbryan the Nightbird, too, died in the battle," Abbot Braumin went on, and he thought he saw a hint of a smile touch De'Unnero's face. "A great loss to all the world."

De'Unnero nodded, though his expression hardly revealed any agreement with the sentiment, more an acknowledgment of Braumin's opinion.

Finally, the abbot did manage to stand up and face De'Unnero squarely. "Where have you been?" he demanded. "We have just passed through our darkest and most confused days—we nearly lost all to King Danube—and we are not even certain of where we now stand within the kingdom or among the populace. And yet, where is Abbot De'Unnero during all of this? Where is the man who will reveal the truth of Father Abbot Markwart's fall?"

"Perhaps it is a truth I did not believe the Church was ready to hear," De'Unnero replied forcefully. He stood back, though, and chuckled. "Markwart erred," he admitted, and those two words coming from the mouth of this man nearly knocked Abbot Braumin off his feet. "As did De'Unnero in trusting him."

"He was possessed by Bestesbulzibar," Abbot Braumin dared to remark. That proclamation brought De'Unnero back to his fine edge of anger, eyes shining dangerously.

"How dare you make such a claim?"

"You just said—"

"That he erred," said De'Unnero. "And so I believe he did. He erred in his obsession with the followers of Avelyn Desbris. Better to let the lot of you play out your philosophies, that your own errors might be laid bare for all to see."

"You come back here to speak such nonsense?" Abbot Braumin asked, walking around the desk, for he did not like the way that De'Unnero was using it as a prop to gain a physical advantage. "If you are of Markwart's mind, then know that your ideas have been discredited."

"Because Father Abbot Markwart was possessed by Bestesbulzibar?" De'Unnero asked skeptically.

"Yes!" the abbot of St. Precious snapped. "By the words of Jilseponie herself!" He didn't miss the flash of anger that crossed De'Unnero's face at the mention of the woman. "She, who survived the fight with Markwart, who went to him spiritually to do battle, saw the truth of the man, saw the alliance he had made with the most foul demon."

De'Unnero began laughing before Braumin finished the sentence. "And you would expect her to say differently?" he asked. "Would she admit, then, that Father Abbot Markwart was possessed by angels?"

"You have missed so much," Braumin replied.

"I have witnessed more than you believe from afar."

"Then where have you been?" the abbot demanded. "As we passed our trials with King Danube and Duke Kalas—now Baron of Palmaris—where was Marcalo De'Unnero? As we began our inquisition into the disposition of Father Abbot Markwart, where was De'Unnero? Did you fear, perhaps, that you would be brought to answer for your crimes?"

"Fear?" echoed the former abbot, the former bishop of Palmaris. "And pray tell me what crimes I might have to answer for, good Abbot. Aloysius Crump?" he asked, referring to a merchant whom he, acting as bishop, had arrested and subsequently executed. "Tried and convicted of hiding gem-stones, when the edict of the Father Abbot was that I should confiscate every one. What then have I done to deserve such words as these? I stood by Father Abbot Markwart, as I was trained to do at St.-Mere-Abelle, as you were trained to do before Master Jojonah poisoned your heart with his silly beliefs. Yes, my friend, I will speak honestly with you and will not be-gin to pretend that I mourn the death of the heretic Jojonah. And, yes, I freely admit that I acted the part of Father Abbot Markwart's second and followed his commands, the orders of the rightful leader of the Abellican Church, as any soldier would follow the orders of King Danube. Am I to be called to account for that? Will Braumin Herde place me under arrest and try me publicly? Who next, then, fool? Will you find those who came with Father Abbot Markwart to St. Precious on his first visit and try them for their actions in taking the centaur, Bradwarden, prisoner? But wait, was not your own dear friend, Brother Dellman, among that group? What of the guards in St.-Mere-Abelle who watched over Bradwarden and the doomed Chilichunks in the dungeons of our home abbey? Tell me, abbot of St. Precious, if you mean to punish them as well." De'Unnero shook his head and laughed wickedly, then came forward to stand face-to-face with the abbot, his eyes locked in a fanatical glare. "Pray tell me, abbot reformer, what you will do with all those brothers and all the townsfolk who dragged your precious Master Jojonah through the streets of St.-Mere-Abelle town and tortured him and burned him at the stake. Are they all guilty, as you hint that I am? Shall we build rows of stakes to satiate your lust for revenge?"

"Markwart has been discredited," Abbot Braumin said grimly and determinedly. "He was wrong, Brother De'Unnero, as were you in following him blindly."

De'Unnero backed off a step, though he continued to hold fast that wicked grin of his, the look he had perfected years before, that made it seem as if he held the upper hand in every confrontation, as if he, De'Unnero, somehow knew more than his opponents could begin to understand. "Even if what you say is true, I expect to be formally welcomed back into the Church," he said.

"You must account for the last months," Abbot Braumin declared, but De'Unnero was shaking his head even as the words came out.

"I must account for nothing," he replied. "I needed time to sort through the tumultuous events, and so I left. Can less be said of Braumin and his cohorts and their flight to the Barbacan?"

Braumin's expression turned incredulous.

"If I am called to account for my actions of the last year, dear Braumin Herde, then know that you and your friends will likewise face the inquisition," De'Unnero said confidently. "Your side won the conflict in Palmaris, that much is obvious, and the victor might write the histories in his manner of choosing; but St. Precious is not so large and important a place when measured against St.-Mere-Abelle, and I, and Father Markwart, did not leave that place without allies.

"I have returned, brother," De'Unnero finished, holding wide his arms. "Accept that as fact and think well before you choose to begin a war against me."

Braumin winced and did indeed begin to reflect on the man's words. He hated De'Unnero as much as he had hated Markwart, but did he really have any kind of a case for action against the man? There were rumors that De'Unnero had murdered Baron Bildeborough, rumors Abbot Braumin believed wholeheartedly. But they were just that, rumors, and if there was any evidence of the crime, Braumin hadn't seen it. Marcalo De'Unnero had

been Markwart's principal bully, a brute who reveled in the fight, who pun-
ished mercilessly those who disagreed with him.

De'Unnero had viciously battled Elbryan, and the wound that had even-
tually brought down the ranger had been inflicted by a tiger's paw, the
favored weapon of this man.

But were De'Unnero's actions in that last fight, when Jilseponie and
Elbryan had invaded Chasewind Manor with the express purpose of killing
the Father Abbot of the Abellican Church, really a crime?

Braumin thought so, but had not Master Francis tried to stop the ranger
from entering Chasewind Manor earlier? Did that make Francis a criminal
as well? Braumin winced again and tried to find some answer. To him,
De'Unnero was indeed a criminal, and he knew that he would not be the
only one who saw the dangerous man that way. Certainly Jilseponie would
do battle with De'Unnero if ever she saw him again—on sight and to the
death.

Then it hit Braumin squarely, the realization that the timing of this
meeting was much more than coincidence. How strange that De'Unnero
had walked back into St. Precious on the same day Jilseponie had left Palmaris for the northland!

Bolstered by the notion that the dangerous man might harbor some fear
of Jilseponie, Braumin Herde squared his shoulders. "I am the abbot of St.
Precious," he declared, "sanctioned by Church and Crown, by King
Danube himself, and backed by Abbot Je'howith of St. Honce and by all
the brethren of St. Precious. I'll not relinquish the position."

"And I am simply cast aside?"

"You left," Braumin insisted, "without explanation, without, many
would say, just cause."

"That was my choice."

"A choice that cost you your appointment at St. Precious," said Braumin,
and then he snorted. "Do you believe that the people of Palmaris or that
Duke Kalas, who has publicly professed his hatred for you, will support
your return to this position?"

"I believe that the choice is for the Church alone," De'Unnero replied
calmly, seeming entirely unshaken by Braumin's blunt attacks. "But the
point is irrelevant, because I have no further designs on St. Precious, or
upon this wretched city at all. I only came here to fill a vacancy at the
request of my Father Abbot. You see my loyalty to him as a crime, but
given the doctrine of the Church, that is a ridiculous assertion. I am confident that if we battled for this position at the College of Abbots—which I
assume will soon be called—I would prevail. My service to St.-Mere-Abelle
cannot be undone by your passions, nor can it be twisted into something
perverse and evil.

"But fear not, too-young abbot, for I am no threat to your coveted post,"
De'Unnero went on. "Indeed, I am glad that you are here; I only hope that

all of the other followers of Jojonah and Avelyn will flock here beside you. Better that you all fester in this place of minor importance, while I attend to the greater workings of the Church in St.-Mere-Abelle."

Braumin Herde wanted to shout out at the man, to call for the guards and put this wretched criminal in prison, but when he considered it all, he knew that he could do little, really, and that any actions he took against De'Unnero now could have very serious implications at the forthcoming College of Abbots, repercussions that Braumin and his friends could ill afford. For De'Unnero, though his title as bishop had been revoked and his stewardship as abbot of St. Precious had been rightfully turned over to Braumin, was still a ranking master of the Abellican Order, a monk of many accomplishments, a strong leader with a place and a voice within the Church.

A very loud and obnoxious voice, Abbot Braumin understood.

Prince Midalis and Andacanavar sat on a large wet rock overlooking the Gulf of Corona, holding stoically against gusting and unseasonably cold ocean winds and stinging drizzle.

"I keep hoping that we will see a sail, or a hundred," Midalis admitted.

"That your brother will send the help you requested?" the ranger asked.

"Two score Allheart knights and a brigade of Kingsmen would bolster our cause against the goblins," Midalis remarked.

"Where are they, then?" Andacanavar asked. "Your brother sits as king in a land that, by all reports, has defeated the threat. Why has he not sent his soldiers to aid in your—in our—cause?"

Midalis honestly had no answer to that. "I suspect that he is embroiled in other pressing matters," he answered. "Perhaps rogue bands of monsters remain."

"Or maybe he has his soldiers busy in keeping order in a kingdom gone crazy," the ranger reasoned, and that raised Midalis' eyebrows.

"I have seen such things before," Andacanavar went on. "The aftermath of war can be more dangerous than the war itself."

Midalis shook his head and stared back out over the dark waters.

"Where are they, then?" Andacanavar asked. "Where are the ships and the brave Allheart knights? Is your brother so deaf to your call?"

Prince Midalis had no answers. Whatever the reason, it was becoming obvious to him that this fight in Vanguard was his alone among the nobility of Honce-the-Bear. He glanced from the cold and dark waters of the Mirianic back to his ranger companion, and took heart in the sight of the great and noble warrior.

For, whether his brother, the King, came to his aid or not, the Duke of Vanguard—the Prince of Honce-the-Bear—knew that he and his people were no longer alone in their fight.

*   *   *

She looked up at the sky and noted the dark, heavy clouds. There would be more rain; every day, it seemed, more stormy weather rolled in from the Mirianic, pounding Falidean Bay and Falidean town, soaking the ground where they had buried poor Brennilee, turning the dirt to mud. That ground had still been hard when they had put the child into it, and some of the men digging the grave had muttered that they hoped they had put Brennilee down far enough to keep her from the rains.

Merry Cowsenfed prayed—prayed mostly that the torrents wouldn't bring up the little box into which they had placed Brennilee. That had happened several times in Falidean town during heavy storms: coffins sometimes rotted through so that you could see the decomposed corpses, floating right out of the ground. Merry stifled a cry and shook her head as her darkest fears and deepest pain led her to imagine the sight of her beautiful, precious Brennilee rotting within that box.

The woman melted down to her knees, head bent, shoulders heaving with sobs. They could rebury the child, she thought.

Yes, soon enough. They could dig up the grave and bury the child down deeper.

Merry Cowsenfed looked down at the rosy spots on her own forearm and nodded. For, yes, she knew, the gravediggers would be working again soon enough.

"Merry!" came a call from the road behind her. Without rising up, the drenched woman glanced back over her shoulder to see about a score gathered there. She couldn't make out many faces, but she did recognize Thedo Crayle and his wife, Dinny, the little Haggarty boy, and one or two others; and from the one thing she knew all those she recognized had in common, Merry could pretty much guess the remainder of the group.

They were the sick of Falidean, people with the rosy spots, and with the awful fever and stomach-churning to follow soon enough.

Merry pulled herself up and pulled her shawl tight about her shoulders, bending her head against the driving rain.

"Ye come with us, Merry," said Dinny Crayle in her gentle voice as she met the grieving woman and put her arms about Merry's shoulders. "We're going to St. Gwendolyn, we are, to ask the abbess to help us."

Merry looked at her, at all the desperate and sick townsfolk, but there was no hope on her strained features. "Ye'll be turned away," she said. "The monks won't be helpin' with the plague. They'll be hidin' from it, as do our kin."

"Cowards all!" one blustery man cried out. "The abbess'll open her door, or we'll knock the damned thing down!"

That brought a chorus of cheers, cries wrought of anger and of determination, but Merry's voice rose above them.

"Ye're knowin' the rules!" she yelled. "Ye got the rosy plague, so ye stay put and make yer peace with God and accept yer fate."

"Damn the rules!" another man yelled out.

"Ye got the plague!" Merry yelled back. "Ye stay put, then, so as ye don't go bringin' it to all the other towns o' the kingdom."

"Damn the rules!" the same man cried.

"But ye know we're to die, then, and horribly," Dinny Crayle said to Merry. "Ye know we're to take the fever and get all crazy, and call out for dead ones, and jerk about all horrible until our arms and legs ache and bruise. And ye'll get the weeps. And then ye'll die, and if ye're lucky, someone else with the rosies'll take the time to put ye in the ground—or might that they'll just drop ye off the road and let the birds peck at yer blind eyes."

A couple of the nearby children started wailing, and so did several of the adults, but mostly, the adults cried that the rules were wrong and that the monks must help them.

"No God'll let us die like that," another woman insisted.

"Forty-three dead in the town already," Thedo Crayle reminded Merry, "forty-three, with yer own Brennilee among 'em. And another fifty've got it. At least fifty, and probably with twice that number gettin' it but not yet knowin' that they be doomed. That's near to a hunnerd, Merry. A hunnerd out o' eleven hunnerd in all Falidean town. Stay put, ye say? Bah to that. The whole town'll fall dead soon enough."

"But might be only our town," Merry tried to reason.

Thedo scoffed. "How many boats've come in since we learned o' the plague? And how many just before that? And where'd it come to us from, if all who got it stayed home? No, good Merry, it's out and was so before it found Falidean town. The rosy's out and runnin', don't ye doubt, and them monks've got to do somethin' about it. We're goin' to St. Gwendolyn, with ye or without ye. We'll get our Abbess Delenia and her sisters and brothers to heal us."

"Brother Avelyn kilt the demon, so they're sayin'," Dinny added, "and if them monks're killin' the dactyl demon, then they're strong enough to kill the rosies!"

Another cheer went up, and the group started down the long muddy road, with Dinny Crayle holding fast to her friend Merry, guiding the woman along. Merry looked back repeatedly at Brennilee's little grave marker, her instincts screaming in protest at the thought of leaving her little girl behind. What would happen to Brennilee if Merry died in some distant land? Who would they put in the ground beside her little girl, or would they even bother to bury Brennilee again if her little coffin churned up? Truly, Merry's heart broke. She didn't believe that the Abellican monks could, or would, help them, but she went along anyway.

Mostly it was sheer weakness, the inability to resist Dinny's pull, the inability to break away from the only comforting hands that had found her stooped shoulders these last days, since she had begun to show signs of the rosy plague.

The group took up a song soon after, a chanting prayer that spoke of the hope and redemption offered by the Abellican Church, that spoke of St. Abelle, the healer of souls, the healer of bodies.

inability to break away from the only comforting hands that had found her stooped shoulders these last days, since she had begun to show signs of the rosy plague.

The group took up a song soon after, a chanting prayer that spoke of the hope and redemption offered by the Abellican Church, that spoke of St. Abelle, the healer of souls, the healer of bodies.

PART TWO

▼

SETTLING

I had to get out of there.

I knew beyond anything else that I had to get out of Palmaris, away from that place of pain and turmoil. It was overwhelming me—all of it. It was paralyzing me with pain and most of all with doubt.

I had to get back on the road to the north, to my home: a simpler place by far. In Dundalis, in all the Timberlands, the pressures of survival overrule many of the trappings of civilization. In the wild Timberlands, where the domain of nature dominates that of mankind, the often-too-confusing concepts of right and wrong are replaced by the simpler concept of consequences. In the wilds of the Timberlands, you choose your course, you act upon that trail, and you accept—for what else might you do?—the consequences of those choices and actions. Had I lost Elbryan to a mistaken handhold while scaling a cliff face rather than in battling a demon spirit, then, I believe, I could have more easily accepted his death. The pain, the sense of loss, would have been no less profound, of course, but it would have been outside the realm of the more personal questions the actual conditions fostered. It would have been a simple reality based upon simple reality, and not a reality of loss based upon some philosophical questions of morality and justice. Would such an accidental loss of my love have been more senseless?

Of that I am not sure, and, thus, I had to get out of there.

My decision to go disappointed many. I have weakened my allies, I fear, and bolstered my enemies. To those looking upon me from afar, it seems as if I chose the easier road.

They think that I am running away. Friends and enemies believe that I have retreated from my fight, have fled from the peril. I cannot completely disagree, for my stance on the larger battle within Honce-the-Bear now seems to me as intangible as the battlefield itself. Are we fighting a demon spirit or the very nature of mankind? Was Markwart an aberration or an inevitability? How many revolutions have been fought by people espousing a more enlightened way, a greater truth, a greater justice, only to see the victors fall into the same human failings as their predecessors?

Yes, I fear I have come to question the value of the war itself.

Perhaps I am running away from the confusion, from the noise of aftermath, that unsettling scrambling to fill the power vacancies. But in the final measure, I am not running away from the greater battle; of this, I am certain. Nor will my road truly be easier. I have come to recognize now that I am charging headlong into the most personal and potentially devastating battle I have ever fought. I am running to

The Enduring Gift of Bestesbulzibar

The day was hot, brutally so, but at least the incessant rains that had so filled the spring and early summer now seemed to be burned away by the brilliant sunshine. Master Francis, his robes flung as wide as he could get them, would have welcomed rain this day, anything to wash the stickiness from his weary body.

He had made the seventy-or-so-mile journey from St.-Mere-Abelle to St. Precious in a couple of days, with magical assistance, but the return trip had been marked by one problem after another. With his escorts, Francis had stopped in Amvoy on the Masur Delaval to gather supplies; but in that small sister city of Palmaris, they had encountered too much misery to ignore, including a group of people wounded in a skirmish with a band of goblins still running wild in the eastern reaches, as well as a little boy who had been kicked by a horse. At Francis' insistence, and over the protests of a couple of the older brothers, the group had spent nearly two weeks in Amvoy, working with their few hematite soul stones to aid anyone in need—and it seemed as if the entire town had come to them!

Now, finally, they were on the road again, but not on a direct route toward St.-Mere-Abelle but rather heading southeast, toward a small hamlet named Davon Dinnishire—a settlement of hardy people who had come south from Vanguard. The remnants of a goblin band had been spotted lurking in the forests near the place, and, though word had gone out to those soldiers hunting the monsters, Francis had learned that none were available to go to the support of Davon Dinnishire.

"It is not our affair," one young brother, Julius, argued. "We have been entrusted with coordinating the College of Abbots at St.-Mere-Abelle, yet we tarry with the business of the military."

Master Francis fixed Brother Julius with a sympathetic expression, and a helpless smile. "Once I walked as you now walk," he said to the young brother, loudly enough for all of those near to him to hear. "Once I walked with the pride that I—that the Church and thus anyone associated with it—was somehow above the common man."

Julius seemed perplexed by the statement and completely off his guard.

"It took the death of Father Abbot Markwart, the destruction of the evil that the man had become—"

"Master Francis!" another of the group interrupted.

Francis smiled again and held up his hand to silence the murmuring of the astonished brothers.

"To go now straight to St.-Mere-Abelle, though we know Davon Dinnishire is in dire need, would be an act of sin, plain and without argument," Francis stated. "It would be a course that the younger and less wise Francis Dellacourt, betrayed by the edicts of Father Abbot Markwart, would surely have followed.

"I am wiser now, my young friend," Francis finished. "I do not speak with God, but I believe now that I better understand the path our faith asks us to walk. And that path now is to Davon Dinnishire." Another of the group started to question that, but Francis cut him short. "I am the only master in the group," he reminded them. "I have served as bishop of Palmaris and as abbot of St. Precious. I walked beside the Father Abbot for many months. This is not an issue I plan to debate with you, Brother Julius, or with any of you," he said, glancing around at all the monks.

There was only a bit of grumbling behind him as he started down the southeastern road once more.

Master Francis walked with honest convictions and a purposeful stride. He did wince once, though, when he heard Brother Julius whisper to another brother that Francis was only delaying because he feared to return to St.-Mere-Abelle and face stern Master Bou-raiy, who would not be pleased at all about the events in Palmaris from the fall of Father Abbot Markwart to the present. There was a grain of truth in that statement, Francis had to admit.

Soon enough, the monks came to the walled village of Davon Dinnishire, running the last mile, using a rising plume of black smoke to guide them. They were somewhat relieved to find that the village had not been completely destroyed. The villagers were forming bucket lines to try to put out the flames.

"Who leads here?" Francis demanded of the first woman he could stop.

The old peasant pointed to a young, strong man of about thirty winters, with reddish brown hair and a full beard, thick arms and a barrel chest, and intense gray eyes that flashed like embers flaring to life every time he barked an order at one of the nearby villagers.

Francis hurried over to him. The villager's gray eyes widened when he recognized the approaching man as an Abellican monk. "I am Master Francis of St.-Mere-Abelle," he introduced himself. "We will help where we may."

"A pity ye wasn't here this morn," the man replied. "If ye'd helped our fight with them goblins, we'd not have so many squirming with pain, and not so many fires to douse. Laird Dinnishire, I am—Maladance Dinnishire o' the Davon Dinnishire clan." He held out his hand, and Francis took it and shook it firmly, but turned back as he did and ordered his monks to get to work.

"The wounded first," Francis instructed, "then go and help with the fires."

"Did ye see the goblins?" Maladance Dinnishire asked. "Somewhere between two and three score run off, by last count."

"And how many came against you?" asked Francis.

"Not many more than that," the laird admitted. "We weren't to run out after them, and they stayed back, throwing fiery arrows and running up to launch their spears. We killed a few, and hurt a few more, but they were just testing our mettle, so to speak."

"They will return," Francis reasoned.

"Likely this same night," Maladance agreed. "Goblins're likin' the dark. But don't ye worry, Master Francis. If they're tryin' to get over our wall, they're dyin' tryin'!"

Francis didn't doubt the town's resolve or strength, for he understood that many of the towns in this region had been badly set upon during the months of the demon war. Many enemy forces had landed along the gulf coast, part of an assault force that had set its eyes upon the greatest prize in all the kingdom: St.-Mere-Abelle. But then the demon dactyl had been destroyed and the monstrous army had lost its coordination. The attack upon St.-Mere-Abelle had utterly failed and, since the powrie fleet had been mostly destroyed and the rest had sailed off, those goblins and powries already on the land had been left with no escape from the region, running off in small marauding bands.

So these townsfolk, farmers mostly, had seen some fighting, he knew. But he knew, too, that even if they fought valiantly, they would suffer further losses, perhaps heavy losses, against so many goblin warriors.

Francis went to work, helping the wounded and fighting the fires. When he was done, some three hours later, the sun was beginning its western descent. He called together those of his brethren he could find, all but a couple still tending the wounded and the ill. All of the monks were drenched in sweat and covered in soot, eyes red from smoke and hands blistered from running with heavy, water-filled buckets.

"Gather your strength, both physical and magical," Master Francis bade them. "The goblins mean to return this night, but we will go out and find them where they camp."

That widened some eyes!

"We are eighteen brothers of St.-Mere-Abelle, trained in fighting and in magic," Francis said.

"We've one offensive gemstone," Brother Julius, who had become somewhat of a spokesman for the rest of the group, interjected, "a single graphite."

"Enough to blind and confuse our enemies that we might spring upon them," Francis remarked with a sly grin.

"You are beginning to sound much like Master De'Unnero," Brother Julius remarked, and his tone showed that he spoke somewhat in jest. But Francis didn't take the comparison that way at all and scowled fiercely at the younger man.

"We have a responsibility to these people," he declared, "to all people who are in need."

As he finished, there came a tumult from down the lane. The brothers turned and saw a monk crashing out of the door of a peasant hovel, stripping off his robes as he ran full speed for the group. "Master Francis!" he called repeatedly. By the time he reached the group, he was wearing only his short cotton underclothing, and to the amazement of the other monks, he grabbed up one bucket of water and doused himself.

"Brother Cranston!" Francis scolded. "We are all uncomfortable in the heat—"

"Rosy plague!" Cranston replied desperately. "In that house . . . a woman . . . already dead."

Francis rushed over and grabbed the man, shaking him. "Rosy plague?" he asked breathlessly. "Are you sure, brother?"

"Red spots with white rings all about her body," Brother Cranston replied. "Her eyes were sunken and bruised, and she had bled from her gums and her eyes, I could see. Oh, but she rotted away!"

Brother Julius came up to Francis and dropped a heavy hand on the master's shoulder. "We must be far from this place at once," he said gravely. Behind him, Francis heard another mutter, "Better that the goblins come back and burn the whole town to the ground."

Francis wanted to shout at the brother, to shove Julius and his words far aside. But he could not dismiss any of the remarks. The rosy plague! The scourge of Honce-the-Bear. Francis' primary duties at St.-Mere-Abelle for years had been as a historian, and so he knew, better than any, the truth of the rosy plague. It had first occurred in God's Year 412, devastating the southern reaches of the kingdom. One in seven had died, according to the records. One in seven. And in Yorkey that number had been closer to one in four.

And yet the plague that had occurred the following century, from 517 to 529, had been even more virulent, devastating the Mantis Arm and spreading across the Gulf of Corona to Vanguard. Ursal had been particularly hard hit. Afterward the record keepers of the day, Abellican monks mostly, had put the death toll at one in three—some had even claimed that half the population of Honce-the-Bear had fallen.

The rosy plague!

How vulnerable Honce-the-Bear would have been then to invasion by Behren, to the south, except that Behren had not been spared either. Francis, of course, had no records of the death toll in that southern kingdom, but many of the accounts he had read had claimed that the Behrenese had suffered even more than the folk of Honce-the-Bear. Now the kingdom was even more thickly populated than it had been before the 517 plague, Francis knew. And now, given the war, the kingdom was even less prepared to handle such a disaster.

So even though Master Francis Dellacourt—the enlightened monk who had learned the truth of Father Abbot Markwart and of the heroes he had once considered enemies, had turned his life down a different road, a road of compassion and of service—wanted to yell against the callous remarks of his brethren, he could not find the strength to do so. Not in that terribly shocking moment, not in the face of the threat of the rosy plague!

But first he had to go and see. He had read the descriptions of the disease, had seen artists' renderings of the victims. Several times since 529, there had been reports of the plague, but they had proven either to be minor outbreaks or simply the mistaken claims of desperate people. He bade his brethren to stay there, except for a pair he sent in search of the three still-missing brethren, and then Master Francis gathered up his strength and strode determinedly toward the hovel at the end of the lane.

He heard weeping and found a pair of children within, looking haggard and afraid. He brushed past them and through a curtain, and there she lay.

> *Ring around the rosy,*
> *Gather bowls of posies*
> *Burn the clothes*
> *And dig the holes*
> *And cover us with dirt.*

It was the first verse of an old children's song, a poem that had been penned sometime around God's Year 412, a song of the attempts to ward off the killer plague by diminishing the rotting stench of its victims with flowers, a song that told the honest truth for those who contracted the illness. " 'And cover us with dirt,' " Francis whispered.

"Get out! Get out!" he yelled at the children. "Out and far away from here. You can do nothing for your mother now. Get out!" He chased the weeping children out before him into the lane; and several townsfolk, Laird Dinnishire among them, came over.

"My brethren and I will go out after the goblins," Francis explained to him. "With luck, they will not return to your town."

"What's wrong in the house?" the concerned laird asked.

Francis looked at the hovel. "Burn it," he instructed.

"What?"

"Burn it to the ground," Francis declared, fixing the man with a determined stare, "at once."

"Ye can'no—"

"Burn it!" Francis interrupted. "You must trust me, Laird Dinnishire, I beg of you. No one is to enter."

The laird stared at him incredulously, and those behind Dinnishire shook their heads and mumbled.

Francis took the laird by the arm and pulled him aside. And then he explained to the man, plainly and honestly, that the goblins were not the worst of their troubles this hot summer day.

"Ye canno' be sure," Dinnishire protested.

"I am not," Francis lied, for he did not want to start a panic, and forewarning, beyond burning the house, would do the folk of Davon Dinnishire little good. "But are we to risk the chance that I am right? The woman is dead, and her husband and children—"

"Husband's been dead two years now," Laird Dinnishire explained. "Killed in a powrie fight."

"Then the children must be taken in elsewhere. Burn the house to its foundation, and then you, and another one or two you can trust, must go and clear the remains of the house and of the dead woman."

Laird Dinnishire stared at him.

"I beg of you, Laird Dinnishire," Francis said solemnly.

"Ye'll keep them goblins off us?" the man asked.

Francis nodded, then went back and gathered up his brethren; and out they went, on the hunt for goblins.

As soon as they reached the trees beyond the farms immediately surrounding Davon Dinnishire, Francis set the group into a defensive formation. Not wanting to diminish his own magical energies any more than he already had done with his efforts in healing the injured townsfolk, he gave the finest hematite to Brother Julius and bade the monk to spirit-walk to search for the goblins.

Julius was dumfounded. He had attempted only one spirit-walk in his years at St.-Mere-Abelle, and that had not gone well—the monk unintentionally had tried to inhabit the body of another nearby student. "I am not so good at such a task," he admitted.

Francis nodded, for he understood well the man's trepidation. Markwart, Avelyn, and Jilseponie had all taken gemstone use to a higher level, where such feats as spirit-walking seemed almost routine. Francis, too, had learned much in his days beside the Father Abbot, and he had forgotten how daunting spirit-walking could be. And how dangerous. He took back the gemstone, then, regretting that he would be using even more of his magical energies, and set off out of body, rushing through the trees, across the small river, and over the wide bluffs.

He found the goblin band almost immediately and counted their number at only thirty. He stayed with them only a few seconds, to get a feel for their organization and readiness, then headed back, taking a circuitous route, which confirmed his suspicions that the rest of the group—another score, perhaps—was spread out among the trees.

"They have done well in choosing and setting up their encampment," Francis explained when he returned to his brethren. Before the details of the terrain were lost from his memory, he bent down and sketched out a rough map in the dirt. "We'll not get anywhere close to the goblins without being noticed."

"Let us turn for St.-Mere-Abelle, then," Brother Julius started to say, but Francis cut him short with an angry glare.

"We need not go to them," Francis went on. "I doubt that they expect any trouble from the townsfolk—it seems more reasonable that they believe the people of Davon Dinnishire will await the next attack from behind the walls of their village. To get back there, the goblins will likely take this route." He indicated the fairly obvious path on his map. "Let us prepare a section of that same path for their march."

The monks headed out at once, coming to a stretch of wide-limbed maples, with a clear and easily traveled path beneath that Francis reasoned the goblins would take, not expecting any ambush. Francis took a good, long look at the area. Never had he been much of a tactician, but rather more of a political animal.

"If I may, Master Francis," said Brother Julius, apparently noting that the man was at a loss. "We put everyone up in the trees, except you, who will travel to the far end with the graphite. Those of us carrying crossbows will arm the weapons." He glanced around and nodded, for more than half the monks did carry crossbows. "The rest will sharpen a stick to use as a spear or take as large a stone as they can carry up into the boughs with them.

"You come out first, reacting to a predetermined event, such as the lead goblins passing a specific tree," Brother Julius went on. The other monks nodded, for they knew Julius had fought with Master De'Unnero, the finest of tacticians, on several occasions, including during the almost legendary slaughter of powries at St.-Mere-Abelle's lower dock gates. "We will expect the flash, and so we will cover our eyes, and then . . ." He paused and smiled grimly, and it seemed to everyone, even to Francis, that Julius—now that he wasn't going to get his way concerning the return to St.-Mere-Abelle—had put his heart into the fight.

A good student of De'Unnero, Francis noted, with just the right attitude.

Soon after, the monks were all in place, settled on their branches, with Francis farther down the lane, behind a large tree.

The minutes became an hour, became two and then two more. Though he was growing as impatient as any, Francis was glad of the delay, of the rest, that he might recover more and more of his magical energies. He didn't really believe that he would kill many goblins with his lightning bolt, but the stronger the flash, the more likely a solid and quick victory.

The sun went below the western horizon, and still the forest remained quiet. Francis understood that the goblins would gain an advantage in the dark, for the night was their favored time, so he was relieved to see Sheila, Corona's bright moon, nearly full, rising in the dark sky.

Still they waited—and Francis hoped that the other brothers remained awake!

And then he nearly jumped out of his boots, for a goblin slipped quietly past him, moving from tree to tree. Francis resisted the urge to chase the creature, understanding that this was a lead scout and that any noise from him would likely ruin their ambush. He took careful note of the goblin's movements, though, for he expected that he would see that one again all too soon.

Soon after, there came a rustling down the trail, and Francis saw the dark forms, trotting easily, crossing the maple grove.

The master took a deep breath, rubbing his hands along the graphite, finding his heart. He harbored no doubt about the course of his actions; he merely feared that he would not be strong enough to see his brothers through this fight, that they would all die out here on the road with so many important messages, of the future of the Church and of the threat of plague, yet to deliver.

In any case, it was too late to change his mind or his plans, Francis deliberately told himself, and so he crouched and focused on the leading goblins, waiting until they reached the appointed spot.

Out jumped Francis, falling to one knee and holding forth the graphite, calling out a single time—the signal for his brothers to shield their eyes—and letting loose a sizzling blast of white energy, a lightning bolt that charred three of the first five goblins, dropping the next bunch writhing to the ground, and stealing the vision of all for the moment—a moment long enough for the Abellican brothers to fire their crossbows and throw their stones and spears down upon the confused monsters, then to leap down to the ground and begin the wild melee—elbows, feet, and fists flying savagely.

And what a rout it seemed, with goblins falling, scrambling, shrieking, and ducking! For a moment, Francis thought the day would be won without damage to his brethren. And indeed, before the first two minutes of fighting had passed, a score and more of the goblins were down, with another score running haphazardly into the cover of the forest.

Francis called out rudimentary commands—cheers more than orders—and he leaped about, graphite in hand, his blood coursing fiercely, his heart pumping furiously, and in that heightened state of energy, confident that he could loose another equally powerful blast of lightning.

Maybe he caught the movement out of the corner of his eye, or perhaps it was just a result of his heightened sense of awareness, but he sensed a movement behind him and spun about, just as the goblin who had earlier passed this spot thrust its spear at his chest. Francis gave a cry of surprise and fear and had no time to do anything but dive aside. He felt the spear tip slash, slip in, and bang against his rib. Had the goblin been carrying a better weapon, that would have been the sudden end of Master Francis Della-court. But the meager spear deflected off the rib and tore a longer but more superficial line as it came out along the side of Francis' chest, lodging in the folds of his thick robe instead of into his flesh.

Francis staggered to his feet, aware that the spear was at his side and that the goblin was no longer holding it. But the vicious little creature was coming fast in pursuit, yellow teeth bared.

Francis didn't try to extract the spear, but shrugged off his robe, dropping it—the weapon with it—to the ground. He brought his left arm into a defensive position before him, then drove his right arm to block and push aside the goblin's first attack. The wretched little creature snarled and drooled, its tongue hanging out of its mouth; and it hardly reacted to the sudden movement as Francis snap-kicked it under the chin, driving its jaws together and nipping off the tip of that pointy little tongue.

The dazed creature staggered backward two steps, and Francis, well trained in the arts martial at St.-Mere-Abelle, came on to take the advantage, pushing aside the skinny goblin's arms, then snapping off a left jab into the creature's face, once and then again. The goblin staggered backward, and Francis fell over it, bearing it heavily to the ground beneath him.

The goblin bit hard into his shoulder, but Francis got his hands around the thing's neck and squeezed with all his strength. It seemed to Francis to last an hour—an hour of fiery pain from the goblin's bite and of horror as the thing squirmed pitifully in his unyielding grasp, arms flailing.

And then it lay still, very still; and even in the moonlight, Francis could see the blackness of death that had come over its face.

Reminding himself that there was still a battle being waged behind him, that other goblins even then might be running at him with cruel spears, Francis wrenched himself away and staggered to his feet.

He saw then that his brethren had performed well, that many goblins were down, and that any of those still near the monks, who had formed into a tight defensive circle, had no chance of gaining any advantage.

But those goblins who had run off had not gone far, Francis saw to his horror. At the left flank, a substantial group of goblins was approaching, spears up and ready to fly.

Francis dove down for his robe, scrambling for the pocket. A moment later, he lifted his hand and reached into the graphite gemstone, calling forth its power. The volley of spears flew in—he heard the cries of his brethren—and the lightning stroke fired off, dropping several more goblins, stunning several others.

On came the Abellican monks, leaping into the goblin ranks, punishing them in close combat with strength and skills no goblin could match.

Francis moved to join the fighting, but found his legs weak beneath him, and when he reached down to feel his chest, his hand came back covered in blood. He was on the ground then, suddenly, alone and vulnerable and expecting another goblin to come up and skewer him.

But then he heard Brother Julius call out his name; and a horde of monks gathered about him, defending him.

Francis reached up and gave Julius the graphite. "Crossbows," he managed to gasp.

The remaining goblins regrouped and came back at the defending monks, but their barrage of spears was met by another blast of lightning and by a volley of more deadly crossbow quarrels. Those surviving goblins ran, scattered, into the forest night.

"How many?" Francis demanded of Julius shortly after.

"Rest, master," Julius replied. "You will be tended by bandage and by gemstone, and will feel stronger in the morning."

"How many?" came the determined question a second time.

"We have downed nearly two score," Julius answered. "They will all be killed, and those remaining have fled without organization and should pose no further threat to Davon Dinnishire."

Francis grabbed Julius by the front of his robe and pulled himself up, so that their faces nearly touched. "How many?" Francis growled.

"Six," Brother Julius replied gravely. "Six are dead, master, and several wounded. We must begin the healing at once."

Francis held the grip for a moment longer, then sank back to the ground. Six brothers killed in a battle that he could have avoided. Master Francis felt breathless, and it had nothing to do with the wound in his side.

He spent a long while—perhaps an hour, perhaps two—lying there, in and out of consciousness, as the other brothers tended his wound with bandages and soul stones. When finally he awoke fully, he learned that another brother had died.

More than a third of his force.

Francis took little comfort in the fact that the number of goblin dead was much more substantial, being consoled only because he knew that he and his brethren had saved Davon Dinnishire from any further attacks—had, for the most part, put an end to this rogue band's troublemaking. He made his slow way about the impromptu encampment, checking on the wounded. Though no anger seemed to be directed specifically his way, he was perceptive enough to understand that more than a few brothers were questioning his wisdom in pursuing this goblin band—queries that, Francis suspected, would be repeated, more forcefully, once he and his companions reached St.-Mere-Abelle.

"Prepare for the road, and we take the dead with us," Francis instructed Brother Julius.

"Straight to St.-Mere-Abelle this time?" Julius asked, a hint of sarcasm in his tone.

Francis glared at him and nodded. "Have you searched the goblins?"

Julius looked at him incredulously. "You expect that they carry treasure?" he asked with a snort. "Their boots were falling off their feet, so worn and decrepit were they."

"I want to know why they were still here," Francis clarified.

"Because they found no escape from the kingdom," Brother Julius replied, rather loudly and sharply. "They, like all the bands still roving this region, were trapped here when the powrie fleet that initially brought them to these shores east of Palmaris was crushed at St.-Mere-Abelle. Where were they to run?"

Francis stared hard at the man. He wasn't sure if Julius was openly second-guessing his decision to fight the monsters, or if the man was simply reeling from the losses. It didn't matter, Francis decided. Though his enemies within the Church might use this incident against him politically once he returned to St.-Mere-Abelle, he knew in his heart he had done right. As Master Jojonah had taken the all-important Barbacan caravan off its course to attack an even more substantial group of monsters for the sake of an Alpinadoran town, so Francis was bound to try to protect Davon Dinnishire.

"Prepare them all for the road," Francis said evenly, not blinking and not backing down an inch. "To St.-Mere-Abelle."

Julius matched the master's stare for a long moment, but then nodded and began calling the camp to order.

Francis, meanwhile, gathered up a burning branch from the small fire the brothers had built, and headed for the pile of goblin bodies. What was he expecting to find? he asked himself repeatedly. Treasure or information that would help him to justify his actions in pursuing this band? Some reward great enough to justify seven dead Abellican brothers?

With anger wrought of guilt, Master Francis pushed among the lice-ridden corpses, kicking them aside. He found a few coins—a pair of gol'bears and some smaller coins—but nothing, as Julius had predicted, that seemed worth the effort of searching the creatures, let alone battling them in the first place. With a helpless sigh, Francis confirmed that the boots of those goblins who were wearing any were ragged things, likely stolen from humans but now worn to shabby pieces. He kicked at one boot, and it fell away, and Francis started to turn back toward his brothers.

But then he noticed something on the goblin's now-exposed foot, and though the coloration was surely wrong—a yellowish blotch inside a circular scar—he recognized the pattern clearly.

Francis bent down low, bringing his torch in for a closer look.

"By God's good graces," he whispered, for he had just seen this same pattern, the pattern of the rosy plague, on the woman in the village. Only on this goblin, the scars seemed healed, as if the creature had overcome the disease. Francis checked the rest of the goblin's body—finding more such scars—then he searched others. To his astonishment, nearly half of the creatures showed remnants of what looked to him like the rosy plague. He would have to research this more closely when he returned to St.-Mere-Abelle, he told himself, to learn if these strange scars were similar to the marks the disease had left on the few human survivors of the plague.

But Francis already had his answer, he believed, and as he followed his assumption along a logical path, he came to understand that the demon dactyl might now be waging another war upon the humans of Honce-the-Bear, a more subtle and more deadly war. Had the demon's minions brought with them the plague?

Francis paused and took a deep and steadying breath, considering his next move carefully. Should he bring one of the infected goblins back to St.-Mere-Abelle? No, he decided almost immediately, fearing the consequences to his precious home if the creature was still spreading the plague. That same thought led him to an even more disturbing possibility: had he and the other brothers contracted the plague by battling the goblins?

"We can check, with hematite," Francis muttered, needing to hear the reassuring words aloud. "We . . . no, the more powerful masters will search for signs when we return."

"What is it, Master Francis?" he heard Brother Julius ask from not so far away.

Francis turned and faced the man squarely, but decided that sharing his disturbing fears at that moment might not be so wise a thing to do. "It is time, past time, for us to return to St.-Mere-Abelle," he answered.

The younger brother nodded and turned away. "We are ready for the road," he announced.

"Brother Julius," Francis called, and the monk turned back to look at him. "Your plan was an excellent one. Without it, the goblins would have overwhelmed us, or, had we left them, would have overwhelmed Davon

Dinnishire. The blood of our dead brethren is not on your hands. I thought you should know that."

"I do, Master Francis," Julius replied in a more accusatory tone. "I do."

The monk turned and walked away, and for a moment, Francis entertained the thought of scolding him publicly for such impertinence. Just for a moment, though. Francis glanced back at the pile of diseased goblins and understood that he had more important issues to attend.

CHAPTER

❖ 10 ❖

Denial of Privilege

A bbot Je'howith fell deeper, deeper into the gemstone, fell into the swirl of its magic and down, down, into its depths. There his spirit found release from the confines of his aged body. To the old abbot, this was the epitome of grace, the closest state one might attain to God while still physically maintaining one's mortal coil. Now he was free of earthly bonds, spirit-walking without physical ailments and limitations, without boundaries.

He saw the woman reclining patiently before him, her hand clutching a sunstone brooch, as he had instructed. Constance Pemblebury was no master of gemstone magic, surely, but with this particular item, she did not have to be. If she felt the battle of wills begin between her and Je'howith, she was to pinch her skin with the enchanted brooch's pin, nothing more, and the antimagic wave would wash the old abbot's intruding spirit out of her.

Je'howith moved closer, fighting the urge to go into her being, to take over her body. That was the danger of spirit-walking—the instinctual desire of the spirit to find a corporeal body, even at the expense of another's spirit.

Je'howith was right beside her now. He reached out his insubstantial hand toward her naked belly—and how he wished he were still of the flesh that he might feel Constance's smooth and delicate skin.

The old abbot washed that impure thought from his mind and focused on the task at hand. He moved even closer, right up to the woman, right into the woman. Now it took all his willpower not to try to possess her immediately. He pushed ahead, searching, searching.

And then he felt it, undeniably: another life, another soul stirring within the woman's womb. Je'howith could no longer resist—his spirit went for the child, joining with the child. It would be so easy to expel this tiny, undeveloped, and unknowing soul! To take the corporeal form! To begin life anew, from the womb, but with the understanding of a previous lifetime's experience!

And then, suddenly, the old abbot was thrown out, expelled so fully that before he even comprehended the change, he was back in his own body, corporeal again, staring, blinking in disbelief as Constance sat up.

"What did you do?" she demanded sharply.

"I—I did as you asked me," Je'howith stammered in reply, and he closed his eyes and shook his head, trying to orient himself.

"You went further," Constance accused, but even as she spoke the words, her expression became perplexed. "You tried . . ." she started to say, but she paused and looked up at Je'howith, and a wry smile came over her.

"Yes, dear Constance," the abbot confirmed. "Your alluring wiles have worked their magic. You carry King Danube's child."

Constance clapped her hands together, then brought them up to cover her mouth, gasping with joy. "It is true," she dared to say.

"Why are you so surprised?" Je'howith asked sarcastically. "Is this not what you wanted? Was this not your purpose ever since you saw your beloved Danube's eye wander the way of Jilseponie Wyndon?"

Constance's expression changed to sternness. "And do you disapprove?" she asked, an accusation as much as a question. "For if you did, then why did you not warn King Danube of my intent?"

Je'howith merely chuckled.

"I fear Jilseponie, but you despise her," Constance went on. "I bear her no ill will, yet you would pay the headsman handsomely to take her pretty head from her shoulders."

Je'howith bowed to her, an admission that her reasoning was sound. "I fear her more than you ever could," he explained. "You fear that she will threaten your little place at Danube's side. I fear that she will topple the world of the Abellican Church."

"And what better way to keep her out of the Church than to involve her in the affairs of the Crown?" reasoned Constance, again in that accusatory tone. "Perhaps Je'howith whispers of Jilseponie in King Danube's ear."

The monk laughed. "Because I would be better off by far if Jilseponie came to Ursal as queen of Honce-the-Bear?" he asked incredulously. "No, my dear Constance, never would I desire that. I am glad that the woman has gone north, far out of the way, and is not meddling in the affairs of either Church or Crown."

"And what of Constance, then, and her condition?" she asked.

Again the old abbot chuckled, belittling the whole thing. "This will not be Danube's first child. Nor, I doubt, will it be his last."

"It?" Constance echoed. "Boy or girl?"

"Most mothers do not wish to be told."

Constance fixed the old man with a devastating glower.

"Boy," Je'howith answered, and Constance clenched her fist with absolute glee. "You assume much if you think this will greatly alter your standing," Je'howith said.

"You know nothing of my relationship with King Danube," Constance replied. "You, not I, assume much."

Je'howith draped his arm about the woman, fixing her with a disarming smile. "Listen to us," he bade her. "We sound as if we are against each other in this matter, when, truthfully, we both share similar goals. The health of King Danube and his kingdom is to our mutual liking, is it not?"

"And how does my situation affect that health, in Abbot Je'howith's thinking?" Constance asked bluntly.

The old man's smile seemed genuine. "Why, Milady Pemblebury, it would not pain me to call you my queen."

Constance returned the smile and nodded, then dressed and took her leave.

Abbot Je'howith, whose world had just been turned upside down in Palmaris, whose position in his beloved Church had been severely strained by his association with the man who lost the battle for the Church, watched her every step. Was she carrying the future King of Honce-the-Bear? Or—even more relevant to old Je'howith, who would not likely outlive young King Danube, would this situation elevate Constance to her coveted position as queen?

"So be it," the old abbot said aloud, and he nodded, unconcerned. He had never truly been at odds with Constance—often he had considered her as Danube's most reasonable secular adviser. He didn't think it likely that Danube would take her as his wife anyway—if he meant to do that, he would have done so long ago.

But still, despite all of his logical arguments telling him that this situation was neither unexpected nor damaging, it nagged at Je'howith until he finally discerned his source of distress.

Again he nodded, his understanding of his own fears coming clearer. Might this situation push King Danube to other action? To the active pursuit of Jilseponie, perhaps, that he might sire a more acceptable heir?

Constance had gotten her wish, the culmination of her pursuit and treachery, but old and wise Je'howith wasn't sure that the woman fully understood the consequences.

A boy, a son for King Danube Brock Ursal! The news should not have surprised Constance, who had been working so long to just that end; and yet, from the moment Je'howith had told her about the child, all the world had seemed to slip out of focus.

She went immediately to her room, to her bed, and reclined there, deep in thought and steeped in joy. She would mother the future King of Honce-the-Bear! This child within her would rise through the ranks of nobility to the very highest level, would bring the name of Pemblebury the stature it had once known, many generations before.

Once, before the unification of the kingdom under King Danube's great-

great-great-great-grandfather, the Pembleburys had been the lords of Wester-Honce, an independent fiefdom. When King Bendragon Coelyn Ursal had unified the kingdom, subjugating Wester-Honce, the Pembleburys had remained an important family; but over the generations that stature, along with the population and importance of Wester-Honce itself, had gradually diminished, to the point where Constance's grandmother had chosen to become a courtesan in order to retain any ties at all to the Throne. Constance's mother, a bastard child of a duke, a distant relation to the family of Targon Bree Kalas, had followed suit, and had taught Constance in the family's new profession.

Constance's child would be the first male in the family for three generations and, given its pedigree, held the promise of restoring all that the Pembleburys once were, and more.

Along with the hopes Constance fostered that morning were more than a few doubts. She understood, even more clearly now that her efforts had worked, that she had forced upon King Danube a delicate and potentially devastating situation. She had played her hand, had taken a great risk, in the hopes that King would remain loyal to her.

Constance took a deep and steadying breath, considering again the potential consequences, the risk that she would be forced from the city, into the circles of lesser nobles, as had both women who had previously become pregnant with Danube's children. A moment of sheer terror gripped her, the sudden certainty that her actions to secure a greater role had thus doomed her to a minor position in a minor court.

It was a passing fear, though, for Constance reminded herself of how badly she had wanted a child. Her childbearing days were nearing their end, but Danube showed little movement toward formalizing their relationship, and so she had been given little choice.

Of course, she could have sought out a different sire, a less complicated union with a lesser noble—many of whom would have been thrilled to take her as wife. But Constance didn't want just any man's child, and had no intention of settling for another whom she did not love. No, she loved Danube, and had loved him since before his wedding to Queen Vivian two decades earlier. He was her friend and her lover, the only man who had ever seemed to genuinely understand her. And now he was the father of her child, and to Constance, nothing in all the world could have been more appropriate.

And so, as she settled in for a long morning's rest, her joy overcame her fears, and she became at ease with the reality of her situation, very pleased that her child, Danube's child, was growing within her.

"Kalas continues to hold the Abellican Church in check in Palmaris and all the northern reaches," King Danube said happily to Je'howith when the old abbot came upon him, later that same day, reclining in his study, sipping fine brandy, and surrounded by the most extensive library in all the world, greater even than the collection of tomes hoarded at St.-Mere-Abelle.

Danube's smile was genuine; he was in fine spirits, and not because of the drink. He was happy to be home again, in the bright summer, and with his kingdom finally settling back into its previous state of calm. He was happy that he could again go riding in the fields around Castle Ursal, that he could enjoy the balls and parties with the many nobles and courtesans. It seemed that the pall of the demon dactyl was finally lifting from his kingdom, and that the upstart brothers of the Abellican Church, often his most bitter rivals, would soon again be huddled within their dark walls.

"I do miss Duke Kalas," the King admitted, and he laughed again when Je'howith, who had never been a friend to the fiery and ultimately secular Duke, frowned deeply. "Perhaps I will be able to invite him home soon enough."

"Do not underestimate Abbot Braumin Herde and his intentions," Je'howith warned.

"Word from Kalas says that Jilseponie has left for the northland," the King replied. "Without her, our friend Braumin will prove much less formidable. And as the darkness recedes, so too will the influence of the Church. The people of Palmaris remember well the oppression of Bishop De'Unnero, I assure you, and his reign of terror suited Duke Kalas well."

"Because Duke Kalas was ever such a gentle man," Je'howith said with obvious sarcasm.

King Danube only laughed again. "It is a fine day, my friend, with the promise of many better days yet to come," he said, hoisting his glass in toast.

Abbot Je'howith assumed a pensive posture; and Danube lowered his glass, looking hard at the old monk, finally catching on that the man's arrival was more than a casual visit.

"I met with Constance this morning," Je'howith remarked.

"And . . ." Danube prompted. "If there is trouble in my court, then speak it plainly."

"She is with child," Je'howith informed him. "Your child. A son, I believe, who will be born next midwinter, unless there are complications."

Danube swallowed hard. "Impossible . . ." he started to say. "Constance is well versed in methods of preventing . . ." He paused there and considered the information, wondering immediately if the conception was accidental or deliberate. Constance had long been his trusted friend and his off-and-on lover for decades—and once she had questioned him directly about his intentions toward her, if he had any beyond their liaisons. . . . But to think that she had purposely tricked him . . .

"These things do happen, my King," Abbot Je'howith said. "You have sired two before—have you forgotten? Many of the courtesans find themselves with child, I assure you, though they do not carry through with the pregnancy."

"Children of mine?" Danube asked, his eyes widening in an accurate reflection of his shock.

Abbot Je'howith began patting his hands in the air to calm the man. "It happens," he said quietly. "They consider their condition and their future. Their places at court, after all, are ones reserved for the most beautiful and the most talented . . . and the ones least burdened. Many courtesans understand well the complications that a child will bring to their lives, a situation that might send them back to a life of poverty and without position."

King Danube settled back in a chair that seemed suddenly not so comfortable to him, and took a hearty swallow of his potent liquor. He didn't like being told of the seedier side of his life, but neither could he deny the truth of Je'howith's observations. When he compared that truth to Constance's present situation, though, he took some comfort. "Constance will not do that," he remarked.

"No, she will not," Je'howith agreed. "I doubt that she views carrying the child of King Danube Brock Ursal as a burden or a cause for tears, unless they be tears of joy."

His tone as he finished made it clear to Danube that the old man fully believed that Constance had become pregnant on purpose; but strangely, to Danube, even that possibility did not invoke his wrath. How many years had Constance Pemblebury stood steadfastly beside him? How many times had she been there to comfort him in days of distress, to reassure him on those few occasions when he was faced with momentous decisions: the pardoning of a condemned criminal or the portioning of rations among communities where starvation seemed inevitable?

"Perhaps she has earned this child," Danube muttered, speaking more to himself than to Je'howith.

"And what, exactly, is this child?" Je'howith asked bluntly, drawing him from his private contemplations. The king looked up at the old man. "You have sired two before, and have done well by the mothers, awarding them comfortable positions and even minor titles for your children," the abbot reminded him. "Yet at the same time, you invoked Refusal of Acceptance, separating them forever from the ruling line, denying them for all time any claims to the throne of Honce-the-Bear. Will you follow the same course with the child of Constance Pemblebury?"

Danube started to reply *Of course*, but the words got stuck in his throat as he considered the reality of the situation, of this woman. He gave no answer, then, but merely blew a deep and contemplative sigh.

"Do you love her?" Je'howith asked.

Danube shook his head, but at the same time, he answered, "I do not know."

"Do you love the woman Jilseponie?" the surprising abbot went on, and how that question widened King Danube's eyes!

"How could you ask such a question?" he responded loudly, but again, Je'howith was patting his hands in the air, motioning for a calm discourse.

"I saw the look in your eyes when you gazed upon her," the abbot replied. "She is beautiful beyond question, a sight to stir the loins of any man, and by deed alone she has made herself fit for the throne—indeed, I would reason that there is no woman in all the world more suited to sit by your side than Jilseponie Wyndon."

Again, Danube found no rebuttal against the sound reasoning. He carried it one step further, though, and reminded himself that perhaps the second woman most fit to be queen would be none other than the woman now carrying his child. The confusion inspired by that realization showed clearly on his face.

"I have delivered stunning news to you, my King," Je'howith said with a bow. "There is no need to make any decisions at this time."

"Soon enough," Danube replied. "The seasons will pass quickly, and Constance's condition will be known before summer's end. Many will whisper and ask questions."

"You need not marry her, obviously."

"But I will need to make a decree concerning her status and that of the child," Danube reasoned. "To invoke Refusal of Acceptance would wound Constance profoundly, something I do not wish to do."

"But something, perhaps, that she has brought upon herself," Je'howith reminded him.

Danube's stern expression showed that he wasn't ready to accept that notion, that he understood that whatever Constance's actions to prevent or allow conception had been, he, too, had played more than a minor role.

"There is also the matter of your brother," said Je'howith, quickly changing the subject.

"And if I do nothing?" Danube asked, for he recognized that Je'howith, as abbot of St. Honce, was among the most knowledgeable men in the kingdom of the affairs of court. "If I simply let events take their place—let the child be born and do not invoke the Refusal, nor openly claim the child—then will the boy become heir to the throne above Midalis?"

Je'howith hesitated a moment, then nodded. "If you die before Midalis and it is commonly accepted that this child is yours, and by a woman who remains at your side, then the child will indeed have some claim to the throne. It will be no easy ascent, I expect, but rather, one strongly contested by writ and, perhaps, by sword. Wars have begun for lesser reasons, my King."

"Then I need to choose, and soon," Danube replied. "Do I wound Constance or enrage Midalis? For either way, it seems as if I am about to bring pain to a friend."

"There remains a third option," said Je'howith.

"I would never ask her to be rid of the baby," Danube insisted.

"No, not that," said Je'howith. "Never that!"

Danube tilted his head, studying the man, convinced that if, as the abbot had remarked, other women had been rid of their unwanted children, then hypocritical old Je'howith, or some other gemstone-wielding monk, had likely played a role in the process.

"You can use a delaying tactic," the abbot went on, "a way for you to let the situation go on and let the passage of time guide you to more decisive and definitive action. This is not without precedent—you can issue a decree of Denial of Privilege, a technical term and legal maneuver that will not deny the child's claim to the throne forever, as you have done with your other bastard heirs, but will, rather, maintain the present status, keeping Constance's child outside the line of succession and keeping your option— or that of Midalis should he succeed you and die childless—for recognizing the child as rightful heir at a future date."

"Denial of Privilege?" Danube echoed.

"A temporary measure that has been used in centuries past," Je'howith answered. "And it is possible for you to even include contingencies that will lift the injunction against the child's becoming king. Let us suppose that you outlive your brother, then die unexpectedly."

"A truly inspiring supposition," Danube said dryly.

"In that case, had you so specified, Constance's child would assume the throne," Je'howith explained.

"And if I decree a Denial of Privilege and Midalis outlives me?"

"Then the child will have no claim to the throne above your brother, and it would be up to him to either assign rights to the child in the event of his childless demise or deny them outright with a formal Refusal of Acceptance."

King Danube settled back again and put his hand to his chin, trying to digest all of these options.

"How much easier it all would be if you, and your brother, had both married and sired proper heirs," the abbot lamented.

Danube glanced up at him, eyes narrow, a poignant reminder to the old abbot that he had indeed been married to Queen Vivian, who had died despite Je'howith's efforts to save her. And those efforts—or at least, the lack of their effectiveness—had in effect split the court of Ursal for many years and were the source of the lingering hatred between Je'howith and Duke Kalas.

Je'howith promptly bowed and turned to leave.

And King Danube Brock Ursal, who had been happily celebrating what he thought would be a return to normalcy, found himself full of questions and turmoil. The delaying tactic sounded most promising, both for sparing

Constance the pain and for placating Midalis, who had never really been close to his brother, the King, but had never been his rival either.

Yes, the Denial of Privilege seemed a promising course; and, in truth, when he looked at things that way, this all didn't seem like such a momentous problem.

However, there was one other complicating factor, an image of another woman, a warrior, a gemstone witch. It was an image King Danube could not shake out of his head.

CHAPTER

❖ 11 ❖

Resting Side by Side

He had a feeling, as he flitted from tree to tree, of true warmth and friendship, a feeling not unlike that he experienced whenever he returned home to Andur'Blough Inninness after one of his forays into the realm of the humans. For Juraviel, the Timberlands region around Dundalis, Weedy Meadow, and End-o'-the-World—the former haunt of Nightbird, the home of both the ranger and Jilseponie—had the same smell and feel as the elven valley. How curious that notion struck the elf now as he moved along the forested hills and valleys, how surprising.

Juraviel was Touel'alfar, of the people. That fact was the primary truth in his long life, the binding code of responsibility and of a specific and shared understanding of all the world and its varied inhabitants. In Juraviel's thoughts, in the thoughts of every Touel'alfar, even the least of friends among his own people—the other elf with whom he could not agree on anything, the elf he found most unpleasant—ranked far above the best of friends he might make among *n'Touel'alfar*, the folk *not* of the people. Juraviel did not question that tenet of his existence—never before and not now—but his feeling warmth as he neared the small human settlement of Dundalis, his feeling almost as if he were going home surprised him.

Perhaps, had he looked more deeply into himself, Belli'mar Juraviel would have noted then that his lines of ingrained reasoning were not in accord with the feelings within his heart.

The elf paused in his travels late one afternoon, finding a high branch of a wide maple where he could settle for a short rest. Soon he was comfortably asleep.

And then, soon after, he awoke to a haunting melody drifting on the evening breeze, echoing through the forest as if every tree were taking it inside in a deep and lingering breath and then blowing it out again for the rest of the forest to share, but altered, only slightly, by the heart of its last host tree.

"The Forest Ghost," Juraviel whispered, and he smiled as he heard the name aloud, the name the humans of Elbryan's first home had bestowed upon the centaur, Bradwarden, and his bagpipes. How many times had young Elbryan and Jilseponie heard that tune? Juraviel wondered. How many times had it been just below their level of consciousness as they drifted off to sleep in their little beds?

And though even Bradwarden was considered *n'Touel'alfar* by his some-what xenophobic people, Juraviel could not deny the comfort he derived from hearing the centaur's song, akin to the comfort he felt from just being in this region once more.

He followed the song slowly and whimsically, pausing to listen or to dance, whenever he found a clearing in the forest canopy that afforded him a beautiful view of the starlit heavens. He knew that the night was young and that Bradwarden often played until very, very late, so he meandered and he wandered. And finally he saw them, the centaur standing atop a bare-topped hillock, his pipes under one arm. Bradwarden was not as wide as other horses Juraviel had seen—certainly not as massive as mighty Symphony—but it seemed to the elf as if his centaur friend were ten feet tall, a gigantic and powerful creature. That such an obvious warrior could play such beautiful melodies struck Juraviel profoundly, the light and dark of Bradwarden's soul, at once ferocious and tender.

Reclining on the grass beside the centaur lay Roger Lockless. It occurred to Juraviel then that the young man, with his slightly angular features and delicate size—the result of a disease that had taken both his parents—seemed as much akin to the elves as to the humans. Not in temperament, though, Juraviel reminded himself. Roger had learned much in the trials of the last couple of years, had grown tremendously from the self-centered boy Juraviel and Nightbird had helped escape from the clutches of a vicious powrie band that had been occupying Caer Tinella. But as far as Juraviel and all the elves were concerned, he still had far, far to go even to approach the level of understanding and reasoning of Jilseponie. And from there, Roger would have far to go to begin to see the truth of the world as Brad-warden or Nightbird could see it; and even those two, despite everything, could never climb beyond the limitations of their kind, could never be any-thing but *n'Touel'alfar*.

Juraviel did like Roger, though, had tolerated him even when he was younger and more foolish, and had worked with him well during the last days of the war against Markwart.

"I cannot wait to see her again," he heard Roger say; and he knew from the expression on the man's face that Roger was surely talking about Jilse-ponie. Was it possible, then, that the woman hadn't even yet come north, and that Roger, perhaps, still possessed the gemstones?

Bradwarden paused. "Ah, but she's takin' her time about it," he said. "It's not but a week o' ridin' for one lookin' to get here from Palmaris."

"She's got friends in Caer Tinella," Roger reminded him.

"And she's got good weather and a road clear o' monsters," the centaur added. "Aye, that's it. Our Pony's not used to walkin' a road clear o' monsters. Got her all confused."

They shared a lighthearted laugh, and not out of any nervousness, for neither seemed the least bit afraid for the well-being of their dear, and ultimately capable, friend.

Juraviel moved stealthily up the hill, a whisper of wind, a roaming shadow. "Perhaps Jilseponie left the road in search of sport," he said. Both his friends jumped in surprise, Bradwarden tossing down his pipes and grabbing up an axe that likely outweighed Juraviel, Roger turning several evasive rolls to the side.

They both settled quickly, and Bradwarden roared out a great cheer, obviously recognizing the elf's voice, even as Roger cautiously called out, "Juraviel?"

The elf stepped out into the clear. "Too long has it been since I have heard the piping of the Forest Ghost," he said. Bradwarden tossed his axe back over his shoulder and skipped down to hoist Juraviel in a great hug.

"And too long since I have heard the complaints of Roger Lockless!" Juraviel added in jest as Bradwarden put him down so that Roger could embrace him.

"And too long since we've seen yerself, elf," the centaur replied. "But I thought ye was for yer home."

"And so I have been in the valley for all these months," Juraviel replied, "and would be still, had not Lady Dasslerond bidden me to return here for—" He paused and waved his hands. "Ah, but that is business that we two, Bradwarden, must discuss later. Nothing so serious that it cannot wait until old friends have had time to share news."

Both Bradwarden and Roger seemed concerned for a moment, until Juraviel's smile melted away any anxieties. "Not much for tellin'," the centaur began. "All three towns are up and full o' folk again."

"Goblins in the area?" Juraviel asked.

"No sign of goblins, powries, or giants," Roger was quick to reply. "We have kept vigilant scouting parties all about the region, and all has been quiet and peaceful."

"We're thinkin' that there's more than a few o' the beasts farther to the north," Bradwarden added. "But we're thinkin', too, that none o' them got the belly for comin' south again."

Juraviel nodded, for it seemed logical enough. These two and Elbryan, along with a contingent of Kingsmen and some renegade monks, had gone all the way back to the Barbacan, after all, hundreds of miles through the Wilderlands, with hardly a sign of the monsters. And Juraviel's own trail had led him in from the Wilderlands to the west, again with no sign of any monsters, except of course in the Moorlands, which had always been thick with goblins. Those goblins, until the coming of the dactyl, had never been a threat to anybody except for those foolish enough to wander into their territory.

Yes, the land was settling again, at long last, into peace, and that fact only made Bradwarden's song all the sweeter.

"And if they do come south," Roger put in at length, "then I'll find them and steal all their weapons, and won't they be easy to chase off then!"

"Unless they have Craggoth hounds," Juraviel said to the boastful man somewhat sternly; and the mention of the powerful powrie hunting dogs reminded Roger of a not-so-pleasant experience.

Bradwarden howled with laughter and Roger's lips got very tight, but Juraviel held the man's gaze with equal intensity; his expression alone poignantly asked Roger who it was that he was trying to impress.

"Well, enough o' the boastin'," Bradwarden said, and he lifted his pipes back to his lips, but paused and nodded to Juraviel. "Ye goin' to tell us what's bringin' ye back here, elf? Or are ye waitin' for us to beg ye?"

"I have become the mentor to another ranger," Juraviel admitted.

"You are bringing another ranger here?" Roger quickly put in, his tone making it seem as if he was not too thrilled about that prospect.

"She is just a child," he explained, "and her path, I assure you, will bring her nowhere near Dundalis."

Roger nodded grimly, but his look turned perplexed. "She?"

"Why are you so surprised?" Juraviel replied. "Do you not believe that a woman can be a ranger?"

"Ho, ho, what!" Bradwarden howled, doing his best Avelyn Desbris imitation. "But wouldn't Pony be kickin' yer skinny backside if she ever heard ye talkin' like that!"

Roger shrugged, conceding the point.

"Indeed, Jilseponie would have been a fine candidate for our training," Juraviel agreed. "Had we known her potential when she walked down the road from the ruined Dundalis, we might have changed her life's path considerably."

This whole topic seemed like a minor point, and nothing to debate, but Juraviel noted that Roger didn't appear very pleased by it all. The elf understood Roger Lockless, particularly the man's minor failings, well enough to recognize the source of that look. "You, too, Roger Lockless, might have found yourself in Caer'alfar, had your situation merited it."

"I could still go and learn," the young man insisted.

"You are at least five years too old," Juraviel explained. "Lady Dasslerond would have no part of bringing an adult human into our land for such training."

"Then *you* teach me," Roger said, only half kiddingly, "while you are here, I mean."

"The training takes years."

"Then just teach me select parts of it," Roger went on. "Teach me that sword dance that Elbryan and Pony . . ." His voice trailed off, his mouth hanging open at the sight of Juraviel, whose lips were thin, and his expression stern, seemingly bordering on the verge of an explosion.

"I'm thinkin' he's sayin' no," Bradwarden remarked dryly.

Roger looked to Bradwarden for support and smiled sheepishly.

"So are ye goin' to tell us, elf?" the centaur prompted. "Ye got yerself a new ranger-to-be, but that's not a reason for ye to come all the way out here to tell me about it."

"She is a rider," Juraviel said, his glare still locked upon Roger, "and I must secure a mount for her." He understood that the young man hadn't intentionally said anything wrong, but the mere mention of *bi'nelle dasada*, the secret elven fighting technique, opened a wound. It was Elbryan's teaching of the secret dance to Jilseponie that had so angered Lady Dasslerond, and, Juraviel believed, that was why Lady Dasslerond felt justified in keeping their child and raising it as a son of the Touel'alfar. Lady Dasslerond's anger, Juraviel believed, was the primary reason guiding her handling of the boy, her keeping Juraviel away from him, her keeping Jilseponie ignorant of his existence. Even more than that, Lady Dasslerond held Juraviel ultimately at fault for Elbryan's teaching Jilseponie the sword dance. Whatever feelings he might have for Elbryan or for Jilseponie, Juraviel couldn't deny the truth of Elbryan's betrayal. The ranger had given something away that was not his to give, and in doing so, he had, to Lady Dasslerond's way of thinking, threatened the very existence of the Touel'alfar.

"We've more than a few fine ponies runnin' about," Bradwarden started to answer, but then a wry grin crossed his face. "Ye're not thinkin' . . ." he guessed.

"A proper mount for a ranger," Juraviel said determinedly.

Roger looked from one to the other, as if trying to decipher their meaning, but then his eyes widened and he stared at Juraviel. "Symphony?" he asked. "You mean to take Symphony away? But—"

"Easy, lad," Bradwarden intervened. "I'm thinkin' that none're takin' Symphony unless Symphony's wantin' to go."

"True enough," Juraviel agreed, "and I am sure that if Symphony is not agreeable, Bradwarden will help me to find another fitting mount."

"Good rider, this one?" the centaur asked.

"To-gai-ru," Juraviel answered.

Bradwarden whistled in admiration.

"Like the pinto horses?" Roger asked. "The ones the Allheart knights ride?"

"To-gai," Bradwarden confirmed. "And they're ponies, not horses, though they're big ones at that, eight hundred pounds o' muscle and on the top side o' fourteen hands. If ye're lookin' to get one of those for yer young ranger, then ye're lookin' in the wrong place."

Juraviel nodded and then decided to let the matter drop; he and Bradwarden could take care of the horse business later on. "Play your pipes, Forest Ghost," he said with a smile. "I have heard enough of the events; now I wish to hear what is in Bradwarden's heart."

The centaur smiled and began his melody once again, while Juraviel reclined on the grass beside Roger. The young man was soon fast asleep, but Juraviel stayed up long into the night, staring at the stars and drinking in Bradwarden's song.

"You were telling Bradwarden that you expect Jilseponie to return to Dundalis soon," Juraviel prompted Roger when the two were walking back through the forest toward Dundalis the next morning. The day was hot and sunny, with not a hint of a wind. Bradwarden had gone off at daybreak to scout the horse herd for Juraviel, and to see if he could find Symphony.

"She may already be there," the young man replied with obvious excitement; and Juraviel, too, was thrilled at the prospect of seeing his dear friend once more. There was something else edging Roger's voice, Juraviel recognized, something beyond simple happiness and excitement.

"Have you seen her at all of late?" Juraviel asked.

"Not since last summer," Roger replied, "not since the day Bradwarden and I brought—Elbryan—I mean . . ."

"The day you brought Nightbird's casket from Palmaris," Juraviel finished for him. "I watched you begin your journey up the northern road."

"That was the worst journey of my life," Roger said, his voice slightly quavering. "I still can't believe . . ."

"He is at rest in the grove?" Juraviel asked. "Beside his uncle Mather?"

Roger nodded, and the elf immediately turned aside from the trail back to Dundalis, heading instead for the grave of his friend, with Roger close behind.

The temperature seemed cooler in the sheltered grove in the forest north of Dundalis. Juraviel, who knew the place well, led the way along the many-forked and confusing trails, for though the grove was not very large, there was a bit of magic about it, a minor illusion placed by Lady Dasslerond herself, using her powerful emerald, when she had come to bid farewell to Mather Wyndon several years after his death.

Juraviel picked the trail with certainty, moving among the somber trees; and soon the pair came to the place, with its side-by-side cairns. They stood solemnly for a long while, staring and remembering—and for Juraviel, who had lived for more than two centuries, that meant remembering two friends, two rangers.

"Tempest was buried there with Mather Wyndon for years until Elbryan earned it from the spirit of his uncle," the elf remarked at length.

Roger cleared his throat uncomfortably, and Juraviel let his look linger on him until Roger offered an explanation.

"We weren't sure which tomb should get the sword," Roger explained. "To me, it was Elbryan's—Nightbird's—weapon, but Bradwarden thought it better if Tempest went back to rest with Mather."

"But the bow, Hawkwing, is with Nightbird?" Juraviel asked somewhat urgently, for that bow, the last the elf's father had ever crafted, had been made specifically for Nightbird.

"With Elbryan," Roger confirmed.

"Fair enough," the elf said, and Roger seemed to relax.

Just for a moment again, Juraviel had to stare long and hard at Roger to get him to open up with his feelings. "I keep thinking that perhaps if I, or we, had found our way into St. Precious earlier—soon enough to get the weapons and deliver them to Nightbird—that the fight at Chasewind Manor might have turned out differently," Roger explained.

"I tried to do just that," Juraviel admitted, hoping to alleviate Roger's guilt. "I was within the abbey when the alarm sounded, when Jilseponie began her determined march across the city. I could not find them, sword or bow."

"They were both within St. Precious," Roger said. He was nodding and did seem relieved. "We found them afterward, locked in a secret place by Father Abbot Markwart. Brother Braumin brought them to Jilseponie, but she bade him to send them north with the caisson, to be buried with Nightbird. I just wish Nightbird had them in his grasp when he went into Chasewind Manor after Pony."

"It was a confused moment," Juraviel agreed. "Much was misplaced." The way he said that and the look he gave to Roger seemed to throw the young man off balance.

"Well, we found them at least," Roger insisted—too eagerly, Juraviel noted. The elf knew then that Roger was hiding something, and, given the man's demeanor when he spoke of Jilseponie's impending arrival and the rumors Lady Dasslerond had told him that the woman's cache of gemstones had not been recovered from Chasewind Manor, Juraviel had a pretty good idea what that might be.

"Yes, and you dispensed them properly," Juraviel agreed. "And never did I doubt that Roger Lockless and Bradwarden would act in any way that was not in the best interests of all."

"We did not know if the Touel'alfar would want them back," Roger explained.

Juraviel looked down at the cairns, at the burial places of two great rangers and of two marvelous elven weapons. He suspected that these cairns might be disturbed in the not too distant future, as a new ranger, heir to the bloodline of Mather and Elbryan, came to claim his territory and his birthright. The boy would have to do battle with the spirit of Mather to win the right to wield Tempest, and likewise would have to face his own father for the right to carry Hawkwing. Lady Dasslerond had better train the child well, Juraviel thought.

"You did well in the aftermath of the tragedy," Juraviel said at length. "It was a confusing time, and much, I suspect, was misplaced." There, the elf thought, he had left Roger an opening.

But Roger didn't take the bait, just shrugged his shoulders.

Belli'mar Juraviel could accept that. To Roger's understanding—to the understanding of all of them, Jilseponie included—the gemstones were neither the province nor the interest of the Touel'alfar. When Jilseponie had thought that she and Elbryan might be killed at St.-Mere-Abelle, she had begged Juraviel to take the cache of gemstones stolen by Avelyn Desbris, the source of Markwart's anger at the pair, and carry them far away to Andur'Blough Inninness. Juraviel had steadfastly refused, insisting that the gemstones were a problem for the humans, not the elves.

How ironic that seemed to the elf, given one of his missions to this place.

"Come," he bade Roger. "I will take you to the northern slope that overlooks Dundalis and you can go see if there is any word from Jilseponie. Bradwarden and I will meet you on the hillock tonight that we might enjoy together a fine meal, fine conversation, and the centaur's song."

Roger followed the elf out of the grove and across the few forested miles back to the village. Juraviel set off as soon as Roger was out of sight, half running, half flying back to find the centaur.

Bradwarden had marked his trail well for the elf, and so Juraviel had little trouble locating him on a long ridge of birch, overlooking a wide field. Below, a herd of wild horses, including the magnificent black, white-booted stallion, grazed. Soon after Juraviel arrived beside the centaur, Symphony picked his head up and turned their way, and the elf caught the glimmer of turquoise set in the stallion's chest, a magical gemstone Avelyn Desbris had placed there to heighten the connection between rider and mount.

"I told him ye mean to take him," Bradwarden remarked. Even as he finished, Symphony galloped their way, skidded to a stop, and reared, front legs pawing the air. Then the horse swung about and thundered off, and the whole herd took up the charge in his wake.

"I'm not thinkin' he's likin' the idea," Bradwarden added dryly.

Juraviel studied the running horse for a moment, the seeming urgency in Symphony's long and thundering stride.

"Symphony's pickin' his own course," Bradwarden went on. "He might be thinkin' that there's work to be done about here."

"Would Symphony consider the fate of his own herd above my needs?" Juraviel asked.

"Sounds like an elf," Bradwarden quipped with a snort.

Juraviel eyed him sternly, which, of course, only made the centaur laugh harder.

"Whatever Symphony might be thinking or feeling, his path is his own to choose, and I'll not try to drag him to Andur'Blough Inninness," Juraviel announced.

Bradwarden snorted all the louder, as if the mere thought of that was absurd—which indeed, Juraviel knew, it was. Even in the days when Nightbird rode Symphony, the stallion knew no master.

"Have you any other prospects?" Juraviel asked.

"Symphony showed me one," Bradwarden explained, pointing down the line to a small, muscular sorrel stallion running near the back of the herd, and not in tight formation like the rest, but lagging and ranging out wide, this way and that. "A two-year-old, and getting a bit edgy."

"Symphony showed you?" Juraviel asked. The elf really didn't doubt that Symphony and Bradwarden were capable of such communication, but he had to wonder at the stallion's intent, if there was any, in picking out one of its own herd.

"He's got the mare smell in his nose," Bradwarden explained, "and it's takin' out all his senses. He even took a run at Symphony. Ye'll be takin' him away or Symphony'll be kickin' him deep into the forest. If the little one's lucky, Symphony won't kill him."

Juraviel nodded, for now it made sense. There were other stallions in the herd besides Symphony, but not many, and apparently none in competition with the great stallion. Juraviel had reservations, though—would this spirited young stallion be too much for young Brynn?—and they showed clearly in his expression.

"Ye take him away from the mare smell, and he'll be a fine one," the centaur said, obviously catching the elf's drift. "Ye might be geldin' him, o' course, though I've never been fond o' that treatment!"

"Will Symphony help us secure him?"

"Oh, I'll get him for ye," the centaur assured him. "I'll have him this very night, though it'll take a couple o' days for me and Roger to break him."

The image brought on by Bradwarden's choice of partners brought a smile to Juraviel. Roger had never been much of a rider, and if this young stallion was as spirited and strong as he appeared, the young man might be finding getting out of bed each morning a bit of a trial.

"Same hill?" Bradwarden asked.

"Sheila will be bright tonight," Juraviel replied. "I will meet you there when she passes her midpoint."

The centaur reached down and hoisted a long length of strong rope, slinging it over one shoulder. He gave a quick salute to Juraviel, then trotted down along the ridgeline, paralleling the course of Symphony and the herd. "I'm hopin' none o' them mares're hot with the smell," he remarked quietly.

"For the stallion's sake or for your own?" Juraviel asked with a laugh, and Bradwarden joined in.

Juraviel thought to go directly to the outskirts of Dundalis then, to listen in on the conversations of unwitting humans and learn what he might about events since the fall of Markwart and also to discern any further information about Jilseponie's progress to the north. He found himself sidetracked, though. Again he found himself standing in the grove before the two stone cairns. Whatever words Juraviel might find, like *n'Touel'alfar*, they did little to relieve his pain at that moment. He remembered Mather, and the man's gallant fall while saving the young Bradwarden from the clutches of a goblin horde—no wonder that the centaur insisted upon returning Tempest to Mather's side. Mostly, though, Juraviel explored the newer, raw wound—the loss of Elbryan. He remembered all his days with the young man, training him, bringing him along in his understanding of the elven way of seeing the world, and teaching him *bi'nelle dasada*. He remembered the night of Elbryan's naming, when the young man became Nightbird the ranger, under a starry sky in Caer'alfar. He contrasted that event with Dasslerond's continuing anger at the man and at Jilseponie, and considered his own initial reaction, anger, upon learning that Nightbird had taught the woman the sword dance. But then Juraviel remembered the first time he had seen the two fighting together within *bi'nelle dasada*, battling goblins on a hillock above a trapped wagon caravan. How beautiful they had been together, how complementary to each other's movements, and how deadly to the goblins. Watching that display, Belli'mar Juraviel had thrown away his anger at Nightbird, had then considered the man's instruction of Jilseponie a gift upon the elven gift, heightening the value of that the elves had given to him.

If only Lady Dasslerond been able to witness such a display!

But she had not, and Juraviel's description of the scene could hardly sway her.

"Rest well, my fallen friend," the elf said. "Keep Hawkwing close to your side until the day that your son comes to claim it."

That last statement brought a smile to Juraviel's face, as he turned and started for Dundalis, but how much wider that smile would have been, he realized, if he were allowed to play some role in tutoring the child of Nightbird.

The elf spent the rest of the day about the outskirts of Dundalis, resting on high branches, and listening to conversations of some of the townsfolk. He fell asleep to dreams of his lost friend and didn't awaken until the moon was high in the clear night sky.

He arrived at the base of the hillock, serenaded by Bradwarden's piping, a short while later. The young stallion was there, tethered to a tree, grazing easily and not even lifting its head to mark the approach of the quiet elf.

He found Roger reclining beside the centaur, much in the same position as the night before.

"Got him," Bradwarden remarked. "Oh, but he's a spirited beastie. Yer little ranger friend is in for some wild ridin'."

"And what about my little friend Roger?" Juraviel asked with a smile.

Roger, who obviously had already been informed of his role, put on a sour look that the elf knew was mostly bluster.

"He'll be sittin' funny for a bit, don't ye doubt," the centaur said with a laugh. "But we'll get the stallion so he'll take a saddle, at least."

"A week?" Juraviel asked. "For I've some business to attend to."

Bradwarden nodded. "I'll break 'em both by then," he said, glancing wryly sidelong at Roger.

The three spent the rest of the night relaxing on the hillock. After Roger had fallen asleep, Juraviel wandered down to the stallion to better inspect him.

With his ragged sorrel coat, he wasn't the prettiest of horses, certainly nothing compared to Symphony, but he was strong and well muscled, with enough inner fires showing in his dark eyes to keep Brynn Dharielle working hard indeed.

Juraviel was back on the road in the morning, leaving Bradwarden and Roger to their work with the stallion. He headed south, shadowing the one road, with a hundred and fifty miles before him. He meant to arrive in Caer Tinella in three days.

❖ 12 ❖

Reciprocation

"There they go," Liam O'Blythe remarked as the line of goblins streamed along the ravine floor below them. "Right along yer big friend's course and right on time."

"Signal the archers," Prince Midalis instructed. "Let us be done with this."

Liam lifted his spear, tipped with a red flag emblazoned with the black cow: the sign of death. Before the man had gone through three waves of the pennant, the eager archers, set along both sides of the ravine, began firing their missiles down upon the running goblins.

Bruinhelde and his kinsmen had caught this band, one of the few remaining anywhere near Pireth Vanguard, as they camped in the forest. Using Andacanavar as scout and as liaison to Midalis and his men, the Alpinadorans had orchestrated this little ambush.

The archers thinned the goblin line, and those monsters sprinting out in front of the main host soon came upon a series of traps, trip lines, and ankle pits, buried spikes, and one deep trench that bottled up the whole retreat. And that, of course, merely gave the archers more time to let fly their arrows, and into a more concentrated group of targets.

Not to miss any of the fun, Bruinhelde and his horde then appeared at the end of the ravine to Midalis's right. The lead Alpinadorans charged out and fell into their hammer-spins, launching a devastating barrage at the nearest goblins.

And still the archers rained death upon the confused and frightened creatures.

Midalis's cavalry appeared at the left end of the ravine, coming in slowly and in tight ranks, spears leveled before them.

"I should be down with them," the Prince remarked, and, indeed, this was the first action of the season in which he had not been leading the way. There had been no time, for Midalis had been at St. Belfour when the call had come in, and the goblin retreat had been on in full by the time he had even reached this spot on the ridge in the center of the ravine's northern side.

"Bah, but they're not even to see any fightin'," Liam replied, "nothin' more than runnin' down a few strays."

The second Alpinadoran line came charging ahead then, closer to the trailing goblin ranks; and again, the huge northern men spun and launched their chain-handled hammers, smashing the closest ranks.

The goblins didn't even try to assume any defensive formation, just scrambled all over one another, howling and screaming and running out of that death pit in every direction. Those climbing up the north and south walls were met by concentrated arrow volleys that sent them skidding back in their own blood. Those going to the east—Midalis' left—were run down and skewered. Those trying to run back the way they had come, to the west, were met by a third hammer barrage.

It was over in a few minutes, and Prince Midalis hadn't heard even a single human cry out in pain. After all the months of fighting, this skirmish, the battle of the Masur Tierman-dae—so named for the dry bed of the stream that had shaped the ravine—was easily the most one-sided of the entire conflict.

It was no accident, Midalis understood. As his warriors and the Alpinadorans had come to know and better trust each other, as they had come to understand each other's fighting strengths and weaknesses, they had learned to complement each other. And now, with the barbarians growing more accustomed to the Vanguard terrain, the combined force was better shaping the battlefields, picking the fights in which they could inflict the most damage and avoiding those that seemed too risky.

The battle of the Masur Tierman-dae had been a complete success, and Midalis confidently expected many more of the same . . . if they could find enough goblins left to kill.

Some movement from behind caught their attention, and the pair turned to see Andacanavar striding up the ridge, deftly picking his course among the tangles of brush and roots. Without a word of greeting, he moved to stand beside Midalis and Liam; and though the two Vanguardsmen were mounted, they did not tower over the huge Alpinadoran.

"I came to this place as soon as I heard of the fight," Midalis explained. "And I feared that I missed it—though it has been choreographed perfectly, a complete rout. But I am surprised to see Andacanavar here. I had thought you would be leading the Alpinadoran ranks."

"Bruinhelde's fight, from beginning to end," the ranger answered. "And your archers and horsemen performed their role perfectly. Look down on the ravine with hope, Prince Midalis, for before you looms the last goblin threat to Vanguard." As he finished, he turned away from the slaughter on the ravine floor to gaze meaningfully at Midalis. When Midalis met his eyes, he understood that Andacanavar referred to much more than regional security.

With this slaughter, the goblins had been eradicated from Vanguard in Honce-the-Bear. But now, Midalis knew, would come the real test. Would the army of Vanguard follow the Alpinadorans north to the southern reaches of their kingdom, to secure those lands, as well?

Midalis wanted to give the ranger his assurances of that cooperation, but he could not; his talks with his countrymen toward just that end had not been met with enthusiasm. He nodded to Andacanavar and remarked, "And all the minions of the dactyl will be on the run before long."

Andacanavar cocked an eyebrow at the obviously evasive remark, but he, too, nodded, apparently accepting the delicacy of the situation.

"Where was Andacanavar, then, to be missin' such a fight as this?" Liam O'Blythe put in. He added, "Does well by Bruinhelde to see him puttin' together such a massacre."

"Business in the north," the ranger answered, and he looked even more intently at the Prince of Vanguard and went on, "arrangements to be made."

Midalis glanced back at Liam and saw the look of concern on the man's face—for he had told Liam of Andacanavar's pending "arrangements." Ironically, it was that expression of doubt, of fear even, that bolstered Midalis in his resolve that this alliance with Bruinhelde's people would not be a passing thing. He turned back to Andacanavar, his face grim, and nodded. "Inform Bruinhelde that I will meet him at the mead hall tomorrow night," he said, "that we might discuss our plans."

The ranger looked back down at the valley, where the last of the goblins were scrambling wildly, only to be run down, skewered by arrows or blasted by Alpinadoran hammers.

"And a fine mead hall celebration it will be," the ranger remarked. He patted Midalis' horse on the neck and trotted back the way he had come, as Midalis and Liam silently watched him go.

When Midalis finally looked away from the ranger, toward his companion, he saw that the distress had not left Liam's expression.

"He moves with the grace of a much smaller man," Midalis remarked, more to break the tension than anything else.

"And quick on his feet, if he went all the way to the mountains and back," Liam agreed, his sharp tone and his reference to the mountains—the expected locale of the ominous arrangements for the blood-brothering Andacanavar had indicated to Midalis—telling the Prince in no uncertain terms that Liam's fears were strongly founded.

"Your concern truly touches me," he said with a chuckle.

Liam didn't smile. "I'm not thrilled with losin' me Prince," he said.

"Andacanavar would not have arranged this trial if he believed I could not survive it," Midalis replied, "nor have I even agreed to partake."

"Oh, ye'll go," Liam continued, nodding his head. "I know ye too well to think ye'd refuse any dare."

That brought another chuckle to Midalis, with the recollections of so many chances he and Liam had taken together as younger men in the wild Vanguard woods. Liam even managed a slight smile of his own then, unable to resist the delicious memories.

"But ye were younger then," Liam said after a moment, "and we was both seein' less to lose."

"I have not agreed," Midalis repeated, bluntly and firmly, and there was truth in his words. He truly had not decided upon the wisdom of accepting the blood-brothering, as Andacanavar had called it. On the surface, it seemed like a wonderful way to strengthen the bond between the Vanguardsmen and the Alpinadorans—Bruinhelde was no minor chieftain among the northern clans! If Midalis and Bruinhelde both survived the blood-brothering trials, they would be bound forever as siblings.

But Midalis knew that by agreeing to such a binding trial, a ritual that would bind not only him but also those who served him, he was in effect signing a treaty with Alpinador—or at least with Bruinhelde's substantial clan. And did he have the right to enter into such a treaty without the knowledge and blessings of his brother, the King? What would happen if Bruinhelde called upon their alliance at some future date, forcing the Prince of Vanguard to send half his troops to the frigid northern reaches of desolate Alpinador to battle some new enemy, a great dragon, perhaps, or invading powries?

On the other hand, Prince Midalis could not deny that Bruinhelde and his clansmen had saved him and his army, had saved St. Belfour, despite their animosity toward the Abellican Church. Could the honorable Midalis ignore the ranger's request for such a binding?

"Haven't ye then?" Liam remarked after a long and uncomfortable silence. "Haven't ye come to see the barbarians as allies? Even as friends, mayhap?"

Midalis stared at him hard, but didn't deny the words.

"Haven't ye figured that we'd be packin' for the roads north, to see if any goblins're needin' chasin' out in Bruinhelde's land?"

"Do you not believe that we owe that much, at least?" Midalis replied.

"Aye," Liam said resignedly and without hesitation. "We're owin' them barbarians too much, by me own figurin'. But I'll be with ye, don't ye doubt."

"Never did," Midalis answered, and he urged his horse into motion and turned back down the ridge.

He and Liam met the rest of the warriors on the field outside of St.

Belfour soon after, the men full of excitement. The monks came out to join in the celebration as well, led by a boisterous Agronguerre bearing barrels of wine and ale and food. They all knew it, without ever hearing it proclaimed officially by Midalis: the goblin threat had been ended this day, and the folk of Vanguard could go about putting their fields, and their lives, back in order.

Midalis took it all in stride, and prepared to let them have this night of rejoicing—or thought he would, at least, until Andacanavar and Bruinhelde arrived. Fortunately, Midalis was among the first to spot them.

The Prince rushed over to the pair and spoke before either of them, particularly grim Bruinhelde, could instigate the conversation about Vanguardsmen going north. "I have promised to meet you in the mead hall tomorrow night," he said.

"You do not invite us to participate in your celebration?" Bruinhelde asked. "Would it have been better for Midalis, then, if we had not fought the goblins this day?"

"Of c-course you are welcome," Midalis stuttered, only then realizing how ungrateful and unwelcoming he had sounded. "You and all of your warriors. I only thought . . . I mean, my friend, you do not wear the face of celebration but one of planning."

"There will be no mead hall tomorrow night," Bruinhelde explained, rather gruffly. But since Midalis was certainly used to gruffness from the man, this did not alarm him greatly. "We leave with the morning light, for the northern trails back to our home."

Liam O'Blythe walked up beside the Prince then, bearing extra mugs of ale, which he offered to the guests.

"You can understand Bruinhelde's desire to be on the road as soon as possible," Andacanavar stated. "He knows not whether any of our fleeing enemies have ventured into his homeland, though we left the passes into the region well guarded."

"Of course," Midalis agreed, and he held his mug up in salute to Bruinhelde. The barbarian looked at the Prince for a moment, then responded in kind.

"Tomorrow will be a sad day for the men of Vanguard," Midalis went on.

"For some," Bruinhelde replied, and Midalis knew he was talking about the brothers of St. Belfour; for though Agronguerre had done well to secure the alliance, the barbarians had remained suspicious of the monks.

"For all," Midalis replied. "Vanguard has not forgotten what you and your warriors have done for us. All in St. Belfour would have perished had not Bruinhelde and his brethren come to the field. We remember."

"Well enough to follow us north?" the Alpinadoran leader asked bluntly.

Midalis sighed. "I had meant to address that issue in detail with my warriors at sunrise," he explained. "Thus, I had planned to speak with you at the mead hall tomorrow night."

"You will come or you will not," Bruinhelde said.

"You are the leader of the Vanguardsmen," Andacanavar said. "Is not your word their law?"

There it was, spoken baldly without any room for evasion. Midalis was indeed the leader, the ruler, was the man who had to make this decision. But Prince Midalis had never been an autocrat, preferring rather to build consensus for his decisions. He almost always sought out the advice of his fellows—Liam, Agronguerre, and others—and always listened carefully to that advice before acting. Now, though, it had been laid squarely upon his shoulders: a great weight, a great decision that could hold grave implications for his beloved fellow Vanguardsmen in the immediate future and for the kingdom of Honce-the-Bear for years to come.

And Midalis had to respond now. Studying the Alpinadorans, he recognized that Bruinhelde had forced this decision as a test more of the man Midalis, than of the Vanguardsmen in general. Given that Bruinhelde and Midalis were about to go through the most intimate of ceremonies, where, according to Andacanavar, they would have to depend fully on each other or perish, the Prince could understand Bruinhelde's desire to see his heart laid bare.

"We shall come," Midalis answered firmly. Liam gasped, but did well, Midalis thought, in quickly composing himself. "Of course we shall! What friends, what allies, would you have made, good Bruinhelde, if we accepted your blood to protect our homes but did not offer our own in return? I do not yet know, however, how many I can bring with me. Our farms and homes have been ravaged by the years of battle, and I must make sure that they are ready to supply us for the next winter."

"Make your plans, then," Bruinhelde offered. "We will await your arrival at the mead hall tomorrow night."

"But ye just said—" a confused Liam started to protest. But Midalis, who understood well the test Bruinhelde had just put to him and was not the least bit surprised by the Alpinadoran leader's reversal, stopped him with an upraised hand.

"I will bring as many as can be spared," Midalis replied. "Now, please join us in our celebration." He turned and waved his hand across, an invitation for the two Alpinadorans, who, with their great height and massive bulk, stood out among the smaller Vanguardsmen.

Bruinhelde looked to Andacanavar, and the ranger nodded and led the way into the host of revelers. Few joined the two barbarians, though many looked their way. After a while, Prince Midalis, fearing that their guests might feel insulted, bade Liam to gather a few friends and go and join them.

"They're all afraid o' sayin' the wrong thing," Liam explained. "Ye do well with Bruinhelde and the ranger, but the rest of us don't know 'em, and aren't sure we're wantin' to know 'em!

"I know what ye're thinkin' to say," Liam quickly added, seeing that

Midalis was about to protest. "And no, me lord, I'm not forgettin' what Bruinhelde and his kin did for us on the field about St. Belfour and in all the fightin' since."

"Then go and make our guests feel welcome," Midalis instructed. Liam turned to do just that, but stopped short.

"Seems another had the same way o' thinkin'," he said, leading Midalis' gaze across to the two barbarians and to Abbot Agronguerre and Brother Haney, who were approaching them.

Midalis set off quickly at once, Liam falling in step behind him.

"Greetings, good Bruinhelde and good Andacanavar," he heard the abbot say. "You remember Brother Haney, I trust."

A group of men cut across Midalis at that moment, stopping him short, and their discussion prevented him from hearing the barbarians' response. He breathed a little easier when he finally managed to get around the group of Vanguardsmen, to find the two monks and the two barbarians seemingly at ease.

"Twenty brothers," Agronguerre was saying as Midalis approached. "I wish it could be more, as I wish that I could travel with you."

"You're not so old," Andacanavar offered to the abbot.

"Closer to seventy than to sixty!" Agronguerre proudly replied, patting his belly under the drawstring of his brown robe.

Andacanavar laughed and winked at that statement, a not-so-subtle reminder that he, too, had seen several decades of life, though he could out-fight any man north of the gulf.

"Me abbot's got to stay in St. Belfour," Brother Haney cut in. "Word's that a messenger's on the way from the south. We lost our Father Abbot—"

"The leader of our Church," Agronguerre explained. Andacanavar nodded, but Bruinhelde just held his stoic, unreadable expression. "And thus, I expect to be summoned to the south, where a new leader will be elected. But with Vanguard apparently secured, my brothers and I wish to help along the road to the north. I would not presume to send Abellican monks into Alpinador, though, without your permission."

"We came to your aid, you come to ours," Bruinhelde remarked, cutting short Andacanavar, who seemed to be beginning another of his many diplomatic interventions. "It is fair and good. Your brothers are welcome, and with my thanks."

Prince Midalis could hardly believe his ears. He and Liam joined the group with a nod, and with the Prince patting Agronguerre on the shoulder.

"They will take gemstones with them," Agronguerre went on, "and will use them against our enemies and to aid the wounded Vanguardsmen. For your own wounded—" Bruinhelde stiffened and Midalis held his breath

"—the choice remains yours to make, of course." Agronguerre continued, "If you desire our healing magic, pray you simply ask."

"No," said Bruinhelde.

"As you will," Agronguerre replied. "I feel that I would be derelict in our friendship if I did not make the offer."

"And a fine offer you've made," Andacanavar put in.

"You will watch over the brothers," Bruinhelde said to Midalis.

"Brother Haney will lead them," Agronguerre remarked, but the barbarian leader wasn't paying him any attention.

"We welcome them as allies against our enemies," Bruinhelde went on. "Not as . . ." He leaned over to Andacanavar and said something in the Alpinadoran tongue, and the ranger promptly translated.

"Not as missionaries."

"Of course," Abbot Agronguerre said with a bow, and he turned to Midalis. "Let us know when you plan to depart. The brothers will be ready." With another bow to the barbarians, he led Brother Haney away.

"It is time for us to return to our own folk, as well," Andacanavar said. "We await you at the mead hall tomorrow night.

"And, Prince Midalis," he added with a sly look, "name a second to command your force. If the opportunity presents itself, perhaps we can make this trip doubly profitable. And, my friend, you never can tell when the spirit shaggoth will win."

Midalis smiled at the remark, but he felt Liam O'Blythe tense at his side, and he knew that his friend was going to try to persuade him against accepting the blood-brothering, probably long into the night.

Finding Sides

"You choose your allies foolishly," Targon Bree Kalas fumed at Abbot Braumin.

"Choose?" Braumin echoed incredulously, and in truth, the churchman shared Kalas' feelings more than the Duke could ever know.

"Bishop De'Unnero is not well liked within the city," Kalas went on.

"Nor within the Church," Braumin said under his breath. They had met by chance at the Palmaris market, but as soon as Braumin had seen Kalas coming, had seen the expression on the Duke's face, he had guessed the source of the man's ire.

"They remember Aloysius Crump," Kalas went on. "Who could forget the sight of the innocent man being roasted alive with your *godly* magic? They remember De'Unnero's actions against their families and friends. And now you are fool enough to parade him before the people? Does your Church invite such disdain?"

Abbot Braumin swallowed hard, forcing himself to calm down, reminding himself not to play into Kalas' hands here in the open. For a brief moment, he had wondered why in the world Duke Kalas, with whom he had been fighting from the very beginning of their respective appointments, would go out of his way to point out the trouble with keeping De'Unnero around. But given the public nature of this place, given the multitude of spectators and the way the Duke had already couched the premise of the conversation, the answer seemed clear. Braumin had gone out of his way to keep De'Unnero's return as secret as possible, though rumors had slipped out. He had begged the former Bishop to keep a low profile, and De'-Unnero, apparently understanding the wisdom of Braumin's suggestion, had done just that.

"Am I to refuse the *former* Bishop entry to St. Precious?" Braumin asked innocently.

"Expel him!" Duke Kalas returned. It struck Braumin then that there was more than political gain motivating Kalas here, there was true hatred for De'Unnero. "Excommunicate him! Why, I would not share the same church with the man!"

"I have not seen you at service in St. Precious, your Grace," Braumin pointed out.

But Kalas snorted, shook his head, and walked away, with every member of his entourage pointedly speaking the name of De'Unnero, along with some unfavorable adjective, as they followed him.

Abbot Braumin stood in the market for a long while, aware of the angry stares coming at him from every angle. De'Unnero had made too many enemies here, he understood, and he dropped the fruit he had picked back into the vendor's cart and started away swiftly for St. Precious, hoping that he might use Kalas' tirade and those angry stares of the peasants to persuade the former Bishop that it would be better for all if he left the city.

Master Francis paused and stared long and hard at the cold walls of St.-Mere-Abelle, brown and gray stone stretching for more than a mile along the high cliff overlooking All Saints Bay. He remembered the first time he had entered the abbey, more than a decade before, a young novice walking through the Gauntlet of Willing Suffering, a row of older brothers armed with wooden paddles.

Still, Francis would have preferred that treatment to what awaited him now within the foreboding place. His news was grim, all of it, from the disaster in Palmaris and the loss of brothers to the goblins outside Davon Dinnishire to, perhaps worst of all, the signs he had encountered of the rosy plague. But even more than that, Francis saw St.-Mere-Abelle now as a reminder of his errors. In that place, he had followed Father Abbot Markwart, had obeyed the man blindly, even when Markwart was torturing the innocent Chilichunks and the centaur, Bradwarden, in the dungeons. Here Francis had not spoken out against the murder—and it was indeed murder, he understood now—of Master Jojonah.

St.-Mere-Abelle—with all its strong stone walls, its sense of majesty and power—reminded Master Francis of his own frailties. And he could not even enter secure in the knowledge that he had put those faults behind him. Oh, he was wiser now, he understood the evil that had possessed Father Abbot Markwart, but it seemed to him that his own courage remained an elusive thing. Perhaps he had been wrong in withdrawing his demand that Jilseponie take over the Abellican Church. He understood and still recognized the problems that such a nomination would have brought, but shouldn't he have fought for it anyway? Shouldn't he have stood up for the right course, whatever the potential troubles?

And yet, Master Francis knew now, looking at the mighty St.-Mere-Abelle, that he could not have done it, could not have nominated Jilseponie. Not then and not now.

With a sigh, resigned to his own sense of failure, Master Francis Della-court led the brothers, the living carrying the dead, across the mile of open field to the front gates of St.-Mere-Abelle.

He was agitated, too much so, he knew, but Abbot Braumin could not contain his frustration. So many great dreams had followed him to this place within the hierarchy of the Church, so many hopes that Nightbird's sacrifice would bolster him and his companions in their efforts to better the Church and better the world.

Yet in the months he had been serving as abbot of St. Precious, Braumin Herde had known only frustration. And while the abbey had done much to aid the inhabitants of Palmaris, had expanded its prayer services consider-ably and had sent out brothers with soul stones on missions of healing, Braumin had made little, if any, progress on any institutional changes at St. Precious. Every one of his plans had run into Duke Kalas, and the man had forced a stalemate.

And now De'Unnero!

The word of the former Bishop's arrival was general throughout the city now, after the public discussion at the market. The prayer services immedi-ately following their meeting had been crowded, but the people had not come into St. Precious for blessings but rather to gossip, to see if they might catch a glimpse to confirm that the hated De'Unnero was back.

Wisely, Marcalo De'Unnero had stayed away, as Braumin had advised. Protestors arrived daily and surrounded the abbey, calling for De'Unnero's expulsion, excommunication, even execution. Braumin understood that Duke Kalas had likely put them up to it, but that hardly mattered—for others had fallen in with the plans, no doubt, and the rage would grow and grow along with the summer heat.

The abbot paced about his office now, wringing his hands, muttering prayers for guidance.

The door opened and Master Visconti poked his head in, then swung the door wide so that De'Unnero could enter before him.

Braumin held up his hand to Visconti, motioning for him to leave.

"Did you expect any different reaction when you returned to the city?" Braumin began curtly, when he and De'Unnero were alone.

De'Unnero snorted, an unimpressed grin upon his face. "I have returned subservient," he said quietly. Braumin noted that there was a tremor in his voice, and it seemed to the abbot as if De'Unnero was engaged in a tremen-dous inner struggle at that moment. "I have accepted your ascension to a position I once held, have I not? A position that I would likely have con-tinued to hold—"

"Master Francis replaced you as abbot long before the fight at Chasewind Manor," Abbot Braumin reminded him.

De'Unnero paused, a telling hesitation to the perceptive Braumin. He was trying to compose himself, the abbot knew, trying not to fly into a rage—and while Braumin surely feared such a rage from this dangerous man, he thought that prodding De'Unnero along in that direction might not be a bad thing.

"You need not recite me a chronology, Abbot Braumin," De'Unnero said, his voice controlled once more. "I understand perfectly well—better than do you, I am sure—all that went on during the last days of Father Abbot Markwart. I understand perfectly well the role I was forced to play—"

"That you eagerly played," Braumin corrected. De'Unnero's dark eyes flashed with anger, but again he paused and suppressed the rage.

"As you will," he said, his dark eyes narrowing. "You were not here, I remind you."

"Except when I was in your dungeons," Braumin retorted. "Except when my friends and I were dragged from the Barbacan, from Mount Aida and Avelyn's shrine, by De'Unnero and his henchmen."

"By Father Abbot Markwart, whom De'Unnero served," the former Bishop corrected, "and by the King of Honce-the-Bear. Have you forgotten? Was not Kalas, the same Duke Kalas who now serves as baron of Palmaris, beside me on that plateau, demanding your surrender?"

"I remember!" Abbot Braumin said loudly and firmly. "I remember, and so do they, Master De'Unnero, former Bishop of Palmaris," he said, sweeping his arm out toward the window. "The people of Palmaris remember."

De'Unnero stiffened; Braumin noted that he clenched one fist at his side.

"They hate you," the abbot went on determinedly. "You represent to them everything that was wrong—"

"They are idiots," De'Unnero interrupted sharply, his tone, the strength of his voice, setting Braumin back on his heels. "Fools all. Cattle and sheep who flock into our pews in the hopes that their minor sacrifice of time will bring them absolution for the miserable ways in which they conduct their lives."

Braumin stuttered over that blunt proclamation for a few moments before coming up with any response at all. "They do not look upon your reign as bishop favorably," he said. "As it was with Father Abbot Markwart—"

"I did not return to fight old battles," De'Unnero insisted, his tone still razor edged—a clear sign to Braumin that his words against him were not falling upon deaf ears.

"Then why did you return, Marcalo De'Unnero?" the abbot asked, matching the man's obvious ire.

"This is my appointed abbey," De'Unnero replied immediately. "My Church."

"I rather doubt that the current St. Precious resembles anything that could be called your Church," Braumin reasoned, "nor Markwart's." He thought that he had touched a nerve within De'Unnero with the blunt statement, but the man's look proved to be one of incredulity and not defensiveness.

"Because you tend to the ills of the populace?" he asked. "Because you comfort them and tell them that God will cure all and will take them into his bosom, no matter how wretched an existence they might live? Because, in your own foolishness and arrogance, you believe that you can cure those ills, that you can make it better for all of them?"

"Is that not our calling?"

"That is a lie, and nothing more!" De'Unnero insisted. "It is not our place to coddle and comfort, but to instruct and demand obedience."

"You do not sound like one who has dismissed the errors of Markwart," Braumin remarked.

"I sound like one who would not compound those errors with the false dreams of paradise," De'Unnero retorted. "Since you apparently insist on such a course, perhaps I should make myself more prominent at prayers and about the city."

"Do your words blot out the reality?" Braumin yelled at him, coming forward suddenly and poking his finger toward the man. "Can you not hear them about our walls? Can you not understand the enemies you have made, Duke Kalas among them? This is not your place, Marcalo De'Unnero. St. Precious is not—"

He ended with a gasp as De'Unnero exploded into motion, reaching his right hand over Braumin's extended arm and jabbing finger. De'Unnero twisted his arm down and turned around, forcing Braumin to turn, bringing himself behind the abbot. De'Unnero had him locked and helpless, one arm up, painfully wrenched behind his back, with the former Bishop's left arm tight across his throat.

"You did not learn your lessons in the arts martial, my friend," De'Unnero purred into Braumin's ear. Braumin could hear the feral, feline growl deep in the man's throat.

"Get out of my abbey and out of my city," Braumin replied, having to gasp for breath with every word.

"How easy it would be for me to reclaim the abbey," De'Unnero went on. "Alas for poor Abbot Braumin, falling to his death down the stairs. Or out the window, perhaps. But thankfully, St. Precious is not in turmoil, for they've another abbot on hand. Pity about the accident." As he ended, he tightened his hold and let go of Braumin's arm, bringing his other arm up beside Braumin's head.

The strength of the man appalled Braumin and made him acutely aware that De'Unnero could break his neck with a simple twist. Still, Braumin fought past the pain and the fear, held his determined course. "Alas for Baron Rochefort Bildeborough," he gasped, referring to the longtime, beloved Baron of Palmaris, a man the populace believed had been killed by a great wildcat, but who those within Braumin's circle believed had been murdered by none other than Marcalo De'Unnero.

De'Unnero growled at the reference. Braumin thought his life was at its end, but then the volatile former Bishop shoved Braumin away.

"You return *subservient?*" Braumin asked skeptically, rubbing his neck and echoing De'Unnero's initial statement.

"Subservient to the truth and the mission of our Church," De'Unnero replied. "But I see that my truth and your own are not in accord."

"Get out of my abbey," Braumin repeated.

"Have you that power, young Abbot Braumin?"

"I am not alone in my feelings toward you," Braumin assured the man. "You are not welcome here—in St. Precious or in Palmaris."

"And will you enlist Duke Kalas into your cause against me?" De'Unnero asked with a snort. "Will you seek the support of a man open in his disdain for the Abellican Church?"

"If I must," Braumin answered coolly. "My brethren in St. Precious, the Duke's soldiers, the people of Palmaris—whatever aid I might find in ridding the city of you."

"How charitable," De'Unnero said, his voice dripping sarcasm.

"Charitable for the people of Palmaris, yes," Braumin replied without hesitation. He looked Marcalo De'Unnero in the eye again and matched the man's intensity. "Get out of St. Precious and out of Palmaris," he stated flatly and evenly, speaking each word with heavy emphasis. "You are not wanted here, and your presence will only weaken the position of St. Precious with the flock we tend."

De'Unnero started to respond, but just spat upon the floor at Braumin's feet and wheeled out of the room.

Master Viscenti entered on the man's heels. "Are you all right?" he asked, obviously flustered and frightened.

"As all right as one can be after arguing with Marcalo De'Unnero," Braumin answered dryly.

Viscenti bobbed his head, his nervous tic jerking one shoulder forward repeatedly. "I do not like that one at all," he said. "I had hoped that he had met his end out . . . out wherever he has been!"

"Brother Viscenti!" Braumin scolded, though the abbot had to admit to himself that he felt the same way. "It is not our place to wish ill on a fellow brother of the Order."

Viscenti looked at him incredulously, his expression almost horrified that Braumin would so name De'Unnero.

And Abbot Braumin understood the sentiment completely. But the truth was plain to him: De'Unnero had not been excommunicated, had not even been charged with any crime against the Crown or the Church. For whatever the rumors might say, the former Bishop owed no explanations and no apologies. How Braumin Herde wished he had some real evidence that De'Unnero had murdered the former Baron of Palmaris!

But he did not, and though De'Unnero had no claim to a position of bishop—which had been formally revoked by King Danube himself—or of abbot—for that title had been taken from De'Unnero formally by Father Abbot Markwart—the man remained a master of the Abellican Order, with a high rank and a strong voice in all matters of the Church, including the College of Abbots that would convene in the fall.

Braumin winced as he considered that De'Unnero might even make a play for the position of father abbot, then winced even more when he realized that several other prominent masters of St.-Mere-Abelle would likely back that nomination.

It was not a pleasant thought.

Marcalo De'Unnero left St. Precious that very evening. Abbot Braumin found little relief in watching him go.

Silence. Dead silence, a stillness so profound that it spoke volumes to Master Francis as he sat at the end of the long, narrow table in the audience chamber used by the father abbots of St.-Mere-Abelle. He had met with Master Fio Bou-raiy soon after his arrival in the abbey and had previewed for the man all that he would tell at the meeting—his entire tale, honestly spoken, except, at the bidding of Bou-raiy, his fears concerning the plague. That news had to be relayed more cautiously and to an even more select group, Bou-raiy had convinced Francis—or at least, had secured Francis' agreement.

Francis had told the rest of his tale in full to the five masters in attendance: the dominant Bou-raiy, the most powerful man remaining at St.-Mere-Abelle; Machuso, who handled all the laymen working in the abbey; young Glendenhook, capable and ambitious, a recent appointee to the rank of master and only in his late thirties; and the two oldest, yet still least prominent among the group, Baldmir and Timminey, men who reminded Francis somewhat of Je'howith of St. Honce, only less forceful and conniving. It occurred to Francis that neither of the pair would even have been appointed to their present rank had not circumstances—the loss of all four of the brothers who had gone to Pimaninicuit, of Siherton by Avelyn's hands, of Jojonah at Markwart's hands, and the untimely deaths of several other older masters over the last couple of years—left them as the only candidates. Both had served as immaculates for more than thirty years, after all, with no prominent reasons to suggest any cause for elevation. At this time, St.-Mere-Abelle was not strong in high-ranking monks.

And at this time, Francis feared, that lack of leadership might prove devastating to the Church.

"Then you agree with the reports we have previously heard that Father

Abbot Markwart's fall, though tragic, was for the ultimate betterment of the Church?" asked Master Bou-raiy, a man in his mid-forties with short and neatly trimmed salt-and-pepper hair, a perfectly clean-shaven face, and a general appearance and demeanor of competence and sternness. What added to the latter attribute was the fact that the man's left sleeve was tied off at the shoulder, for he had lost his arm in an accident working the stone-cutting. No one who knew Fio Bou-raiy would consider him crippled in any way, though.

"Father Abbot Markwart lost sight of much in his last days," Francis replied. "He told me as much with his last breath."

"And what of Francis, then?" Bou-raiy said, narrowing his eyes. "If Markwart strayed, then what of Francis, who followed him to Palmaris to do his every bidding?"

"Master Francis was—is but a young man," Master Machuso put in. "You ask much of a young brother to refuse the commands of the Father Abbot."

"Young, yet old enough to accept an appointment as master, as abbot, as bishop," Bou-raiy was quick to reply.

Francis studied him carefully, recognizing that Bou-raiy hadn't been pleased that Markwart had overlooked him when choosing Francis to serve as his second.

"And now we have an even younger man holding title as our principal in the important city of Palmaris," scoffed Glendenhook.

"It was a difficult time," Francis said quietly. "I followed my Father Abbot, and perhaps erred on more than one occasion."

"As have we all," Master Machuso replied.

"And I have since relinquished those titles Father Abbot Markwart bestowed upon me," Francis stated.

"Except that of master," Glendenhook interjected; and it seemed to Francis as if the young and fiery master was serving as Bou-raiy's mouth-piece. With his barrel chest and curly blond hair and beard, and a snarling attitude, Glendenhook was an imposing sort.

"I would likely have been nominated for the position by this point in any case," Francis calmly went on, "a position that I believe I have earned, with my work, including organizing the expedition to the Barbacan to learn the fate of the demon dactyl. I keep the title because it, unlike the position of bishop—which is no more, in any case—and that of abbot—of which there can only be one, in any case—does not preclude the appointment of others more deserving."

"And yet, we now have a former heretic serving in your previous place at St. Precious," Glendenhook remarked.

"A man falsely accused of heresy," Francis replied, "a man who had the courage to refute Father Abbot Markwart when I, and others in this room, did not." He noted that Machuso and the two older men were nodding their agreement; but Bou-raiy stiffened, and Glendenhook seemed as if he was about to spit. "I urge you to accept and offer your blessings to Abbot Braumin Herde, as have King Danube and Abbot Je'howith of St. Honce. And I urge you to accept with open hearts the nomination of Brother Viscenti to the position of master."

"It seems a proper course," Machuso remarked, looking to Bou-raiy.

"And if we do not so accept the nominations, of either man?" Master Bou-raiy asked.

"Then you risk dividing the Church, for many will stand beside them, and I will advise them to hold their posts."

That bold statement raised a few eyebrows.

"This is not our domain, Master Bou-raiy," Francis went on. "We here at St.-Mere-Abelle, in the absence of a father abbot, must allow the brothers of St. Precious to appoint whomever they believe acceptable, as long as it is within the guidelines of our Order, as it would seem for both Braumin Herde and Marlboro Viscenti. The brothers of St. Precious have chosen Braumin Herde; and thus he is empowered to nominate and elevate Brother Viscenti to the position of master. We could recall Viscenti to St.-Mere-Abelle, of course, since this was his appointed abbey, and then void the promotion, but to what end? We would only then be weakening an already difficult position in Palmaris, where King Danube has given Duke Targon Bree Kalas, no friend of the Church, the barony."

Again there was a long period of silence, with even Glendenhook looking to Bou-raiy for guidance. The older man struck a pensive pose and stroked his hand over his hairless chin several times, staring at Francis, never blinking.

"What of the woman, Jilseponie?" Glendenhook asked, looking to both Francis and Bou-raiy. "Declared an outlaw and heretic."

"More a candidate for mother abbess," Francis remarked. The sudden, horrified expressions from all of the others, even his apparent allies, reminded him of the battle that nomination would have brought upon the Church!

"No outlaw," he said. "It was Father Abbot Markwart himself who once so named her; and who bore her out to me, unconscious after their titanic struggle; and who admitted to me that she had been right all along. She is neither outlaw nor heretic, by the words of the very man who so branded her."

"Perhaps further investigation—" Master Glendenhook started to say.

"No!" Francis roared at him, and again, he was greeted by stunned expressions. "No," he said again, more calmly. "Jilseponie is a hero to the people of Palmaris, to all who live north of the city, and to many others, I would guess, who only heard of and did not witness her deeds. She is in the highest favor of King Danube, I assure you, and any action we take against her, even actions within our province such as excommunication, will only bring scorn upon our Church, and perhaps bring the armies of the King, as well."

"Strong words, brother," Bou-raiy remarked.

"You were not there, Master Bou-raiy," Francis replied calmly. "If you had witnessed the events in Palmaris, you would think my words an understatement, I assure you."

"What of her gemstones?" Bou-raiy asked. "The considerable cache stolen by Brother Avelyn? It is said that they were not found after the battle."

Francis shrugged. "It is rumored that the stones were consumed in the fight against the Father Abbot."

More than a few whispers began at that statement, mostly of doubt—and Francis had a hard time making the case here, since he, too, believed that the stones had been pilfered.

Bou-raiy settled back in his chair once more, and signaled to Glendenhook to be quiet just as the man was about to begin the argument anew.

"So be it," Bou-raiy said at length. "Braumin Herde, through his courage and the simple good fortune of having his side prevail, has earned a post—one that we could not easily fill without weakening our own abbey even more. If he deems it necessary to promote Brother Viscenti, then let him have his way. I must admit my own relief in having both of them, and Brothers Castinagis and Dellman as well, out of St.-Mere-Abelle."

"Hear, hear," Master Glendenhook applauded.

Francis let the uncalled-for slight slip by, relieved that Bou-raiy would take that one insult as satisfying enough and let the promotions stand without argument.

"As for the woman Jilseponie," Bou-raiy went on, "she can go in peace, and let the wisdom of the ages judge her actions, good or bad. We have not the time nor the resources to pursue the battles waged by Father Abbot Markwart. However," he warned in the gravest of tones, "Jilseponie would be wise not to keep those stones, for whatever justification she might have found in holding them during the reign of Markwart is past now."

Francis nodded, understanding the complications that would indeed arise if Jilseponie had the stones and began using them in the northland. Bou-raiy would never stand for it, though Francis wondered what, indeed, the man might do about it. Francis had seen the results of Jilseponie's frightening march through Palmaris on her way to Markwart.

"We have more important issues to contend with, anyway," Bou-raiy continued, leaning forward in his chair, a clear signal that he wanted to move the meeting his way. "There is the little matter of filling, and efficiently, the vacancy at the top of our Order. We have discussed this long before your arrival, of course, Master Francis, and already have planned to summon a College of Abbots in Calember, as you advised us today.

"Brothers," he went on solemnly, pausing and looking at each of the other five in turn. "We must be united in this. It is no secret that Olin of Bondabruce will make a claim for father abbot. I have known Abbot Olin for many years and consider him a fine man, but his ties to Behren disturb me."

"What of Master Bou-raiy?" Glendenhook immediately put in, and again Francis got the distinct impression that the man was speaking for Bou-raiy, as if the two had planned this little exchange.

"With all due respect," Master Machuso put in calmly and, indeed, respectfully, "you are but five years in the title of master, Brother Bou-raiy. I would not oppose such a seemingly premature ascension to the highest position under other circumstances—"

"He is the finest master remaining within the Church!" Glendenhook snapped. Bou-raiy remained very calm and waved the man to silence, then motioned for Machuso to continue.

"Even if we were all to stand united behind you, you cannot expect to have any chance of winning the nomination against Abbot Olin," Machuso explained. "And where, then, would that leave us? Abbot Olin would ascend to the position of father abbot, and he would not come to serve as such viewing any of us in a favorable light."

Again Glendenhook started to respond, but Bou-raiy cut him short.

"True enough, good Master Machuso," he said. "Who among us, then, do you advise? Yourself?"

Machuso narrowed his eyes a bit, Francis noted, for Bou-raiy's tone, though his words were in agreement, was somewhat condescending. The gentle Machuso quickly let the insult pass, and then replied with a laugh.

"Then who?" Bou-raiy asked, holding his hand up. "Tell us, Master Francis, was this matter discussed among the brethren in Palmaris? With Abbot Je'howith? Yes, perhaps Je'howith will try for the position, but I warn you that any intentions you might be holding in that matter will not bring the Church together. Je'howith is far too—"

"Tied to King Danube, and to the troubled days of Father Abbot Markwart's end, to be acceptable," Francis interrupted. "But, yes, we did indeed discuss the matter at length, to find a candidate who would prove acceptable to all in the Church, one who would heal us and bring us back together, of one mind and one purpose."

"And that choice?"

"Agronguerre of St. Belfour, it would seem," Francis replied.

"An excellent man, of fine reputation," Master Machuso said enthusiastically.

"Indeed," Master Timminey agreed.

"Why do you say, 'it would seem,' brother?" Bou-raiy asked Francis.

"I do not know that Abbot Braumin Herde knows the man well enough to agree to the choice," Francis admitted.

"And Abbot Je'howith?"

"It was Je'howith who suggested Abbot Agronguerre," Francis explained.

Bou-raiy settled back in his chair, again in that pensive pose, again rubbing his hairless chin. Francis saw the disappointment, even anger, flash across his face—particularly in his gray eyes—more than once, but he was clearly a man in control of his emotions, and the dark cloud was but a temporary thing.

To the left of Bou-raiy, Glendenhook seemed even more agitated, rubbing his thumbs across his fingers, even chewing his lip. They had hoped that all the brothers of St.-Mere-Abelle, particularly all the masters, would rally behind Bou-raiy, but Machuso's grounded response had thrown those hopes out in short order.

Francis looked back to Bou-raiy, could already see the man coming to terms with the developments. Likely, he was thinking that Abbot Agronguerre was an old man, probably with less than a decade of life left, compared to Olin, who was barely into his fifties and in fine health. Yes, Francis came to recognize, Bou-raiy was thinking that it might be wise to throw his weight behind Agronguerre, virtually assuring the man of election. He could then make himself indispensable to the new Father Abbot, working himself into the position of heir apparent.

Yes, Bou-raiy was going to agree with this, Francis realized, and the cause for Abbot Agronguerre was not hurt at all by the fact that Masters Bou-raiy and Olin had never been friendly.

"We will take the issue under advisement," Bou-raiy decided, "with each of us, and the other masters of St.-Mere-Abelle, coming to his own decision on the matter."

"Agronguerre of St. Belfour is a fine choice," Machuso said, offering a wink to Francis.

"Indeed," Master Timminey said again, with even more enthusiasm.

Francis glanced over at Baldmir to see if he might even get a third supporter, but the old master's head was drooping, his rhythmic breathing showing that he was fast asleep.

"Now, to the last matter we must herein discuss," Bou-raiy said, his voice growing grave and dark. "We suffer greatly at the loss of so many promising brothers."

"As do I," Francis replied.

"Yet you chose to pursue the goblin band and attack," Bou-raiy maintained, "when you obviously could have avoided the conflict."

"At the price of a village," Francis reminded.

"You have explained as much," Bou-raiy replied, holding his palm toward Francis, ending the debate. "This, too, we must take under advisement. We will appoint a brother inquisitor to study the matter."

Francis nodded: this was not unexpected, and he was confident that he would be exonerated.

"Vespers will begin within the hour," Bou-raiy said before Francis could continue with the only remaining part of his tale—that concerning the rosy plague. Baldmir stirred, and, as one, the gathered masters looked out the western window at the setting sun. "Let us go now and prepare."

As soon as he finished the sentence, the other brothers, except for Francis and Bou-raiy, began sliding back their chairs, and that unquestioning obedience confirmed to Francis that Fio Bou-raiy had strengthened his position considerably at St.-Mere-Abelle in the days since Markwart's departure for Palmaris.

Francis, too, then started to rise, but Bou-raiy subtly motioned to him to hold back. In a matter of moments, the two were alone.

"I have secured all of those brothers who returned with you," Bou-raiy explained.

"Secured?"

"Separated them from their peers," Bou-raiy explained, and Francis' face grew tight. "That we might ensure their understanding of what they have seen."

"Concerning the plague," Francis reasoned.

"Concerning a sick woman and a scarred goblin," Bou-raiy corrected.

"I am not unversed in matters of the rosy plague," Francis curtly replied.

"Nor do I doubt your claims," Bou-raiy was quick to respond. "But, dear brother, do you understand the implications of your discovery? Do you realize the problems, the panic, the ostracism, the stonings, perhaps, that such information could propagate if it became generally known throughout the land?"

"That is why I only quietly relayed my beliefs to Laird Dinnishire," Francis replied.

"Yet you would have those fears spoken openly at St.-Mere-Abelle."

"We are the chosen of God," Francis reasoned, "the shepherds of the common folk, the protectors. . . ."

Bou-raiy snorted, shaking his head. "Protectors?" he echoed skeptically. "Protectors? There are no protectors against the rosy plague, Master Francis. Are we to protect the people by alarming them?"

"Warning them," Francis corrected.

"To what end? That they might see death coming? That they might live in fear of their neighbors or of their own children?"

"We are to sit quietly, then, and take no action?" Francis asked.

"I do not doubt your observations, though I caution you that many other diseases resemble the rosy plague," Bou-raiy explained. "And perhaps this is some other sickness, since the goblins apparently escaped the disease alive. Yes, we shall take precautions here at St.-Mere-Abelle, and perhaps we will send word to the other abbots that they, too, might open their gates only to a select few."

Francis, full of frustration, rose quickly, his chair sliding out behind him.

"What about them?" he demanded, swinging his arm wide, as if to encompass the whole world.

Bou-raiy, too, rose from his chair, slowly and deliberately, hand planted firmly on the table and leaning forward, so that even though he was nearly ten feet away from Francis, the younger man felt his presence. "We do not know that it *was* the rosy plague," he said. "And if it is indeed, then we do not know how widespread it is, or will become. You are versed in the history of the plague, you say. Then you know that there have been instances when it has scoured the world and other times when it struck in select places, then disappeared of its own accord."

"And how are we to know which this will be, if we lock ourselves inside our abbeys and open our gates only to a select few?"

"By the passage of months, of years," Bou-raiy answered solemnly. "Knowledge is not power in this matter, my friend, for our knowledge of the spreading plague, if it comes to that, will give us no power to slow it or to stop it."

"The plague can be slowed," Francis argued. "If those who are diseased remain apart from others—"

"This is something the people know already," Bou-raiy reminded him. "And, in truth, it is a matter more for the King's soldiers than the brothers of St.-Mere-Abelle. You know the old song, I presume, rhyme and verse. You know what it says about the efficiency of gemstone magic against the rosy plague."

Indeed, Master Francis Dellacourt knew the old words well, the old words of gloom and of complete disaster.

> *Help to one in twenty*
> *Dying people plenty*
> *Stupid priest*
> *Ate the Beast*
> *And now can't help himself.*
>
> *Praying people follow*
> *Into graves so hollow*
> *Take their gems*
> *Away from them*
> *And cover them with dirt!*

"One in twenty," Francis admitted, for in all those times past, the best efforts of those brothers strongest in the gemstone magic had produced healing in one in twenty of those afflicted whom they treated. And the number of brothers who were then themselves infected because of their healing attempts actually outweighed the number of those healed!

"So what are we to do?" Master Bou-raiy said, and for the first time since his return, Francis noted some true empathy in the man's strong voice. "But you fear too much, I believe," he went on, patting Francis' shoulder. "You have been through such trials, brother, that I fear you are overwhelmed and in need of rest. Perhaps what you witnessed were signs of the plague, and perhaps not. And even if it is so, it may be no more than a minor outbreak, afflicting a village or two, and nothing more."

"You did not see the faces of the dead woman's children," Francis remarked.

"Death is a common visitor to Honce-the-Bear," Bou-raiy replied, "in one form or another. Perhaps it has been much too common a visitor these last years—certainly our own Order has buried far too many brothers."

The way he finished that sentence reminded Francis none too gently that, because of Francis' choice, they were about to bury seven more.

"We will wait, and we will watch, and we will hope for the best," Bou-raiy went on. "Because that is all we can do, and because we have other pressing business, duties to the Order and to the people, that we can perform."

"Behind closed gates," Francis remarked with sarcasm.

"Yes," Bou-raiy answered simply, and to Francis, that matter-of-fact, callous attitude hit hard right in the heart, a poignant echo of another prominent brother he had recently buried.

❖ 14 ❖

Trappings of Reputation

Pony rode her wonderful Greystone along beside the wagon, chatting with Belster as he rolled and bounced along. The back of the rig was full of supplies—food and drinks, some extra clothing, and the kegs and other implements they'd need to rebuild Belster's tavern in Dundalis, which they had just agreed would be named Fellowship Way.

The pair were in a fine mood this sunny day, approaching Caer Tinella after a leisurely two-week journey from Palmaris, one marked by long visits with one grateful farming family after another or quiet nights beside a fire under the starry sky.

For Pony, the weight on her shoulders had lessened as soon as she had left the turmoil of Palmaris behind her. Now she didn't have to worry about politics and secret alliances, didn't have to consider the implications of her every move. Up here, she was not Jilseponie, hero of the demon war, slayer of evil Markwart. Up here, she was Pony, just Pony, the same little girl who had grown strong and happy in Dundalis with Elbryan before the coming of the goblins; the same warrior who had stood beside the ranger to protect the folk and the lands from the demon hordes.

Here, she was not moving her horse carefully through the throngs of people crowding the markets, but rather was riding him freely, feeling his muscles beneath her as he thundered along. Often, she would take him out across a field beside the road, for no better reason than to let him gallop, to feel the freedom and the wind. She had brought a saddle with her, but more often than not, she rode Greystone bareback.

She went off on yet another such jaunt, heading across a long, narrow field. She spotted a downed tree lying in a tangle of brush, its trunk suspended more than half a man's height from the ground.

"Ho, what are ye thinking?" Belster called, seeing her smile spreading wide, even from twenty feet away.

Pony didn't answer other than to urge Greystone into a canter and put him in line.

She heard Belster's complaints that she was a "crazy child," but they seemed to come from far away as the wind roared past her ears. And then she heard nothing as she took the horse in, so intense became her focus, picking her spot.

Up Greystone went, rounding his muscled neck and shoulders, and Pony rose to a half seat, her hands resting on his neck, her legs clamped tight about Greystone's flanks, her body in perfect balance. As soon as they landed, she turned her horse back toward the road, where she spotted Belster, the portly innkeeper shaking his head and giving one great resigned sigh after another.

"Ye're to get yerself killed, girl," he said as she trotted past.

Pony just laughed and asked Greystone for a canter, aiming at the fallen tree again.

And then a third time and a fourth, while Belster simply kept the wagon rolling.

Pony caught up to him a few minutes later where the road wound around a small hillock.

"Caer Tinella," the innkeeper announced, pointing north to where a feather of smoke drifted into the air.

Pony slowed Greystone to a walk, cooling him down. Soon after, she dismounted, tying Greystone to the back of the wagon and taking a seat beside Belster.

"Done yer fun, then?" the innkeeper asked.

"Just beginning," Pony replied, "especially if my guess about that town is right."

"Ah, the woman Kilronney," Belster replied, referring to a dear friend of Pony's, a soldier from the Palmaris garrison who had helped her when she had been separated from Elbryan.

Pony had seen the woman only once since the last battle. Imprisoned in Chasewind Manor, under the kinder hand of King Danube, Colleen Kilronney had been well on her way to recovering from the wounds she had received during her battles beside Pony. But still, when Pony had at last found her after the deaths of Elbryan and Markwart, Colleen was scarred, physically and within her heart. She had resigned her position with the Palmaris garrison, despite a plea from her cousin Shamus—another friend of Pony's—and from Duke Kalas himself.

In that brief meeting, all that Pony had gleaned from Colleen was that she was tired and heading north to Caer Tinella.

It didn't take Pony and Belster long to find Colleen; the first villagers they encountered directed them to a small cottage on the northeastern side of town. Pony left Belster behind, riding Greystone quickly to the place, then jumping down and running to the door.

Her eagerness and excitement diminished considerably when Colleen Kilronney answered, for she seemed now a mere shell of her former self.

Once she had been square-shouldered and strong, but now her shoulders sagged. Once her eyes had flashed with eagerness for battle, but now they seemed almost glazed. Even Colleen's red hair seemed duller, as if the whole woman had faded.

Pony held her hand out, and Colleen, a wide smile growing on her face, reached for it, with her *left* hand, holding her right arm noticeably tight to her side.

"What have you done?" Pony asked, hugging her friend, but taking care not to pain her obviously injured right arm.

"Bad place for catching a sword," Colleen replied, still managing to smile. She led Pony into her modest cottage, offering her a seat at a small round table, then sitting beside her friend. "Ye're looking well," she said. "Are ye gettin' past the pain?"

Pony sighed. "Will I ever?" she asked. Colleen put a hand on Pony's shoulder—again, her left hand—and rubbed her.

"Let me see that wound," Pony said, reaching into her pouch and bringing forth the soul stone.

"Oh, but they're lettin' ye keep one now?" Colleen asked. "Or did ye just take the thing?"

Pony helped her to slip her tunic off, and she winced in sympathetic pain when she saw Colleen's wound, scabbed now but a vicious slash across the top of her biceps.

"Two weeks old," Colleen explained. "Thought I was to lose the arm."

Pony put a finger over the woman's lips, then dropped her hand down onto the cut, rubbing the tender flesh. At the same time, she peered into the soul stone, deeper and deeper into the swirling gray of the hematite, letting herself fall into its magic. She made a connection to Colleen's wound, sent her consciousness into the woman's torn muscles.

And then Pony took the injury back to herself, absorbed it with her being. She felt a moment of excruciating pain, but held to her purpose, enveloping, absorbing the wound, and then using her own strength and the soul stone to heal the tears and make the scars into healthy flesh once more.

Then Pony withdrew her spirit, but not before lingering a bit to try to get a sense of the woman's general health. She wasn't thrilled with what she sensed there, for it seemed to her as if Colleen's physical being was somehow depleted, worn out.

A moment later, Pony opened her eyes to see Colleen already flexing her arm, working it in small circles, apparently without pain.

"I was thinkin' o' comin' to ye for just that medicine," the woman remarked, flashing her smile, "but I expected that ye'd be too busy for helpin' the likes o' meself."

"Never that!" Pony assured her. She wrapped the woman in a hug again, and this time, Colleen returned it with both arms.

"You have not been feeling well," Pony remarked when they sat back again.

"I took more of a beatin' than I knew," Colleen confirmed. "I'm just needin' the rest, is all."

"And the new wound?" Pony asked. "It does not seem that you are finding much rest."

"A bigmouthed son of a drunken powrie," Colleen replied, "a man named Seano Bellick. Used to be with the Palmaris garrison, same as meself, and we never did like each other much. He's living in Caer Tinella now, and nothing but trouble, I tell ye. We had a bit of a disagreement in Callicky's pub."

"A *bit* of a disagreement?" Pony echoed. "He nearly cut your arm off!"

"Got me good," Colleen admitted.

"Where can I find him?" Pony asked.

"Just provin' himself the better," Colleen said, waving the notion away. "And so he was, but if I'd'a catched him in me better days—"

"It will heal," Pony promised.

"Mendin' already, and hardly hurtin' since ye went at it with yer gemstone," Colleen agreed. "Might that ye should wait a bit in town, so that ye can put Seano's heart back in his chest after I'm done cuttin' it out."

They had a good laugh, but for Pony, it was bittersweet. The Colleen she had first met in Dundalis would indeed have paid back Seano Bellick—or any man for that matter—but Pony recognized that Colleen would not prove to be much of a match for any seasoned warrior now. That notion stung Pony, for Colleen had taken that initial, and lingering, beating during their flight from Palmaris, from Markwart and De'Unnero, only for the sake of Pony.

"Will ye be stayin' long?" Colleen asked. "Or are ye runnin' right out for Dundalis?"

"I wish you would join me."

"I've got me own home here," Colleen said with a shake of her head. "We been through this before. Ye got yer own place and I've got mine. Oh, I'll come and see ye, don't ye doubt—might even set me sights on Dundalis for a home. But not now."

Pony didn't press the point. "I'll need an introduction to the mayor, or whoever it is that leads Caer Tinella."

"That'd be Janine o' the Lake," Colleen replied, "a fine woman. But what're ye thinkin' to do that ye're needin' to bother her?"

Belster O'Comely poked his head in the door then, and gave a great shout at the sight of Colleen, then stalked across the room and gave her a hug. "So did ye convince her to go north with us?" he asked Pony.

"I already told her that I'd not be runnin' across the wilds with a drunk like Belster O'Comely beside me," Colleen replied, and both she and Belster laughed heartily.

Their comfort and familiarity gave Pony pause. Colleen and Belster didn't know each other all that well, yet they seemed to be chatting like old friends. Might there be some real feelings there, buried beneath a jovial façade?

"But ye will come up and see us?" Belster asked.

"By the pigs, I will!" Colleen replied.

"Good enough then," said Belster. "I'll put a bottle o' me best boggle aside for that fine day."

"Go get it now, and we'll make this one a fine day," Colleen suggested, but before Belster could reply, he found Pony shaking her head.

"I need to speak with Janine," she said.

"So ye said, but ye didn't tell me why."

"We will set up a healing tent," Pony explained, "to tend to all those in need."

"For whatever ails them?" Colleen asked skeptically. "Boils and corns, a cut here and a sore belly there?"

Pony nodded, and Colleen's expression was one of incredulity.

"Them monks're allowing it?" she asked.

"The monks have no power to stop it," Pony said.

Within the hour, Belster and Pony had set up a tent in the small square at the center of Caer Tinella, and word had been sent out through the town and to the neighboring town of Landsdown. Folk came filtering in, slowly at first, only those who already knew Pony and her exploits. But as it became recognized that she was performing miraculous healing, the line at the tent grew and grew.

So many folk of the two towns came—mostly with minor injuries or ailments, but one with a serious tear near the knee and another quite sick from eating rotten food—that Pony agreed to spend the night at Colleen's and continue the healing for a second day.

Pony and Belster caused quite a stir in the region and caught the attention of all, including a trio of rough-looking fellows, former soldiers, and another, quieter watcher, unseen among the boughs.

That quiet watcher paid heed to the other three and heard much of their suspicious remarks, particularly when one said, "She should be south, far south of Palmaris, where they're finding the rosy plague."

Late the second afternoon, Pony and Belster loaded up their wagon and set out again for the north. The weather was clear and warm, the breeze gentle; the pair took an easy pace, enjoying the sights and smells of the summertime forest. And indeed, it seemed obvious to Belster that his companion was in a much better mood now than when they had set out from Palmaris.

"Findin' a bit o' heart, are ye?" he asked her as the late-afternoon shadows stretched across the path before them.

Pony glanced over at him, not really understanding.

"With the gemstones, I mean," Belster explained. "Ye did yer work with more of a smile than I seen on ye for months, girl."

Pony shrugged, admitting nothing to Belster. To herself, though, she did consider the innkeeper's words, and carefully. She felt good about the work she had been doing since leaving Palmaris, felt as if she was making a bit of difference in the world—though not on the scale that Brother Braumin or King Danube had envisioned. Not changing the world itself, for that, she had come to believe, was beyond anyone's control. But what she was doing now was changing a little corner of the world, the lives of a few, and with beneficial results. So yes, Pony's mood had lightened considerably.

They declined the offer of some farmers to sleep in their barn as twilight descended, and instead went a bit farther down the road, out of sight of any houses. When Pony spotted a small clearing beside the trail, she pulled the wagon up for the night and untied the horses, setting them out to graze, while Belster prepared a fine meal from the food the grateful people of Caer Tinella had given them.

Soon the pair were relaxing and eating, staring up at the stars and listening to the night songs of the forest.

"This was our time," Pony remarked, drawing Belster's attention from the last tidbits of stew. "Nightbird's time," Pony explained. "We would sit for hours, watching the sunset and the last glows of daylight, watching the stars growing brighter and more numerous."

"It'll get easier," Belster promised.

Pony looked up at the stars and blinked back her tears. She could only hope so.

She fell asleep soon after, but as on every night since Elbryan's fall, she had a fitful, not restful, sleep. When she opened her eyes to find that it was still dark, she was neither surprised nor alarmed. She lay there for a moment, wondering what, if anything, had awakened her.

Greystone nickered—not a quiet, restful sound but one with a slight element of alarm.

Pony lifted herself up on her elbows and glanced over at the tethered horses. To the untrained eye, everything would have seemed fine, but Pony's warrior instincts told her that something was amiss. Perhaps it was the way Greystone now stood, muscles tensed as if preparing to bolt at the slightest provocation. Or maybe it was the nighttime sounds, or lack thereof, about her, the forest creatures watchful.

Pony stood up quietly, staying low in a crouch and strapping her sword, Defender, to her waist. She reached for her soul stone, thinking to fly out to scout the area, but before she could even begin, she noted a movement down the road a bit, a humanoid shape, a large man perhaps, moving deliberately toward their camp.

Many possibilities crossed Pony's mind; many things screamed out at her to keep her on her guard. Why was anyone out at this late hour? And why would anyone be alone on the road north of Caer Tinella at any time of day? Or was this man alone? Greystone was behind Pony, at a good distance, while the approaching man was in front of her; and yet the horse had apparently sensed his presence.

She kept all those disturbing thoughts in proper perspective, buried them beneath the confidence of years of battle experience, and she slowly rolled onto her side, not wanting to present a clear target to any archers who might be nearby. She tucked one leg under her so that she could get up in a hurry, and put her hand on her sword hilt.

The form came closer, walking with a determined stride and swinging something—a battle-ax, perhaps—in one hand.

"That will be close enough, sir," Pony said suddenly, and the man jerked to an abrupt halt.

A long moment of silence passed, and then the large man laughed and brought his arms about, slamming his weapon against the flat of a metal shield.

"What?" Belster groaned, rolling.

"Stay down," Pony instructed him. She rose up to a crouch, inching toward the man and glancing all about, expecting that he had allies nearby.

"Are you the friend of the fool Kilronney?" the man bellowed, that alone giving Pony a good idea of who this might be.

"And if I am?" Pony replied, as she neatly kicked at one of the smoldering branches on the fire. She slipped low and grabbed it up, giving a shake so that the breeze brought a flare of life to it. By the time she had taken two steps, the end of the branch was aflame, giving her a better view of the man—and him, and any allies he might have, a fine view of her.

He didn't seem very old—mid-thirties perhaps—but his curly hair was more silver than its previous blond, as was his full beard. He wore a sleeveless jerkin, showing hardened, muscled, hairy arms, with leather bracers about his wrists. Even more notable to Pony, the man's shield was battered and torn, and his axe head was notched from previous encounters.

"Seano Bellick," she remarked casually, moving closer to the man and tossing the burning branch to the ground at her side—anything to make it more difficult for any hidden associates the man might have to get a clear shot at her.

The big man laughed.

"Who's here?" Belster called from behind.

"Stay back, near the wagon," Pony instructed sharply.

"Ah, you got nothing to fear from me," Seano Bellick said. "I come to talk, not to fight, and I fight fair."

Pony's expression clearly revealed her serious doubts about that. There was very little this man could say to calm her, she realized, for he had injured her dear friend, and Pony almost hoped he would wade in and take a swing with that cumbersome axe of his.

"Talk then," she said grimly.

Seano Bellick gave a great belly laugh. "A spirited one, eh?" he said.

"You could have spoken to me in the town," Pony retorted. "My whereabouts were no secret."

Bellick shrugged. "Well, I found you now."

Pony didn't blink, didn't return her hand to Defender's hilt, confident that she could draw and thrust before the man could take a step.

"You got quite the reputation about here," Seano said. "Fighting goblins and powries and even giants, so it's said about Pony."

"Jilseponie," the woman corrected, and Seano bowed.

"So it's said about *Jilseponie*," he remarked. "And now you come into town and fix the torn fingernails and the blisters and the bad-food stomach. Making a name for yourself."

Pony wanted to argue that if he really thought she had done, and was doing, all that in the hopes of making a name for herself, that he was sorely mistaken; but she quickly came to the conclusion that this thug wasn't worth the time to explain—and wouldn't begin to understand her, anyway.

Seano nodded his head. It was quite clear to Pony where this was going, though she had no intention of making it easier for the man by instigating any action.

"I doubt not that the reputation is well earned, Po—Jilseponie," Seano said. "And that makes it all the sweeter for me. Take out that fancy sword of yours and show me what you been showing goblins."

"Walk away," Pony replied. "I've got nothing for you, Seano Bellick. Not half the reputation you seem to think you can earn this night and not enough wealth to make a fight worth your time or effort. Put up your ugly axe and walk away, south to Caer Tinella or into the deep forest where a bear can take you, if that is your pleasure."

"Nothing I want?" Seano echoed skeptically. "Why, taking you down'd make the name of Seano Bellick feared from Palmaris to Caer Tinella, would make Duke Kalas know what a fool was Bildeborough for cutting me out before he got killed."

The words hardly surprised Pony.

"Nothing I want?" Seano said again, even more incredulously. "Why, you got a magic gemstone, girlie. A prize most appreciated by all of them about, now that you've shown what it can do."

"And know that you have no power with it," Pony remarked.

"But others will be wanting it," Seano snapped back, his agitation obviously increasing. "And others'd pay for it with good gold. And, besides, if I got your stone, then others'll know I took it from you, that you didn't give it to me agreeably.

"So give it over and save me the trouble, and yourself the pain, of me taking it from you," he finished, flashing a nearly toothless, ugly grin.

Pony paused for a long moment, sizing the fellow up. Still she kept Defender in its sheath. "I expect that my reputation is not nearly as impressive as you make it sound," she answered slowly and very calmly, "at least, not to you."

"I've a bit of a reputation of my own," the big man replied.

"One I know well," Pony answered. She took a deep, steadying breath, clearing out her anger and replacing it with simple pragmatism and generosity. "Seano Bellick," she said, again in calm and perfectly controlled tones, "while I'd dearly love to pay you back for the pain you have caused to my friend—"

"Another tough girlie," he interjected snidely.

Pony winced, thinking that Colleen, if she had been in top fighting form, would have had little trouble with this braggart. "I choose to fight not at all with humans," she went on. "The world is full of enough enemies without us making war on each other. So, with that in mind, I offer you now, indeed I beg you, to put up your axe and walk off."

"Give me the gemstone and away I go," Seano said.

Pony slowly shook her head. "Do not do this."

"Are ye all right, girl?" Belster called. Pony couldn't afford even the slightest bit of her attention for the innkeeper, and so she ignored the remark, her focus squarely on Seano.

"Take out your sword," the big man said.

"Walk away."

"Last warning."

"Walk away."

Predictably, Seano Bellick roared and leaped at Pony, and her sword snapped out in the blink of Seano's eye, stabbing ahead, forcing the man to rise to his tiptoes, suck in his gut, and skid to an abrupt halt. To his credit, Seano improvised well, slashing his axe to hold Pony back, then advancing as he came across with a wicked backhand slash, and then a third straight-across slash, to hold Pony at bay while he regained his balance and took a defensive posture.

A sudden thought came to Pony to go for her soul stone, to fall into its depths and invade this thug's mind, overpowering his will and forcing him to run off. "No," she answered that pacific notion as Seano roared and came on again, feigning a downward chop, then falling back slightly, then stutter-stepping suddenly ahead, launching a wicked slash that missed the backing Pony. "No," Pony said again, more determinedly, coming to the realization that she didn't want to chase him off, that she wanted to pay him back for his treatment of Colleen, and even more than that, that she wanted to use this deserving target to unleash all of her months of pent-up frustrations.

"No, don't you run off, Seano Bellick," she whispered. The big man eyed her skeptically and attacked again—missing again as the nimble woman skittered back, one, two, three steps, always in perfect balance.

Seano paused and stared at her, and Pony understood, for the man had never seen anyone moving in battle quite the way she did. This was *bi'nelle dasada*; and in it, the only movement in the retreat was in the legs, while the torso remained balanced and on center. Elbryan had often referred to this forward-and-back skittering as spiderlike, an appropriate description to Pony's thinking.

"You're a quick one," Seano bellowed, "but one blow of my axe will split you in two!"

Pony didn't bother to respond, didn't even blink. Seano howled all the louder and banged his axe head against his metal shield. Even as that clang sounded, the big man exploded into a charge, holding his shield up.

Pony's responding thrust slipped her sword tip around to the inside of the shield, but it seemed to Seano that he had gained an advantage. On he came, shoving his shield forward to put Defender out of the way, then swiping his axe across viciously.

Pony ducked it, then ducked the ensuing backhand. By the time Seano came with the third vicious slash, she had slipped out to the side, out of his reach.

Now she suddenly had the advantage, and she stabbed ahead with Defender, forcing Seano to alter the angle of his next backhand to fend off the rushing blade. He did this beautifully—even Pony nodded her appreciation for the cunning parry—though he nearly lost his awkward weapon in the process. Then he rolled his shield arm forward, putting the defensive barrier between himself and Pony once more.

She hit that shield with three sharp raps, Defender's fine silverel blade creasing it twice and cutting a small line in the metal on the third slash.

Seano flashed his toothless smile, but there was a wince there, Pony recognized, for the battering had likely stung his shield arm.

"You should have one of these," the man taunted, lifting his shield.

Pony hit the metal again, hard, and then jumped back as Seano's heavy axe swiped harmlessly across.

"Just slows you down," she replied confidently. To illustrate her point, she launched her first real attack, sliding forward with three quick steps and coming in with a hard thrust that got inside the blocking shield. She had him beaten with the move, but couldn't go too deep with the cut, for Seano's axe was quickly swinging her way again. Pony did manage to stick the man in the belly, enough to draw blood through the newest hole in his ragged tunic.

"I'll make you pay for that!" he promised, and he came on in a rage.

Pony kept back from the first swing and backhand, ducked the second as she slipped in past his hip, reversing her grip and scoring another minor hit. She rushed by, then dropped to roll ahead of the next backhanded axe swing.

She came up in time to pick off Seano's next cut with a neatly angled diagonal parry, so that his axe slid out and down.

And then she had him, or would have, had not a noise to the side and Belster's cry distracted her. She told herself repeatedly that she shouldn't be surprised to see that Seano had brought a couple of friends—both holding bows.

"You are the better fighter," Seano admitted, "for what good that'll do you."

"Did you not claim that you fight fair?" Pony protested.

"And so I did," said Seano. "But now I'm not fighting. No, girlie, now I'm thieving, so just be handing over that gemstone, and me and me friends will be on our merry way."

Pony eyed him and made no movement to retrieve the gemstone or to put up her sword.

"My archer friend can get your companion where he's sitting," Seano remarked.

"Belster," Pony called.

"I see them," the innkeeper replied. "A pair with bows."

"Are you clear to their aim?"

"Got a wagon right beside me," Belster explained.

Seano gave a chuckle. "Are you to make it more difficult, then?" he asked. "More's the pity. To think that my friend will have to take you down."

Pony reached into her pouch and pulled forth the hematite, and Seano put a greedy hand out for it.

She didn't immediately turn it over, but stood there, staring at the gemstone, sending her thoughts into it, accepting its magic and blending that energy with her own.

And then she came out of her body, with enough magical strength to focus her thoughts into something tangible, to project an image of herself, elongated, twisted, and demonic. That horrifying image appeared before the two archers, issuing a hellish shriek, the specter's mouth opening wide.

The two archers fell back, crying out, and tripped over their own feet trying to run back into the forest.

"What?" she heard Seano Bellick cry, and she rushed back into her body, coming on guard immediately, and not a moment too soon; for the big man, apparently sensing some kind of betrayal, leaped forward, his mighty axe leading, a straightforward, downward chop aimed for Pony's forehead.

Purely on instinct, and faster than Seano could have believed possible, the woman's warrior reflexes took over. She lunged suddenly, her sword tip meeting the descent of the axe, chipping into the wooden handle just below the head, before Seano could gain any momentum.

In the same fluid movement, Pony disengaged, retracting her blade but an inch, then slipping it under Seano's axe and rotating her arm across and down, taking Seano's weapon along for the ride.

The man should have let go, surrendering the weapon, but he hadn't even really registered the parry yet, let alone the counter, and soon his arm had rotated in and down.

Pony slipped her blade free and brought Defender up over the axe handle and quickly across. And then she fell back, sputtering, as blood splashed across her face.

It had all happened in the blink of an eye, and Seano Bellick's weapon—and the hand still holding it—fell to the ground.

The big man howled, throwing his shield aside and falling to his knees, clutching his wrist, trying to stop the spurting blood.

After the instant of shock, Pony knew that she could not pay him any heed. She turned and started to sprint toward the spot where the archers had been, but she hadn't gone two strides before the pair reappeared, bows drawn and ready.

Pony slowed, staring hard at the men, noting the trembling of their fingers, studying every aspect of them, body and weapon, in an attempt to find a way. She didn't think it likely that either would hit her, so unnerved they seemed, and yet . . .

"Are you still intent on this fight?" she asked sternly, walking slowly but deliberately toward the pair. She was balancing here, measuring a guess against practicality. One line of reasoning told her to stay back, that the darkness and the distance would make their shots all the more difficult. A second line of thought told Pony to intimidate these already unnerved men to the maximum, make them see their doom, shake them so badly that they could hardly loose an arrow, let alone hit anything.

Then she caught a glimmer from their metal arrowheads.

"Ye give us the stone and we're on our way," the smaller of the pair demanded, his cap, a triangular huntsman's affair, pulled low, accentuating his dark eyes. He was the more dangerous of the two, Pony noted, the steadiest of hand and, likely, the better shot.

"I will give you nothing," Pony replied, "but will take from you more than your hands, I promise!" She ended with a hiss and a flourish with her arms, and the larger man cried out and ran away, but the smaller growled and let fly his arrow.

As soon as he did, the man screeched and grabbed at his face, a great convulsion racking his frame. And then he dropped to the ground.

Pony didn't see it, focusing instead on the arrow's flight, aimed straight for her heart and too fast for her possibly to deflect. She did instinctively bring her sword across, and with hardly a conscious effort, sent her fears into Defender, a sword so named because of the line of small magnetites, lodestones, set into its guard.

In response those magnetites sent forth their waves of attracting energies, grabbing at the metal arrowhead, altering its course enough so that the guard intercepted it and held the missile fast.

Stunned, Pony looked down at the sword, at the arrow held there, the arrow that, she knew, would have skewered her.

Then she looked back to the archer, lying very still. Had his own friend shot him? "Belster?" she called.

"Are ye all right, girl?" he asked from over by the wagon. Pony knew then that he had played no part in this. Confused, Pony went to the archer, lying facedown, and she grew even more perplexed, for the man showed no wound on his back.

Crouching beside him, her eyes scanning the forest for signs of trouble, her ears trying to tune away from Seano Bellick's continuing wails, the woman rolled the archer over.

He was dead, still clutching his face, his hand over his left eye. Pony pulled that hand away and found her answer in the form of a tiny arrow shaft, protruding from the torn socket.

"Juraviel?" the woman whispered hopefully, turning, her eyes going up to the boughs.

CHAPTER

❖ 15 ❖

Across the Gulf

It was a lump of rock in the middle of nowhere, bound on one side by the Gulf of Corona and on the other by the ferocious and cold water of the great Mirianic Ocean. A hundred people called this island, Dancard, home, mostly soldiers serving the Coastpoint Guards at Pireth Dancard, the twin-towered fortress rising above the surf.

They were hardy folk here, making their living harvesting the great strands of kelp and fishing. They suffered storms and giant sharks, and had repelled a sizable powrie attack in the demon war. But even when they talked of that heroic battle, the folk of Dancard did so with a stoic attitude, without excitement. Hardy and dour, pragmatic and accepting their lot in life, the folk of Dancard—soldier and civilian alike—depended upon themselves and each other, and were not very trusting of visitors. But neither were they hostile, and they had taken in the *Saudi Jacintha* for repairs and had helped resupply the ship, though Captain Al'u'met had not even asked for that much.

Brother Dellman was glad to be leaving, though, as the ship glided out of the one harbor along the island's treacherous coast. The *Saudi Jacintha* had been out of Palmaris for more than a month, and had expected to be in Pireth Vanguard by this time, but bad luck and some broken rigging had forced the ship to limp into an unplanned stop in Dancard.

"A stern group of men and women," remarked Captain Al'u'met, a tall and straight man with the dark skin and woolly hair indicative of his Behrenese heritage. Al'u'met was indeed a rarity in Honce-the-Bear, particularly this far north. While there was a sizeable Behrenese quarter in the dock area of Palmaris, few of the dark-skinned southerners were ever able to find any employment beyond simple manual work, if they were fortunate enough to find any work at all; and no Behrenese, outside the region near Entel, the very southernmost city of Honce-the-Bear, had risen anywhere near as high a level as captain of a sailing ship. There was nothing typical about Al'u'met. He was Abellican, not a follower of the yatols of his home-

188

land, and was among the most impressive men Brother Holan Dellman had ever met, a man who commanded respect upon mere sight.

"They have to be to survive, I suppose," Brother Dellman replied.

"Good folk," Al'u'met added with a nod, then he turned from the taffrail and headed forward, the young monk right behind.

"How long before we see land?" Dellman asked.

"You can see it right now if you look behind us," Al'u'met said with a chuckle, but the humor was lost on poor Dellman and on several of the other crewmen who had heard the remark, for they were all weary of staring out at empty ocean. Captain Al'u'met cleared his throat and explained, "Two weeks if the wind stays steady, but once land is in sight, we'll not have far left to run, for our course is straight to Pireth Vanguard now."

Brother Dellman leaned on the rail and stared ahead. "So be it," he said, reminding himself silently of the solemn duty Abbot Braumin had put upon him. He would be the abbot's principal adviser this fall, when the votes would be cast for the new father abbot. He was to take a measure of Abbot Agronguerre, and his judgment upon the man alone could well determine the course of the Abellican Church.

With that in mind, Brother Holan Dellman offered no complaints—to Al'u'met or to anyone else.

And so it went, day after day, until, just under a week later, the crewman in the crow's nest called out, "A sail! Due north."

Brother Dellman looked up from his deck cleaning. He saw Al'u'met stride by, heading for the prow, and so he followed in the dark man's wake.

"The same one?" he asked, for the *Saudi Jacintha* had been trailing a ship for a couple of days before she put into Pireth Dancard. It had been barely a speck on the horizon at first, though the swift *Saudi Jacintha* had closed the distance considerably, enough for the lookout to get a decent view of the small vessel, an older ship with a single mast and a bank of oars. As the *Saudi Jacintha* had neared, those oars had set to work, keeping their distance.

"Not many sail this part of the gulf," Al'u'met answered, "at this season or any other." He looked up at the crow's nest. "What do you make of it?" he called.

"Single square sail," the crewman answered.

"Same as before?"

"Under no flag that I can see," the man confirmed.

Al'u'met looked at Dellman. "I suspect it is the same ship," he said. "Though why an old square-rigged reme would be out so far from the coast, I cannot begin to guess."

Dellman looked up at the *Saudi Jacintha*'s sails, full of wind, and figured they'd have their answers soon enough.

*   *   *

"Yach, a chaser!" came the cry from the lookout on that square-masted reme.

Dalump Keedump kicked a bucket across the deck and stormed to the taffrail, cursing at every step.

"Yer friend Duke Kalas," another powrie, Dokie Ruggs, grumbled, storming to the rail beside the powrie leader. "Set us out 'ere to die, 'e did!"

"We're not knowin' that!" the powrie leader screamed. "Could be a trader or one bringin' supplies to that castle we passed, and now, mighten be goin' to another up north."

"Yach, but ye're hopin', and not believin' yer own words," Dokie Ruggs answered, and several others nearby nodded in agreement. "It be Kalas, I say. Sent us out here in this leaky tub and sent that one out behind to put us to the bottom, 'e did!"

"She was flyin' a flag o' Palmaris," another remarked.

"Half the stinkin' boats o' the human lands fly the flag o' Palmaris," Dalump argued.

"It be Kalas," insisted Dokie. "She'd o' had us afore, if she hadn't blown her rigging, and now she'll catch us for sure. And us without a way to even fight back!"

Dalump Keedump leaned heavily on the rail to consider his options—and those seemed very few to the powrie leader at that time. He wasn't certain that Dokie Ruggs and the others had it right, for he trusted Duke Kalas, somewhat. He and his fellows had performed well for the man, and with their help, Kalas had secured his position in Palmaris. But there was simply no reason for Kalas to have gone to the trouble of giving Dalump and his fellows a ship, then chasing them all the way across the Gulf of Corona to sink them. Kalas could have let them all die in the dungeons of Chasewind Manor, without anyone knowing about it.

No, Dalump Keedump wasn't convinced that his frightened kindred were right, but still, whatever this ship might be, it represented danger. What might she do, even if she was just a trader, if she found a barely seaworthy old bucket like this one thick with powries? And powries unable to defend themselves! Every human sailor had reason to hate powries.

Dalump looked over his shoulder at the empty water before his creaking old ship, then looked back to the southern horizon, though the sail of the pursuing ship wasn't visible from the deck yet. The powrie leader knew that he'd have to send his fellows to the oars again, and soon, bending their backs to compensate for the meager power the little square sail was providing.

That notion gave Dalump some hope, though, for none in all the world could row as strong and as long as a powrie, and he had a crew whose lives depended upon it.

*   *   *

The *Saudi Jacintha* closed very slowly over the next few days, close enough to see that the other boat's oars were hard at work. On the morning of the fifth day, the lookout informed Al'u'met that the reme had turned more to the east, and the captain, curious as to why this boat was so intent on staying ahead of his ship, which flew no war flags, ordered his crew to follow. Soon after, the square-masted reme turned back to the north.

"They are trying to avoid us, obviously," Al'u'met informed Brother Dellman.

"And to no harm," the monk replied, trying to stay focused on his critical mission here, though he, too, was more than a little curious about the strange reme.

Al'u'met considered the man's reply for a few moments, then nodded. "If she turns again, we'll not pursue," he said, "though I am not fond of allowing such a ship to sail the gulf without some explanation."

"My dear Captain Al'u'met, you are not in service to Duke Bretherford," Dellman said lightly, referring to the King's man who commanded the Honce-the-Bear naval forces.

"But I am in service to all other traders who sail the region," Al'u'met replied, "as are they to me and my crew. It is a brotherhood out here, my friend, one that we all need to survive against the unspeakable power of the Mirianic. But my debt to you and your brethren is no less—well do I remember the services your allies performed for my people on the docks of Palmaris, when all the rest of the world seemed against us. I will deliver you, as promised, and as soon as I may. Perhaps I will find our reme friend on my return from Vanguard."

Brother Dellman bowed and went back to his voluntary duties on deck. Every so often, he glanced northward, shielding his eyes from the glare off the water, and once or twice he thought he saw the distant sail.

They lost sight of the ship the next morning, when a thick fog came up. The wind was light, and it took the fog a long time to dissipate. When at last it was clear again, the reme, as much oar-powered as wind-driven, had moved out of sight.

Captain Al'u'met, Brother Dellman, and all the rest of the crew tried to put it out of mind, as well.

And so the days slipped past, and the wind came up strong again, and sure enough, the square sail appeared at the edge of the horizon once more.

But the weather was worsening, and they found that night full of rain and the next morning full of fog yet again, and when it at last cleared, the next evening after that, the captain and crew were greeted not by a distant sail, but by a distant light, high above the water.

"Pireth Vanguard," Al'u'met informed Dellman and all the others.

The next morning, the *Saudi Jacintha* floated beside the long wharf of the northernmost Honce-the-Bear fortress.

*   *   *

Another ship put in that morning as well, but into a sheltered bay some five miles north. The powries had pushed the old reme to her limits, and now she was badly in need of some repairs to oars and to mainmast. The bedraggled powries, rowing hard for a week and a half, needed the respite, as well, and more important, to Dalump Keedump's thinking, needed some real weapons, something they could throw from a distance at the pursuing ship or any others they might find on the open Mirianic. Also, the Weathered Isles, the powries' home and goal, were a long way away, and a few supplies would surely raise the morale of Dalump's overworked and underfed crew.

Perhaps that pursuing ship would discover them here and come in for the kill. Dalump and his tough powries didn't fear humans, not even the Allheart knights, and while they had no heart for fighting them out on the open water—not in this rickety and defenseless ship, at least—they'd be more than happy to do battle on land.

But for that, too, they'd need weapons, something Duke Kalas had flatly refused to provide—not even a spear for sticking fish. So now half the weary crew went to work with renewed vigor, cutting branches and fashioning crude bows and spears and clubs, while others worked to ready the ship, and still others went out to scout the region.

Dalump didn't say it, but he and all the others were also hoping their scouts might happen upon a cluster of houses, scantily guarded, where the crew might find some fun at the expense of a few wretched humans.

The docks were quiet that morning; with the inclement weather and a few days of fine catches before it, the Vanguard fishing fleet had not ventured out in force.

The *Saudi Jacintha* had been guided in by a pair of soldiers, wearing the red uniforms of the famed Coastpoint Guards. The two started somewhat, seeing a Behrenese man piloting the craft, but their trepidation was tempered a bit when they noted an Abellican monk standing beside the captain, chatting easily.

As soon as the *Saudi Jacintha* was secured to the wharf and its gangplank lowered, the captain and Brother Dellman made ready to disembark. "Permission to go ashore?" Al'u'met asked.

"Granted, for yerself and the brother," one of the soldiers answered. "Warder Presso will want to speak with ye before giving a general invitation."

"Fair enough," said Al'u'met, and he and Dellman moved off the ship and followed the pair up a long stairway carved out of the stone cliff, into Pireth Vanguard and to the office of Warder Constantine Presso.

"Al'u'met," the warder said as soon as the pair entered. He rose and came around his desk, obviously familiar with the Behrenese captain. "How long has it been, my old friend?"

"Back in the days when you served at Pireth Tulme," Al'u'met replied, "long before the war."

They shook hands warmly, and Al'u'met introduced his old friend to Brother Dellman.

"I have brought him for a meeting with Abbot Agronguerre," Al'u'met explained. "Many tidings from the south, some wondrous, some painful."

"We have heard rumors, but nothing substantial," Presso replied. "Know that, at last, and through the tireless work of our Prince Midalis, the goblin scum have been cleansed from our land."

Al'u'met nodded. "We will tell our tale in full to Abbot Agronguerre," he said. "I believe that Warder Presso would also be welcomed at that meeting, if he was so inclined." He looked to Brother Dellman as he spoke, deferring to the man but making it quite clear that he trusted Presso implicitly.

"If he is a friend of Al'u'met, then welcome he is," the monk said with a respectful bow.

"To St. Belfour, then," Warder Presso said, and he led the way out of the office, giving orders to his men to make Al'u'met's crew most welcome, and to get a detail inspecting the ship.

The trio rode comfortably in the warder's carriage through the woodlands to the small clearing and the stone structure of St. Belfour. Abbot Agronguerre was quite busy this day, but he and Brother Haney made time for them.

"The College of Abbots will convene in Calember," Brother Dellman explained as soon as the formal introductions were ended. "We will take you there in the *Saudi Jacintha*, if you please."

"Three months?" Agronguerre asked, looking mostly to Al'u'met. "That is a long time in a fine season for a trader to be tied up, is it not?"

"I am indebted to your—to my—Church, Abbot Agronguerre," Al'u'met explained, "and mostly to those who bade me to bring Brother Dellman here and to deliver both of you to St.-Mere-Abelle. It is a service I, and my crew, willingly offer."

"Most generous," said Abbot Agronguerre. "But perhaps the second part will prove unnecessary. If I am to go to the College, as surely I am, then I will need transport back soon after, and better if it is a Vanguard ship, that it can dock the winter through at Pireth Vanguard."

Al'u'met looked to Dellman, but the young brother wasn't prepared to answer that logic at that time.

"We will discuss it at length," Al'u'met said, "but no need for haste. Let us tell you of the events in Palmaris and in the southern part of the kingdom, momentous events indeed."

"Father Abbot Markwart is dead," Agronguerre remarked, "so said one trader who came through. Killed by a man named Nightbird and the woman Pony."

"Jilseponie," Brother Dellman corrected. "Elbryan Wyndon, known as Nightbird, and his wife, Jilseponie, who is often called Pony."

"And they are outlaws?" asked the abbot.

"Nightbird was killed in the battle," Dellman explained. "And far from an outlaw, Jilseponie is now hailed as the hero of the kingdom."

Abbot Agronguerre wore a perplexed expression indeed!

Brother Dellman took a deep breath, collecting his thoughts. He had to go back to the beginning, he realized, to bring this man through the last tumultuous year in the southern reaches of Honce-the-Bear, and the western stretch, all the way through the Timberlands and up to the Barbacan and the miracle at Mount Aida.

The three Vanguardsmen listened intently, leaning forward so far in their seats that they seemed as if they would topple onto the floor. Brother Haney repeatedly brought his right hand up before his face, making the gesture of the blessing of the evergreen, particularly when Dellman told of the events at Mount Aida, at Avelyn's grave, when the blessed arm of the martyred brother shot forth waves of energy to utterly destroy the horde of goblins that had trapped Dellman and his companions on that forlorn plateau.

And Agronguerre, too, made the sign of the evergreen when Brother Dellman told of the final battle at Chasewind Manor, of the fall of Markwart—from grace and from life.

When he ended, the three Vanguardsmen sat there silently for a long, long time. Brother Haney looked to his abbot repeatedly, deferring to Agronguerre's wisdom before he voiced his own thoughts.

"Where is this woman Jilseponie now?" the abbot asked.

"She went home—to the Timberlands and a town called Dundalis," Al'u'met explained. "There lies her husband."

"An impressive woman," Agronguerre remarked.

"You cannot begin to understand the depth of her heroism," Al'u'met was pleased to reply. "In the time of Bishop De'Unnero and the last days of Father Abbot Markwart, my people were being persecuted brutally in Palmaris, and Jilseponie stood strong beside us, risking all for folk she did not even know. There is a goodness there, and a strength."

"None is stronger in the use of the sacred gemstones," Brother Dellman remarked, and both Agronguerre and Haney gasped and made the evergreen sign.

"Both the Church and King Danube himself recognized it within her," Al'u'met went on. "She was offered both the barony of Palmaris and a high position within your Church, as abbess of St. Precious, or even . . ." He paused and looked to Dellman.

"There was talk of nominating her as mother abbess of the Abellican Church," Dellman admitted. "Proposed by Master Francis Dellacourt—"

"Markwart's lackey," Agronguerre interrupted. "Well I know Brother

Francis from the last College of Abbots. I found him most disagreeable, to be honest."

"Master Francis has seen the error of his ways," Brother Dellman assured him. "He saw it on the face of his dying Father Abbot, and heard it in the last words, of repentance, that Markwart spoke to him."

"It has been an interesting year," Abbot Agronguerre said with a profound sigh.

"I should like to meet this Jilseponie," Warder Presso remarked.

"She once served in your Coastpoint Guard," Brother Dellman told him, and the Warder nodded appreciatively. "Indeed, she was at Pireth Tulme when the powries invaded, perhaps the only survivor of that massacre."

That widened Presso's eyes, and he stared hard at Dellman. "Describe her," he demanded.

"Beauty incarnate," Al'u'met said with a chuckle.

Dellman was more specific, holding up his hand to indicate that Pony was about five foot five. "Her eyes are blue and her hair golden," he said.

"It could not be," Warder Presso remarked.

"You know her?" Al'u'met asked him.

"There was a woman at Pireth Tulme who went by the name of Jill," Presso explained. "She had been indentured into the King's army— something about a failed marriage with a nobleman—and had worked her way into the Coastpoint Guard. But that was years ago."

"A failed marriage to Connor Bildeborough, nephew of Baron Bildeborough of Palmaris," Brother Dellman explained, smiling, for he knew that they were indeed speaking of the same remarkable woman. "A marriage that could only fail, since Jilseponie's heart was ever for Elbryan."

"Amazing," Warder Presso breathed.

"You do know her, then," said Agronguerre.

Presso nodded. "And even then, she was impressive, good Abbot. A woman of high moral character and strength of heart and of arm."

"That would be her," said a smiling Al'u'met.

"We can decide on your passage at a later date," Brother Dellman said to Abbot Agronguerre. "In the meantime, I have been instructed to spend the summer in Vanguard, and truly, I do wish to see this wondrous land."

"And you are most welcome, Brother Dellman," said the congenial Agronguerre. "There is much room here at St. Belfour, and with so many brothers off in the north with Prince Midalis, an extra set of hands would greatly help."

"And Captain Al'u'met and his crew will stay with me at Pireth Vanguard," said Warder Presso. "I, too, find myself shorthanded, with many soldiers on the road with my Prince."

"And when do you expect their return?" Al'u'met asked.

"We have heard rumors that it will be soon," Presso replied. "They ventured to southern Alpinador with the barbarian leader Bruinhelde and the ranger Andacanavar, repaying the northmen for their aid in our struggles."

"An alliance with Alpinador?" Captain Al'u'met asked skeptically.

Warder Presso shrugged. "That is a story for another day, I suspect," he answered when there came a soft knock on Abbot Agronguerre's door.

"Vespers," the abbot explained, rising. "Perhaps you would lead us in our prayers this evening, Brother Dellman."

Dellman rose from his chair and bowed respectfully. He stared at Agronguerre, continuing to take the measure of the man. If first impressions meant anything at all, though, Dellman suspected that he would indeed be recommending that Braumin Herde and the others nominate this man for the position of father abbot.

CHAPTER

❖ 16 ❖

Too Much Akin

"One returning brother after another," Master Bou-raiy said with obvious sarcasm as Marcalo De'Unnero walked into his office in St.-Mere-Abelle. "First Brother—oh, do pardon me, it is Master Francis now—comes in unexpectedly, and now our pleasure is doubled."

De'Unnero wore a smirk as he studied the man. Bou-raiy had never been a friend of his, had resented him; for, though younger, De'Unnero had been in greater favor of Father Abbot Markwart, and, through deed after deed, had elevated himself above Bou-raiy. Their rivalry had been evident to De'Unnero soon after the powrie fleet had come to St.-Mere-Abelle. De'Unnero had distinguished himself in that fight, while Bou-raiy had spent the bulk of it at the western wall, waiting for a ground invasion that had never come.

De'Unnero wasn't surprised to find that Bou-raiy had used the power vacuum at St.-Mere-Abelle to further his own cause; who else was there, after all, to take up the lead at the great abbey? So now Bou-raiy, a man long buried under Markwart's disdain, had stepped forward, with that lackey Glendenhook at his heels.

"Two masters—former bishops, former abbots, both—returned to bolster St.-Mere-Abelle in this time of trial," De'Unnero said.

"Bolster?" Bou-raiy echoed skeptically, and he gave a sarcastic laugh. De'Unnero pictured how wide that smile might stretch if he drove his palm through Bou-raiy's front teeth. "Bolster? Master De'Unnero, have you not listened to the whispers that hound your every step? Have you not heard the snickers?"

"I followed Father Abbot Markwart."

"Who is discredited," Bou-raiy reminded him. "Both you and Francis found your zenith under Markwart's rule, that is true. But now he is gone, and will soon enough be forgotten." He paused and shook his head. "Offer me not that scowl, Marcalo De'Unnero. There was once a day when you outranked me here at St.-Mere-Abelle, but only because of Father Abbot Markwart. You will find few allies among the remaining masters, I assure you, even with Master Francis, if what I have heard about his admission of error is true. No, you have returned to find a new Church in the place of the old—the old that so welcomed a man of your . . . talents."

"I'll not defend my actions, nor recount my deeds, for the likes of Fio Bou-raiy," De'Unnero retorted.

"Deeds inflated in your recounting, no doubt."

That statement stopped De'Unnero cold, and he stared hard at the man, felt the primal urges of the tiger welling inside him. How he wanted to give in to that darker side, to become the great cat and leap across the desk, tearing this wretch apart! How he wanted to taste Fio Bou-raiy's blood!

The volatile master fought hard to keep his breathing steady, to restrain those brutal urges. What would be left for him if he gave in to them now? He would have to flee St.-Mere-Abelle and his cherished Order for all time, would have to run and exist on the borderlands of civilization, as he had done over the last months. No, he didn't want that again, not at all, and so he fought with all his willpower, closing off his mind to Bou-raiy's continuing stream of sarcastic comments. The man was a gnat, De'Unnero reminded himself constantly, an insignificant pest feeling the seeds of power for the first time in his miserable life.

"You are nearly ten years my junior," Bou-raiy was saying. "Ten years! A full decade, I have studied the ancient texts and the ways of man and God longer than you. So know your place now, and know that your place is beneath me."

"And how many years more than Master Bou-raiy have Masters Timminey and Baldmir so studied the ways of man and God?" De'Unnero asked with sincere calm, for he was back in control again, suppressing the predator urge. "By your own logic, you place yourself below them, and below Machuso and several others as well, and, yet, it is Bou-raiy, and none of the others, who now sits in the office of the Father Abbot."

Bou-raiy leaned back in his chair, his smile widening on his strong-featured face. "We both understand the difference between men like Machuso and Baldmir and men like us," he said. "Some were born to lead, and others to serve. Some were born for greatness, and others . . . well, you understand my meaning."

"Your arrogance, you mean," De'Unnero replied. "You separate brothers along whatever lines suit your needs. You claim ascendance above me because of experience, yet rebuff the notion in those who would so claim ascendance over you."

"They would not even want the responsibility of the position," Bou-raiy replied, coming forward suddenly, and again, De'Unnero had to hold fast against his surprise and the sudden killer urge it produced.

"And do you intend to have your stooge, Glendenhook, nominate you for father abbot formally at the College of Abbots?" De'Unnero asked bluntly. "They will destroy you if you so try, you know—Braumin Herde and Francis, and the newest master, Viscenti," he said with a derisive chortle. "Je'howith and Olin, and Olin's lackey, Abbess Delenia. They will all stand against you." He paused for dramatic effect, though he realized there would be little surprise in his proclamation. "As will I."

Bou-raiy sat back in his chair again, obviously deep in thought for a long, long while. De'Unnero thought he understood where the man's line of reasoning might be leading, and his suspicions were confirmed when Bou-raiy announced, rather abruptly, "They will back Abbot Agronguerre of St. Belfour, as will I."

Yes, it made perfect sense to De'Unnero. Bou-raiy knew that he'd never defeat Agronguerre, and so he would throw all his influence behind the gentle Vanguardsman, the *old* Vanguardsman, in the hopes that Agronguerre would do for him what Markwart had done for De'Unnero and Francis. The difference, though, was that Bou-raiy was much older than either Francis or De'Unnero had been when Markwart had taken them firmly under his black wing. Thus, when old Agronguerre died—likely within a few years—Bou-raiy would be right there, the heir apparent, and with all the experience and credentials to step in virtually uncontested.

"Abbot Agronguerre is a kind man of generous nature," Bou-raiy said unconvincingly, for though the words were accurate, De'Unnero understood that those qualities of which Bou-raiy now spoke so highly were not admirable in his eyes. "Perhaps our Church is in need of exactly that at this troubled time: a man of years and wisdom to come into St.-Mere-Abelle and begin the healing."

Marcalo De'Unnero knew this game, and knew it well. He almost admired Master Bou-raiy's patience and foresight, and would have said as much to him—except that he hated Bou-raiy.

De'Unnero went about his business acclimating himself to the daily workings of St.-Mere-Abelle. Bou-raiy didn't oppose him at all, to his initial surprise, and even allowed him to step back in as the master in charge of training the younger brothers in the arts martial.

"Your left arm!" De'Unnero cried at a second-year brother, Tellarese, at training one damp morning. The master stormed up to him and grabbed his left arm forcefully, yanking it up into the proper blocking position. "How do you propose to deflect my punch if your arm hovers about your chest?"

As he finished, the obviously weak man's arm slipped down again, and

De'Unnero wasted not a second in a snapped jab over that forearm and into Tellarese's face, knocking the man to the ground.

With a frustrated growl, the master turned about and stalked away. "Idiot!" he muttered, and he motioned for another of his students, a first-year brother who showed some promise, to go against Tellarese.

The two squared off and exchanged a couple of halfhearted punches, more to measure each other than to attempt any real offense, while the other ten brothers at the training exercise tightened their circle around the combatants, keeping them close together.

When Tellarese's arm came down yet again and the first-year brother scored a slight slap across his face, De'Unnero stormed back in and tossed the first-year brother aside, taking his place.

"I th-thought to counter," Tellarese stuttered.

"You offered him the punch in the hope that you might then find an opening in his defenses?"

"Yes."

De'Unnero snorted incredulously. "You would trade your opponent a clear shot at your face? For what? What better counter might you find than that?"

"I only thought—"

"You did not think!" the frustrated De'Unnero yelled. Once, he had been the Bishop of Palmaris, a great man with a great responsibility, one that he had performed to perfection. Had Markwart defeated Elbryan and Jilseponie on that fateful day in Chasewind Manor, then he, De'Unnero, would have been in line to become the next father abbot. Once, he had hunted Nightbird, the famed ranger, perhaps the greatest warrior in all the world. He had faced off against the man squarely and fairly, and, to his thinking, had bested him.

Once, he had known all of that glory, and now, now he was teaching idiots who would never, ever, be able to defend themselves against an ugly little goblin, let alone a real opponent.

All that frustration rolled out of Marcalo De'Unnero as he slapped Tellarese across the face with his right hand, and then, when the man put his hand up to block that hand, De'Unnero hit him harder across the face with the left, an obvious and easy response.

And when pitiful Tellarese, always a step behind, brought his other arm up to block, dropping his first guard, De'Unnero slapped him hard again with his right hand.

"If I had a dagger, would you let me stick it deep into your belly in the hope that you would then find an opening to slap me?" De'Unnero asked, and he hit Tellarese again, and then again, and when the man finally put both his hands up to protect his head, De'Unnero punched him in the belly. When his hands came instinctively down as he doubled up a bit, De'Unnero slapped him once and again across the face.

He heard the other students groaning and gasping in sympathy for poor Tellarese, but that support for the weakling only spurred the angry De'Unnero on even more. His blows came harder, and more rapidly, and then, suddenly, he stopped.

It took Tellarese a long time to even peek out from behind his raised arms, and then, slowly, slowly, he uncoiled.

"I did not understand," he said quietly.

"And do you now?" De'Unnero asked him, and his voice seemed to the others to carry a strange, almost feral quality.

"I do."

"Then defend!" he said, leaping into a fighting stance.

Tellarese's arms came up into proper position, and De'Unnero rolled his shoulder, several times, feigning punch after punch.

To his surprise, Tellarese launched a punch of his own, a left jab, that somehow got through and clipped De'Unnero's face. The younger brothers encircling the pair, though they tried to hold it back, gave the beginnings of a cheer.

De'Unnero's arm came forward with blinding speed, swiping hard across Tellarese's face, and—to Tellarese's horror, to the horror of those looking on, to the horror of De'Unnero himself—leaving four distinct gashes across the young brother's face.

De'Unnero immediately dropped his arm to his side, letting his voluminous sleeve fall back over his feline limb. How had that happened? How, when, had he lost control?

And over this!

"There are times when you allow a strike to gain a strike," he growled at the stumbling, dazed Tellarese, spinning to take in the whole group. "When I know that my strike will be decisive, I might allow a minor hit," he improvised; for in truth, Tellarese's lucky punch had surprised De'Unnero almost as much as learning that his arm had transformed into a tiger's paw. "But beware! When you employ such a strategy, there is no room for error. You must be certain of your opponent's weakness and of your own ability to deliver the final blow. Your lesson is ended this day. Perform the course of obstacles a dozen times, each of you, then run the length of the abbey wall three times. Then retire and consider this lesson!"

He started away, wanting nothing more than to crawl into his room and hide for the remainder of the day, but he stopped, seeing the expressions of stunned horror on the faces of the other students. He turned back to see Tellarese down on one knee, holding his face, but hardly stemming the dripping blood flow.

"You two," De'Unnero said to the two nearest brothers. "See to his wounds or take him to Master Machuso, if necessary. And when he is bandaged, the three of you complete the lesson."

And with that, Marcalo De'Unnero went back to his small room, closed the door tightly, and wondered, wondered, how this thing had happened. So distressed was he that he missed the vespers.

"Allies?" De'Unnero asked Master Francis doubtfully later that evening, when Francis arrived uninvited at his door.

"We once served the same Father Abbot," was all that Francis would admit.

"The man who fell," De'Unnero replied. "And now are we to fall with him? Or are we to stand together, my *friend*, Master Francis?" His tone showed his words to be obviously a jest. "You and me against all the rest of the Church?"

"You make light of this, which tells me clearly that you underestimate the danger to us, and to any others who stood with Markwart," Francis replied coldly. "The Church has changed, Master De'Unnero, has shifted away from Markwart and his heavy-handed tactics. I suspect that Marcalo De'Unnero, whose primary fame stems from his ability to train brothers in the arts martial, will either change his mannerisms or find his role greatly diminished in the new Abellican Church."

"Would you have me suckle at Fio Bou-raiy's teat?" De'Unnero snapped back.

"Master Bou-raiy will not lead the Church," Francis answered. "But do not underestimate his influence within St.-Mere-Abelle. When I returned from Palmaris, I, too, was surprised by how deeply he had entrenched himself. To go looking for a fight with the man is not wise."

"Why did you come to me?" De'Unnero demanded. "When has Francis called De'Unnero a friend?" It was true enough; even in the days of Markwart, Francis and De'Unnero had not been close, not at all. If anything, they'd been rivals, vying for whatever positions came open as Markwart ran roughshod through the Church hierarchy.

"I came here only to advise," Francis replied calmly. "Whether you take that advice or not is within your province. This is not Markwart's Church any longer. I expect that Braumin Herde and the other followers of Avelyn and Jojonah will have their day now."

De'Unnero snorted at the absurdity.

"Even Father Abbot Markwart admitted his failure concerning Avelyn Desbris," Francis explained.

"His failure in not bringing the man, and the man's followers, to swifter and more severe justice," De'Unnero interjected.

"His failure in admitting the truth," Francis went on determinedly. "The tale that is widely accepted by the people of Honce-the-Bear is that Avelyn—with help from Jilseponie and Elbryan; the centaur, Bradwarden; and the Touel'alfar—destroyed the demon dactyl."

"And how has this tale been proven?" De'Unnero asked. "By the words of outlaws?"

"Outlaws no longer," Francis reminded. "And the story is confirmed by the presence of Avelyn's mummified arm, protruding from the rock at blasted Mount Aida. You have, perhaps, heard of the miracle at Aida?"

"The silly tale of goblins reduced to mere skeletons when they tried to approach those huddled at the all-powerful hand?"

Now it was Francis' turn to chortle. "Not so silly when spoken by an abbot who witnessed the event," he said; for, indeed, Abbot Braumin had been among those saved by the miracle at Aida.

"This is foolishness and nothing more," De'Unnero said with a sigh, "mere fantasy, put forth to further the ambitions of eager young men."

"Whatever you may think of it, whatever I may think of it, the people of the kingdom, and many of those within the Church, have decided in Braumin Herde's favor," Francis remarked.

"And how does Master Francis view the exploits of Avelyn Desbris, and Master Jojonah after him?" De'Unnero asked, a sly edge creeping into his voice. "And how does Master Francis view the supposed miracle at Aida?"

"Your test of me is irrelevant and foolish," Francis answered.

"Yet I would know the answer," De'Unnero was quick to reply.

"I have heard two sides of the story of Avelyn Desbris, and there is some truth in both versions, I would guess," Francis said noncommittally. "As for Master Jojonah, I do not agree that he deserved his fate."

"You did not speak in his favor," De'Unnero remarked.

"I was only an immaculate brother then," Francis reminded, "with no voice in the College of Abbots. But you are right in your accusation nonetheless, and my silence is something I will have to live with for the rest of my years."

"Have you, too, lost the belly for the fight?" De'Unnero asked.

Francis didn't justify that nonsense with an answer.

"And what of the miracle, then," De'Unnero pressed. "Does Francis believe that the ghost of Avelyn returned to slay goblins?"

"Your sarcastic tone reveals that you have not been to Aida," Francis answered. "I have. I have seen the grave, the mummified arm, and I have felt . . ." He paused and closed his eyes.

"What, Master Francis?" De'Unnero pressed, his words sounding more like a sneer than a question. "What did you feel at Mount Aida? The presence of angels? God himself come down to bless you as you groveled before a fallen heretic?"

"I went there with complete skepticism," Francis shot back. "I went there hoping to find Avelyn Desbris alive, that I could drag him back to Father Abbot Markwart heavily chained! But I cannot deny that there was an aura about that grave site, a sense of peace and calm."

De'Unnero waved his hand dismissively. "Next you will be nominating Brother Avelyn for sainthood," he scoffed.

"Abbot Braumin will beat me to that, I would guess," Francis said in all seriousness. De'Unnero nearly spat with disgust.

"Oh, wondrous time!" the fierce monk said with absolute sarcasm. "To live in the age of miracles! What joy I have found!"

Francis paused for a long time, staring at the man, nodding. "I came to you simply to explain what I have observed," he said at length, "to warn you that the Church as you knew it no longer exists. To bid you to temper your fires, for in this Church such actions as your wounding Brother Tellarese will not be looked upon with favor. This is not Markwart's time, nor are kingdom and Church under siege by the minions of the demon dactyl. Take heed, or do not. I felt obligated, for all that we went through side by side, to tell you these things, at least, but I'll take no responsibility for your decisions."

De'Unnero was about to dismiss him, but Francis didn't wait, just turned and stormed away.

Despite De'Unnero's flippant attitude, the words of Master Francis resonated deeply within the troubled man. He could scoff and spit and respond with sarcasm, but the simple truth of Francis' observations cut deeply.

He went to bed with those thoughts in mind and found little sleep—and certainly nothing restful—for his tossing and turning was filled with dreams of his slashing his way through lines of praying brothers with his tiger's paws. Terrible dreams, with the blood of young brothers splattering him, covering him, while he yelled at them, telling them that they were wrong, that they were weak, and that their weakness would be the end of the Abellican Church. And when they wouldn't listen, when they turned away from his ranting to continue their idiotic prayers, De'Unnero slashed them and tore them and felt their hot blood all over his neck and face.

He awakened, covered in sweat, and on the floor, wrapped in his bedsheets, long before the dawn. Immediately he looked at his hands—and nearly fainted with relief to find that they were still hands and not feline paws. Then, his relief lasting only a split second, De'Unnero started patting himself and rubbing his neck and face, feeling for blood.

"Just a dream," he told himself, for he felt only sweat. He climbed back into his bed and started straightening the blankets, but before he had settled down, he realized that he would find no further sleep this night.

He went to the abbey's east wall instead, overlooking All Saints Bay, and there watched the sunrise, the slanting rays turning the dark Mirianic waters a shimmering red.

He had thought that he was coming home when he had left Palmaris and the fools at St. Precious, but now he understood the painful truth. He hadn't changed—at least, he didn't believe that he had—but St.-Mere-Abelle surely had. This was not his home any longer, he knew, and he wasn't even certain if this was truly still his Church or his Order. Marcalo De'Unnero had not been overly fond of Father Abbot Markwart. Certainly he hadn't been the man's willing lackey, as had Francis. No, he had argued with Markwart at many turns, and had followed his own course on occasion, to the frustration of the tyrannic Father Abbot. But at least with Markwart, the Church had known stability and a direct code of conduct. In his last days, Markwart had brought purpose to the Church, had aspired to bring the Abellican Order to new and greater heights of power—thus the appointment of a bishop in Palmaris, a move to take power for the Church from the King unknown in Honce-the-Bear in several centuries. Thus Markwart's decree that only members of the Church could possess the sacred gemstones.

Yes, for all the differences he might have had with Father Abbot Markwart, De'Unnero agreed in principle with the man's policies. But what might he, and his Church, find now with Markwart gone, with no clear-cut and powerful leader to take his place? Even worse, how strong would the idiot Braumin Herde and his followers become, using the image of Jojonah burning at the stake to bolster their position among the more softhearted brothers, and proclaiming a "miracle" at Mount Aida?

De'Unnero didn't like the prospects, and honestly, given his inability to deal with Master Bou-raiy, didn't see any way in which he could turn the tide.

He leaned on the wall, staring at the sparkling red waters of All Saints Bay, and wondered how far his beloved Church would fall.

The approach of footsteps some time later brought him from his contemplations, and he turned, and sighed, to see Francis and Bou-raiy marching his way.

"Brother Tellarese will be some time in healing," Bou-raiy announced.

"It was but a minor wound," De'Unnero replied, turning away from him.

"Or would have been, had it not been inflicted by cat's claws," said Bou-raiy. "It is full of pus and required Machuso to work on the man with a soul stone for half the night."

"That is why we have soul stones," De'Unnero dryly answered, never taking his gaze from the bay. To his surprise, Bou-raiy came up right beside him, leaning on the wall.

"We have heard rumors of trouble in the south," he said, his voice grim; but still De'Unnero did not look his way. "Rumors of the rosy plague."

Even the reference to that most dreaded disease didn't stir De'Unnero. "Someone cries plague every few years," he replied.

"I have seen signs of it," Francis interjected.

"Signs that you compare with pictures in an old book?" came De'Unnero's sarcastic response.

"The other masters and I have decided that we must send someone to investigate these claims," Bou-raiy explained.

Now De'Unnero did look at the man, his eyes narrow and threatening. "All the other masters?" he asked. "Where, then, was I?"

"We could not find you this morning," Bou-raiy answered, not backing away from that threatening glare.

De'Unnero turned it upon Francis. "Leave us," he instructed.

Francis made no move to go.

"Pray, leave us, Brother Francis," De'Unnero more politely requested, and Francis gave one concerned look to Bou-raiy, then walked off a bit.

"And you have decided that I should be the one to go and investigate," De'Unnero said quietly.

"Perhaps it would be better if you were to leave the abbey for a while, yes," Bou-raiy answered.

"I am not bound by your edicts," said De'Unnero, standing straight and, though he was not a tall man, thoroughly imposing.

"It is a request backed by every master at St.-Mere-Abelle."

"Francis?" De'Unnero asked, loudly enough so that the man could hear.

"Yes," Bou-raiy answered.

That brought a chuckle from De'Unnero. He couldn't believe how quickly Bou-raiy had acted, seizing upon the injury of Brother Tellarese to turn against him. He should have seen it coming, he realized. His climb to power had left many sour faces in its wake.

"I can get the immaculate brothers also to agree with the request," Bou-raiy said.

"Now I am to take my orders from immaculate brothers?" De'Unnero was quick to answer, "or from troublesome and jealous masters who fear, perhaps, that I will shake their comfortable world?"

Bou-raiy looked at him curiously.

"Yes, Master Fio Bou-raiy has carved out a comfortable niche for himself in the absence of Markwart and others," De'Unnero went on. "Master Fio Bou-raiy fears that I will come in and upset his coveted position."

"We have already had this argument," Bou-raiy said dryly, obviously seeing where this was heading.

"And we will have it again, and many times, I suspect," said De'Unnero. "But not now. I was just thinking that perhaps it would be better if I left St.-Mere-Abelle for a while, and if the masters wish that course to be to the south, then so be it."

"A wise decision."

"But I will be back for the College of Abbots, of course, a loud voice indeed," De'Unnero promised. Then more quietly, so that Francis could not hear, he added, "And I will watch the course of the nominating carefully, I assure you, and if Agronguerre of Belfour is to win, then I will back him as vehemently as Bou-raiy, and I will become indispensable to the man, as I was to Father Abbot Markwart."

"Abbot Agronguerre is no warrior," Bou-raiy remarked.

"Every father abbot is a warrior," De'Unnero corrected, "or will be, as soon as he learns of the undercurrents among those he should most be able to trust. Oh, he will be glad of my assistance, do not doubt, and he is not a young man."

"Do you really believe that you could ever win the favor of enough in our Order to win a nomination as father abbot?" Bou-raiy said incredulously.

"I believe that I could prevent Bou-raiy from achieving the position," De'Unnero stated bluntly, and to his delight, his adversary's lips grew very thin.

"A fight for another day," De'Unnero went on. He looked past Bou-raiy, drawing Francis' attention. "You have an itinerary planned for me, no doubt?" he asked.

"Presently," a startled Francis answered.

"Soon," said De'Unnero. "I wish to be out of here before midday."

And he walked away, considering again this Church he had returned to find, this hollow shell, in his estimation, of what Markwart might have achieved. Yes, he would willingly go to the south, but not on any search for the plague. He would go to St. Gwendolyn, perhaps, or all the way to Entel, if time allowed, and seek out allies among the more forceful brethren of the southern abbeys. How would Abbot Olin react upon hearing that the ascension of Agronguerre to father abbot was all but assured?

Olin and De'Unnero got on well together, and he knew that Olin would not likely be pleased with the events occurring in the Church, as the man had been glad that Jojonah was put to the stake. And he knew from the previous College of Abbots that Olin—and Abbess Delenia, as well—were no friends to Bou-raiy.

Yes, De'Unnero mused, on the road he could stir up some trouble; and in his estimation, any chaos he might bring to this present incarnation of the Church—this pitiful Order that tried to find a hero in Avelyn Desbris, a heretic and murderer, and in Jojonah, who had admitted treason against St.-Mere-Abelle—could only facilitate positive changes.

Marcalo De'Unnero had been a political animal for most of his adult life, and he understood the implications of his path. And he knew, if Bou-raiy and Francis and the others did not, that Braumin Herde and his ill-advised friends could well split the Abellican Church apart. De'Unnero would wage that battle earnestly and eagerly, and if he had to burn St.-Mere-Abelle itself down to the ground, then he would do so in the confidence that he would rise atop the ashes.

He made one stop before receiving his itinerary from Francis, a visit to one of the lower libraries, where he slipped one of the few copies of a very special ocean chart into the folds of his robes.

His steps out of St.-Mere-Abelle were even more eager than the hopeful ones that had led him back to the place a few days before.

*   *   *

From the wall of St.-Mere-Abelle, Master Bou-raiy watched the man go. His own thoughts concerning the Church that morning were not so different from those of this man he considered an enemy. Logically, it seemed to Bou-raiy as if the appointment of Agronguerre—an event that seemed more and more likely to him—should signal the beginning of the healing process. Agronguerre was known for just the kind of gentleness and compassion that would be needed within the wounded Church; and Bou-raiy's remark to the surprised De'Unnero that the ascension of Agronguerre might be exactly what the Church needed at this time was not made in jest, nor for any subtle political reasons.

It seemed obvious and logical, and Bou-raiy was certain that enough abbots and masters would see it that way to elect the man easily.

But when he looked deeper than the seemingly obvious logic, Fio Bou-raiy couldn't help thinking that this great living body that was the Abellican Church was now like some giant crouching predator, motionless in the brush, hushed and ready to spring.

And again—his thoughts ironically along the same lines as those of his avowed enemy De'Unnero—Fio Bou-raiy wasn't sure at all that he wanted to head off that predator's spring.

❖ 17 ❖

Pilfering Old Friends

"**A**arrgh! Put it back! Put it back!" Seano Bellick roared. He fell to his knees, grabbing at his bloody stump, his hand lying a few feet away, still clutching the handle of his axe.

Pony walked right by him, paying him no heed. "Belli'mar Juraviel?" she called. "Are you about? Or another of the Touel'alfar, then? To be sure, I know that arrow!"

"What're ye talkin' about, girl?" Belster O'Comely asked, coming around the wagon.

"My hand!" Seano howled. "Put it back, I say! Use your magic, I beg you!"

"I cannot put your hand back on your arm," Pony said sharply, turning on him with a snarl.

"You must!"

"There is no such magic!" Pony scolded, and it took all of her willpower to stop her from walking over and kicking the ugly brute in the face.

Seano Bellick wailed pitifully, still clutching at his torn stump. He reached for the hand with his remaining one, but recoiled as his fingers neared it, too afraid to even touch the gruesome thing. And he had to bring his hand back to his stump, for as soon as he let it go, the blood started spurting all over again.

"I'll bleed out!" the man cried. "Oh, but you killed me! Oh, you witch woman! You killed me!"

Belster walked up beside Pony, the two staring at the pitiful sight. "What're ye thinkin'?" Belster asked, for Pony made no move, either for her gemstone or for any bandages. She just stood there, staring at Seano Bellick as the man's lifeblood trickled forth.

"Girl?" Belster asked, after a long moment passed without her showing any intention of responding.

"Bleeding out," Seano said, his voice weaker, breaking with sobs.

"I believe that Belli'mar Juraviel or one of his kin is about," Pony said to

Belster, turning away from Seano. "The archer was felled by a Touel'alfar arrow, right through the eye."

"What of it?" Belster asked, motioning toward Seano.

"Am I not worthy of your healing, good woman?" Seano pleaded. "You then," he said to Belster.

"Are ye to be judgin' them ye mean to heal?" Belster asked in all serious-ness, but to Pony's back, for she'd started away, looking up at the trees in hopes of catching a glimpse of Juraviel.

That comment stung Pony and she turned fiercely.

"I'm not sayin' ye shouldn't be," Belster explained. "I'm just askin' so ye can get it clear in yer own head. Ye got one lookin' for healin', and needin' yer healin', and ye got the healin', but are ye to tend only those ye're thinkin' deservin'?"

"I cut them just to fix them?" Pony asked.

Belster gave a shrug.

He wouldn't commit to an answer, but the question alone had given her his opinion of the matter, of course, had held a mirror up before Pony's anger so that she could clearly see that growling expression upon her own face.

She had the power now of life or death over Seano, and over so many. The gemstone, the gift of God, bestowed that upon her, and thus was she to play in the role of God, as judge of the man and all the others? She nearly laughed aloud at the absurdity of it, but she went for her soul stone and moved close to Seano.

Before she fell into the magic of the gem, she looked the man straight in the eye and promised coldly, "If ever you try to steal from me again or to hurt me or any of my friends or any other innocent person, I will hunt you down and we will replay this fight. My gemstone cannot attach a severed hand, nor, I promise you, can it attach a severed head."

Pony went into the stone and sealed up the blubbering Seano's wound in short order.

"What say you, Juraviel?" she called to the boughs. "Would the Touel'alfar have shown such mercy?"

"The Touel'alfar would have properly finished the job in the first place," came the answer of a melodic, and most welcome, voice. "A thrust through the heart, perhaps, and certainly nothing as messy as you have shown.

"The third archer has long fled," the still-unseen elf informed her. "Have Belster send this fool along down the south road, and then you come out into the forest to the north, that we might speak privately."

Pony looked plaintively at Belster.

"Must have somethin' important to tell ye, then," the innkeeper remarked, and he moved for Seano Bellick. "Come on, ye great feeder of the pig. Get ye back to Caer Tinella, where ye can tell 'em all that ye met with Pony, and met with disaster. Aye, that's the way of it, ye met with the disaster named Pony!"

"Well put," Pony remarked sarcastically, and she walked northward, as Belster half walked and half carried the shocked Seano south.

"Did I do well, then?" Pony asked Juraviel when she finally spotted the elusive elf siting on a bare branch a dozen feet off the ground.

"In fighting or in healing?" Juraviel asked.

"Both."

"If that clumsy thug gave you any trouble in battle, then surely I would have questioned Nightbird's sanity in ever teaching you *bi'nelle dasada*," the elf replied. Even as he spoke the words, Pony noted that there was indeed some strain behind his jovial façade. "In healing him, you did as I knew you would."

"What would Belli'mar Juraviel have done?" Pony asked.

"I would have killed him cleanly in the first place, as I said," the elf answered matter-of-factly, with that cold and calm pragmatism that almost always crept into the thinking of any of the unforgiving Touel'alfar.

"But if you did not," Pony pressed, "if you found yourself in the same situation as I just faced, would you have tended his wound?"

Belli'mar Juraviel spent a long while honestly considering the question. Certainly many of his kin, Lady Dasslerond among them, would have let the man die—elves showed no mercy to any *n'Touel'alfar* whose actions labeled them as enemies. "I would have been sorely disappointed in you if you had let the fool die," was all the answer that Juraviel would give. "And so would you, a profound failing within yourself, a clear contradiction of that which you are, one that would have haunted you for all your days."

It was Pony's turn to pause and reflect, and she found herself nodding her agreement, glad indeed that she had not let Seano die. "Are you to sit up there all the night?" she asked suddenly. "Or are you to come down here and give an old friend a hug she sorely needs?"

How Belli'mar Juraviel wanted to go to her and do just that! He even started propping himself off of the branch. But two words, *rosy plague,* echoed in his mind. He had no idea, of course, if there really was such a plague beginning in the human lands, had no evidence except for rumors coming from an unknown source about some problems far in the southland.

But for Belli'mar Juraviel, this moment sang out to him as another critical choice in his life's course. If there was a plague, and Pony had contracted it, and, in going to her, Juraviel brought it upon himself, then what would happen to Andur'Blough Inninness? Could the elven population, so tiny, survive such a plague?

Belli'mar Juraviel weighed the odds that Pony was so infected, and they seemed long indeed. Very long. But he was Touel'alfar, and she was not. It came down to something as simple as that.

And there was one other thing that Belli'mar knew, whether he admitted it to himself or not: if he went down to Pony and hugged her, if he allowed himself to recognize the deep and abiding friendship between them, the love that had bound him to the sides of Elbryan and Pony all the way to the dungeons of St.-Mere-Abelle and back, then how could he not tell this woman of the child now living in Andur'Blough Inninness? Her child, Elbryan's child.

"You have a soul stone," he remarked suddenly, needing to change the subject. "Where are your others?"

Pony shrugged. "I hardly care," she said honestly. "Nor is the Church overly concerned. More gemstones will find their way out of the abbey coffers."

"You have heard this?" Juraviel asked, and he truly wanted to know. If the magical gemstones began flowing out of the various abbeys, the implications to the Touel'alfar could be significant and dire.

"I sense it," Pony answered. "The era of Markwart, and the centuries of policies that led to the creation of such an animal as he, has ended, and the era of Avelyn will soon begin."

"You believe that Avelyn would be careless with the stones?"

"I believe that Avelyn would put them where they could do the most good," Pony answered confidently. "As he did with the turquoise he gave to Symphony, to heighten the bond between the horse and Elbryan."

Juraviel let it go at that, understanding Pony's mind in this, and knowing that any further answers from her would be nothing more than conjecture. Juraviel understood, and was even a bit envious, of the motivations behind those avowed followers of Avelyn: a generosity and clear mission to make all the world a better place. But Juraviel was more pragmatic and realistic than to believe that their plans would be realized so easily. The gemstones were power, pure and simple, and letting that kind of power out into the world could have many more disastrous side effects than those people blinded by compassion could ever foresee.

Humans did not live a long time, Juraviel reminded himself. They considered a mere century as more than a lifetime, and so they often acted short-sightedly; humans would do that which helped immediate situations, often to disastrous effect for future generations.

But Belli'mar Juraviel was not human; he was Touel'alfar and had seen the birth and death of several centuries. Pony's words now only strengthened the elf's feelings on that which he had to do and made Juraviel wonder honestly if Lady Dasslerond hadn't foreseen this impending change in Church policy.

"I tell you this last thing because I am your friend," Juraviel said.

"Understand well the gift that Nightbird gave to you; it is, among my people, as high an honor as can be bestowed."

"*Bi'nelle dasada,*" Pony reasoned a moment later.

"It was not his to give," Juraviel explained. "And he should not have done so, not even to you, without Lady Dasslerond's permission."

Pony didn't even begin to know how to answer that surprising remark.

"And it is not yours to give," Juraviel went on, his tone turning grave. "I have sworn that you will not, and based upon my trust in you, Lady Dasslerond allowed you to live," Juraviel said. Each word he spoke made Pony's blue eyes open a bit wider in sheer astonishment. "I pray that you do not betray that trust."

"I would never," the woman breathed.

"So I told my lady," said Juraviel. "And I would not even have told you of this, except that I fear that you do not understand the power of that gift and the need that we have to keep it secret."

"Never," Pony agreed.

"Belster returns," the elf announced, seeing the man bouncing up the path toward Pony.

"His archer friend found him down the road," the innkeeper said to Pony when she turned to regard him. "I think the fool dropped his bow when ye chased him off. Pity for the two o' them if they find highwaymen waitin' for them down the way a bit!"

Ironic and fitting, Pony thought, and she turned back to the tree and Juraviel.

But the elf was already long gone.

By the time he neared Dundalis, Juraviel was certain that he had left Pony and Belster far, far behind. Pony had come after him, once, on that first night after he had left her with Belster. Using the soul stone, the woman had flown out of body, covering miles in seconds. Juraviel had felt her presence, and keenly, had even heard her telepathic call—and not just her feelings, but actual words, asking for an explanation.

But the elf had pretended not to hear, or at least, not to hear well, so that he had merely whispered farewell several times and kept on his speedy way. Soon, Pony had given up the chase.

Truly, the dismissal of his friend was tearing Belli'mar Juraviel apart, as was the secret of the child being trained in Andur'Blough Inninness. The entire result of the demon war was not as Juraviel had hoped or predicted. First he had lost one of his very best friends, Tuntun of the Touel'alfar, in the bowels of Aida. And then Nightbird had fallen. And now this. Juraviel had envisioned himself sitting on a hillock with Bradwarden and Nightbird and Jilseponie, trading stories and listening to the centaur's song. It was a fantasy Juraviel had played out in his mind a hundred times, and now that it could not come to pass, it was a continual emptiness, a pang he felt forever within his heart.

All that he could hold against that pang, all that he could use to battle back, was the truth of his heritage. He was Touel'alfar, and would have out-lived Nightbird and Pony, and their children's children's children.

Barely three days after his encounter with Pony, Juraviel found himself in the forest of the Timberlands again, following the song of Bradwarden, and found the centaur and Roger at their favorite hillock under the starry sky. Juraviel noted with interest that the stallion, too, was nearby, tethered to a tree at the base of the open mound.

"Taked ye long enough," the centaur remarked, lowering his pipes, and Roger came up on his elbows.

"Sooner than agreed," Juraviel replied. "We said a week, and yet only six days have passed. Will you need the seventh to finish preparing the horse?"

Roger's groan was telling indeed.

"No, he's as good as he's to get for now," Bradwarden answered. "A fiery little beastie, don't ye doubt. Ye'll be findin' yer road a spirited run, but he'll take a saddle, at least."

"Then I will be gone before the dawn," the elf announced, surprising both his friends.

"In a hurry, are ye?"

"I am not out for pleasure, but on an errand for my lady," Juraviel explained. "She bade me return with all haste, and so I shall."

Roger looked from Juraviel to the centaur curiously. "Are you coming up for a drink, at least?" he asked, for Juraviel had stopped halfway up the hillock, and showed no signs of coming any closer.

"Presently," the elf answered. "I have a bit more to do to prepare for the road. I met Jilseponie on the road north of Caer Tinella." Roger perked up at that. "She and Belster should arrive within a few days."

And with that, the elf skittered off into the forest. In truth, he had nothing left to prepare—he would find his supplies along the road—but he wanted to minimize his contact with any potential plague carriers, his friends included.

Bradwarden's song went on for a long, long time, and so in tune was it with the natural surroundings that Juraviel hardly noticed when the last delicate notes drifted into nothingness. But when he did register the silence, the elf knew that it was time for him to move, and quickly.

He went back to the hillock, and took comfort that Bradwarden, who never seemed to sleep, wasn't about. Up he went, to find Roger snoring contentedly beside the orange embers.

He found the gemstones, as expected, in Roger's belt pouch—a ruby and a soul stone, a lodestone and a graphite, and several others—and wasted no time in pocketing them. He did glance back once, stung by a pang of guilt—Roger was his friend, after all—but then, remembering who he was and the needs of his people, the needs of *the people*, he moved swiftly down the hillock and untethered the horse, then walked off into the dark forest.

"Way before the dawn, by my countin'," he heard Bradwarden's voice soon after, for though Juraviel could easily have gotten away from the region without being noticed by anyone, the centaur included, Bradwarden could certainly track a horse.

"The sooner I begin, the sooner I find my home," Juraviel replied calmly.

The centaur came into view a few steps down the trail behind him, and started to catch up, but Juraviel held up his hand, motioning for Bradwarden to stay back.

"What're ye about, elf?" Bradwarden asked.

"I am in a hurry, as I explained," Juraviel replied.

"No, it's a bit more than that," Bradwarden reasoned. "The Juraviel I know doesn't refuse an offer of a drink with his friends."

"I had preparations—"

"The Juraviel I know would be askin' his friends for help, then, if his preparations were so important," Bradwarden interrupted, as he came forward a few strides. "The Juraviel I know wouldn't have left Pony and Belster on the road, but would've spent the extra couple o' days walkin' with them, whatever his lady Dasslerond might be needin'. So what're ye about, elf? Are ye to tell me or not?"

Juraviel thought on that for a long moment. "You take care, Bradwarden," he said in all seriousness. "On the road south, I heard rumors of the rosy plague."

"Oh, by the demons, ye say."

"I know not if there is any truth to those words—more likely, they were the utterances of a gossiping fool and nothing more," the elf went on. "But I can ill afford to take the chance, any chance, of bringing the plague back to my people."

Bradwarden shook his head in frustration, but then looked at Juraviel and nodded.

"You take care of Roger and Jilseponie, as well," the elf said. "I fear that if the rumors of plague prove true, then this might be the last time I see you—any of you. Know that if the land becomes ill with plague, the Touel'alfar will secure our borders and none will leave for many years."

Again, Bradwarden merely nodded.

"Farewell," Juraviel said.

"And to ye," Bradwarden replied, and Belli'mar Juraviel left him there, in the forest that suddenly seemed all the darker.

Pony and Belster arrived in Dundalis right on schedule, the portly innkeeper driving the wagon and Pony riding Greystone. What a splendid sight she seemed to the folk of the Timberland community, many of whom owed their lives to the heroic deeds of this woman in the days of the demon armies. The whole town turned out to see the pair, cheering; and Pony, though embarrassed, felt indeed as if she had come home.

And leading all the cheers was Roger Lockless, his smile so wide that it seemed as if it would take in his ample ears.

"We've been waiting and waiting," he explained. "Belli'mar Juraviel told us that he found you north of Caer Tinella, but I had hoped you would arrive sooner, give that strong horse of yours a bit of a workout."

"An easy road, for we've nowhere else we need to be," Pony answered. "Just as I prefer."

Roger's expression was curious for just a moment, but his smile soon returned. "No one built upon the foundation of the old Howling Sheila," he explained. "We knew that you'd return."

"Olwan Wyndon put down that foundation," Pony answered, her voice somber. How well she remembered that particular place! When the monsters came to sack Dundalis, when Pony was but twelve years old, she had crawled under that foundation to escape the swords and spears and fire. She had emerged after the carnage, to find that all of the town, all of her family and all of her friends, were dead or missing. She and Elbryan alone had survived the catastrophe.

But Dundalis had been rebuilt, and that foundation had supported yet another structure, Belster's Howling Sheila tavern.

And then Dundalis had been sacked again.

The memories showed Pony the best of human spirit, the resilience, the ability to fight on and on. Why wasn't she now feeling that way? Where was her fighting spirit, her willingness to accept the losses and rebuild everything?

Perhaps some things could not be recovered, she mused, staring at the foundation and wondering if perhaps she should not have come back to this place. Here was the legacy of the Howling Sheila, a foundation of cold stone; and out there, not so far away, was another legacy, a cairn of cold stone.

"Are you all right?" she heard Roger ask, but it seemed to her as if his words came from far, far away. "Pony?"

She felt his hands on her shoulders, and only then understood that her shoulders were trembling, and that she was clammy and weak.

Then Belster was there beside her, holding her arm to support her.

Pony reached deep inside and shook away the fit. "I should have eaten more at breakfast," she said to Belster, smiling sheepishly.

The innkeeper looked at her and politely nodded, but Pony knew, of course, that he had seen right through her little lie. Belster had come to know her so very well over the last year, and he understood the source of her distress.

"Fetch some food!" Roger called to the townsfolk. "As fine a meal as we can prepare." He started to point out a couple of men to set to the task, but Pony put her arm on his and held it low.

"Later," she said.

"Nonsense," Roger argued. "We will prepare the finest—"

"Later," Pony said again, more forcefully. "I have something I must do."

"Are ye sure, girl?" Belster asked, and Pony turned back to face him, took a deep breath, and nodded.

"I'll start setting up, then," Belster said.

"Roger will help you, I am sure," Pony, who wanted to do this thing alone, replied, and she looked to Roger again and patted his arm, smiling.

Then she went to Greystone and pulled herself into the saddle. She headed out of town at a swift trot, up the north slope, then walked the horse slowly down the fairly steep incline into the pine groves and the thick white caribou moss.

When she came out the other side of that dell, she had Greystone at an eager canter, running through the forest.

"She's knowin' the woods as well as any," Bradwarden insisted when a frantic Roger came to him later on, wailing that they had to find Pony. "As well as any human might," the centaur corrected with a sly wink.

"She's been gone for hours," Roger explained.

"And I'm thinkin' that she'll be doin' many o' these little rides out alone over the next few weeks. Can ye no' guess where's she's gone to, boy, and can ye no' be figurin' why she wanted to go there alone?"

Roger looked at him curiously at first, but finally a light of recognition came over him.

"You are sure that she's all right?" he asked.

"I'd be worryin' about any monsters that might've found the girl," Bradwarden said with a hearty chuckle. "Ye gived her back her gemstones, didn't ye?"

Roger's expression spoke volumes to the perceptive centaur.

"What're ye thinkin', boy?"

"I don't have them," Roger admitted.

Now it was Bradwarden's turn to wear the confused expression. "Ye said ye did," the centaur protested. "Ye even showed 'em to me!"

"I did have them, but they're gone!" Roger tried to explain.

"Gone?"

"I had them a few days ago, but I woke up one morning to find my pouch empty."

"Ye're sayin' ye lost a clutch o' magic that could flatten a fair-sized town?" Bradwarden cried. "Ye lost a clutch o' gems that a hunnerd merchants'd willingly give over all their gold to get their hands on?"

"I had them, and then I did not," Roger insisted.

"And ye didn't think to say anythin' when the thief might still be about?" Bradwarden roared at him.

"I think I know who took them," Roger replied quietly.

"Well, we'll go and have a talk with the ..." The centaur stopped, catching a hint of what might be going on here. "When d'ye say ye lost the damn things?"

"Three mornings ago."

"The night after ..." Bradwarden paused and shook his head. It made no sense. Juraviel? Their elven friend stole Pony's gemstones?

"Either Juraviel took them or someone else stole up the hillock that night after we had gone to sleep," Roger insisted.

Truly, Bradwarden had no answers for that. He knew well enough that no one had come up that hillock to steal from Roger. And yet, unless the man was lying, those gemstones had disappeared on that very night—the very night Belli'mar Juraviel made his hasty retreat from the region.

"It might be that them monks found a way to magically come and get the damn things," the centaur said unconvincingly, for both he and Roger knew well that if there was such a manner of retrieval, Father Abbot Markwart would surely have discovered it and used it to get the cache of stones back a long time ago.

"I don't even know what to tell Pony," Roger admitted.

"Has she asked for them?"

"No."

"Is she even knowin' that ye got the damn things?"

"I don't think so."

"Then tell her not a thing until she's askin'," Bradwarden advised. "I'm thinkin' that the girl's got enough weighin' down her heart at this time."

"More than you know," Roger replied. "I was talking with Belster earlier and he told me all that Pony walked away from in Palmaris. They offered her everything, the barony, the abbey. Everything. And she just walked away."

Bradwarden eyed the man and marked well his tone. "And ye're thinkin' she chose wrong?"

"After all we went through?" Roger replied, his frustration creeping into his voice. "After all the fighting and all the dying? After Elbryan gave his very life for a better world? And we could have that world, we—Pony could make it all worthwhile."

"I'm seein' a new side o' ye, to be sure," the centaur remarked, and that set Roger back on his heels a bit.

"I fought alongside everyone else," the man protested when he got his bearings back.

"Never said ye didn't," Bradwarden replied. "But by me own thinkin', ye was fightin' more for Roger than for any paradise in yer thoughts."

Again, the man had to pause for a bit to consider any response he might give, for Roger understood that the centaur spoke honestly and accurately. All through the early days of the war, Roger had indeed been a selfish warrior, considering every action based mostly on what fame it might bring to him.

Elbryan had shown him the error of his ways, as had Juraviel, with typical elven bluntness. Only now, however, with Bradwarden so clearly pointing it out, did Roger begin to understand the depth of the change that had come over him. Only now did he consciously recognize that Elbryan had died for a reason, for something bigger than his own life and bigger than Pony's life. And, to Roger's complete surprise, he found himself frustrated and disappointed that Pony had chosen to run away when all the city was being offered up to her, when, with a few words and a few actions, she could have made a profound change upon Palmaris, a change for the better, a change that would give meaning to their sacrifices made in battling first the demon and its minions and then the demons that had infected the Abellican Church.

And she had run away!

"But aren't ye being tough on the poor girl?" Bradwarden remarked.

"She should not be here," Roger replied. "Or at least, she should not be planning to stay. There is too much to do, and time will work against us if we do not act."

"Against us?" the centaur echoed doubtfully. "I'm not seein' Roger Lockless doin' much work in Palmaris. I'm not seein' Roger Lockless doin' much work at all!" He ended with a laugh, a great belly laugh; but Roger, too perplexed by these revelations concerning his feelings, didn't join in.

"Ah, but ye're bein' too hard on her," Bradwarden explained.

"The opportunity—"

"And what good might she be doin' if her heart's not in it?" Bradwarden promptly interrupted, and his voice grew more grim then, and more serious. "Ye lost a friend, and so ye're stingin', and wantin' to put a meanin' to it," the centaur explained. "And so ye should be, and so should we all. But Pony's lost more than a friend."

"I loved Elbryan," Roger started to protest, but Bradwarden was laughing at the absurdity of the statement, and Roger couldn't honestly disagree. Comparing his relationship with Elbryan to the one the ranger shared with Pony was indeed absurd.

"She's needin' time to heal," the centaur said after a bit. "She's needin' time for rememberin' who she is and why she is, and for findin' a reason to keep on fightin'."

"How long?" Roger asked. "It's been a year."

"A torn heart can take a sight longer than a year," Bradwarden said quietly, solemnly, his voice filled with obvious sympathy for his dear friend Pony. "Ye give her the time, and it might be that she'll go back and begin the fight anew."

"Might be?"

"And might not be," the centaur said plainly. "Ye can't be tellin' someone else what fights they're wantin' to pick, and ye can't be arguin' the worth o' fightin' to one who's not seein' it."

"And if she chooses not to continue?" Roger asked. "What value, then, of Elbryan's death?"

"Ask yerself," the centaur replied. "Ye're so quick to be makin' it Pony's fight, and easy enough for ye, sittin' up here in the Timberlands. Where's Roger, then? I'm askin'. He's lettin' his friend go cold in the ground, and not doin' a thing to bring a value to Elbryan's death."

"I was not offered the barony or the abbey."

"Ye weren't lookin' for the offer," Bradwarden said. "Ye could've ridden the last fight to some power, if ye so chose."

"I came north with you," Roger protested, "to bury Elbryan."

"And ye could've been back in Palmaris before the summer was half finished," Bradwarden scolded. "Are ye mad at Pony, boy? Are ye really? Or is it yerself that's botherin' yerself?"

Roger started to answer, but stopped short and stood staring out at the forest, wondering, wondering.

"Pony's needin' a friend now, and needin' us to let her do all that she's needin' to do without our judgin' her," Bradwarden remarked sternly. "Ye think ye can do that?"

Roger looked him right in the eye, considered the question carefully and honestly, then nodded.

A chill wind came up that evening, and Pony honestly wasn't sure if it was a natural thing or a consequence of this cold place. In either case, how fitting it seemed to her as she stood before the two cairns in the grove north of Dundalis, a place that would have left her cold on the hottest of bright summer days.

She only glanced at the older of the graves, the resting place of Mather Wyndon, Elbryan's uncle and the first Wyndon ranger. She couldn't help but picture the body under those stones, disturbed first by Elbryan on that dark night when he had earned Tempest, the elven sword, and then again more recently by Bradwarden and Roger, when they reinterred the weapon beside its original owner.

And Pony couldn't help but picture Elbryan, and the mere thought of her love lying cold in the ground nearly buckled her knees. He was there, under those rocks, with Hawkwing, the magnificent bow Belli'mar Juraviel's father, Joycenevial, had crafted for him during his years of training with the Touel'alfar. He was there, with eyes unseeing and a mouth that could not draw breath. He, who had so often warmed her in his gentle but strong embrace, was there, alone and cold, and there was nothing, nothing that she could do about it.

All of her young life had been marred by loss. First her family and friends—all of them save Elbryan—had been murdered by goblins and giants. Then her companions at Pireth Tulme—men and women she hadn't considered friends but with whom she had forged a working relationship—

had been slaughtered by the attacking powries. Then the Chilichunks, who had shown her only love, had perished in the dungeons of St.-Mere-Abelle.

Then Paulson, Cric, and Chipmunk and Tuntun and Avelyn, dear Avelyn, all lost on the road to Mount Aida. And her child, torn from her womb by the demon Markwart. And finally—in an act that had saved her life, surely—she had lost Elbryan, her lover, her best friend, the man she had intended to grow old beside.

It didn't get easier, these confrontations with death. Far from hardening her heart to future losses, each death seemed to amplify those that came before.

She pictured them now, all of them, from Elbryan to Avelyn to her father, walking past her as if in a dream, moving close in front of her but never seeing her or hearing her plaintive calls. Walking, walking away from her forever.

She reached out and tried to grab Elbryan, but he was an insubstantial thing, a formed mist and nothing more, and her hand passed right through him. He was an image, a memory, something lost.

Pony blinked open her eyes and didn't even try to hold back the tears that rolled down her cheeks.

CHAPTER

❖ 18 ❖

Friendships Fast

"I hadn't thought we'd be seein' our home again so soon," Liam O'Blythe remarked to Prince Midalis as they trotted their mounts at the lead of a long column making its way through the muggy air of the Vanguard forest. They had gone north with Bruinhelde and his clan only to be met by barbarian scouts reporting that southern Alpinador was clear of monsters, that not a sign of any goblins or powries had been seen in many, many weeks. And so, with Bruinhelde's approval and a knowing wink and a nod from Andacanavar, the men of Vanguard had turned about, heading back to their homes to erase the scars of the demon war.

Andacanavar had come back to the south, as well, though he had taken a roundabout route and they hadn't seen him in a couple of days. With Midalis' blessing, the ranger had decided to haunt the region of Vanguard for the rest of the summer, to learn what he could about his southern neighbors in the hopes that he could further bridge the chasm between the two peoples. The ranger had also elicited from Midalis the Prince's promise that, when he returned home in the autumn, Midalis would accompany him.

There remained the not so little matter of the blood-brothering.

"Pireth Vanguard!" the point scout called back.

"Well, she is still standing, then," Midalis remarked. A few moments later, rounding a bend and cresting a rise in the trail, Liam and Midalis came in sight of the fortress, its towers stark against the heavy gray sky hanging over the Gulf of Corona behind it.

Before they entered the fortress, the pair noted that a trader was in port, but it wasn't until Midalis saw Warder Presso running toward him that he realized something unusual was going on. The battle-weary Prince was relieved indeed to learn the Warder's news, to learn that nothing sinister had happened in the days since their departure.

Still, a monk visiting from Palmaris, come to take Abbot Agronguerre
back to St.-Mere-Abelle, was no small matter; and though he was tired and
hot and dirty, Prince Midalis decided that he should go straight to St.
Belfour to meet the man. Liam, of course, willingly followed; and the two
were joined by Captain Al'u'met, who was riding Warder Presso's own fine
horse. On the trails to the abbey, Al'u'met told of the happenings in Palmaris yet again; and as they nodded, hanging on every word, both the
Prince and his adviser came to understand why Midalis' brother, the King,
had not responded to their request for soldiers.

"I had heard rumors that the Father Abbot had died," Midalis said when
Al'u'met finished. "But never would I have believed that such turmoil and
treacherous circumstance surrounded that tragic event."

"The kingdom will be long in recovering from the scars of the demon
dactyl," Al'u'met said grimly. "Perhaps the Church will choose its next
leader wisely, to the benefit of us all."

"Ye're seein' benefit in anythin' the Abellican Church's doin'?" Liam
O'Blythe asked the dark-skinned southerner bluntly.

"I am Abellican," Al'u'met explained, "and have followed that path to
God for many decades."

"I only meant—"

Al'u'met stopped him with a smile and an upraised hand.

"When will they convene the College of Abbots?" Midalis asked.

"I am bid to transport Brother Dellman, Abbot Agronguerre, and any
entourage the abbot chooses to bring, to St.-Mere-Abelle in the autumn,"
Al'u'met explained. "They will convene in Calember, as they did last time."

Midalis started to answer, but then paused and considered the words
carefully. "This Brother Dellman," he asked, "who sent him?"

"Abbot Braumin of St. Precious."

"I do not know the man," Midalis replied, "nor have I ever heard Abbot
Agronguerre mention him. He is young?"

"For an abbot, very much so," Al'u'met explained. "Abbot Braumin has
earned his rank by deed, and not by mere age. He stood with Nightbird and
Jilseponie, even under promise of torture by the Father Abbot. He would
not renounce his beliefs, though his refusal seemed as if it would surely cost
him his life. Brother Dellman, too. A fine young man, by my estimation."

Al'u'met started to take the conversation that way, but Midalis would not
let him, more concerned with the one thing that nagged at him, just below
his consciousness, about this visit.

"Why have you come so early?" he asked plainly.

"It is a long voyage, and one unpredictable," Al'u'met explained. "The
weather was not so foul, and yet we had to put in at Dancard for repair."

"You could still be in Palmaris dock," Midalis countered, and he noticed
the concerned expression come over Liam's face, and realized then that he

might be giving away his suspicions. "You could have waited out the rest of the month in the south and still have had more than enough time to come up here, fetch Agronguerre, and return to St.-Mere-Abelle."

"I could not chance the weather," Al'u'met answered, but Midalis saw right through that excuse. Every sailor along the gulf knew well that the late-spring weather was much more treacherous than that of late summer and early autumn. Not only had Al'u'met come up prematurely, but he had done so against the conventional wisdom of the gulf sailors.

What was it, then? Prince Midalis wondered. Why had this protégé of the new abbot come running all the way to Vanguard with an invitation that could have been delivered by any one of the many traders that would venture here over the next month and a half? And certainly a man as prominent as Abbot Agronguerre would have had little trouble in finding his own passage south. Following that same line of thought, it struck Midalis that it made more sense for the abbot to use one of Midalis' ships, and not go south with Al'u'met, that he might return before the winter season set in deep.

Unless Abbot Braumin and his cohorts weren't expecting Agronguerre to return to Vanguard any time soon, Midalis reasoned; and it occurred to him then that this was much more than an invitation. He had a difficult time holding his smile in check all the rest of the way to St. Belfour.

They arrived late in the afternoon, and met immediately with Brother Dellman, Abbot Agronguerre, and the ever-present Brother Haney. Dellman told his tale yet again, more quickly this time, since the Prince had already heard all of Al'u'met's contributions. What most interested the Prince, and what he made Dellman repeat several times and elaborate on, were the parts concerning his brother's actions in the city.

Brother Dellman took care to paint King Danube in a positive light, and it was not a hard task for the young monk. He explained that Danube had wisely held back to allow Elbryan and Jilseponie to settle their war with Markwart. "He understood that this fight was about the soul of the Church more than any threat to his secular kingdom," Dellman explained. "It was the proper course for him to take."

Midalis nodded, not surprised, for ever had his older brother been wise in the ways of diplomacy; and one of the primary lessons they both had learned at a young age was never to engage the kingdom in a fight that did not directly involve them.

"His wisdom after the battle was no less," Brother Dellman went on, resisting the temptation to offer the glaring exception of Danube's choice for the new baron, installing the hostile Duke Kalas instead of a more diplomatic soul. "He begged Jilseponie to take the barony."

That raised Prince Midalis' dark eyebrows and those of Liam O'Blythe, as well.

"If you knew the woman, you would better appreciate the correctness of that choice," Captain Al'u'met put in.

"Then I will have to make it a point to meet this most remarkable woman," Prince Midalis sincerely replied.

"You will not be disappointed," said Warder Presso, which caught all of the Vanguardsmen by surprise. "If she is the same woman, Jill, who served with me at Pireth Tulme many years ago, then you will be duly impressed."

"A pity that she'll not be at the College of Abbots," Agronguerre remarked.

"An invitation will surely be extended," said Dellman. "And just as certainly, Jilseponie will refuse. She has gone north, back into the Timberlands, to heal her heart. Better will all the world be if that process is successful and Jilseponie returns to us soon!"

His obvious enthusiasm and sincerity had all the heads bobbing in agreement, and had all of those who had not met the woman—including Warder Presso, who had not seen her in years—anxious indeed to gaze upon this growing legend.

They talked long into the night, informally, mostly trading anecdotes of their experiences during the war. Abbot Agronguerre excused himself from vespers, and allowed Brothers Haney and Dellman to do likewise, so that they could continue this most productive and enjoyable meeting. When finally they ended, past midnight, there had been forged an honest friendship between them all, and all the secular guests were invited to remain at the abbey for as long as they desired.

Still, Brother Dellman was surprised indeed when Prince Midalis bade him to hold back a moment while all the others filed out of the abbot's audience chamber.

"I find it curious that you have come up here so early," the Prince explained.

"We simply wanted to make sure that the message of the College of Abbots was properly delivered and in a timely enough manner for Abbot Agronguerre to make his preparations," Brother Dellman replied.

"That could have been done in an easier and more convenient manner," the Prince observed.

Brother Dellman shrugged, having no practical answer and not wanting to get into the discussion at that time.

"You are a good and trusted friend of the new abbot of St. Precious," Midalis observed.

"Abbot Braumin Herde," Dellman replied. "I traveled with him across the land, running from Markwart and running toward Avelyn. I was beside him at the miracle of Aida, and again beside him when he was taken captive by Markwart, and by the King's soldiers."

"And now, with Markwart dead and discredited, the new abbot of St. Precious, your friend Braumin Herde, will have a strong voice at the College, yes?"

Brother Dellman considered the strange question for a moment, then just shrugged.

"The tide flows in his favor," the Prince observed. "He who was instrumental in the fall of Father Abbot Markwart, he who leads those of the other philosophy, Avelyn's philosophy, will certainly be heard clearly at the College of Abbots."

"If the other abbots and masters are wise, they will listen to Abbot Braumin's every word with great care," Brother Dellman remarked.

"And does Abbot Braumin intend to try for the highest position in the Church?"

That set Dellman back on his heels. "Forgive me, my Prince, but it is not within my province to discuss such matters."

"Of course," said Midalis. "Yet you said that he was a young man—too young to be so nominated and elected, I would guess, given my understanding of your Church."

"You know much of us," replied Dellman, who was growing increasingly uneasy with this whole train of conversation.

"But perhaps Abbot Braumin has set his sights toward nominating another for the position of father abbot," Prince Midalis said. "Perhaps he, like many others, no doubt, is seeking a person who will lead the Church in a better direction."

"That would be his charge, my Prince," Brother Dellman said, "as it is now the charge of every abbot and every master."

A wry smile came over the handsome young Prince's face. "And so, given that, would not this young abbot send out his most trusted friends to study those likely candidates?" he asked.

"Again you ask of me that which I cannot answer," Dellman replied, which, of course, was an answer in itself, and one that pleased Prince Midalis greatly.

"I will say this to you without any personal motives," Midalis offered. "If you and your friend the abbot are indeed thinking that Abbot Agronguerre might be a proper selection for that most important position within your Church, then know that I second that nomination with all of my heart. He is a wonderful man, a man of diplomacy—his work in quelling the trepidations of the Alpinadoran leaders in our recent truce was marvelous and generous—and, foremost, a man of God. I have never truly considered myself overreligious, good Brother Dellman, but when I hear Abbot Agronguerre speaking—and always his words come from the truth that is in his heart—I know that I am hearing the will of God."

"Strong words," Brother Dellman gasped, for they were indeed, words that would border on heresy if Midalis were speaking them with any intent of personal gain! And yet, in looking at the man, in considering the situation faced by both Church and State, Dellman understood that the Prince was speaking from his heart.

"If you are considering Abbot Agronguerre for nomination, then look as deeply as you may," Prince Midalis went on. "For surely, the more familiar you become with Abbot Agronguerre, the more firmly you will desire him as your new father abbot. This I know, Brother Dellman, for I have served beside the man for many years and have not once found error in his ways. Oh, I have not always agreed with his choices; but even for those over which we were at odds, I knew that his choice had come from a logical and consistent philosophy, one based on the highest and most noble traditions of your Church."

"I will consider your words carefully, Prince Midalis," Brother Dellman answered.

"Then you admit that you are here for more reasons than to deliver an invitation?" Midalis asked with that wry grin again.

Brother Dellman, too, couldn't help but smile. "Forgive me, my Prince," he answered yet again, "but it is not within my province to discuss such matters."

Midalis laughed aloud and clapped Dellman on the shoulder as he walked past, collecting the man in his wake.

Dellman retired to his room soon after, but was far too excited to even think about sleep. He paced his small room, digesting all that he had learned, thinking that Abbot Braumin had been wise indeed to send him to this place, and that the Abellican Church might soon elect the leader it needed to get through this dark time.

Abbot Agronguerre hustled down to the front courtyard of St. Belfour a couple of days later, when he learned that a most unexpected visitor had arrived, seeking audience with him and with Prince Midalis, who was still within the abbey. Along the way, the abbot managed to find Haney and Dellman, and bade them accompany him, though he didn't pause long enough to fill them in on the details.

As soon as they came in sight of the courtyard, the source of the abbot's nervous excitement became clear—in the nearly seven-foot frame of mighty Andacanavar.

"Greetings, friend Andacanavar," Agronguerre said, huffing and puffing to catch his breath. "Good tidings, I pray, bring you to us at this time. You remember Brother Haney, I am sure, and let me introduce to you a visitor from the south, Brother—"

"Holan Dellman," Andacanavar interrupted, and both Haney and Agronguerre looked curiously from the ranger to their southern brother.

"Greetings again, Andacanavar of Alpinador," Brother Dellman remarked, and Agronguerre detected a bit of nervousness along with the obvious familiarity.

"We have both walked a long road, it would seem, to come to the same place," the ranger said with a grin. But it seemed to Agronguerre as if Andacanavar, too, was straining to be polite. These two had a history, he realized, and one that had not been without conflict.

Indeed, Dellman and the ranger had met first spiritually, and not physically. Dellman had gone along with Master Jojonah, then Brother Francis and other brothers from St.-Mere-Abelle on their caravan journey to the Barbacan to investigate the demise of the demon dactyl. Their road had taken them through Alpinador, and after a fight with monsters outside of one Alpinadoran village, Brother Dellman, scouting out of body, had found that they were being shadowed by Andacanavar. Master Jojonah had then sent Brother Braumin out to the man spiritually with soul stone magic, to quietly suggest that he should turn around and go home. Failing that, Braumin had been instructed to possess the man and walk his body back to the southland.

But Andacanavar, stronger of will than the monks could ever have expected, had turned the tables, had walked through the spiritual connection to possess Braumin, and then had used the monk's physical body to go into the encampment and learn more about the brothers.

The two had come to terms over their misunderstanding, but still there remained some tension between them—and between the ranger and Braumin's supporters, who had seen their leader magically and spiritually overwhelmed by the man. The act of possession was among the most distasteful products of gemstone magic, a rape of the spirit; and two who had known such intimate battle as that would never, ever forget it.

"I had thought you to be back in Alpinador, with Bruinhelde," Abbot Agronguerre remarked.

"Bruinhelde is not back in Alpinador, either," the ranger explained, slowly turning his gaze away from Brother Dellman. "We found the road clear."

"We heard as much," replied Agronguerre. "My brethren returned to us several days ago, and glad we were to learn that Alpinador was spared the trials of the demon dactyl."

"We fought our share," Andacanavar informed him. "But good tidings indeed that the threat to our homeland had ended. And yet it was tidings of further war that brought us back to the south, soon after Prince Midalis and the others left us."

A shadow crossed over Abbot Agronguerre's chubby face.

"Prince Midalis is here, by the reports," the ranger remarked. "Take me to him that I have to tell my tale but once."

They found Midalis eating his breakfast on the flat top of the abbey's northwestern tower. Predictably, Liam O'Blythe was there as well; and it occurred to everyone there, Liam included, how similar the man and his relationship to Prince Midalis was to that of Brother Haney and his relationship to Abbot Agronguerre. Both had been born peasants, and through deed alone had risen to important, if little recognized, positions, for both were sounding boards for their respective leaders, confidants who first heard the policies the men would institute. Both were younger than the men they followed, protégés of sorts: one the likely successor as abbot of St. Belfour, the other already appointed an earl, and likely in line for the duchy of Vanguard.

Midalis seemed no less surprised by the ranger's appearance than Agronguerre had been. He wiped his mouth quickly and rose from the table, moving fast to greet the man away from the plates of half-eaten food, and subtly motioning for Liam to clear up the mess.

"Tidings of war, so says Andacanavar," Abbot Agronguerre said immediately. "And Bruinhelde and some of his warriors have returned, as well."

"Trouble?" Midalis asked the ranger.

"So says one of our scouts, who spoke with one of your own," the ranger informed him. "To the east of here, in a rough bay. A boat put in, a boat full of powries."

"Barrelboat," Midalis reasoned.

"Not so," Andacanavar replied. "A masted ship. They put in to the bay, but did not, it seems, know the waters well, for when the tide went out, their boat came down hard to the rocks and mud. So you have got powries again, my friend, and so we came down to join in the fun of being rid of the wretched bloody caps."

They rode out in force from St. Belfour soon after, Abbot Agronguerre in his coach leading the same twenty brothers who had just returned from Alpinador, plus Dellman and Haney. Beside them went Midalis, Liam, and Andacanavar. Their numbers swelled five times over when they crossed through the town of Vanguard and the fortress, where Warder Presso and Al'u'met came out to meet them, along with many of the Pireth Vanguard soldiers. After a brief meeting to try to determine the exact location of this bay, Al'u'met returned to the *Saudi Jacintha* and, after bringing aboard some more of Warder Presso's archers, put out, shadowing the marching army to the east.

With Bruinhelde and his warriors already in place in the east, and another two towns to cross through, where more volunteers would join, it seemed as if this would be one battle where the odds, at last, favored Midalis' side.

"Prop it, pull it, and peg it!" Dalump Keedump roared at his crew, and the powries did just that, tugging the heavy lines, bringing the boat up the ramp an inch, and then pegging the crank to hold it in its new position.

They had come in for repairs and supplies, and perhaps a bit of sport, but—curse their luck—the tide had dropped too low for the heavy boat, and had damaged the hull.

"Prop it, pull it, and peg it!" the powrie boss cried again enthusiastically, for they were making progress now in getting the ship repaired and in getting themselves on the way home. Dalump had led a raid upon a nearby village, a few farmhouses clustered together, and though—to the dismay of all the fierce bloody caps—there were no humans about to slaughter, they tore down the walls of the buildings and found enough rope and other supplies to come back and complete their repairs. Now, with the front half of the boat clear of the water, the crack in her hull visible and seeming not too severe, Dalump figured they could be back out to sea with the next high tide.

"Prop it, pull it, and peg it!" he cried again and again, the boat creaking out of the water more and more. "Yach, but we'll be back to our home in short order, lads, and then we'll turn about with another army to go and pay back the dog Kalas!"

And so it went, the growling, untiring powries bending their backs and pulling hard.

Midalis was not surprised to see them, for his scouts had reported that about three families of refugees were on the road. Still, the image of his people being uprooted yet again by monsters brought a fire into the young Prince. He'd see them back to their homes and give them a few powrie heads to stake about the grounds for decorations.

"Me Prince!" cried the man trotting beside the lead wagon, a sturdy farmer of about forty winters, and he ran forward and fell to one knee before Midalis.

"Have powries so chased you from your homes?" Midalis asked.

"And would've burned us in our homes, don't ye doubt, had not some o' his kin—" he indicated Andacanavar "—come to rouse us."

Midalis gave a resigned chuckle. "It would seem that I, and my people, are in Bruinhelde's debt yet again," he remarked to Andacanavar.

"Blood-brothering erases all debt," the ranger replied with a wink.

"Come, and let us be quick," Midalis said to his men, "before Bruinhelde and his men take all the fun from us." He turned back to the farmer. "You need run no farther," he explained. "I will leave some soldiers and brothers with you for your protection. Camp here and wait—and for not too long, I would guess—before we signal you that you may return to your homes."

"If there's anything left o' them," the man remarked.

"And if not, then we will help you to rebuild them!" Prince Midalis replied with enthusiasm.

They picked up their pace after that, quick-marching all the way out to the east, to the bay. The Prince, who knew well the region, decided to take a northerly route and approach the bay heading south, where they would come in sight of the place high on a wooded cliff, overlooking the water.

"I will find you there," Andacanavar promised; and the ranger ran off, seeking Bruinhelde and his kin so that the attack might be coordinated.

"There are the beasts, and what's left of the houses," Liam O'Blythe remarked when they got to the spot, to see the powries hard at work at their impromptu, but wonderfully constructed, dry dock.

"They are cunning fellows," Prince Midalis replied, and he looked up and noted that Brother Dellman, in particular, wore a surprised expression.

"You know of them?" he asked the young monk.

"It may be that we chased this same boat across the gulf," the brother explained.

"They are trying to get home," Abbot Agronguerre remarked.

"A pity for them," Midalis said grimly. There was no argument from the soldiers and the monks or from the Vanguardsmen who had suffered so terribly at the hands of the vicious bloody caps. "Set your archers all along the cliff," he instructed Warder Presso. "Tell them to pick their shots carefully and to wait for the signal." Midalis turned to Abbot Agronguerre. "I pray you do the same with your crossbowmen and any gemstone magic you wish to throw at our enemies. I doubt that you will be needing much energy with the soul stone when this battle is finished."

Abbot Agronguerre nodded his agreement with the tactic and the assessment. As far as they could see, the powries numbered less than a score, and Agronguerre doubted that any would even survive the first volley.

Andacanavar returned to them a few minutes later, explaining that Bruinhelde and his force were in position just to the southwest of the dry dock, in the trees at the western edge of the little bay's mouth, ready to strike.

Midalis looked to Liam, who ran off at once, assembling a force to complement the barbarians'.

"Bruinhelde has more than enough men to finish this task," Andacanavar assured the Prince. "When they break from the forest edge, rain your death upon the powries, and it will be finished."

"This is Vanguard," the Prince replied. "My men should be among the attacking force."

"We've not the time," the ranger explained, pointing down to the dry dock. "It seems that we've come upon our enemies at the last moment. They are preparing to leave, and Bruinhelde will not allow that!"

"Nor will Captain Al'u'met," Brother Dellman added, and all eyes turned his way, to see him smiling widely and looking out past the bay, to the open gulf. And there, around the western lip of the bay, they all saw the sails of the *Saudi Jacintha*, as the boat glided to intercept the powries' craft.

Apparently, Bruinhelde and his kin spotted those sails as well, and, not knowing their intent, decided to make sure that those powries already landed found no reinforcements. Or, Midalis mused, perhaps the barbarian leader was just trying to make sure that he and his brethren did indeed find all the fun!

Whatever the case, the barbarian horde came crashing out of the brush, howling wildly, launching their chained hammers.

Prince Midalis leaped up and cried out, and down went the devastating volley, arrows and crossbow bolts and streaks of lightning.

Dalump Keedump recognized his doom clearly enough when the barbarian horde, a hundred strong at least, came roaring out of the forest, and that fear was only multiplied when death rained down upon his companions from above.

Fortunately for the powrie leader and a couple of his associates, they were tucked in close to the boat at that moment, with the bulky craft between them and the archers, and thus escaped the volley.

Dalump ordered his minions—those few still standing!—to meet the charge, but he held back the two beside him and motioned for one to go up on the ship with him and for the other to run forward and cut the line.

The powrie could only hope that his foolish soldiers would keep the barbarians busy long enough for him to get out into the bay.

"They're running!" Midalis cried as the powrie boat slid down the dry dock to splash into the water. The powrie who had cut the line ran wildly along the beach, trying to keep up, and when he found that he could not, he dove down in the sand and grabbed up the rope, getting pulled along.

Midalis' archers focused their next shots on that sliding dwarf, and when he hit the water, all around him turned crimson.

Bruinhelde, too, cried out against the escape, and he rushed around those few charging powries, letting his able companions cleave the dwarves down, while he ran full out down the beach.

Already the boat's square mainsail was filling with wind, but Bruinhelde's long stride got him close enough. He dove into the water and snatched the trailing rope, pulling himself along its length.

From up above, the archers and the monks focused their missiles and their magic at the deck of the boat, but no clear targets could they see. The craft, groaning and creaking, began its turn for the bay mouth.

"Al'u'met will get them," Midalis remarked. "Keep putting arrows across the deck," he instructed Liam.

"Hold them!" Agronguerre overruled the Prince. The abbot pointed down to the water, indicating Bruinhelde, working hard to get to the boat.

"Go for the sail, then!" Midalis commanded. "And keep your shots high!"

*   *   *

Dalump Keedump kept his head low, cursing and spitting as yet another thunderous lightning bolt flashed overhead, ripping a line in one sail. But then the ship lurched as it came about, its sail filling with a strong breeze, rushing in diagonally from behind.

"Yach, catch us if ye can!" the powrie shouted, but his words died in his mouth when he looked forward and saw the *Saudi Jacintha* closing fast, her deck crowded with archers.

"We got to quit," the other powrie said.

"And go back to a human jail?" Dalump answered, and he slapped his companion on the back of the head. "Yach, I'll go to the bottom o' the bay afore I'll sit in a smelly dungeon again!" With that, he tied off the wheel to keep her sailing straight and rushed forward, dragging his reluctant companion beside him, howling curses at the approaching ship.

"Come on then, ye dogs! I'll give ye a hit or ten!"

Bruinhelde tugged furiously, pulling his body closer and closer alongside the speeding craft. The rope was tied off in front, but the thought of following that course daunted the barbarian, for he'd surely drown in the prow waves before he ever dragged himself out of the water. Besides, the deck was low.

Bruinhelde wrapped one arm tightly about the rope, then pulled in the slack behind him. He coiled the loose end and tossed it up, looping it on a spur along the railing, then caught it as it came back down. He nearly lost his grip altogether when he let go of the towing end and jerked to the end of the slack on the other piece of rope, but again, with sheer determination and strength, the powerful barbarian drove on. Soon he was back to the spot where he had thrown the rope, and then, with a great tug, he came out of the water, scrambling up the side of the boat.

He peeked over to see only two powries, and both of them up front, with their backs to him.

Bruinhelde drew a long dagger from his belt and pulled himself up higher.

"Hold your shots," Al'u'met instructed his many archers as the boats continued to close.

The powrie curses came at him, along with a flying club, as Dalump launched the missile. "I'll ram ye to the bottom with me!" the powrie promised.

"Take them out," Captain Al'u'met said grimly, and the bows bent back and the arrows flew.

Unfortunately, at that same moment, Bruinhelde appeared, charging hard at the powrie pair.

The barrage dropped Dalump Keedump and his powrie companion. Behind them, Bruinhelde went down.

The mood in the two distinct camps on the beach that night was somber indeed. Abbot Agronguerre, along with Brothers Dellman and Haney, went to the Alpinadoran encampment, offering their bandages and services.

Captain Al'u'met, all apologies, accompanied Prince Midalis, Liam, and Andacanavar, to join the Alpinadoran council.

"We did not see Bruinhelde," the captain explained, and Andacanavar translated, with equal sincerity, for his excited kinsmen. "Else we would have held the shot and let him finish the powries."

One Alpinadoran answered gruffly, using words that none of the Vanguardsmen understood, and then another agreed. When Andacanavar turned back to the Vanguardsmen, he offered a comforting wink.

"Bruinhelde was injured in battle," the ranger explained. "There is no shame in that. As for your error, they do not doubt your honesty, though I will admit that they are surprised, as am I, to see a man with skin so dark."

Captain Al'u'met bowed low.

"We all pray that Bruinhelde will survive his wounds," Prince Midalis offered.

"He is made of tougher stuff than you understand, if you fear that he will not," Andacanavar determinedly replied.

"He's unconscious," Brother Haney remarked. "He'll not even know."

Abbot Agronguerre stared hard at the younger brother. "And what think you, Brother Dellman?" he asked. "Should I use the soul stone upon our friend Bruinhelde, though he has forbidden me to do so with any of his warriors?"

"I do not know enough of the situation or the history to make such a judgment," Dellman deferred.

"Without the magic, he might well die," Haney argued. "And if Bruinhelde's to die, then all of our gains with Alpinador these last months might be for naught. Andacanavar takes little of the praise for the friendship, giving it to Bruinhelde."

"True enough," Abbot Agronguerre conceded.

"So you will go to him with the soul stone?" Brother Dellman asked.

Abbot Agronguerre paused for a long moment and stroked his hand against his chin. "No," he decided. "No, whatever the cost, then so be it. I'll not take the man's soul for the sake of his body; and to use the hematite, in Bruinhelde's thinking, I would be doing just that. Let us continue our conventional work upon him and let us pray."

Brother Dellman stared long and hard at Abbot Agronguerre at that moment, and the old monk, obviously feeling that gaze upon him, turned a questioning stare the brother's way.

"If we are to hold any friendship with Alpinador, then it must be a bond forged in truth and in respect," Agronguerre explained. "It will bring me great sorrow if Bruinhelde, so wise for one of his heritage, passes from our world this night, but greater would my regret be if I dishonored the bond of friendship."

In that moment, Brother Dellman knew. Beyond any doubt, he knew this man would become the next father abbot of the Abellican Church, a nomination Dellman would wholeheartedly embrace.

They waited a long time beside Bruinhelde's bed, bandaging him. Brother Haney finally managed to cut through the shaft of the last arrow, its tip embedded deeply in the barbarian's hip. They could not dare to try to extract it, not without gemstone magic assistance, but at least now the whole of it was contained within the man.

Another hour passed, and Bruinhelde seemed to be resting more comfortably. He even opened one eye, to find Agronguerre close to him.

"It hurts," the abbot remarked, and Bruinhelde gave a slight nod.

"Good Bruinhelde, I offer this only in the truest sense of friendship," Agronguerre said, and he held the soul stone up before the barbarian's blue eyes.

And those eyes widened—in horror, it seemed to Dellman. Bruinhelde's breath came in rasps and he shook his head violently, though every movement seemed to pain him greatly.

"Then we'll not!" Abbot Agronguerre assured him, grabbing him to hold him steady. "Only on your word would we ever presume such a thing. Fear not!" He knew that Bruinhelde was only partially understanding him, but the man seemed to relax somewhat.

Soon, Bruinhelde was asleep.

At Agronguerre's bidding, Brother Dellman went to the barbarian council tent to inform them of the progress. When he arrived, he found an embarrassed Midalis holding a flag, the pennant of Bretherford, Duke of the Mirianic, his brother's naval commander.

"It was indeed the same ship we chased across the gulf," Captain Al'u'met explained. "An Ursal ship, no doubt, likely fresh out of Palmaris."

"How can this be, Brother Dellman?" Midalis asked, and the monk swallowed hard. On his way over, he had passed the lines of powrie bodies stretched on the beach, and he was fairly certain that he recognized at least one of the dwarves, an orange-bearded creature he had seen on a misty morning, taken prisoner in the last Palmaris battle, from the western fields.

"Duke Kalas," he remarked, and all eyes turned his way. He started to tell the tale of the fight that long-ago morning, and of the Duke and his brilliant Allheart knights marching the powries in from the field.

"An escape from the Palmaris dungeons?" Prince Midalis asked incredulously.

That notion seemed like the only possible answer; and yet, it, too, seemed impossible. How could a small band of powries break out of the fortress known as Chasewind Manor and somehow commandeer a sailing ship out of Palmaris' busy and well-guarded port?

Then it hit Dellman, like a slap in the face. Why hadn't he and Al'u'met heard of any such escape, or theft of a ship, before they left, since the powries had obviously sailed out just ahead of them? And even beyond that, why hadn't the powries been summarily executed after the battle on the western fields, as had been announced and would certainly have been proper?

And why, Dellman wondered—and he wondered, too, why he hadn't thought of this those many weeks before—hadn't any of the Allheart knights been even slightly injured in that fight? They were great warriors, to be sure, perhaps the best in Honce-the-Bear, but the powrie numbers had been much greater that day—so proclaimed the victorious Duke—and that battlefield hadn't even been prepared properly.

"No escape," Dellman blurted, shaking his head incredulously, for the alternative stuck in his throat. He started to go on, to admit his suspicions that these particular powries had been in league with Duke Kalas, but he looked at the Prince standing before him, and then at the barbarians hanging on his every word, and wisely changed his mind.

"No escape from the dungeons," he said with clear conviction. "Likely these dwarves were being transported—back to Ursal, I would presume— for proper execution or interrogation, when they overwhelmed the crew of the ship and turned her back for the open waters."

Andacanavar promptly translated, and the other Alpinadorans nodded their agreement. When the young brother looked back to his own country-men, though—particularly at Midalis and Al'u'met, he saw the obvious doubts shadowing their expressions.

Al'u'met spoke those concerns clearly on the return journey to the Van-guardsmen encampment. "We would have heard of any transport of pris-oners," he reasoned. "Duke Kalas would have made a grand spectacle of it, an occasion for furthering his own glory."

"You do not speak as one enamored of the Duke of Wester-Honce," Prince Midalis said with a chuckle.

"I heard many recountings of his return to the city with his prisoners," Al'u'met argued. "If these were indeed the same dwarves, and they were being taken out of Palmaris, then Duke Kalas would have done so with fanfare."

"Fair enough," the Prince replied. "Then they did escape from the dun-geons of Palmaris."

"Or they were released," Brother Dellman remarked. "An agreement between the Duke and the powrie leader?"

"You have reason to believe this?" Midalis asked sharply.

"Duke Kalas has been a friend to King Danube, the Prince's own brother, for all their lives," Liam O'Blythe said to Dellman, a clear warning to the man to take care with his words.

"A prisoner exchange, perhaps," Dellman remarked. "Whatever the case, I cannot dismiss my suspicions that if these powries sailed out of Palmaris, they did so under the guidance of the Duke or one of his high-ranking associates."

Midalis mulled that blunt statement over for a moment, then nodded. "I know not if I agree with your assessment, Brother Dellman, but I am glad that you did not speak of such possibilities in the presence of our barbarian friends. Andacanavar, and particularly Bruinhelde, have a much simpler understanding of how to deal with these monsters. One does not parlay with powries or goblins or giants. One kills them and moves on to the next."

"I am not sure that I disagree with that philosophy," Dellman remarked.

"But we do know that the world is a much more complicated place than that," Midalis went on. But though he spoke the words firmly, it seemed obvious to Dellman that he wasn't thrilled at the possibility that one of his brother's closest advisers and friends, the commander of the most elite force in the Honce-the-Bear military, was somehow in league with bloody caps. "If your suspicions have grounds, then I am certain that Duke Kalas had his reasons, and that those reasons were to the benefit of the kingdom," Prince Midalis finished.

To the benefit of the kingdom over the benefit of the Church? Brother Dellman wondered, for he remembered well how much Duke Kalas had gained in popularity after that *saving* battle on Palmaris' western fields and how well Kalas had then used his popularity against Abbot Braumin in their constant squabbles.

Midalis and his soldiers, Al'u'met and his crew, Agronguerre and the brothers of St. Belfour, and Andacanavar and the Alpinadorans kept a solemn vigil over Bruinhelde for the next few days.

And then, one quiet afternoon, the barbarian leader came out of the tent, limping badly but with the same determined expression that had earned him the position of respect among his clansmen.

Once again, Brother Dellman was reminded of how wisely Abbot Agronguerre had chosen, for Bruinhelde made a point of going to the old monk and warmly clasping his hand. Agronguerre had been spoken of as a potential healer for the wounded Church, and it seemed to Dellman as if they could not have found a better candidate.

The Alpinadorans hosted a great mead hall celebration that night—it never ceased to amaze the Vanguardsmen just how much of the drink these men could carry around with them!

All were in attendance, a night without tension, as Bruinhelde made a point of dismissing any thoughts of blame against Al'u'met or his men.

Brother Dellman, like everyone else in attendance, drank heartily, and it seemed to him as if his mug was more quickly filled—by both Brother Haney and Liam O'Blythe—than any of the others. He thought little of it, though, just enjoyed the drink; and by the time Liam and Haney came to him and took him by the arms, explaining that he looked as if he needed a walk in the nighttime air, the young brother was in no condition to argue.

They brought him out and walked him along the beach, down to the shore, and there they remained for a long time, as the moon Sheila made her slow pass overhead and the roars of laughter and cheers from the mead hall gradually diminished.

Leaning on the powrie boat, Dellman started to nod off, but then awakened, harshly, as Liam O'Blythe splashed a mug full of cold seawater in his face.

"What?" the monk sputtered.

"We know that ye came out to tell us o' the College," Brother Haney began, and only then did Dellman begin to understand how in league these two truly were. "And to take us there, so ye say."

"But what else're ye for, Brother Dellman?" Liam O'Blythe insisted.

Dellman, still groggy from the drink, looked at them both incredulously.

"Oh, tell us, ye fool, and be done with it," Brother Haney prompted. "Ye came to spy on Abbot Agronguerre, didn't ye?"

"Spy?"

"What're ye about, Brother Dellman?" Haney went on. "Ye tell us or we'll put ye in the water."

Dellman straightened and blinked the grogginess out of his bloodshot eyes. "Indeed," he said indignantly, eyeing the young Haney directly.

"Not to be hurtin' ye, just to cool ye off a bit," the other monk replied.

"Ye came to see what he was about," Liam O'Blythe reasoned. "That's me thinkin', and me Prince's, too. So what're ye about, mysterious Brother Dellman? Why'd yer abbot send ye halfway around the kingdom?"

Dellman merely shrugged, and his lack of denial spoke volumes.

"And what will ye tell yer abbot?" Brother Haney demanded, coming forward, but he hesitated, for now Brother Dellman was grinning.

"I will tell Abbot Braumin that Abbot Agronguerre is as fine a man as his reputation makes him out to be," Dellman explained. "I will tell Abbot Braumin that his nomination of Abbot Agronguerre for the position of father abbot would be a great service to the Abellican Church." There, he had said it, and he almost wondered if the dumstruck Brother Haney would simply fall over in the sand.

"Vanguard's loss'll be yer Church's gain, then," an equally stunned Liam O'Blythe remarked.

"Does he know?" Brother Haney asked.

"No, and you are not to tell him!" Dellman instructed. "I believe that Abbot Agronguerre should be informed of the entirety of the plan to nominate him by one more worthy and knowledgeable than either you or me. Abbot Braumin, or old Je'howith of St. Honce, perhaps."

"Suren he's got his suspicions, as we had ours," Liam reasoned.

Dellman nodded. "And he will know the truth of it, soon enough," he said. "Now promise me that you will say nothing to him."

Both men nodded, Haney wearing a silly grin, and that led to a toast, and to another, and when they ran out of mead, Liam O'Blythe ran back to the tent to fetch more, that their private celebration could continue long into the night.

CHAPTER
❖ 19 ❖

Practical Indifference

Master Bou-raiy had offered to send several younger brothers with De'Unnero on his journey, but he had flatly refused, both because he didn't need any of Bou-raiy's lackeys reporting back on his every move, and because he desired speed.

And Master De'Unnero knew how to travel fast. He fell into the weretiger, became a great cat under the glow of Sheila, and covered the miles more quickly than he might have even if he had been riding a fine horse. All those traveling hours were a trial for the monk, though, as every scent of every type of prey, of conies and deer, of cattle and sheep—and mostly of humans—drifted his way. He knew that to give in, to feast even upon the flesh of a squirrel, would defeat him, would allow the great feline spirit that had found its way into his corporeal form to take over his sensibilities: he would hunt down and devour a squirrel, and before he awakened again would find himself covered in human blood. He knew it, and so he fought it. And De'Unnero, so strong of will, again conquered the spirit of the weretiger.

He used the form of the great cat for transportation only, and in that guise covered as much as seventy miles in a single night. His first destination, on order of the masters of St.-Mere-Abelle, was to be St. Gwendolyn by the Sea, an important abbey, the fifth largest of the Abellican Order and the one housing the only women in the Order, the Sisters of St. Gwendolyn, named for a relatively minor martyr of the third century. De'Unnero's plan was to remain at St. Gwendolyn for as short a time as possible, then to catch a sailing boat out of the abbey's docks along the Mantis Arm coast, sailing south for Entel and St. Bondabruce, the residence of powerful Abbot Olin. De'Unnero was confident that he could get more cooperation and alliance from the man than from anyone at St.-Mere-Abelle, and so he was anxious to get there before Olin sailed for the College of Abbots. He thought he could make it if he could find seaborne transport at St. Gwendolyn.

After a week of hard travel, when he at last came in sight of St. Gwendolyn by the Sea, a white-walled abbey of soaring minarets, Master De'Unnero abandoned his plan, and knew from the scene about the abbey that all future plans would also be altered.

Inevitably.

For there, spread about St. Gwendolyn's grounds, De'Unnero saw the truth of Honce-the-Bear's future, saw the sickly masses huddled under torn tents in dirty robes, all the area about them full of waste and refuse and dead bodies.

That first image of the tarnished fields about St. Gwendolyn burned into the heart and soul of Master Marcalo De'Unnero, assaulted him as the worst, the very worst, sight he had ever witnessed, a prophecy of abject doom and despair, the proof positive that God had altogether abandoned his land and his Order.

No, the master thought. No, God had not deserted his Church, but his Church had surely deserted the ways of God. This foolishness with Avelyn, the murderer, the thief; this insistence—even by those who did not believe in Avelyn or Jojonah, or in the humanistic, sympathetic, and pathetically weak message that was being attributed to them—that the former, and perhaps the latter, as well, would be canonized! This ascension by Braumin and his cohorts to positions of almost dictatorial powers in the Order— voices they earned only because they happened to be on the right side when the secular forces of the kingdom destroyed the figurehead of their opposition! This general belief that the Abellican Church had to become a great nursemaid to the populace!

Yes, that was it, De'Unnero understood. The new Church leaders wanted to become as nursemaids, and so God was now showing them the folly of their beliefs, the weakness of their softened hearts. De'Unnero knew the old songs and children's rhymes. Like every brother indoctrinated into the Abellican Order, he had learned of the efforts of previous generations to try to heal those afflicted with the rosy plague, knew that only one in twenty could be healed, and that monks seeking such miracles would contract the disease and die, on the average of about one in seven attempts.

"Would Avelyn Desbris be among those running out with soul stone in hand?" De'Unnero asked himself, and he knew the answer well— knew that Avelyn, if he were alive and at St. Gwendolyn, would be out in that field even then, working tirelessly to try to save someone, anyone. Avelyn would be too ill to continue his efforts within a week or two, and he would be dead soon after. "Yes, Avelyn, and when you had died in such a manner, when they had thrown your body on the pyre so that your rotting flesh could not pass the disease to others, would they then call you a saint or a fool?"

In that moment, up on that bluff overlooking the field of wretches,

Marcalo De'Unnero saw things very clearly, saw the foolishness that had invaded his beloved Order, the selfishness of Pride and Arrogance, among the most deadly of sins, that had come into the seemingly generous hearts of those brothers calling for humanistic reform.

That was not the Church that Markwart had envisioned or had striven toward as father abbot. And though, in truth, Marcalo De'Unnero had been no enthusiastic supporter of many of Dalebert Markwart's visions, thinking them limited in scope, he recognized that the man had at least attempted to keep the Church on its rightful and righteous course, a path toward leadership, not friendship, toward instruction and not hand-holding.

They were the brothers of Saint Abelle, the mouthpieces of God, those whose concerns had to be the souls and not the bodies, whose compassion had to focus on the afterlife, not the present life. People suffered and people died every day, and in every conceivable horrible way. But that was not important, in De'Unnero's vision. Preparation for inevitable death was a process of cleansing the soul while the body rotted away; and this new vision of the Church, these hints that the errors of Avelyn would be ignored, that the man might be made a saint, this notion that the sacred gemstones were not exclusively the province of the Abellican brothers, that they were meant to alleviate the suffering—the physical and not the spiritual suffering!—all of it, screamed at Marcalo De'Unnero that his beloved Church had not only turned down the wrong fork in the road but also had turned completely around and was walking the path toward the demon dactyl and not toward God.

Marcalo De'Unnero knew at that moment of epiphany what he had to do, or at least, what he had to fight for. But how might he begin to bring it about?

He looked more carefully at the scene spread before him, at the scores, no hundreds, of huddled wretches, and at the long bed of various flowers— a tussie-mussie bed, it was called—that had been planted in front of the gates of St. Gwendolyn. The scholar brothers and the secular healers of the day, and of generations past, had come to the conclusion that the plague was spread mostly by the rotting smell of its victims; and the scents that could most effectively block that deadly odor were certain combinations of the various aromatic flowers.

De'Unnero glanced behind him, to the road that led to the main square of Gwendolyn village, which he saw nestled in a dell north of the abbey. He could picture the scene along Gwendolyn village's avenues, people walking with nosegays, smaller versions of the same floral combinations. People walking about with that telltale look of despair, of utter terror.

He kept his human form now, but De'Unnero ran full out down that road and into Gwendolyn. He purchased a nosegay from a market, flourishing despite—or actually, because of—the pall that lay over the town. Then he ran back to the bluff overlooking the field. For the first time since he had left St.-Mere-Abelle, De'Unnero wished that he had taken some gemstones, something to help get him by that desperate crowd, or to clear the way before him. Lacking that, the master fell into the tiger yet again, grimacing with the pain as his lower half transformed into the shape of the great cat, with muscled, powerful legs that could propel him away from any danger in an instant.

He checked the folds of his robes to ensure that the transformed limbs could not be seen, then went with all speed down onto the field, trying to circumvent the rabble. They came at him, the pitiful things, shuffling and wailing; but De'Unnero outran most, and when some circled to block his path to the monastery, the monk leaped on tiger legs, clearing them easily, landing lightly and running on, toward the tussie-mussie bed.

"Hold fast!" came the cry from the wall, and De'Unnero paused long enough to see several crossbowmen leveling their weapons his way. "None to cross the posies!"

"I am Master De'Unnero of St.-Mere-Abelle, you fool!" the monk roared back, and he charged on, right through the flower bed.

He heard the archers cry out again, to a couple of peasants chasing him, and then, to his satisfaction, he heard the click of their crossbows and the agonized cries behind him. At last, he thought, brothers with the courage to do the right thing.

The main gate of St. Gwendolyn swung wide and the portcullis beyond it cranked up, up, and De'Unnero skittered through, his smile wide, prepared to congratulate the brothers of St. Gwendolyn for their vigilance and willingness to do that which was right.

But he paused, stunned, for the scene inside the abbey courtyard nearly mimicked that without! Several brothers and sisters were stretched out on the ground under makeshift tents, moaning, while others peeked out at De'Unnero from various doors and windows or looked down upon him from the parapets. The portcullis behind the master slammed down.

"Where is Abbess Delenia?" De'Unnero barked at the nearest apparently healthy brother, a crossbowman on the parapet beside the gate tower.

The young monk shook his head, his expression grim. "We are without our abbess, all of our masters, and all but one sovereign sister," he explained. "Fie the rosy plague!"

De'Unnero winced at the grim news, for St. Gwendolyn had not been thin of high-ranking monks, as were some of the other abbeys. At the last College of Abbots, Delenia had brought no fewer than five masters and three sovereign sisters with her, and she had told De'Unnero personally that she had three more sisters nearing promotion to that rank, the equivalent of master.

"We unafflicted number fewer than fifty," the monk continued. "The plague caught us before we understood its nature."

"And how many have gone out to try and cure those diseased upon your field?" De'Unnero demanded. Though he was wounded by the near-complete downfall of St. Gwendolyn by the Sea, he transferred that pain into anger and neither sympathy nor sadness.

The monk shrugged and started to look away.

"How many, brother?" De'Unnero demanded, and a twitch of his legs lifted him up the twelve feet to the parapet, to stand before the stunned man. "That is how it entered your abbey, is it not?"

"Abbess Delenia . . ." the man stammered, and De'Unnero knew that his presumption had hit the mark perfectly. Never had Abbess Delenia failed in matters of sympathy, a weakness that De'Unnero considered general in her gender. She could debate and argue with the best minds in the Abellican Order, and she had been a friend to Abbot Olin; but De'Unnero had always considered Delenia sympathetic to Avelyn and even more so to Jojonah, for she had shown no stomach for watching the heretical master burn at the stake in the village of St.-Mere-Abelle.

"Convene all the healthy brothers and sisters in the abbess's audience chambers," the master instructed the scared young monk. "We have much to discuss."

Merry Cowsenfed walked past her stunned, sobbing companions to the body lying in the tussie-mussie bed, a man who had come to the field outside of St. Gwendolyn only three days before. He had lost his wife and two of his three children to the plague; and now his third, a young daughter, had begun to show the telltale rosy spots. Thus the desperate man had ridden hard, and then when his horse had faltered, had run hard, carrying the child nearly a hundred miles to get to St. Gwendolyn.

He wasn't even afflicted with the plague.

How ironic, it seemed to Merry, to see the healthiest one of the bunch of them lying dead on the flowers. She bent down and turned the man over, then spun away, dodging the flying blood, for the crossbow quarrel had broken through his front teeth, tearing a garish wound through the bottom of his mouth and into his throat.

Then Merry heard the cries, the pitiful screams of a child barely strong enough to hold herself upright. She came at the body then, barely five years old, half walking, half crawling, begging for her da. Merry intercepted the child, scooped her in her arms, and carried her away, motioning, as they went, for some others to go and collect the body.

"There ye go, child," Merry cooed softly into the frantic girl's ear. "There ye go. Merry's got ye now and all'll be put aright."

But Merry knew the lie, as well as anyone alive. Nothing would be put aright; nothing *could* be put aright. Even if the remaining monks—that new one who ran through the field, perhaps—came running out and offered a cure for them all, nothing would be put aright.

How well Merry Cowsenfed knew the awful truth! She looked down at her bare arm, at the scars left over from her fight with the rosy plague. She had been the one in twenty who had been saved by the monks and their work with the soul stone. Abbess Delenia herself had tended to Merry.

"One in twenty," the woman said, shaking her head. The monks had come out to tend dozens, dozens, yet only Merry had survived thus far. And so many of those brave and generous monks were now dead, the woman mused. Delenia and the sovereign sisters who had used their magic to help those from Falidean town. All dead, every one.

Delenia had pronounced Merry cured, and there had been great cries of rejoicing from the abbey walls, and Merry had been invited to go inside and pray. But the battered and weary woman understood the ridiculousness of the abbess' claims that she was healed, knew that nothing could be farther from the truth. Her body had survived the plague, perhaps, but her heart had not. She refused the invitation, preferring to stay out on the field with the rest of the group that had come in from Falidean town.

They were all dead now, Dinny and Thedo and all the rest, dead like her Brennilee, and not even in the ground with a proper coffin. No, just burned on the pyre—the first ones who had died, at least, for the pitiful folk had later run out of wood. The more recent deceased had merely been rolled into a hole in their dirty clothes, food for the worms.

Merry looked about the field now, at the empty eyes, the pleading expressions, at all of those who wanted so desperately that which Merry had found. They wanted the monks to come out and tend them, to take the disease away, because they thought that then everything would be put aright.

It would not, Merry knew, not for her and not for them. The rosy plague had come and destroyed her world, had destroyed their world, and nothing would ever be the same.

An older woman, bent and nearly choking on her own phlegm, came up and offered to take the child from Merry, but Merry refused, explaining that she'd tend this one.

The child died that same night, and Merry gently put her on the cart that came by to collect the bodies.

"She was the one ye should've tried to save, ye fools!" a frustrated and furious Merry yelled at the abbey walls a short while after that. She stood behind the tussie-mussie bed, shaking her fist at the silhouettes of the monks up on the parapets. "Ye fix the children, and they'll heal, body and soul. Ye don't be wastin' yer time with the likes o' me, ye fools! Don't ye know that I've got hurts yer stones canno' find? Oh, but where are ye, then? Ye've not been out o' yer walls in days, in weeks! Are ye just to sit in there and let us all die, then? Are ye just to stand on yer walls and shoot us dead if we come too close? And ye're calling yerself the folk o' God—bah, but ye're just a pack of scared dogs, ye are!"

"Who is the hag?" De'Unnero asked one of the other brothers, the trio standing atop the abbey gate tower, looking out over the field.

"Merry Cowsenfed of Falidean town," the young monk answered, "the only one saved by Abbess Delenia and the others."

"And no doubt at the cost of Delenia's own life," De'Unnero quipped. "Fool."

Raised voices from the courtyard behind and below turned the pair about.

"The sick brothers are not so pleased," the young monk remarked.

"They are without options," De'Unnero replied, for at the meeting of those still healthy within St. Gwendolyn, the master from St.-Mere-Abelle had forced some difficult but necessary decisions. All of the sick monks were to leave the abbey ground, to go out on the field beyond the tussie-mussie bed with the other diseased folk. De'Unnero had offered to bring the tidings to the sick monks personally, but several of the remaining sisters had asked to do it. Now they were down in the courtyard, carrying their warding posies before them, telling their sick brethren that they must be gone.

The argument continued to swell, with more and more of the diseased monks crowding by the sisters, shaking their fists, their voices rising.

"Surely you see the reason for this," De'Unnero called down to them, turning all eyes his way.

"This has been our home for years," one brother called back at him.

"And the others of St. Gwendolyn have been your family," De'Unnero reasoned. "Why would you so endanger your brethren? Have you lost all courage, brother? Have you forgotten the generous spirit that is supposed to guide an Abellican monk?"

"The generous spirit that throws sick folk out into the night?" the monk answered hotly.

"It is not a duty that we enjoy," De'Unnero replied, his voice calm, "nor one that we demand lightly. The salvation of the abbey is more important than your own life, and to that end, you will leave, and now. Those who can walk will carry those who cannot."

"Out there, without hope?" the brother asked.

"Out there, with others similarly afflicted," De'Unnero corrected.

There was some jostling in the crowd, a few shouts of protest; and the sisters who had delivered the tidings fell back, fearing a riot.

"I will offer you this one thing," De'Unnero called down, and he pulled a gemstone from the small pouch in his robe, a gray stone he had just taken from St. Gwendolyn's minor stores.

"Take this soul stone out with you and tend one another," De'Unnero went on. He tossed it down to the closest ailing monk. "You will show it to me each night, and inform me of its every possessor, for I will have it back."

"When we are all dead," the young brother reasoned.

"Who can speak God's will?" De'Unnero replied with a shrug, but it was obvious to him, and to all the others, that this group was surely doomed. They might find some comfort with the soul stone, but never would any of them find the strength to drive back the rosy plague. "Take it and go," De'Unnero finished, and his voice dropped low. "I offer you no other choice."

"And if we refuse?"

It was not an unexpected question, but the master's response certainly caught more than a few of the onlookers by surprise. He reached over to one of the nearby young brothers and pulled the crossbow from the man, then leveled it at the impertinent diseased monk. "Begone," he said calmly, too calmly, "for the good of your abbey and your still-healthy brethren. Begone."

The monk puffed out his chest and assumed a defiant pose, but others near him—correctly reading the grim expression on Master De'Unnero's face, understanding beyond any doubt that the fierce master from St.-Mere-Abelle would indeed shoot him dead—pulled the man back.

Slowly, without enthusiasm and without hope, the ailing brothers and sisters of St. Gwendolyn collected those who could no longer stand, gathered all the warm blankets and clothing that they could carry, and began their solemn procession out the front gates of the abbey.

"The walk of the dead," the young monk standing on the parapet beside De'Unnero remarked.

All the monks expelled from St. Gwendolyn were dead within the week, their demise hastened, De'Unnero regularly pointed out, by their feeble attempts to alleviate the suffering of one another. "It is akin to diving into the mud to help clean a fallen brother," De'Unnero explained to all of the healthy brethren at one of their many meetings. "Better would they be if they found healthy hosts that they might use the soul stone to leech the strength."

"But how many peasants might then become ill?" one of the sisters asked.

"If a hundred peasants gave their lives to save a single brother, then the reward would be worth the cost," De'Unnero insisted.

"And how many brethren sacrifices would suffice to save one peasant?" the same sister asked.

"None," came the harsh answer. "If one Abellican monk saved a dozen peasants but forfeited his own life in the process, then the cost would be too high. Do you place no value on your training? On your years of dedication to the highest principles? We are warriors, do you hear? Warriors of God, the holders of the truth, the keepers of the sacred stones."

"Beware the sin of pride, brother," the sister remarked, but before she had even finished the sentence, the fierce master was there, scowling at her.

"Do you believe that you can save them all, sister?" he asked. "Do you so fear death that you must try?"

That set her back a bit, as she tried to sort through the seeming illogic.

"We will all die," De'Unnero explained, spinning away from her to address the entire gathering, the remaining monks of St. Gwendolyn. "You," he said to one young monk, "and I, and he and he and she and she. We will all die, and they will all die. But we bear the burden of carrying the word of God. We must not be silenced! And now, when the world has gone astray, when our Church has wandered from the holy path, we—you brethren and I—who have witnessed the folly, must speak all the louder!"

He stormed out of the room, full of fire, full of ire, stalking through the courtyard and calling for the portcullis to be lifted and the gate to be thrown wide.

Outside, he found Merry Cowsenfed wandering about the flower bed, like some sentinel awaiting the arrival of death.

"With all them other monks dead, have ye and yer fellows decided to come out and help us again?" she asked hopefully when she spotted De'Unnero. "Ye got to help Prissy first, poor little one—"

"I came for the soul stone and nothing more," De'Unnero replied sharply.

Merry looked at him as if she had been slapped. "Ye can't be forgettin' us," she said, her voice barely a whisper. "The abbess and her friends—"

"Are all dead," De'Unnero reminded her. "Dead because they refused to accept the truth."

"The truth, ye're sayin'?" Merry questioned. "Is it yer own truth, then, that I should be dead and buried? The plague had me thick," she said, raising one bare arm to show the master her ring-shaped scars.

"The soul stone," De'Unnero insisted, holding out his hand.

"Ye got more o' them things inside, more than ye could need," Merry argued. "We're wantin' only the one."

"You could not begin to use it."

"We'll find one that can, then," said Merry. "If yerself and yer fellow monks aren't to help us, then ye got to at least let us keep the stone. Ye got to at least let us try."

De'Unnero narrowed his gaze. "Try, then," he said, and he looked to another nearby fellow, one obviously quite sick with the plague. "Go and fetch . . . what was the name?"

"Prissy," Merry answered. "Prissy Collier."

"Be quick!" De'Unnero snapped, and the man ran off.

He returned a few moments later, bearing a small girl, two or three years old. Gently he laid her on the ground near Merry, and then, on De'Unnero's wave, he backed off.

"She's near to passin'," Merry remarked.

"Then save her," De'Unnero said to her. "You have the soul stone, so invoke the name and power of God and rid her of the plague."

Merry looked at him incredulously.

"Now!" the monk roared at her.

Merry looked all around, very conscious of the growing audience, the many sick folk looking on from a distance and the many monks now lining the abbey's parapet and front gate tower.

"Now," De'Unnero said again. "You desire a miracle, so pray for one."

"I'm just a washerwoman, a poor—"

"Then give me the stone," De'Unnero said, holding forth his hand once more.

Merry reached into her pocket and did indeed bring forth the stone, but she didn't give it to De'Unnero. She clutched it close to her bosom and fell to her knees beside poor, sick Prissy. And then she began to pray, with all her heart and soul. She invoked every prayer she had learned as a child, and made up many more, words torn from her heart. She kissed the soul stone repeatedly, then pressed it to Prissy's forehead and begged for God to let her and the girl join, as she had done with Abbess Delenia.

Merry prayed all through the rest of the day and long into the night. Tirelessly she knelt and she prayed, and tirelessly did De'Unnero stand over her, watching her, judging her.

The dawn broke and Merry, her voice all but gone now, begging more than praying, still cried out for a miracle that seemed as if it would not come.

Prissy Collier died that morning, with Merry sobbing over her. After a long while, De'Unnero calmly reached down and helped the woman up.

"The soul stone," he said, holding forth his hand.

Merry Cowsenfed seemed a broken woman, her face puffy and blotchy, streaked with tears. Her whole body trembled; her knees seemed as if they would buckle at any moment.

But then she straightened and squared her sagging shoulders. "No, ye canno' take it from us," she said.

De'Unnero tilted his head in disbelief and a wry smile came over him.

"It did no' work with Prissy, but it will," Merry insisted. "It has to work, for it's all we got."

As she finished, she felt the sudden, burning explosion as De'Unnero's tiger paw swiped across her face, tearing the flesh. She felt the sharp tug on her arm next, saw her hand fly out and fly open.

Then she was falling, falling, and so slowly, it seemed!

The last thing Merry Cowsenfed saw on the field outside St. Gwendolyn was Marcalo De'Unnero's back as the monk callously walked away.

CHAPTER

❖ 20 ❖

The Bringer of Dreams

Down south, it was still autumn, but up here, in Alpinador and on the slopes of a steep mountain, winter had set in.

The stinging winds and snow hardly seemed to bother Andacanavar as he led Bruinhelde and Midalis. The ranger walked lightly, despite his years, despite the storm, as if he were more spirit than corporeal, as if he had somehow found a complete unity and harmony with nature—something made even more painfully obvious to poor Prince Midalis, trudging on, plowing through the snow up to his knees.

Bruinhelde's steps were even more strained, for the barbarian leader had not fully healed, and never would, the embedded arrowhead grinding painfully against his hipbone. Still, he had no trouble pacing Midalis, who was not used to such climbs nor such heights, for they were nearly two miles higher than Pireth Vanguard now, approaching the cave of the snow-crawler, the spirit shaggoth.

Finally, Andacanavar stopped and shielded his eyes with his hand, pointing to a windblown, rocky spur up ahead. "The opening," he announced.

Midalis came up beside the ranger, staring hard, but he could not make out any opening in the snow and rocks.

"It is there," Andacanavar assured him, seeing his doubtful expression.

"The home of the spirit shaggoth?"

The ranger nodded.

"How do you know?" the Prince asked.

"Andacanavar has walked this range for many years," Bruinhelde put in, catching up to them.

"But how do you know that the beast is still alive?" Prince Midalis asked. "How many years have passed since you have seen the creature?"

"As long as men are alive, the spirit shaggoth is alive," the ranger answered confidently. "With haste, now," he said, starting away, "before the night catches us on the open face."

There was indeed a cave entrance up ahead, though Midalis was practically on top of it before he even discerned it. Andacanavar led the way in, and they had to crawl beneath the low-hanging rock ceiling for some distance, along a dark, winding corridor—something that didn't bring much comfort to the Prince, with a legendary monster supposedly residing just within!

They came into a chamber, dimly lit by daylight creeping in through a small opening where the overhanging rock of the western wall overlapped a bit but did not join with the western edge of the floor. It was a small room, barely large enough for the three to get apart without bumping elbows, with only two exits: the one they had crawled through and another tight tunnel across the way, this one ascending at a steep angle.

Andacanavar methodically went about his preparations, building a small fire near that tunnel. He produced a hunk of venison, a thick and juicy steak, and set it on a spit above the fire, then sat back, fanning the smoke, letting the aroma of cooking meat drift up the natural chimney.

"Whetting his appetite," the ranger explained with a wink.

From his large pack, the ranger then brought forth the items the pair would need: two pairs of iron spurs, which angled downward rather than backward; a palm-sized ornate item of flint and steel; a metal pole tipped on both sides by lengths of chain; a pair of javelins, specially crafted to hook to the free end of each chain; and finally, reverently, a disc-shaped object wrapped in deerskin. The ranger put this on the ground before the three of them and spoke several prayers in his own tongue as he gently unfolded each layer of leather.

Prince Midalis stared at the revealed item curiously, at the beauty of the thing in light of the knowledge that it had been crafted by the fierce Alpinadorans. It was a burnished wooden hoop, holding within it what seemed like a spiderweb set with dozens and dozens of crystals, or diamonds, perhaps. In the very center, and suspended back from the web, was a single candle.

"What is it?" he dared to ask.

"Your only hope of getting out of there alive," the ranger answered with a wry grin. He lifted the hoop and the flint and steel, and with a flick of his fingers, created a spark that ignited the candle. Then he turned to face the other two, with the candle flame pointing toward him.

Slowly, Andacanavar moved the hoop, left and right. The crystals caught the candle's flame and reflected it and brightened it and bent it into different colors so that Bruinhelde and Midalis felt as if they were sitting in the middle of a brilliant rainbow.

"Behold Towalloko," the ranger said, and quietly, so that his voice did not break the mounting trance, "the bringer of dreams."

"Towalloko," Midalis repeated softly, and he was falling, falling, deeper and deeper into the web of colors and images, his mind soaring from the cave on the side of the mountain to a different place, a quieter and more peaceful place.

With a puff, Andacanavar blew out the candle, and Midalis' eyes popped wide as if he had just awakened from a restful sleep. He stared at Towalloko, trying to piece it all together. There was magic here, he knew, gemstone magic; and Andacanavar had spoken of the hoop as if it were one of the many Alpinadoran gods. And yet the Alpinadorans rejected the sacred stones outright and completely. Midalis furrowed his brow at the apparent contradiction. He stared hard at Andacanavar, seeking some explanation, but the ranger only smiled knowingly, and went back to sorting the many items.

Then the ranger explained, in precise detail, the procedure for this task that lay before the two leaders. The ritual of blood-brothering had ancient traditions in Alpinador, ever since the tribal ancestors, who worshiped the spirit shaggoth as the mountain god of snow, had captured the beast in this cave. Once, the feat of riding the creature had been a passage of manhood for every tribal youngster, but as the years had passed with many, many of the adolescent boys losing their lives or limbs in the attempt, the ritual had been moved to a more remote and even more special place in Alpinadoran culture, the blood-brothering.

This blood-brothering between Midalis and Bruinhelde, Andacanavar explained, would be the first in over a decade.

"And how did the last one end?" a clearly worried Midalis asked.

Andacanavar only smiled.

"You are not to harm the shaggoth," the ranger explained a moment later, "in no way, not even at the cost of your own life."

Bruinhelde nodded, his jaw set, but Midalis gave a doubtful smirk.

"Not that you could bring harm to the great beast anyway," Andacanavar said, his tone somber, "not even if you brought fine weapons in there with you. This is a test of your courage, not your warrior skills, and a test of your trust in each other. If either of you fails, then you both will surely die, and horribly."

Midalis wanted to remark that he doubted Andacanavar would risk such a loss, but he held the thought and considered, then, that the ranger would not do this thing, would not bring them here and risk so very much, if he didn't trust both Midalis and Bruinhelde. The Prince turned to regard this giant man who would become his blood-brother. In truth, he didn't care much for stubborn Bruinhelde, found him driven by honor to the point of callousness, but he did trust the man would keep his word. And in battle, in any test where he had to depend upon the honor of an ally, Midalis couldn't think of another man, except perhaps Liam, with whom he would rather be allied.

"Are you prepared to begin?" the ranger asked solemnly; and both men, after a glance at each other, nodded.

Andacanavar took a small pot out of his seemingly bottomless backpack, and then produced packets of various herbs from his many belt pouches. He poured them all together in the pot, added a little snow, and set it over the fire. Soon a sweet aroma filled the small chamber, permeating Midalis' consciousness with rainbow dreams and blurring images.

He felt light, as if he could glide on mountain winds. He felt sleepy, and then strangely energetic. He watched Andacanavar's movements as if in a dream, as the ranger took the venison off of the spit, then unhooked one chain from the metal center bar and skewered the venison upon it. He re-attached the chain and handed it to Bruinhelde. Then the ranger, with a final salute to both men, crawled back into the tunnel that had brought them to this chamber and began to sing softly outside.

Bruinhelde gathered a pair of spurs and began tying them on his heavy boots, and Midalis did likewise; then, without even a glance at the Prince, Bruinhelde collected the rest of the items and began crawling up the steep tunnel. Midalis, feeling as if he was simply floating up the shaft, followed closely.

The Prince couldn't see much through the smoke, but he sensed that Bruinhelde had exited the chimney, and then heard the barbarian's sharp intake of breath, as if in fear.

Fighting his own fears, reminding himself that Bruinhelde was depending on him, Midalis clawed up the last ten feet of tunnel, pulling himself onto the floor of a higher chamber, beside the barbarian. Midalis followed the man's gaze across this larger chamber to a light-colored mound on the floor. Midalis at first thought it was a pile of snow.

But then it moved, uncoiled, coming toward them slowly, sniffing. As his eyes adjusted to the light, Midalis could make out more and more of the creature—this shaggoth spirit—and it took every ounce of will he could muster not to simply dive back down the tunnel!

It resembled a great centipede, perhaps ten times the length of a man and thrice as thick, its wormlike torso gleaming white, with one line of glowing bright orange along its back. Even from this distance, Midalis could feel the heat of that stripe and realized that the spirit shaggoth used that hot strip to help it burrow under the snow.

It kept its monstrous head off the ground as it clattered toward them, its single, bulbous, black insectlike eye glittering eagerly from the middle of its flat face, and its many legs skittering. Midalis shivered at the sight of the creature's ample teeth: great elongated fangs and tusks, too large to be contained even by its considerable mouth.

"We go now," Bruinhelde whispered, and he thrust one of the chains into Midalis' hand. The Prince looked at it curiously for just a moment; but Bruinhelde was already moving, so he, too, leaped up, working rapidly to take up the slack.

The spirit shaggoth sprouted small white wings from the sides of its upper torso, beating them furiously to lift its head farther off the ground, raising its front quarter up, like one of the great hooded snakes of Behren.

And that eye! That glittering eye! Looking right through him, Midalis believed. He nearly lost all hope then, nearly threw himself on the ground before the mighty creature that it could kill him swiftly.

But Bruinhelde kept moving, and the barbarian's calm allowed Midalis to keep his wits about him. A moment later the pair, swinging their chains in unison, sent the skewered venison steak flying out before them, to land on the ground near the spirit shaggoth.

The creature eyed the meat curiously. Midalis heard it sniffing again and recognized the spirit shaggoth's nose was a mere hole in its face right below the bulbous eye.

"What if it does not strike the meat?" Midalis asked quietly, working, fastening his javelin to the free end of his chain, as was Bruinhelde.

The spirit shaggoth began to sway, back and forth. Hypnotizing movements, back and forth, back and forth. Andacanavar had warned them about this, had told them that to stare into that eye was to forget all plans, was to freeze in the face of the spirit shaggoth and be devoured.

Midalis glanced at Bruinhelde and saw the barbarian was standing perfectly still, staring at the creature. The Prince lashed out, punching the barbarian's shoulder. Then he and Bruinhelde both jumped in terror as the spirit shaggoth struck, taut muscles propelling the head forward with blinding speed at the venison and the bar, snapping it up.

"Now!" Bruinhelde yelled. Both he and Midalis launched their javelins past the spirit shaggoth's head, which was up high again, to the floor behind. Bruinhelde immediately brought forth Towalloko, snapping flint against steel to light the wick. Then he ran before the great beast, holding out the bringer of dreams, turning the ring slowly, slowly.

Prince Midalis knew what he was supposed to do—run past the distracted monster, scoop up one chain as a rein, and mount it, straddling the orange line of fire to catch the other chain. He knew that the sooner he went, the better their chances of success, and silently screamed at himself to move. But he couldn't bring his legs to action.

"Go!" Bruinhelde called to him.

Midalis tried to move. He thought of the disaster this day would bring if he did not go—if, because of his cowardice, Bruinhelde was killed, or they both were forced out in disgrace. What loss to Honce-the-Bear, to Vanguard, which had been saved by the Alpinadorans.

Yes, that was it, the image of St. Belfour besieged, of the goblins closing in on Midalis' small force. Surely those creatures would have destroyed the Vanguardsmen had not Bruinhelde and his clansmen come to their aid.

Now Midalis was running low in a crouch, his spurs crunching into the ice-covered floor or sparking whenever they struck bare stone. He tried to keep his movements fluid, to make no abrupt move that would break the swaying spirit shaggoth from its Towalloko-induced trance.

He came around the side of its swaying neck and saw the first chain on the floor. Then it seemed to him as if everything was happening in a dreamlike fog, his own motions slow, so slow! He gathered up the chain and leaped for the spirit shaggoth's back, planting one foot on the bony ridge separating the outer segments from that glowing orange stripe. Midalis didn't even consider the plain good luck that kept his foot securely in place, for to slip here and fall upon that superheated back would have melted the skin from his bones! Nor did he even consider his next motion, but quickly swung his free leg over that glowing stripe and planted his foot on the opposite bony ridge, then reached down low and scooped up the other chain.

Then he saw the many bones littering the chamber—whitened skulls and charred leg bones—and the Prince nearly froze in horror.

But he growled away his fear. In a moment, he was standing straight, holding the chains, frantically taking up the slack.

The spirit shaggoth turned suddenly to the left and reared even higher; and Midalis, thrown off balance, fell forward and just managed to throw his arm out and stop himself, his chest and face barely an inch from the glowing stripe.

He realized that Bruinhelde was moving, heading for a side exit, holding forth Towalloko, luring the creature out.

They went down a corridor and came out on a long, snow-covered ledge, with a thousand-foot drop to Midalis' left and a towering cliff face to his right. Now Bruinhelde scrambled out of the way, and Midalis was on his own.

Immediately, the spirit shaggoth began to tug and buck, but Midalis held the reins, keeping the creature's head high.

The Prince heard the wind in his ears as the creature ran down the length of the ridge, scattering the snow from the rock, its hundred feet clacking on the stone. At the far end, the Prince tugged hard on the right rein, bringing the creature around in a dizzying turn, and before he had even oriented himself, he discovered that they were almost back to Bruinhelde.

Now the barbarian put up Towalloko again, entrancing the creature. Prince Midalis found getting off the beast was even more trying than getting on, out here in the wind, where one slip could burn his leg or send him flying to his death.

He managed it somehow and went to Bruinhelde, taking Towalloko, keeping the mesmerizing rainbow working.

He retreated into the creature's chamber as Bruinhelde rode the beast the length of the precipice and back again, and was ready to catch the creature's attention and hold it as the barbarian dismounted and joined him.

Out of breath, hardly believing what they had just done, the pair slowly backed toward the chimney.

Without warning, the candle went out; the mesmerizing rainbow hues were no more.

Midalis knew beyond doubt that the creature would strike at Bruinhelde. He knew, too, that he could escape in a wild slide down the steep tunnel. But how could he do that to this man, his new brother?

He leaped in front of Bruinhelde—or tried to, for the barbarian, harboring the same thoughts, tried to leap in front of him at the same moment. They crashed together, Midalis' forehead smacking Bruinhelde's shoulder, their knees crashing together, and then they stumbled, certain that they were doomed.

The spirit shaggoth inexplicably missed the strike, as if their sudden movements and collision had confused it.

The pair scrambled all over each other, pushing each other toward the downward-slanting tunnel, then falling into it together, bouncing and tumbling, and finally crawling out the lower opening, to find Andacanavar waiting for them.

"A fun ride, then." The ranger laughed at the disheveled pair, for Midalis' forehead was bleeding and Bruinhelde was holding one knee. "We could go up and ride it again."

"With all our blessings," Midalis said, holding out Towalloko. "You go."

But Andacanavar only laughed again and led them out of the cave.

Midalis hardly noticed the first part of their descent, for he was lost in a haze of smoky dreams. Then, as his thoughts cleared, he found himself with a most profound headache, could feel his pulse throbbing in his temples. At first, he thought it the result of the collision with Bruinhelde, but when he looked at him, he found that the barbarian was similarly rubbing his head.

The herbal smoke, Midalis reasoned; and a strange notion occurred to him then. How much of this experience had been real and how much had been hallucination? Was there even really a creature within that cavern? And if so, was it as they had seen it, so terrifying, so mighty? Yes, that was it, Midalis thought. This whole experience had been naught but an elaborate deceit!

"What are you thinking?" Andacanavar asked, seeing Midalis' perplexed expression; but then the ranger exploded in laughter, and so did Bruinhelde.

Midalis stared at them both curiously.

Andacanavar, laughing still, produced a small sheet of polished metal and held it out to the man. "Your face," he explained.

Midalis took the mirror and held it up before him, then gasped and had to reconsider his assumption.

For the Prince's face was bright red, burned by his close encounter with the spirit shaggoth's back.

"You have some ugly monsters in Alpinador," Midalis remarked.

"We say the same of your women," Bruinhelde replied; and they laughed again, all three.

"You are brethren now," Andacanavar remarked in all seriousness.

Midalis and Bruinhelde nodded—each had willingly risked his own safety to save the other. Even in that moment of victory, the Prince wondered how his natural brother would feel about the newest addition to the family.

"I'm only eight years in the Church," Brother Haney said to Liam O'Blythe and Brother Dellman as they walked along the docks of Pireth Vanguard, toward the waiting *Saudi Jacintha*. "There be two brothers older than meself in all of Vanguard, not counting Abbot Agronguerre."

His doubts touched Dellman, for he had heard the rumors that had named Haney as Agronguerre's choice for abbot, if he was indeed elected father abbot. Haney wasn't of the correct age, of course, wasn't even a master, but such premature appointments were not unusual at all in Vanguard, where brothers were few. On occasion, St.-Mere-Abelle had been forced to send a master north to replace a fallen abbot. Given the turmoil in the southland these days, and the absence of masters and other high-ranking brethren, Dellman thought that unlikely. And if Abbot Agronguerre did indeed become father abbot, then his faith in Haney would likely secure the man's ascent as abbot at St. Belfour.

"Will ye come back to us?" Liam O'Blythe asked Dellman.

"My course is not my own to decide," the brother answered, then quickly added, "but if given the chance to name my road, it will indeed include Vanguard. Perhaps I will take my first appointment as master in service to Abbot Haney of St. Belfour." It was just the right thing to say, a remark that widened a smile on Brother Haney's face, and just the right time to say it, for they had come to the gangplank leading aboard the *Saudi Jacintha*, with Captain Al'u'met looking across at them approvingly. The three, their friendship forged that night on the beach, and grown since, joined hands then.

"Would that we had a jigger o' single malt to toast," Liam said with a wink.

Dellman looked at him curiously. "I have but one fear of returning to Vanguard," he said seriously, drawing concerned looks from his companions.

"I fear that I will begin to speak like you!" Dellman explained, and all three broke down in laughter and fell into a great hug.

"Ye do return to us, Brother Dellman," Brother Haney remarked as the man started up the gangplank. Dellman glanced back over his shoulder and nodded sincerely, for he had every intention of doing just that.

*   *   *

"And if I do not return—" Abbot Agronguerre began to Prince Midalis, the two standing in a side room off the docks of Pireth Vanguard while the *Saudi Jacintha* was readied for leaving.

"Then Brother Haney will be named as abbot of St. Belfour," the Prince assured the monk. "We are no strangers to succession, my friend. Is there an abbey more independent than St. Belfour in all Honce-the-Bear?"

"More renegade, perhaps," the abbot answered with a laugh, but his visage quickly sobered. "It pains me to leave Vanguard."

Prince Midalis, whose own heart was equally tied to this wild and beautiful land, understood. "You are called to serve, and there could be no better choice."

"We do not know the outcome," Agronguerre reminded him.

"But we do," the Prince insisted. "Your Church is not so foolish a body as to ignore the obvious. You will become the next father abbot in a month's time, and the world will be a brighter place because of it, though Vanguard will suffer without your wisdom."

"Somehow, I think that Vanguard will survive," the abbot remarked dryly. It was his turn to give a congratulatory pat on Midalis' shoulder.

It was true enough. Bruinhelde and the ranger had gone back to Alpinador, and the barbarian leader, though walking with an even more pronounced limp now, had left as a friend of Midalis, their bond forged in battle and in blood-brothering. It seemed obvious to all that the potential for true peace in Vanguard had never been greater. The way was open now for friendships among the people of the two countries, permission granted by respective leaders. A Vanguardsman who saw an Alpinadoran walking the southern roads could invite the man in for a meal and a bed without fear now, and an Alpinadoran who completed a successful hunt could now go south to find trade with the Vanguardsmen. Midalis and Bruinhelde had done all that up on that mountain, in the cave of the spirit shaggoth. They had become as brothers, bonded forever, and by extension, had bonded their kingdoms together.

Of course, the Prince continued to wonder with more than a little trepidation how his brother would receive these tidings, but it was a fear he easily suppressed. Vanguard was his responsibility—Danube had made that point all too clear by sending no help in their struggles against the demon's minions—and thus, it was his province to forge such necessary bonds. He still didn't understand the barbarians and their fierce culture, and didn't pretend that he did. But he did know, beyond doubt, that his beloved Vanguard was more secure, and that his people would live better lives because of the alliance.

"The world has changed much," Agronguerre remarked.

"For the better," Midalis replied.

"Perhaps," said the man who would be father abbot. "The passage of time will show us the truth. I wonder, though, need it take a war to bring about such change? Are we men creatures of habit, locked into routines and rituals that have long since lost their purpose, that have long since degenerated into worthlessness?"

"That is a proper question for any father abbot to ask," said Midalis. "That is the question of a visionary, of one not complacent with that which is but who seeks that which can be."

"I remember well when Father Abbot Markwart burned Master Jojonah at the stake," Abbot Agronguerre explained. "The man's one crime was to disagree with that which was, to seek that which he thought could be."

"You said that he allowed criminals into St.-Mere-Abelle."

Agronguerre shrugged. "Criminals?" he asked skeptically. "The woman Jilseponie, who has since been declared a hero, who came with Nightbird to rescue the centaur, Bradwarden, one of those who battled and destroyed the demon dactyl."

"Father Abbot Markwart could not have known that at the time of Master Jojonah's demise," Midalis reasoned.

"Could not, or would not?" Abbot Agronguerre replied, and he gave a resigned sigh. "I am not a visionary, I fear; and if they believed that I was, I would not now be considered for the position of father abbot."

"Then you will show them the truth," Midalis replied, but Agronguerre gave him a skeptical look, an expression that showed Midalis that the old monk wasn't certain of what that truth might be.

"You will follow your heart always," the Prince insisted. "You will do that which is best, not for you, but for your Church and for the world. That is my definition of a man of God, and the very best quality that anyone could ask in a father abbot."

To those claims, Agronguerre had no response, nor any doubts. He smiled warmly at his friend—this young, but so wise, Prince—and gave the man a hug, then turned for the docks and walked the first steps of the most important journey of all his life.

CHAPTER

❖ 21 ❖

Calm Captain in
a Stormy Sea

The mood was somber that Calember at St.-Mere-Abelle, where all the abbots and masters and many of the immaculate brothers had gathered for their second College of Abbots in recent years. That first College, wherein Markwart had declared Avelyn a heretic and had burned Avelyn's primary follower, Master Jojonah, at the stake, had been marked by excitement and action, with rousing speeches and grand rhetoric. But this one, though the times seemed more peaceful and the future in many ways more promising, was a quiet yet foreboding event. Two noteworthy absences—that of Abbess Delenia of St. Gwendolyn and that of Master Marcalo De'Unnero—had set the grim tone, especially when De'Unnero's messenger, a peasant, had arrived with the news of the tragedy at St. Gwendolyn.

Abbot Braumin and Master Viscenti spent their first hours at the great abbey enjoying a reunion with Brother Dellman, and it didn't take Dellman long to convince them that Abbot Agronguerre was indeed the best choice for the position of father abbot. Dellman spoke mostly of Agronguerre's easy temperament and of the man's handling of Bruinhelde and the other Alpinadorans.

"I have spent several months with the abbot," Dellman finished, "and I am certain that he was no lackey of Markwart. No, when Abbot Je'howith told you that Agronguerre was not pleased with the handling of Master Jojonah, he was speaking truthfully."

Abbot Braumin looked at Viscenti, who was nodding enthusiastically. "Abbot Agronguerre, then," he remarked, "and may God grant him the wisdom to lead us through these difficult days." Abbot Braumin patted Dellman's shoulder, thanking him for a job well done, and then rose to leave—to confer with Master Francis and then with old Je'howith, who had only arrived an hour earlier, obviously exhausted.

261

"There is yet another matter we must discuss," Brother Dellman remarked, his tone grave.

Abbot Braumin turned, studied the man for a moment, then took his seat.

Brother Dellman began this part of his report dramatically, throwing a bright red beret, a powrie's infamous bloody cap, on the table before his two companions. "It concerns Duke Kalas," he began.

As expected, Abbot Agronguerre of St. Belfour was quickly nominated and elected father abbot. Abbot Braumin and his followers backed him enthusiastically, as did old Je'howith and Master Francis, along with Bouraiy and Glendenhook and several others from St.-Mere-Abelle.

Abbot Olin of St. Bondabruce of Entel was not pleased, but as Abbess Delenia was dead, he could rally no real support for his own cause. Delenia's self-appointed successor, De'Unnero, surprisingly backed Olin in absentia, but that only seemed to hurt the man's chances even more.

So on a cold morning in God's Year 827, on the very first vote of the College, Abbot Fuesa Agronguerre of Vanguard became Father Abbot Agronguerre of the Abellican Church, the second most powerful man in all Honce-the-Bear.

He ascended the podium to offer his acceptance speech to moderate applause. Even his most fervent backers had voted for him only because they believed him to be a peacemaker, a fence-mender, someone who could appease both that group rooted in the traditions of the Church as expressed by Father Abbot Markwart and those followers of Avelyn Desbris, determined to reform what they saw as tragic flaws in the Church.

"As you know, I have spent almost all my long life in Vanguard," Agronguerre said, measuring his words carefully, after he had completed the formal regards to his hosts and a recitation of the virtues of Abbot Olin, his only competition for the position, that went on for nearly five minutes. "Many of you might wonder, then, if that experience—or lack of experience—might prove a detriment to me as I seek to lead the Church that is mostly based outside that isolated region. Put those fears in a hole deep and dark, I pray. Vanguard is not so different a place from St.-Mere-Abelle, and living among the small numbers of people up there has provided me an understanding of the world at large.

"I have served the Prince of Honce-the-Bear for many years now," Agronguerre went on, "as fine a man as I have ever known. With his guidance, the folk of Vanguard have forged an alliance, a bond of necessity, with the barbarians of Alpinador." That news brought more than a few surprised expressions and more than a few gasps and groans. The Abellican Church had a long and disastrous history with the Alpinadoran barbarians. Many times, the Church had sent missionaries, had even established minor chapels inside Alpinador; and every one of those excursions had ended disastrously, with missionary monks never heard from again.

"Our ways, our beliefs, our entire lives are very different from those of our northern neighbors," Agronguerre went on, "and yet we found strength in unity against the minions of Bestesbulzibar, curse his very name; and from that necessary moment of peace, we found more to agree upon than ever we would have believed possible. And so I see our current situation within our own Order. We are faced now with the task of understanding the tragedy of Father Abbot Markwart, his reign and his demise, and with understanding the truth of Mount Aida, and of Avelyn Desbris. How widely opinions differ on this point and on this lost brother, Avelyn! Some would proclaim him saint; others, heretic. But there is a truth out there, my brethren, one that we, as a united Church, must discover and embrace, wherever it leads us."

He went on for many minutes, recalling his own anger at the fate of Jojonah, speaking of Abbot Braumin and the others who claimed to have witnessed the miracle at the blasted mountain. He spoke of the relationship of Church and Crown, of the encroachment made on both independent forces in the battle-torn city of Palmaris, and the continuing struggle that Abbot Braumin now faced with Duke Kalas.

And then Agronguerre, after a pause and a most profound sigh, came around to the most pressing issue of all. He asked for a moment of silent prayer for Abbess Delenia, who had been a friend to so many of those in attendance and who had served the Church with honor and distinction for more than three decades.

"It appears that our hour of darkness has not yet passed," he said quietly. "Upon its discovery by Master Francis, the other masters wisely dispatched one of their own to the south to investigate rumors of the return of the rosy plague. Well, my brethren, those rumors seem well-founded. Master De'Unnero has reported the disaster at St. Gwendolyn, where the plague has devastated the ranks of our brethren, where pitiful refugees have crowded the fields around the abbey, begging for relief that we have no power to give. Let us pray, each of us, that the plague is restricted to that region, that it will not encompass the world as it did in centuries past, and that its presence in our time will be short indeed."

He finished with a recitation of the entire litany of prayers, where all the gathered brothers joined in, and then opened the floor for comments.

And how they came pouring in, opinions from every quarter concerning how the Church should deal with the rosy plague. Some called for the complete isolation of the Mantis Arm—though Francis was quick to remind them that Davon Dinnishire lay between St.-Mere-Abelle and Palmaris, far from there. Others called for the immediate isolation of every abbey, barring the doors, holding masses outside with presiding monks standing atop gate towers and the like.

On and on it went, with no practical answers, only suggestions wrought of abject terror. Father Abbot Agronguerre listened to them all attentively, hopefully, but all that he came away with was the understanding that this budding crisis was far beyond them, was something that only God could alleviate. The last call of that day, from the Father Abbot at the podium, was for all of them, for every brother in the Abellican Church and the few remaining sisters, to pray for guidance and for relief.

It seemed a meager weapon to the gathering of a Church that had just battled the armies of Bestesbulzibar, to monks who had used mighty gemstone magic to fell giants and powries by the score.

But it was all they had.

"I was no better a guest than you were a host, Father Abbot," a blushing Brother Dellman responded after Agronguerre spoke highly of him to Abbot Braumin that evening after vespers.

"You were more than a guest," the new Father Abbot replied. "In your short time in Vanguard, you became as family to us of St. Belfour."

Dellman searched for a reply, but merely bowed his head.

"Which is why I have asked you to join me at this time," Agronguerre went on to Dellman and particularly to Abbot Braumin.

"Brother Dellman's integrity and graciousness come as no surprise to me, Father Abbot," Braumin Herde replied, but there was an edge to his voice, telling Agronguerre that he understood where this was leading.

Given that, the Father Abbot got right to the point. "I know how valuable a companion Brother Dellman has been to you," he said, "and I do appreciate your work in Palmaris at this troubled and delicate time, but I have answered the call of my Church at great risk to St. Belfour. Brother Haney, who will soon become abbot of St. Belfour, is an excellent man indeed, and I could not have asked for a more suitable replacement."

"But . . ." Abbot Braumin prompted, looking at Dellman.

"He is all alone," Agronguerre answered. "Almost all the other brothers at St. Belfour are young and inexperienced, and though Prince Midalis is certainly a friend of the Church, the new alliance with the barbarians of Alpinador will place great demands on the abbot of St. Belfour. I think it prudent to give our young abbot a strong ally and a voice of experience and wisdom."

"Surely there are others m-more qualified than I," Brother Dellman stammered, obviously overwhelmed. His tone showed that he was not upset about the request, just stunned. "Masters from St.-Mere-Abelle."

"Abbot Braumin," Father Abbot Agronguerre said with a great sigh, "I know not in which of the masters here I can place my trust. Nor do I know any of them well enough to guess if they could tolerate the hardships of Vanguard. Master Francis comes to mind, of course, for he seems the most worldly of the group, but I believe from all that I have heard—from your own Brother Dellman—that I should keep Master Francis close at hand for a time."

"An assessment with which I heartily agree," said Braumin.

"Then?" Father Abbot Agronguerre asked. "Will you lend your friend Brother Dellman to Brother Haney and St. Belfour?"

Braumin turned to Dellman. "What say you, brother? This is your life we are discussing, after all, and I would say that you have earned your choice of abbeys. Will you return with me to St. Precious or sail north for Vanguard?"

Dellman seemed completely at a loss. He started to answer several times, but stopped and merely shook his head. "Which would be of greater service to my Church?" he asked.

"St. Belfour," Abbot Braumin said before the new Father Abbot could answer. He looked directly at Dellman as he spoke, staring into the younger man's eyes, showing his sincerity.

Dellman turned to the new Father Abbot and nodded. "I go where my Church most needs me, Father Abbot," he said. "And, truly, I would be glad in my heart to spend more time in Vanguard, to learn more of the folk and of the good brothers of St. Belfour."

"I will sorely miss him in Palmaris," Abbot Braumin remarked. "Brother Dellman was among the wisest of advisers and the most steadfast of supporters during the ordeal of Father Abbot Markwart's last days."

"You make my heart glad, then," the Father Abbot said, "and this will not merely be to the benefit of St. Belfour and our friend Brother Haney. Up there in wild Vanguard, you will attain the rank of master very quickly, perhaps within a few months."

"I am not nearly prepared," Brother Dellman replied.

"You are more prepared than most who attain the rank," Abbot Braumin was quick to put in, "and more prepared than I, certainly, in the role God has now chosen me to play."

"Vanguard is not thick with brethren," the Father Abbot said. "And St. Belfour at this time, as in so many times, is without masters. I will send word to Brother Haney to rectify that situation as soon as he is established as abbot."

Abbot Braumin nodded his agreement, his smile wide; and Brother Dellman, too, was beaming.

"Now for a less pleasing matter," Father Abbot Agronguerre announced. He rose from his chair, motioning for Abbot Braumin alone to follow him into an adjoining room, where several masters and abbots were waiting, including Francis, Bou-raiy, Glendenhook, and Machuso.

"I had asked Abbot Je'howith to join us, as well," Agronguerre remarked to them all, taking his seat at the head of the table and motioning for

Braumin to sit right beside him—again a subtle but distinct hint about his attitude concerning the last days of Markwart's reign. "But he has already departed, well on his way back to Ursal and St. Honce."

Abbot Braumin nodded, recognizing that he understood that departure better than did the new Father Abbot. Braumin knew, and Je'howith knew, that they now had gathered to discuss the disposition of Marcalo De'Unnero. Abbot Je'howith, so tied to Markwart, certainly wanted no part of this potential battle.

And it did become a battle, immediately.

"He has declared himself abbot of St. Gwendolyn," Master Fio Bou-raiy spouted angrily, "an unprecedented act of arrogance."

"Or of necessity," Master Machuso, ever the peacemaker, put in.

"St. Gwendolyn is traditionally led by an abbess, not an abbot," one of the lesser abbots argued.

"That may be true enough," Father Abbot Agronguerre conceded, "but by Master De'Unnero's words, there are no suitable women to take the position at this time. All but one of the sovereign sisters are dead, and the remaining one has become ill."

"Or had her heart removed by a tiger's paw," Master Bou-raiy remarked under his breath but loud enough for several seated near him, including Agronguerre and Braumin Herde, to hear.

"Interim abbot, then?" Machuso innocently asked.

"No!" Bou-raiy flatly declared, pounding his fist on the table. He turned to Agronguerre. "Deny him this, I beg of you. His record is one of destruction, and if the plague is thick in the southland, St. Gwendolyn will be key to holding the common folk loyal to the Church."

Surprised by the forcefulness of the master's argument, Agronguerre looked to Abbot Braumin, who, in turn, motioned to Master Francis. "You served beside him," Braumin said. "You know him better than any other in this room."

Francis narrowed his eyes as he stared hard at Braumin, obviously not pleased to be so put on the spot. "We were never friends," Francis said evenly.

"But you followed him to Palmaris and served in positions vacated by Master De'Unnero," Father Abbot Agronguerre reasoned.

"True enough," Francis conceded. "Yet I want it made clear here before I speak my opinion that you all understand that I harbor little friendship for Master Marcalo De'Unnero and that I would have preferred to remain silent on this matter.

"But I have been asked, and so I will answer," Francis went on quietly. "Master De'Unnero's record in Palmaris was less than exemplary. The people there would not have him back, I am sure."

"They would have him on a gallows," Abbot Braumin remarked.

"Indeed, I requested that he leave the city because his mere presence within St. Precious was bringing us disdain that bolstered Duke Kalas."

"But Master De'Unnero is not known in the region of St. Gwendolyn," Master Machuso pressed. "Can we presume that his actions in Palmaris were at the explicit instructions of Father Abbot Markwart and, thus, are mistakes that will not be repeated?"

"A dangerous assumption," Master Glendenhook replied.

"Am I to replace him?" Agronguerre asked distastefully. It was obvious to all in attendance that the gentle man did not want his first official act in office to be one of division. And yet, given the mood of all around him, of masters as diverse as Bou-raiy and Francis—obviously not in any alliance— what choice did Father Abbot Agronguerre have?

"Recall him," Master Bou-raiy said determinedly. "We will not find it a difficult task to find a more suitable abbot or abbess for St. Gwendolyn, I assure you."

That call was seconded by many about the table, including Abbot Braumin, who made a note to speak with the new Father Abbot at length about his true feelings concerning Marcalo De'Unnero—the man, in Braumin's honest opinion, who posed the greatest threat of all to the Abellican Church.

Father Abbot Agronguerre took in all the nods and calls with a resigned nod of his head. Yes, the year would end on a grave note, Agronguerre realized, and given the confirmation of the rosy plague, he doubted that the next year would be any better.

PART THREE

▾

THE QUIET
YEARS

Where is the balance, I wonder, between community and self? When does the assertion of one's personal needs become mere selfishness?

These are questions that followed me to Dundalis, to haunt me every day. So many hopes and dreams were placed upon me, so many people believing that I somehow magically possessed the power to change their world for the better. If I had fought that battle, I believe that not only would I have accomplished little, and perhaps nothing lasting, but also I would have completed the destruction of myself that the wretch Markwart began in the dungeons of St.-Mere-Abelle when he murdered my parents; that he continued on the field outside Palmaris, when he stole from me my child; and then, in Chasewind Manor, when he wounded me deeply and when he took from me my husband, my love. This was my fear, and it chased me out of Palmaris, chased me home to a quieter place.

But what if I was wrong? What if my efforts might have had some impact upon the lives of so many deserving innocents? What obligation, what responsibility, is then incumbent upon me?

Ever since I first witnessed Elbryan at his morning routine of bi'nelle dasada, *I longed to learn it and to understand all the lessons that he had been taught by the Touel'alfar. I wanted to be a ranger, as was he. But now, in retrospect, I wonder if I am possessed of that same generous spirit. I learned the sword dance, and attained a level of mastery in it strong enough to complement Elbryan's own, but those other qualities of the ranger, I fear, cannot be taught. They must be a part of the heart and soul, and there, perhaps, is my failing. Elbryan— no, not Elbryan, but Nightbird—so willingly threw himself into my battle with Markwart, though he was already grievously wounded and knew that doing so would surely cost him his very life. Yet he did it, without question, without fear, and without remorse because he was a ranger, because he knew that ridding the world of the demon that possessed the Father Abbot of the Abellican Church was paramount, a greater responsibility than that of protecting his own flesh and blood.*

I, too, went at Markwart with every ounce of my strength and willpower, but my motive at that time was not generosity of spirit but simple rage and the belief that the demon had already taken everything from me. Would I have been so willing to begin that battle if I understood that it would cost me the only thing I had remaining? If I knew that Elbryan, my dearest husband, would be lost to me forever?

I doubt that I would.

And now, with all those questions burning my every thought, I came north to the quiet Timberlands to find peace within myself. But this, I fear, is yet another of life's twisted and cruel paradoxes. I am moving toward inner peace now—I feel it keenly—but what awaits me when at last I attain that level of calm? When I find the end of turmoil, will I find, as well, the end of meaning? Will inner peace be accompanied by nothing more than emptiness?

And yet, what is the other option? The person who strives for peace of community instead of inner peace must find just the opposite, I fear, an unattainable goal. For there will always be trouble of one sort or another. A tyrant, a war, a despotic landowner, a thief in the alley, a misguided father abbot. There is no paradise in this existence for creatures as complex as human beings. There is no perfect human world, bereft of strife and battle of one sort or another.

I know that now, or at least I fear it profoundly. And with that knowledge came the sense of futility, of running up a mud-slick steep slope, only to slide back over and over again.

Will the new Father Abbot be any better than the previous one? Likely, since those electing him will be cautious to seek certain generous qualities. But what about the next after that, and after that? It will, it must, come back to Markwart, I fear; and, given that, how can I see anything more than the futility of sacrifice?

And, given that, how can I agree with Elbryan's gift of his own life?

And so here I am, in Dundalis, the place quiet and buried in deep snow as the world drifts into God's Year 828. How I long for seasons far past, for those early years when Elbryan and I ran about Dundalis, oblivious of goblins and demons and men like Father Abbot Dalebert Markwart!

Perhaps the greatest thing of all that has been stolen from me over these years was my innocence. I see the world too clearly, with all of its soiled corners.

With all of its cairns over buried heroes.

—JILSEPONIE WYNDON

❖ 22 ❖

Playing Trump

The snow was deep, the northern wind bitterly cold, but Abbot Braumin showed a distinct spring in his step as he approached the gates of Chasewind Manor.

The sentries at the outer gate held him in check for a long while, as he expected, and didn't even offer him the meager shelter of their small stone gatehouse nor any of their steaming tea. No, they merely eyed him, their stares as cold as the north wind; and Abbot Braumin, despite his fine mood, had to wonder if he could ever repair the damage Duke Kalas had done to the relationship of Church and Crown in Palmaris.

A short while later, the abbot was finally admitted to the main house, and there he was made to sit and wait yet again, as the minutes became an hour, and then two. Braumin took it all in stride, whistling, singing some of his favorite hymns, even coaxing one flustered servant into an impromptu penitence session.

That session—certainly not a welcome thing in the court of Duke Targon Bree Kalas—was interrupted almost immediately by Kalas' aide, bidding the abbot to enter and commence his business with the Duke.

Abbot Braumin muttered a little prayer for himself, begging forgiveness for so using the unwitting servant, and promised to attend his own penitence session once he returned to St. Precious.

"Good morn, God's morn, Duke Kalas," Braumin said cheerfully as he entered the man's study.

Kalas peered up at him from behind a great oaken desk, his expression one of pure suspicion.

Braumin took a long moment studying that scowl. It was no secret about the city that the Duke had been in a particularly foul mood of late; and Braumin could guess the source of that discontent. Many of Ursal's nobles were no doubt wintering in Entel or at Dragon Lake, a favored winter palace, while he was stuck up here, in the bitter Palmaris winter, alone and without any close friends.

Even many of the stoic Allheart knights were beginning to shows signs of discontent, of homesickness.

"It is morning," Kalas replied gruffly, shuffling some papers and nearly overturning his inkwell, "and I suppose that every morning is God's to claim."

"Indeed," Braumin said, intentionally making his tone annoyingly chipper.

"Whatever concept of God one might hold," Duke Kalas continued, narrowing his eyes.

"Ah, the purest concept of all," Braumin answered without the slightest hesitation. He tossed a rolled parchment on the desk in front of Kalas.

Still eyeing Braumin suspiciously, the Duke picked it up and slipped the ribbon from it. He snapped it open with a swift, sudden movement, his eyes scanning, scanning, while he tried to hold his expression steady. Then, finished, he simply dropped the parchment back to his desk and sat up straight, folding his hands together on the desk before him. "A chapel for Avelyn Desbris?" he asked.

"In Caer Tinella," Abbot Braumin said cheerfully, "with the blessing of new Father Abbot Agronguerre—a good friend of your King's brother, I understand."

Kalas, well aware of Prince Midalis' relationship with the Abellican Church in Vanguard, didn't blink. "How steady is your Church, Abbot Braumin," he remarked. "First you claim Avelyn a heretic, now a saint. Do you so sway between good and evil? Do you worship God today and a demon tomorrow, or in your eyes are they, perhaps, one and the same?"

"Your blasphemy does not shock me, Duke Kalas," Braumin replied, "nor does it impress me."

"If you believe that I have any desire to impress you, or any of your clergy leadership, then you do not understand me at all," came the confident and firm answer.

Abbot Braumin gave a slight bow, conceding the point, not wanting to go down this tangent path.

"I have no jurisdiction over Caer Tinella," the Duke of Wester-Honce went on. "You should be throwing your writ upon the desk of Duke Tetrafel of the Wilderlands."

"I need not the permission of the Crown or any of its representatives to begin construction of the chapel of Avelyn in Caer Tinella," Abbot Braumin returned.

"Then why come here?" asked Kalas. "Do you mean to taunt me by flaunting the expansion of your Church? Or to convince me, perhaps, that your way—the Light of Avelyn, I am hearing it called—is the one true way, and that Markwart and all the evil he wrought was but an aberration, a corrected mistake?"

"I inform you of the construction of the new chapel in Caer Tinella merely as a courtesy," Abbot Braumin answered. "I intend to use masons from Palmaris for that work, and for the expansion of St. Precious."

Kalas was nodding, obviously bored, and it took a long moment for that last part to even register. He snapped his glare up at Abbot Braumin, his eyes again going narrow and threatening. "We have already settled this matter," he said.

"What is settled in one moment might be altered in another," Braumin replied.

Kalas just stared at him.

"There is new information," the abbot said.

"You have found a way around the law?" Duke Kalas asked skeptically.

"You decide," Abbot Braumin replied, with equal confidence. "Brother Dellman told me of a most unusual encounter up in Vanguard, Duke Kalas: a battle fought with powries."

"Not so unusual in these troubled times," Kalas replied, glancing at the lone sentry in the room, an Allheart knight, standing at attention to the side of the great desk.

Abbot Braumin studied the Duke carefully, looking for any signs of unintentional personal betrayal, as he continued. "Apparently, these powries had some trouble with their ship."

"A barrelboat?"

Now it was Abbot Braumin's turn to glance at the Allheart knight, then questioningly back to Kalas.

The Duke caught the cue. "Leave us," he instructed the knight. The man looked at him curiously, but then snapped a chest-thumping salute and strode from the room.

"Palmaris ship," Braumin said bluntly as soon as the door had closed, and he paused and let the notes of that devastating information hang in the air. Kalas did shift in his seat then, and Braumin imagined the man fighting an inner struggle at that moment. Should he feign ignorance? Or should he concoct some wild tale of escape?

The Duke folded his hands but did not sit back comfortably in his chair, a clear sign to Braumin that his words had intrigued the man and, perhaps, had scared him.

"A curious thing," Braumin went on, his tone now casual. "Brother Dellman insists that he recognized one or two of the powries."

"They all look alike, so I have observed," Duke Kalas said dryly.

"Though some might carry remarkable scars or wear distinctive clothing," Abbot Braumin remarked.

Duke Kalas sat very still, staring, probing; and Braumin knew that he had hit the man squarely, that Brother Dellman's beliefs about the origins of the powrie band in Vanguard had been right on the mark. And now, given

Kalas' reactions, Abbot Braumin knew that the powrie band had not escaped from Palmaris. Duke Kalas had a secret, a very dark one.

"And where does your Brother Dellman believe he once saw these same powries?" Kalas asked, again in dry and seemingly unconcerned tones. But again, a subtle shift in his seat betrayed his true anxieties.

"He cannot yet be certain," Abbot Braumin replied, emphasizing the word "yet." "He envisions a misty and drizzly morning. . . ." He let his voice trail off, the threat to Kalas hanging obvious and ominous.

The Duke stood up suddenly. "What games do you play?" he asked, walking to the side of his desk to a brandy locker with, Braumin noted, a rather large sword hanging over it. The Duke poured himself a drink and motioned an offer to Braumin, who shook his head.

Kalas swirled the liquid in his glass a couple of times, then slowly turned, half sitting on the edge of the locker, his expression calm once more.

"If you have more to say, then speak it clearly," he bade the abbot.

"I doubt there will ever be more to say," Braumin replied. "I will be too busy with the construction of the chapel of Avelyn in Caer Tinella and with the expansion of St. Precious."

There it was, laid out clearly and simply.

Duke Kalas sat very still for a long while, digesting all of the information, sipping his drink, then swallowing it suddenly in one great gulp. He threw the glass against the wall, shattering it, and rose up so forcefully that the heavy locker skidded back a few inches.

"You have heard of the word 'extortion'?" he asked.

"You have heard of the word 'politics'?" Braumin came right back.

Kalas reached back and above him and tore the sword from the wall, bringing it out before him. "Perhaps a personal meeting with your God will teach you the difference between the two," he started to say, but he stopped, staring curiously, as Abbot Braumin presented his hand forward, palm up, revealing a small dark stone, a graphite, humming with power.

"Shall we see which of us God chooses to take and instruct this day?" he asked, a wry, confident smile on his face; though in truth, his guts were churning. Braumin Herde had never been a warrior, nor was he overproficient with the gemstones. With his graphite, he could bring forth a small bolt of lightning, but he doubted it would do more than slow fierce Kalas for a few moments, and perhaps straighten a bit of the curly black hair on the man's head.

But still, Braumin was not surprised by this sudden turn, not at all. His quiet accusation against Kalas was no minor thing, after all!

And so he was ready for this moment, had prepared himself extensively, and he stood perfectly still, hand up firm.

"You play dangerous games, Abbot Braumin."

"Not so, Duke Kalas," Braumin replied. "We each use whatever means we must to further that cause in which we believe. The revelation of a supposed dark secret, perhaps, or a battle on a foggy morning."

"And what cause will you further?" Kalas spat.

"St. Precious will be expanded," the monk replied. He lowered his hand as Kalas lowered his sword.

"That is all?"

"That is all." Braumin Herde didn't add "for now," but he saw from Kalas' sour expression that the Duke understood the implication well enough. Abbot Braumin had a heavy sword now, hanging in the air above the head of Duke Targon Bree Kalas, and Kalas' own inability to dismiss the hints as preposterous were all the proof that Braumin needed to know that what Dellman suspected was true: Duke Kalas of Wester-Honce, perhaps the closest adviser in all the world to King Danube Brock Ursal himself, had utilized powries, wretched bloody caps, in his quest to strengthen the power of the Throne in Palmaris.

Abbot Braumin's step as he exited Chasewind Manor soon after was— surprisingly to him—not as boisterous as the ones that had brought him to the place, though he had the signed approval for St. Precious' expansion tucked safely under one arm. No, Braumin found the whole business of coercing Duke Kalas a most distasteful affair, and he prayed that he would never, ever have to repeat it.

But he would visit the man again, if need be, the abbot assured himself. His life had purpose and a direct path, and he swore then on the soul of Master Jojonah—his mentor, his dearest friend—that he would continue the good fight.

"Lady Pemblebury approaches," the sentry in the hall announced.

Abbot Je'howith crinkled his old face at the proclamation, but King Danube couldn't hold back a smile.

"You have not made the open declaration yet," Je'howith reminded him. "Whispers speak that the coming child is yours, of course, but word has not been sent, nor has your decision concerning the status of the child."

"I did not know that anything was required of me," Danube replied sarcastically, for he was the king, after all, and his word, whatever that word might be, was law in Honce-the-Bear.

"I only wonder what your brother might come to think if those whispers reach his ears," Je'howith said; and that did indeed give Danube pause. "The new Father Abbot is of Vanguard, and a friend to Midalis. It seems likely that the region will be more closely tied to the rest of the kingdom now, with Agronguerre leading the Church."

"And perhaps those of your Church are not well versed in discretion," Danube retorted.

"The only brother who returned to Vanguard from the College of

Abbots was young Dellman, no friend of mine, I assure you," Je'howith came back. "If Brother Dellman has brought news of Constance Pemblebury's condition, then he learned it from someone else."

"The same Dellman from Palmaris?" King Danube asked, for he remembered well Braumin Herde and his little group of imprisoned companions.

Je'howith nodded.

"The same Dellman who is friend to Jilseponie?" King Danube asked.

Abbot Je'howith raised an eyebrow at that and at the way Danube spoke the woman's name. Apparently, that little spark Je'howith and others had seen up in Palmaris continued to burn. Constance, beginning her eighth month of pregnancy, would not enjoy the sight of that simmering flame.

Constance Pemblebury entered the room then, waddling more than walking, one hand supporting her lower back. Her look was not one of a woman in pain, though, but of a woman fulfilled and in bliss.

King Danube went to her immediately and brushed aside her attendant, taking her by the arm and guiding her to a seat in the audience room's only chair: the throne.

How ironic, old Je'howith mused.

"You do realize, my King," the old monk said, grinning wryly, "that the Church must openly frown on our monarch producing a bastard child."

King Danube turned and scowled at Je'howith, but Constance laughed. "How unprecedented!" she said with complete sarcasm, and then she groaned and winced.

Danube turned to her immediately, feeling her swollen belly, putting a gentle hand to her forehead. "Are you all right?" he asked.

Je'howith studied the man, his movements, and the tone of his voice. Gentle, but not loving. He did care for Constance, but Abbot Je'howith recognized at that moment that Danube would not likely marry the woman, not while images of the fair Jilseponie danced in his head.

Constance assured him that she was feeling quite well, and Je'howith seconded that sentiment, guiding the doting Danube away from her. "She has two months yet to go," the old abbot reminded him.

"And then comes our child," Constance remarked.

"My son," Danube agreed, and again Constance beamed.

To hear Danube speaking of the child with such obvious pride fostered her hopes, Je'howith realized. And what of those hopes? the cleric wondered. What course would King Danube take once the child, his son, was born? Would he employ the Denial of Privilege, as they had discussed, or would he be so overwhelmed by the birth of this child that he would accept it openly?

Wouldn't Prince Midalis be thrilled if that came to pass!

Je'howith couldn't contain a chuckle, though when Danube and Constance looked at him, he merely shook his head and waved his hand dismissively. In truth, the old abbot hardly cared which way King Danube chose to go concerning the child. Certainly, if he did not disavow the child's bloodline rights, the kingdom could be in for a difficult and messy transition, but that would not likely affect Je'howith, who would probably be long dead by that time. And if King Danube did openly accept the child, keeping the babe, and thus, Constance, at his side, then the possibility of Jilseponie ever getting close to Je'howith's beloved Ursal seemed even more remote.

In either case, this situation could be getting all the more interesting in about two months' time.

Abbot Je'howith fought hard to contain another chuckle.

Abbot Braumin was surprised and quite pleased to see the visitor to St. Precious that day. He was a handsome man of about Braumin's age, with a slender but hardened frame and alert dark eyes that took in every detail of the room about him. He was a military man, obviously, trained in readiness.

The snows had continued heavy that winter, but word had come to Abbot Braumin that Duke Kalas had left Chasewind Manor, and the city altogether, for a trip to the south. And now this, an old friend, the return of a good man who had shared some very important moments in Braumin Herde's life. Yes, the year was off to a grand start.

"Shamus Kilronney," the abbot greeted him warmly. "I heard that you had resigned your post in the Kingsmen and traveled south."

"Not so far south, my friend, Brother—Abbot Braumin," Shamus Kilronney replied. He looked around appreciatively. "You have done well, and are deserving of all that has befallen you of late."

Braumin accepted the kind words with a nod and a smile. Shamus had been with him on that journey to the Barbacan, when the goblins had encircled them, closing in. Shamus Kilronney had stood tall and proud, prepared to die, when the miracle of Avelyn's upraised, mummified arm had sent forth waves of energy to destroy the goblin horde.

Shamus had been beside Braumin again on a second occasion in that same place, when King Danube and Father Abbot Markwart had marched in with their respective armies to take them as prisoners.

In truth, the two men hardly knew each other, and yet they had forged a deep bond in trials shared and miracles witnessed.

"The sky is thick with snow," Abbot Braumin remarked. "Why does Shamus Kilronney return to us at this unlikely time?"

"Duke Kalas bade an Allheart knight named Mowin Satyr to serve in his stead while he returned to the court at Ursal at the summons of King Danube," Shamus explained. "Satyr is an old friend of mine, and he knew that I have family within the city, so he bade me to come and aid him."

"Colleen?"

"She is north, in Caer Tinella, I have heard," Shamus replied.

"Well, I am glad that you have returned," Abbot Braumin said, motioning for the man to follow him to more comfortable quarters. "You may be aware that the relationship between Church and Crown in Palmaris has not been a good one since the events at Chasewind Manor."

"Duke Kalas has never been fond of the Church," Shamus remarked, "at least not since Queen Vivian became ill and died, and the brothers of St. Honce could do nothing to save her. You will find Mowin Satyr more agreeable, I believe."

"For however long he might serve."

"It could be some time," Shamus explained. "That is why I have come to you. Duke Kalas claimed that he was summoned to Ursal, but none of those remaining at Chasewind Manor know anything about that. Nor, according to Mowin Satyr, is he planning on returning to the city any time soon, perhaps never."

Abbot Braumin couldn't help but smile and shake his head. He couldn't believe how effective his hints concerning the powries had been, further confirmation to him that Kalas had indeed engaged in some sort of under-the-table dealings with the bloody caps. He poured himself a glass of wine and one for Shamus, then handed it over.

"To a better relationship between Church and Crown," he toasted, lifting his glass, and Shamus was quick to tap it with his own.

"I wonder," Abbot Braumin mused aloud a moment later. "Perhaps there is something more you might do for me, my friend, if you are willing."

"If I might," Shamus said.

"Inquire of your friend Mowin Satyr of a battle that was fought on the western fields before King Danube departed the city, around the Calember before last."

Shamus looked at him curiously.

"He will know the fight," Abbot Braumin assured the man, "a quick and easy victory over a powrie band."

"I will ask," Shamus agreed, looking at the monk curiously. "But I say this now, my friend Abbot Braumin, I will not serve as a spy for St. Precious. I have come back to Palmaris because an old friend needed me, and I will do all that I can to bring a better peace between you and whoever is ruling at Chasewind Manor. But I will play no role in this continuing intrigue between St. Precious and Chasewind Manor."

"Fair enough," Abbot Braumin replied. He lifted his glass in toast again, and again, Shamus Kilronney was quick to tap it with his own.

Yes, God's Year 828 was off to a grand start.

❖ 23 ❖

Doc'alfar

Too many wonders have I seen! the man wrote, the edges of many parchments hanging raggedly about his open pack. *Oh, for the eyes of one man to so engulf the splendor of the untainted world! What a true blessing God has bestowed upon me, humble Tetrafel, to grant me these visions. And the world will long remember me, I am sure, for when the kingdom of Honce-the-Bear engulfs these western Wilderlands, the wonders they will see—the gigantic waterfalls, the majestic mountain peaks, the forests so thick that beneath their canopy dwells eternal twilight—will be made all the more wondrous by their recollections of these, my words.*

The Duke of the Wilderlands glanced up from his parchment to scan the workings of his encampment, the many servants and soldiers going about their typical late-afternoon routines, preparing the tents and the meals, setting up the perimeter guard—and that line of sentries had proven most necessary in the three years Tetrafel and his fellow explorers had been out far to the west of Ursal, in untamed, unmapped lands, seeking a direct pass through the towering Belt-and-Buckle Mountains into the To-gai steppes of western Behren. King Danube desired a direct trading route with the To-gai clansmen, without the costly interference of the Behrenese merchants.

The initial reluctance of Tetrafel, a man of nearly fifty years, who spent more time on a large pillow than on a horse, to accept the offered mission had been washed away by a grander vision that had come to him. He would be the explorer who opened up the vast western Wilderlands, a region known to be rich in natural resources, towering trees, and coveted peat. Once Danube had agreed to send along a large contingent of soldiers—nearly a score now traveled with the Duke—and a similar group of servants—several men and a few young women who would also see to other needs—Tetrafel had recognized the opportunity to bring himself a bit of immortality.

Now, after three years, the man did not regret his decision, not on this particular day, at least, when he and his companions had easily traveled nearly twenty miles along a huge river—a river the Duke planned to name the Tetrafel—to find, at its end, the most tremendous, stupendous waterfall they had ever heard tell of: Tetrafel Falls, of course.

There had been troubles in the three years, mostly in the form of huge bears, great cats, and other beasts. They had found one tribe of goblins, but their superior training and weaponry enabled them to summarily destroy the ugly creatures; and a fairly indelicate disease had caught up with them several times. But after three years, they had lost less than a handful of their band, including just two soldiers.

All that they had to do now, Tetrafel realized, was find a pass through the mountains when spring opened the trails, and then return to Ursal, heralded as the greatest explorers of the modern age, their names, Duke Timian Tetrafel's at least, etched in tomes and stamped indelibly upon natural and majestic wonders. And finding that pass did not seem like such an impossibility, now that they had gone even farther west, to a point, Tetrafel believed, where crossing the mountains would put them in western To-gai. The peaks were not nearly as towering here, and were wider spaced. The higher elevations still showed snowcaps, though down in the foothills, the winter here was no worse than in Ursal, with the occasional inch or two of snow, but inevitably followed by milder weather that soon cleared the ground.

They were not in sight of the great River Tetrafel now, but they could hear the thunder of the distant falls. For their campsite, they had chosen a small clearing within a ring of towering pines, high natural walls so thick that they blocked out the light of Sheila completely as the moon rose in the east; and they knew that they would see only the slightest hints of the glowing orb until she climbed high in the sky, nearly directly overhead.

The camp was quiet and organized, with the occasional bursts of laughter from one quarter or another, or more embarrassing sounds from under the boughs of a nearby pine, where a soldier and a servant had stolen off to pass the hours. Dinner was not an organized and set event in Tetrafel's camp, but rather a personal option of wandering over to the large cook pots and scooping a bit of broth, or walking by one of the many spits and tearing a limb from whatever creatures the huntsmen had managed to bag that particular day.

Secure in his sentries and satisfied that he had entered enough in his all-important diary that day, Duke Tetrafel headed for the cook fires. He started for one of the pots, but changed his mind and went to the roasting deer instead, tearing off a huge hunk of meat, dropping as much to the ground as found its way to his mouth.

His actions were not unnoticed.

In a tree not so far away, and well within the set perimeter of the encampment, a pair of slender, white-skinned, blue-eyed humanoids with hair the color of ravens' wings, sat quietly—perfectly quietly—upon a pine branch, studying the scene before them.

They care nothing for the creatures they slay, one of them motioned to the other in an intricate combination of hand gestures, eye movements, and facial and body expressions.

Nor for the spirituality of the mating dance, the other, equally disgusted, returned, a point made even more acute by the grunting sounds from a copulating couple on the ground beneath them. *They are killer animals and nothing more.*

The other nodded his agreement. *"Twick'a pwess fin,"* he whispered in the tongue of the Doc'alfar, a language not unlike that of the Touel'alfar, distant, unknown cousins of the wingless, white-skinned elves.

"Twick'a pwess fin," the other echoed in agreement, which translated into "a fitting end."

Then they were gone, as silently as they had arrived, slipping past the lumbering sentries with no more noise than a shadow.

"Curse the rotten luck," one sentry muttered, for the wind shifted later that night, bringing the fine spray thrown high into the air by the distant falls over the field and the encampment.

"Not so bad," his companion replied from a short distance away. "Stay close to the pines; they'll keep ye dry."

"A warm bed in Ursal'd keep me drier," the first returned. "Are we ever to get back there?"

"The Duke's seeing a chance to put his name on mountains," the second replied. "But we're all to gain, and if we find the pass, Tetrafel's promised us enough gol'bears to each buy a grand house."

The other nodded, and that promise did seem to warm his weathered bones. But the spray continued, filtering through the trees as a fine, cold mist. And then a foul, rotting odor accompanied it.

"Now what's bringing the stink?" the first sentry asked, crinkling his nose.

"Smells like a carcass," said the other. "Could be a great cat coming back from a hunt. Get on yer guard now!"

And they both did, setting arrows to their bowstrings and peering into the gray, misty moonlight.

The stench got worse, filling their nostrils, making their eyes run; and then they saw a shape, not of a great cat, but of a humanoid—a man, it seemed—walking stiff-legged through the mist and the sparse underbrush.

"Hold where ye are!" the first sentry commanded. "Ye got two bows aiming at ye!"

Now they did recognize the approaching form—he was barely a dozen strides away—as a man, skinny and grizzled, with long hair and a huge beard. He had to have heard the command, they knew, but he kept on coming in that stiff-legged gait, his arms straight out before him.

And he was filthy! Covered in dirt, or peat, and smelling like a rotting and dirty carcass.

"Hold now! I'm warning ye!" the sentry commanded.

He kept on coming; and the sentry, a trained and seasoned soldier, followed his orders to the word and let fly his arrow. It hit the approaching man's chest with a dull splat, and burrowed in deep, but the man kept coming, didn't even flinch!

"I hit him! I hit him!" the confused sentry protested; and now his companion let fly, a shot that took the intruder in the side, just below the rib cage, a shot from a bow so strong of pull that the arrow disappeared completely into the body, its tip breaking through the other side.

The approaching man flinched, the sheer force of the blow knocking him a step sideways. But he kept on coming, coming, his arms outstretched, his expression blank.

"Awake! Awake!" the second sentry yelled, falling back through the wall of pines toward the camp. His companion, though, didn't retreat, but drew out his heavy sword and leaped ahead.

The approaching intruder didn't change his speed or his route, coming straight in; and the soldier exploded into motion, bringing his sword up and over, cleaving one of those reaching arms above the elbow, severing it easily.

A bit of blood rolled out, but more than that came a sickly greenish white pus.

The soldier knew then the horrible truth, understood the stench to be a mixture of peat and rot, the sickly smell of death, but tainted even more with earthen richness. He knew then that he was fighting not a man but a corpse! Gagging, horrified, he fell back; but the zombie caught his sword in its bare hand as he turned, in a grip tremendously strong.

He screamed out—somehow he found his voice enough to make noise—and tugged and tugged at the sword, then gave it up altogether and tried to scramble away. But as he turned, he saw them, dozens and dozens of walking dead, coming through the mist. Overwhelmed, he stumbled and went down.

He cried out again as the one-armed zombie fell over him, grabbing him by the elbow, crushing his joint in its iron grip. He shouted and flailed, beating the thing about the head and shoulders, to no avail.

But then his companion was beside him again, and with one mighty swing, he decapitated the zombie.

Still it held on stubbornly. The other soldier, seeing the monsters approaching from everywhere, it seemed, hacked wildly at that clasping hand, severing it, too. He pulled his friend to his feet and dragged him to the pines, but the man was still screaming, for that severed hand was still clutching him!

*   *   *

Duke Tetrafel rubbed his bleary eyes and peeked out from his bedroll. The sight of the encampment, of the panic, brought him wide awake, and he scrambled to his feet.

"Attack! Attack, my Duke!" one nearby soldier cried to him, running forward, bearing Tetrafel's sword belt.

Tetrafel struggled to clasp it on, turning, trying to keep up with the dizzying scene.

"The dead, they are!" screamed a sentry crashing through the pine wall. "The dead've risen against us!"

"From the forest, from the forest!" another yelled. The pines all about the small clearing began to shake, and the monsters strode through, in that stiff-legged gait, their peat-covered arms out straight before them. From the back of the camp came a horrified cry that turned Duke Tetrafel about. A pair of sentries scrambled through the pine wall, but got yanked right back in, grabbed and tugged so hard that one of them left one of his shoes behind.

The screams that followed were, perhaps, the most awful sound Duke Tetrafel had ever heard.

"Form a defense!" the captain of Tetrafel's contingent cried, and his men moved back near the fire, forming a ring about it, with the servants and their Duke behind them.

The zombie ring closed slowly, ominously.

"Go for their heads," cried one of the sentries who had first encountered them.

But then, above the tumult, they heard a melodic song, a gentle, sweet harmony of beautiful, delicate voices, drifting on the evening breeze, singing in a language that they did not know, something preternatural, a sylvan song of an ancient forest. As if on cue, the zombies stopped and lowered their arms.

The wind blew a bit stronger, as if flowing with the song.

"What is it?" more than one man asked anxiously.

"Be still," Duke Tetrafel told them all. "Allies, perhaps."

Between the men and the zombies, the ground began to tremble and then to break apart, and then . . .

Flowers sprouted. Huge flowers, with great petals shining silver in the moonlight, the likes of which the men of Honce-the-Bear had never seen.

And the smell of them! Overwhelming, overpowering, burying even the stench of the zombies.

An inviting smell, Duke Tetrafel thought, compelling him to lie down and rest, to close his eyes and sleep. Yes, Tetrafel realized, he wanted nothing more at that moment than to sleep. He saw several of his companions go down beside him, nestling comfortably on the ground, and without even registering the movement, he found himself on his hands and knees, having trouble, so much trouble, even keeping his head up.

"Get up!" He heard the captain's voice from far, far away. "All of ye! They're coming on again! Oh, get up, ye fools!"

And then he heard the cries and the shouts, the swoosh of cutting blades, the hum of bowstrings.

And then he heard . . . nothing at all, just felt the warmth of a deep, deep sleep.

Duke Tetrafel woke up as if in a dark nightmare. The fog clung to the ground all about him—not a watery mist like the one from the falls, but an opaque, soupy blanket. He was sitting now, tightly bound with his hands behind him around a small stake. He was in a forest, still, but not the same one, as far as he could discern; for instead of the thick rows of pines, the trees about him now were mere skeletons, black and twisted and leafless.

Groans to either side of him made him glance about, to see many of his party, similarly seated and bound, in a neat line, which told him that these stakes had been purposely placed, that their captors, whoever they might be, were skilled at this.

"Where are the others?" he asked one soldier near him.

"They took them!" came the nervous, completely unsettled reply. Duke Tetrafel followed the sweating man's gaze to a pair of smallish, very slender creatures walking toward them. Flanking the duo came several of the walking dead.

Trying hard to ignore their horrid escorts, Tetrafel studied the pair carefully, their creamy white skin and penetrating blue eyes that seemed to glow with an inner sparkle. They wore dark-colored robes, the cowls back, and at times seemed to simply disappear into the landscape, except for their exposed heads. Tetrafel tried to sort things out. These weren't merely small humans, he knew, and that was confirmed as they neared and he noted their pointy ears and angular features.

"Touel'alfar?" he asked, for he had heard some tales of the elves, mostly children's fireside stories.

The two robed figures froze at the word, glancing at each other with obvious rage.

"Doc'alfar!" one of them said sharply. He strode over and hit Duke Tetrafel with a backhanded slap across the face that nearly left the man unconscious. He could hardly believe that a creature so lithe and small had hit him so damned hard!

By the time Tetrafel had recovered his senses, the two robed Doc'alfar had selected their next victim, a woman seated several places to the Duke's right. They motioned to her and turned away; and their unthinking, unquestioning servants moved to her, pulling her free of her bindings and hoisting her up. She cried pitifully, and her legs would not support her, but that hardly mattered to the zombies. They kept moving, holding her fast; and if she did not work her legs to keep up, they dragged her along.

"What are you doing with her?" Duke Tetrafel demanded, and when the two robed Doc'alfar didn't even glance back, he turned to the soldier next to him. "What are they to do with her?"

"To the bog with her," the man replied grimly. "Watch yer own fate, me Duke."

Duke Tetrafel stared back into the fog, to the receding figures, seeming like ghosts now.

He saw the Doc'alfar pause and pour various liquids over the squirming woman, and then watched the zombies drag the woman to the side, and then up a small platform that he had not noticed before, for in the fog it had seemed like just another of the many twisted trees.

The zombies took her, screaming and sobbing, out to the end of the platform and held her there; and all of her wriggling and screaming and kicking did her no good at all.

The two Doc'alfar began chanting, one after another, their melodic voices filling the wind with sound, complementing each other perfectly. Gradually, their song blended together, until they were chanting in one voice. Others, unseen among the trees and in the fog, joined in, Tetrafel realized after a while; and the whole forest seemed to be singing.

What garish ritual is this? the Duke wondered. Was it religious?

And then, abruptly, all sound, even the woman's sobs, stopped, as if compelled by one of the Doc'alfar, the lithe creature thrusting his arms up into the night air, his voluminous sleeves falling back to show his white, slender arms. All the world seemed to pause, as if the creature had stopped time itself.

And then the zombies pushed the woman forward, and she screamed as she fell, breaking the spell.

Tetrafel could barely make her out through the shifting fog, buried to her waist in the bog, scrambling and crying; her movements only made her sink down even farther.

"Oh, help me!" she cried, sinking slowly, slowly. "Help me. I don't want to die! I don't want to be one o' them zombies!"

It went on and on, for several agonizing minutes, the woman unable to get out and being dragged down, slowly, slowly. The Doc'alfar began their song again, a prayer of sacrifice, apparently, drowning the woman's shrill, horrified cries. Soon that song was the only noise carried on the wind.

When it was over, the Doc'alfar methodically headed back again, their zombies in tow, and despite the shouting protests, they selected another, a soldier this time; and all the man's vicious fighting proved to be of no avail as the zombies dragged him away.

Duke Tetrafel could hardly breathe! What horror had he stumbled upon, out here beyond civilization? He knew then, as they all did, that the woman's assessment of her fate was correct, that through some magical ceremony, he and all his party would be given to the bog, then returned to the Doc'alfar as unthinking, undead servants!

He thought of all his work, of all the glory, of his aspirations for immortality. Now he would find that immortality, but in no way he had ever wanted!

"They'll go off for a bit after the second," the soldier next to him whispered harshly. "Two at a time, they do, and then they're away for a bit."

Tetrafel instinctively struggled with his bindings. "Too tight," he replied to the man, trying hard to keep his voice steady, to not cry out in fear.

"But I've got me post loose," the man replied.

The chosen soldier went into the bog then. At first they heard nothing, the man apparently facing his death bravely, but then, as the thick, wet bog rose to his neck, he began to scream out in protest, and then to cry. And then . . . silence.

As the soldier beside the Duke had predicted, the Doc'alfar and their zombies disappeared soon after, melting into the fog.

The man gave a grunt and a great tug, and he fell over onto his side, his head right behind the seated Duke. Tetrafel strained his neck to glance back, wondering what good that movement might have done.

The soldier opened his mouth and stuck out his tongue—a tongue pierced by a stud set with a small gray stone.

"Magical," the man explained, "a gift from a friend, put in to put a spark in the ladies, if ye get me meaning."

"What are you babbling about?" Duke Tetrafel replied rather loudly, and he glanced back as if he expected a host of zombies to rise up and throttle him.

"Ye might feel a bit of a charge, a spark," the soldier explained. Before the Duke could even ask what the soldier was talking about, he did indeed feel a sharp sting on his wrist. He didn't protest, though, for he felt, too, that the rope holding him had loosened, the binding burned by the electric charge.

Tetrafel pulled his hands free and fell over the soldier, working furiously at the man's bindings. Then he was free, too, and the Duke moved to the next in line, a servant woman, who was crying wildly. He had just finished with her bindings and moved to the woman beside her when he realized that the song had begun again, and he turned back to see ghostly forms appearing in the fog.

With a cry of terror, Duke Tetrafel abandoned the woman and ran off into the night.

He heard the screams of those still tied, or of those who had just begun to flee and were not quick enough, as they got hauled down and dragged back.

A part of Tetrafel demanded that he go back, that he die with these men and women who had served so well beside him for these three years. A noble part of him screamed at him to face his fate bravely.

But he pictured the zombies, the horrid peat-covered undead, and he ran on. He wanted to go back, but he could not. His legs kept moving. He fell hard and scraped his face, but he scrambled right back up and ran on, into the fog.

Others were running in the fog-enshrouded forest, he knew; and pursuit was all about—the heavy dragging steps of the zombies and, even more dangerous, the nimble Doc'alfar, some running in the boughs above.

Duke Tetrafel ran until his legs ached and his breath would not come, and then, driven by the sheerest horror, he ran on and on and on. For all of his life, he ran. For his eternal soul, he ran.

The sun rose before his eyes, and still he ran, and he thought for a moment that it had all been only a terrible dream.

But he knew better, knew the truth. And Duke Timian Tetrafel of the Wilderlands, a nobleman of the court of King Danube Brock Ursal, a man who had planned to engrave his name in the histories of his people and upon some of the greatest natural monuments in all the world, crumpled into the grass and wept.

Tetrafel met two other soldiers of his band that day, men as frightened as he. There was no talk of returning to try to save any of the others; there was little talk at all.

They just ran on and on, to the east, to lands where the dead did not rise out of peat bogs.

More than three weeks later, the three came back into the somewhat civilized lands of Wester-Honce, and a week after that, riding in the back of a farmer's sleigh, Duke Tetrafel arrived home in Ursal. The very next day, Duke Kalas returned to the city, vowing never to go back to wretched Palmaris.

A week later, King Danube's son was born to Constance Pemblebury.

CHAPTER

❖ 24 ❖

The Brothers Repentant

"You hate everything, and everyone," Sovereign Sister Treisa insisted, coming forward and poking her accusing finger De'Unnero's way. Outside the abbey, spring had passed its midpoint, and the number of pitiful, plague-ridden, desperate folk had swelled once more, adding to the sovereign sister's foul mood. She was the one remaining sovereign sister at the abbey, and thus had become the spokeswoman for all fifteen of the sisters still alive at St. Gwendolyn.

The man, the self-appointed abbot of the devastated abbey, glanced around, his smile wry, reminding Treisa that she was not among friends here in his office. Several brothers of St. Gwendolyn, converts to De'Unnero's definition of the Abellican faith, desperate men seeking answers, lined the room.

Treisa backed off a step and followed the abbot's gaze about the room, staring incredulously at the faces of men she had once considered her brothers. What a different abbey she had found when she had hastily returned after hearing of the demise of her friend and mentor Abbess Delenia and several others! What a different place was St. Gwendolyn, with Marcalo De'Unnero as abbot! That had been De'Unnero's first tactic, she understood, separating the remaining brothers from the remaining sisters of St. Gwendolyn. He had installed a patriarchal, male-dominated order here in the one abbey that had been established to see to the religious ambitions of those few women who managed to earn, through bribery of rich fathers or through sheer, undeniable goodness, a place in the Church.

"You claim that the followers of Avelyn brought the plague to us," she said, quietly but not meekly.

"Plausible," the abbot replied calmly.

"Unproven," Sovereign Sister Treisa retorted.

"Plausible," De'Unnero repeated. "And if we are to believe that the plague is a punishment from God, as we know it must be, then the proof lies before you."

Treisa stared at him curiously, not catching the link.

"With the murder of Father Abbot Markwart, the Abellican Church has shifted its purpose and its direction," De'Unnero explained; and it was clear to Treisa that he was preaching to his followers more than explaining to her. "Rumors from the College of Abbots hint that the process to canonize Avelyn Desbris will begin this very year. Canonization? The man murdered Master Siherton of St.-Mere-Abelle—I was there and remember well! The man stole a huge treasure of sacred gemstones and ran across the world as an impostor brother, ignoring law and commands to cease and return. Canonization? Saint Avelyn?"

"Is not the process one of investigation?" Treisa asked, but De'Unnero scoffed at her before she finished.

"It is political," he argued, "a way to placate the masses who have become very afraid—a way to fabricate a hero, that those who seek personal gain might raise that hero's name in their own honor." He paused and eyed Treisa suspiciously. "Such was the canonization of St. Gwendolyn."

The woman gagged and nearly choked on that proclamation! Many in the Church throughout the last centuries had secretly questioned the ascension of Gwendolyn to sainthood, some claiming that impurities had been overlooked, others arguing that the woman, a healer and then a warrior of the third century, should have been dismissed simply because she had not recognized her place as a member of the fair sex. But rarely, if ever, had anyone within the Church so publicly denounced Gwendolyn or any other saint!

Treisa looked around for support against the blasphemer, but she found her brothers of St. Gwendolyn, men she had served beside piously for years, standing firm with the monster from St.-Mere-Abelle.

"How can you claim to be of the faith and yet doubt?" De'Unnero asked dramatically, storming about the room and waving his arms. "Witness the trials that have befallen the world, the suffering, the death! We are the guardians of the word of God, the guides to holiness. If the world is fallen to ruin, then we of the Abellican Church cannot diminish our part in it. No, we must accept the blame, and use it as guidance to right our straying road."

"Is that not what the new abbot of St. Precious claims to do?" Treisa dared to remark.

De'Unnero laughed. "Do you not understand, sovereign sister?" he asked. "It was the error of Avelyn that began all this. The theft and the murder."

Several of the St. Gwendolyn brothers shook their fists and cheered their agreement. This place was becoming dangerous, Treisa realized, and from more than the plague!

De'Unnero went on and on, railing against Avelyn and Jojonah, against Braumin Herde and the traitor Francis, and against anything or anyone not in agreement with his philosophy. He ended, standing right before the incredulous Treisa, his eyes wild; and she shrank back, fearing that he would strike her.

"Go to your room, sister," he said quietly, "or go wherever your heart leads you. I am the abbot of St. Gwendolyn now. I will give you a short while to adjust to that reality. But I warn you, here and now and in front of all these witnesses, if you cross me, I will demote you. I will push you back within the Order, until you find yourself performing tasks with the first-year sisters. Discipline alone will get us through these dark times, and I'll not have that compromised by Sovereign Sister Treisa."

He turned and waved at her to leave.

And she did, after letting her gaze linger about the room to the gathered brothers—to the followers, it seemed, of Marcalo De'Unnero.

As De'Unnero expected, Treisa gave him no trouble over the next couple of weeks. The abbot went about his days in the humid air solidifying his grasp on those eager young brothers seeking answers to a world gone crazy. He continued his tirades against his enemies, including Fio Bou-raiy in the customary mix, and each of his increasingly excited speeches was met with increasingly excited applause.

But De'Unnero knew that it could not go on forever, knew that his position of abbot had not been, and would not likely be, sanctioned. Thus, he wasn't surprised at all one muggy morning when one of the brothers hustled into his office to announce that Masters Glendenhook and Machuso of St.-Mere-Abelle had arrived, along with a contingent of twenty brothers, several immaculates among them.

"Shall I bring them?" the brother asked.

De'Unnero started to nod, but then changed his mind. "Not here," he explained. "I will meet them in the courtyard.

"And brother," he added as the younger monk turned to go, "let the word go throughout the abbey, that all may bear witness to this."

"Yes, my abbot," the young monk said, and he ran out of the room.

De'Unnero lingered there for a long while. He wanted to make sure that he gave his followers ample time to get out there to watch this event, as Glendenhook and the others from St.-Mere-Abelle no doubt tried to exert their will over that of the brethren of St. Gwendolyn. Yes, this would be a critical moment for him, De'Unnero knew: the moment when he learned the truth of the courage and loyalty of his followers.

He came out into the courtyard, not in the decorated robes of an abbot, but in his normal, weathered brown robes, hood thrown back. There stood Glendenhook and Machuso, flanked by the other brothers of their abbey, all scowling and trying to appear intimidating.

Marcalo De'Unnero was rarely intimidated. With a nod to his many watching followers, he strode across the courtyard to stand before the two visiting masters.

"If you had better announced your intentions, I could have better prepared the abbey," De'Unnero remarked casually, almost flippantly.

"Perhaps we would be better served in your private offices," Master Machuso said softly.

"Why so, Master Machuso?" De'Unnero loudly replied.

"We have come on official business of the Abellican Church," Master Glendenhook said firmly, "sent by Father Abbot Agronguerre himself."

"Ah, yes," De'Unnero replied, walking about, glancing up at his friends and followers lining the courtyard wall. "And how fares the new Father Abbot? I trust that my *in absentia* vote was counted."

"Recorded and noted," Master Machuso assured him.

"And still Abbot Agronguerre counted more votes than did Abbot Olin?" De'Unnero asked, again loudly; and his words made Glendenhook glance about suspiciously, for he understood that De'Unnero's announcing that he had voted for Olin would bolster his popularity among the brethren of St. Gwendolyn, who had many ties to Olin's Entel abbey.

"Indeed," Master Glendenhook added dryly. "Agronguerre of St. Belfour was well supported by many different factions within the Church. Thus, he is the rightful father abbot, whose word initiates canon law. Now, good Master De'Unnero, may we retire to a more private setting and conclude our business efficiently?"

"I doubt that your business and my own are the same," De'Unnero replied.

"My business concerns you," Glendenhook insisted.

"Then speak it plainly!" De'Unnero demanded angrily.

Glendenhook stared at him long and hard.

"You have come to inform me that I am recalled to St.-Mere-Abelle," De'Unnero stated, and several of the gathered St. Gwendolyn brothers gasped.

Glendenhook continued to glower.

"And what of my appointment as abbot?" De'Unnero went on. "Sanctioned, or not? Not, I would guess, else how might I be recalled?"

"You were never *appointed* as abbot of St. Gwendolyn!" Master Glendenhook shouted.

"What say you, brethren?" De'Unnero was calling out before the visiting master even finished the declaration.

"Abbot De'Unnero!" one young brother cried; and then others joined in, howling their approval for this man they had accepted as their leader.

Master Machuso came forward and took De'Unnero by the elbow—or at least tried to, for the fiery master yanked away from him.

"Do not do this," Machuso warned. "We are sent with the strictest of orders and backed by all of the power of St.-Mere-Abelle."

De'Unnero laughed at him.

"Master De'Unnero is not your abbot!" Master Glendenhook called loudly, addressing all the gathering. "He is needed in St.-Mere-Abelle, in the court of the new, of *your* new, Father Abbot."

"While we twist," cried one young brother.

"A new abbot will be appointed presently," Glendenhook assured the man, amid the murmuring of discontent. "You have not been forgotten, nor is your plight of minor concern."

"Of no concern at all, then?" De'Unnero was quick to quip.

Glendenhook just looked at him and sighed profoundly.

The crowd about them began jostling then, some brothers coming down from the parapets, others hanging back but shaking their fists. Glendenhook looked back, to see his escorts from St.-Mere-Abelle shifting nervously and glancing all about—until they saw him. He gave a nod and produced a gemstone; and all of his brethren—except for Machuso, who started praying—did likewise.

"You are a bigger fool than even I believed, if you allow this to continue," Glendenhook said quietly to De'Unnero. "Did you think that Father Abbot Agronguerre would not anticipate this from you?"

"Fio Bou-raiy, you mean," De'Unnero said coldly; and he was not laughing, not smiling at all. He held up his hand, and those brothers who had begun to approach stopped in their tracks. The tense pose held for a long while, Glendenhook and De'Unnero staring, staring, neither blinking.

"Do not do this, I beg," came Machuso's soothing old voice.

De'Unnero broke into a chuckle, a sinister, superior, and threatening sound. "You have come for St. Gwendolyn," he said, "and so she is yours. You have come for Marcalo De'Unnero, but he, I fear, is not yours. No, Master Glendenhook. I see the road before me, the path where I might preach the true word of God, rather than the petty and self-serving proclamations issuing forth from St.-Mere-Abelle. My path," he said loudly, moving out and reaching with his voice for his many followers, "our path," he corrected, "is not within the shelter of a secluded abbey, oblivious even of the cries of those dying of the rosy plague right outside our doorway. No, our path is the open road, that our words might reach the ears of the needy peasants, that they might find again the course of righteousness!"

Cheers went up from every corner of the courtyard, and Glendenhook and the others from St.-Mere-Abelle could only watch and groan. Glendenhook tried to appeal to the brothers of St. Gwendolyn, but De'Unnero's words drowned out his, in both volume and impact.

Finally, an outraged Glendenhook looked back directly at De'Unnero, his eyes full of hatred.

"You came here seeking the abbey, and so St. Gwendolyn is yours," De'Unnero said innocently.

"Do not do this," said Glendenhook, and his tone was nothing like the begging, pleading words of Master Machuso, but one dripping with threat. "You go against Church doctrine here, walking a dangerous road."

"And who will rise up against me?" De'Unnero asked. "Against us? Your friend Fio Bou-raiy, the lackey of gentle Agronguerre? The King? No, brother, we recognize the truth of it all now. We understand that the Church has stepped from that truth, and we will not be deterred from the righteous road."

"Master De'Unnero!" Machuso cried, horrified.

"Join with us!" De'Unnero offered suddenly and apparently sincerely, "before all the world is fallen into darkness. Help us put the Church aright, and thus end the misery of the plague."

Glendenhook stared at him incredulously.

"Now is the time for action and not words," De'Unnero insisted.

"You believe the plague to be a punishment from God?" Glendenhook whispered harshly.

"On a deserving populace," De'Unnero growled back at him, "on those who have forsaken the truth."

"Absurd."

"Obvious," De'Unnero countered. "I see it, and they see it." He swept his arm about to encompass the gathered brothers of St. Gwendolyn. "We know the truth and we know the source—and no edicts from Father Abbot Agronguerre will sway us from that path."

"You cannot—" Master Machuso started to say, but Glendenhook knifed an arm across the older man's chest, bidding him to be quiet.

"You risk the wrath of Father Abbot Agronguerre and all the masters of St.-Mere-Abelle," Glendenhook warned.

"And you, Brother Glendenhook, risk the wrath of Marcalo De'Unnero," De'Unnero said evenly, moving right up to the man, his posture and the set of his eyes and jaw a poignant reminder to Glendenhook of the reputation of this monk, Brother Marcalo De'Unnero, widely accepted as the greatest fighter ever to walk out of St.-Mere-Abelle, ever to train in the Abellican Order. "Which of us, then, do you believe in the worse situation?"

The question obviously unnerved Glendenhook profoundly. The man held a gemstone in his hand—a graphite likely, or perhaps even a lodestone. But he'd never try to bring up the magic, De'Unnero knew with confidence, because Glendenhook realized that De'Unnero could kill him with a single, well-placed blow. No, Glendenhook would never find the courage to take such a risk.

"Take your abbey and be glad that I deemed our path to be out there," De'Unnero said quietly, staring unblinkingly with each word. "We are beyond you now, all of us. We will follow the true course of the Abellican Order, that perhaps our actions will inspire others—even Master Glendenhook, perhaps—to walk beside us."

"You have gone mad," Glendenhook remarked.

"As much has been said of many prophets," De'Unnero was quick to respond. He held up his hand, then, and all about him hushed. "To the road!" De'Unnero demanded with a powerful signaling movement, and the brothers of St. Gwendolyn gave a cheer and led the way to the front gate.

"If you try to stop us, you may prove victorious," De'Unnero said calmly—too calmly! "But I warn you that I will come for your throat first and foremost." He finished and lifted one arm, revealing that it was no longer a human arm but the paw of a great tiger.

Master Glendenhook watched De'Unnero and nearly every one of the remaining twenty-seven brothers of St. Gwendolyn walk out of the abbey gate soon after, all the brothers bending to scoop up flowers as protection against the plague.

And then they walked away, from St. Gwendolyn and from the Abellican Church.

And so on that day, the fifth day of summer in God's Year 828, the Brothers Repentant were conceived, led by Marcalo De'Unnero, the former abbot of St. Precious, the former Bishop of Palmaris, the former abbot of St. Gwendolyn, and the greatest warrior ever produced by the Abellican Church.

CHAPTER

❖ 25 ❖

Summer Heat

"What news from Palmaris?" Duke Kalas asked, sitting astride his short and muscular pinto To-gai-ru pony.

King Danube, riding a taller snow-white gelding, turned to regard the man, but it was Constance Pemblebury, trotting her chestnut up between them, who was first to answer.

"Is it midweek already, then?" she asked sarcastically, for they all knew well that the week had just begun. "Is not that question normally reserved for midweek and the end of the week?"

Duke Kalas glared at the woman, but Constance only laughed and kicked up an even swifter pace, outdistancing her fellow riders across the manicured, hedge-lined field behind Castle Ursal.

"I have heard not a word from our friends in the northern city," King Danube replied to the original question, "nor do I care."

"Nor should you, my King," said Kalas. "The folk of Palmaris are a difficult lot, and made all the harder by their recent experiences in war and in civil strife. If you commanded me back to the place, I would renounce my title of duke of Wester-Honce!"

That made King Danube raise an eyebrow, but he merely nodded; for Kalas had made it quite clear to him from the very first day he had returned to Ursal the previous winter that he had no intention of going anywhere near the wretched city of Palmaris again.

"Still," Danube remarked, "I do wonder about my legacy."

"Your legacy?" Kalas asked incredulously, purposely dramatizing his surprise. "You defeated the demon dactyl and the demon Markwart, who overran the Abellican Church. You—"

"Let us not exaggerate the role that I played in either event, my friend," Danube said. "Indeed, I understand that I will be thought of fondly in decades hence, but there are other matters that I see before me now. Perhaps the strife in Palmaris, and much of the discontent that often rumbles about Ursal's avenues, is the result of too many people too close together. We both know, after all, how disagreeable some are by their very nature."

He ended with a chuckle, and so Kalas joined in.

"Perhaps it is time for us to consider the expansion of Honce-the-Bear's borders; and in that regard, Palmaris might prove a very important location," King Danube reasoned.

"The Timberlands?" Duke Kalas asked doubtfully.

"Impossible, by treaty, and I do not mean to leave a legacy as one who dishonored his word," King Danube replied. "But there are many places in between Palmaris and the Timberlands. The Church has recognized this small town—Cacr Tinella by name, I believe—and with the mood of the folk in the north, perhaps we should look in that direction, as well."

"I pray you do not act rashly," Kalas said, "or hastily. The north is much glamorized today because of yesterday's events; but in the end, it remains a savage and untamed place, filled with savage and untamed folk."

"I hear well your words," said King Danube, "but I'll not leave Palmaris without a proper and strong baron at this time."

Kalas' expression dropped and his shoulders sagged.

"Oh, not you, my friend," King Danube said with a laugh. "Nay, even if you were so inclined, I value your advice too much to send you back across the kingdom and away from my side. But there is another Duke, recently returned to my court, whose province actually extends beyond Palmaris to the north and the west."

"Tetrafel," Kalas easily reasoned. "But is he recovered?"

"Nearly well enough, I would say," replied Danube. "He has even begun talking of rewriting his lost journal, though I doubt that any of the maps he draws from memory will prove of much use to future expeditions. But if our Duke is determined to immerse himself in his work, then what better place for him than Palmaris? I will allow him to spend the season in Ursal, recovering, and then I will afford him a strong contingent of supporters for his journey, and in truth, I doubt that Abbot Braumin will prove too difficult to manage."

Duke Kalas nodded and even managed a smile, but given his own experience in Palmaris, he doubted those last words strongly.

The hamlet of Juniper in the rolling green hills of southern Honce-the-Bear, the county known as Yorkey, was a quiet and unassuming community. Not an old cluster of houses, Juniper traced no deep roots into the past but was, rather, a fairly new community, a place where any settler might step right into the highest social circles, and where new folk were not generally treated with suspicion and derision.

Thus, many of the less acceptable wanderers of southern Honce-the-Bear found their way to Juniper, to a place even they, the unwanted, the different, might call home.

That made Juniper a growing community, and, when the brothers of St. Gwendolyn mentioned the place to De'Unnero, a prime target for the Brothers Repentant.

They came one wickedly hot late-summer afternoon, in a line single file, heads down, dressed in their thick woolen Abellican robes with the hoods pulled low, chanting, chanting for forgiveness of their sins and for the sins of all the men in all the world.

De'Unnero led the procession to the small town's central square, the brothers forming a semicircle behind him as he threw back his hood and began his cry to the people. "I am Brother Truth!" he declared. "Hear my words if you value your life and your eternal soul!" Like any other town in Honce-the-Bear in God's Year 828, entertainment was not often found, and a charismatic speaker was a rarity indeed. Soon, the entire village of Juniper had turned out to watch the spectacle.

And what a show De'Unnero and his fanatical followers gave them! The self-proclaimed Brother Truth spoke of the sins of some unnamed man in some unnamed community, and one of the brothers ran forward, stripping off his robes so that he was clothed only in a white loincloth, and prostrating himself on the ground before De'Unnero.

Another brother rushed up with a short, three-stranded whip, and on De'Unnero's orders, proceeded to give the prone brother twenty vicious lashes, drawing deep lines of blood on the man's back.

On and on it went, with De'Unnero's followers, the Brothers Repentant, accepting the sins of the world into their own flesh and blood, and then beating those sins away.

When at last, after more than three brutal hours, De'Unnero's cries diminished, when every Repentant Brother had shed his blood and tears, the show was over. But to the crowd, that was unacceptable; and now, on De'Unnero's cue, it was their turn to proclaim their sins, and more important, to proclaim those sins of their neighbors, openly.

And the Brothers Repentant went at the offending peasants with even more vigor than they had lashed each other.

When two men were accused of an "unnatural friendship," they were beaten into unconsciousness and then publicly castrated. When a young boy was accused of stealing a neighbor's chickens, De'Unnero forced the boy's own mother to cut off his hand. And she did it! Because the folk of Juniper knew of the rosy plague and did not doubt this holy Abellican brother who had come to them to tell them why the plague had arisen, and more important, how it could be put down.

The last order of business in Juniper came long after sunset. The Brothers Repentant were still in the public square, completing their ritual with an orgy of self-flagellation, when De'Unnero spotted a dark-skinned Behrenese among the onlookers. The heathen was dragged forward to face the fierce master.

"Who is your God?" De'Unnero demanded.

The man didn't answer.

"Chezru?" the master asked, naming the deity of the Behren yatols. "Do you fall to your knees to worship Chezru?"

The man didn't answer, but he was trembling visibly now, as De'Unnero walked around him, slowly, scrutinizing his every aspect.

"Deny him," De'Unnero instructed the man when he came around to face him squarely once again. "Publicly denounce Chezru, here and now, as a false idol."

The man didn't answer.

"If you'll not do it, then you have already answered my first question," De'Unnero said slyly. "Denounce Chezru, I say! Name him as the betrayer of souls."

One of the other Brothers Repentant rushed up, as if to tackle the man, but De'Unnero held him back.

"We see the plague growing in our lands," the master explained to the frightened dark-skinned man. "We know its source: the errant course of worship. Denounce Chezru now, I warn you, else you reveal yourself as a heretic and, thus, a sire of the plague."

That last statement seemed to bolster the poor Behrenese man. He took a deep breath and looked evenly at De'Unnero. "You beseech me to abandon my soul to save my flesh," he said in his thick Behrenese accent. "That I cannot do."

"Hang him!" came one cry, but De'Unnero stifled it, and all subsequent ones.

"Where are his people?" the master asked loudly. Then he had his answer; and he was pleased to learn that an entire enclave of Behrenese were living on an old farm just outside Juniper.

"Bring him," he instructed his Brothers Repentant, and the Behrenese man was dragged away. On went the procession, through the night, torches in hand. They encircled the large farmhouse and saw the frightened faces—old folks and children included—peering out at them through the windows.

De'Unnero ordered the Behrenese out of the house, but they refused.

"Who is your God?" he called to them. "Do you serve the Abellican Church or the Chezru chieftain of your homeland?"

No reply.

De'Unnero signaled to two brothers flanking him, each brandishing blazing torches, to approach the house.

"You will answer me or we will burn your house down around you!" De'Unnero roared. "Which Church do you serve?"

The door slid open and an old, weathered, dark-skinned man walked out, moving slowly but steadily toward the volatile monk.

He looked to the Brothers Repentant holding the other Behrenese. "Let him go," he demanded.

They ignored him, and he followed their gazes to the ringmaster.

"Begone from here," the old man said to De'Unnero. "Our home is this, fairly taken and rebuilt. No explanations do we owe you."

"You are yatol," De'Unnero accused, for that was the religion of the southern country, and he knew from the dark-skinned man's accent and inflection that he had not been long in Honce-the-Bear.

The old man squared his shoulders.

"Name the Abellican Church as your Church," De'Unnero demanded. "Accept St. Abelle as your savior and our God as your God!"

"Our faith we will not renounce," the man said proudly, lifting his gaze so that he could address the crowd. But then he was down on the ground, suddenly dropped by a heavy punch delivered expertly by Marcalo De'Unnero. And then he and the other man were sent running, chased by Brothers Repentant brandishing whips. Those angry monks chased the two Behrenese right up to the house, cracking their whips, forcing the dark-skinned men to seek refuge inside.

"Burn them in their house," De'Unnero instructed, and the rest of the Brothers Repentant surged forward with their torches, setting the house ablaze on all sides, taking care to quickly engulf any potential exits.

The screams soon followed, pleading and begging, but the Brothers Repentant did not heed those cries and shed no tears for the heathen Behrenese, for they, like the followers of Avelyn, were to blame for delivering the rosy plague upon the land. They, with their sacrilegious rituals—which De'Unnero insisted included the sacrifice of kidnapped fair-skinned babies—were not innocent. Nay, by the cries of De'Unnero, whipping all the gathering, even the secular peasants, into a fury and a frenzy: the Behrenese were akin to minions of the demon dactyl.

De'Unnero called up all the rumors of Behrenese horrors, relentlessly condemning the dark-skinned southerners. His moment of highest triumph came shortly thereafter—the house burning wildly, smoke billowing into the nighttime sky—when one Behrenese woman somehow managed to elude the fire and run out, only to be hunted down by the folk of Juniper, the crowd stirred by De'Unnero's tirade. They caught her and dragged her down, beat her and kicked her, and carried her back to the inferno. Howling with rage and glee, ignoring her pitiful screams, they threw her back into the fire to be consumed.

The Brothers Repentant left Juniper a torn and battered place the next day, moving out across the rolling fields of southern Honce-the-Bear. Behind them, they left fifteen dead and scores maimed and scarred. And yet, to some at least, they left as heroes, as the holy brothers who would defeat the rosy plague. Indeed, the number of Brothers Repentant grew by four that day, young, strong men of Juniper wanting to join in the war against sin, against the plague. Men willing to accept the responsibilities of mankind's sins onto their own shoulders.

Men willing to suffer.
And to kill.

"She is with child again," Abbot Je'howith announced to King Danube and Duke Kalas on the day after the autumn equinox, after his examination of Constance Pemblebury. "Another son."

King Danube smiled; Kalas laughed out loud. "Thus the heir and the spare," the Duke said.

Danube looked at him directly. His first instinct was to lash out at his rather callous and blunt friend, but he held the words in check. Duke Kalas had a right to be questioning the status of the children, Danube realized, given that he had not yet publicly announced the Denial of Privilege for Merwick, his first son with Constance, now nearly seven months old.

"We will see if that is to be," the King replied, and calmly.

Kalas paused, and pondered the reply carefully. "You have invoked Refusal of Acceptance before," he reasoned, "but not with one as close as Constance. Do you plan to marry her?"

Now it was Abbot Je'howith's turn to laugh, a cackling sound that turned both sets of eyes upon him. "Indeed, my sovereign," he said, "do you plan to marry Lady Pemblebury? As your adviser in matters spiritual, I have to inform you that these conceptions, unless immaculate, do not set such a fine example for the rabble."

All three had a good laugh at that, and Danube was glad for the dodge. He knew that he had to make some serious decisions, and soon, but truly he was torn. He did care for Constance, and dearly, and did not want to bring her pain in any way. But still, that image of another beautiful and spirited woman stayed bright in his mind.

They let it go at that for the time being, and Je'howith skulked back to his abbey, while Kalas escorted Danube on their daily ride across the fields, enjoying the luxuries his by birthright, the pleasures that accompanied exalted station.

Those pleasures would prove short-lived.

The news of the summer riot in the hamlet of Juniper and of similar outbursts along the farmlands between Ursal and Entel didn't reach Castle Ursal until the next week, ironically, the very same day that the first victim of the rosy plague was confirmed within the city.

The mood in Danube's audience hall—where Danube, Duke Kalas, Constance, and the baby Merwick, awaited the arrival of Duke Tetrafel and Abbot Je'howith—was somber, a far shift from the carefree revelry among the nobles throughout the previous season. Suddenly the world seemed a darker place, and whatever reprieve the nobles of Danube's court had experienced after the fall of the dactyl and its minions and the shake-up within the Abellican Church, seemed fast diminishing. None of them had experienced the rosy plague before, of course, but they knew well the histories, the devastation the sickness had wrought upon their kingdom on several occasions in centuries past.

"It is the plague!" came the cry, and Duke Tetrafel entered the room, out of breath from his long run through Castle Ursal. "It is confirmed, my King. The rosy plague!"

King Danube motioned for the man to calm down and take one of the seats that had been placed about before the throne. With a glance to the side, to see young Merwick at play with some game pieces, Tetrafel seated himself right before Danube.

"I have just spoken with one of the brothers of St. Honce," Tetrafel started to explain, but Danube raised his hand to cut the man short.

"We have already been informed," the King explained. "I spoke with Abbot Je'howith earlier this morn."

"The rosy plague!" Tetrafel said, shaking his head. "What are we to do?"

"What can we do?" Duke Kalas answered. "Lock our doors fast and tight."

"And continue with the business of ruling," King Danube added. "For you, Duke Tetrafel, that means completing your reconstruction of your lost diary. All that you and your team toiled for in the west must not be lost to the ages."

Duke Tetrafel winced, obviously pained by the memory. "Even the Doc'alfar?" he asked quietly.

"Especially the Doc'alfar," King Danube answered. "These are potential enemies, and I plan to know about them, all about them."

Duke Tetrafel nodded.

"But you'll not continue your work here," the King went on. "I need you to serve as my eyes and ears and mouth in Palmaris."

Tetrafel winced again. "But the plague, my King," he protested.

"Chasewind Manor is secure," Duke Kalas added, "and comfortable. You will find all that you need there, and as much security from the plague as can be found here—as can be found anywhere in all the world, I fear."

"Duke Tetrafel," King Danube started formally, seeing that the man remained unconvinced, "I have great plans for the north, for the wild lands north of Palmaris, many of which fall within your province. We will delay those plans, no doubt, while the rosy plague runs its devastating course, but when the sickness has passed—and always, it passes—I intend to turn my eyes northward, to Palmaris and beyond. To Caer Tinella and all the way to the Timberlands.

"It will be the greatest expansion of Honce-the-Bear since the conquest of Vanguard, and I will need you, the greatest explorer of our day, to lead the way. So go to Palmaris with all haste. Duke Kalas has prepared his journal from his months there. Rule wisely and always with an eye toward the glorious future that you and I will find."

The appeal proved more than successful. Duke Tetrafel rolled forward off his chair, to one knee before Danube. "I will not fail in this, my King," he said, bowing his head. Then he came up, saluted, and left the room in a hurry, nearly running over Abbot Je'howith in the process.

"One so old as that should not be so excitable," Je'howith remarked, walking in, the others noticed, with a more pronounced limp this day.

Je'howith took Tetrafel's vacated seat and leaned back, though he didn't seem as if he could get comfortable at all. The old abbot's sullen expression was as clear an answer to the intended first question as Danube needed.

"It is true then," the King stated. "The rosy plague has descended upon Ursal."

"And with more vigor to the east," Je'howith replied.

"A minor outbreak?" Constance spoke hopefully, her gaze going to her child as she asked the question.

"Who can tell?" Je'howith answered. "There have been occasions when the plague has appeared, but quickly dissipated, and others . . ." He let it end there, with a shake of his head.

"And in either case, what good is your Church, Abbot Je'howith?" Duke Kalas put in, the enmity between the two wasting no time in rearing up, as it did at every council session. "Will your abbots close their abbey doors, that they do not hear the pleas of the dying? Will they block their tiny windows, that they do not see the suffering of the people they pretend to lead to God?"

Abbot Je'howith perked up at those remarks, sat up straight and tall and narrowed his eyes. "We will indeed bolt our doors against the populace," he admitted. "And so shall you, Duke Kalas, and you, King Danube. We cannot battle the plague; and so we must, all of us, try to hide from it as we may."

"And what of the peasants out in the streets?" Duke Kalas went on dramatically, though it was obvious that he had no logical side in this debate, for even Danube was nodding his agreement with Je'howith's words.

"They will try to hide, as well," Je'howith answered, "And many will be caught and will die, and horribly, because that is God's will."

Duke Kalas stood up so forcefully at that proclamation, at the notion that any god might be involved in the rosy plague, that his chair went flying behind him.

"Anything that you cannot explain or control you claim as God's will," he accused.

"Everything in all the world is God's will," Je'howith retorted.

"Like the coming of the demon dactyl?" Kalas asked slyly, sarcastically, given the accepted theory that the previous Father Abbot of the Abellican Church had fallen under the spell of the demon Bestesbulzibar.

Je'howith only shrugged and turned away from the Duke, facing the King instead. That action surprised Kalas—and Danube and Constance as well—for usually the old abbot seemed to enjoy the verbal sparring with Kalas as much as the Duke did.

"There are other issues we must discuss," Danube said gravely, "concerning your Church. Have you heard anything of these so-named Brothers Repentant?"

"Only as much as yourself, my King," Je'howith answered. "A rogue band, and not sanctioned by Father Abbot Agronguerre."

"And their leader?" Danube asked. "This Brother Truth?"

Kalas snorted at the ridiculous title.

"I know nothing of him," Je'howith replied.

"They travel from town to town," Duke Kalas remarked angrily, moving beside Danube. "They decry the sins of man and beat each other senseless— no difficult feat, I would guess, for ones so fanatically committed to the Abellican Church."

"Spare me your foolish comments," Je'howith said dryly.

"Would that it ended there," said King Danube. "They seem to be seeking enemies of the Church, or, at least, of their version of the Church. On two occasions, they have persecuted Behrenese."

"I have heard as much."

"And does this alarm you?" King Danube baited, for he knew that Je'howith, like most Abellicans, held little love for the heathen southerners.

"What would you have me say?" the old monk replied.

"Do you understand that Honce-the-Bear trades with Behren?" King Danube said. He, too, stood up, and motioned for Duke Kalas to move aside. "Have you so quickly forgotten the turmoil caused by Bishop De'Unnero, when he began a similar persecution of the Behrenese in Palmaris? Ambassador Rahib Daibe nearly suspended trade, and threatened war. Perhaps your Church considers the persecution of heathens no matter of import, my old friend, but I do not desire to thrust my kingdom into another war!"

His voice rose with his ire. All in the room—Constance and Kalas and Je'howith, and even his infant son—looked at him incredulously. Rarely had they seen King Danube Brock Ursal, as even-tempered as any man alive, so animated and flustered.

"My Church is not to blame for the rosy plague," Abbot Je'howith said quietly.

"But if your Church complicates the trouble—" Duke Kalas started to warn, but Danube cut him off with a sharp wave.

"I warned you and the others in Palmaris to put your house in order," Danube said.

"As we have!" Je'howith protested. Now he, too, rose from his seat, though shakily, to get on even footing with his adversaries. "Father Abbot Agronguerre is a fine man; and despite the words of Duke Kalas here, you cannot dispute that Abbot Braumin Herde has done a fine job in bringing order to the devastated city of Palmaris."

"Devastated by your Church most of all," said Kalas. But Danube hushed him again, this time with a sharp wave and then a threatening look.

The King blew a long sigh then, and sank back into his chair. How quickly the darkness had descended on him and on his kingdom! A few days before, he was celebrating a successful and peaceful summer and the news of another son, and now, suddenly, it was as if he and his kingdom had been thrust back into the midst of turmoil.

"The Brothers Repentant are not sanctioned?" he asked calmly.

Je'howith shook his head. "We know nothing of them, nor would we applaud their efforts."

"Nor are they unprecedented," Constance Pemblebury unexpectedly put in, and the other three looked to her. "In time of great desperation, such cults often reveal themselves. In the first onset of the plague, the Brothers of Flagellation—"

"Yes, yes," Je'howith agreed. "In desperate times come desperate measures."

Danube rubbed his eyes and sighed again. "See that they are not, and are never, sanctioned," he warned Je'howith, "or risk war between Church and Crown."

Je'howith nodded, and wasn't particularly worried, for he knew Father Abbot Agronguerre well enough to understand that the man would never agree to such actions as were being attributed to this rogue band.

"Is there nothing that we can do against the plague?" Danube asked softly.

Je'howith shook his head. "We can hide," he answered.

On that sour note, the meeting adjourned, with Je'howith retiring to his private quarters in St. Honce but only after issuing orders to all his brethren that they were no longer to go out among the peasants and that the great oaken doors of the abbey were to remain bolted and guarded. In addition, all but the essential civilian workers at St. Honce were dismissed that day, sent home and told not to return.

Within the week, the brothers of St. Honce had blessed and laid a tussie-mussie bed outside their walls and a second outside the closed gates of Castle Ursal. Reports of the plague continued to grow within the city, as Je'howith knew it would, as it always had in crowded areas during previous outbreaks.

By the end of the following week, crowds of sufferers appeared outside the walls of both abbey and castle. Wails rent the night air regularly: mothers, mostly, finding the telltale red spots on the limbs of their children.

Abbot Je'howith watched it all from the narrow window of his room, high in the main tower of St. Honce. How old he felt, and how weary! Weary of everything, of his fights with Duke Kalas—arguments where the frustrated

King Danube now seemed to be leaning more in favor of Kalas. Weary of the philosophical war he had waged within his own Church. Weary of upstart young brothers—who was this Brother Truth?—who thought they understood the truth of the world but surely did not!

Abbot Je'howith had found purpose after the fall of Markwart in Palmaris in the form of simple survival and of protecting the memory of the former Father Abbot. How moot that seemed now, with the rosy plague spreading fast across the land, a horror that would bury even the terrible memories of the demon dactyl.

Je'howith looked around him at the ancient stone walls, aware of the very real possibility that he would never again see the world outside this sanctuary, this prison. On its previous visits to Honce-the-Bear, the rosy plague had stayed a decade or more. The members of the Abellican Church would turn inward for the duration, would begin the great debates about the universe anew, the purpose of Man and of life itself, the nature of God, the reality of death.

Je'howith, too old and too tired and too certain that he had no answers, wanted no part of it.

He heard the cart men then, as twilight descended, walking the streets of Ursal in their black robes and masks, calling for the folk to bring out their dead.

Je'howith knew that soon enough those carts would make extra trips and would be overloaded at every one.

"Bring out yer dead!"

The words cut profoundly into old Abbot Je'howith, a poignant reminder of impotence and futility.

"Bring out yer dead!"

He shuffled to his cot and, weary of it all, lay down.

It began as a numbness in his arm, a tingling that spread gradually throughout his shoulder and upper chest. His last meal, he presumed, disagreeing with his old bowels.

But the numbness changed to a burning sensation, general at first, but becoming more and more focused about his heart, and the old man understood.

He lay there, frantic but helpless, doubting that he could even find the strength to walk out of his room. He turned his head and stared at his night table. He had a hematite in there, he recalled through the waves of pain. Perhaps he could use it to contact another brother. . . .

A darker thought came to old Je'howith, a recent memory of his examination of Constance Pemblebury. He had used the soul stone to enter her body, her womb, had seen the unborn child and felt its warmth and its spirit. He could expel that spirit, he realized. He could use the soul stone to send his spirit into Constance's womb, to take the body of the unborn babe.

To be reborn as the son of the King!

Je'howith clutched his chest as another sharp wave of pain washed over him.

As soon as it abated, his hand moved for the night table.

But then he recoiled, considering more clearly the course he had devised, recognizing the immorality and wrongness of it! How could he think to do such a horrible thing? He had spent his whole life in the service of God, and though he had made mistakes and though he had often failed, he had never done wrong purposefully! And certainly he had never entertained the idea of something as sinful as this!

With a growl against the pain, Abbot Je'howith did indeed reach over and pull forth the soul stone, bringing it close to his burning heart. He fell into the swirls of the gem, not to attack the spirit of Constance's unborn child, not even to contact another brother.

No, his time here was over, the old abbot understood. His weariness of it all was, he believed, a call from God that it was time to come home.

The old abbot replayed most of his life in those last few minutes, most of all the final years, when Markwart had gone astray and Je'howith had, out of fear and darker intentions, willingly followed him. He wondered, given the many turns, if he would truly find redemption at the end of this final road.

He wondered, and not without trepidation, what redemption might be.

Abbot Je'howith closed his eyes for the last time.

CHAPTER

❖ 26 ❖

Unfamiliar Faces with Familiar Expressions

"Complain, complain," Roger chided Pony. "You'll see Colleen, and you know that you want that! We start tomorrow."

Pony, astride Greystone at the top of the north slope leading out of Dundalis, just waved him away; and off Roger went, skipping as much as trotting, thrilled that he had finally convinced Pony to go to Caer Tinella with him.

Pony couldn't hide her smile as she watched her friend go. Roger had pestered her all through the summer, but she had steadfastly refused. He wanted her to go all the way to Palmaris with him, and finally, she had relented enough to agree to journey halfway, to Caer Tinella and their friend Colleen.

Looking past Roger, Pony noted the town that had served her so well as a sanctuary. She had been here about a year, and in that time had found some measure of peace. She spent her days working in Fellowship Way beside Belster O'Comely, who was usually too busy chatting with the townsfolk— mostly his very best friend, Tomas Gingerwart—to get any real work done. Pony, though, had been happy enough in just keeping to herself, going about her routines, taking solace in the ordinary work of ordinary days.

And now Roger wanted to upset everything, wanted to pull her back to the south, where, she feared, those memories waited for her. He had worn her down, and she had agreed; but now her smile faded as she wondered if she could hold to that agreement!

She gave a sigh and turned away, for she had another appointment to keep that day. She prodded Greystone slowly down the other side of the ridge, the northern descent, and into the wide pine vale thick with white caribou moss. This, too, was a place of memories, but good ones mostly, of her youth with Elbryan in the days before the goblins.

Pony rode through the vale and into the forest, trotting her horse easily and stopping occasionally for a break or simply to bask in the solitude. This was her refuge, the place where she could forget the troubles of the wider, civilized world. She didn't fear any large animals, no cats nor bears, nor was she afraid that any remnants of the demon's monstrous minions might still be about. No, Pony's only fear was of a different sort, of memories wrought by the foolishness of men, the reminder of how little she had accomplished, of how futile her dear Elbryan's death had been.

She stopped at the appointed spot, a secluded stream-fed pond not so far from the grove that held Elbryan's grave. Bradwarden wasn't there yet, so she hopped down from Greystone and kicked off her shoes, dropping her feet into the comfortably chilly water.

A long time passed, but Pony hardly cared that the centaur was late. She lay back in the leaf-covered grass, splashing her feet, remembering the good times and putting the bad far, far away.

"I'd throw ye in for the fun of it, if I didn't think the chill'd kill ye," came the centaur's voice, some time later, rousing Pony from a restful sleep.

She looked up at the sky curiously. "Noon?" she asked with sarcasm, for that had been their appointed hour and the sun was now low in the western sky.

"Midday, I said," the centaur corrected. "And since I'm to bed after the turn of midnight, and asleep until late in the morn, this is close enough, by me own guessin'!"

Pony threw a handful of leaves at him, but the autumn wind got them and sent them fluttering in all directions.

"Ye got to learn to look at the world proper, girl." Bradwarden laughed.

"A world I'll be seeing more of soon enough," Pony replied.

"Aye, I saw yer friend Roger and he telled me as much," said Bradwarden. "He finally got to ye, did he? Well, ye know how I'm feelin' about it."

"Indeed," Pony muttered, for Bradwarden had been pestering her to go to the south with Roger almost as much as Roger had.

"Ye can't be hidin' forever, now can ye?"

"Hiding?" Pony snorted. "Can you not understand that I simply prefer this place?"

"Even if ye're speakin' true—and I'm thinkin' that ye're tellin' yerself a bit of a lie—then ye should get out beyond the Timberlands once in a bit and see the wider world."

"If Roger had his way, I would be spending the whole of my winter in Palmaris," Pony remarked.

"Not so bad a thing!" Bradwarden bellowed.

Pony looked at him doubtfully. "Life here is peaceful and enjoyable," she replied after a while. "I've no desire to leave, and do so only as a friend to Roger, who does not wish to travel the road to Caer Tinella alone. I cannot understand his restlessness—he has all that he wants right here."

That brought a belly laugh from the centaur. "All that he's wantin'?" he echoed incredulously. "And what're ye thinkin's here for the boy? The sun's shinin', girl. Don't ye feel it in yer bones and in yer heart?"

Pony stared at him for a long moment, then remarked, "In my bones, perhaps."

Bradwarden laughed yet again. "Aye, in yer bones alone, and there's a part o' Roger's problem!"

Pony stared at him curiously.

"He's a young man, full o' spirit and full o' wantin'," the centaur pointed out the obvious. "There be only two single women in all the three Timberland towns, and one's still a child and showing no hints of love."

"And the other is me," Pony reasoned. "You don't believe that Roger . . ." she started to ask, her voice showing her alarm.

"I believe that he'd love ye with all his heart if ye wanted it," Bradwarden remarked. "But, no, girl, ye rest easy, for Roger's not thinkin' on ye in that way. He's too good the friend, for yerself and for yer Nightbird."

Pony rested back in the thick carpet of leaves, considering the words. "Roger's going to Palmaris to find a wife," she stated more than asked.

"A lover, at least, I'd be guessin'," the centaur replied. "And can ye blame him?"

That last question, and the rather sharp tone in which it was delivered, made Pony glance up at Bradwarden curiously.

"Have ye so forgotten what it's feelin' like to be in love?" the centaur asked quietly, compassionately.

"Spoken from you?" Pony asked with more than a little sarcasm, for, as far as she knew, Bradwarden had never been enamored of any other centaurs; as far as Pony knew, there weren't any other centaurs in all the world!

"It's a bit different with me own kind," the centaur explained. "We've ways to . . ." He paused, obviously embarrassed, and cleared his throat, a great rumbling sound like boulders cascading down a rocky slope. "We go to find our lovin' once a five-year, and no more. A different love each time, or mighten be the same. And when the mare's with young, then she's to rear and raise the little one alone."

"So you never knew your father," Pony reasoned.

"Knew of him, and that's enough," Bradwarden said; and if there was a trace of regret in his voice, Pony couldn't detect it.

"But yer own kind," the centaur went on, "now, there's a different tale to be telled. I been watchin' yer kind for too long to be thinkin' that any of ye might find happiness alone."

Pony eyed him squarely, for that remark had been a clear shot at her, she believed.

"Oh, ye'll find yerself wantin' again, perhaps, and might that ye won't," the centaur replied to that look. "But ye've known love, girl, as great a love as me own eyes've e'er seen. Ye've known it, and ye can feel it still, warmin' yer heart."

"I feel a great hole in my heart," Pony stated.

"At times," said the centaur with a wry smile. The mere fact that Bradwarden could get away with such a look while speaking of Elbryan confirmed to Pony that there was indeed a measure of truth in his words. "But the warm parts're meltin' that hole closed, by me own guess.

"Still, ye've known that love, as Belster once did, and so ye two have yer memories, and that's a sight more than Roger's got."

Pony started to reply but held the words in check, considering carefully the centaur's reasoning, and deciding that it was indeed sound. Roger was lonely, and was at an age and an emotional place where he needed more than friends. Bradwarden was right: up here in the Timberlands, the choices for a young man were not plentiful.

Pony lay back and put her hands behind her head, staring up at the late-afternoon autumn sky, clear blue and with puffy white clouds drifting by. She did remember well that feeling of being in love. She felt it still, that warmth and closeness, despite the fact that her lover lay cold in the ground. She wondered then, and perhaps for the first time since the tragedy at Chasewind Manor, if she would ever find love again. Even more than that, she wondered if she would ever want to find love again.

She stayed with Bradwarden until late in the night, listening to his piping song. On her way back to Dundalis, she stopped by the grove and the two cairns, and paused there for a long time, remembering.

The next morning—still tired, for she had not returned to her bed until very late indeed—Pony rode Greystone beside Roger, who was riding an older mare he and Bradwarden had taken from Symphony's herd, down the road to the south. An easy week of riding later, the pair trotted into Caer Tinella.

They found Colleen at her house, the woman looking even more feeble and battered than she had when Pony and Belster had stopped in the town on their way to Dundalis. Still, Colleen found the strength to wrap Pony and Roger in a great hug.

"I been thinkin' o' goin' to Dundalis," she explained, pushing Pony back to arm's length and staring admiringly at her, "soon as I'm feeling the better, I mean."

"Well, we saved you the journey," Pony offered, trying to look cheerful.

Colleen put on a sly look. "Ye paid him back good, didn't ye? Seano Bellick, I mean."

Roger looked curiously at Pony. "He came at us in the night," she explained. "I tried to convince him to leave."

"Oh, ye convinced him, I'd say," Colleen said with a chuckle, and she turned to Roger and explained. "Cut off his axe hand, she did, and put an arrow into his friend's eye! Seano come through here the next day, howlin' in pain and howlin' mad. The fool run right through, and all the way to Palmaris—though I heared he got killed on the road."

"Not much of a loss to the world, then," Pony remarked.

"Can't know for sure," Colleen explained, and she had to pause for a long while, coughing and coughing. "We've not been gettin' much word from the south of late—farmers gettin' in their crops and all."

"Do you know if Brother Braumin remains as abbot of St. Precious?" Pony asked.

"Aye, and he's all the stronger because Duke Kalas ran off last winter, back to Ursal," Colleen replied. "Me cousin Shamus sent word to me. He's back in the city, workin' with the man who's holding court as baron. They're lovin' Abbot Braumin in Palmaris."

"It will be good to see him again," Roger remarked.

"Ye're passin' through, then?" Colleen asked.

"Roger is, but I came to see you," Pony replied.

"Good timin' for ye," Colleen said to Roger. "There's a caravan goin' out for Palmaris tomorrow."

"I had hoped to visit longer than that," said Roger.

"But they're sayin' a storm's comin' fast," Colleen answered. "Ye might want to get on with that caravan if ye're lookin' for a safe road to Palmaris."

Roger looked to Pony, and she shrugged. They had known from the beginning that this moment would soon be upon them, where they parted ways, and perhaps, by Roger's own words, for a long, long time.

"Ye go and see Janine o' the Lake," Colleen instructed. "She'll get ye fixed up with the drivers."

They chatted a while longer, and Colleen set out some biscuits and some steaming stew. Then Roger hustled away, following Colleen's directions to the house of Janine of the Lake.

"Why are you still ill?" Pony asked bluntly, as soon as Colleen closed the door behind Roger.

Colleen looked at her as if she had just been slapped. "Well, ain't that a fine way to be saying hello," she replied.

"An honest way," Pony retorted. "When I left you here before, you were ill, but it seemed easily explained, with the recent fight against Seano Bellick and with all that you have endured these last years. But now . . . Colleen, it has been a year. Have you been sick all this time?"

Colleen's frown withered under the genuine concern. "I had a fine summer," she assured Pony. "I don't know what's come over me of late, but it's nothing to fret about."

"I would be a liar, and no friend, if I told you that you looked strong and healthy," Pony said.

"And I'd be a liar if I telled ye I felt that way," Colleen agreed. "But it'll pass," she insisted.

Pony nodded, trying to seem confident, but she rolled her hematite through her fingers as she did, thinking that she might find need of the soul stone before she left Caer Tinella.

Roger left with the caravan the next day, for it was the last scheduled caravan of the season and many of the farmers were predicting early snows. The young man tried again to convince Pony to go with him, to no avail, and then he fretted about her getting caught here in Caer Tinella by early winter weather.

But Pony told him that she wasn't overconcerned, that she and Greystone could get home whenever they decided it was time to go. And then, remembering well Bradwarden's words to her about why Roger had needed to leave, she bade the young man to be on his way and made him promise to give her fond greetings to all of her friends back in Palmaris.

Truly, Pony had no intention of leaving anytime soon. Her original plan was to accompany Roger here and spend a couple of days, and then return to Dundalis; but with Colleen looking so fragile—even worse, Pony believed, than the previous year—she simply could not walk away.

As predicted, winter did come early to the fields and forests north of Palmaris, but by that time, Roger and the caravan were safely within the walls of the port city on the Masur Delaval.

He went straight to St. Precious when he arrived in the city, though the hour was late; and it was good indeed to be back beside Abbot Braumin and Brothers Viscenti and Castinagis. They laughed and told exaggerated tales of old times. They caught each other up-to-date on the present, and spoke in quiet tones their hopes for the future.

"Pony should have come with me," Roger decided. "It would do her heart good to witness the turn in the Abellican Church, to learn that Avelyn's name will no longer be blasphemed."

"We do not know that," Master Viscenti warned.

"The brothers inquisitor will arrive soon to question us concerning the disposition of Avelyn and the miracle at Mount Aida," Abbot Braumin explained. "Their investigation will determine the fate of Avelyn's legacy within the Church."

"Can there be any doubt?" Roger asked. "I was there at Aida beside you. As pure a miracle as the world has ever known!"

"Hold fast that thought," Brother Castinagis piped in. "I am sure that the brothers inquisitor will find your voice in time."

They talked easily all that first night until they drifted off, one by one, to sleep. And then they spent the better part of the next day together, reminiscing, planning, and again long into the night, until Abbot Braumin was called to a meeting with Brother Talumus and some others.

Roger went out alone into Palmaris' night.

He made his way to a familiar area and found, to his delight, that a new tavern had been erected on the site of the old Fellowship Way, the inn of Graevis and Pettibwa Chilichunk, Pony's deceased adoptive parents.

The place had been renamed The Giant's Bones, and when he entered, Roger understood why, for lining the walls as macabre support beams were the whitened bones of several giants. Huge skulls adorned the walls, including the biggest of all set on a shelf right behind the bar. The lighting, too, reflected the name: a chandelier constructed of a giant's rib cage.

Roger wandered through, studying the creative decorations and the unfamiliar faces wearing all too familiar expressions. The tavern, this place, The Giant's Bones, was very different from Fellowship Way, he thought, and yet very much the same. Roger listened in on a few conversations as he made his way to the bar, words he had heard before, in a different time.

They seemed happy enough, these folk, though Roger heard a few of the typical, predictable complaints about taxes and tithes, and he heard low and ominous murmurs at one table about some plague.

But, in truth, the more he listened and the more he looked, the more Roger felt comfortable in the tavern, the more it felt like home.

"What're ye drinking, friend?" came a gravelly voice behind him.

"Honey mead," Roger replied, without turning.

He heard the clank of a bottle and glass, then came the same voice. "Well, what're ye looking at, girl, and why ain't ye working?"

Roger glanced back then, to see the grizzly-bearded innkeeper pouring his drink and to see, more pointedly, a familiar face indeed, staring back at him from behind the bar.

"Roger Lockless," Dainsey Aucomb said happily. "But I wondered if I'd ever see ye in here again."

"Dainsey!" Roger replied, reaching forward to share a little hug and kiss over the bar.

"Ye spill it, ye pay for it," the gruff innkeeper said, and Roger leaned back.

"Oh, ye're such a brute, ye are, Bigelow Brown!" Dainsey said with a laugh, and she swatted the man with her dishrag. "Ye'd be showin' more manners, ye would, if ye knew who ye was shoutin' at!"

That made Bigelow Brown look at Roger more carefully, but before he could begin to ask, Dainsey hustled about the bar and took the slender man by the arm, escorting him across the room. She shooed a couple of men from a table and gave it to Roger, then went back and retrieved his honey mead.

"I'll come by whenever I can find the time," Dainsey said. "I'm wantin' to hear all about Pony and Belster and Dundalis."

Roger smiled at her and nodded, and he was glad indeed that he had come back to Palmaris.

True to her word, Dainsey Aucomb visited Roger often, and often with refills of his honey mead, drinks that she insisted were gifts from Bigelow

Brown, though Roger doubted that the tavern keeper even knew he was being so generous. They chatted and they laughed, catching each other up on the last year's events; and before he realized the hour, Roger found that he was among the tavern's last patrons.

"I'll be done me work soon," Dainsey explained, delivering one last glass of honey mead.

"A walk?" Roger asked, pointing to her and to himself.

"I'd like that, Roger Lockless," Dainsey answered with a little smile, and she went back to the bar to finish her work.

It was a fine night for a late walk. A bit cold, perhaps, but the storm that had hit farther north had barely clipped Palmaris, and now the stars were out bright and crisp.

Dainsey led the way, walking slowly and talking easily. They went around the side of the tavern and down an alley, where, to Roger's surprise, they found a ladder set into the tavern wall, leading up to the only flat section of roof on the whole structure.

"I made 'em build it like that," Dainsey explained, taking hold of one of the rungs and starting up. "I wanted it to be the same way it was when Pony was workin' here."

Roger followed her up to the flat roof; she was sitting comfortably with her back against the warm chimney by the time he pulled himself over the roof's edge.

"This was Pony's special place," Dainsey explained, and Roger nodded, for Pony had told him about her nights on the roof of Fellowship Way. "Where she'd come to hide from the troubles and to steal a peek at all the wide world."

Roger looked all about, at the quiet of the Palmaris night, up at the twinkling stars, and over at the soft glow by the river, where the docks, despite the late hour, remained very much active and alive. He surely understood Dainsey's description, "to steal a peek at all the wide world," for it seemed to him as if he could watch all the city from up here, as if he were some otherworldly spy, looking in on—but very much separated from—the quiet hours of the folk of Palmaris.

He heard a couple on the street below, whispering and giggling, and he gave a wry smile as he caught some of their private conversation, words that they had meant for no other ears.

He could see how Pony so loved this place.

"Is she well?" Dainsey asked, drawing him from his trance.

Roger looked at her. "Pony?" he asked.

"Well, who else might I be talkin' about?" the woman asked with a chuckle.

"She is better," Roger explained. "I left her in Caer Tinella with Colleen Kilronney."

"Her cousin's back in Palmaris, working beside the new baron now that Kalas' run off," Dainsey put in.

Roger walked over and sat down beside her, close enough to share the warmth of the chimney.

"She should've stayed," Dainsey remarked, "or I should've gone with her."

"There's not much up there," Roger told her honestly. "That's what Pony needed for now, but you would have found life . . . tedious."

"But I do miss her," Dainsey said. She looked over at Roger, and he could see that there was hint of a tear in her eye. "She could've stayed and ruled the world. Oh, she's such a pretty one."

Roger stared at her earnestly, looked deep into her delicate eyes in a manner in which he never had thought to look before. "No prettier than Dainsey Aucomb," he said before he could think, for if he had considered the words, he never would have found the courage to spout them!

Dainsey blushed and started to look away, but Roger, bolstered by hearing his own forward declaration, grabbed her chin in his small hand and forced her to look back at him. " 'Tis true," he said.

Dainsey stared at him doubtfully. "I gived ye too much o' the honey mead," she said with a chuckle.

"It has nothing to do with the drink," Roger declared flatly and firmly.

Dainsey tried to turn away again, and started to laugh, but Roger held her with his hand, and stifled her chuckles with a sober and serious look.

"Ye never said so before," she said quietly.

Roger shook his head, having no real answer to that. "I do not know that I ever looked closely enough before," he said. "But 'tis true, Dainsey Aucomb."

She started to say something, then started to chuckle, but Roger came forward and kissed her gently.

Dainsey pushed him back to arm's length. "What're ye about, then?" she asked.

Now it was Roger's turn to blush. "I—I—I do not know," he blurted, and started to turn away.

But Dainsey Aucomb gave a great laugh and grabbed him hard, pulling him in for another kiss, a deeper and more urgent kiss.

The early snow didn't stay for long, and soon after, the road to Dundalis was open again. But Pony couldn't leave, because Colleen had not improved. Far from it; the woman was looking more drawn and weary with each passing day. Pony had offered to try to help her with the soul stone several times, but Colleen had refused, insisting that it was just an early season chill and that she'd be rid of it soon enough.

But then one morning when she went in to check on Colleen—an oddity, since the woman, despite her sickness, was always up before Pony and preparing her breakfast—Pony found her drenched in sweat in bed, too weak to even begin to stand.

Pony pulled down the heavy blankets to try to cool the woman down.

And then she saw them, on Colleen's bare arm, round red splotches about the size of a gol'bear coin and ringed in white.

"What?" Pony asked, lifting the arm to better see the strange rings.

Colleen couldn't answer; Pony wondered if she'd even heard the question.

The rosy plague had come to the northland.

CHAPTER

❖ 27 ❖

A Thousand,
Thousand Little Demons

"It's the rosy plague, I tell ye," the old woman said decisively. She was examining Colleen from afar, and she was backing with each word now that she had seen the telltale rings. She reached the door, her mouth moving as if she were trying futilely to find some words strong enough to express her horror, and then she slipped out into the daylight.

Pony rushed outside behind her. "The rosy plague?" she echoed, for she had no idea what that might be. Pony had grown up on the frontier in the Timberlands. Her mother had taught her to read well enough, but she had never studied formally, and she had never heard of the plague.

"Aye, and the death of us all!" the old woman wailed.

"What about my friend?"

"She's doomed or she's not, but that's not for yerself to decide," the old woman answered coldly.

"I have a gemstone," Pony said, producing the hematite. "I have been trained in the use—"

"It'll do ye no good against the rosy plague!" the old woman cried. "Ye'll just get yerself kilt!"

Pony eyed her sternly, but the wrinkled old woman threw up her hands, gave a great wail, and ran off, crying, "Ring around the rosy!"

Pony went back inside, scolding herself for even consulting the town's accepted healer, instead of just fighting the disease with her soul stone. She moved up beside Colleen, who was lying on her bed, and took the woman's hand in her own. She could feel the heat emanating from Colleen, could feel clammy wetness on her frail-looking arm. What a different woman this was from the warrior who had accompanied Pony throughout her trials! Colleen had been strong—stronger than Pony, surely, with thick arms and broad shoulders. But now she seemed so frail, so tired, so beaten. Pony felt more than a twinge of guilt at the sight, for Colleen's downslide had begun on the journey in which she had accompanied the outlaw Pony north out of Palmaris. De'Unnero, half man, half tiger, had caught them on the road, had downed Pony, and then had beaten Colleen severely. She had gotten away, for De'Unnero's focus was Pony and not her, but Colleen had never really recovered.

And now here she lay, feverish and frail in her bed.

Pony put aside her guilt and focused on correcting the situation, focused on the all-important hematite, the soul stone, the stone of healing. Deeper and deeper she went into the gemstone's inviting gray depths, into the swirl, her spirit leaving her body behind. Free of material bonds, Pony floated about the bed, looking down upon Colleen and upon her own physical form, still holding the woman's hand. She focused her thoughts on Colleen, and could feel the sickness, a tangible thing; could feel the heat rising from Colleen's battered body; could sense that the very air was tainted by a sickly smell of rot.

At first that stench, the sheer wrongness of it, nearly overwhelmed Pony, nearly chased her right back into her own body. She understood at that moment why the old woman had run off wailing. For a moment, she wanted to do nothing more than that same thing. But she found her heart and her strength, reminded herself that she had faced Markwart, the embodiment of Bestesbulzibar itself, in this same spiritual state. If she left Colleen now, then her friend would certainly die, and horribly, and soon.

She could not let that happen.

Colleen was her friend, who had stood with her against the darkness of the demon dactyl.

She could not let that happen.

Colleen's descent to this point had begun when she was fighting beside Pony, in a battle that Colleen made her own for the sake of friendship and nothing more.

She could not let that happen.

With renewed resolve, as determined as she had ever been, the spirit of Pony dove into Colleen to meet the sickness head-on. She found it immediately, general in Colleen's battered body, like some green pus bubbling up all through her. Pony's spiritual hands glowed with healing fire, and she thrust them down upon the sickly broth of the rosy plague.

And indeed, that green pus melted beneath her touch, steamed away into sickly vapors! Pony pressed on determinedly, pushed down, down. She had beaten back the spirit of the demon; she could defeat this.

So she thought.

Her spiritual hands pressed into the greenish plague as if she were pushing them into a pot of pea soup—a deep pot. Soon the plague all about those two areas where she focused her healing closed in around her arms, grabbing at her, a thousand, thousand tiny enemies seeking to invade her spiritual arms, to find a link to her physical form. Pony pressed and slapped, but the soupy disease slipped down before her and rolled over her glowing, healing hands, attacking relentlessly. Pony had battled perhaps the greatest single foe in all the world, but this was different. This time, her enemies, the little creatures of the rosy plague that had invaded Colleen's body, were too many to fight, were too hungry and vicious.

They would not wait their turn to war with Pony but came at her all at once, attacked the spiritual hematite link without regard. She knew she was killing them with her healing hands—by the score, by the hundred, by the thousand—but only then, to her horror, did she realize the truth: they were multiplying as fast as she was destroying them! She moved frantically, desperately, intently focused, for she had to be. To let up for one moment was to allow the rosy plague into her own body. If even one of these tiny plague creatures got into her, it would begin the frantic reproduction process within its new host.

She knew that, and gave everything she could possibly offer into the gemstone. Her hands glowed even brighter, a burning, healing light.

But the plague was too thick and too hungry, and soon Pony realized that she was slapping at her own arms, desperate to keep the vicious little creatures out of her. Before she could even register the change, the connection with Colleen was severed; and a moment later, Pony found herself sitting on the floor beside the bed, instinctively slapping at her arms.

A few moments later, she slumped back against the wall, exhausted and overwhelmed and unsure of whether or not any of the vicious little creatures had found their way into her body.

She crawled back to Colleen and pulled herself up by the woman's side.

Her efforts had done nothing at all to alleviate the woman's suffering.

"She's flagging us, but not coming any closer," the watchman explained to Warder Presso. The two stood on the rampart of Pireth Vanguard, overlooking the wide Gulf of Corona, observing a curious ship that had sailed in just a few minutes before. The ship had come close to Vanguard's long wharf, but then, when a group of soldiers had gone down to help her tie in, she had put back out fifty yards.

The distant crew had then called something about delivering a message to the new abbot of St. Belfour, but when the soldiers had inquired of the message, the sailors had insisted on seeing the warder of the fort.

"She's not carrying any standard of Honce-the-Bear," Presso remarked, studying the vessel, obviously a trader. "But she's got the evergreen flying," he added, pointing to the lower pennant on the aft line of the mizzen mast, the white flag with the evergreen symbol of the Abellican Church. "Agronguerre, likely, sending word to Abbot Haney."

"But why aren't they just saying it, then?" the nervous soldier asked. "And why won't they come in? We've asked them over and over."

Presso, more skilled in ways politic, merely smiled at the ignorant remark. Knowledge was power, to the Church and the Crown, and so messages were often secret. Still, this visit to Vanguard seemed especially strange this late in the season, with the cold winter wind already blowing down from Alpinador. And for the crew of this ship to be apparently intent on turning about seemed preposterous. Even if they meant to cross the gulf only halfway and dock at Dancard, the journey could take several days, and one of the gulf's many winter storms could easily put them under the waves.

Strange as it seemed, Presso could not deny the sight before him, and so he hurried down the long winding stairway outside the fortress, making his way to the low docks and his men.

"They want to send it in on an arrow," one explained.

Presso looked around, spotting an earthen embankment not so far away. "Go and tell them who I am," he bade the soldier. "Have them put their message there, and on my word as a warder in the Coastpoint Guards, assure them that it will be delivered, unread, to Abbot Haney at St. Belfour posthaste."

"They should just come in and deliver it themselves," the soldier grumbled, but he saluted his warder and ran down the length of the long dock, calling to the ship.

A moment later, an arrow soared off the boat, thudding into the earthen embankment, and the soldiers retrieved it as the ship bade them farewell and turned fast for the south.

Constantine Presso then surprised his men by announcing that he would deliver the message personally. An hour later, he arrived at St. Belfour and was announced in the audience chamber of the new abbot, who sat comfortably behind his modest desk, with Brother Dellman sitting off to the side.

"From Father Abbot Agronguerre, I would assume," the warder explained after the informal greetings. "I believe that is his seal." He tossed the rolled parchment on the desk before Haney.

"Unopened?" Haney remarked.

"As we were bid by the ship that delivered it," Presso explained. "By arrow, I must add, for they would not dock."

That made Haney turn a curious, somewhat nervous glance over Brother Dellman.

"I thank you for delivering it, Warder Presso," he then said, "and for holding the confidence, as you were requested."

"But I ask that you open it now, in my presence," the warder surprised the abbot by saying.

Haney glanced at Dellman again, and both turned curious gazes over Presso.

"The manner of delivery brings me as much worry as it does you, my friends," Presso said, trying not to be mysterious. "Open it, I pray. I'll stand back, on my word, but if the news is grave, and if it concerns Pireth Vanguard or Prince Midalis, then you must inform me immediately."

That seemed fair enough, and so Abbot Haney, with Brother Dellman coming up right beside him, broke the seal. "Promotion to master for you?" Haney wondered aloud, smiling at his friend and close adviser.

Dellman smiled, too, but both of the men turned their lips down quickly into most profound frowns when Haney unrolled the parchment.

"Grave news," Warder Presso said, seeing it clearly from their expressions.

Abbot Haney was trembling as he handed the parchment to Presso, who took it, thinking that perhaps their dear friend Agronguerre had died.

When he read the words, a warning about the rosy plague, the warder—who was a friend of Agronguerre's and admired the man greatly—wished that his initial fears had been correct.

"I trust that you will be discreet with this information," Brother Dellman remarked. It struck Presso from the look that Dellman gave Haney that he wasn't pleased that his abbot had so readily turned over the letter. "If we are too quick to spread this grave news, it could cause panic."

"And of course, only King's men and Church members should be so privileged," Warder Presso said, voice dripping with sarcasm.

"That is not what I said."

"But is it not what you meant?"

"Enough," Haney demanded of them both. "Deliver that at once to Prince Midalis, I pray you, Warder Presso," he instructed. "If he wishes to meet with us that we can coordinate our efforts to spread such dire news, then, of course, I—we," he added, glancing up at Dellman, "will be available."

Presso nodded, gave a slight bow, then started to turn, but paused and looked back at Dellman. "Forgive me, brother," he said sincerely. "Blame my surly words on my surprise at reading such unexpected and tragic news."

"And my own for so responding," said Dellman with a polite bow.

Prince Midalis met with Abbot Haney that same evening, but not before issuing a general blockade of Pireth Vanguard. No ships were to be allowed in, not even to the long dock, and no goods unloaded.

Abbot Haney agreed, and the next morning, the two leaders broke the devastating news to the general population of Vanguard. Also, that same day, Midalis sent runners north to alert the Alpinadorans of the pending disaster. And thus was the northeastern quarter of Honce-the-Bear shut down.

Visitors were no longer welcome in the land that prided itself on camaraderie and friendship.

The cart slogged along trails that were mud where the sun hit them and ice where it did not. Greystone tugged at the harness without protest, eager to please the driver, Pony.

And she urged the horse on with all speed, though she tried to pick as smooth a path as she could find. Behind her, wrapped in blankets but cold and miserable nonetheless, Colleen Kilronney groaned and coughed.

Pony tried to block out those pitiful sounds and focus on the road ahead, the road south to Palmaris, to St. Precious, to somewhere Pony might find someone and some way to help her mortally ill friend.

She glanced west, to the dark clouds that had risen over the horizon as the afternoon had drawn on, and second-guessed her decision to set out from Caer Tinella. She little feared weather this early in the season if it was just herself and Greystone, but how would she keep Colleen warm if the snows forced them off the road? And surely her friend would not survive a cold, wet night.

And so she rode on, after the sun went down, and wishing that she had a magical diamond that she might light the path before her!

Later on snow began to fall and a cold, cold wind rushed down; and Pony wished even more for that magical diamond, that she could call a warming glow to comfort her poor friend.

She set a torch blazing and drove on, trying to outrun the storm, to get far enough south so that it would be a more gentle event, rain, perhaps.

But the snow kept falling, wet snow, clumping on the wagon and wheels, weighing down Greystone's load. It settled over the trail, making the ice even more slippery and more treacherous in the dark.

Pony knew that she could not stop. She had seventy miles of road before her to get to Palmaris, Colleen's only chance. Gently but firmly she bade Greystone continue, and the valiant horse trudged along.

The night deepened and the snow continued, accumulating on the road, making progress more difficult, bringing a bright sheen to poor Greystone's blond coat. Pony knew that she had to press on, but knew, too, that if she did, Greystone would likely fall over and die. She and her horse could not make it alone.

She pulled up at the side of the trail and brought her torch back, tucking the blankets tightly about Colleen, trying to keep her as warm as possible. Then she ran to Greystone and unhitched him and walked him, trying to cool him down slowly and safely.

And all the while, she wondered what she could do next. How could she save Colleen?

Her soul stone seemed the only answer. Perhaps she could reach out and find some nearby help. Of course, if she was honest with any nearby farmers or woodsmen, they wouldn't likely come anywhere near her or Colleen. Perhaps she could swap a horse with them, though she'd hate to part with wonderful Greystone.

She came back to the wagon then, deciding that the soul stone was her only option. She reached into her pouch and produced the hematite, and fell into it immediately, using its magic to free her of her corporeal form. For a moment, she thought of going at Colleen's tiny disease demons again, but the memory of the previous encounter left her weak. So she went out, searching, searching.

And she found her answer—her wonderful, amazing answer—in but a few moments, as she encountered another spirit, strong and natural: the thoughts of magnificent Symphony, nearby and running hard toward her. Pony felt the horse keenly, understood so clearly that it was indeed Symphony, and recognized clearly Symphony's intent to come to her aid. She suspected that she had touched the turquoise bond with her hematite reach, and a miraculous bond it was!

She rushed back into her corporeal form, then over to Colleen, lighting a fire, tucking in her blankets, kissing her on the forehead and telling her that it would be all right.

Symphony arrived soon after, snorting and pawing the ground. Pony wondered if she could manipulate the harness and rope so that both horses could pull the wagon, but she gave up on the idea quickly, mostly because she sensed Symphony's impatience, almost as if the horse understood her needs and was assuring her that he could fulfill them.

She harnessed him up and tied Greystone to the back. Though the snow continued, even intensified, the wagon was rolling again, and swiftly, with Symphony plowing forward.

A dull sunrise came and went, and still they rolled on. Soon they came to muddier ground, and the snow became cold rain, and still they rolled on.

Symphony pulled tirelessly, through the morning and into the afternoon, and then, amazingly to Pony, she saw the farmhouses increasing in number along the rolling hills, and knew that she would see Palmaris over the very next rise.

Down they went, gaining speed with the goal in sight. The guards at the city's northern gate motioned for the wagon to stop, and Pony called out to them to let her pass. "Without delay!" she cried. "I am Jilseponie Wyndon—you know me—and you know the person I carry to the healing doors of St. Precious. Colleen Kilronney, she is: a friend to any soldier of Palmaris!"

The soldiers bustled about and seemed unsure what to do, until one of them took careful note of the black, white-booted stallion pulling her wagon, and cried out, "Symphony!" They knew then that it was indeed Pony returned to them, and they threw the gates wide. Several mounted their own horses and led Pony's wagon through the winding streets of Palmaris, clearing the road all the way to the doors of St. Precious.

The brothers who met the unexpected caravan reacted with equal fervor, bringing Abbot Braumin and the other leaders, Viscenti, Talumus, and Castinagis, in short order.

Pony saw the bed of flowers laid out in front of the abbey, half buried by wet snow, most of them dead. Shaking her head, she came down from the wagon and fell into Braumin's arms. "Help her," she pleaded, and then, overcome with exhaustion, Pony collapsed.

She awoke in a plain but comfortable cot, dressed only in a long white shirt, but covered by many thick blankets. She was in the abbey, she recognized by the narrow, rectangular window and the plain, gray stone walls. A shaft of sunlight streaming in through that narrow window told her that the storm had ended.

Pony pulled herself out of bed and went over to the window, looking out to the Masur Delaval and the rising sun. Only then did she realize that she had slept for the better part of an entire day, and only then did she remember the harrowing journey through the dark night and the snow.

She searched for her clothes, but, finding none, wrapped a blanket about her and charged out of the room. She knew the layout of St. Precious well from her days there after the fight at Chasewind Manor, and so she ran straight off for Abbot Braumin's office.

He was there, along with Viscenti and Talumus, arguing over some philosophical point concerning the origin of Man and how the Original Man had become diversified into the various races: Alpinadoran, Bearman, Behrenese, and To-gai-ru.

That conversation ended abruptly when Pony came crashing through the door.

"Jilseponie," Abbot Braumin said. "How good it does my heart to see you awake and well. Ah, yes, your clothing—"

"Where is she?" Pony asked.

Abbot Braumin looked at her curiously for just a moment, and then a cloud passed over his face. He looked at his two companions, nodding for them to leave the room.

They both did so without question, Viscenti pausing only long enough to drop a comforting pat on Pony's shoulder.

Then the door shut hard behind her, and Pony nearly jumped off the floor. Hardly able to draw breath, she asked again, more somberly, "Where is she?"

"She is very ill," Abbot Braumin replied, standing up and coming around the desk. He moved near Pony, but she visibly stiffened and so he sat instead on the edge of his desk.

"Is?" Pony echoed. "Then she is still alive."

Abbot Braumin nodded. "But not for long, I fear."

Pony started to respond, but nearly choked as Braumin's blunt response registered fully.

"She is afflicted with the rosy plague," Braumin said quietly. "The red spots, the fever . . . there can be no doubt."

Pony was nodding with each word. "I was told as much already," she said.

"But you do not understand what that means, I fear," Braumin replied, "else you would not have driven so hard to bring her here."

Pony stared at him incredulously. "Where, then?" she asked. "Where am I to bring one so ill if not to St. Precious Abbey? Who am I to turn to for help if not Abbot Braumin Herde, my friend?"

Braumin put his hand up in the air as she spoke the words—words obviously painful for him to hear. "The rosy plague," he said again. "Do you not know the song?"

Pony stared at him curiously, and Braumin began to sing the children's rhyme.

> *Ring around the rosy,*
> *Gather bowls of posies*
> *Burn the clothes*
> *And dig the holes*
> *And cover us with dirt.*
>
> *Help to one in twenty*
> *Dying people plenty*
> *Stupid priest*
> *Ate the Beast*
> *And now can't help himself.*
>
> *Praying people follow*
> *Into graves so hollow*
> *Take their gems*
> *Away from them*
> *And cover them with dirt!*

Pony continued to stare, but the words began to sink in, began to ring in her heart the truth about her doomed friend. "Where, then?" she asked weakly.

Braumin came forward and wrapped her in a tight hug. "You make her comfortable, as much as possible, and you say good-bye," he whispered.

Pony let that hug linger for a long, long while, needing the support. Finally she pushed Braumin back far enough so that she could look into his compassionate face. "Where is she?" she asked quietly.

"There is a house not so far from here that already knows the plague," Braumin started to explain.

"She is not within St. Precious?" Pony asked, her voice rising with her surprise.

"I could not," Braumin answered. "I should not have let you in so soon after you spent such intimate time with her."

Pony's eyes widened.

"But I could not refuse you," Braumin went on. "Never that! And yet you must understand that I had to send several brothers to you with soul stones, to search your body for signs of the plague. Still, I should not have let you in, in accordance with Abellican canon."

Pony's eyes stayed very wide.

"Did you not understand the words of the rhyme?" Braumin asked, turning away from her with a withering glare. "One in twenty we may help, but one in seven will afflict the tending monk. The words are true. We of the Order, even with the gifts of God's gemstones, cannot wage battle against the rosy plague."

"One in twenty, you say," Pony replied, a distinct edge to her voice. "Will you not, then, try? For Colleen? For me?"

"I cannot. Nor can any of my brethren. Nor should you."

"Is she not your friend?"

"I cannot."

"Did she not stand strong with us against the darkness of Markwart?"

"I cannot."

"Did she not escape De'Unnero, to spread news of my capture and of the march to the north?"

"I cannot."

"Did she not suffer imprisonment without denouncing us, or Avelyn, or any of the principles that we held dear?" Pony continued to press, coming closer with each statement, so that she was, by this time, leaning heavily over the desk, staring Braumin in the eye from a distance of less than a foot.

"I cannot!" Braumin answered with even more emphasis. "It is our law, without exception."

"It is a bad law," Pony accused.

"Perhaps," said Braumin, "but one without exception. If the King of Honce-the-Bear became ill with plague, the Abellican Church would offer only prayers. If the Father Abbot became ill with plague, he would be forced out of St.-Mere-Abelle, beyond the tussie-mussie bed." Braumin settled back, his voice going low and somber. "There is but one exception I would make. If you, Jilseponie, became ill with plague, I would abdicate my post and my calling, take one soul stone in hand, and would go to you with all my heart and soul."

Pony just stared at him, too stunned by this unbelievable information even to find the words to respond.

"But even if I was successful, even if you proved the one in twenty, then I would be banished for my actions and not allowed back within my abbey until after the plague had abated," Braumin explained, "a decade, perhaps. By that time, I would likely have met with my own death. And if not, it is even possible that I would be branded a heretic for offering such false hopes to the general population. This is much larger than you or me, my friend. It is a matter of the very survival of the Church."

"I am going to Colleen," Pony remarked.

"Do not," said Braumin.

"What stones might I combine with hematite to help shield my work?"

"There is nothing," Braumin said bluntly, his tone rising. "Hematite will bring you to the disease, and there you will succeed if you are fortunate and its hold is not great, fail if moderate, and fail utterly, and sicken yourself, if it is thick within the victim."

Pony considered those words carefully in the context of what she had found awaiting her previous delving into the tortured body of Colleen Kilronney. Could the plague be any thicker within a living person? she had to honestly wonder, shivering at the mere memory of her encounter with the disease.

"I cannot bring her here," Pony said calmly.

Abbot Braumin, though his expression was pained, shook his head.

"And you cannot go with me to her."

Braumin winced even more, but again he shook his head.

"And what will you do through all the years of plague, then?" Pony asked sharply. "Will you remain in your abbey behind locked gates, discussing the origins of the various human races?"

"That and other matters philosophical," the abbot explained. "It is long tradition within the Church that times of plague are times of retreat for the brothers, to discuss and debate the greater questions of existence."

"While the world suffers."

Abbot Braumin seemed wounded. He sighed deeply. "What would you have me do?"

"I know the path before me," Pony answered.

"And it is one that I again bid you not to walk," Braumin replied. "You are more likely to die trying to help her than to give her any aid."

"I have already tried with my soul stone," Pony replied honestly, "and failed utterly."

"Then why go?"

Pony stared at him, disappointed in Braumin for the first time since she had met him. *Then why go?* she echoed incredulously in her mind. To hold her, of course, and talk to her, to comfort her and to say farewell! How could generous Braumin not see so obvious a duty? How could he place tradition over compassion?

"I will have my clothes, and be gone," Pony answered.

Braumin nodded, then paused for a brief moment and moved behind his desk, pulling open a drawer. He produced a small sack. "One of every gemstone available at St. Precious, including the very same cat's-eye circlet you once wore," he explained, handing it over to Pony. "In times of plague, the folk may be driven mad. You might need these for protection."

Pony took the sack, but stared at Braumin skeptically.

"Also, since I know your heart, and doubt not your talent, I hold a hope that you will again prove our savior, that you will find a gemstone combination that will prove effective against the rosy plague. God be with you, Jilseponie." He hugged her and kissed her on the cheek, then he led her out to retrieve her possessions.

They said good-bye at St. Precious' front gate.

Pony found Colleen in bed, feverish and delirious, calling out for her cousin Shamus. The woman tending her, another plague sufferer, just shook her head when Pony entered the building, even telling Pony that she should not be there.

"Ye're just to kill yerself for mercy," she said.

Pony sighed and pushed past her, going to her friend. She wiped Colleen's brow and whispered calming words into her ear.

Not words about letting go, about going to the other side, though. Pony wasn't ready to quit fighting just yet. She had little privacy, for there were three other plague victims in the same room, all near death, and in the other rooms of the house languished more people in various stages of illness.

Pony pulled open the sack and gently dumped the gemstones on the floor before her, rolling them, sorting them. She took up the serpentine first, considering the shield the gem allowed her to bring up against fire. Might that shield also defeat the intrusions of the plague? For Pony honestly believed that if she could do that, if she could keep the little plague demons away from her own body and spirit, and could thus concentrate wholly on attacking the disease within the victim, she would have much better results.

She held the serpentine and the soul stone. It didn't seem like the answer to her, for she understood the nature of the fire shield and didn't believe that it would stop anything other than fire, just as sunstone could block magic but nothing else. Still, she looked at Colleen, at the shine of sweat on her forehead, the redness in her half-open eyes, her swollen tongue, and knew she had to try.

In she went, serpentine first and then hematite. And then out of her—hopefully—protected body, her spirit went into the green muck of the plague within poor Colleen.

Five minutes later, Pony was on the floor, exhausted and frantically slapping her arms, hoping that none of the plague demons had managed to get into her.

The serpentine shield had done nothing at all.

Pony prayed for guidance. She used the hematite, not to go back to Colleen, but to find a deeper level of concentration, to find the spirit of Avelyn, seeking near-divine guidance.

An image flashed in her mind of that upraised hand at Mount Aida, and for a moment she thought the spirit of Avelyn had come to her and would guide her, would show her the gemstone combination to defeat the rosy plague.

Her spirits sagged a moment later, though, for there was nothing—no answers, no hope.

She fiddled with the stones again, arranging them in various groups and trying to figure out a combination of magical properties that would defeat the plague. She tried serpentine again with hematite and ruby, the stone of fire, wondering if there was some way she could bring up some type of spiritual fire that would burn at the green morass.

Again, she wound up on the floor, desperate and even more exhausted.

And on the bed, Colleen continued to deteriorate.

She went at Colleen a third time an hour later, this time using hematite and a warm and bright diamond.

Nothing.

Colleen Kilronney died later that night, in Pony's arms, though she didn't know that Pony was holding her. Watching that final agony, followed at last by peace, Pony knew in her heart that there was no magical combination of gemstones.

She knew, too, however, that she would not allow herself to run behind tussie-mussie beds and locked gates, as had Braumin Herde and all the Abellican Church.

She stayed with Colleen all through the morning, until the cart man passed by the house, ringing his bell and calling for the dead.

She found that the doors at St. Precious would not open for her. Abbot Braumin came down to the gates, and in truth, he could not bear to keep her out and offered to let her enter.

But Pony refused, understanding the complications for her friend, not wanting to trade on her friendship with the man to force him against Church edict, no matter how mistaken she believed that edict to be.

"Fare you well, my friend," she said sincerely to Braumin. "Perhaps we will meet again in this life, in happier times, that I might argue your present course."

Braumin managed a smile at her generous words, for her disappointment was not hard to see on her fair face. "We will meet again, if not here, then in heaven, with Avelyn and Jojonah and Elbryan. Go with my blessings and my love, Jilseponie."

Pony nodded and walked away, having no idea where she might next turn. She wanted to go back to Dundalis, but worried that such a journey might prove too difficult at that time even for mighty Symphony.

She found herself wandering near familiar places, avenues she had known through her teenage years, and then again after her return to Palmaris. It all seemed strangely quiet to her, as if the people were hiding in their homes, afraid of the rosy plague. One place in particular caught her attention: the Giant's Bones, a tavern built on the location of her longtime home. Fearing her own emotions but unable to resist, she entered the place, to find it, like the streets, nearly empty, with the notable exceptions of two very familiar and very welcome faces.

Roger and Dainsey nearly knocked her over in their joy at seeing her, Dainsey crying out her name repeatedly and hugging her so tightly that she could hardly draw breath.

"You decided to follow me here," Roger remarked, a smug smile on his face. "And now, with winter settling in, you're stuck here for months!"

That made Dainsey grin excitedly, as well, but Pony's reply erased their smiles.

"I brought Colleen into the city because I could not help her," Pony explained. "She died this morning."

"The rosy plague," Dainsey reasoned.

"The city has the smell of death," Roger added, shaking his head. He moved over to Pony then, offering her another hug, but she held him back and took a deep and steadying breath.

"Come with me to the north," she bade Roger, "back home, where we belong. Both Symphony and Greystone came south with me." She paused as she noted Roger's look over at Dainsey, and then it hit her. It became quite clear to Pony that these two—Roger and Dainsey!—were more than just friends.

"How long?" she started to ask. "How . . ." But she stopped and moved closer to Roger, granting him that hug then, truly glad to find that her friend had found such a worthwhile companion as wonderful Dainsey Aucomb.

But her happiness for Roger lasted only the few seconds it took for her to remember the circumstances that had left her walking the empty streets of Palmaris.

CHAPTER

❖ 28 ❖

What Miserable Wretches
We Mortals Be

I t was spring in Honce-the-Bear, but hardly did it seem like a time of
life renewing.

Francis leaned heavily on the stone wall of St.-Mere-Abelle,
needing the support. Beyond his shadow, beyond the window—which was
no more than a rectangular opening in the stone—he saw them.

Dozens of them, scores of them, hundreds of them. Ghostly figures
walking slowly through the morning mist that blanketed the field west of
the abbey, huddled under blankets and rags against the chill that still bit
hard in the springtime night. So beaten and battered were they, so emaciated, that they seemed like skeletons, this collection of pitiful souls outside
the abbey seemed like a gathering of the walking dead.

And the brothers of St.-Mere-Abelle could do nothing for them. Oh, the
monks threw some coins, clothing, blankets, and food, mostly as payment
for work performed by the plague-ridden sufferers. On Master Bou-raiy's
suggestion, Master Machuso had hired the gathered plague victims to plant
this year's huge tussie-mussie, a massive flower bed that would continue on
and on as far as the victims could plant, that might span the mile of ground
fronting St.-Mere-Abelle's western wall.

Francis watched some of them, those with the strength remaining,
laboring along the base of the wall, digging in the ground with rotting fingers. The monk bumped his head against the unyielding stone, not hard,
but repeatedly, as if trying to thump the frustrations out of his skull.

"What miserable wretches we mortals be," he recited gravely, the
opening line to an old verse written by a poet deemed a heretic in the fifth
century.

"Calvin of Bri'Onnaire," came the voice of Fio Bou-raiy behind him, and
Francis turned, startled. "Strong words, brother."

Francis noted the one-armed master, flanked by Father Abbot Agronguerre.

"Fitting words," he replied to Bou-raiy, "for who in this time is not considering his own mortality?"

"Calm, brother," Father Abbot Agronguerre bade Francis.

"He who believes in God does not fear death," Bou-raiy promptly and sternly replied. "Calvin of Bri'Onnaire's words were wrought of fear, not contemplation. He knew that he was a sinner, who faced excommunication by the Church for the lies he spread, and thus grew his fear of death and his bitterness toward all things Abellican. It is well documented."

Master Francis chuckled and shook his head, then closed his eyes and in a voice thick with gravity and sincere emotion recited Calvin's "*Mortalis*," the verse that had sealed the poet's fate at the stake.

> *What miserable wretches we mortals be*
> *To build our homes in sheltered lea,*
> *To build our hopes in sheltered womb*
> *Weaving fancies of the tomb.*
>
> *What wretched souls we mortals be*
> *To bask in false epiphany,*
> *To see a light so clear, so true,*
> *To save us from the fate we rue.*
> *Deny the truth before our sight*
> *That worms invade eternal night,*
> *That maggots feed within the skin*
> *Of faithful pure, devoid of sin.*
>
> *Oh what hopeful children mortals be!*
> *Castles in air, grand barges at sea,*
> *Bed of clouds and angels' song,*
> *Heavenly feasting eternity long.*
> *What mockery made of endless night!*
> *That prayer transcends truth and hope denies sight!*
> *That all that we know and all that we see*
> *Is washed away by what we pray must be.*
>
> *So tell me not of eternal soul*
> *That flees my coil through worm-bit hole.*
> *For when I die what is left of me?*
> *A whisper lost to eternity.*

"I know the tale, brother," Francis finished, opening his eyes to stare solemnly at Bou-raiy, "and I know, too, that '*Mortalis*' was considered a work of great introspection when Calvin presented it to the brothers of St. Honce in the time of plague."

"The time of contemplation," Master Bou-raiy corrected.

"It was only when Calvin went out among the people, reciting his dark works, that the Church took exception," Francis remarked.

"Because some things should not be spoken openly," said Bou-raiy.

Francis gave another helpless chuckle.

"Brother, you must admit that we are the caretakers of the souls of Corona," Father Abbot Agronguerre put in.

"While the bodies rot," Francis said sarcastically.

Master Bou-raiy started to jump in, but the Father Abbot held him back with an upraised hand. "We do what we can," Agronguerre admitted. It was obvious to Francis that the man was agonizing over the dark happenings in the world about him. "Calvin of Bri'Onnaire was condemned not for his words but for rousing the common folk against the Church, for preying upon their fears of mortality. That is the challenge before us: to hold the faith of the populace."

A smile grew upon Master Francis' face as he considered those words— and the irony behind them. "There is a woman out there among them," he said, "one-eyed and horribly scarred on her face and neck, with the rings of plague scars all over her arms. They say she tends the sick tirelessly; I have heard that many of the victims have called out for her beatification on their deathbeds."

"I have heard of the woman, and expect that she will be investigated when the time for such tasks arrives," Father Abbot Agronguerre replied.

"Even your canonization of Brother Avelyn has been put off," Bou-raiy had to add.

Francis didn't even bother to spout the retort that came immediately to his lips: that he would hardly consider himself a supporter of Avelyn Desbris, let alone a sponsor for the wayward brother's canonization!

"It is also whispered that this peasant woman is no friend of the Abellican Church," Francis went on. "According to her, we have deserted her and all the other victims of the rosy plague. And there is the other rumor that says it was an Abellican brother who wounded her face outside St. Gwendolyn, a brother with a hand that resembled a cat's paw. Would you wager a guess about his identity?"

He ended with heavy sarcasm, but it was lost on the other two, neither of whom were overfond of Marcalo De'Unnero. De'Unnero and his Brothers Repentant, by all reports, were laying waste southern Honce-the-Bear, inciting riots, even murdering some unfortunates who did not fit their particular description of a proper Abellican. Even more disconcerting to all the leaders at St.-Mere-Abelle was that when Father Abbot Agronguerre had sent a messenger by ship to Entel to warn Abbot Olin about the Brothers Repentant and to offer Olin the full backing of the Church if he chose to confront them openly, Agronguerre had received a reply that seemed to condone Brother Truth more than condemn him. The other abbey in Entel,

the much smaller St. Rontlemore, had been faithful to the spirit of Agronguerre's warning, but Olin of Bondabruce had seemed ambivalent at best.

"We cannot end their suffering," Fio Bou-raiy stated flatly, moving to
stand right before Francis, "and all that we might accomplish in trying
would be to destroy the last bastions of security against the rosy plague. In
this time, God alone will choose who is to live and who is to die. Our duty,
brother, is to ensure that those who die do not do so without hope; to
ensure that those unfortunate victims understand the truth of what awaits
them beyond this life; for in that hope, they can come to accept their
mortality."

" 'So tell me not of eternal soul that flees my coil through worm-bit
hole,' " Francis replied.

"Master Francis," said Agronguerre, having heard enough. He, too,
walked over, pushing past Bou-raiy. "I warn you in all sincerity and in all
generosity, as your father abbot and as your friend, to guard well your
words. Master Bou-raiy speaks realistically of our role against the rosy
plague. We are the caretakers of souls more than of bodies."

"And the caretakers of hope, perhaps?" Francis asked.

"Yes."

"And when do we stop asking the question of what the populace might
believe and begin asking the question of what we, honestly, believe?"
Francis asked.

The two brothers looked at him curiously.

"I know when, and so do you," Francis went on. "It will happen to each
of us in turn, as we contract the plague, perhaps, or come to sense, whatever the cause, that our personal end is near. Only then will we, each of us,
honestly confront that greatest of mysteries. Only then will we hear the
words of Calvin of Bri'Onnaire, or like words."

"You seem to be confronting them right now," Master Bou-raiy observed.

"Because I look out at them," said Francis, turning back to the small
window, "and I wonder at my place in all this. I wonder at the morality of
hiding behind our walls and flower beds. We, the possessors of the sacred
stones—of hematite, the soul stone of healing. There lies an incongruity,
brother, of which I cannot make sense."

Father Abbot Agronguerre patted Francis' shoulder comfortingly, but
Fio Bou-raiy's face screwed up with a jumble of emotions, disgust mostly,
and he turned away with a snort.

Pony, Roger, and Dainsey arrived in Caer Tinella amid a mélange of late-
spring scents, with mountain laurel and other flowers blooming bright and
thick. A cruel irony, Pony thought, for in Palmaris, in all the cities of
Honce-the-Bear to the south, the plague grew thicker by the day, the
vibrancy of life dulling under the dark pall, the springtime scents overcome
by the smell of rot.

All three had been invited by Abbot Braumin to stay within St. Precious, and Pony most of all had understood the generosity of that gesture. St. Precious was a veritable fortress now, and not even the new baron of Palmaris, an arrogant duke named Tetrafel, had been allowed entrance when he had gone to speak with Abbot Braumin. But Braumin did not forget his friends.

Pony believed that Roger and Dainsey would accept the offer—certainly Dainsey had shown great excitement when Braumin had called it out to them through the newly constructed portcullis backing St. Precious' main gate. And, in fact, Pony had hoped that her friends would accept: that they, at least, would become insulated, somewhat, against the darkness. For her, it was never a question. Something within her recoiled against the thought; she could not run and hide in the abbey while so many suffered and died.

And yet, there was nothing she could do to help them, she had come to painfully realize over the few months she had spent in Palmaris. First Colleen and then a succession of others had died in her arms; and so many times Pony knew that she had barely escaped her encounters with the plague with her health intact. After one devastating defeat after another, she wanted only to go back home, to Dundalis.

She felt a combination of pleasant surprise and trepidation when Roger and Dainsey had opted to go north, though only as far as Caer Tinella, rather than retreating into the abbey.

They found that the plague had not come strong into Caer Tinella, though one man had contracted it and had died out in the forest somewhere, for he'd understood his responsibility to the community when the rosy spots appeared and had walked away into the wilderness to die alone.

Colleen's house was still deserted, and so Roger and Dainsey, with the blessing of Janine of the Lake and the other town leaders, claimed it as their own.

"You are certain you will not come to Dundalis with me?" Pony asked them soon after they had settled into the place, with Pony getting restless for the road home.

"Dainsey has friends here and so do I," Roger answered, and he wrapped Pony in a great hug. "This was my home, and I feel the need to be home, as do you."

She pushed him back to arm's length and looked him over. "But promise that you will return and visit me and Bradwarden," she said.

Roger smiled. "We'll both go north," he answered, "perhaps before the end of the season, and in the fall, surely, if not before!"

They shared another hug and Pony kissed him on the cheek. That very night, under the cover of darkness, she rode out of Caer Tinella on Greystone, with Symphony trotting along beside them.

She made Dundalis in five days, on Greystone, for Symphony had run off into the forest to rejoin his herd. His departure reminded Pony of how extraordinary the stallion's arrival beside her on the road south had been. What had brought him to her? How could a horse so perfectly understand the needs of a human being?

Perhaps it had something to do with the turquoise gemstone Avelyn had put into the horse's breast as a gift to both Elbryan and Symphony, she mused, or perhaps there had been something special and extraordinary about Symphony even before that. Whatever the case, Pony knew well that had it not been for the stallion, she and Colleen and likely Greystone, as well, would have died on the road between Caer Tinella and Palmaris in the snowstorm.

Word had reached Dundalis of the rosy plague, Pony discovered as soon as she rode in, for she found herself assaulted by anxious questions from every corner, a group of men rushing out to meet her.

"Yes," she told them all. "The plague is thick in Palmaris."

They all backed away from her at that answer, and Pony merely shrugged and rode to Fellowship Way and Belster O'Comely. Other than the growing fear of the plague, Pony found that things had not changed much in Dundalis. She found Belster busily wiping the bar, and how his smile widened when he saw her!

He rushed around the edge of the bar and wrapped her in a great hug and bade her to tell him of all her adventures.

His smile disappeared, of course, when Pony told him of Colleen, but he managed another smile at the thought of Roger and Dainsey together, for Belster loved both of them dearly.

"I thought ye dead, girl," the innkeeper admitted, "when the season turned and ye did not return." He shook his head, a tear growing in his eye. "I feared the weather or the plague."

"Fear the plague," Pony admitted, "for it grows thicker with each passing day, and none of us, even up here in the Timberlands, is safe from it. And once it has you . . ." Now it was Pony's turn to shake her head helplessly. "I could do nothing for Colleen but hold her while she died."

Belster reached back over the bar and brought out a bottle of his strongest liquor, and poured Pony a large shot. The woman didn't normally drink anything stronger than wine, but she took the glass and swallowed its contents in one gulp.

It was going to be a long and difficult time.

Pony went out to the grove that night, to be with Elbryan, to wonder if he would be there for her when death called to her. After her encounters with the rosy plague, Pony was feeling quite vulnerable, and she honestly doubted that she'd find her way through this plague alive.

Those grim thoughts held her fast through most of the quiet night, until a familiar song drifted on the evening breeze: the harmony of Bradwarden.

So familiar with the forest about Dundalis, so at home out here on a warm night, Pony found her way toward the centaur easily enough—until the music abruptly stopped.

"Bradwarden?" she called, for she knew she was close to him.

She waited a few moments but received no answer. She reached into her pouch and sifted through the gemstones Braumin had given her, finding a multifaceted, perfectly cut diamond. She called out the centaur's name again and brought up a tremendous light, filling all the area.

"Ow!" came a yell from the brush to the side. "Well, there's a good one for me eyes, now ain't it?" Bradwarden added.

Pony focused on the voice, and finally managed to sort out the silhouette of the centaur's human torso lurking in the shadows.

Pony smiled and decreased the light, and started to move toward Bradwarden. But so too did the centaur move, one step away for every one Pony took toward him, and she sensed immediately that there was something terribly wrong here.

"What is it?" she asked, and she stopped, turning to get a better angle to see her friend.

"Twenty strides away, that's the rule," Bradwarden remarked, "centaur strides and not yer little baby human steps."

Pony considered the words for just a moment, her face screwed up in confusion, but then she got it. "The plague," she said evenly.

"Thick in the south, I'm hearin'," Bradwarden confirmed.

Pony nodded. "Palmaris is in turmoil," she explained. "So is Ursal, by all reports."

"Dark days," the centaur remarked. "Can't be runnin' to Aida to blow up this enemy."

Pony increased the diamond's light again subtly, trying to get a better view, concerned suddenly that her friend might not be well.

"The plague's not found me," Bradwarden explained, catching on.

"I do not know that it can affect a centaur," Pony said.

"Oh, but it can!" Bradwarden replied. "Nearly wiped away me folk time before last, and so we found the rule: twenty strides and not a step closer."

"From anyone who has the plague," Pony finished.

"To anyone at all," the centaur corrected firmly, "except the horse, o' course. Horses can't catch the damned thing and can't give it to others."

"But if someone is not afflicted—" Pony started to say.

"How're ye to know?" the centaur demanded. "Ye can't know, ye know. Ye might have it, or ye might not. Ye'll not know for sure until ye sicken or ye don't."

Pony paused, sorting it all out. "So you are saying that you will not come within twenty centaur strides of anyone at all?" she asked. "Of me?"

"It's the way it's got to be," the centaur answered. Pony caught the slight quaver in his voice, but just a slight one, and one that did little to diminish his firm resolve.

"Have you joined the Abellican Church, then?" Pony asked sarcastically. "They lock their doors and hide in their abbeys while the world outside dies."

"And if one o' their own gets it, they send him out, not to doubt," the centaur added.

"They do," Pony answered. "Cowards all!"

"No!"

Bradwarden's tone surprised her, as straightforward and determined as she had ever heard from the typically blunt centaur.

"Ye call 'em cowards, but I'm thinkin' them wise indeed," Bradwarden said after a short pause. "What're they to do, then? Come out and die? Wallow in the misery until the misery grows in them?"

"They could try something!" Pony insisted. "Anything! What right have they to hide themselves away?"

"Not a right, but a responsibility, I'm guessin'," said the centaur. "Ye don't know, me friend—ye can't know, for yer type o' folks don't keep so long a memory. Not long enough, anyway. Do ye know the tidin's the plague will bring? Do ye know the riotin' and the fightin' and the dyin'?"

Pony straightened and stared at him, but had no answer.

"Yer friends open their abbeys and half o' them'll die from the plague, and doin' no good in the process," Bradwarden remarked. "And the other half'll likely die in the fightin', for the folk'll blame them monks afore long, don't ye doubt! Happened before and will happen again! They'll blame 'em and they'll burn down their abbeys and they'll stake 'em up. God's not with them now, they know, and so they'll blame them who think they speak to God."

That set Pony back on her heels a bit, for she realized that she hadn't really considered all the implications here. She hated Braumin's choice, the Church's choice, but was there a logical, even necessary reason behind their seeming cowardice?

Suddenly Pony felt very much alone in a very large and dangerous world, a place that had grown beyond her ability to manipulate, even to understand. She looked at her distant friend plaintively. "Play for me," she bade him, her voice barely a whisper.

"Aye, that I can do," the centaur replied quietly, and he took up his pipes and began a soulful melody, a quiet, melancholy tune that seemed to Pony to cry for all the world.

Braumin heard the rumble of thunder, and thought it curious, for the sky beyond his little window seemed bright and sunny. Even as he began to catch on to the truth, he heard the cries from a brother in the corridor.

Braumin rushed out, nearly colliding with the man.

"Fighting in the streets!" the young brother cried. "Brothers and peasants! Call out the guard! Call out the guard!"

Braumin rushed by the frightened young brother, through the corridors of St. Precious, across the inner courtyard and to the front wall, where he found Talumus and Castinagis on the ramparts, gemstones in hand. Flanking the two were several other brothers, all holding crossbows.

Braumin Herde scrambled up the ladder to join his friends. He heard another thunderstroke before he even got up there, followed by screams, both angry and agonized.

"There!" Brother Talumus cried, pointing down a long avenue to a group of about a score of robed brothers hustling toward St. Precious, waving gemstones, a host of peasants pursuing them and flanking them along other avenues.

"From St.-Mere-Abelle?" Brother Castinagis asked, for none of St. Precious' brethren were out of the abbey at that time.

"Raise your crossbows!" Talumus cried, the running brothers and the pursuing throng closing in.

"No!" said Abbot Braumin, and all eyes turned upon him. "We'll not kill the folk of Palmaris," he declared.

"They will overrun the brothers!" Talumus argued.

But Braumin remained adamant. He noted that Talumus held a graphite gemstone, and he took it from the man and marked the approach. "Open the portcullis and have brothers ready to swing wide the gates," he ordered Talumus.

Master Viscenti joined them then, carrying an assortment of stones, graphite among them.

"We have to defeat the flanks," Braumin explained, pointing to the avenue that ended in the courtyard to the left of the abbey. "Kill none, but strike the ground before them to hold them back."

"Run, brothers!" Castinagis cried to the approaching group. Both Braumin and Viscenti began falling into their gemstones then, exciting the magical energy. Three lines of people came rushing toward the abbey: the central, led by the running brothers, and ones on either side, curling in to seal off their escape into St. Precious. Those flanking lines turned the last corner and began the last run to spill into the courtyard before the gates.

Abbot Braumin loosed his lightning bolt to the right, followed by Viscenti's lesser strike to the left. Braumin's bolt struck a building, a farrier's shop, rattling the windows and sending several horseshoes flying wildly. Viscenti's bolt hit the cobblestones of the road and ricocheted up, catching the leading peasants squarely in the face and hurling them to the ground. Viscenti could only pray that he hadn't harmed any too badly.

"The doors! The doors!" Castinagis screamed a moment later. St. Precious' front gates swung wide, and Brother Talumus and a dozen other brothers rushed out to escort the line of running brothers into the abbey.

They didn't get in easily, though—Talumus and the others had to kick and punch through a group of stubborn peasants, swatting them away.

Finally, with several people down and wounded before the gates, and two brothers bleeding badly, St. Precious was secured.

From the rampart, Abbot Braumin could only watch and shake his head helplessly. He noted a group of city soldiers along the avenue to the right, making no move at all to secure the situation.

He wasn't surprised.

Braumin went down to the inner courtyard then, to greet his unexpected visitors. By the time he arrived, they had pulled back their hoods. Some were being tended for minor wounds, others were simply bent over, trying to catch their breath.

Braumin looked them over curiously, for though many were not young men, he didn't recognize any of them—except one.

"Master Glendenhook?" he asked, moving near to the man.

"Greetings, Abbot Braumin," Glendenhook replied.

"Why are you out of St.-Mere-Abelle?" Braumin asked incredulously. "Why are you here?"

"We are the brothers inquisitor," another monk answered in the thick accent of southeastern Honce-the-Bear—from Entel, likely. "We've come to investigate claims of a miracle at Mount Aida performed by Avelyn Desbris."

Abbot Braumin swayed as if a slight wind could have knocked him over. "The building of the chapel of Avelyn was halted," he replied, "by order of Father Abbot Agronguerre."

"It would be foolish to expose ourselves in such a manner as to dedicate a new chapel," Master Glendenhook replied. "But the canonization of Brother Avelyn must go forward. A full investigation."

Abbot Braumin heard Talumus and Viscenti and others about him give a cheer, but he just stared at Glendenhook curiously.

"The people need a hero at this dark time, would you not agree, Abbot Braumin?" Glendenhook remarked. "Perhaps Brother Avelyn will withstand the scrutiny of the process and become that hero."

It didn't make much sense to Braumin at that time. He knew that Glendenhook was tied closely to Master Bou-raiy, certainly no friend to the memory of Avelyn Desbris. At the College of Abbots, when Markwart had condemned Master Jojonah for following Avelyn, Bou-raiy had been a huge supporter of Jojonah's execution.

"Let Avelyn's name be put forward and let all the world rejoice," Master Glendenhook added, and he seemed sincere.

But when he looked at Glendenhook's smile, Abbot Braumin couldn't help but question that sincerity.

Something just didn't seem right.

CHAPTER

❖ 29 ❖

The Second Gift

"Abbot Hingas desires audience, my liege," the castle guardsman reported to King Danube.

Duke Kalas, sitting at the side of the room, snorted derisively. He had no love for Hingas, the interim abbot of St. Honce, whom he thought a complete fool. Kalas didn't care much for any member of the Abellican Church, of course, but in the case of Abbot Hingas, several others of King Danube's court, Constance among them, had to agree with him.

"He has come to complain about the broken windows again, no doubt," said Constance Pemblebury, who had her back to the others, sitting modestly and feeding Torrence, her second son, who was now six months old. Merwick moved excitedly about her chair, setting up little wooden blocks, then kicking them all over the room.

"Or to talk about the weight of a soul," Kalas remarked, "of how it is lighter than the very air about us and so it floats, floats, to heaven." His voice rose an octave as he spoke the words, sarcastic and derisive.

"Your Majesty?" the poor sentry asked.

King Danube rolled his eyes.

"No!" Kalas yelled at the sentry. "Out with him! Out! Send him back to St. Honce and tell him to suffer the rocks and the taunts. Tell them all to suffer, for the good of the world, and when they have finally appointed an abbot, a real abbot, let him come and beg audience with the King."

The fiery Duke's tirade didn't surprise the others, of course, but the intensity of it this time certainly made Danube and Constance look at each other with concern.

"Better off is Je'howith," Constance remarked dryly, and even diplomatic King Danube couldn't deny a chuckle at that.

"In the grave and at peace from Duke Kalas," Danube said.

"Did you wish to speak with the idiot?" Kalas asked, clutching his heart as if their words had wounded him.

343

"Likely you did me a favor," King Danube replied, pulling himself from his chair and walking over to the window.

Below him lay Ursal, quiet, awaiting winter. Every family had at least one victim now, so it was reported; and many houses lay dark and still, full of death, with no one to go in and retrieve the bodies.

Such was King Danube's beloved capital that late autumn of God's Year 829. It should have been among the happiest times of Danube's life. The demon and its minions had been shattered; the Church, always a nagging rival to the Throne, had been pushed into disarray; and his dear Constance had given him two sons: sons whom he was beginning to think of as heirs to his throne—though, of course, he'd have to speak with his brother at length about that possibility.

Yet, here he was, buttoned up within the prison that Castle Ursal had become, a fortress against the misery of the plague, though that most insidious of enemies had found its way even into these fortified halls, forcing the expulsion of two servants and a guard.

So far, though, none of his closest friends had been afflicted; and for that, King Danube mumbled a little prayer of thanks as he stood solemnly at the high window, looking out over his wounded kingdom.

Not much of a blessing, perhaps, but in this dark day, any light at all seemed a good thing.

The snow held off in the northland until after the turn of winter, but when it did come to Dundalis, it did so in fury, with drifts covering the entire sides of houses and burying the fences of the corrals.

Soon after, and still before the turn of God's Year 830, the weather calmed enough for Pony to attempt venturing out. And truly, she needed the time alone, at the grove and Elbryan's cairn, her great retreat from the events of the world.

She saddled Greystone and walked out of Dundalis, up the north slope and along the rim of the vale filled with caribou moss and pines, for the edges of the dale were windblown and nearly clear, while the dell itself was deep in snow. She found the trails within the forest easier going than she had anticipated, though the snow was often halfway up Greystone's legs, and on several occasions, Pony had to dismount and lead the horse along.

She had left early in the morning, and a good thing it was, for it was nearing noon when she at last came to the sheltered grove. The rolling hills and sharp ravines nearby were too deep and too slick, so Pony had dismounted again and tethered the horse in a windblown clearing, walking in the last quarter mile.

Two sets of hoofprints, running the length of the last field and right into the grove, alerted her that she was not alone. At first, she thought that it might be Bradwarden and Symphony—for who else would be out here on such a day—but then she saw a third track, the boots of a rider, beside the line of hoofprints.

Shadowing the forest line for cover, Pony did a complete circuit of the grove. She spied a lone rider in the distance, sitting quietly along the tree line, bundled under mounds of furs.

Now she fell into her hematite, using its depths to release her spirit from her corporeal body. She went out to the rider first, and determined on her way that he had a companion, who was within the grove—her grove!—and the mere thought of that made her angry.

The rider was a man of about Pony's age, rugged but handsome, with a dark, two-week beard and sparkling, alert eyes. Something about him seemed familiar to Pony, but she could not place it.

Not wanting to linger for fear of being discovered, she turned her spirit and swept into the grove, passing insubstantially among the trees.

She found the other man standing before the twin cairns—grave markers that had been recently cleared of snow. He was a giant of a man, with long, somewhat thinning, flaxen hair, eyes the color of a clear northern sky, and a sword strapped diagonally across his back.

And what a sword—the largest Pony had ever seen! A sword that could cleave through any blocking shield, through any blocking tree, and cut the opponent in half!

The man started, glancing about, suddenly on the alert; and Pony realized that he had somehow sensed her presence. In the span of a single thought, she was back in her body, blinking her eyes, orienting herself to the physical world about her.

She paused, waiting a few moments, and when no call came from the grove and when the giant man didn't emerge, she picked a path that would keep her out of sight of the waiting rider, and slipped across the field, one hand on Defender, the other in her gemstone pouch, rolling both graphite and lodestone between her fingers.

She moved stealthily, perfectly quiet, from shadow to shadow, as Elbryan had taught her. Still, before she was within ten paces of the man, he called out, "You should not be sneaking up on me so, good woman. It makes me edgy."

He turned slowly, a wry smile showing on his bearded face. His hands remained at his side, making no movement toward that incredible sword.

"A bit far out of town in such a season as this, are you not?" the man asked.

"What do you know of it?"

"I know that Dundalis is the closest town, and a hard morning's march in this deep snow," the man answered. "And I know that Weedy Meadow is another twenty miles from that."

Pony cocked her head, staring at him curiously. How could he know so

much, without her being aware of any such man in the area? And what of
Bradwarden? The centaur knew, or claimed to know, of everything that
moved in the forest. And yet, Pony had not heard from Bradwarden in
many days, and even that had been no more than the piping song carried on
a favorable evening breeze.

"What are you doing here?" Pony asked firmly, watching the man
closely. If he went for that sword, she intended to lay him low with a lightning stroke.

The big man shrugged. "Paying my respects," he said.

"To whom?" Pony's words came out unintentionally sharp. Who was
this man to presume that he could walk unannounced to Elbryan's grave?

"To fellow rangers," the Alpinadoran replied, and Pony's jaw dropped.

"To Nightbird, and to Mather before him," the ranger went on. "Word
reached me of his demise, and so I owed him this visit, though the road was
long and difficult."

"Who are you?"

"I was thinking of asking you the same thing."

"Who are you to stand uninvited and unannounced before my husband's
grave?" Pony replied, clarifying much.

The big man nodded and smiled. "Jilseponie Wyndon, then," he said.
"Pony to her friends. Companion of Nightbird to the end." He bowed
respectfully. "I am Andacanavar of Alpinador, elven-trained, as was your
husband. The full story of the tragedy in Palmaris came to me by the way
of Brother Holan Dellman of the Abellican Church, who now serves at
St. Belfour in Vanguard."

Pony was shaking her head, hardly able to believe the man, but the mention of Brother Dellman, her friend, put her at ease. Too much so, she realized a moment later, when she head a voice behind her.

"And I am Liam O'Blythe," it said, and Pony spun to see the man who'd
been on horseback near her—near enough to have jumped her before
she could use her gemstones or draw her sword, and how foolish that made
her feel.

But this man, too, bowed politely, respectfully, and made no move
against her.

"We did not know that you were again in this area," Andacanavar went
on, "else we would have sought you out."

"Though we plan on making as little contact with the folk of this region,
or any other region outside Vanguard, as possible," Liam said.

Pony looked at him curiously, and then at his huge companion. "You
would find that the folk of the Timberlands are not so quick to judge based
on heritage," she said.

"Not that," Andacanavar explained. "We have heard news of the rosy
plague."

"True words," Pony said.

"And thus we do not wish to bring it with us back to Vanguard or to Alpinador," Liam said. "But enough of my intrusion," he went on, and Pony realized that the ranger behind her had given him a signal to be gone. He left with another bow, moving gracefully, with a warrior's balanced gait, and Pony turned back to regard the ranger.

They talked easily, like old friends, for more than two hours. Pony did most of the talking, answering Andacanavar's many questions about Elbryan. The ranger wanted every detail of every story, wanted to hear Pony imitate her lover's laugh and describe his wry grin to the dimple. Andacanavar listened to her with obvious amusement, smiling and laughing often.

How quickly the afternoon passed, and Pony realized that she would have to be on her way if she hoped to make Dundalis before dark.

"The signs are telling me that tomorrow will be another fine day," the ranger said to her. "Will you come back to this place, then, and speak with me again?"

Pony looked at him, seeming unsure.

"I will tell you more about the elves, and more about that which helped to form your Nightbird into the man you loved," Andacanavar promised.

"Then I will return," Pony said with a smile.

That night, in her bed in the small room above Fellowship Way, Pony was visited by dreams of Elbryan more vivid than any she had known since his death. Unlike some of her previous dreams of her husband— reenactments of that final battle mostly, and horrible things—these were pleasant, warm memories that made Pony awaken with a smile.

She was up early, working quickly through her chores at the tavern, then promising Belster she would return by dark and rushing out. She found Andacanavar and his friend at the grove again; and again, the smaller man left them. Untrue to his promise, though, Andacanavar bade Pony again to do the talking, to tell him even more of Nightbird.

And she complied eagerly, pouring out her heart, telling about her separation from Elbryan and all those years apart, when he was with the elves, and she in Palmaris and later in the King's army. She told of their journey to the Barbacan to do battle with the demon dactyl—Andacanavar liked that part most of all!—and of their work against the minions of the demon upon their return south. She told of the journey to St.-Mere-Abelle to rescue Bradwarden, and then she told the Alpinadoran ranger, in solemn tones, tears streaking her cheeks, of the final battle against Markwart, when Elbryan gave his life to save her and to rid the world of Bestesbulzibar.

When the sun began its swift descent, Pony realized that she had to go.

"Tomorrow?" Andacanavar asked her.

"That you can tell me again of the Touel'alfar?" Pony asked sarcastically, for the ranger had spent the entire day asking question after question.

"I will," the ranger promised. "I will tell you of the many tests a ranger in training must master. A marvelous race are the Touel'alfar. Adaptable and—"

Pony laughed aloud. "That is not a word I would use to describe them," she said.

"But they are!" Andacanavar protested. "Why, they had to concoct an entirely different fighting style for me, to accommodate my size and strength."

"Different than *bi'nelle dasada*?" Pony asked, and that set the big man back on his heels.

"What would you know of that?" he asked.

Pony glanced to the side, to see the ranger's companion returning to the grove.

"I know the sword dance," Pony whispered. "I know it well."

Andacanavar looked at her, his face showing both surprise and concern. "What would you know of it, then?" he asked.

"Nightbird—Elbryan—taught it to me," she explained. "The sword dance. All of it. We fought together in movements perfectly complementary."

That raised Andacanavar's bushy eyebrows, and he nodded and said, "hmm," repeatedly.

"Lady Dasslerond was not pleased," Pony admitted, then she laughed. "Not at all!"

"I say this not in jest, my friend, but I suspect that the lady considered quieting you in the most extreme manner possible," the ranger replied.

"I doubt you not at all," Pony replied in all seriousness. "I suspect that Belli'mar Juraviel intervened on my behalf, and that, because of him, the lady trusts that I will keep well the elven secret."

"No small faith!" said Andacanavar. "Are you the new ranger of the Timberlands?" he asked jokingly.

But Pony's face remained serious. "Belli'mar explained that such a thing would not be possible, that I was too old to be considered for the training," she said.

"But they let you live and keep well their secret, and that is no small thing!" Andacanavar said with a great laugh, and Pony joined him.

"Then that weapon strapped at your hip is for more than show?" the ranger asked a moment later, a wry look crossing his face. "Liam fancies himself a bit of a swordsman," he said. "You think you might show me?"

Pony considered the challenge for a moment. She thought that she should refuse, remembering her promise to Belli'mar Juraviel to keep the sword dance private and secret. And yet, this was a ranger bidding her on, one who knew the dance, obviously.

"What is it?" Andacanavar's companion asked, seeing the questioning expressions as he walked up to the pair, dropping a wild turkey he had shot beside him.

"Right here?" Pony asked Andacanavar. "It is crowded with trees."

"Does not the dance take the entire battlefield into consideration?" the ranger asked.

"What battlefield?" asked the smaller man.

"Your battlefield," Andacanavar replied, standing up and brushing the snow from his doeskin breeches. "Yours and hers. Our new friend has told me some interesting things about her background, and I would like to test her here and now."

"Then the battlefield is your own," the other man protested.

Andacanavar gave a laugh. "My fighting style is too disparate from that which she claims for me to take any measure. Come then, Liam, draw your sword and dirk and let the woman have her way with you."

The man looked at Pony curiously, to see her brushing the snow off her breeches and then drawing a truly beautiful, slender sword.

He nodded. "Be gentle," he said to Pony.

"Never in all my life," she replied, and she turned sideways, on guard, her left foot back, her right leg before her. She rocked over her knee, finding her balance.

"And if I unintentionally hurt her, will you chop me down, Andacanavar?" the smaller man asked.

The ranger gave a chuckle—and he meant it, for just from Pony's stance, Andacanavar understood that his companion's fears were not likely to come to fruition.

"I will try not to cut you, and expect the same," the man said. "First blood, if it comes to that, first advantage if not."

Pony didn't bother to answer, just rocked back and forth, feeling her balance, remembering her many training sessions with Elbryan, working the dance naked in the morning light, remembering the many fights she had won beside her lover, their movements too harmonious, too synchronous, for any enemy to stand against them.

She felt *bi'nelle dasada* flowing through her again, for the first time since that awful day, but instead of bringing back all the bad memories and fears and sense of loss, it felt to Pony as if she were with her lover again. It felt wonderful!

"Are you ready?" she heard her opponent ask. From his tone, she realized that he must have already asked that question several times.

She smiled and nodded, and Liam came on suddenly, a side slash with the sword, followed by a sudden short dagger thrust.

Pony easily had Defender in line to parry the slash, then angled her sword the other way, abbreviating the dagger move.

The man smiled, obviously impressed. Pony came on suddenly, a lunge and thrust that became a sideways slap that sent his sword wide, followed by another quick step forward, Defender's tip coming ahead briefly, then angling down, parrying his dagger parry before it could begin.

The man was quick, though, and he brought his sword back in, recovering from his surprise, and went on the sudden forward attack.

But the sword dance was flowing mightily through Pony, filling her with a joy she had feared she would never know again. On came Liam's sword thrust and dagger thrust, but Pony skittered back, her legs working fast, her upper body hardly moving at all, in perfect balance.

Liam came on even farther, seeing that she was running out of room, with a clump of birch trees close behind.

Pony backed right up to them, and as her opponent closed, she came forward with a thrust—a measured thrust, for she ended it abruptly, her left hand catching hold of the birch behind her, all her momentum shifting suddenly, so that she spun around the bending tree.

"Well done," her opponent congratulated her. But before he even finished his salute, sword to forehead, he had to launch his weapon out in a desperate parry, for Pony leaped through the birch tangle and came on once again—thrust, thrust, thrust.

He parried each stroke in succession, barely, and now found himself backing fast, and with far less balance than Pony had shown.

She pressed her advantage, rushing forward, sword stabbing for his belly, for his chest, for his face, and then his belly again, and with his using both his weapons frantically to fend off her blows.

Now her momentum had seemingly played out, and she should have retreated into a defensive stance again, but she did not, instead coming forward even more aggressively.

It appeared as if she had erred, and her opponent, obviously no novice to battle, took the initiative and the offensive, easily parrying one unbalanced thrust and reversing his footing, coming forward fast, sword leading, dagger following in two commanding thrusts that hit . . .

Nothing.

And Liam stopped, stunned, for in his flurry he had blocked his own vision and now he couldn't even locate his opponent!

Then he felt the tip of a sword against the back of his neck, just under his head, and he froze in place.

"I would call that an advantage!" Andacanavar roared. Liam dropped sword and dagger and shrugged.

"No blood, I pray," he said to Pony as she walked by, staring intently into her deep blue eyes.

"It will heal," she promised, and she sheathed Defender and moved beside the ranger.

He nodded approvingly.

"Nightbird gave you a great gift," he remarked.

Pony nodded her agreement, for right then, feeling that tingling power of the sword dance coursing through her, she gained an even greater appreciation of the gift.

"Was that all he taught you?" Andacanavar asked.

Pony looked at him, not understanding. How could she begin to list all the things that she and Elbryan had taught each other, or had learned together?

"Your hesitance alone answers my question," the ranger said. "He did not teach you, and so I shall. Tomorrow."

Pony looked at him skeptically.

"Trust me on this, woman," the ranger bade her. "You will find more than you expect, I promise." He paused and held Pony's stare for a long time, while her expression went through skepticism and trepidation and then into some measure of hopefulness.

"Tomorrow?" he asked again.

"Early," Pony promised, and she gathered her things and took up Greystone's reins and walked away.

"A remarkable woman," Andacanavar's companion, who was not Liam O'Blythe, remarked as Pony and Greystone disappeared into the forest.

"Skilled and determined, and a feast for a man's eyes," the ranger replied, looking down at his friend. "I told you last night that she would beat you, and easily."

"Brother Dellman described her as beautiful," the ranger's companion remarked, "and I do not think that our friend Dellman makes that observation often of women."

"His words could not begin to tell the whole truth of her," Andacanavar replied, and he gave his companion a sly look. "Beauty enough to make any man swoon."

"And are you not a man?" came the next question.

"Too old for her, but I'm thinking that she is about your own age."

The man, so easily defeated in the sword fight, only shrugged and smiled.

"Was that good enough for you?" Andacanavar called out to their newest companion, as Bradwarden trotted into the grove, though he stayed the proper distance from the humans, as centaur law demanded in times of the plague.

"She left with a smile," the centaur admitted, "one I've not seen on that beautiful face o' hers in a long while."

"Rangers have a way of doing that to beautiful women," Andacanavar said with a wink.

"Her pain's deep," the centaur remarked seriously.

"And tomorrow it might be deep again," Andacanavar replied, "for she will be meeting her lover again. It will hurt, no doubt, but it is a pain she is needing."

"I wouldn't've asked for yer help if I didn't think ye'd be helpin'," Bradwarden said.

"And glad we are that you did," said the ranger's companion. The tone of his voice, wistful, even enchanted, made Bradwarden and Andacanavar look at each other and wink knowingly.

"I see it all the time," the centaur mumbled to Andacanavar.

Once again, Pony found her dreams filled with pleasant memories of her lover, of sword dancing and making love, of long walks in the forest or just sitting and talking on a bare hillock, hearing Bradwarden's song.

She awoke in a fine mood and once again rushed through her chores and out of Dundalis, riding Greystone as hard as the trails would permit back to the sheltered grove.

She found Andacanavar there alone, waiting for her, but she found that Bradwarden was not far away, for his piping filled the crisp winter air with warming notes.

"When I hear the centaur's song, it feels like Elbryan is still with me," Pony said wistfully. "He and I used to listen to that song when we were children, living in Dundalis."

"He is still with you!" Andacanavar roared. "Of course he is!" He looked all about, as if expecting a ghost to materialize nearby, and then a curious expression appeared on his face. "Did he not teach you anything of the other gift?" he asked. "The more important gift of the Touel'alfar?"

Pony looked at him curiously.

"Oracle," Andacanavar explained.

Pony nodded; she should have known. "He once tried," she explained, "that I might better contact the spirit of another friend lost to us. But I did not need it, for Avelyn was with me at that time. I could feel it."

"But now you need it."

Again Pony fixed him with a skeptical and curious expression.

"You do not believe that Nightbird, your Elbryan, is still with you," Andacanavar explained. "You are not even certain that he has found the next level of existence, or even if such a level truly exists. Oh, yes, Avelyn was with you, you say, but was it really his spirit, or was it just your own hopes and memories of him?"

Pony stared at him hard, feeling uncomfortable suddenly, feeling as if his words were a bit too intimate.

"That is your fear, I say," the ranger declared. "And because of it, you cannot get past your mourning."

"You assume much."

"I read well," Andacanavar corrected. "And the message is clear upon your face whenever you speak of Elbryan." He dusted the snow off his pant legs and stood up, bending and holding out his hand to Pony. "Come," he said. "Let me show you the other gift of the Touel'alfar, the one that will free you."

"Lady Dasslerond—"

"Is not here, now is she?" Andacanavar replied. "And if she allows you to live with the secret of *bi'nelle dasada*, then know that she has already passed judgment upon you, and that it is a favorable one. Come on, then. The weather will not hold another day and I've a long road before me."

Skeptical still, Pony accepted the large man's hand, and he pulled her up to her feet with hardly the slightest effort.

He had already prepared the cave, a hollow at the base of a great elm, for he had used the place extensively to contact the spirits of both Elbryan and Avelyn. He explained the process to Pony, carefully, then helped her into the hole.

She found that Andacanavar had set a log at one end, for her to sit on, and had propped a mirror against the opposite wall, facing it. He barely let her orient herself to the surroundings before he dropped the blanket over the opening, darkening the cave so that Pony could hardly make out the shapes.

But that was the way of Oracle. As Andacanavar had instructed, she took her seat upon the log and stared hard into the mirror, thinking of Elbryan, remembering their times together, and then her thoughts drifted deeper, deeper, until she was far into meditation, not unlike that which she used to enter the sword dance, not unlike that which she used to fall within the magic of a gemstone.

And then she saw him, her love, a shadow moving about the mirror.

"Elbryan," she whispered, and the tears came freely. "Can you hear me?"

She didn't get any audible response, nor did the dark shadow move, but Pony sensed a warmth suddenly and knew that her lover was with her.

But not close enough for her liking, and she shifted forward, even coming off the log seat, but her movement broke her level of concentration and the image faded—or maybe it had never really been there. Maybe it was a trick her heart had played upon her imagination.

No, that wasn't it, Pony realized. He had been there, in spirit. Truly.

She settled back on the log, thinking to fall again into the trance, but only then did she realize how much time had passed. And she had to be out of the grove long before dark.

She went to the cave opening and pushed aside the blanket, blinking repeatedly at the relatively bright afternoon light.

"Did you find him, then?" asked the ranger, seated comfortably nearby, his black-haired companion beside him.

Pony nodded. "I think . . ."

"Do not think too much, lass," said Andacanavar. "Feel."

He came over then and pulled her out of the hole.

"Your road is back to Dundalis," the ranger remarked, "and fast, for a storm will come up tonight, I am sure."

"And your own road?"

"Back to the east," the ranger replied.

"And the storm?"

"Not much of one for one from Alpinador," the ranger replied with a laugh. "We'll find a difficult road, no doubt, but one that we can manage."

Pony stood and stared at the huge man for a long time, realizing then that, though they had known each other for only a few days, she was going to miss him very much. "You said that you would teach me," she argued.

"And so I have," the ranger replied. "You said that you think you saw your lost lover, and that is better success than one can ever expect for their first tries at Oracle. You'll get more tries, for I'll leave the mirror in place. It will become easier—you will begin to teach yourself—and then you will know, my friend. You will know that you are not alone, and that there is a place of peace awaiting us after this life. And when you know that, truly, and not just hope it, then you will be free."

Pony stared at him curiously, not really knowing what to make of him and his promise.

The cynical part of her remained doubtful that even Oracle could take her to such enlightenment, but another part of her, a very private and very big part, prayed that he was right.

"The covering should be over that window, brother," Master Fio Bou-raiy said when he came upon Francis in his room, staring out the window at the western fields.

Francis turned about to face the master, his face a mask of pain. "To keep out the cold?" he asked. "Or the sounds of the misery?"

"Both," Bou-raiy answered, his expression grim. He softened it, though, and gave a sigh. "Will you not join us in the mass of celebration for the new year?" he asked.

"For what will we pray?" Francis asked sincerely. "That the plague stays outside our walls?"

"I've not the heart nor the time for your unending sarcasm, brother," Bou-raiy replied. "Father Abbot Agronguerre asked me to come and tell you that we are soon to begin. Will you join us?"

Francis turned and looked back out the window. In the field beyond, he saw the fires—meager fires, for they had little to burn. He saw the dark, huddled silhouettes of the miserable victims moving about the encampment, the many makeshift tents set up in the mud and snow.

"No," he answered.

"This is a required mass," Master Bou-raiy reminded him. "I ask once more, will you not join us?"

"No," Francis answered without hesitation, not bothering to turn to face the man.

"Then you will answer to Father Abbot Agronguerre in the morning," Bou-raiy said, and he left the room.

"No," Francis said again. He considered the night, the last of God's

Year 829. He knew that the turn of the year was mostly a symbolic thing, the imposition of a human calendar on God's universal clock. But he understood, too, the need for such symbols, the inspiration that a man might draw from them. The strength and resolve that a man might draw from them.

Brother Francis Dellacourt, an Abellican master, walked out of St.-Mere-Abelle that night, while the rest of the monastery sang in the mass in celebration of the New Year. He pulled a donkey behind him, the beast laden with mounds of blankets.

Across the frozen and long-dead tussie-mussie bed he went, into the muddy field, into the cold wind blowing back off All Saints Bay.

Many curious gazes settled upon him, and then a woman came out of the darkness to stand before him. Her face was half torn away, a mask of scars, and she tilted her head, regarding him with her one remaining eye.

"Do ye reek o' the plague then?" Merry Cowsenfed asked.

Brother Francis came forward a step and fell to his knees before the woman, taking her hand in his own and pressing it to his lips.

He had found his church.

She talked and chatted with him easily, bouncing her ideas off him, and her fears; and though he never answered, Pony knew beyond doubt that he was truly with her again, that there was a sentient, conscious spirit of Elbryan out there, ready to help her sort out her feelings and her fears.

This was no trick of magic, she believed, no trick of imagination, and no imparting of false hopes. This was Elbryan, her Elbryan, within the mirror, looking at her, knowing her, and she him.

She found her strength there, though the world about her continued to darken, because there, in that hollow beneath the elm, in that mirror, Jilseponie Wyndon had found her church.

PART FOUR

THE LONG
ROAD

How easy it is for a person to overwhelm herself merely by considering too big a picture. I have spent many, many months despairing over my inability to find a balance between community and self, fearing selfishness while becoming paralyzed by a world I know to be too far beyond my, or anyone's, control.

What point was fighting the battle if the war could not, could never, be won?

And in that confusion, compounded by the purest grief, I became lost, a wandering, aimless person, searching for nothing more than peace. That peace I found in Fellowship Way, with Belster beside me, and with Bradwarden's tunes and the ultimate serenity of the starry sky to calm my nights.

But those are frozen moments, I have come to know, little pieces of serenity in a storm of chaos. The world does not stop for the stars; the errors of mankind continue, and the dangers of nature are ever present. There is no end of turmoil, but far from a terrible thing, I have come to see that turmoil—change—is what adds meaning.

My lament was that perfection of society was not attainable, and I still hold by my words: There is no paradise in this existence for creatures as complex as human beings. There is no perfect human world bereft of strife and battle of one sort or another. I have not come to see a different truth than that. I have not found some magical remedy, some honest hope for paradise within the swirl of chaos.

Or perhaps I have.

In considering only the desired destination, I blinded myself to the road; and there lies the truth, there lies the hope, there lies the meaning. Since the end seemed unattainable, I believed the journey futile, and there was my error—and one I will forgive myself because of my fog of grief.

No one can make the world perfect. Not Nightbird. Not King Danube. Not Father Abbot Agronguerre, nor Father Abbot Markwart—and I do believe that Markwart, in his misguided way, tried to do just that—before him. No one, nor any one group, be it Church or Crown. Perhaps the perfect king could bring about paradise across the land—but for only a few short blinks in the rolling span of time. Even the great heroes, Terranen Dinoniel, Avelyn Desbris, and my own dear Nightbird, will fade in the fog of the ages, or their memories will be perverted and warped to suit the needs of current historians. Their message and their way will shine brightly, but briefly, in the context of history, because we are fallible creatures, doomed to forget and doomed to err.

Yet there is a point to it all. There is a meaning and a joy and a hope. For while perfection is not attainable, the glory and the satisfaction lie along the road.

And now I know, and perhaps this is the end of grief, that such a journey is worth taking. If all that I can accomplish is the betterment of a single day in the life of a single individual, then so be it. It is the attempt to do what is right—the attempt to move myself and those around me toward a better place—that is worth the sacrifice, however great that sacrifice must be.

Yes, I have lost my innocence. I have lost so many dear to me. Every day, I see the cairn of Elbryan. He was a ranger. He walked the road toward paradise with his eyes wide open and his heart full of hope and joy. He gave everything, his very life, trying to make the world a better place.

Futile?

Not to the people he saved. Not to the mothers and fathers who still have their children because of him. Not to the people of Caer Tinella, who would have died in the forest at the hands of the goblins and powries had it not been for Nightbird. And had Avelyn not given his life in destroying the physical manifestation of Bestesbulzibar, then all the world would be a darker place by far.

Perhaps this is the end of my grief, for now when I look upon the grave of Elbryan, I know only calm. He is with me, every step of my own road.

That road is out of Dundalis, I know, out of the hiding place called Fellowship Way, to those places where I am needed most, whatever the personal price.

Yes, I see the world clearly, with all its soiled corners, with all of its cairns for buried heroes.

There is work yet to be done.

—JILSEPONIE WYNDON

CHAPTER

❖ 30 ❖

Fight On

"Nothing but sickness and death," Belster O'Comely said with disgust, waving his hands and his bar rag about dramatically. He wasn't playing to any grand audience, though, for he and Pony were the only two in Fellowship Way at this early hour. "What's in yer head, then?"

Pony looked at him, her face masked in the perfect expression of calm. "It is my place now," she replied.

"Yer place?" Belster echoed. "Didn't ye spend all yer breath in pullin' me up here?"

"And I did need to come up here," Pony tried to explain, though she knew that the journey she had walked to get to this point was something quite beyond her pragmatic friend. "And we have carved a good life out of Dundalis."

"Then why leave?" Belster asked simply.

"I am needed in the south," Pony said, for about the tenth time that morning.

Belster put on a contemplative expression and pose. "So—just so I'm sortin' it out right—ye're wanting to come north when all the world's bright in the south, and now ye're wantin' to go south, when the darkness of the plague has swallowed the whole of it?" The portly man shook his head and snorted. "Chasin' darkness, are ye, girl?"

Pony started to reply, but stopped, realizing that she had little to say against that interpretation of her actions. From Belster's point of view, from the point of view of anyone who had not walked her recent spiritual path, it seemed that she was doing exactly that—chasing misery and darkness.

"Ye're goin' to get yerself sick and dead, is all," Belster finished, and he wiped the rag hard across the bar.

Pony grabbed his arm and stared up at him, forcing him to look her directly in the eye. "I might do just that," she said in all seriousness. "And I might go down there and do no good at all for anybody. But—can you not understand?—I have to try. I have been given this gift with the gemstones, a gift that the Abellican brothers claim is a direct calling from God. Am I to deny that? Am I to huddle with the hoarded gemstones while people around me suffer and die?"

"That's what them monks do," Belster reminded.

"And they are wrong," Pony insisted.

"The gemstones won't fix the rosy plague," Belster said. "Ye did try, with Colleen and with others when ye were in Palmaris. Have ye forgotten that already?"

"I will never forget," Pony grimly replied.

"Then why're ye pretendin' that ye don't know better?" Belster demanded. "Ye fought the plague and it beat ye. Ye fought it again and it beat ye again—and ye're not the first to wage this battle. Them monks, they know the truth of it, and they admit the truth of it, and that's why they stay behind their walls."

"No!" Pony interrupted. "They hide because they are afraid."

"Because they're smart."

"Afraid," Pony said again, firmly. "They hide because they have found no answer and fear the consequences of trying. If Avelyn thought along those same lines, would he have ever gone to Mount Aida after the demon dactyl? If Nightbird thought along those same lines, would he have joined me in my fight against Markwart?"

Belster started to respond, but Pony knew what was coming and cut him short. "Yes, they are both dead," she said before he could. "But think of what might have happened if they had not tried, if they had not gone against their fears and won a battle that none believed they possibly could."

Belster gave a great sigh of surrender.

The door to Fellowship Way banged open then, for the first time that morning, and a young man, Harley Oleman, crashed in, obviously agitated.

"It's here! It's here!" he cried. "The rosy plague's found us!"

Pony looked at Belster.

"Jonno Drinks," Harley Oleman explained. "Jonno Drinks' got the rings!"

"Ye wanted yer fight," Belster said quietly to Pony. "Seems like it found ye here."

Pony dropped her hand into her gem pouch and produced the deep gray hematite, the soul stone, holding it up before Belster. "A fight that I am more than ready to wage," she said determinedly. She headed for the door, motioning for Harley Oleman to follow her.

"He should be put right out," Harley started to say, turning to plead with Belster as he did, for it was perfectly obvious that Pony wouldn't be seeing things quite that way.

Pony knew Jonno Drinks, though not well, but even if she didn't know him at all, it wouldn't have been hard for her to figure out which cottage belonged to him. A crowd had gathered outside the small shack, many cursing and demanding that the man walk out of the house and out of their town.

They quieted considerably when Pony came through their ranks, casting stern glances at each and every one. "Compassion is salvation," she reminded them. "Woe to you if you get the plague and die, but all the more woe to you if that happens after you have shown such cruelty to your fellows."

And after the woman they held up as a great hero put them in their place, Pony stunned them even more by striding right up to Jonno Drinks' door, and after a sharp rap to let the sick man know she was coming, right into the house.

She heard them before she closed the door behind her, some whispering that she, too, would have to be forced out of town.

She ignored them. Her fight lay before her, not behind—with the rosy plague and not with her fellow townsfolk.

She found Jonno Drinks in bed, feverish and with those same hollow, pleading eyes that had faced her in Palmaris. She was surprised at how advanced the plague already seemed in the man, and wondered if he had been hiding it for a while—and feared the consequences to the rest of Dundalis if that was the case.

"One battle at a time," she reminded herself, and she clutched the soul stone tightly, bringing forth its magic to free her from her corporeal form, and then spiritually diving right at the man.

An hour later, Pony sat on the floor beside Jonno Drinks' bed, thoroughly exhausted and sometimes slapping at her arms as if the little plague creatures were all about her. For all of her determination and all of her strength, she had done little to push back the plague in the man, she knew, and had once again nearly been overwhelmed.

The worst part was that she had believed she was making some progress at first, pushing through the green soup that was the plague, but then it had come at her, and viciously, and only her great power with the soul stone had kept the tiny demons at bay. A lesser gem user would have likely been overwhelmed by Jonno's disease.

And so she believed that she had survived another encounter, but for Pony, that was hardly a victory.

She fell asleep right there, beside Jonno Drinks' bed.

She awoke many hours later, when the sun was low in the west. She felt somewhat refreshed and turned back to Jonno, soul stone in hand, thinking to do battle one more time.

She found the man resting comfortably, though, and decided against the course. Let him sleep and let her gather even more strength before the next fight. She must be better prepared for that fight, she realized; should find some answers between now and then.

Pony pulled open the gemstone pouch and considered the myriad stones in there, searching for a combination, searching for some answer that would not come.

But then she thought of Elbryan and of Avelyn, of those heroes who had gone before, and she thought she knew where she might get some answers.

She came out of the house swiftly, wanting to get to Oracle before nightfall. The crowd was still there—nearly all the town now—waiting, waiting, like the specter of death itself.

"He dead?" one man asked.

Pony shook her head. "We are fighting," she replied, and she noted that every one of them fell back at her approach.

"He should be put out of town," another man, farther in back, remarked.

Pony stopped and glared in his direction. "Hear me well," she said, her tone deathly cold. "If you, if any of you, think to harm Jonno Drinks, or think to put him out of town, then I will hunt you down."

"Easy, girl," said Belster, coming forward through the mob and reaching out to take Pony's arm.

But she pulled away from him forcefully. "I mean every word," she warned. "Leave him be, in his house. Surround the place with flowers, if that will bring you some measure of comfort, but do not harm him in any way." The manner in which she spoke the words, so calmly, so determined, combined with that prominent gem pouch and that marvelous sword strapped on her hip, caused many a face to blanch. These people knew Jilseponie and knew her well—well enough to fear her should they provoke her wrath.

To heighten the effect, a moment later, powerful Symphony thundered into town, galloping down the road.

Pony looked at the horse with awe—it was as if he had read her mind, yet again, and had come rushing to her aid. She had to wonder how great the connection between her and Symphony had become, how powerful the magic of the turquoise set in the horse's breast truly might be.

Those were questions for another day. She grabbed Symphony by the mane and leaped up, rolling into position atop him.

And off they went. Pony didn't even have to guide the horse, for he seemed to know her destination well. Before the sun went down, she was at the grove, at the little hollow at the base of the elm, settling in to talk with the spirits.

She called to Elbryan, she called to Avelyn, but what she found instead, whether in her mind or in that other dimension she believed existed behind the mirror, was an image of the world before the human kingdoms, a preternatural world of great beasts and exotic plants, of ragged clans of men living under pine boughs or in caves: a world before the Abellican Church, before civilization itself.

Before human civilization, for there were races far older than Man.

And there was something else, Pony realized as she examined that strange sensation of times long past: the rosy plague. It was older than the kingdoms, older than the Church, older than mankind.

Perhaps the answer lay in the past, in those whose memories were longer than the records of mankind.

Another image came to Pony then, but surely in her head, in her fairly recent memories, when she and Elbryan had camped on the side of a mountain in the west, staring down at an opaque veil of fog, with Andur'Blough Inninness, the valley of the Touel'alfar, hidden beyond it.

Later that night, back in her room at Fellowship Way in Dundalis, Pony went into the soul stone again, with all her strength—not to attack Jonno's plague this time, but to fly out across the miles, to the west, to the elves.

In mere minutes, she came to mountain passes she had walked once before, with Elbryan. Had she been walking now, she realized, she never would have found the specific trails to the well-hidden elven valley, but in her spiritual form, she was able to soar up past the peaks, getting a wide view of mountains majestic. Still, it took Pony a long, long time to sort out that maze of mountains, to find, nestled in one wide vale, a familiar opaque blanket of magical fog.

She went down to the mountain slope above that blanket and paused. She knew that the elves had set an enchantment upon the place to prevent unwanted visitors—and anyone who was *n'Touel'alfar* was considered an unwanted visitor!—but she had no idea if their magical wards extended into the realm of the spirit. She spent a long time studying that veil, and she did indeed sense danger there, even for her in this form.

Perhaps she could flow through the mountain, she thought, down through cracks in the stone that would bring her into the elven valley underneath the poisoned carpet of fog. She studied the rock beneath her, picking her path. Then she stopped abruptly, shifting her attention; for there, rising out of the fog, was the most beautiful creature she had ever seen, an elven woman with golden eyes and golden hair, with features angular yet soft, and perfectly symmetrical. She was dressed in flowing robes of the palest green, trimmed with golden lace, and a crown of thorns adorned her forehead. Pony knew before a word was spoken that this was Lady Dasslerond standing before her.

The elf held up her hand, and Pony saw the sparkle of a green gem within, and then she felt the waves of magic rolling over her spirit and body, as if the miles themselves were somehow contracting to bring her wholly to this place.

Pony knew that she could resist that magic, could fight back, and her instincts almost led her to do just that. But she held back and trusted in the fair Lady of Caer'alfar.

A strange sensation washed over Pony, and she felt as if she were corporeal again—corporeal and standing on the slope just above the elven valley, hundreds of miles from Dundalis.

"I would have been disappointed if you did not seek us out," Lady Dasslerond remarked. "And I have been disappointed in you before, Jilseponie Wyndon."

The words caught Pony off guard, and she looked at the elf curiously.

"Your actions in Palmaris were not unknown to me," Dasslerond went on. "I am not fond of assassins."

Pony knew then that the elf had to be talking about her attempt on Markwart's life, a shot with the lodestone from a rooftop far away.

"Better for all the world if I had succeeded, then," Pony replied without hesitation.

"But better for Jilseponie?"

"Better for Nightbird!" Pony retorted, and that seemed to set Dasslerond back on her pretty little heels a bit.

The elf paused, then nodded. "I expect much from one who has learned *bi'nelle dasada*," she said.

"I understand my responsibilities," Pony replied. "The sword dance will not be shared with anyone."

"So Belli'mar Juraviel has told me, and so I believe," Dasslerond said.

"But I did not come to you to speak of the sword dance," Pony went on, feeling the tug of her magic and fearing that exhaustion would overtake her and send her careening back to Dundalis—if that's where her physical form remained. "Our lands are thick with a disease, the rosy plague."

"This is known to me."

"You and your people have battled this disease before," Pony reasoned, "or at least, you have watched the humans battle against it."

Dasslerond nodded.

"Then tell me how to fight it," Pony pleaded hopefully. "Show me the wisdom of the ages, that I might bring some hope to a world grown dark!"

Dasslerond's expression dropped, and with it, Pony's hopes. "That wisdom is already known to the Abellican brothers and to your King," she explained.

"To hide?"

"Indeed."

"As you and your people will hide?"

"Indeed," said the lady of Caer'alfar. "This plague is the affair of humans, and we intend to keep it that way." Pony's expression hardened into a sneer, but Dasslerond continued undeterred. "We are not numerous," she explained, "nor do we procreate quickly. If the rosy plague found us in our home, it could destroy all that is left of the Touel'alfar. I cannot take that chance, whatever the cost to the humans."

Pony bit her lip—and felt the physical sensation as if she were indeed corporeal.

"This I will give you, and only this," Dasslerond went on, and she reached her other hand out from within her robes, showing a parchment to Pony. She let go of the parchment and gave a gentle puff, and it floated across the expanse on magical winds into Pony's waiting hands.

"A poultice and a syrup," the lady of Caer'alfar explained. "They will not cure the plague—nothing that I know of in all the world will do that—but they will bring some relief to, and extend the life of, those afflicted."

Pony glanced down at the parchment, recognizing some names of herbs and other plants. "Why were these mixtures not known before?" she asked.

"They were," Dasslerond replied, "in the time of the last plague. The memory of Man is not long, I fear."

Pony glanced down at the parchment again, not knowing if it would return with her to Dundalis and wanting to remember well the recipes.

"That is all I can do," Lady Dasslerond said suddenly, drawing Pony's attention back. "You must now leave from this place. Perhaps we will survive this time, and if so, then perhaps we will meet again. Farewell, Jilseponie Wyndon." And she held up her hand and that sparkling emerald gemstone.

Pony held up her hand, as well, trying to make the lady pause long enough for her to commit the recipes to memory; but then, suddenly, she felt the waves of emerald magic and she was flying, flying, across the miles, soaring faster than the wind out of the mountains, away from Lady Dasslerond's secret domain and back to her own room in Fellowship Way in Dundalis.

She was there for just a moment, in body and in spirit, and then, overwhelmed by magical exhaustion, as if Dasslerond had somehow tapped into her own energies to bring about the more complete physical teleportation, she collapsed into unconsciousness.

Belli'mar Juraviel was waiting for Lady Dasslerond just beneath the opaque veil of mist. He nodded his approval and his thanks, for in truth, he had little idea of how sternly Dasslerond would treat their uninvited guest.

"You wanted to tell her," he remarked slyly.

Dasslerond fixed him with a puzzled expression.

"About her child," Juraviel said with a hopeful smile.

But that grin could not survive Dasslerond's ensuing glower. "Not at all," the lady said determinedly, and Juraviel knew that his hopes and his guess were misplaced.

"She has no child," Lady Dasslerond added; and she walked past, back down to the world of the Touel'alfar.

Belli'mar Juraviel stood on the mountain slope for a long, long while, wounded by the unyielding coldness of his lady. He had thought that he had found a chink in her armor, a weak link in her great coat woven of duty; but he knew now that he was wrong.

He thought of the young ranger in training, Aydrian, and wondered if the boy would ever know the truth of his mother or that she was still very much alive.

"Aydrian," Juraviel said aloud, an elvish title that meant "lord of the skies," or "eagle." Lady Dasslerond had allowed Juraviel finally to name the boy, and had approved of his lofty choice wholeheartedly—yet another signal to Juraviel that Lady Dasslerond thought this young lad could aspire to the epitome of the profession, could become the perfect ranger. Only one other ranger in the history of the training had been given the title Aydrian, the very first ranger ever trained in Andur'Blough Inninness.

That ranger had gone on to live a long, though fairly uneventful, life; and since that time, no one had ever presumed to give the name to another young trainee.

But this one was different. Very different and very special.

Juraviel just wished that Dasslerond would involve Jilseponie with the lad, for her sake and, more important, for the sake of the child.

When Pony awoke, she found, to her relief, that it had not all been a dream; for in her hand she held the parchment given her by Lady Dasslerond. She didn't understand the magic that had worked the physical transportation of her corporeal body—or at least some of it—and then of the parchment.

But that was a question for another day, for a day when the rosy plague was beaten. She still had no solution, no cure, but at least she had a weapon now. She looked down at the parchment and nodded her relief to find that neither the poultice nor the syrup required any ingredients that could not be readily found. It also struck her that many of the ingredients were flowers, including many of those commonly found in the monks' tussie-mussie beds. Perhaps there was something to those old tales of posies and the like.

Armed with her parchment, Pony rushed downstairs, to find that it was morning again, and late morning at that.

"I thought ye'd sleep the whole of the day away," Belster remarked, and the grim edge to his voice told Pony of his deeper fears: that this time, the rosy plague had caught her.

"Gather your friends," Pony said, scampering over to the bar and placing the parchment before the startled innkeeper. "We need to collect all these things and put them together quickly."

"Where'd ye get this?"

"From a friend," Pony replied, "one who visited me in the night, and one we can trust."

Belster looked down at the beautiful script on the page, and, though he could barely read, the delicate lines of calligraphy certainly gave him some indication of who that nighttime visitor might have been.

"Will it work?" he asked.

"It will help," Pony answered. "Now be off and be quick. And find one who can scribe copies, that we might send them to the south!"

Later that same afternoon, Pony knelt beside the bed of Jonno Drinks. She had lathered his emaciated, racked body with the poultice and had spooned several large doses of the syrup into him. And now she had her soul stone in hand, ready to go in and do battle with her newest allies beside her.

She found the plague waiting for her, like some crouched demon, wounded by the elven medicines. But that wound only seemed to make the tiny plague demons even more vicious in their counterattack, and Pony soon found herself slouched on the floor, overwhelmed and exhausted.

Jonno Drinks was resting more comfortably, it seemed, but Pony knew that she had done little to defeat the plague, that she and her elven-made allies might have bought the poor man a little comfort and a little time, but nothing more.

Still, she went at the plague again the next day, and the next after that, fighting with all her strength, again trying various gemstone combinations.

Jonno Drinks was dead within the week, leaving Pony frustrated and feeling very small indeed.

CHAPTER

❖ 31 ❖

Saving Potential Saints

Abbot Braumin's eyes widened when his door swung open and Timian Tetrafel, Duke of the Wilderlands, Baron of Palmaris, stormed in, a very agitated Brother Talumus right on his heels.

"I tried to keep him out," Talumus started to explain.

"Keep me out indeed!" Tetrafel boomed. "I will raze your walls if ever I find the doors closed to me again."

"The abbey is closed," Abbot Braumin said, working hard to make his tone calm, to show complete control here.

"And the streets are full of dying people!" Tetrafel yelled at him.

"That is why the abbey is closed," Braumin replied, "as should be Chasewind Manor—none to enter and none to leave."

"I am watching my city die about me," Tetrafel fumed, "and I have had to expel several servants and soldiers from my own house these last three weeks! It will catch us in our holes, I say!"

"A situation more likely if we come out of those holes," said Abbot Braumin, "or allow others in."

"Are you not hearing me?" the Duke cried. "The rosy plague has entered my house."

Abbot Braumin stared long and hard at the man, trying to be sympathetic but also holding fast to his pragmatism. "You should not have come here," he said. "And you, Brother Talumus, should not have let him in."

"He had an army with him," Talumus protested. "They said that—"

"That we would tear down your doors," Tetrafel finished for him. "And so we would have done just that. Thrown St. Precious open wide for the masses to come in." He walked over to the room's one window and tore the curtain aside. "Can you not see them down there, Abbot Braumin?" he asked. "Can you not hear their misery?"

"Every groan," replied Braumin, in all seriousness and with not a hint of sarcasm in his words.

"They are afraid," said Tetrafel, calming a bit. "Those who are not afflicted fear that they soon will be, and those who are . . . they have nothing to lose."

Braumin nodded.

"There are fights all around the city," the Duke went on. "Those few ships that do come in cannot find anyone to help unload their cargoes. The farmers who come in with crops find themselves assaulted almost as soon as they pass through the city gates, the mobs of miserable, helpless victims fighting for food they can no longer afford to buy."

Abbot Braumin listened carefully, understanding then the fears that had brought Tetrafel so forcefully, and so unexpectedly, to St. Precious. The plague continued to intensify in Palmaris, ravaging the city; and Tetrafel was afraid, and rightly so, that the city could explode into rioting and mayhem. Braumin had heard rumors that the city guardsmen were not overfond of their new ruler, and no doubt Tetrafel was having trouble controlling them. Thus Duke Tetrafel, coming into St. Precious with such fire and self-righteousness, was in fact guided by simple desperation. The city had to be put in line or suffer even worse, and Tetrafel was afraid that he could not rely on the soldiers to carry out his orders.

"All that you say is already known to me," Braumin said, after Tetrafel finished his long rant.

"Well, what then do you intend to do about it?" the Duke asked.

Braumin put on a puzzled expression. "I?" he asked.

"Are you not the abbot of St. Precious?"

"Indeed, and as such, I am not the magistrate in control of Palmaris' streets," Braumin replied. "That is your jurisdiction, Duke Tetrafel, and so I suggest that you put your soldiers to work quickly. As for me and my brethren, we will continue our course, offering masses from the walls."

"And hiding behind the walls," Tetrafel muttered sarcastically.

Braumin let the remark pass. "We are the guardians of the spirit, not of the body," the abbot went on. "We have no power over the rosy plague; and the best that we can do is lend comfort—from a safe distance, yes—to those afflicted. To ease their passage from this life."

Tetrafel stuttered over several intended replies, and wound up throwing his hands up in disgust. "The healers of the world!" he cried, storming out of the room.

Abbot Braumin motioned for Talumus to close the door behind the departing Duke. "I am sorry, abbot," Talumus explained. "I would not have allowed him admittance, but I feared that his soldiers would take down the gates."

Braumin was nodding and patting the air comfortingly. "Find Viscenti and Castinagis," he instructed. "Work with them to triple the watches at the front gates. If Duke Tetrafel returns, deny him admittance."

"And his soldiers?"

"Keep them out," Abbot Braumin said grimly, "by whatever means necessary. By lightning stroke and fireball, by crossbow quarrel and hot oil. Keep them out. St. Precious is not to be violated again, at any cost."

Talumus stood as if struck for a long while, staring wide-eyed at Braumin— and Braumin knew that it was as much his tone as his words that had so caught the young man off guard. But this was not the time for squeamishness, Braumin knew, not the time for weakening convictions. Their duty in a time of the rosy plague was simply to survive, to hold the secrets and teaching of their faith secure for the world when the darkness at last lifted.

Still, he saw them now, with the curtain torn away from his window: the miserable wretches huddled and shivering, though the day was warm.

For kindhearted Abbot Braumin Herde, the sight nearly broke him.

The young monk came out of St.-Mere-Abelle solemnly, the walk of the dead. He carried a large pack, stuffed with food and other supplies, but the parting gift of the Abellican brothers to this poor, frightened, plague-infested young man hardly seemed to suffice.

As he had been ordered, he crossed the tussie-mussie bed; and as soon as he did, the other plague victims knew that he, too, had become one of them. They came to him and crowded about, as much to see what he had in his pack as to offer their sympathy.

That craven desperation only made the poor young monk even more upset, and he pushed people away and cried out.

And then one peasant woman with half her face torn away approached him, and her smile was too genuine and too comforting for the monk to mistrust her. She took his hand in her own, patted it and kissed it gently, then led him through the gathering.

He saw a fellow brother then, though he hardly recognized Master Francis, with his beard and long, dirty hair. Francis recognized him, however, and he patted the young brother on the shoulder. "I will come to you this very night," he promised, and he showed the young brother a soul stone. "Perhaps together we can banish the plague from your body."

Glad that his frightened brother was calmed somewhat by the pledge, Francis patted him again on the shoulder and nodded to Merry Cowsenfed, who led the monk away.

Francis had other matters to attend at that time, but when he glanced back toward the abbey, he saw a vision he could not resist, a one-armed monk dressed in a robe of flowers, standing just inside the alcove before St.-Mere-Abelle's great gates, on the safe side of the tussie-mussie bed.

"Begone, beggar," Fio Bou-raiy said when Francis came over to face him across the flower bed.

"How far the mighty have fallen, then," Francis replied, and a flicker of recognition crossed Master Bou-raiy's face at the sound of that familiar voice. Bou-raiy moved closer to the tussie-mussie bed and peered intently at the hunched figure across the way, wearing still the robes of an Abellican monk, though they, too, like Francis, had weathered the winter and spring badly.

"Still alive?" Bou-raiy asked with a snicker.

"That, or I am the specter of death come to warn you of the consequences of your cowardice," Francis replied sarcastically.

"I would have thought that the plague had taken you by now," Bou-raiy went on, seemingly unperturbed by Francis' unyielding sarcasm. "Any little rings about your body, Master Francis?"

"None," Francis answered defiantly. "But if the plague does find me, then I know it to be God's will."

"A fool's consequence, more likely," Bou-raiy interrupted.

Francis paused, then nodded, conceding the point. "I have saved one already," he replied. "My life for the reward of another's life."

"The life of an Abellican master for the life of a lowly peasant," Bou-raiy retorted, obviously unimpressed.

"Perhaps I will save even more," Francis went on, and he held up the soul stone.

"You are ahead of the odds already," Bou-raiy replied. "One in twenty, brother, and one in seven will poison you."

"I have treated scores," Francis stated.

"And saved only one?"

"Too many are far too advanced in the plague when they arrive," Francis tried to explain, though he wondered why he even bothered trying to reach this stubborn brother.

"And what of Brother Gellis?" Master Bou-raiy asked, motioning in the direction where the newest addition to the plague camp had gone. "First signs. Can Francis the hero save him?"

Francis shrugged calmly.

"And what of the other three monks who have left St.-Mere-Abelle?" Bou-raiy asked slyly, for he knew well enough their fate.

Francis had no answer. Indeed, three other plague-afflicted brothers had come out of the barricaded abbey, and all three had died within two weeks. Francis had tried to save them, had worked with them, joining their spirits within the magic of the hematite, but to no avail.

"It would seem that you have survived longer than the old poems predict," Master Bou-raiy conceded, "but also have you failed to heal as many as the old poems predict. Perhaps you are not going at this task with all your heart, brother."

Francis just glared at him.

"Father Abbot Agronguerre would allow you to return to us," Bou-raiy then said, taking Francis by complete surprise. "Of course, you would have to spend a week within the gatehouse, secluded, and that even after several brothers had probed your spirit with soul stones. But if you remain plague free, then you will be back in the fold, brother, back to your position of master, and none will judge your indiscretions."

Now Francis stared at the man incredulously, wondering why Bou-raiy would even relay such an invitation. Surely Bou-raiy would be happier if Francis dropped dead of the plague there and then!

But when he thought more carefully about it all, Francis understood the master's seeming enthusiasm about his possible return, and suspected that Bou-raiy might even have suggested the invitation to Father Abbot Agronguerre. Because if Francis gave up his mission and walked back into St.-Mere-Abelle, he would be bolstering the Church canon concerning the plague, would be admitting that this enemy was far beyond the power of the monks and their gemstones even to be faced.

Hadn't the former Father Abbot Dalebert Markwart used those same tactics against his enemies? Against Jojonah and his followers? Hadn't Markwart, in fact, offered that same sweet honey—forgiveness, even redemption, back in the Abellican fold—to hold Francis to his side after Francis had inadvertently killed Grady Chilichunk on the road from Palmaris?

"Do you see that woman?" Francis asked, pointing across the field to a woman walking with a limp and a stooped back and carrying two pails for water. "Her name is Merry Cowsenfed," Francis explained. "She came from Falidean town, far to the south, by way of St. Gwendolyn. She, too, is scarred with the rings of the rosy plague, but Abbess Delenia went to her and healed her."

"And Abbess Delenia is now dead," Bou-raiy reminded him. "And St. Gwendolyn is a mere shell, being run by but a handful of minor sisters."

"But they tried," Francis explained emphatically. "And because Abbess Delenia had the heart to try, Merry Cowsenfed is alive. Now, you will argue that her life is not worth that of a single Abellican, let alone an abbess, but look at her! Watch her every move! The woman, this peasant that you would so easily disclaim and allow to die, is beatified by her every action. A hundred years hence, there may well be a new saint, Saint Merry, who would have died unnoticed had not Abbess Delenia tried. You cannot place value upon people because of their temporary station in life, brother. That is your error, the arrogance that allows you to justify your decision to hide behind thick stone walls."

Master Fio Bou-raiy stared long and hard at Merry Cowsenfed as she made her slow, deliberate way across the field. Then he turned back to Francis; and for a moment, just a split second, Francis thought that he had gotten through to the stubborn man. But then Bou-raiy snorted and waved his hand, and whirled about, his flower-sewn robes flying wide.

Francis just put his head down and walked back out to his people. As he had promised, he went to the newest addition to the plague camp, the

exiled young Brother Gellis, that very night, and together, they fiercely battled the rosy plague within the monk.

For only the second time in the few months Francis had been outside, he
believed that he was making strong progress against the disease, but then,
one morning, Gellis awoke with a scream, his body racked by fever.

He died that same afternoon.

Francis walked with the bearers as they carried his emaciated body to the
pyre for burning. He noted that his fellow monks were watching that procession from St.-Mere-Abelle's wall, prominent among them Fio Bou-raiy,
with his flowered robe and his grim expression.

He and Francis locked stares from across the distance for just a moment,
but it was not a harmonious joining of mind and spirit.

CHAPTER

❖ 32 ❖

Safeguarding

I
t felt so good to have the wind on her face again—not the limited breeze that whistled through Castle Ursal's windows, but the wide and strong wind, blowing across the fields, bending trees and grass, carrying the scents of the summertime flowers.

Constance Pemblebury urged her horse on even faster, a full gallop, despite the cries of protest from Danube and Kalas behind her. She needed this moment, this brief, too-brief escape from the grim realities of the rosy plague. King Danube had arranged it, had cleared a wide path to the gardens, lining them with vigilant Allheart knights so that he and his two friends could at last enjoy a morning outside the castle, out of sight and sound of any of the miserable plague victims. Danube had hoped that Merwick and Torrence would accompany them as well—he had even rigged a seat to put behind Constance's saddle for Torrence—but Constance, though more than ready to take this chance for herself, would in no way allow her children out of the relative safety of the castle.

Constance felt her hair waving out behind her, felt as if she had escaped the very bonds of Corona itself. But then she had to slow, for she was approaching the far end of the rectangular garden, Allheart knights were warning her back, and Danube and Kalas were calling out to her.

She brought her horse to a trot and heard the approach of the two horses behind her. It was easy enough for her to turn in her sidesaddle and glance back at the King and Duke, and she did so with a wistful and mischievous smile. "Why haven't we done this a thousand times?" she asked.

Before either of the two men could answer, though, there came a tumult from the other direction, from the near end of the garden; and all three looked to see a mob of peasants bursting through the Allheart ranks, crying out for their king.

"Ye must save us!" It started as a plea.

"Where's our God? Why's he not hearing ye, me King?" Then the voices

376

rolled in together, as if the whole mob had taken on a single heart and voice. From begging to questioning to, at last, and predictably, anger.

"Ye've abandoned us! Ye're lettin' us rot!"

The Allheart knights rushed around on their horses, trying to stem the tide; and under normal circumstances, they would have easily controlled the ragtag peasants. But nothing was ordinary about this scene—for the mob was too wild and uncontrolled, for these were people with absolutely nothing left to lose: people who would even, at some basic level, prefer the lance of an Allheart knight now compared to the slow and agonizing death they were facing. Also, the knights themselves didn't attack with vigor, for they understood that these were plague victims, walking poison. To strike one was to wear the blood of one; and then even a noble Allheart knight could find himself on the other side of this line.

"Run him again, and swiftly!" Duke Kalas called to Constance. Before the stunned and emotionally wounded King Danube could begin to react, quick-thinking Kalas grabbed the King's horse's bridle and pulled the beast in a turn with his own, then reached back and swatted Danube's horse a sharp crack on the rump.

Off they flew, all three, running fast for the southern gate of Castle Ursal, leaving the mob behind, and approaching, Danube saw to his dismay, a line of archers preparing their deadly volley.

"Bobbed arrows alone!" he commanded, referring to the practice, headless arrows the archers often used in Castle Ursal's wide courtyard.

"But, my King—" the leader of the brigade began to protest. Danube shot him such a scowl that the words stuck in his throat.

Satisfied that the brigade would do as he commanded, Danube thundered away for the southern gate, urging his horse into a rough lope and running purposely on the cobblestones now, the sound of the hooves drowning out plaintive and angry cries from the field behind.

An upset and dejected Danube sat on his throne later that day, his hands out before his face, fingers tapping.

"Only a handful were seriously injured," remarked Duke Kalas, sitting next to him. "Only one peasant was killed."

"Your Allhearts performed with their usual brilliance," Danube offered, but that recognition hardly seemed to brighten his mood. "Though I fear we'll not know the full extent of the disaster until weeks have passed," he added, a clear reference to the fact that several of those Allheart knights might have become exposed to the rosy plague in the riot.

And all of it, both men understood too clearly, was due to the fact that the King merely wanted a day out in the sunshine, a day out of the tomb that Castle Ursal had become.

"We should be looking to the greater fortune of the day," said Constance, standing a short distance away. Behind her, Merwick and Torrence played in the bliss of youthful ignorance, making toys out of relics, smudging priceless tapestries, laughing and crying with equally fervent passion. "Had we not reacted as swiftly as we did, it is possible that all three of us would have found ourselves in the midst of the plague-ridden."

"They would not have unhorsed us," Duke Kalas said with a fierce and determined look.

"Would they have had to?" Constance answered. "Or would the King of Honce-the-Bear soon be facing the same executioner as they?"

It was true enough, and no one had an answer against it. The plague victims had come close to the King himself, far too close.

"We will not be able to do such a thing again," Danube announced. Kalas, whose stress had grown with each passing day, scowled all the more. "We were foolish even to go out there at this time."

"The plague has never been thicker about Ursal's streets," Duke Kalas admitted grimly.

"And whether we take chances or not, there remains the possibility of its finding a way into our house," Constance added. Both Kalas and Danube eyed her curiously, for her tone showed that her statement was leading to something more.

"These are dangerous times," she said, moving closer, but pointedly glancing back at her two children as she did, "more dangerous to the Throne of the kingdom, I would argue, than ever was the dactyl or its evil minions."

King Danube nodded, but wasn't so certain of that. Of course, he had never shared the little secret of Father Abbot Markwart's vengeful spirit making several threatening visits to his private bedchambers. On the surface though, and except for that one point, Constance's argument was well taken. The dactyl's war, for all its terror and trouble, never got anywhere near Ursal, but remained in the northern reaches of the kingdom.

The plague, on the other hand, loomed all about Castle Ursal's walls.

"I am not certain that this latest plague is not another manifestation of the dactyl's evil minions," King Danube did argue.

"For all of our cautions," Constance went on, "for all the soldiers lining the walls, and for all the thickness of those walls themselves, we cannot guarantee that the plague will not find us, any of us. And if it does, even if it is you, my King, then all the monks in all the world will likely prove useless against its workings."

Duke Kalas snorted loudly at that statement, for he had long ago determined the Abellican monks to be useless against any sort of illness. Was it not a disease, after all, and one far less powerful than the rosy plague, that had killed young Queen Vivian? And that right before the eyes of Abbot Je'howith?

"I thank you for the cheerful warning," Danube said dryly. "But in all truth, Constance, this danger has been known to us since the beginning."

"Then why have you taken no steps to solidify the kingdom in its event?" the woman bluntly asked.

A puzzled King Danube stared at her.

"Merwick and Torrence," Duke Kalas said quietly, catching on, and before King Danube could pick up on that, he went on. "The line of succession is already in place. Have you forgotten Prince Midalis of Vanguard?"

"We do not even know if my brother is alive," Danube admitted before Constance could reply. "We have had no word from Vanguard in many months."

"Surely if he had fallen, then word would have been passed south," Kalas argued.

Danube nodded. "Probably," he admitted, "but we cannot be certain, nor can we be certain that my brother is not now lying feverish in a bed, heavy with plague."

Kalas sighed.

"It is the truth, if an unpleasant one," King Danube added, then he turned to Constance. "What solution do you see?" he asked, though it was obvious to him and to Kalas what she was hinting at.

Constance eyed the King directly, then turned her gaze, taking his with her, toward her—toward their—two children.

Duke Kalas gave a laugh. "How fortunate," he muttered sarcastically.

But King Danube wasn't seeing things that way at all. "How fortunate indeed," he echoed, but in a very different tone. "And our experience this day reminded me of how fragile is our existence." He rose from his chair and walked deliberately toward Constance. "You are my witness in this, Duke Kalas," he said solemnly.

"Yes, my King," came the obedient answer, for even stubborn Kalas knew when he could not push the boundaries with his friend.

"In the event of my death, the throne passes to my brother, Prince Midalis of Vanguard," Danube said formally. "In the event that Prince Midalis is unable to ascend the throne, then Merwick, son of Constance, son of King Danube Brock Ursal, shall be crowned King of Honce-the-Bear, and a regent shall be appointed from the dukes of the land to oversee the kingdom until he is old enough and trained enough to assume the responsibilities of the Throne.

"Beyond Merwick, the title and claim lie with young Torrence, again under the tutelage of a properly appointed regent. And I should like you, my friend Kalas, to serve as that regent if you are able."

Constance beamed but said nothing; nor did Duke Kalas, who wore a very different expression, somewhat of a cross between amusement and disgust.

"Go and fetch the royal scribe," Danube instructed Constance, "and the abbot of St. Honce and any of the other noblemen who are about the castle. We will make this proclamation again, in full witness and with all the propriety demanded of such a solemn occasion."

Constance was gone in the blink of an eye.

"I hope she made you as happy in the moment of conceiving the children as you made her now," Duke Kalas remarked. Danube turned a dangerous stare on him, warning him that he might again be crossing the very thin line that separated the words of a friend to a friend from the words of a Duke to his King.

"I am weary of the road, my friend," Prince Midalis told Andacanavar as the two at last came into the more familiar reaches of Vanguard, nearing home. "I do not understand how you can live such a nomadic life."

"It is the way of my people," Andacanavar explained. "We move to follow the caribou herds and the elk, to escape winter's bite in the far north and summer's plague of insects in the south."

Midalis nodded and smiled, obviously unconvinced of the benefits of such a life.

"This road was more lonely than most," the ranger went on. "Few contacts, out of necessity. Trust me, my friend, you will enjoy another such journey someday, after the plague has passed, when we can dine with the farmers along the road or speak with the hardy woodsmen of the Timberlands across a tavern table."

"And perhaps we shall do just that," said Midalis. "But for now, I am glad to be home."

Soon after, the pair came in sight of St. Belfour, walking their mounts along the trail climbing to the lea that lay before the abbey.

And then they saw them, the refugees, strewn across the lawn before St. Belfour. Miserable, plague-ridden wretches, many near death.

The rosy plague had beaten Prince Midalis back to his homeland.

"Would that I was born with a womb," Duke Kalas snickered as Constance walked by him later that night in a torch-lit corridor in Castle Ursal, "and all the charms to catch a nobleman's fancy."

Constance glared at him, but he relieved the tension with a burst of laughter. "I blame you not at all," Kalas went on.

"And I do not appreciate your sarcasm," she coldly replied. "Can you deny the responsibility of my decision? Would you have Honce-the-Bear without a proper line of succession should King Danube die?"

Kalas laughed again. "Pragmatism? Or personal gain?"

"Can they not be one and the same?"

"I am not angry with you, dear Constance," the Duke explained. "Jealous, perhaps, and filled with admiration. I believe that you became

pregnant by King Danube deliberately, both times. You conceived Merwick on the barge south from Palmaris, when you knew that another
woman had caught Danube's oft-wandering eye." He noted that Constance
did wince a bit at the reference to Jilseponie. "And so you struck your love
coup, and brilliantly, and you have patiently awaited the time to gain the
declaration that you hold so dear."

Constance stood, steel jawed, staring at him, not blinking.

"You used those tools and weapons available to you to insinuate yourself
into the royal line," Duke Kalas stated bluntly, and he gave a great bow and
swept his arm out wide. He staggered a bit as he did, and only then did
Constance catch on that the man might have indulged himself with a few
potent drinks.

She started to comment on that, but stopped herself. How could she
judge Kalas at this unsettling time, after the terrifying incident in the
garden? In truth, Constance, too, would have liked to spend that night
curled up with a bottle!

"You can think whatever you wish of me," she said instead calmly, "but I
do love him—"

"You always have," Duke Kalas replied. "And do not misunderstand me,
for I'll say nothing to King Danube to change his mind or his course, nor do
I consider that course ill for Honce-the-Bear."

"You judge me," Constance accused, "but I do love him, with all of my
heart."

"And he?"

Constance looked away, then shook her head. "He does not love me,"
she admitted. "He'll not even share my bed any longer, though he pro-
claims that we remain friends—and indeed, he treats me well."

"He asked you to ride today," Duke Kalas said, and his voice took on a
different, sympathetic tone.

"Danube has always held me dear as a friend," Constance said. "But he
does not love me. Never that. He loves the memory of Vivian. He loves . . ."

"That woman," Kalas finished, his voice low. "The hero."

His obvious enmity surprised Constance. She was no friend of Jilseponie
Wyndon's, of course, but it seemed from Duke Kalas' tone that he cared
for the woman even less than she. Wounded pride, Constance figured, for
hadn't Jilseponie refused his advances in Palmaris?

But then Kalas surprised her even more.

"Pity the kingdom if King Danube finds his love," he said.

Constance stared at him curiously.

"The marriage of Church and Crown," Kalas said dryly, "the end of the
world."

"If you feel that way, then it is good that you do not oppose me," Constance said after a long and considering pause. She gave a little snicker and
started away.

"A pity that you have no connections in Vanguard," came Kalas' voice behind her, and she stopped and turned on him suspiciously. "Else you could eliminate the last barrier to your glory."

Duke Kalas bowed again and wisely ran away.

His remark had been said in jest, Constance knew, but still, she could not help but retrace the actions that had brought her to this point. She was not without guilt, but that was only a minor twinge against the reality of her current situation. The kingdom was better off for her deliberate course, and now Constance had insinuated her bloodline, her children, into the royal line. Even if neither of her sons actually got to the throne, their children would remain in the line of ascent, and so on throughout the coming generations.

One day in the future, near or far, Constance Pemblebury would be remembered as the Queen Mother of Honce-the-Bear.

CHAPTER

❖ 33 ❖

The Abandoned Flock

He looked at his lover and blamed himself. There was no avoiding it. Dainsey had wanted to come back to Palmaris for a visit—the plague had arrived in all force in Caer Tinella, anyway—but Roger had argued against the course.

But he hadn't argued strenuously enough, and the two had traveled south. Now, less than a month later, Dainsey stood beside him on wobbly legs, her eyes sunken and listless, her brow beaded with the sweat of a fever, her body marked by rosy splotches ringed in white—though Roger had taken great pains to cover the woman enough to hide those telltale marks before venturing here to St. Precious.

Still, it would not be enough, he knew, to get them through the gatehouse. They had been admitted over the tussie-mussie bed immediately, for Abbot Braumin's invitation to them remained in force. However, inside the gatehouse came a second test, where several monks, trained with soul stones, sent out their spirits to inspect any who would cross into the abbey.

With that uncomfortable scrutiny ended, Roger now could only wait and hope.

The minutes stretched on and on, and Roger understood that if the monks had failed to detect the illness, they would have already let them in. No, they knew the truth of it, he realized, and had gone to speak with Abbot Braumin.

Roger knew what was coming even as the small panel slid away at the end of the narrow gatehouse corridor, and the grim face of a brother appeared beyond.

"You may enter, but the woman cannot," came the voice—a voice that Roger recognized.

"She is my heart and my soul, Brother Castinagis," Roger argued.

"She is thick with plague," came the reply, firm but somewhat tempered by compassion. "She cannot enter St. Precious. I am sorry, my friend."

"I want to speak with Abbot Braumin."

383

"Then come in."

Roger looked at Dainsey. "What of her?" he asked.

"She cannot enter," Castinagis said again. "Nor can she remain within the gatehouse. Send her back out, beyond the flower bed."

Roger considered the course. Things beyond that flower bed were not pretty, with plague victims milling about and—since the town guard would come nowhere near them—lawlessness abundant. He had to take Dainsey back to their rented room at The Giant's Bones, he knew.

"Tell Abbot Braumin that I will soon return," he said to Castinagis, lowering his voice to show his anger. "Alone."

"If you go back beyond the flower bed, then you will be subjected to another spiritual inspection before you are allowed to enter the abbey," came Castinagis' unyielding response.

"I will be gone but a few minutes," Roger argued.

"A few seconds would be too long a time," came the answer, and the panel at the end of the corridor slammed shut.

Roger's heart sank with that sound. He had hoped that he, as a personal friend of Braumin's, would find some assistance here, some of the compassion that St. Precious was not lending to those other unfortunate victims. He had hoped that his connections with the powerful churchmen would save Dainsey.

But now, even though he hadn't yet uttered one word to Braumin, Roger was being forced to face the truth, the fact that not Braumin, not Viscenti, not any of them, would do anything at all to help Dainsey, that her affliction would bring to her the same end as everyone else so diseased.

It took Roger a long while to find enough strength to lead his dear Dainsey back out of St. Precious. Never in his life, not even when he had been caught by Kos-kosio Begulne of the powries, had he felt so helpless and so wretched.

"There's not many goin' into the city o' late," the ferry pilot said to the leader of the curious group of men as they neared the Palmaris wharf. They wore robes like those of Abellican monks, except that theirs were black with red hoods instead of the normal brown on brown. "Den o' sickness, it is!" the pilot said ironically with a cough.

"Do you think you can hide from it?" the leader of the group, Marcalo De'Unnero, said to the man, his voice a tantalizing whisper. "The rosy plague is a punishment from God, and God sees all. If you are a sinner, my friend, then the plague will find you, no matter how deep a hole you find to climb in."

The pilot, obviously shaken, waved his hands and shook his head. "Not a sinner, I ain't!" he cried. "But I'm not wantin' to hear ye no more."

"But hear me you must!" De'Unnero said, grabbing the man by the front of his dirty tunic and lifting him up to his tiptoes. "There is no place for you to hide, friend. Salvation lies only in repentance!" he finished loudly, and all the hundred red-hooded men behind him, the Brothers Repentant—their numbers swollen by the rush of eager townsfolk to join their ranks, for they, after all, by De'Unnero's own words, held the secret to health—cheered wildly.

"Repent!" De'Unnero yelled, and he drove the man to his knees.

"I will, I will!" the terrified pilot replied.

De'Unnero lifted his other hand, which was now the paw of a tiger, so that the pilot could see it clearly. "Swear fealty to the Church!" he demanded. "The true Church of St. Abelle, the Church of the Brothers Repentant."

Eyes wide at the sight of the deadly appendage, the poor pilot began to tremble and cry, and he even kissed De'Unnero's hand.

Behind De'Unnero, the Brothers Repentant howled for blood. They began jumping so violently that the ferry rocked dangerously. They began punching each other; several stripped off their black robes and walked through the rest of the gathering, accepting slap after slap so that their bare skin reddened.

"We are your salvation," De'Unnero said to the trembling man.

"Yes, master."

"Yet you took our money for passage," De'Unnero went on.

"Kill him, Brother Truth!" several men yelled.

"Take it back!" the pilot begged, pulling his purse from his belt and thrusting it into De'Unnero's hand. "I swear, Brother Truth, if I'd'a known, I'd not taken a copper bear. On me mum's soul, I swear."

De'Unnero took the purse and eyed the pilot dangerously a bit longer. Then he shoved the man down to the deck. "Get us in to dock," he said disgustedly, and he moved forward. The city was coming into clear view now, the buildings showing through the morning fog.

His anger was feigned, though, for in truth, the former Bishop of Palmaris was in a fine mood this particularly sweet day. He and his ferocious brood had swept across the southland, all across Yorkey, scouring town after town of infidels, and taking care to avoid any Abellican abbeys—with the sole exception of Abbot Olin's St. Bondabruce. As De'Unnero had guessed, Olin had been quite sympathetic to his cause, and while the man hadn't openly endorsed the Brothers Repentant, hadn't even let them into his abbey, neither had he opposed them and he had secretly met with De'Unnero. That meeting had gone wonderfully, as far as De'Unnero was concerned, for he hadn't missed the intrigue on Olin's face when he had hinted that he might know the way to Pimaninicuit, the far-off isle holding the treasure equivalent of the hoards of a hundred, hundred kings on its gem-covered beaches.

But those were thoughts for another day, the fierce master knew. For now, before him lay the most coveted jewel, the city of his greatest triumph and greatest defeat. Here lay Palmaris, mighty Palmaris, thick with the plague and ripe for the words of the Brothers Repentant.

Marcalo De'Unnero had not forgotten the treatment the folk here had given to him, nor the stern words of Abbot Braumin when the fool had expelled him from the city.

No, De'Unnero had not forgotten anything about Palmaris, the city in which all of this trouble with the plague had really begun. The city where Markwart and the old ways had been abandoned for this new foolishness. The city that embraced Braumin, and thus Jojonah and thus Avelyn and their insane ideas that the Church should be the healer of the common folk.

De'Unnero spat as he considered the irony of that goal. Where were the healers of the common folk now, this kinder and more compassionate Church? Hidden away, by all reports, behind thick walls and stinking flower beds.

Their cowardice would be their undoing, De'Unnero knew. Their cowardice would deliver the desperate, abandoned people of Palmaris to him, would make them heed his words of potential salvation.

Then Abbot Braumin and his foolish friends would come to understand what their errant beliefs had bought them.

Yes, this was a particularly sweet day.

Roger suffered through the indignity of another spiritual rape in the gatehouse of St. Precious, then stormed out when at last he was cleared to enter.

"Where is Abbot Braumin?" he demanded of Brother Castinagis, who was again manning the gate.

Castinagis snorted and shook his head, patting poor Roger to calm him. "He will see you," he assured the man, but Roger shoved him away.

"He will hear me!" Roger retorted. "And woe to those who turned Dainsey away!" Roger turned and stomped off, heading for the main building and the office of his friend.

"Abbot Braumin already knows," Brother Castinagis called softly behind him, stopping Roger in his tracks. "He knew even as we were inspecting you and the woman, even as we were following his orders that no one enter St. Precious without such inspection. He knew that your woman friend was turned away before it ever happened. Do not look so surprised, Roger! Have you forgotten that similar treatment was afforded Colleen Kilronney when Jilseponie brought her to our door?"

"B-but . . ." Roger stammered, and his thoughts were all jumbled. "I am your friend."

"Indeed," said Castinagis, with no trace of sarcasm, "a valued friend, and it pains me, as I'm sure it pains Abbot Braumin, that we cannot help your woman companion. Do you not understand? This is the rosy plague; we have no weapons against it."

"What am I to do?" Roger asked. "Am I to sit by and simply watch Dainsey die?"

"You would be wiser by far to stay here with us," came a soft voice behind them. Roger turned to see his old friend Braumin Herde emerging from the building. The man had aged noticeably in the last year, the first signs of silver streaking his curly black hair, and deep lines running out from the sides of his eyes. "There are plague houses which will make your Dainsey comfortable. I can arrange it. You need not return to her."

Roger stared at him incredulously.

"There is nothing you can do for her," Braumin went on. He moved closer and tried to put a comforting arm on Roger's shoulder, but Roger danced away. "And contact with her greatly endangers you."

"There must be some answer. . . ." Roger started to argue, shaking his head.

"There is nothing," Abbot Braumin said sternly. "Only to hide, and you must hide with us."

"Dainsey needs me," Roger argued.

"You will do nothing more than watch her die," Castinagis said.

Roger turned back to him, his expression grim and determined. "Then that is what I must do," he declared. "I must watch her die. I must hold her hand and bid her farewell on her journey."

"Those are a fool's words!" Castinagis cried.

Roger started to shout back at him, but he hadn't the strength. He stuttered over several beginnings, but then just threw his hands up and wailed. Then, his legs giving out beneath him, he fell to his knees, sobbing. Both monks rushed to him immediately.

"I will arrange for her care," Abbot Braumin promised.

"You will stay with us. Among friends," Castinagis added.

Roger considered their words, their good intentions, for a brief moment; but any comfort or hope they tried to impart was fast washed away by an image of Dainsey, Roger's dear Dainsey, the woman he had come to love so dearly, lying feverish on a bed and calling out for him.

That was a cry that Roger Lockless, whatever the potential danger, could not ignore.

"No!" he growled, and he stubbornly pulled himself up to his feet. "No, if you cannot help her, then I will find someone else who can."

"There is no one," Braumin said softly. "Nothing."

"Then I will stay with her," Roger snarled back at him, "to the end."

Castinagis started to say something, but Abbot Braumin cut him short with a wave of his hand and a nod. They had seen this behavior before, of course, in Jilseponie, and so it was not unexpected that one who was not of the Church could not see the greater good against the immediate pain.

Roger started to walk away but stopped suddenly and wheeled about. "I wish to marry her," he said—and it was obvious that the thought had just then come into his mind—"formally, before the eyes of God."

"She cannot come here," Brother Castinagis said.

"Will you do that much for me, at least?" Roger asked Braumin. "Perform the ceremony from across the tussie-mussie bed." He stared hard at his friend.

Castinagis, too, looked at Braumin.

"I would prefer that you not return to her," the abbot of St. Precious said. "You ask me to sanction a union that cannot last out the rest of the summer."

"I ask you to confirm our love before God's eyes as something sacred, for that it is," Roger corrected. "Can you not even do that much for me?"

Abbot Braumin spent a long time thinking it over. "If I believed that there was some chance that I might convince you to abandon this lost cause, then surely I would," he said at last, "but if you are determined to remain beside the poor woman, then better that it be a union sanctioned by God. Go and bring her to the tussie-mussie bed, and be quick, before I become convinced that I, too, am playing the part of the fool."

Roger was on his way before Braumin even finished.

CHAPTER

❖ 34 ❖

Angry Sheep

"Do not," Francis warned the irate man with wild, bloodshot eyes and telltale rings on his bare arms. The monk stepped in front of the man, blocking his path to the tussie-mussie bed and St.-Mere-Abelle, for Francis understood all too clearly that the brothers atop the wall with crossbows and gemstones were very serious about killing him if he approached.

"You cannot hope . . ." Francis started to say, but the wild man, the man who had just watched his only son carted off to the common grave, wasn't listening. He came forward like a charging bull and swung his heavy arms furiously.

Too furiously, and Francis, well trained in the arts martial, ducked the blow and hooked the arm as it swept above him, pushing it down and, with a simple step and twist, put himself behind his attacker. Before the outraged commoner understood what hit him, Francis had the man's right arm bent up behind his back, while Francis' left arm was across the man's neck. Despite his great rage, the man was helpless.

The man tried to pull straight ahead, but Francis slipped one foot in front of him, and down they went, heavily, Francis landing atop the face-down commoner.

"I'll kill ye all!" the man raged. "I'll kill ye to death! I will! I will. . . ." His voice trailed off as he broke into sobs. "I will."

"I understand," Francis whispered. "Your son . . . I know your pain."

"How could ye?" came a question from behind.

"What're ye or any o' yer stinkin' monk friends knowin' o' anythin'?" demanded another. Francis felt a boot come down heavily on the small of his back.

And then they fell over him, only a pair of men, but many others were cheering them on. They tore Francis free of the sobbing man and brought him up roughly. Though he managed to get in one quick punch against one man and a pair of sharp kicks to the other's shin, he knew that they had him caught—and understood that others would come help them if he wriggled free.

"Get him and kill him!" one man cried.

"Death to 'em all!" shouted another. Then the mob swirled about Francis, and then . . . parted, for shoving her way through it came Merry Cowsenfed, cursing and spitting with every step. When one man gave a particularly loud and threatening shout Francis' way, Merry promptly smacked him across the face.

"What're ye all gone mad?" she screamed, her unusual ire calming the crowd. "This one's been helping us every day, and came out to us healthy! Can any o' the rest of ye say that ye'd be so generous if ye didn't think ye yerself had the plague already? Ah, but what a lot o' fools I got meself caught up with! To be hittin' so on poor Brother Francis!"

The murmuring of the crowd died away, each person turning to the next, as if waiting for instructions.

Then the two men holding Francis roughly pushed him free. "Bah, Merry's right," said one. "This one ain't done nothin' earnin' him a beatin'." He turned ominously toward St.-Mere-Abelle. "But them others . . ." he snarled, and the crowd erupted into ferocious cheers behind him. The man Francis had downed clawed his way back to his feet and reiterated his hatred for the Abellican monks.

Again, Francis rushed to the forefront. "They have crossbows and gemstones!" he pleaded. "They will kill you all before you ever get near the wall. And look at that wall! How do you plan to get over it? Or through it? A team of To-gai-ru ponies could not run a ram through that door, I promise you!"

Every point he made was perfectly valid, every one enough of a detriment to turn aside any reasonable person. But these were not reasonable people. No, they had lost everything, and in the pain and hopelessness of that moment, Francis's words rang hollow.

And so they started off, and so did Brother Francis—but not physically. The monk reached into his pouch and clenched his hand about his soul stone, falling into its magic, freeing his spirit from his body. He went right for the apparent leader of the mob, the man who had torn him from the grieving father.

He did not want to possess the man, but Francis did send his spirit into him. And once inside the man's thoughts, the monk began to impart images and sounds of slaughter, of men running, screaming, while magical fires bit at them and peeled away their flesh. He showed the man a scene of bodies piled twenty deep atop the tussie-mussie bed. He showed . . .

And then the connection was broken, suddenly, Francis' spirit sent careening back to his body. He blinked his eyes, working hard to recover from the shock, fearing that the slaughter had already begun.

But the mob was still there, hardly moving, just staring at their leader, who stood openmouthed, staring blankly at the towering wall and at the deadly monks standing atop it.

Merry Cowsenfed was at his arm all the while, tugging hard and pleading with him to turn about.

The man, seeming unsure, glanced back at Francis.

"They will kill you," Francis explained, "every one of you."

The man closed his eyes and clenched his fists at his sides, but whatever the level of rage within him, he could not ignore the simple fact that they had no chance even to get anywhere near their enemies. No chance at all.

The man growled and lifted his clenched fists into the air, but then he walked back from the tussie-mussie bed—the battle line, it seemed—and roughly jostled through the crowd.

Francis breathed a profound sigh of relief, but he soon became aware that many of those around him weren't very happy with this outcome. Some cursed and shook their fists at him, though most did turn back, grumbling and shaking their heads.

In Francis' estimation, they had just avoided a complete slaughter. He sighed again and nodded to Merry, then turned to find a wrinkled old woman, her face as sharp as Yorkey cheese, glaring at him.

"Bah, but ain't ye spittin' pretty words," she said. "Is that why they sent ye out, Brother Francis o' St.-Mere-Abelle? To talk pretty and keep us walkin' dead folk in our place?"

Francis couldn't find the words to answer her.

"Bah, who's carin' about ye, anyway, Brother Francis the saint," she said with sincere disgust. "Ye're soon to catch the rosies, if ye ain't already, and soon to be put in the ground."

Far from disputing her or yelling at her, Francis stood there and accepted the judgment and the looks of all those who had turned from St.-Mere-Abelle's fortified gate.

And he accepted, too, the old crone's prediction, for Francis honestly believed that the last one he had tried to cure had beaten him back, and more.

Francis was fairly convinced that the plague was growing within him.

"Perhaps our dear Brother Francis serves a purpose after all," Fio Bou-raiy said to Father Abbot Agronguerre, the pair watching the spectacle from the wall. "For them, I mean," Bou-raiy elaborated with slight snicker. "A pity if they came against us."

"You sound as if you would enjoy such a sight," the Father Abbot observed. Fio Bou-raiy shuffled nervously, reminding himself that he and this Father Abbot he so desperately wanted to impress were not often of like mind.

"Not so," he replied. "And forgive me, Father Abbot. It is only that I feel so helpless in these circumstances. There are times when I wonder if God has deserted the world."

"Indeed," said an obviously unconvinced Agronguerre, raising an eyebrow. "Take care, for you are spouting words akin to that of our dear misguided Brother De'Unnero."

"I only mean—"

"I know what you mean, and what you meant," Agronguerre interrupted.

A long and uncomfortable silence followed.

"How fare the brothers working on the herbal poultices and syrups that Brother Francis bade us to make?" Agronguerre asked at length. "The ones that came down from the Timberlands—from Jilseponie, we believe?"

"They had all the ingredients available," Bou-raiy answered. "I suspect that the compounding is nearly complete."

"If it is not, then add brothers to the work," the Father Abbot instructed, "as many as it takes to get those concoctions out to the desperate people."

"They will not cure, by Abbot Braumin's own words, relayed to us directly from St. Precious, and to him from the very source of the recipes: the woman Jilseponie, so he said."

"But they will help," Agronguerre tartly replied. "And they will help to make the people understand that we are doing all that we can. Brother Francis stopped their charge this time. Next time, I fear, we will be forced to use more drastic measures, and that I do not desire.

"And your observation concerning Brother Francis was quite correct," Agronguerre went on. "He does play an important role—more so than you apparently recognize. Look upon him and be glad for him. His choice in this has been a blessing to the Abellican Church as much as to the peasants he so magnificently serves."

"Surely you do not agree with him," Master Bou-raiy snapped back without hesitation.

Father Abbot Agronguerre turned away from the man without answering, looking back over the desolate field and the wretched refugees, clearly torn by the sight.

"Father Abbot!"

"Fear not, for I am not intending to open St.-Mere-Abelle to the plague victims," Agronguerre replied solemnly, "nor have I any designs of walking out of our gates to join dear Francis on the field. But neither can I find fault with the man for his choices. No, I admire him, and fear that the only reason I am not out there beside him is because . . ." He paused and turned back to face Fio Bou-raiy squarely. "Because I am afraid, brother. I am old and have not many years left and am not afraid of death. No, not that. But I am afraid of the rosy plague."

Fio Bou-raiy thought to argue strongly against Francis, to label the man a fool and his course one of disaster for the Church if his example was held up in a positive light, but he wisely bit back the words. He held no fears that Abbot Agronguerre would prod others to follow Brother Francis, nor that the man would go out on the field himself; and though he didn't want Francis praised in any way for his foolish actions, he recognized that to be a small price to pay. For Brother Francis would be dead soon enough, Fio Bou-raiy believed, yet another example of the folly of trying to do battle with the rosy plague.

"It is pragmatism that keeps you here, Father Abbot," he did say quietly.

"Is it?" Agronguerre asked with a snort, and he turned and walked away.

A frustrated Fio Bou-raiy turned back to face the field and leaned heavily on the wall. He spotted Francis then, again at work with his soul stone on some unfortunate victim. Bou-raiy shook his head in disgust, and he did not agree with Father Abbot Agronguerre at all on this point. No, he saw Francis as setting a bad example for the Church, reinforcing the belief of the ignorant peasants that the Church should be more active in this time of desperation.

Fio Bou-raiy slapped his hand against the thick stone wall. They would get the poultices and syrup out soon, but he almost hoped that it would not be soon enough, that the peasants would come at St.-Mere-Abelle wildly. No, he didn't really want to kill any of them, though he figured that to do so would actually prove a blessing to the poor, unfortunate wretches. But if it did happen, Fio Bou-raiy decided that his first shot, with lightning or with crossbow, would not be aimed at any ignorant peasant. No, he would target a certain troublemaking Abellican brother.

"Do it!" King Danube demanded, as harsh a command as he had ever given to Duke Kalas.

"You would jeopardize the goodwill toward the Throne for the sake of—" Kalas tried to argue.

"Do it, and now!" King Danube interrupted. There was no room in his tone for any debate. "With all speed."

Kalas glanced to the side, to Constance Pemblebury.

"With all speed and with all heart," King Danube said.

Kalas saluted his King with a thump to his chest, a formal acceptance of command that did not often occur between the two friends, then turned sharply on his heel and stormed out of the room, his boots clacking loudly with every step.

King Danube looked over at Constance and sighed.

"It pains Duke Kalas greatly to do anything of benefit to the Abellican Church," she said, trying to calm him.

King Danube nodded and closed his eyes, remembering all too well the source of Kalas' pain and resentment, remembering Vivian, his queen. But then, before he could fall too deeply into the trance of long-ago memories, he blinked his eyes and shook his head resolutely. His duty as king now was clear to him: to protect St. Honce as strongly as he would protect Castle Ursal, and though the brothers within the abbey might be able to contain the peasant horde now threatening riot at their gates, it was incumbent upon the Crown to make a strong showing of support for the Church.

There was no room for argument, and no time for debate.

He and Constance sat quietly for a few minutes, each digesting the sudden but not unexpected turn of events.

And then came the cries of outrage, the explosion of the mob, and then a crackle of thunder.

"They are going against the abbey," Constance observed.

And then they heard a different sort of thunder, the rumble of horses' pounding hooves, and the peasants' cries of anger soon shifted to wails of pain and terror.

The pair in the throne room understood well enough that the Allheart knights had charged out with their typical, brutal efficiency, understood that the threat to St. Honce had just come to an abrupt end.

King Danube glanced over at Constance and saw the pained, weary look upon her face. This was taking such a toll on all of them. The seclusion, the helplessness, the necessary and exhausting shows of strength.

"You should go and spend some time with Merwick and Torrence," Danube offered.

"Duke Kalas will soon return, and his mood will be all the more foul," Constance replied.

Danube nodded, knowing the truth of that observation. "Go and play," he insisted. "Duke Kalas is a member of the court and the appointed leader of the Allheart knights. He will do as I instruct, and do so properly, or he will be relieved of his command."

Constance raised her eyebrows, her expression skeptical.

And that, too, Danube understood all too well. In this time of great discontent and frustration, replacing Duke Kalas would not sit well with the Allheart knights, who truly loved the man. But Danube knew, as well, that it would never come to that. Kalas was stubborn and his hatred of the Abellican Church could not be underestimated, but in the end and above all else, he was Danube's man, a true friend. He and his knights had performed beautifully outside St. Honce, no doubt; and he and Danube could quickly put that distasteful errand behind them.

Constance, after a moment, seemed to come to the same conclusion, for she rose from her seat and walked past King Danube, giving him a kiss on the cheek, and then made her way out of the room.

Duke Kalas appeared within minutes.

"Near to fifty dead," he announced grimly, "trampled on the streets."

"And your knights?" Danube asked.

Kalas scoffed, as if at the notion that any of his magnificent Allhearts could even be wounded by the likes of a mere peasant.

"Then we did as we had to," the King went on. "We defended St. Honce, as our agreement with the Abellican Church demands, and we reminded the peasants that even in a time of plague the laws must be obeyed."

If only it were that simple! Danube silently added, for though he remained stern and solid, and though he believed in his proclamation, the reality that his prized Allheart knights had just slaughtered fifty of his own people offended him profoundly.

And offended Kalas, too, Danube noted, as the man walked past him and took the seat Constance had vacated, dropping his chin to his palm and staring blankly ahead.

Outside, on the streets, occasional cries of outage, of betrayal—by both the monks and the peasants—resonated grimly in their ears.

The rallying shouts ended abruptly as Marcalo De'Unnero, the self-titled Brother Truth, shoved through the ranks of the Brothers Repentant and the gathered peasants of Palmaris, and charged down the lane the short distance to where the Behrenese had gathered.

The dark-skinned southerners had come out in response to the shouts of anger, a group of men and women asking for nothing but to be left alone at their dockside homes in peace. But Brother Truth had spoken, had proclaimed the mere presence of the Behrenese as a source of God's anger, as a source of the rosy plague.

The nearest Behrenese man lifted a weapon, a gaff, at the charging monk, but De'Unnero skidded to an abrupt stop and snap-kicked the underside of the shaft, launching it far and wide. In the same motion, the expert fighting monk brought his leg down and to the side, caving in the knee of the next closest southerner. Then, still without ever bringing his foot back to the ground, De'Unnero brought his leg back, kicking his first opponent in the gut, doubling the man over.

De'Unnero dropped his foot and pivoted it, lifting his other foot as he turned, angling it to slam the Behrenese in the chin, snapping his head violently to the side and dropping him facedown on the stone.

Then he felt the weretiger roaring within him, screaming to be let loose that he might devour and destroy all who stood before him. He almost complied, almost fell into the beast, but then his consciousness screamed out even louder that to reveal that side of himself in this city—this city that had lost its beloved Baron Bildeborough to such a cat!—would surely spell his defeat. He fought with all his willpower, concentrating, concentrating, and actually took a slight hit from one of his pitiful opponents, so distracted was he.

But then he had the urges put down, and he leaped ahead, spinning and kicking. He landed right before one man, who, apparently thinking he had the monk vulnerable, brought a huge axe straight up over his head.

De'Unnero hit him with a left, right, left, right, left, right, square in the face, and the axe fell to the ground behind the stunned man. He started to drift down, but vicious De'Unnero hit him again in the face—left, right, left, right, left, right—all the way down to his knees. There the Behrenese remained, kneeling and beyond dazed, and De'Unnero leaped in the air and came down with a double stomp on the top of the man's chest.

He heard the crack of backbone.

De'Unnero threw his arms up high, fists clenched, and roared in victory; and then he looked around and saw the hundred Brothers Repentant and twice that many common Palmaris citizens driving hard against the Behrenese, overwhelming them with sheer numbers, dragging them down and beating them to death.

But even more satisfying to Brother Truth was the spectacle of the Palmaris city guard, sitting astride their horses down at the end of a lane, a force large enough to successfully intervene. They did not; they sat and they watched, and the Brothers Repentant swept the Behrenese enclave away, killing those they could catch and burning down every structure that had housed any of the dark-skinned folk.

Borne on Wings of Desperation

"It's Roger!" Pony said happily to Belster, when she recognized the man driving the wagon that was rolling into the southern end of Dundalis. Her smile disappeared almost as soon as it began to spread, though, as she took note of the form beside her friend, slumped and huddled under a heavy cloak, though the day was quite warm.

It was Dainsey, Pony knew, and she could guess easily enough why the woman was so postured.

"She's got the plague," Belster remarked, obviously deducing the same thing. "Why'd the fool bring her here, then?"

That uncharacteristically bitter statement brought a scowl to Pony's face, and she showed it to Belster directly.

He shook his head, showing embarrassment for the callous remark but also holding fast to his anger. Pony could understand that well enough; Dundalis had remained relatively free of the dreaded disease thus far, but one victim could change all that, could send the rosy plague rushing through the town like a fire. Those who knew the oral histories of the plague had claimed that entire villages, even fair-sized towns had simply disappeared under the deadly sweep of the disease.

But, without even talking to Roger, Pony also understood why he had come. She could see the look on his face as the wagon approached, an expression sad and panicked, a desperate and hopeless plea.

Some people went out to Roger, calling greetings, but he waved them back from the wagon. "A safe distance!" he cried, and every one of those villagers wore at first a perplexed expression but one that inevitably fast turned to horror.

They knew; everyone in the kingdom knew.

Then Roger spotted his dear friend, the last hope of his beloved Dainsey. "Pony," he called weakly.

She rushed up to the wagon and grabbed the bridle of the draft horse, stopping the beast.

"Stay back," Roger warned. "Oh, Pony, it is Dainsey, sick with the rosy plague!"

She nodded grimly and continued past the horse and onto the wagon's bench. She gently lifted the edge of Dainsey's hood, reaching in to feel her forehead.

Dainsey's teeth were chattering, but she was hot to the touch.

Pony sighed. "You've tried your best, but you are tending her in the wrong manner," she explained, pushing back the hood, untying the cloak, and pulling it off Dainsey's frail-looking shoulders.

"I tried. . . ." Roger started to reply. "I went to Palmaris, to Braumin, but he . . ."

"He turned you away," Pony finished grimly.

Roger just nodded his head.

"Well, you will not be turned away here," Pony promised, and she gently lifted Dainsey into her arms—and how light she was! "Follow me to Fellowship Way," she instructed.

"You can cure her?" Roger asked.

Pony couldn't ignore the flicker of hope that came into his voice, the light that suddenly brightened his face. She wanted to say that she could—how she wanted to tell Roger that!—but she knew that false hope could be a more devastating thing than no hope at all, and she could not lie to Roger.

"I will try," she promised, turning to slip down the side of the wagon.

Roger grabbed her by the arm, and she turned to see his desperately pleading face.

"This is the rosy plague, Roger," she said softly. "I have had no luck at all in battling it thus far. None. Everyone I have attempted to heal is dead. But I will try."

Roger sucked in his breath and stood, wavering, for a long moment. Then he collected himself and nodded.

True to her promise, Pony brought Dainsey into her private room above Fellowship Way, gathered her hematite, and went at the disease with all her strength and determination. As soon as her disembodied spirit entered Dainsey's battered body, though, she knew that she had no chance. The plague was thick in the woman, thicker than Pony had ever seen it before, a great green morass of disease.

She tried and she tried, but inevitably wound up fighting the wretched stuff away from herself and gaining no ground at all in actually helping Dainsey.

She came out of the gemstone trance a long while later and slipped off the side of the bed. Her legs wouldn't hold her, so exhausted had the battle made her, and she slumped heavily against the wall, then slid down with a thump to the floor. She heard Roger call out to her, and then he was there, beside her.

"What happened?" he asked repeatedly. "Did you defeat it?"

Pony's expression spoke volumes. Roger slumped to the floor, fighting hard against the sobs.

Pony gathered her own strength—she had to, for Roger—and went to him, dropping her hand on his heaving shoulder.

"We do not surrender," she assured him. "We will use the herbal poultices and syrups on her, as many as we can make. And I will go back to her with the gemstone. I promise I will."

Roger looked at her squarely. "You will not save her," he said.

Pony could not rightfully disagree.

They huddled on the field before St. Belfour as they huddled before all the other abbeys in Honce-the-Bear, the pitiful plague victims praying for help that would not come. For the rosy plague, in all its fury, in all its indifference to the screams of the suffering, had come to Vanguard.

Inside St. Belfour, the scene was no less one of distress. The plague hadn't crept into the halls of the abbey yet, but for the brothers of St. Belfour—gentle Brother Dellman and all those trained under the compassionate guidance of Abbot Agronguerre—witnessing such horrendous suffering in their fellow Vanguardsmen was profoundly upsetting. After the initial reports of the plague in Vanguard had filtered into St. Belfour, Abbot Haney and Brother Dellman had huddled in Haney's office, arguing their course of action. The two had never truly disagreed, yet neither had they been in a state of agreement, both of them wavering back and forth, to help or not to help. They knew Church doctrine concerning the rosy plague—it was written prominently in the guiding books of every Abellican abbey— but these were not men who willingly turned their backs on people in need. And so they argued and they shouted, they banged their hands in frustration on Haney's great desk and thumped their heads against the walls.

But in the end, they did as the Church instructed; they locked their gates. They tried to be generous to the gathered victims, tried to persuade them to return to their homes; and when that failed, they offered them as many supplies as they could spare. And the crowd, understanding the generosity and much closer to the brethren of the region than were the folk of many southern cities to their abbeys, had complied with Abbot Haney's requests. The gathered victims had formed two groups, with a distinctive space in between them so that the monks could go out on their daily tasks, mostly collecting food—much of which would be turned over to the plague victims.

Still, for all the cooperation and all the understanding on both sides of St. Belfour's imposing wall, Haney and Dellman remained miserable prisoners, sealed in by the sounds of suffering, by their own helplessness.

Every day and every night, they heard them.

"I cannot suffer this," Dellman advised his abbot one morning. He had just come from the wall, from viewing the bodies of those who had died the previous night, including two children.

Abbot Haney held up his hands. He had no answers, obviously; there was no darker and more secluded place to hide.

"I will go out to them," Brother Dellman announced.

"To what end?"

Now it was Dellman's turn to shrug. "I pray that you will afford me a single soul stone, that I might try, at least, to alleviate some of the suffering."

"Ye're knowin' the old songs, I trust," Abbot Haney replied, but he was not scolding. "And ye know where the Church stands concernin' this."

"Of course," Dellman replied. "The chances are greater that I will become afflicted than that I will actually cure anybody. I, we, are supposed to lock the gates and block our ears, sit within our abbeys—as long as we do not contract the plague—and speak of the higher aspects of life and of faith." He gave a chuckle, a helpless and sarcastic sound. "We are to discuss how many angels might kneel upon our thumbnails in ceremonies of mutual prayer, or other such vital issues."

"Brother Dellman," Abbot Haney remarked, before the man could gain any momentum.

Dellman relented and nodded, understanding that his friend was as pained by all this as he was.

They stood facing each other quietly for a long while.

"I am leaving the abbey," Brother Dellman announced. "I cannot suffer this. Will you give me a soul stone?"

Abbot Haney smiled and turned his stare to the room's only window. He couldn't even see out of it from his angle, for the opening was narrow and the surrounding stone wall thick; and even if he could have seen through it, the view was of nothing but the trees of the hills behind St. Belfour. But Haney didn't actually have to see outside to view the scene in his mind.

"Do not leave the abbey," he said quietly.

"I must," said Dellman, shaking his head slowly and deliberately.

"Ye canno' suffer this," said Hancy, "nor can I. Don't ye leave the abbey, for we'll soon throw wide our gates and let the sufferers in."

Dellman's eyes widened with shock, still shaking his head, even more forcefully now at this unexpected and frightening proclamation. "Th-this is something I must do," he stammered, not wanting to drag his brethren down his own chosen path of doom. "I did not mean . . ."

"Are ye thinkin' that I'm not hearin' their cries?" Haney asked.

"But the other brothers . . ."

"Will be gettin' a choice," Haney explained. "I'll tell them me plans, and tell them there's no dishonor in takin' a boat I'm charterin' for the south, for the safety o' St.-Mere-Abelle. Let them go who will—they'll be welcomed well enough by Abbot Agronguerre in the big abbey. And for St. Belfour, we'll make her a house o' healin'. Or of tryin', at least." He rose from his seat and came around the desk, nodding his head for every shake that Dellman gave of his. When he got close to the man, Dellman broke down, falling over Haney and wrapping him in a hug of appreciation and relief. For Holan Dellman was truly terrified, and Haney's bold decision had just lent him strength when he most needed it.

"You should not be here, my friend," Prince Midalis said to Andacanavar when the ranger arrived unexpectedly at Pireth Vanguard. "Our fears have come true: the plague is thick about the land. Run north to your home, my friend, to the clean air of Alpinador."

"Not so clean," Andacanavar said gravely, and Midalis understood.

"I have no answers for you," he replied. "We have recipes for salves and the like that will ease the suffering, so it is said, but they'll not cure the plague."

"Perhaps the winter, then," Andacanavar said. "Perhaps the cold of winter will drive the plague from our lands."

Prince Midalis nodded hopefully and supportively, but he knew the grim truth of the rosy plague, and he suspected that the fierce Alpinadoran weather would only make the plague even more terrible for those suffering from it.

She went at the plague again, and was again overwhelmed. She tried different gemstone combinations—and many of the previous ones—and was again and again overwhelmed. They used the salves and the syrups and their prayers, all to little or no avail. Pony quickly came to realize that she would not save Dainsey, and also strongly suspected that this infection, so brutal and complete, would be the one to get her, that her attempts with Dainsey would spell her doom. And yet she understood that she could not stop trying. Every time she looked at Roger's heartbroken expression, she knew that she had to try.

One evening after her latest miserable attempt, the exhausted Pony rode Greystone out of Dundalis to the north, to the grove and the little hollow she used for Oracle. She was going to Elbryan this night, as much to inform him that she believed she might soon be joining him as to garner any particular insights. She just needed his spirit at that moment, needed to know in her heart that he was close to her.

Such a dark night was coming on by the time she got to the hollow that Pony had to set a candle just outside the opening, using its meager light to give her enough of a view of the mirror to recognize the shadowy images within that other realm. She sat back and half closed her eyes, her focus solely on the mirror, her heart leaping out in a plaintive call to her Elbryan.

And then she was comforted, for he was there, in the cave with her.

And then she was confused, for Elbryan's shadowy silhouette faded, replaced by another indistinct image, one that Pony could not make out for a long, long while.

And then it came clearer to her, combining with memories of a long-ago time in a faraway place.

Avelyn's hand.

"She's clear to the stream, and that's where ye should be settin' yer camp," Bradwarden said to Pony.

"And you will look beyond it tonight, while I am at work with Dainsey?" the woman asked.

The centaur gave her a scowl. "Ye get yerself some sleep tonight," he demanded. "Ye been runnin' yerself straight for the five days since we left Dundalis. Ye got Symphony tired, and that's not a thing I've seen done before."

Pony started to argue, but wound up just nodding her head, for his words were true. She had gone straight back to Dundalis after her vision at Oracle, had roused Roger and Dainsey, and then had gone out from the town, sending her thoughts wide and far for Symphony, magnificent Symphony, the only horse in all the world strong enough to get her and Dainsey to the Barbacan and Mount Aida in time to save poor Dainsey.

The horse had come to her almost immediately, as if he had been waiting for this very moment, as if Symphony—with that intelligence that was not human but seemed in so many ways to be beyond human—had known that he and Pony would make this journey.

Perhaps that was exactly it, Pony dared to believe. Symphony had been intimately connected to both Elbryan and Avelyn through the turquoise gemstone. Perhaps those same spirits that had imparted the image to Pony at Oracle had done the same to Symphony through the continuing magic of the turquoise.

Pony had to believe that, for the sake of Dainsey and of herself and of all the world.

They had set out that same night—and wasn't Roger heartbroken when Pony explained without room for debate that he would not be joining them, that Greystone, for all his strength and desire, could not begin to match the pace they needed to set with Symphony. Two days north of Dundalis, Pony had found unexpected assistance when they had come upon Bradwarden; and the centaur, with the strength and stamina of a horse and the intelligence of a human, had agreed to scout the fields and trails ahead of them long into each night, then report back to her on the best and fastest course.

And how swiftly Symphony, though carrying both Pony and Dainsey,

had run that course. Pony had aided Symphony's effort with the malachite—
magically lightening the load—and with the hematite—spirit-walking and
leaching some of the strength from creatures, deer mostly, along the road,
then imparting it to the stallion. Now, five days out, they had covered hundreds of miles. The ring of mountains that marked the Barbacan was already
in sight.

It was a good thing, too, Pony knew. For though she had spent every
night with Dainsey, using the soul stone to try to beat back the edges of the
encroaching plague, and though she had coated the woman in salve, Dainsey
was nearing her bitter end. She couldn't even reply to Pony anymore, spent
her days and nights in delirium. Her eyes rolled open and closed, unseeing;
her words, when she said anything, were jumbled and confused. Dainsey
could die at any moment, Pony knew; so she could only pray that the woman
would live long enough to get to the flattened top of Mount Aida, and that
Pony's interpretation of the vision would prove correct.

The thought of going back to Roger with news that Dainsey had died
nearly broke her heart.

They traveled to the stream and set camp. Bradwarden lingered about
the area for a while, then disappeared into the forest to scout the road
ahead. To Pony's surprise, he returned a short while later, looking none too
pleased.

"Goblins," he said. "Ye knew we'd meet up with the scum."

"How many?" she asked, scooping up her sword and buckling it about
her waist, then checking her pouch of gemstones.

"Small tribe," Bradwarden asked. "I might be finding a way around
them."

Pony shook her head. "No time."

"Now what're ye thinkin'?" the centaur asked. "If ye go in there
throwin' yer fireballs, then ye're likely to bring hosts o' the creatures down
upon us. I'll find us another road."

"No time," Pony said again grimly. She tossed blanket and saddle on
Symphony, tightened the girth, and mounted.

"Goblins killed Elbryan's uncle Mather," Bradwarden said suddenly.
"As fine a fighter as—"

"He did not have these," Pony replied, jingling her purse of gemstones—
and she put her heels to Symphony's flanks and the great stallion leaped away.

She wore the cat's-eye circlet around her forehead and so had little
trouble seeing in the dark. She followed the lone trail available and soon
noted movement among the branches of a tree: a pair, at least, of goblins
doing sentry duty for the campsite in a small clearing beyond.

Pony hit the tree with lightning, the resonating thunder shaking the
stunned and blinded creatures from the limbs.

Pony rode right by them, into the clearing. "Begone from this place!" she cried. Symphony reared as she pulled Defender from its sheath—though, in truth, her other hand clutched the weapons, serpentine and ruby, that she intended to use.

"Begone! Begone!" she cried again in warning.

Goblins howled and shouted, ran all over and screamed curses at Pony, who was now, along with her horse, glowing blue from the serpentine fire-shield. And then one of the miserable creatures rushed out from the side and launched a spear Pony's way.

The woman ducked and parried it with her sword, barely deflecting the missile harmlessly high. But the goblins gained confidence from the bold attack and came on, howling.

Pony loosed a fireball, the concussive force blowing goblins from their feet—charring some, setting others ablaze to roll roaring in agony and terror. Those not injured by the fire blast scrambled back to their feet: some running off; others standing still, confused and terrified; and still others stubbornly charging at the woman again.

Pony lifted her hand, her magical energies wrought of rage, and altered the magic of the gemstone, now shooting a line of fire at the nearest creature, engulfing it in flames. A shift of her arm and another goblin became a living torch.

And then a third, and now most of the goblins who had been charging skidded to a stop and wheeled about, running, screaming, into the forest night.

When Pony got back to her encampment, she found Bradwarden still standing on the edge, keeping watch over poor Dainsey.

"Subtle," the centaur remarked, for even here, Pony knew, her display had been visible.

"Effective," she promptly corrected. "You can go and scout out the northern road now."

Travel was easy the next day, with not a sign of goblins—living goblins—anywhere to be found. Pony rode Symphony into the foothills before dark and found a campsite among a tumble of boulders.

Bradwarden caught up to her sometime later, though he remained far away.

"Are you to go ahead again this night?" she asked.

The centaur looked to the steeply inclining trail doubtfully. "Too many rocks, too many hills, and too many little ravines," he answered. "I'd walk right by a host o' the creatures and never see 'em. And I'm not for the climb," he added, "nor should ye be bringin' Symphony—he'll slow ye down more than help ye."

"Wait here, then," Pony replied, "with Symphony. I'll take Dainsey alone tomorrow."

"Long way for carrying," Bradwarden remarked.

Pony nodded. So be it.

They were long gone before first light, earlier than Pony had planned, for the night had been difficult on poor Dainsey. She was restless now, clawing at her clothing as if trying to escape somehow from that which she knew was coming.

And coming fast, Pony understood. She had seen people die—far too many people—and she realized after the turn of midnight that Death had come calling for Dainsey. And so she had set out, first on Symphony and then, when the trails became too difficult for the horse to serve any purpose, Pony turned him loose. She hoisted the woman onto her back and trudged on, forcing step after step as the minutes became an hour.

On she went stubbornly, pausing only for short rests. On one such break, she lay Dainsey down gently, thinking the woman asleep.

But then Dainsey's eyes opened wide.

"Dainsey?" Pony asked, moving close, and she realized that Dainsey was not hearing her, was not seeing her. She waved her hand right before those eyes—oh, those eyes!

Nothing. Dainsey did not see her at all.

The woman began to thrash about, her arms waving.

"No, no," Pony said. "No, damn you, Death, you cannot have her! Not now! Not after all this way!"

But she knew. The end was upon Dainsey. Pony glanced all about desperately; small sounds escaped her throat, feral and angry, for they were but a hundred feet or so from the break in the mountain pass, and from that spot, she would be able to see Mount Aida and the plateau that held Avelyn's mummified arm. How could Death, how could God, have been so cruel as to let them get this close, a mile perhaps, from their goal?

"No, no," Pony said over and over, and hardly thinking of the movement, the woman tore at her belt pouch violently. Gemstones fell all about the ground, but one did not escape Pony's grasp. A gray stone, a soul stone.

She went into it, flew out of her own body, and charged into Dainsey's battered form. The plague was all about her, then, the stench and the images of rot.

Pony attacked, and viciously, her rage preventing her from even considering her own welfare. She tore at the soupy morass, slapped it down, scraped it from Dainsey's lungs. She fought and fought, throwing all her strength fully against the tiny demons.

And then she was done, sitting to the side, crying.

Dainsey was still alive—Pony had bought her some time, at least. But how much? And how could she hope to go on, for she could barely lift herself off the ground?

She did get up, though, and she went to Dainsey and, with a growl, lifted the woman into her arms, half carrying her and half dragging her, up, up, until she reached the summit of this pass, breaking through the ring of the Barbacan. There before her loomed Mount Aida, a mile perhaps to the plateau and Avelyn's arm. Only a mile! And with several hundred miles already behind her.

But she couldn't hope to make it, not now; and already Dainsey was showing signs that Death had come calling once more, that the reprieve was at its end.

"Malachite," Pony whispered, and she looked all about, then realized that the gem must be on the ground with the others back down the path. She set Dainsey down again, and turned to get it, but stumbled, exhausted, and went down hard. She started to rise, so stubbornly, but understood that it was over, that even if she could find the gemstone quickly, she'd never find the strength to use it to any real effect.

It was over.

CHAPTER

❖ 36 ❖

The Ghost of Romeo Mullahy

They walked through the streets as unobtrusively as possible, making the daily run for supplies down to the dock section before the sunrise. This day, though, they had learned of the riot in that area, of many Behrenese beaten, even murdered, and all at the hands of this strange cult, the Brothers Repentant.

The five monks had lingered longer than they had planned and now understood, to their alarm, that they would not get back into St. Precious before daylight. They moved with all speed in their flower-sewn robes, like walking tussie-mussie beds. They moved to each street corner carefully, peeking around, making sure that they would not rush onto the next lane into a host of plague victims. Those folk of Palmaris weren't pleased with the Abellican Church at that time.

Brother Anders Castinagis, leading the group this morning, breathed a little easier when the wall containing the secret back entrance of St. Precious at last came into view. He could have brought his brethren around in a wide loop to avoid being seen by the host encamped before the abbey, but Castinagis figured that such a delay might prove even more dangerous. He led them, then, across the boulevards to the side of the square.

Cries rang out behind them, but Castinagis wasn't overconcerned, for he had known before this last expanse that they would not make the run without being spotted. But he was confident, too, that he and his four companions could get through the back door before any of the roused plague victims got anywhere near them.

They hustled off, trotting along the wall toward the door, glancing back confidently.

They should have looked ahead.

Coming around the corner at the back of the abbey, running fast and with obvious purpose, came a host of black-robed, red-hooded monks.

Castinagis skidded to a stop. He saw the crack of the concealed door—a

407

portal that would not be noticed by anyone who didn't know it was there—and measured the distance immediately against the speed of the approaching band.

He dropped his supply-laden pack, crying for his brethren to do the same, and sprinted away, calling out for the door to be opened.

And it was, a crack, and Castinagis could have gotten there ahead of the approaching Brothers Repentant, but his companions could not, he recognized, and so he burst right by the door, meeting the charge of the leading red-hooded monk. "Get in!" he cried as he went.

Anders Castinagis was a fine fighter, a big and strong man with fists of stone and a jaw that could take a punch. He had trained well at St.-Mere-Abelle, was graduated from the lessons of arts martial near the top of his class.

He did not know that now he was about to battle his instructor.

He came in hard, thinking to knock the leading attacker back, hit him quickly a few times, then wheel back to join his brethren inside.

His surprise was complete when the first punch he threw, a straight right, got picked off cleanly, a hand snapping up under his wrist, catching hold and easily turning his arm over. Castinagis tried to ward with his free left hand as his opponent came forward, right hand positioned like a serpent's head aiming to strike his throat.

But then, suddenly and unexpectedly, the red-hooded monk brought his straight-fingered hand out to the side, then kicked Castinagis' twisted elbow, shattering the bone. As Castinagis moved his free hand down to grasp at the pain, that serpentlike hand snapped in against his exposed throat.

He felt himself falling, but then he was caught, a strong hand clamping tightly over his face, and he knew no more.

Marcalo De'Unnero thought to drop his catch when he noted the fighting by the back door of St. Precious. His brethren had run past him and the monks from inside the abbey, knowing a brother to be trapped outside, had come pouring out to meet the charge.

Also, farther back but closing fast, came the angry mob, throwing stones and shouting curses. And behind them came the clatter of hoofbeats, of city guardsmen, De'Unnero knew.

It was all too beautiful.

He hoisted the half-conscious monk up under his arm and dragged him down one side alley, and many of his brothers followed.

And so began the impromptu trial of Anders Castinagis, with De'Unnero, Brother Truth, holding him up as an example of the errors of the world, an Abellican monk who, like all the brown-robed churchmen, had fallen from the path of God and had thus brought the rosy plague down among them all.

The plague victims wanted to believe those words—needed someone to blame—and they came at poor Castinagis viciously, spitting at him and kicking at him.

Over by the abbey, there came the sound of a lightning stroke, and even more general rioting.

That would have been the bitter end of Anders Castinagis, but then a contingent of horsemen, city guard, turned into the alleyway and came charging down, scattering plague-ridden peasants and Brothers Repentant alike.

De'Unnero thought to make a stand against them, thought to leap astride the nearest horse and kill the soldier, but he understood that this was not a fight he wanted. He wasn't personally afraid, of course, but thus far the soldiers of Palmaris—and thus, implicitly, the Duke serving as ruler of the city—had not hindered the Brothers Repentant from their orations and their occasional attacks on the Behrenese. Better not to make them an enemy, the cunning De'Unnero understood.

He leaped out of the way of the nearest approaching soldier and yelled for a general retreat. There was no pursuit, for the soldiers likewise did not wish to do battle with De'Unnero and his group. No, they were merely acting as the law required them, to protect an Abellican brother.

From the end of the alley, the fierce monk watched the soldiers scoop up the battered form of Anders Castinagis and turn back for St. Precious, forming a tight, defensive ring about the monk and warding the angry peasants away.

De'Unnero smiled at the sight. He knew that while many were dying each day of the plague, the numbers of the discontented, of the outraged, would continue to swell. He knew that he would find many allies in his war against the Abellican Church—no, not the Abellican Church, he mused, for it was his intent to reestablish that very body in proper form. No, this incarnation of his beloved Church more resembled a Church of Avelyn, or of Jojonah.

He would remedy that.

One abbey at a time.

One *burned* abbey at a time.

"It was De'Unnero," Castinagis, lisping badly from a lip swollen to three times its normal size, insisted. "No one else could move like that, with such speed and precision."

"Rumors have named him as the leader of the Brothers Repentant," Abbot Braumin replied with a sigh.

"Then we expose him to the people of Palmaris," Viscenti chimed in eagerly.

The door of the audience chamber banged open then, and a very angry Duke Tetrafel stormed into the room.

"How did you—" Abbot Braumin started to ask.

"His soldiers had just helped us, abbot," came a nervous remark from behind the Duke, from the brother who had been charged with watching the gate that day.

Abbot Braumin understood immediately; Duke Tetrafel had used the leverage of his soldiers' intervention to bully his way into the abbey. So be it, Braumin thought, and he waved the nervous young sentry monk away.

"You submitted to the gemstone inspection, of course," Braumin remarked, though he knew well that the Duke most certainly had not.

Tetrafel scoffed at the absurd notion. "If your monks tried to come to me with that stone of possession, my soldiers would raze your abbey," he blustered.

"We are allowed our rules and our sanctuary," Braumin replied.

"And did my soldiers not just allow several of your monks to get back into that sanctuary?" Tetrafel asked. "Your friend Brother Castinagis among them? He would have been killed in the gutter. Yet this is how you greet me?"

Braumin paused for a long while to digest the words. "My pardon," he said, coming around the desk and offering a polite bow. "Of course we are in your debt. But do understand that we have set up St. Precious as a sanctuary against the rosy plague, and to ensure that we must spiritually inspect everyone who enters. Even the brothers are subjected to such inspections, myself included, if we venture out beyond the tussie-mussie bed."

"And if it was discovered that you had become afflicted with the plague?" Tetrafel asked suspiciously.

"Then I would leave St. Precious at once," Abbot Braumin replied without the slightest hesitation and without any hint of insincerity in his voice.

Tetrafel chuckled and stared at the abbot incredulously. "Then you are a fool," he said.

The abbot only shrugged.

"And if I became afflicted?" the Duke asked slyly. "Would I, too, be denied admittance to St. Precious? And if so, would you and your brethren come out to tend to me?"

"Yes," said Braumin, "and no."

Tetrafel paused a moment to clarify the curt responses, then a great scowl crossed his face. "You would let me die?" The soldiers behind the Duke bristled.

"There is nothing we could do to alter that."

"The old songs of doom proclaim that a monk might cure one in twenty," Tetrafel argued. "Would not twenty monks then have a fair chance of saving their Baron and Duke?"

"They would." Again, Abbot Braumin kept his response curt and to the point.

"But you would not send them," Duke Tetrafel reasoned.

"No," answered the abbot.

"Yet I risk my soldiers for the sake of your monks!" the Duke snapped back, and he was having a hard time masking his mounting anger.

"We can make no exceptions in this matter," Braumin replied, "not for a nobleman, not for an abbot, not for the Father Abbot himself. If Father Abbot Agronguerre became so afflicted, he would be cast out of St.-Mere-Abelle."

"Do you hear your own words as you speak them?" Duke Tetrafel roared. "Could you begin to believe that the lives of twenty minor monks were not worth the gain of saving a duke or even your own Father Abbot? Pray you then that King Danube does not become so afflicted, for if he did, and if your Church then did not come to his aid with every Abellican brother available, then the kingdom and the Church would be at war!"

Abbot Braumin seriously doubted that, for it was not without precedent. Furthermore, while it pained gentle Braumin to watch the suffering of the common folk, Tetrafel's point was lost completely on him. In his view of the world, the life of a single brother, even a novitiate to the Abellican Church, was worth that of a duke or a king or a father abbot. As were the lives of every commoner now suffering on the square outside St. Precious. Yes, Braumin Herde cursed his helplessness daily, but he was glad, at least, that he was not possessed of the arrogance that seemed to be a major trait among the secular leaders of the kingdom.

"I have your words and your thoughts now," Duke Tetrafel fumed. "I see your perspective all too clearly, Abbot Braumin. Understand that I now relinquish all responsibility for the safety of your brethren if they venture outside St. Precious. Exit at your own peril!" And he turned and stormed out of the room, sweeping his soldiers up in his wake.

"That went well," Castinagis lisped sarcastically.

As if to accentuate the point, a stone bounced off Braumin's window, clattering for a second, then falling harmlessly away. All day long, since the near riot at the back door, the peasants had been throwing rocks and curses at the abbey.

"We have lost the city," Abbot Braumin remarked.

"We could send word to St.-Mere-Abelle for help," Viscenti offered.

Braumin was shaking his head before the man even finished. "Father Abbot Agronguerre has his own troubles," he replied. "No, we have lost the hearts of those in Palmaris, and cannot regain them short of going out with our gemstones among the people."

"We send out salves and syrups, blankets and food, every day," Castinagis interjected.

"And it is not enough to placate those who know they are dying," said Braumin.

"We cannot go out to them," Viscenti reasoned.

"Then we weather the plague within our abbey," Abbot Braumin decided, "as it has been in the past, as we have done thus far. We will continue to send out the salves and other supplies as we can spare them, but if the peasants—led by the Brothers Repentant, no doubt—come against us, then we will defend St. Precious vigorously."

"And if we lose the abbey?" Castinagis asked grimly.

"Then we flee Palmaris," Braumin replied, "to Caer Tinella, perhaps, where we might establish the first chapel of Avelyn."

"That course was denied," Viscenti remarked.

Braumin shrugged as if that fact wasn't important. "Perhaps it is time we think about establishing the Church of Avelyn, in partnership with the Abellican Church if they so desire, a separate entity altogether if they do not."

The strong words raised the eyebrows of the other two brothers in the room, and Braumin, too, understood the desperation of such a course. The Church would never agree to such a split, of course, and would likely declare Braumin a heretic—again—and excommunicate any who sided with him. But they wouldn't come after him, Braumin knew, at least not until the time of plague had passed. And in those years, it was quite conceivable that he, with a more generous attitude toward the terrified peasants, might establish himself so securely that the Abellican Church would think it wiser to just let him be.

Those fanciful thoughts continued to roll in Braumin's head for a long while, long after both Viscenti and Castinagis had taken their leave. But in the end, they didn't hold, for Braumin recognized them as the course of a desperate fool. His current problems were not the making of a new Church—indeed, he and his comrades had pushed the Church in a direction favorable to Avelyn and Jojonah, favorable to his own beliefs. The current problem was the plague, pure and simple, and even if Braumin successfully managed to go and establish his coveted chapel, even if he split from the Abellican Church altogether and began his own religion, what would be the gain? The rosy plague would still be among them, and Braumin would still be helpless against it.

Another rock thudded against the abbot's wall.

He glanced that way, toward the window, and tuned in to the curses and shouts being hurled against his abbey. No, he would not run away. He and his brethren would defend St. Precious from all attacks, and vigorously, as he had instructed. If all the city came against them, then all the city would be destroyed, if that is what it would take.

Braumin hated his own thoughts.

But he wouldn't deny the truth, nor the righteousness, of them.

Pony knelt over Dainsey, holding her hand and talking comfortingly to her, trying to give her some dignity and some sense that she was loved and was not alone at this, the end of her life. How bitter it all seemed to Pony, to fail here, just a mile from her destination, though in truth, she doubted that even if she could get to Avelyn's arm, it would do Dainsey any good. The poor woman was too far gone.

"Let go, Dainsey," she whispered, wanting the woman's misery, her obvious fear and pain, to end. "It is all right to let go."

If Dainsey heard her, she made no indication, but Pony kept talking, kept hoping that she was doing some good.

Then a strong hand grabbed Pony's shoulder and pulled her up to her feet. She glanced back to see Bradwarden, right beside her, holding the pouch of gemstones she had left far back down the path.

"What?" she started to ask.

"Ye get her up on me back and climb yerself up with her," the centaur explained. "I'll get ye to the top o' Mount Aida."

"B-Bradwarden, the plague," Pony stuttered.

"Damn it to the dactyl's own bed!" the centaur roared. "I'd rather be catchin' it and dyin' than to keep away and watch me friends sufferin'!"

Pony started to argue—that generous nature within her thought immediately to protect her unafflicted friend. But who was she to so determine Bradwarden's course, or anyone's for that matter? If she was willing to take such risks with her own life as to dive spiritually right into the disease as it ravaged Dainsey, or even complete strangers, then how could she presume to warn Bradwarden away?

Besides, she didn't disagree with him. There were indeed fates worse than death.

She helped Bradwarden to get Dainsey in place on his strong back, and then she climbed up behind her.

"All this time, you have helped, but from a safe distance," Pony observed. "Why now?"

"Because I trust ye, girl," the centaur admitted. "And if ye're thinkin' that ye can heal the plague at the arm, and if ye're hearin' that from Avelyn and Nightbird themselves, then who might I be to be arguin'?"

Pony considered the words and merely shrugged.

"I'll keep it as smooth as I can," the centaur promised.

"She is feeling nothing," Pony replied. "Speed is more urgent than comfort. Fly on!"

And Bradwarden did just that, pounding along trails that he knew all too well. He came down the side of the Barbacan ring, onto the expanse leading to Mount Aida, fields growing thick with new grasses after the devastation of Avelyn's fight against Bestesbulzibar. Then up, up, went Bradwarden, running along familiar trails.

"I'll be coming up on the south face," he explained. "It's a quicker run to the plateau, but I'll not be able to get up the last climb to the place with ye."

"I may need you there," Pony remarked.

"And I'll join ye as soon as I can get meself to the other side," Bradwarden promised.

On they went. They came to places where Pony had to dismount and run along beside, and one cliff where Pony found the strength to use the malachite, levitating both Bradwarden and Dainsey up behind her and saving many hundreds of yards of winding trail.

"Off ye go," the centaur announced, skidding to a stop when they arrived at the last expanse. Pony brought Dainsey around, and Bradwarden hoisted her seemingly lifeless form up over the short rise, laying her atop the flat plateau, then helping Pony up beside her.

"I will get you up with malachite," the woman started to say, but Bradwarden waved the notion away.

"I'll be joinin' ye soon enough," he explained. "Ye save yer strength for Dainsey's last fight." And he turned and thundered away, along the trails that would bring him to the other side of the plateau and an easier route to the top.

Pony turned and stared at the mummified arm of Avelyn Desbris, standing strong out of the very rock of the blasted mountain. In the final explosion that had destroyed the mountaintop and the physical form of Bestesbulzibar, Avelyn had thrust that arm skyward, holding Tempest and the bag of gemstones for his friends to find. For some reason that Pony did not understand, that arm had not rotted, nor had the continual wind worn it away. It appeared just as she had found it those years before, without the sword or the stones, and she couldn't deny the comfort she felt in merely viewing it.

She gathered up Dainsey in her arms and walked over to the arm, laying the woman on the ground gently before it.

Now what?

Pony knelt before the arm and began to pray, to Avelyn, to Elbryan, to anyone who would give her the answers. Before her, Dainsey continued to squirm uncomfortably, fighting against the seemingly inevitable end.

Pony prayed harder. She took out her soul stone and fell into its magic, then soared boldly into the rot that was Dainsey Aucomb. Might she find better results here, in this sacred place?

Pony attacked.

And was beaten back.

"No!" she cried when she came out of the gemstone trance, sitting on the ground helplessly before Dainsey, who was now writhing in the very last moments of her life. "No! It cannot have been a lie!"

"This is my covenant with you," came a voice behind her, and Pony whirled about—to see a young monk, Romeo Mullahy, standing behind her.

But he was dead! Had died in this very place, throwing himself from the rocks rather than accept capture at the hands of Father Abbot Markwart.

Pony stammered a few incomprehensible syllables.

"Whosoever tastes the blood of my palm shall know no fear from the rosy plague," Mullahy said.

Pony reached for the man—and her hand went right through him! It was Romeo Mullahy, his ghost at least, and he was far less than corporeal!

Pony played back his words desperately.

"But ye're dead!" came a cry from farther back, Bradwarden climbing onto the plateau.

Pony looked at Mullahy's insubstantial hands for the blood.

"I spoke for Avelyn," he explained. "This is the covenant of Avelyn."

Pony snapped her gaze back to the mummified hand, to see, to her surprise and her delight, that there was indeed a reddish liquid upon the palm.

Dainsey cried out then, as Death reached for her. Pony reacted faster, reaching down and lifting her face to Avelyn's hand, pressing Dainsey's lips against the palm.

The effect was immediate and stunning, for Dainsey went limp but not in death. No, far from that, Pony knew; Dainsey was—so suddenly—more comfortable than she had been in many days!

Pony laid her down gently before the arm, then she, too, leaned in and kissed the bloody palm—and that blood seemed not to diminish in the least.

She felt the warmth all through her body, and knew then for certain that she had contracted the plague from her work with Dainsey, that it was within her, beginning to gather strength.

But no longer. Pony felt that implicitly.

Whosoever tastes the blood of my palm shall know no fear from the rosy plague.

Pony looked down at Dainsey, who was resting and breathing easily. She glanced back to Romeo Mullahy, but the ghost was already gone, its message delivered.

Bradwarden came up to her.

"Ye got blood on yer lips," he remarked.

"Avelyn's," Pony tried to explain, shaking her head. "The taste of his blood grants freedom from the plague, so said—"

"The ghost of Mullahy," the centaur finished. "I seen him jump meself, back then when Markwart and King Danube came to catch us. Hit them rocks hard."

"How can it be?" Pony asked.

Bradwarden laughed aloud, shaking his head with every rolling bellow. "I'm not for disbelievin' anythin' comin' out o' that arm," he said, and then he paused for a moment, staring from Pony to the still-bloody hand. "Are ye goin' to take some with ye, then?"

Pony, too, looked at the hand. "I cannot," she explained, and indeed, in her heart, she knew. She understood all of it now. "It is the blood and it is this place."

"What're ye thinkin'?" Bradwarden asked suspiciously. "We're a long way from yer homeland."

Pony just turned a determined look his way.

"That Mullahy ghost tell ye that?"

"No," Pony answered with perfect calm. "The spirit of Avelyn did, just now."

Bradwarden and Pony stared at each other for a long while, then the centaur came in low and kissed the bloody hand.

CHAPTER

❖ 37 ❖

The Vision

Symphony ran as never before, bearing Pony straight to the south, thundering down the roads to Dundalis. Bradwarden carried Dainsey now, who was recovering with each passing minute, but the centaur couldn't begin to pace Symphony and Pony. Even when Symphony had been carrying both women on the trip to the Barbacan, Bradwarden had to run on much longer each night to keep up.

But Pony couldn't wait for her two friends. Now that she knew Dainsey to be out of danger and was confident that no goblins would surprise the cunning centaur, her purpose shifted to the wider world, to all the plague victims who had to know the truth of Avelyn's arm. A thousand variables rolled about in Pony's head. Would her newfound immunity against the plague allow her to begin a general healing process throughout the southland? Would plague sufferers begin to make the pilgrimage to the wild Barbacan? How would Pony protect them from monsters and animals, from the weather as the season turned to winter? And what of food? Would she offer blind hope to thousands only to have them starve on the road to the north?

Too many questions, too many dire possibilities. But none, Pony pointedly and repeatedly reminded herself on that wild run to the south, were nearly as dire as the reality that the folk of the kingdom now knew, the reality of the rosy plague and so many dying with each passing day.

With each passing minute, she told herself; and she used the malachite as much as she could to lighten Symphony's load; and she used the soul stone to catch some of the strength from nearby deer and other animals, giving it to Symphony; and she used the cat's-eye circlet to see in the dark, then transferred those images to Symphony so that the run could continue long after sunset.

On one such night, in the light of Sheila, Pony found a solitary form standing vigil on the ridge north of Dundalis; and she was not surprised, but her heart was warmed.

"Greetings, Roger," she called, urging Symphony ahead.

The man nearly fell over trying to get to her. "Tell me!" he cried. "Where is Dainsey?"

"With Bradwarden, some miles behind."

"Did you get to the B-Barbacan?" Roger stuttered, hardly able to speak the question. "Did Avelyn . . ."

Pony slipped down from Symphony's back, and when she turned, her beaming smile was all the answer Roger Lockless needed. He exploded into motion, wrapping Pony in the tightest hug she had ever felt, his shoulders shaking with sobs of joy.

They were in Dundalis soon after; and there Pony, strengthened by the miracle of Avelyn's blood, fought the rosy plague.

Her spirit entered the body of an afflicted man. But now she held no fear of it at all. None. It could not latch on to her spiritual arms as she attacked the disease, scraping it from bone and organ, her healing spiritual touch dissipating the greenish disease.

She stayed with the afflicted man for a long time, moving to every edge of his being, fighting and fighting wherever she found sickness.

Finally, exhausted but satisfied, Pony made her way to her own body. She sat back, her eyes closed, reorienting herself to her corporeal form.

"I am healed!" she heard the man cry, and then came a host of responding cheers.

Pony blinked open her eyes, to find Roger and Belster and Tomas Gingerwart and many, many other folk of Dundalis gathered in the room or just outside the window. And all of them were cheering for her, for her healing of this man.

But Pony knew the truth of it. "You are not cured," she told the man bluntly. The cheering stopped immediately, and the man seemed as if he would topple out of his bed. "I have granted you time, a temporary reprieve, but there is only one way for you to be truly cured."

She paused and looked around, to find them all, every man and every woman, hanging on her every word.

"You said that Dainsey was cured," Roger dared to remark.

"You must travel to the Barbacan," she explained, "to the flattened top of Mount Aida and the arm of Avelyn Desbris. You will see blood in his palm. Kiss it, taste it, and you need not fear the rosy plague anymore."

"The Barbacan?" the man replied, his face bloodless. All about him, people began repeating that question, that name.

Pony understood their terror. Along with the fact that the Barbacan was a place of legendary evil that had been home of the latest incarnation of the demon dactyl, the difficulty of that northern, wild road gave them all pause. Again that tumult of questions, simple logistical problems, assaulted her thoughts. They had to go to the Barbacan, everyone afflicted—and even those who were not yet caught in the grasp of the plague would do well to make the journey.

But how?

Pony went back to Fellowship Way soon after, needing rest. The towns-folk had asked her to lead them to the Barbacan, and she had told them that she would answer them in the morning, but in truth, she had known her answer all along. She could not go back now. No, her road must continue to the south, to Caer Tinella and to Palmaris, at least. The word had to be spread far and wide.

She knew the only hope for making this miracle known to the whole land: she would have to enlist the aid of the King's soldiers and the Abellican brothers. All of them.

Even if she accomplished such a thing, though, how could she secure the northern road so that the pilgrimages could begin at once?

For every passing minute brought pain and grief, every passing day made the pile of corpses grow larger.

Pony fell asleep with those disturbing thoughts in mind, trying to work out the speech she would make to Braumin and the others, to King Danube and Duke Kalas, trying to figure out some way that Bradwarden and Belster could find aid to begin the first pilgrimages. She woke up sometime later, the night still dark, the dawn still far away.

She had her answer.

Pony fell into the soul stone once more, freeing her spirit from its corporeal bonds, then flying, flying across the miles to the west.

Soon after, she came to a place where she knew that she was not welcome, but she called out anyway for the lady of the land.

A few minutes passed; Pony considered plunging through the misty veil that covered Andur'Blough Inninness, invading the elven homeland with her spirit. But then, suddenly, she felt a pull and recognized that Lady Dasslerond was using the magic of her emerald gemstone to bring more of Pony's corporeal form to the place, that they might speak more clearly.

And then the lady of Caer'alfar was before her, glaring at her dangerously. Pony noted that many other Touel'alfar were about, and that those she caught sight of were carrying their deadly little bows. Instinctively, she reached down and felt her own body, recognizing that she was solid enough for Dasslerond's archers to truly harm her.

"We have already had this discussion," the lady said sternly. "Our borders are closed, Jilseponie, to you and to all others of your race."

"The situation has changed," Pony started to say.

"No, it has not!" Lady Dasslerond insisted, narrowing her golden eyes. "The plague is a problem for the human kingdoms. We'll not let it, or you, touch Andur'Blough Inninness. Now begone from this place—I will release your body and I expect your spirit to follow. On pain of death, Jilseponie, your spirit must follow."

"I have found a cure!" Pony yelled at her, and that did cause the lady's eyes to open wide.

"At the Barbacan, the arm of Avelyn," Pony began to explain, "the same arm that brought forth the miracle and killed the goblins. The palm bleeds, Lady Dasslerond, and that blood, the blood of Avelyn, confers immunity to the plague."

"Our community has not been touched by the plague," Dasslerond replied. "Why, then, do you come to tell us?"

"Because you must know, for if the plague does find your valley, you can survive," Pony replied.

Lady Dasslerond thought for a moment, then nodded. "Perhaps we misjudged your return," she admitted. "You have our gratitude for this information. Should we find that we need it, we will heed your words."

"But I need your help," Pony boldly went on. "The folk will begin their march to the Barbacan, by the dozens, the score, the hundreds. Until King Danube and the Abellican monks get their people in place, that will be a road fraught with danger, I fear. With goblins and starvation."

"What do you expect of the Touel'alfar?" Dasslerond asked, a tightness coming back to her voice.

"I expect nothing," Pony replied, "but I beg of you that you lend aid in this time of our need. A host of elves would greatly aid that necessary journey. Your people could chase away the goblins, even could leave food along the road, and would never have to make contact with the pilgrims. You could—"

"Enough!" Dasslerond interrupted. "Your point is made."

"And is my plea heard?"

The lady made no movement, no shake of the head and no confirming nod.

"Begone from this place, Jilseponie," she ordered after a short while.

Pony started to argue, but she felt a sudden tug as her body separated yet again from her spirit and sped back to her room in Dundalis. She blinked her spirit eyes open to find that Dasslerond had already receded into the misty blanket of fog. She thought to follow, to demand an answer, but Pony understood it all too clearly: if she did go down there, Lady Dasslerond would use her emerald to bring her body back, and then she would be killed.

Bradwarden and Dainsey arrived in Dundalis the next morning, to find the folk already preparing to make a pilgrimage to the north. How they cheered Dainsey, many running over to give the miraculously cured woman a big hug, though it was obvious that Roger didn't want to share her with anyone!

"I'm going to need you to lead them back to the Barbacan," Pony said to Bradwarden when she found her way to him.

"Bradwarden and Roger and me," Dainsey said, her eyes sparkling.

Pony shook her head. "I need you," she explained to the woman. "We must go south, to Palmaris, perhaps farther, to show them the miracle, to begin the pilgrimages."

"South, then," Roger said.

"But north for you," Pony said to Roger. He started to protest, but her simple logic cut him short. "You have not yet entered the covenant of Avelyn," she reminded.

"I do not want to be away from Dainsey," said Roger, and he and his wife stared lovingly at each other.

"You will have your time together," Pony promised, "but not now." She grabbed Dainsey by the arm and pulled her away from the man. "You ride Greystone, and I, Symphony."

"Now?" Roger asked. "This very minute? She has just returned, weary already from the road. And we have not even found the chance to—"

"And every minute we wait means that another person will die," Pony said. "That is the truth, is it not? And measured against that truth, does Roger still believe that we should tarry here in Dundalis?"

The man looked at her plaintively, then turned his loving gaze back to Dainsey. But then he sighed and kissed his wife. "You and Pony go with all speed," he said.

"Not Pony," Jilseponie stated, more out of reflex than any conscious thought. Both Roger and Dainsey looked at her curiously, wondering if she had changed her mind, if she had decided that Dainsey must go south alone while she went back to the Barbacan. Pony looked up at them, her expression as determined as any either of them had ever seen.

"Jilseponie," she declared, "not Pony. Pony was a woman who lived quietly in Dundalis. I go south as Jilseponie."

Roger thought about that for a long moment, then nodded. "A fine road and a fast horse to both Dainsey and Jilseponie, then," he said. "Go with all speed."

They did just that, riding out of Dundalis only a few minutes later.

"I told ye she'd find her heart," Bradwarden remarked to Roger as they watched the pair gallop away.

"Off to save the world," the dejected man said with more than a little sarcasm.

"She lit her fires." The centaur laughed. "Now she's ready to go and fight, beside Braumin, against the plague. Against the Duke, if he's not hearin' her, and against the King himself, if she has to. Ye remember her walk across Palmaris when she had enough o' the fool Markwart?" Bradwarden said with a laugh.

Roger stared hard at the centaur. He did indeed remember that journey Jilseponie had made across the city. All who witnessed the bared power of the angry woman remembered it well, and would not soon forget.

"Why're ye lookin' so wounded?" Bradwarden asked, clapping Roger hard on the shoulder. "Weren't ye the one complainin' when she came back to us after refusin' both city and Church? Well, boy, ye got what ye wanted!"

"Maybe she can make a difference," Roger admitted.

"To herself, at least," said the centaur, and Roger looked at him curiously. "Ye need yer purpose in life, lad," Bradwarden explained. "Without it, ye got nothin'. She's seein' her power now, and clearly, and knowin' the responsibility that power's bringin' to her. If she doesn't use it, or at least try, then she'll be failin' her very purpose, and that's a wound ye canno' heal."

"You think she'll beat them all?" Roger asked.

"I'm not knowin' if ye ever can, nor is Pony," Bradwarden admitted, "but ye can beat 'em one at a time, beat 'em back and go on as best as ye can. Pony'll do good for the kingdom, don't ye doubt, and for the little folk who got no hope. A hunnerd, hunnerd will live better, or live at all, because of her workin's, and how can Pony ignore that callin'?"

"Jilseponie," Roger corrected.

They came toward him, toward him, smelling of peat, their lifeless eyes staring at him, envious of his warmth. He tried to run—always before he had been able to escape—but this time, the walking dead had come to him in greater numbers and seemingly in coordinated fashion. Whichever way he turned, they were there, reaching for his throat with stiff arms.

He kicked out at one, spun and punched the face of another zombie—though the horrid creature showed no sign that it had felt the blow.

He dropped and scrambled desperately, pushing through.

But they crowded around him, a wall of rotting, dirty flesh, and he had nowhere to run.

He called out for his companions, but then realized that he had no companions, that he was on his own.

And so he tried to fight, briefly, but then he was down on his back, the walking dead looming over him, coming down at him . . . down at him.

Duke Tetrafel woke up with a shriek, clawing at his bedsheets so wildly that he wound up on the floor in a tumble of blankets. He continued to scream and thrash for some time, until the haze of dreams flitted away, revealing the dawn, the secure dawn in Chasewind Manor.

He sat there on the floor for some time. The dream was not new to him, had followed him all the way across Honce-the-Bear every night since his expedition had been savaged by the little folk and their host of zombies.

But this time, for the first time in his dreams, he had found no escape. This time, for the first time, the walking dead had caught him. Duke Tetrafel pondered that disturbing notion for some time, until the door of his room banged open and one of his attendants came rushing in.

"My Duke!" the man cried. "Are you murdered?"

Tetrafel chuckled and held up an arm to keep the concerned fool at bay.

To his surprise, though, his signal, while stopping the attendant, only seemed to make the man grow even more concerned. He stood a few strides away, gawking openly, and then, to Tetrafel's further astonishment, he began shaking his head and backing away.

"What is it?" the Duke asked, but the man did not—seemed as if he *could* not—respond. He continued backing, almost to the door.

"Speak up, fool," Tetrafel demanded. "What is—"

The man turned and bolted from the room.

Still on the floor amid the tumble of blankets, Tetrafel stared at the open door for a long time, wondering.

And then it hit him, and then the variation of his too-common dream made perfect sense. Slowly, slowly, he brought his arm back in and turned it over.

Rosy spots.

His screams came even more loudly than before.

Abbot Braumin rubbed his hands together nervously as he walked along the quiet corridors of St. Precious. The day had not been good, not at all, with devastating rumors rolling along the unruly streets of Palmaris. And now this news, of a secret visitor that Viscenti had considered important enough to be admitted to the abbey—quietly and after a thorough gemstone inspection.

The abbot came to the door and paused, taking a deep and steadying breath, trying to find his heart. He pushed through, to find Shamus Kilronney waiting for him.

"Brother Viscenti claims that you are packed for the road," the abbot said, trying to keep his tone lighthearted.

"As long a road as I can find, my friend," Shamus said, coming forward and offering a handshake to the abbot. "I have seen too much of all this. I have no heart left for it."

"Palmaris will be a lesser place without you," Braumin remarked.

"Palmaris will be a place of catastrophe whether I remain or not," Shamus corrected. "You have heard the rumors?"

"I hear many rumors every day," said Braumin. "I cannot begin to sort fact from fancy."

Shamus nodded and chuckled, and Braumin knew that the man understood his evasiveness for what it was. He had indeed heard the specific rumor to which Shamus Kilronney must be referring, and his obvious dodge made that truth quite clear.

"It is more than rumor," Shamus said gravely. "Duke Tetrafel has the plague and is even now in a fit of panic at Chasewind Manor."

"As he should be," Braumin said with sincere sympathy.

"He will turn his eyes outward from his insecure sanctuary, will look to St. Precious for aid," said Shamus.

"He and I have already discussed—"

"None of that will matter," Shamus interrupted firmly. "His desperation will lead him to your gates, do not doubt." He held his hand up to stop Braumin's forthcoming, expected response. "And you will turn him away. I am leaving, my friend. I cannot suffer this catastrophe any longer."

That last statement, linked with Shamus' insistence that Tetrafel would come for help, explained it all to Braumin. The catastrophe to which Shamus was referring was not the plague itself but the coming storm when Duke Tetrafel realized that St. Precious would not help him. Shamus was foreseeing—and quite logically, it seemed to Braumin—the chaos that would ensue within the city, the all-out riot, even warfare, between Tetrafel and the abbey. To Braumin's thinking, the brothers of St. Precious had already lost the city, a situation made even more dangerous by the arrival of De'Unnero and the Brothers Repentant. If Duke Tetrafel, instead of merely remaining neutral, actually put his muscle behind De'Unnero and the roused populace, then St. Precious would be hard pressed indeed!

"Where will you go?" Braumin asked his friend.

"North, perhaps," Shamus answered, "to Caer Tinella, and maybe farther—maybe all the way to the Timberlands."

"Is there nothing you can do to help us?" Braumin asked somberly.

"Is there nothing you can do to help Duke Tetrafel?" Shamus replied.

Abbot Braumin looked around, then rolled his eyes and shook his head helplessly. "Then pray for us, my friend," he said.

Shamus Kilronney nodded, patted Braumin on the shoulder, and turned to go.

Abbot Braumin could not bring himself to judge the man, for in truth, he wished that he might run away with Shamus.

CHAPTER

❖ 38 ❖

A Miracle for Francis

Francis slapped futilely at the green swamp of plague that bubbled up all around his arms. He knew that this woman, too, was near death, but he could hardly bear the thought of watching yet another one die, the third in three days.

And so he fought, if not to buy some time for the poor infected woman, then to buy some time for his own shattered sensibilities.

Francis didn't notice that the plague within this woman did not attack his spiritual presence with any vigor, and so he didn't pause to wonder about this change and its implications.

He came out of his battle soon after, having done little good. He stared down at the poor woman, so close to death; and then, as he turned to leave, he found all the world suddenly spinning.

Francis hit the ground facedown.

Huffing and puffing with every running stride, Father Abbot Agronguerre hurried to the front gate tower, where Bou-raiy, Machuso, Glendenhook, and many others had gathered. He pushed through the crowd of brothers to get to the wall, and peering over, beyond the tussie-mussie bed, he saw the spectacle that had so attracted them.

There lay Brother Francis, his head propped up by the one-eyed woman of whom so many demanded beatification.

"The plague has found Brother Francis," Master Machuso softly explained.

"Ring around the rosy," Master Bou-raiy said dryly. "The old songs do not lie."

There came murmurs of assent from all about, with many hands moving through the evergreen gesture.

Father Abbot Agronguerre stared long and hard out over that misty morning field, thoroughly frustrated. He had been living vicariously through Francis, he understood, had been saluting the man's courage and his few triumphs, and also, that greatest triumph of all: that he had been out among the plague victims working tirelessly, yet for all these months, had found miraculous immunity to the dreaded disease.

But now, in the blink of an eye, it seemed, all those notions of miracle had been washed away. There could be no doubt, even looking at him from this distance. Mere exhaustion alone had not felled Brother Francis.

"This is why we follow the precepts and heed the words of the old songs," Fio Bou-raiy went on, turning as he spoke, as if making a speech to the whole gathering. "Our gift from our brothers who came before us lies in the wisdom that they passed down to us, and what greater fools are we if we do not heed their words!"

Again came the murmurs of assent, but it all sounded very wrong to Father Abbot Agronguerre. Not wrong in a practical matter, for he knew he would not run down then and there and throw wide the abbey gates. But wrong in a spiritual sense, in the very tone of Bou-raiy, excited and justified, and in those palpable sighs of relief from all gathered here in the relative safety behind thick stone walls and tussie-mussie aromas.

"Does it please you to see Brother Francis downed?" Agronguerre asked suddenly, the question, as it registered, widening Bou-raiy's eyes with surprise and bringing a gasp of near disbelief from Glendenhook. Even Machuso shifted uncomfortably.

But Agronguerre would not relent so easily. "Every one of you take heed of Brother Francis and the sacrifice that he made," he said forcefully, letting his gaze drift from surprised brother to brother. "If in your hearts, even secretly, you foster some relief, some justification of our course, in seeing Brother Francis stricken ill, if somewhere deep in your heart and soul you believe the man a fool deserving of such a fate, then I expect you at the sacrament of Penitence this very day. We hide because pragmatic Church doctrine demands it of us, but we, every one of us, should wish that we are possessed of such courage as Brother Francis', that we are possessed of such compassion and generosity. We can look out upon him now, knowing that his end is near, and feel justification, or we can look out upon him now and feel sadness in losing a heroic brother."

He finished with a deep breath, then, with a final look at Fio Bou-raiy, stormed out of the gate tower, needing the security of his own chambers.

Inside the gate tower, the mood was more somber and reflective, with many brothers murmuring and shaking their heads.

"So will you go to Penitence?" Master Glendenhook asked Bou-raiy.

The older master scoffed at the notion. "Brother Francis was guided by emotions that I cannot discredit," he said, loudly enough to draw the attention of all the gathering, "but he erred in his thinking."

That seemingly direct contradiction to what the Father Abbot had just said brought murmurs of surprise, even a few gasps.

"Believe not my words, for they are but opinion," Bou-raiy went on, turning and sweeping his arm toward the spectacle beyond the wall. "Believe what you see before you. Brother Francis ignored doctrine because his heart was weak, because he was unable to suffer the wails of the dying. Nay, we cannot argue his emotions, but there before us lies the truth of his course. Perhaps his compassion and generosity, great gifts both, will grant him some measure of mercy in the eyes of God, whom he will soon meet; but he will need that mercy because he refused to accept the greater responsibility that has been thrust upon us—that legacy of constancy, of protecting the Church itself, and not our own fragile selves, against the onslaught of the rosy plague.

"Follow Francis, all of us, to the fields and to the grave?" he asked dramatically. "Aye, and then, in our weakness, do we plunge the future world of Corona into complete and utter darkness!"

His departure was not less forceful or dramatic than Agronguerre's.

Master Glendenhook, along with everyone else, watched Bou-raiy storm away. He had just witnessed the prelude to a titanic struggle, Glendenhook believed, for it seemed obvious to him then that his friend Fio Bou-raiy would not back down, would fight Agronguerre to the very end if the sight of fallen Francis began to weaken the old Father Abbot's resolve.

An image of Agronguerre lying on the field in place of Francis came to Glendenhook's mind then, and with new Father Abbot Fio Bou-raiy watching the spectacle from the security of St.-Mere-Abelle.

At that particular moment, it seemed quite plausible.

Brother Francis awakened to what he thought was the sound of angels singing, a chorus of joyous and beautiful harmonies fitting of heaven. When he opened his eyes, he saw that it was indeed.

Scores of pitiful plague-ridden peasants ringed him, their hands joined together, their voices blended in chanting prayer. He recognized some who had been too weak even to stand earlier the previous night; but with the support of their neighbors, they were standing now and smiling, every one, despite their pain.

Francis rolled to his side and with great effort managed to stand up, turning slowly, slowly, looking into the eyes of his angels, sharing their love and returning it with all his heart.

A fit of panic hit him then suddenly, as he realized that he did not have his precious soul stone. He glanced all around at the ground, hoping that someone from St.-Mere-Abelle had not sneaked out and stolen away with it.

But then, as if in answer to the plaintive expression upon his face, a frail and scarred, one-eyed little woman shuffled toward him with her hand extended, the gray stone upon her upraised palm.

"Thank you, Merry," Francis whispered, taking the stone. "My work is not yet done."

"They're praying for yerself, Brother Francis," Merry replied. "Every one's sending ye his heart. Ye take yer stone and work upon yer own troubles."

Francis smiled, but knew that was impossible, even if he had been so inclined, which he was not. He knew that he had the plague, and understood that it was growing ravenously within him, but Brother Francis was not bothered terribly by that harsh reality.

"We're all singing for ye, Brother Francis," Merry Cowsenfed went on. When he looked more closely at her, Francis realized that she had tears rimming her eye.

Tears for him! Francis had a hard time catching his breath. He could not believe how profoundly he had touched these poor people, could not believe that they so cared for him. He looked at them, looked at the dying, at people he could not save, at people who knew that he could not save them. And they were crying, for him! And they were praying, for him!

"We're not to let the rosy plague take ye, Brother Francis," Merry Cowsenfed said determinedly. "We'll pray to God, we'll yell at God! He's not to be takin' ye from us! Don't ye fear, we'll get ye yer miracle!"

Francis looked at her and offered the most sincere and warm smile that had ever found its way onto his often troubled face. No, they would not save him, he knew beyond doubt. He felt the sickness in him, bubbling and boiling. He could do nothing against it, even with his soul stone, and neither could they. It would take him, he knew, and deliver him to the feet of God for judgment.

For the first time in a long, long while, Brother Francis Dellacourt did not fear that judgment.

"We'll get ye yer miracle!" Merry Cowsenfed said again loudly, and many people joined in that cheer.

They didn't understand, Francis realized. They would indeed give him his miracle, but not the one for which they were now praying.

They would indeed give him his miracle—they already had.

CHAPTER

❖ 39 ❖

Primal Rage

He heard the cries, the angry shouts, and the sound only spurred him on. As he approached the abbey, he heard the rattle of armor and the clatter of horses.

Marcalo De'Unnero slowed his pace, and so, too, did the Brothers Repentant behind him, figuring that the soldiers of the Duke Tetrafel had come to restore order yet again. Still, he continued toward the abbey, hoping that he might find some opportunity to make life a little more miserable for Braumin Herde and the other heretics who had stolen St. Precious.

Turning into the square, De'Unnero's eyes brightened considerably, for he saw that the soldiers—and it seemed as if the entire city guard had turned out—were not impeding the peasants in any way. In fact, many were cheering on the ragged rabble as they, one after another, charged the abbey and launched stones at its unyielding walls.

It was a situation that seemed to De'Unnero to be on the verge of severe escalation.

He turned to his fanatical brethren. "Our call has been heard at last," he said eagerly. "The hour of our glory is upon us. Let us go to them, our flock, and lead them against the heretics!"

The Brothers Repentant squealed as one, raising fists into the air and charging out onto the courtyard before St. Precious, their red hoods over their heads, their black robes flying out behind them.

De'Unnero was taking a chance, and he knew it. The soldiers, he believed, would not stop him and his followers. Not this time.

"The Brothers Repentant," Anders Castinagis said with a growl. "Marcalo De'Unnero."

Braumin Herde watched the mounting insanity, the growing riot. "Duke Tetrafel is over there," he said, motioning across the way, to where a decorated coach could be seen behind the line of stern-faced soldiers. "He allows this."

"He is angry and afraid," Brother Talumus remarked.

"He is a fool," Castinagis added.

"Can we not just reveal him?" Brother Viscenti asked nervously. "De'Unnero, I mean. They hate him. Surely they'll not follow him if they know . . ."

"They fear the plague more than they hate De'Unnero," Abbot Braumin reasoned, shaking his head. "We can reveal him, and likely that will weaken his hold over some. But it will do little to help us in the end, for this riot was incited not by the Brothers Repentant but by Duke Tetrafel."

The blunt inference, though it made perfect sense, unnerved them all.

"I told you before that we had lost the city," Braumin went on. "Now, before us, we have the proof."

"They'll not get through our walls," Brother Castinagis said determinedly. "Not if all the Duke's soldiers charge our gates."

"We will beat them back," Viscenti started to agree.

"No," said Braumin Herde. "No, I will not have the walls of St. Precious stained with the blood of terrified peasants."

"Then how?" Brother Castinagis asked above the tumult that ensued from the abbot's surprising statement. Had not Braumin, after all, already determined that St. Precious would defend itself against all attacks?

Abbot Braumin nodded, his expression showing the other monks that he knew something they did not—that he, perhaps, had found an answer. "Restraint, brothers," he finished and he left them, walking briskly down the corridor leading toward his private chambers. After a confused look at the others, Marlboro Viscenti quickly followed his old friend.

He caught up to the abbot inside the private antechamber, finding Braumin fumbling with the keys to his desk drawer—the one containing most of St. Precious' gemstone stash.

"So you will arm the brothers," Viscenti reasoned as his abbot slid open the all-important drawer. "But you just said—"

"No," Braumin corrected. "I will not have the blood of innocents staining our walls."

"But then . . ." Viscenti started to ask, but he stopped short as he saw the abbot take only a single stone from the desk, a gray stone.

"I will go out to them," Abbot Braumin explained, "to Duke Tetrafel, bearing the stone of healing."

"To what end?" a horrified Viscenti asked.

"To try," Braumin replied. "If I go to him and try to help, perhaps they will relent their attacks upon our walls."

He started to leave, but Viscenti jumped in front of him.

"They will not!" the nervous little man insisted. "And when you go out and try to heal Tetrafel—only to fail, likely—you will be adding more fire to

De'Unnero's dragon breath. He will claim that if God were really on your side, your attempt to heal the Duke would have been successful."

"But he claims the wisdom of the true God, yet does not heal," Braumin reasoned.

"But he does not claim that he can heal," Viscenti replied without hesitation. "He says only that the plague will continue as long as the Church remains astray."

Abbot Braumin shook his head. "I will go to Tetrafel," he announced to Viscenti, and to Talumus and Castinagis, who had just arrived outside of his open door. "Perhaps I will fail, but I will try, at least."

"Because you are a coward," Viscenti said forcefully behind him. Braumin stopped short, stunned by the uncharacteristic outburst from the normally timid man. The abbot slowly and deliberately turned, but the expression he found staring at him was unyielding.

"You are," Viscenti growled.

Braumin shook his head, his expression incredulous. He was about to go out of the abbey, after all, and confront the rosy plague. How could this man construe that to be an act of cowardice?

"You go to Duke Tetrafel, though you know it to be wrong, because you are afraid that he will send his soldiers against us, or at least that he will not stop the peasants from a full riot against us."

"They will not get through!" Brother Castinagis declared. "Not if all the city converges at our front gates!"

"But that is the fear, do you not see?" Viscenti went on, hopping excitedly right up to Braumin. "You are afraid of the very measures you determined that we must take to defend the abbey. You would not preside over such a slaughter! No, not that!"

His sarcastic tone set Braumin even farther back on his heels.

"But when you go out and fail, they will come anyway," Viscenti went on, "led by De'Unnero, if not the dying Tetrafel, and then we will have to fight on without your leadership. You are a coward," Viscenti repeated, and he was trembling with every word. "You know what we must do, but you'll not have the blood on your hands."

Braumin glanced back curiously at Castinagis and Talumus, to find them staring at him coldly.

"And it will only be worse for us, then," reasoned Viscenti. "For how shall we justify our refusal to come out and help them, all of them, if you have broken ranks to go to the Duke? What words shall we use against the peasant curses when you have, by your actions, told them that we who remained within the abbey are merely cowards?"

That struck Braumin to his very core, as poignant a reminder of the reasons behind Church doctrine as he had ever heard. He surprised the three onlookers then, because he started to chuckle—not a mocking laugh, but one of the purest helplessness.

"So you have shown me the error of my ways, my friend Viscenti," Braumin remarked. "I cannot go out to them, to him." He shook his head helplessly as Viscenti sprang forward, wrapping him in a great hug.

"But we'll not aggressively deter our attackers," Braumin instructed. "We shall hold them back as we must, but with limited magic only. A stunning stroke, perhaps, but not a killing one, if that can be avoided."

Castinagis didn't seem pleased with that, but he nodded his agreement.

Shamus Kilronney came into Caer Tinella to find the place infested with plague, but also to find, to his surprise, an aura of hope and determination about the common folk. These were not people preparing to die, Shamus Kilronney realized, but ones preparing to fight. To his continued surprise, Shamus saw that those afflicted with the plague were not being ostracized and told to leave but rather were being embraced by those seemingly unafflicted. While this generous compassion touched him, he honestly wondered if the folk of Caer Tinella had all gone crazy.

He met with Janine of the Lake, the appointed mayor of the town, soon after.

"Got it meself," Janine explained, and she rolled up her blouse sleeve to show the telltale rosy spots, all over her arm. "Thought me time o' living was growing short."

"Thought?" Shamus echoed skeptically, and he instinctively recoiled from the diseased woman.

"Thought," Janine said firmly, fixing the man with as determined a stare as he had ever seen. "Now I'm knowing better, knowing a way to fight back and to live."

Shamus continued to match her stare, his skeptical expression hardly relenting.

Janine gave a great belly laugh. "Thought!" she said again. "But then Pony—no, she's wanting to be called Jilseponie now—came to us and showed us the truth."

Shamus winced, thinking, perhaps, that his old friend Jilseponie might have seen too much of the dying and the suffering, that she, like the Brothers Repentant, might have discovered some false insight into the causes of the rosy plague.

"She cured Dainsey Aucomb, she did," Janine insisted against his unrelenting stare. "Took the plague right out o' her."

Shamus didn't blink. He knew that a person could be cured of the plague with the gemstones, but he knew, too, that such cures were rare indeed. While he was glad to hear that his friend Jilseponie was still alive, he did not dare to believe that she had become all-powerful with those gemstones. No, Shamus knew of the fate of his cousin Colleen, who had died in Jilseponie's arms.

He knew better.

"And she has cured you, as well?" he asked.

Janine gave another laugh. "She chased the plague back a bit," she explained, "but not cured, no."

"Then you are still sick."

Janine nodded.

"But you just spoke of a cure," the increasingly frustrated man blurted.

"So I did, and so Jilseponie found one," Janine quietly and calmly explained, "but not here. No, here she can give ye a bit o' rest from the fighting, but to get yerself truly cured ye must be walking, me friend, all the way to the Barbacan and Mount Aida, to the hand o' the angel and the healing blood. We're readying for just such a journey—the whole town's going north—and the three Timberland towns're already on the road to Aida."

"What?" Shamus asked helplessly, shaking his head and screwing his expression up into one of pure incredulity, as if the whole thing sounded perfectly preposterous. "Where is Jilseponie?"

"Went to Landsdown to help 'em out over there and to get them ready for the road," Janine replied.

Shamus was on the road in a few minutes, riding hard for Landsdown, the sister village of Caer Tinella, a cluster of houses but an hour away.

When he entered the town, he saw a great gathering in the central square, where a tent had been hastily erected. A line of plague victims had formed in front of it, while other people, apparently healthy, rushed about, loading wagons with supplies.

Though he certainly had no desire to go anywhere near the plague-ridden victims, Shamus suppressed his revulsion and his fear and walked along the line until he could see the front of it, where a woman, a familiar face indeed, worked on them, one by one, with a magical gemstone.

Shamus moved up beside Jilseponie, who was deep into the magic, working on a young boy, and patiently waited. A few minutes later, Jilseponie opened her eyes, and the boy smiled widely and ran off. The next sickly plague victim shuffled forward.

Jilseponie glanced to the side, and her expression brightened considerably when she saw her old friend. She held up her hand to motion the next victim to wait a moment, then stood up—with great effort, Shamus noted—and came forward to offer a friend a hug.

Shamus stiffened at the touch, and Jilseponie pulled him back to arm's length, laughing knowingly. "You have nothing to fear from me," she explained. "The rosy plague cannot touch me now."

"You have become the great healer of the world?" Shamus asked with more than a hint of sarcasm.

Jilseponie shook her head. "Not I," she explained.

Shamus looked to the line of the sick, to the boy Jilseponie had just apparently helped, who was working hard with some others loading a wagon.

"I do nothing that any brother trained with the gemstones could not do," Jilseponie said.

"I have seen their work against the rosy plague," Shamus corrected. "They can do little or nothing, and are so terrified that they hide themselves behind their abbey walls."

"They have not kissed the hand," she answered, and she took her seat, motioning for the next sufferer to come forward. She glanced up at Shamus once more, to find him wearing a perfectly incredulous expression.

"Why do you doubt?" she asked him. "Did not you yourself witness a miracle at the arm of Avelyn?"

"But not against the plague."

"Well, I have so witnessed such a miracle against the plague," Jilseponie answered firmly. "I brought Dainsey to Avelyn, and she was as near to death as anyone I have ever seen. There is blood on his hand—perpetually, I believe—and the taste of that blood brought life back into her body. I saw it myself, and knew that when I, too, kissed the hand, I needed no longer fear the rosy plague."

"And so they are going, all of them?" Shamus asked.

"All of them and all the world," Jilseponie answered.

"But how do you know?" the man pressed. "The blood? Will it continue? Will it truly heal?"

Jilseponie fixed him with a perfectly contented and confident smile. "I know," was all that she answered, and she went back to her work, brushing her hand over the feverish forehead of the woman patiently waiting, then lifting the soul stone to her lips.

"We must talk later," Shamus said. Jilseponie gave a slight nod, then fell into the magic of the stone.

A very shaken Shamus Kilronney walked out of the tent, straight to the tavern across the way. The place was empty, but Shamus went to the bar and poured himself a very potent drink.

Jilseponie joined him there later, looking quite exhausted but quite relaxed.

"They should all survive the journey," she explained, "or at least, the plague will not take any of them on the road to Aida." She turned down her eyes. "Except for one," she admitted. "He is too thick with the plague, and even if I were to work with him all the way to Aida, which I cannot do, he could not possibly survive."

Shamus stared at her, shaking his head. "You seem to have figured it all out," he remarked.

"I was told," Jilseponie corrected. "The spirit of Avelyn, through the ghost of Romeo Mullahy, showed me the truth."

Shamus hardly seemed convinced, but Jilseponie only shrugged, too tired to argue.

"So, you can now help to heal the people?" Shamus asked. "Because you tasted the blood and are now impervious to the plague?"

Jilseponie nodded. "I can help them," she said, accepting the glass Shamus handed her. "Some of them, at least. But so could any other brother who has kissed Avelyn's hand. I need not fear the plague anymore, and that freedom allows me to fight it back in most people."

"But not in those terribly afflicted," Shamus reasoned.

Jilseponie shook her head and swallowed the drink. "For many it is too late, I fear," she explained, "and every day I tarry, more will die."

Shamus' expression turned to one of horror. "You accept that responsibility?" he asked.

"If not me, then who?"

He still just stared at her.

"I will not go north with them—they leave in the morning," she went on. "But you should go. Indeed, you must—both to help protect them and to kiss the hand yourself." She looked deeply into Shamus' eyes, her pleading expression reminding him of who she was and of all that they had gone through together. "Bradwarden leads the Timberland folk. Shamus should help lead the folk of these two towns.

"And Shamus should remain in the northland," Jilseponie continued. It was clear to him that she was making up plans as she went. "To stand guard with whatever force he can muster. To keep the road to the Barbacan clear for those who must make the pilgrimage."

Shamus Kilronney, who had traveled the long, long road to the Barbacan, scoffed at the notion. "You will need the King's army for that!" he insisted.

"I intend to enlist the King's army," Jilseponie answered, her tone so strong and grim that Shamus rocked back in his chair and found, to his absolute surprise, that he did not doubt her for a second. But that only reminded him of another pressing problem.

"Palmaris," he said gravely. "The people are rioting, and Duke Tetrafel encourages it. For he, too, has contracted the plague, and Abbot Braumin can do nothing to help him."

Jilseponie nodded, seeming hardly surprised, and not overconcerned.

"The folk are being prodded, too, by the Brothers Repentant," Shamus explained, "a group of wayward monks claiming that the plague is a result of the Church going astray, away from Markwart and toward Avelyn."

Jilseponie did wince a bit at that information.

"They are led by Marcalo De'Unnero, so I have been told," Shamus went on. He poured another strong drink, for he could see, without doubt, from her stunned expression and from the way the blood drained from her face, that she surely needed one.

*   *   *

Stone after stone slammed against the wall or soared over it, making those few monks on the outside parapet duck for cover.

Down in the square below, De'Unnero and his black-and-red-robed brethren ran all about, urging the rabble on.

And on they came, shouting curses, throwing stones, and hoisting make-shift ladders up against the abbey walls. Another group charged the front gates, a huge battering ram rolling along between their two lines.

"Abbot Braumin!" Castinagis cried from up front, for the abbot had bidden the monks to use all restraint. With that battering ram rolling at them, though, they had to act fast.

"Defend the abbey," Braumin agreed, his voice a harsh whisper, and he turned and walked away.

He heard the sharp retort of a lightning stroke behind him, heard the cries of pain and of outrage, heard the continuing rain of stones, and heard, above all else, the voice of Marcalo De'Unnero, rousing the crowd to new heights of frenzy.

For hours they assaulted the abbey; for hours, the monks drove them away. Wherever a ladder went up, a brother was on the spot, pushing it away; while others launched magic crossbow bolts, even hot oil, at the would-be invaders. Dozens died at the base of St. Precious' ancient stone wall, while scores more were wounded.

The next day, they were back again, even more of them, it seemed; and this time another force accompanied the Brothers Repentant and the angry peasants. The sound of great horns heralded the arrival of Duke Tetrafel and his soldiers, all of them outfitted for battle.

Abbot Braumin was on his way to the front wall even before the messenger came running for him. "It is the Duke," the younger brother tried to explain as they hurried along. "He has brought an army and claims that we must surrender our abbey!"

Braumin didn't answer, just hurried on his way, arriving at the parapet above the front gate tower beside his three closest advisers.

"Abbot Braumin!" came the cry from the herald standing at Tetrafel's side.

"I am here," Braumin replied, stepping forward into plain view—and well aware that many of Tetrafel's archers had likely just trained their arrows on him.

The herald cleared his throat and unrolled a parchment. "By order of Duke Timian Tetrafel, Baron of Palmaris, you and your brethren now secluded within the abbey are declared outlaws in the city of Palmaris and are ordered to vacate St. Precious posthaste. Because Duke Tetrafel is a generous and noble man, you will not be prosecuted, as long as you depart the city this very day and promise not to return!"

Abbot Braumin stared hard at Tetrafel all through the reading, purposely keeping all emotion off his face.

"We have spoken of going to Caer Tinella to open the chapel of Avelyn," Vis\!centi remarked.

Braumin turned and stared at him, but shook his head determinedly. "Duke Tetrafel!" he cried out powerfully. "You have no jurisdiction here and no power to make such demands."

The herald started to respond, but Tetrafel, obviously still possessed of some amount of vigor, grabbed the man and pulled him back. "All the city has come out against you!" he yelled at Braumin. "How can you claim the rights of a Church when you have no followers?"

"We did not give you the plague, Duke Tetrafel," Abbot Braumin bluntly answered.

"But you did!" came a cry from the side, from De'Unnero. He ran out before the gathering, waving his arms at the crowd. "They did! Their sacri\-lege has brought the vengeance of God upon us all! Unseat them and He will be contented, and the plague will lift from our lands and our homes!"

"Duke Tetrafel!" Braumin called out. "We did not give you the plague, nor have we the power to cure your sickness. But how many times have the brothers of St. Precious—"

"Out!" the Duke interrupted, leaping out of his carriage and stumbling forward. "Out, I say! Get you gone from that building and from my city!"

Abbot Braumin stared down at him; his cold expression gave the fright\-ened and angry man all the answer that he needed.

"Then you are besieged, I say!" Duke Tetrafel declared. "If the night has passed and you have not fled the abbey and the city, then know that you leave your walls at your own great peril. Besieged! And know that our patience is not great. Your terms of surrender worsen with each passing hour!"

Braumin turned and walked away. "If they come on again, defend the abbey with all necessary force," he told his friends. "And, please, for my own peace of mind, if the opportunity presents itself, strike Marcalo De'Unnero dead."

Castinagis and Talumus nodded grimly at the request, but Viscenti, more familiar with De'Unnero's reputation, blanched at the mere thought of it. He watched Braumin go back into the abbey and wondered if he had been foolish to talk his friend out of going to Duke Tetrafel's aid, wondered if they should not take the offer and vacate Palmaris at once. All of them, every one.

Viscenti looked back to the courtyard, to see De'Unnero leading a prayer session with hundreds—no, thousands!—of folk gathering about the square, lifting their voices in response to his own. The Brothers Repentant filtered through the crowd, enlisting allies.

No, this would be no traditional siege, Viscenti knew. The outraged peasants would come at them again and then again, until St. Precious was no more than a burned-out husk of broken stone. And what would happen

to the brothers? he wondered. Would they be dragged through the streets
and tortured to death? Burned at the stake, perhaps, like poor Master
Jojonah?

He heard the prayers and, more clearly, the words of anger, the promises that the brothers of St. Precious would pay for bringing the plague
upon them.

A shudder coursed down Viscenti's spine. He did not sleep at all that night.

"Here they come," Brother Talumus said grimly to the monks standing
at his side between the outer wall parapets a few mornings later. He knew,
and so did the others, that this would be the worst assault yet. Duke
Tetrafel had declared a siege, but in truth, the actual attacks against the
abbey had increased daily, for the common folk, roused by De'Unnero and
with many of them plague-ridden and thus short of time, had no patience
for any lengthy siege.

A hail of stones led the way, followed by the ladder bearers and many
with makeshift grapnels attached to long lengths of rope. A group stubbornly picked up the battering ram, which had been repelled three times
already—the last time with a dozen peasants toting it slain—and started
toward the main gate, cheering with each grunting stride.

Monks scrambled along the outer wall, some with gemstones, some with
crossbows, some with heavy clubs or knives. They threw lightning and shot
quarrels, pushed aside ladders and slashed ropes.

A hail of arrows soared in just above the wall. Several brothers dropped,
some groaning, some lying very still.

"Tetrafel's archers!" Brother Talumus cried, scrambling in a defensive
crouch. "Lightning to the back! Lightning to the back!"

Abbot Braumin rose up bravely down the line, graphite in hand. He
brought forth a streaking white bolt, slamming into the archer line, scattering men. He started to duck back for cover, but saw a figure he could not
ignore: De'Unnero, rushing madly among the charging peasants, cheering
them on to certain death.

A second bolt, much weaker in intensity, erupted from Braumin's hand,
but De'Unnero saw it coming, and with the reflexes of a cat, he skipped
aside, just getting clipped on one leg.

With a yell that sounded more like a feral growl, the wild monk charged
the abbey.

Braumin glanced all about, seeking the rope or ladder that De'Unnero
might use, and in his distraction, he did not note that the monk's strides
resembled more the gallop of a tiger than the run of a man. Hardly missing
a step, De'Unnero came to the base of the wall and leaped up, up, clearing
the twenty-five-foot height, catching hold of the crenellated wall and pulling himself up with frightening agility and ease right before the stunned
Braumin.

He hit the abbot with a blow that dropped him to the stone. A pair of brothers rushed De'Unnero, but he dipped, thrust one leg out and tripped one, then pushed the tumbling man off the parapet and down to the courtyard; then he rolled under the lunge of the second, catching the scrambling man on his shoulder. De'Unnero's left hand snapped in with a sharp blow to the monk's throat and then, with hardly an effort, he flung the man right over the wall.

The unfortunate monk was still alive when he hit the ground outside the abbey. The peasants fell over him like a flock of ravenous carrion birds.

A third brother approached De'Unnero, loaded crossbow out before him.

De'Unnero locked his gaze, studied his eyes, and anticipated every movement, and even as the man squeezed the trigger, the powerful tiger legs twitched, launching De'Unnero skyward. The bolt crossed harmlessly beneath him.

De'Unnero came down, exploding into a charge that had the crossbowman helpless. He hit the man repeatedly, his fists smashing bone, and this monk was dead before he ever went over the wall.

Still more monks charged the savage warrior, heedless of their doom, thinking only to protect their fallen abbot. De'Unnero went for Braumin and rolled him over as he raised his fist for the killing blow, wanting Braumin to see it coming.

A lightning bolt hit the weretiger in midchest, sending him rolling over the wall. He landed lightly—miraculously to the stunned peasants!—and shook away the stinging pain.

He could not go right back up, for many monks had then converged on the area, many of them with crossbows and all of them aiming his way.

De'Unnero quickly melted back into the crowd.

Despite that setback, the rabble came on furiously, scaling the walls, pounding at the doors. The brothers responded with everything they possessed, but their magic was fast weakening and their numbers, though they took care to stay protected, continued to dwindle under the rain of arrows from Tetrafel's archers.

Abbot Braumin, dazed from the punch and bleeding from the nose—but refusing any help from a brother with a soul stone—looked around at the confusion, at the sheer mass of people coming at the abbey, at Tetrafel's deadly archers raining death from the back of the square, and he knew.

St. Precious would fall this day, and he and all of his brethren would be executed.

She heard the too-familiar sound of battle as she approached the northern wall of Palmaris, the cries of rage and of pain, the slash of steel, the thunder of magical lightning and a deeper, resonating sound: a battering ram thumping against a heavy gate.

Jilseponie urged Symphony into a faster trot, trying to get a bearing on it all. She noted that no soldiers manned the wall, that the gates were closed but apparently unguarded.

"Open!" she cried, now urging Symphony into a canter. "Open for Jilseponie!"

No response.

She knew then that it was St. Precious under attack, and the absence of city soldiers made it apparent to her that Shamus' warning about Duke Tetrafel was on the mark.

"Come in with care, as you may," she said to Dainsey, who rode Greystone beside her. Jilseponie slowed Symphony just enough so that she could fumble within her gemstone pouch, pulling forth several stones, and then she sent her thoughts to him, straight on, asking him for a full and flying gallop.

And flying it was indeed, for as they approached—the horse not slowing at all but taking confidence in his rider—Jilseponie activated the malachite. Squeezing her legs and urging Symphony into a great leap, they went up, up, lifting nearly weightlessly into the air, their great momentum keeping them flying forward, rather than merely levitating.

Over the wall they went, but Jilseponie didn't then relinquish the magic. Her thoughts, her energy, flowed into the stone powerfully, keeping them aloft. She liked the vantage point, and the image she might bring this way to the battlefield.

But how to steer? And how to maintain speed if Symphony's strong legs couldn't contact the ground?

Another thought—Avelyn-inspired, she knew—came to her, and she reached into her pouch and took out another stone, a lodestone. Jilseponie fell into this one, as well, looking out across the city, to the raging battle she could now see over at St. Precious abbey. She focused on the abbey, on the great bell hanging in the central tower. She felt the metal distinctly through the stone, and while ordinarily she would have gathered that attraction into the lodestone, building energy until she could let it fly as a super-speeding missile, this time she used the attraction to bring the stone and the bell together; and as she was holding the stone, and she and her mount were nearly weightless, they flew off toward the tower.

Jilseponie saw the insanity clearly, and the image nearly had her turning herself right around and running off to the sanctuary of the northland. A wild mob seethed about the base of the abbey walls. Up on the parapets, men were being hurled to their deaths, brothers pulled down and torn apart, lightning bolts and arrows and crossbow quarrels killing in numbers that would humble the total felled by the rosy plague!

She brought up a third stone then, her energies not diminishing in the least as the rage rose within her. She was fully into the magic—levitating, magnetically "flying"—and now both herself and her great horse were limned in a bluish white glow, a serpentine fire shield.

Over the battleground she soared, reversing the lodestone energy to break her momentum to slow her, even to angle her out above the main square and the bulk of the fighting. Some heads turned up to regard her, but most, too engaged in the battle, didn't notice.

But then everyone noticed indeed! For Jilseponie brought forth the powers of the ruby: a tremendous, concussive fireball that rocked the ground beneath their feet, that shook the walls of St. Precious more violently than the battering ram ever could. Then she loosed a tremendous lightning strike, angling it for the bell tower, the great gong immediately following the thunderous report.

Duke Tetrafel's archers turned their bows toward her, but not one had the heart and courage to fire. On the abbey walls, the brothers of St. Precious stared in awe, knowing, as each came to recognize the rider, that their salvation was upon them.

Down went Jilseponie and Symphony, onto the square, the horse neighing and stomping the ground.

"What idiocy is this?" Jilseponie demanded, and the battlefield had gone so quiet that she was heard in every corner. "Is not the rosy plague a great enough enemy without us murdering each other? What fools are you who diminish yourselves to the level of powries and goblins?"

Men about the square shied away from her, some ducking, some falling to their knees in fear.

"They are to blame!" one of the Brothers Repentant cried.

"Silence!" Jilseponie roared, and she lifted her handful of gemstones in the man's direction and he scrambled away.

But another brother did not similarly run, but rather came forward deliberately, slowly pulling back his hood, his intense gaze locked upon her. "They are to blame," he said with perfect calm.

Jilseponie had to fight hard to maintain her seat in that moment of recognition, of painful memories and the purest hatred. For she knew him, indeed she did. Despite the long hair and the beard, she recognized Marcalo De'Unnero as clearly as if they had both suddenly been transported back to that fateful day in Chasewind Manor.

"They follow a demonic course," De'Unnero added, still approaching.

"They follow Avelyn," Jilseponie replied.

The man smiled and shrugged, as if she had just agreed with him.

Jilseponie growled and pulled her gaze from the man. "Hear me, all of you!" she cried. "Avelyn was your savior in the time of Bestesbulzibar, and so he is again!"

"Avelyn brought the plague," the leader of the Brothers Repentant, the self-proclaimed Brother Truth, declared.

Various shouts, of hope and of denial, came at her; but Jilseponie hardly heard them, as De'Unnero continued to approach. She understood then that she would not reach them with any effect as long as this figurehead stood before them, denying her every claim.

And at that moment, Jilseponie hardly cared. Suddenly, at that moment, the scene about her mattered not at all. Not the fighting, not even the suffering. No, all that mattered to Jilseponie at that moment was this figure coming toward her, this murderous monster who had begun the ultimate downfall of her dear Elbryan. She swung down from Symphony, dropping all but one of her gemstones back into her pouch, and in the same movement, drew Defender.

De'Unnero continued to smile, but slowed his approach. "Avelyn is a lie," he said.

"Says Marcalo De'Unnero, former bishop of Palmaris," Jilseponie returned. Many in the crowd gasped, telling her that she had guessed correctly: not many in attendance knew the true identity of the man.

"The same Marcalo De'Unnero who murdered Baron Rochefort Bildeborough, and his nephew, Connor," Pony declared. This time, the gasps were even louder.

"Lies, all!" Brother Truth cried, holding his outward calm. "Baron Bildeborough was killed by a great cat, so say the witnesses and all those who investigated his death."

"A creature that can be replicated through use of the gemstones."

"No!" De'Unnero yelled back before that thought could gain any momentum. "The gemstone may replicate but a limb of the cat, perhaps two if the wielder is strong enough. But that is not the tale told by the scene of Baron Bildeborough's death, and so your claim is the preposterous lie of a desperate fool!"

Pony looked around at the crowd, the uncertain and very afraid peasants. She could not begin any trial here, she realized, could not possibly slow all this down enough to turn the tide against De'Unnero.

"Let them decide their course later," she said to the man. "Let us finish our private business here and now." And she waved Defender before her, a motion for the dangerous monk to be on his guard.

With a laugh most sinister, De'Unnero shrugged off his robes and fell into a fighting stance, circling, circling to Pony's left.

"Do not!" Jilseponie heard Abbot Braumin cry from behind. "You do not know the power of—" She held up her hand to silence the man; nothing would deter her from this fight. Not now. This was the man who had wounded Elbryan, who had, in fact, brought about his death in his subsequent battle with Markwart. This was the man who had brought the crowd against St. Precious, without doubt, the symbol of all that Jilseponie despised. This was the man, and no doubt, Jilseponie meant to wage this fight.

Quicker than she could believe, De'Unnero leaped forward, his left arm going under Defender, then coming up and out to keep the sword wide, while his other hand came straight in, a heavy punch aimed for Jilseponie's face. She thought that he would measure her, would take some feinting strides and punches, and so she was caught somewhat off guard, and had to skitter back defensively, taking a clip on the face as he followed the punch through to the end.

The fight would have been over, then and there, for De'Unnero continued ahead, launching another right, then a straight left, then another right.

But Jilseponie knew *bi'nelle dasada*, had mastered much of the dance—particularly the straightforward charge-and-retreat routines—perfectly, and she managed to elude the charging monk long enough to get her sword in line and force him back.

Now she came forward, a sudden charge and thrust; but De'Unnero, so agile—too agile!—leaped into a sidelong roll that forced Jilseponie to turn. By the time she had, he had already come inside her sword reach, and she had to skitter into another desperate retreat.

Only for a moment, though, for she slid down to one knee, under a wild right hook, disengaging Defender from the blocking arm, then slashed the sword across.

Up went De'Unnero, tucking his legs. Jilseponie stopped and pulled the sword in, then thrust straight out, and De'Unnero had to throw his hips to the side to dodge.

He rolled right about that pivot, lifting one leg high, then stomping down; Pony threw her free arm out to block—and then fell back, tucking the bruised limb in against her side.

She didn't let the pain deter her and retreated only a couple of steps before reversing and thrusting, charging ahead several fast strides, angled to keep up with De'Unnero, and thrusting again. Then it was the monk's turn to clutch a wounded limb, a torn forearm.

But if Jilseponie thought that she had any advantage, then she didn't understand the fiber of Marcalo De'Unnero. With a feral growl, he came on, his hands working a blur of circles in the air before him—a blur that Jilseponie didn't dare thrust her sword into, for if she missed any mark, he would certainly disarm her or at least deflect Defender out too far to the side. On he came, hands working a defensive frenzy and every so often launching a straight jab; legs working furiously, keeping perfect balance, and every so often launching a kick for her face.

And Jilseponie was backing, backing, trying to sort out the blur, trying to find some opening. She called to Elbryan then, to guide her.

But he was not there or could not answer. It was only herself against this man, this monster, and she understood clearly at that moment that she was badly overmatched. How she wished she hadn't so depleted her magical energies! How she wished she could activate serpentine and ruby and burn the skin from De'Unnero's bones!

Out came a jab, and she had to slash Defender to turn the punch away, and only then did Jilseponie realize that she had been duped.

Down went De'Unnero, throwing his leg out wide, sweeping it forward, catching the retreating woman on the ankle and tripping her.

She fell with enough balance to prevent any real injury, but again, the monk leaped ahead too quickly and stood towering over her.

She couldn't get Defender in line this time. She noted then that the man's arm had become that of a great tiger.

For Marcalo De'Unnero, this was the moment of complete triumph, of full circle. Jilseponie would die, there and then, and all threat that the followers of Avelyn would somehow push back his brethren would die with her.

For he was the victor, he was the one who would stand among the masses, sending them with renewed fury against the diminishing defenses of St. Precious Abbey.

He had sensed that, had sensed the kill, even as his foot connected with her ankle, sending her tumbling to the cobblestones. He had smelled her blood, had felt the tiger awakening within him. The woman was good— very good—and he knew that he would get only one strike in before she managed to come back on the defensive. But he had the great beast within him; his paw carried lethal claws.

He would need only one strike.

He started his swipe, her neck open to him. She could not possibly bring her sword in line, could not begin to roll out of death's way.

But she opened her other hand and a missile fired out, a small gemstone homing in on the metal in the one piece of jewelry Brother Truth wore: an earring dangling the evergreen symbol of the Abellican Church.

The magic stone drove up against the side of De'Unnero's head, tearing away his ear. His attack became a shriek as he brought his arm in reflexively to grab at the wound.

Jilseponie rolled back, setting her feet under her and coming up; and De'Unnero, too, retreated, howling with pain and outrage.

"Deceiver!" he cried.

"Tell me when I claimed to fight you fairly," she spat back.

"Deceiver!" he cried again.

"I did not use magic until you did!" Jilseponie yelled back. She came forward with a thrust, and De'Unnero leaped aside.

It churned in him, boiling, boiling, the primal rage, the primal beast. His head burned with pain; his brain swirled with red rage. He had won! He had victory right in his grasp, his clawed, tiger's grasp!

He hardly felt the transformation, the crackling and reshaping of bone, the beast overwhelming his control. He knew that he should not, must not, allow this! Not out here, in front of all the folk, not so soon after Jilseponie had just declared him the murderer of Baron Bildeborough!

But he couldn't stop it, not with the blur of pain, the red wall of outrage.

His senses heightened; he saw Jilseponie, her horse behind her, rearing and neighing.

He heard them, all of them, gasping, and then crying out against him.

Desperation had given her the strength to launch the lodestone, but only luck had brought it into such a sensitive area as his ear. She produced another stone now, a graphite, but Jilseponie knew that the thunderbolt she brought forth from it would be of little real effect. Her magical energies were now depleted to the point where she doubted that her bolt would even slow the charge of this terrifying, tremendous cat.

She would have to use Defender alone to stop him; and when she considered the sword, magnificent as it was, Jilseponie realized that she was in dire trouble.

But De'Unnero didn't charge; and suddenly, she realized that their personal battle had come to an abrupt end. Tetrafel's archers had their bows low and level but not aiming at her; the cries from the peasants all about her did not call for her death.

No, De'Unnero had revealed the truth of himself to the folk of Palmaris, had shown them that he had been the murderer of their beloved Baron Bildeborough.

They knew now the truth of Brother Truth.

The great cat sprang—not at Jilseponie, but by her, breaking into a sprint. A volley of arrows followed, some hitting the mark; but on De'Unnero ran, away he leaped, clearing the dodging and ducking peasants, breaking for the city's outer wall with a host of arrows, of crossbow bolts from St. Precious, of charging horsemen, right behind.

Jilseponie stood calm through the storm, held her ground, and turned her attention away from the fleeing tiger toward the more important adversary.

Duke Tetrafel was there, staring back at her from the window of his decorated coach.

Pain and rage, primal hunger and blind hatred all swirled in his mind, along with abject despair at the deep-buried but deep-seated realization that he had failed. He had gone from victory to complete defeat in the blink of an eye, and now he was revealed and banished forevermore.

He charged for the wall, hearing the pursuit, feeling the pain of a dozen stinging arrows that had burrowed under his black-striped orange coat. Fear and rage alone kept him moving, running, running, for the northern gate.

He saw a woman on a familiar horse, but he couldn't stop to tear out her throat, to feast upon her warm blood. He had to get to the gate—and through the gate.

No, the great cat realized, and he quickly turned down a side alley. Not to the gate. The horsemen could follow him through the gate, and he was fast tiring. He was a predator, built for short bursts of speed, and he was sorely wounded, but those horses could run and run.

He headed for the wall again, but not near any gate. The pursuit closed, closed, but De'Unnero used his last remaining strength to get to the base of the wall and to leap high and far.

Another arrow caught him in midflight.

He landed heavily on the field outside, slumping to the ground, but then pulling himself back up and dragging his punctured body away into hiding.

He felt the darkness closing all about him, could hear the rasp of death and feel the cold and merciless hand closing in.

CHAPTER

❖ 40 ❖

Cynicism Laid Bare

They stood in the square, watching the soldiers galloping in pursuit of the fleeing monster.

Jilseponie didn't follow. She just stood there, beside Symphony, open and exposed and vulnerable, out of magic and exhausted. She looked across the way to the remaining Brothers Repentant and the hordes they held back, to the line of soldiers still sitting ominously on their chargers, to Duke Tetrafel, staring at her from the window of his coach, his expression indecipherable.

Slowly, she dared to glance back at St. Precious, to see the monks holding stoic vigil, some with gemstones, some with crossbows, some flanking a great black kettle steaming with hot oil. There stood her friend Braumin Herde staring back at her with a mixture of respect and love, gratitude and fear.

For she was out there, in the calm valley between two great waves; and those waves, despite what she had just done, despite that she had shown the folk of Palmaris the truth of Marcalo De'Unnero, seemed destined to crash together one more time.

By the time Jilseponie looked back across the way, Duke Tetrafel had stepped out of his carriage. She could see the slump of his shoulders, the dark blue under his eyes. Yes, he had the plague; she could smell it thick about him even this far away.

"The brothers of St. Precious did not cause this," Jilseponie said loudly, sweeping her gaze quickly about all the crowd, but then quickly refocusing it on Tetrafel. "The plague is not the work of men, nor is it the scourge of an angry God."

"So you claim!" shouted one of the Brothers Repentant from the side. "So you must, for you have led the way against God!" He came forward as he spoke, prodding his finger at Jilseponie. Her responding look was one of perfect calm and confidence, and perfectly cold; and the man, who had just

447

seen his adored leader beaten away by this dangerous woman, gradually calmed and slowed.

"They are innocent," Jilseponie said to Tetrafel when the threat of the irate brother had passed.

"They hide while the people suffer and die!" the Duke came back.

"As did you, until you learned that the plague was within your own body," she replied. "I do not judge you, Duke," she quickly added, seeing the soldiers all about him bristle at the accusation. "Nor can I, can any of us, judge all the folk who so hide from the plague—monk or soldier, brother or even father—who out of fear for the rest of his family must put a victim out of his house."

"But you never hid from it!" came one cry from the crowd; and Jilseponie recognized the speaker as one of the attendants at the house where Colleen had died.

"But that was my choice to make," Jilseponie quickly answered, before any negative comparisons could be drawn concerning the brothers of St. Precious. "As it was yours, Duke Tetrafel."

The clump of hooves to the side alerted Pony that Dainsey Aucomb and Greystone had at last arrived at the square.

"But take heart!" Jilseponie cried. "For our salvation is upon us, and there is the proof!" She pointed at Dainsey as she finished, then looked back to the crowd to see a great mixture of expressions, and many of them verging on uncontrollable excitement.

"Duke Tetrafel, will you come with me inside the abbey, to meet with Abbot Braumin, that I might explain my revelations to you?"

The sick man stared at her hard.

"A trick!" cried another of the troublesome Brothers Repentant. "A deception to take the heart from our fight!"

Jilseponie didn't even glance the man's way. "You have the plague and will die," she said bluntly to the Duke. "I cannot help you, nor can the brothers within the abbey. But there is an answer, a cure for your sickness, and I know how to reach it."

"Then tell us!" came a cry from the crowd, a plea echoed many times over.

Jilseponie held up her hand. "It will take all of us to do this thing," she shouted back. "It will only work if Duke Tetrafel agrees." And she settled her gaze upon him again as she finished, putting the weight of a thousand desperate prayers squarely on his sickly shoulders. "Will you come in with me?" she asked again. "On my word, you'll not be harmed nor detained."

"Your word?" Duke Tetrafel echoed skeptically, glancing past her to the brothers of the abbey.

"Mine as well," said Abbot Braumin.

The monks about him shifted nervously, staring at him with disbelief. Jilseponie could not enter the abbey, by his own words, unless she submitted to thorough inspection to ensure that she was not afflicted, and Duke Tetrafel, of course, could not be admitted at all, for he was obviously ill with plague.

"We will meet at the gate," the abbot clarified, "on opposite sides of a tussie-mussie bed we will lay out within the tower antechamber."

"A hero to the end," Duke Tetrafel muttered, loudly enough for Jilseponie to hear, but in truth, that arrangement seemed perfectly suited to her needs.

"All of you stay back," Tetrafel said to his soldiers and to the common people. He sucked in his breath and strode forward, then walked with Jilseponie and Dainsey to St. Precious' front gates. It was some time before the monks had the flowers in place within the gatehouse, but soon after, the doors swung open.

Abbot Braumin and his advisers, Viscenti, Talumus, and Castinagis, stood across the flower bed from the trio.

Now it was Jilseponie's turn to take a deep breath. This was her moment, a critical one for the fate of all the world.

She told them the story, all of it, of Dainsey and Roger, of her trip to the Barbacan with Bradwarden and Dainsey, of the ghost of Romeo Mullahy—which made Master Viscenti gasp fearfully—and of the second miracle of Aida.

"I, too, have kissed the hand of Avelyn," Jilseponie finished. "Thus, the rosy plague cannot touch me."

The expressions coming back at her from across the tussie-mussie bed ranged from joyful Master Viscenti, hopeful Brother Talumus, skeptical Brother Castinagis, and, even worse than that, something beyond skeptical, sympathetic Abbot Braumin. Beside Jilseponie, Tetrafel was more animated, was grabbing at the hope she had just offered to him.

"Then you are my angel," he said, taking Jilseponie's hand in his own. "You will take this wretched disease from my body!"

Jilseponie turned to him, trying to find the words to explain to him that, while there was indeed an answer, a true hope, she was not the source of his, or anyone else's, cure.

"The plague is not always fatal," Abbot Braumin interrupted. Jilseponie and Tetrafel both turned to regard him, for the manner in which he had spoken those words showed that he believed Jilseponie's "revelation" to be nothing so spectacular. "People have been cured, though it is rare," the abbot went on.

"Then why do you hide behind your walls?" Duke Tetrafel demanded.

"One in twenty, so say the old songs," the abbot calmly replied. "One in twenty might be helped, but one in seven will afflict the helping brother. We hide because those numbers, learned through bitter experience, demand that we hide."

Tetrafel trembled and seemed on the verge of an explosion.

"This is different," Jilseponie put in. "Dainsey was not helped by me—indeed, I tried and was repulsed, again and again."

"Perhaps you had more success than you believed," suggested Braumin.

Jilseponie was shaking her head before he ever finished the words. "I had no effect, and was, in fact, afflicted by my efforts. Yet the plague is not within me any longer and cannot enter this, my body purified by the blood of Avelyn. It is real, Ab—Braumin. It is real and it is up there, at the Barbacan, the cure for the plague for those who can make the journey, the armor that can turn it aside without fail."

Now it was Braumin's turn to shake his head, but that only made Jilseponie press on more forcefully.

"You doubt, as many doubted your own tale of a miracle at Mount Aida," she reminded him. "I speak of ghosts and of blood on a hand long petrified. I speak of a miraculous recovery by a woman who had already begun her journey into Death's dark realm. And so it is difficult for you to dare to hope." She paused and stared at the abbot intently, even came forward onto the tussie-mussie bed. "You know me, Braumin Herde. You know who I am and what I have done. You know of my attributes and of my failings. False hope has never been among those failings."

"The bell! The bell!" came a cry, echoing along the corridors and the ramparts. "The bell!" the excited young brother cried again, scrambling down beside the abbot and the other leaders of the abbey. "My abbot, the bell!" he stammered, pointing back toward the abbey's central bell tower. The man hardly seemed able to stand, so overwhelmed was he.

"What is it, Brother Dissin?" Braumin demanded, putting his hands on the man's shoulders, trying to hold him steady.

"The bell!" he cried again, tears flowing down his cheeks. "You must see it!"

Even as he finished, more cries came from the back of the abbey, shouts of "A sign!" and "A miracle!"

Castinagis, Talumus, and Viscenti started off that way. Braumin turned to regard Jilseponie and saw that she and her two companions were boldly crossing the flower bed. He started to motion for them to stop but found that he could not—found, to his surprise, that he had come to believe that something extraordinary was indeed happening here, something that he could not and should not deny.

Together they ran into the abbey, up the stone stairs, along a corridor, down another and up another set of stairs, and into the bell tower. They had to push past many brothers—monks who were so overwhelmed that they hardly seemed to notice that Duke Tetrafel, a man infected with the rosy plague, was crowding among them.

Up the winding stairs, they climbed and climbed, coming at last to the highest landing, in plain view of the great bell of St. Precious, the bell Jilseponie had struck with a lightning bolt to herald her arrival in Palmaris.

And there, scorched into the side of the old metal, was an unmistakable image: an upraised arm clenching a sword at midblade.

Braumin's jaw fell open. He turned back to the woman. "How did you ..." he started to ask, but the question fell away, for it was quite obvious that Jilseponie was every bit as stunned and confused as he.

He was tired and he was dirty, and he knew that if he wasn't already afflicted with plague, then he soon would be. But Brother Holan Dellman would not surrender his work, not with so many people dying about the grounds of St. Belfour Abbey.

Nor would Abbot Haney, nor any of the other brothers who had chosen to remain within the structure after the decision had been made to open wide the gates. Three of those brothers had died, and horribly, of plague contracted through their futile healing efforts, and not a single person had been healed, though many lives had been extended somewhat by the heroic efforts.

Even that grim reality had not deterred Haney, Dellman, and the others from the course they knew they must pursue. Nor was Prince Midalis, ever a friend of the common folk, hiding away in his small palace in the complex at Pireth Vanguard. For he, like the monks, could not suffer the cries of the dying.

Midalis had not taken ill yet, but Liam was showing the beginnings of the plague.

Holan Dellman headed for his darkened room, wanting nothing more than to fall down into unconsciousness. He had heard the news of Liam's illness that same morning, soon after he had begun his work with the sick at St. Belfour, and that news, more than his efforts with the sick, had taken the strength from him. How he wanted to go to the man and comfort him! How he wanted to focus all his healing energies on that one man, now, early on, before the plague had taken solid hold of him!

But Dellman could not do that, could not place the fate of his dear friend above that of the others. That was not the way of his faith or of his God; and as much as he had come to love Liam O'Blythe during his time in Vanguard, Holan Dellman loved his God above all else.

But that didn't stop his very human misery at the news.

He collapsed onto his small cot, buried his face into the blankets, and tried to block out all the world.

And then he sensed her, and, with a start, he jerked about and he saw her.

Jilseponie, standing in his room, looking back at him.

Holan Dellman bolted upright. "How did you get here?" he asked. "Did the ship—"

Dellman stopped, suddenly realizing that this was not Jilseponie physically before him, was something less substantial. He gasped, trying to find his breath, and retreated across the cot, eyes wide, his head shaking, his body trembling.

"We have found the answer, Brother Dellman," Jilseponie said to him, in a voice half audible and half telepathic.

Holan Dellman understood spirit-walking, of course, but he had never seen anything this extreme. His first thought was that Jilseponie had died and that her ghost had come to him. But now he realized that this was spirit-walking taken to a level that he had never before seen.

"Brother Dellman!" she said to him, more insistently, and he understood that she was trying to steady him, that her time, perhaps, was not long here in Vanguard.

"Where are you?" he asked.

"In St. Precious," she answered. Her voice seemed weaker suddenly, and her answer was more a feeling than words, an image of a place that Holan Dellman knew well. So, too, came her next communication—an image of a flat-topped mountain, of a mummified arm protruding from the stone.

"Go there, all the sick and all the well," Jilseponie said. "Go and be healed."

Jilseponie's spirit image vanished.

Brother Dellman sat there, gasping, for a long while. Then, no longer exhausted, he ran out to find Abbot Haney.

"They all must go," Jilseponie said to Tetrafel and Braumin when they met later that day in St. Precious Abbey. "The ill and the healthy, in coordinated fashion and with your soldiers to protect them."

Duke Tetrafel, only then beginning to digest the overwhelming logistics of the proposition, hesitated. "I will send some soldiers," he agreed.

"All of them!" Jilseponie argued, her tone showing no room for debate. "Every man and woman. And you must send word to Ursal, telling King Danube to open the roads to the north, to call out the entirety of his army to wage this war as completely as he would if the goblins had returned."

"And you, Abbot Braumin, must send all of your brothers, as quickly as possible, using all the magic available to you, to the Barbacan," she continued. "Once you have tasted the blood of Avelyn, then you, too, might begin to aid those making the journey to Aida without fear of becoming ill."

"But you cannot cure me," Duke Tetrafel argued, "by your own words."

"But I can help to battle the plague, to push it back long enough so that, perhaps, you will survive the journey to the mountaintop, and there be healed."

"You are so certain of all of this?" Braumin asked somberly; and Jilseponie nodded, her expression serious and grim.

"We must have soldiers and monks lining the road, all the way from Palmaris to the Barbacan," she explained, "supply camps, with food and with bolstering healing, with fresh horses, and with soldiers to guide the newest group of pilgrims to the next site."

"Do you understand the difficulties?" Duke Tetrafel asked skeptically.

"Do you understand the implications if we fail in this?" Jilseponie shot back, and that surely silenced the skeptical, plague-infected man.

"You went to Dellman?" Braumin Herde asked.

Jilseponie nodded. "Vanguard is alerted. For now, they must determine their course."

"And you will similarly go to the Father Abbot at St.-Mere-Abelle?" Braumin asked.

Jilseponie thought on that for a few moments, then shook her head. "I will go in body to St.-Mere-Abelle, along with Dainsey. I will face them directly."

Braumin, too, paused and mulled it over, then nodded his agreement. "They will not be easily convinced," he said, remembering his previous meeting with Glendenhook and understanding well the doubting, cynical nature of powerful Fio Bou-raiy.

"We need them," Jilseponie said. "All of them. All of the brothers of your Church. They must go to Aida and protect themselves, then work tirelessly to aid those who will follow them to that holy place."

"Palmaris first," Duke Tetrafel demanded.

Jilseponie nodded. "Let our work begin, now, out in the square."

And so it did, with Jilseponie working with the soul stone, bolstering those sick plague victims who would head out that very day, while the soldiers and the other healthy pilgrims began readying the many horses and wagons.

While Braumin and the others, on Jilseponie's own orders, could not offer direct aid to the plague sufferers, they did work with soul stones, leeching their own strength into Jilseponie, bolstering her efforts.

She worked all the day and all the night. Several, she found, were beyond her help, were simply too thick with plague for her to offer any real relief. They would not make the journey, could not hope to survive the road, even if she went along with them, working on them all the way. She did not turn them away, though, and tried to enact some measure of relief, at least, upon them.

That very night, magically and physically exhausted but knowing that every minute she delayed likely meant the death of another unfortunate victim, Jilseponie and Dainsey Aucomb set out from Palmaris. Instead of taking the normal, slow ferry across the Masur Delaval, the pair were whisked across the great river by Captain Al'u'met on his *Saudi Jacintha*.

Also that very same night, Abbot Braumin and every brother of St. Precious began their swift pilgrimage to the north, using gemstones to lighten the burden on their horses, using gemstones to illuminate the trail before them and to scout the area spiritually, using gemstones to leech the strength from nearby animals, as some of them had learned on their first trip to the Barbacan.

They meant to get there as quickly as possible and return, stretching their line along the road to offer aid to the pilgrims.

Braumin Herde remained doubtful, though he trusted Jilseponie implicitly, and marked well the seemingly miraculous image burned into the bell at St. Precious. But too much was at stake here for the gentle monk. He could not allow his hopes to soar so high, only to learn that Jilseponie had erred, that there was no miracle to be found or that it had been a onetime occurrence, a blessing for Dainsey Aucomb.

What would happen in that instance? the abbot had to worry. What might the peasants or the Duke and his soldiers do if they discovered that they had traveled all the way to the Barbacan, no doubt with many dying along the road, chasing a false hope?

He shuddered at the thought but reminded himself of the character of the messenger. When he had last seen Jilseponie before her return to St. Precious, he had given her an assortment of gemstones and had prayed that she would again prove the light against the darkness. Now she had returned to him with just that claim, and his own doubts of her had laid his cynicism bare before him.

What friend was he if he did not believe her?

What holy man was he if he could not see past his earthly cynicism and dare to believe in miracles?

CHAPTER

❖ 41 ❖

Despite Herself

"We cuts 'em, and that horsie-man leading them won'ts help 'em!" Kriskshnuck, the little goblin, said with a toothy sneer. "Cuts 'em and eats 'em!"

His companions bobbed their heads eagerly, for down on the trail, in clear sight of them, came the line of folk from Dundalis and the other Timberland towns—the first pilgrim group that had set out for the Barbacan.

For the goblins who had swarmed back into the area just south of the mountainous ring, this seemed like an easy kill. The goblins knew this rugged land, where the humans did not. They'd hit the fools on the road, and repeatedly, whittling at their numbers and their resolve, setting them up for the final, overwhelming assault.

And as more and more goblins joined in, their numbers now swelling to over three hundred, it did indeed seem as if that assault would be overwhelming.

Kriskshnuck couldn't keep all of the eager drool in his mouth as he and his companions scrambled down from the ridge, excited to give their reports to their waiting kin. Halfway down the rocky outcropping, though, one of those other goblins cried out in pain.

"Ow!" the wretched little creature yelped. "A bee stinged me." And then, "Ow! Ow!" over and over, and when Kriskshnuck looked back, he saw his companion swatting futilely at the air, waving and jerking spasmodically, before giving one final howl and falling over onto the stone.

Before Kriskshnuck could begin to ask, another of his companions began a similar dancing routine, and then the third of the group.

Kriskshnuck was smart, as goblins go, and so he asked no further questions but just turned and sprinted and scrambled to get out of the area. He got over one ridge, across the flat top of a huge boulder, then down a short cliff face. He turned and started to run, with only twenty feet of open ground separating him from the relative safety of a tree copse.

He felt the first burning sting on his thigh, and looked down to see a

455

small shaft protruding from the muscle. He limped on and got hit again, on the hip, and again after that, in the belly.

Doubled over, clutching his belly with one hand, his thigh with the other, Kriskshnuck scrambled on.

"The trees," he said hopefully, thinking his salvation was at hand. But then he saw them—small forms sitting among the boughs of the closest trees, leveling bows his way.

A volley of small arrows blasted the goblin to the ground.

King Danube stared down at the parchment in disbelief. It had been penned by a trader whose ship had put into Ursal's port that morning, a message that had been shouted down the Masur Delaval, ship to ship, in advance of a formal ducal declaration.

Danube looked up at his advisers, Constance and Kalas, both of whom had seen the parchment before bringing it to him; and their grim expressions accurately reflected one half of the emotions battling within him.

"This could be our salvation," he reminded them.

"Tetrafel is plague ridden and willing to chase any hope," Duke Kalas argued.

"The false hope," Constance was quick to put in. She winced as she considered her own sharp tone, a reflection, perhaps, of her petty fears that Jilseponie had once more come to save the world.

"Can we be so certain?" the King asked. "And we are still days away from the official ducal declaration, dispatched under Tetrafel's own hand."

"Many advance writs prove inaccurate," Kalas reminded him, his tone making it fairly obvious that he was hoping that to be so in this case, as well.

But Danube didn't think so, and he shook his head slowly. "Too important," he remarked.

"Many of the callers are likely as desperate as poor Timian," Constance argued. "Plague ridden themselves or a member of their family, perhaps."

King Danube looked down at the writ again, reading it slowly. Duke Tetrafel was on his way to the Barbacan, it said, along with the entire garrison at his disposal, and most of the folk of Palmaris. How could even desperate callers confuse an event on a scale such as that?

"The particulars might be confused, but the general message of the writ will likely prove accurate," King Danube decided.

"You believe that Timian Tetrafel would be fool enough to turn over his garrison to Jilseponie Wyndon?" Kalas asked incredulously.

"If she has found the answer, then he would likely see that as an obvious course."

Constance snorted and turned away.

"Let us make our plans on the assumption that the particulars of this writ are correct," Danube offered.

"That a cure has been found?" Duke Kalas asked, shaking his head with every word. "Are we to tell that to the desperate thousands in Ursal? What riots might we cause, and what of the cost to the Throne if we are proven wrong?"

"Not that far," King Danube corrected. "We will await Timian's official writ before deciding upon any such course as that. But let us assume that the lesser particulars, the desertion of Palmaris by soldier and citizen alike, are indeed accurate. What, then, must we do?"

Kalas' breathing came in hard rasps, and Constance continued to stare across the room, shaking her head. If those particulars were true, then the implications to Danube could be grave indeed. If Timian Tetrafel had turned the garrison of Palmaris over to Jilseponie, or had sent them out in accordance with Jilseponie's words, then this event could prove politically disastrous for an inactive King Danube. But if Danube fell in with his often unpredictable Duke, and turned his army and his citizenry into the hands of the woman, and her apparent "cure" proved invalid, then the disaster would be multiplied tenfold.

"We could send a small force—Duke Bretherford's sailors, perhaps—sailing north to investigate," Kalas offered.

"And by the time they can return to us, the season will be past, and the roads north closed," King Danube argued. "And the winter will claim many lives that otherwise might have been saved."

Constance turned on her heel. "It sounds as if you have already thrown your faith in with the woman," she said sharply, and she and Danube stared at each other long and hard.

"We are all desperate for an end to the plague," Duke Kalas quietly put in, acting in the uncustomary role of mediator.

"Ready the soldiers for the road," Danube ordered.

"But, my King . . ." Kalas started to argue, and Constance chimed in, as well.

But Danube, expecting such an outburst, was already patting his hand calmly in the air. "I did not command you to begin the march," he clarified, "only to ready the troops in case we so decide. And let us send for Abbot Hingas, that we might learn the disposition of the Church on this matter. The situation at St. Honce and the other abbeys will likely prove even more tentative than our own, for the majority of the folk have come to single out the Church and not the Crown as the source of the plague."

Rain fell, but it hardly dampened the mood of the Timberlands folk, for the mountains of the Barbacan loomed before them, less than a day's march away. Roger Lockless and Bradwarden knew how to get through those mountains; and from there the trip to Mount Aida, to Avelyn's hand and to salvation, would be an easy one indeed.

Roger was up front with Bradwarden that morning, scouting the road carefully, for the centaur had caught a strong scent of goblin and feared that the little wretches were about.

They feared they would encounter a large tribe, an army of the creatures, but the first goblin they actually saw was no threat at all.

It was lying dead on the side of the trail.

Roger went over to inspect the body, prodding it with his foot, then rolling it over. He saw many puncture wounds on the creature's face, neck, and chest—very similar to injuries he had witnessed before.

Immediately his eyes went up to the nearby trees, scouring the boughs.

"What're ye about?" Bradwarden asked. "What killed the little beastie?"

"Arrows," Roger answered, walking about and still looking up. "Little arrows. Elv—"

"Elvish arrows," came the answer from the shadows of one tree, a melodic voice that Roger had heard only once before, but one that he surely recognized.

As did Bradwarden. "Dasslerond?" the centaur asked with a surprised laugh. "Is that yerself, then?"

"Greetings, Bradwarden," Lady Dasslerond answered. "It is good to see you again, though I am surprised to find you in the company of humans in this time of illness."

"Goin' to find an old friend," the centaur answered. "Ye heared o' Avelyn?"

"Jilseponie has told us," Dasslerond answered.

"So ye've been to the arm?"

No answer came back, and Bradwarden understood the elves well enough to let that particular matter drop.

"You will find the road open all the way to Mount Aida," Lady Dasslerond said to the pair.

"Were many o' the goblins about, then?" the centaur asked.

"Not enough," came another, even more familiar elvish voice. "I still have many arrows in my quiver." Belli'mar Juraviel hopped down to the lowest branch on a wide-spreading elm, in clear sight of Roger and Bradwarden. Roger started toward him, but the elf held up his hand and warned the man back.

"We have cleared the road and will remain in place for a short time longer," Lady Dasslerond explained. "But this road is for humans to travel and for humans to guard, and we will be on our way back to Andur'Blough Inninness before the turn of the season."

"Well, ye have our thanks, then," Bradwarden remarked, bowing his human torso respectfully. "And take the goodwill o' Avelyn with ye."

"Straight on to Aida," Lady Dasslerond said, aiming her comment at Roger. "And know that the road will be clear for your return through this region."

"There will be many more following us," Roger started to explain.

"They are already on their way," Juraviel put in, "from Caer Tinella and Landsdown—from Palmaris, even, for Jilseponie has passed through the city. Braumin and his brethren will likely find you before you have traveled far out of the Barbacan, and the new Baron of Palmaris, along with a host of soldiers, will be along not far behind."

Roger and Bradwarden beamed at the news.

"Ah, but Pony's a good girl," the centaur remarked.

"And Dainsey," Roger was quick to add. He turned back to tell Juraviel of the new love that had come into his life, but he found that the ever-elusive elf was already gone, vanished completely into the canopy. He called out several times but was not answered.

The pair went back to the caravan, then, and told them that the way was clear.

That night, they camped on the high ground of the mountainous ring, with Mount Aida in sight. The next day, the first pilgrims found the arm of Avelyn and tasted the blood in the fallen man's palm.

Roger was first to it, following Bradwarden's instructions, and as soon as he entered the covenant with Avelyn, he knew, beyond doubt, that the rosy plague could not touch him.

"It is a fool's journey!" Constance Pemblebury scolded.

King Danube continued to dress in his traveling clothes, strapping his sword belt about his waist.

"What if this is no answer?" Constance continued. "To what dangers do you, in the name of compassion, expose yourself? What price to the kingdom?"

Danube had heard all the arguments before, repeatedly, since he had announced that he and a great force would go out from Ursal, to Palmaris and perhaps, he hinted, even beyond. He fixed Constance with a calm stare and managed a smile. "If this is the answer, then I must be present at the beginning of it," he tried to explain. "What king am I if I hide in Castle Ursal while the potential salvation of all the world comes to fruition in the north?"

"We have hidden in Castle Ursal for all these months," Constance reminded. "Torrence has never been outside these walls."

"And too long it has been!" Danube retorted. He started to leave the room, but Constance rushed around him, blocking the way.

"You are weary of it all, I know," she said, "as are we all. But we must hold strong for the sake of the kingdom."

"Duke Tetrafel has turned his garrison over to Jilseponie," Danube reminded her. "He has emptied Palmaris on her proof that the miracle has been found."

"He is desperate."

"That may be true, but I know, as do you, that I cannot sit back and allow this to happen without me. Many soldiers will be needed to secure the road north; and if this is indeed the answer, then that road will become even more traveled."

"The brothers of St. Honce are not even ready to commit to departure yet," Constance argued, and it was true enough. Abbot Hingas had heard of the supposed miracle, even claimed that Jilseponie had visited him spiritually and bade him to join the pilgrimage to the north. Yet he and his brethren would not commit to such a journey at that time.

King Danube paused and took a deep breath, then grabbed Constance by both shoulders, holding her rock steady. "I believe in this," he said. "I have to. And if it is indeed the salvation of Honce-the-Bear, then I must preside over it. For the good of the people and of the Crown."

"You believe in this?" Constance asked somewhat sharply. "Or in her?"

That took Danube a bit by surprise, for it was the first revelation of Constance's jealousy of Jilseponie, a somewhat stunning revelation given the enormity of the consequences beyond personal relationships.

He stared at Constance for a long while, not blinking, not letting her pull free of his somber gaze. "I must do this," he declared, and he firmly but gently moved the woman out of his way and walked out into the hall.

Duke Kalas, looking none too pleased, but dressed for the road, was waiting for him.

"Duke Bretherford's ships are ready to depart," he said. "The roads are secured all the way to the docks."

"Then let us be off at once," Danube replied, and he started down the hall, sweeping Kalas up in his wake.

"My King!" came the call behind them, turning them both.

Constance leaned heavily on the doorjamb. "You walk off into peril," she explained. "You must name your successor."

Danube stared at her curiously, surprised by such a request. He had gone off on many perilous journeys without ever issuing such a formal declaration. His confusion was short-lived, though, for then he understood that, before this time, there had never been any decision that needed to be made.

"I will return," he said to Constance, not wanting to have to speak the obvious aloud, not wanting to wound the woman.

"I demand this, for the good of the kingdom," Constance said loudly.

King Danube felt Kalas' stare boring into him, but he did not take his own gaze off Constance. "In the event of my demise, my brother, Prince Midalis of Vanguard, will assume the throne," Danube stated clearly. "I will have that formally recorded before I depart Castle Ursal."

Constance's look shifted subtly, to show the flush of anger behind her mask.

King Danube turned and walked away.

Duke Kalas stood staring at Constance for a long while. "Patience," he said when Danube was too far away to hear. "Merwick is not nearly ready."

Constance glowered at him for just a moment, then retreated into the room and slammed the door.

Kalas, who was also against leaving Ursal at that time, but who more readily understood his place and acceded to the wishes of his King, couldn't contain his chuckle as he hurried off to catch Danube.

CHAPTER

❖ 42 ❖

Redemption

The sight that loomed before Jilseponie when she and Dainsey came in view of St.-Mere-Abelle made her memory of the suffering in Palmaris pale in comparison. Scores of tents had been erected on the bleak plain before the great abbey; and it seemed to Jilseponie as if there were a score of sick people for every tent.

Hundreds of them, the walking dead, moving listlessly about the dreary landscape.

"So many," Dainsey Aucomb whispered at her side.

Jilseponie nodded, but she knew the truth of this scene. St.-Mere-Abelle was a fairly isolated place, with no real cities anywhere near—the closest was Palmaris, some eighty miles to the northwest. And still, the grounds teemed with the sick, flocking here from all over the region, no doubt, coming to this greatest bastion of the Abellican Church, dying on the field before the walls of the Father Abbot.

How many more had died on the road? Jilseponie wondered. Likely as many as had arrived here.

The mere thought of it nearly overwhelmed her; in that moment of despair she wanted nothing more than to turn Symphony and pound back toward Dundalis and Fellowship Way, toward the hole she had once dug for herself. She had to stop herself, close her eyes, and conjure an image of Avelyn's arm.

"Too many," she whispered back to Dainsey. She kicked her heels into Symphony's flanks and the great stallion leaped away, galloping down across the field.

Many eyes followed the two riders as they wove their way across the wretched encampment, toward the front gates of the abbey. Jilseponie felt like a sailor on a vast sea; the abbey walls seemed a distant island.

But no refuge, that place, she knew.

She meant to tear those walls down.

*   *   *

462

Brother Francis paced slowly before St.-Mere-Abelle's tussie-mussie bed, feeling his legs weaken with every step.

He wanted them to see this.

He was exhausted now, beyond belief. He had the soul stone in his pocket, and he had considered spirit-walking, having his spirit violate the sanctuary of St.-Mere-Abelle.

Yes, like a ghost, he wanted to haunt them.

He wanted them to see this.

He rolled the stone in his fingers now, knowing that he had missed his chance, for Francis couldn't possibly find the strength to enter its magic now, to separate spirit from body.

He could hardly even find the strength to call out "Bou-raiy!" at the wall.

And his legs were tiring fast and his breath was becoming harder and harder to find.

They had to see this, had to bear witness to the end of Brother Francis, to learn that he faced that end courageously and with the conviction that he was right!

But now he was no longer walking, was, suddenly and without even realizing the movement, not even standing. He managed to roll over a bit, to see the wall, and he took some comfort in the forms he noted up there. He couldn't make them out through his failing eyes, but he sensed that they were watching him, that they were pointing.

They knew, and they would tell Bou-raiy.

Taking comfort in that, Francis turned his attention to the tussie-mussie bed, bathing himself in the aromas, losing himself in the colorful sights and fragrances. He felt as if those very smells might lift him up, up, might separate his soul from his body as surely as would the hematite. He could float on a cloud of aromas to God, to a judgment that he no longer feared.

He hardly heard the horses gallop up to a stop a short distance behind him, hardly heard the gathering crowd—and surely they were gathering, led by Merry Cowsenfed, several hundred people coming to say farewell to Brother Francis of St.-Mere-Abelle.

It would have made Francis happy, if he had known.

Jilseponie knew before she ever moved beside the man that he—like several of those she had encountered in Palmaris, like one she had found on the road here to St.-Mere-Abelle—was beyond her help, that even if she went to him with all of her magical strength, she would buy him only a few minutes or hours, and those he would spend in pain.

She knew by his emaciated form, lying listlessly, that the plague had won this particular fight. She knew by the look in his eyes that he was seeing as much on the other side of death as in the material world.

Jilseponie would never have recognized the man had she not heard his name as she had crossed the field. When last she had seen Francis, he had been strong and stout, even a little portly, clean-shaven and with hair neatly cropped. Now he was a ragged thing! His hair and beard had grown wild, had thickened as his body had thinned.

She went to him and knelt beside him, and took up his hand in her own.

He stared at her for a long while, seeming not to recognize her.

"Greetings, Brother Francis," she whispered. "I have heard of your work here, of your courage and compassion."

Francis continued to stare at her curiously, and then a smile widened on his face, a light of recognition. "Jilseponie?" he asked.

She nodded and reached for her soul stone, though she doubted she could even get into the magical energy in time for Francis.

Francis' smile turned down suddenly. "Can you forgive me?" he asked, his voice a rasping thing, for a discernible rattle came from his chest with every word and every breath.

Jilseponie paused and looked back at him curiously.

"Your brother," Francis remarked, "Grady Chilichunk. I was the one."

Jilseponie moved close to him, trying to suppress a scowl.

"I killed him," Francis admitted, "on the road from Palmaris. It was an accident . . . I did not mean . . ."

Jilseponie put her finger against Francis' lips to quiet him. That battle seemed so far removed now, that hatred so irrelevant to the current situation.

"Forgive me," Francis said again. "We were all so confused then, and all so wrong."

"And now you see the truth?" she asked him.

Francis' smile returned, but then he winced and closed his eyes. Jilseponie started to reach for her soul stone again, but, as if he had read her mind, Brother Francis reached over and held her arm. "I go without fear," he whispered, and it seemed to Jilseponie as if he were speaking more to himself than to her.

"I do not fear justice," he finished, never opening his eyes, and those were the last words that Brother Francis Dellacourt of St.-Mere-Abelle would ever utter.

It hurt Jilseponie more than she would ever have believed to watch this man die. She held little fondness for Francis, had once been his avowed enemy; and even in those last days when she had been with him in St. Precious after the fall of Markwart, even when he had declared that she should become the mother abbess of the Abellican Church, she had not been overfond of him.

And he had died peacefully, contentedly, it seemed; and yet, to her surprise, Jilseponie found that his passing had wounded her.

She gently removed his hand from her forearm and placed it over his chest, then slowly rose and turned, first to regard the teary gathering of plague sufferers and the one-eyed woman who led them, then to turn and face the dark and foreboding walls of St.-Mere-Abelle. It took her a while to steady herself, to get over the emotional shock of looking at this place.

The place that had served as prison for Bradwarden. The place where her adoptive parents had died horribly.

She took another steadying breath, reminding herself of her purpose and her need, and she forced her gaze to drift up, up, to the dark, cloaked forms standing along the wall. She took Dainsey's hand and walked toward them.

"Francis is dead?" came a call down, a sharp voice she did not recognize.

"He is," Jilseponie answered.

The snort that she heard next seemed to her one of derision.

"They never was likin' him much for comin' out to us," came a voice from behind. Jilseponie turned to see the one-eyed woman standing there. Behind her, the others were gathering up the body of Francis, wrapping it lovingly in sheets.

"They put him out when he came down with plague?" Jilseponie reasoned.

The woman shook her head. "He came out of his own doin'," she answered, "and not a sign o' the plague in him. And he worked with them," she added, turning back to motion to the crowd of the sick. "All of 'em. And he helped one or two afore the plague caught up to him. Ah, a good man was Brother Francis. A saint, I say! But them on the wall don't know it." She spat on the ground. "Bah, they're not knowin' anythin' but their own scaredness. Won't come out and will shoot us dead, any of us, if we walk across their precious flowers."

Brother Francis, a saint. The incongruous notion rolled around in Jilseponie's mind as she stood there, staring at his body being borne away by the peasants. His last words, the proclamation that he did not fear justice, weighed more heavily on her, then. Had Francis truly found the light and the truth? Was his contentment at his death as real as it had seemed? Could he so understand that he had redeemed himself, and thus, need not fear the judgment of his God?

Jilseponie turned back to look at the monks on the wall, and many more had come up by then, no doubt to watch the last journey of their brother.

"I need to speak to the Father Abbot," she called to them.

"You cannot come in," came the reply from that same, sharp voice, and in a purely condescending tone.

Jilseponie looked at the great doors of the abbey, her hands going reflexively to the gemstones hanging at her belt. "Ah, but I could if I wanted to," she muttered under her breath. She looked back up at the wall, at the harsh speaker, and only then did she note that one of the monk's sleeves was tied off, as if he was missing an arm.

"I will speak to him in the gateway, from across the tussie-mussie bed," she said.

The monk scoffed at her and started to turn away.

"Do you know who I am?" she cried out, stopping him in midturn. "I am Jilseponie Wyndon of Dundalis, friend to Avelyn Desbris, friend to Braumin Herde, wife of Nightbird! I am she who destroyed the demon of Father Abbot Markwart!"

The monk walked back to the edge of the wall and leaned out through the break in the battlement, peering at her intently.

"Tell Father Abbot Agronguerre that I have come bearing the most urgent news," she went on. "The most urgent."

"Tell me, then," the monk replied.

"Bid him meet me by the tussie-mussie bed," Jilseponie continued, ignoring the man's command. "If you wish to hear my tale, then join him. I've not the time to tell it more than once." Then she turned away, gathering the one-eyed woman and Dainsey in tow and walking toward the other peasants.

The monk called out several times to her then, mostly cries for her to stop and explain herself and a threat or two that he would not bring Agronguerre to meet with her.

But Jilseponie wasn't playing that game with him. Not then. Not with so much obviously critical work right before her.

"Tell me your tale," she bade the one-eyed woman, for she knew that this one had somehow survived the plague and had, subsequently, come to be the leader of this tent city.

Soon after, while she tended yet another in the long line of plague sufferers that Merry Cowsenfed had ordered for her, the great gates of St.-Mere-Abelle swung open. In the archway across the tussie-mussie bed stood several brothers, flanked, Jilseponie noted, by monks armed with heavy crossbows. She motioned for Merry Cowsenfed to join her.

"Keep them quiet and in line," she explained. "I will be back soon enough."

"I seen them that ye healed," Merry started to spout, so obviously thrilled.

"Not healed," Jilseponie quickly corrected, "no, not that. That will come later, as I told you, and from one much greater than I." She patted the woman on the shoulder, then motioned for Dainsey to follow her and strode over to her side of the tussie-mussie bed.

"We have heard much of your good work, Jilseponie Wyndon," greeted the largest man there, an older monk who seemed to Jilseponie as if he could be Belster O'Comely's father. "I am Father Abbot Agronguerre, formerly of St. Belfour. It pains my heart greatly to learn that you are with plague."

"Not I," Jilseponie replied immediately.

"But you tend to the victims," the Father Abbot reasoned.

"And soon to find the same fate as Francis, no doubt," the one-armed monk beside him remarked.

"The plague cannot touch me," Jilseponie replied, "for I have tasted of the blood of Avelyn's covenant. Thus I can tend them with the soul stone without fear that the plague demons will attack me, and thus am I more effective in the tending."

"You will heal them all?" the one-armed monk asked, his tone half skeptical and half sarcastic.

"I will heal none, likely," the woman replied, "but I will make many strong enough for the road, for the journey they must now undertake." She paused, trying to measure the level of interest as it crossed all their faces. "To the Barbacan, to Avelyn," she explained. "There they will be healed."

The one-armed monk snorted and started to respond, but Agronguerre put his arm up before the man, silencing him.

"It is true, Father Abbot," Jilseponie went on, staring at him. "This woman—" she pulled Dainsey forward "—is my living proof. I took her to the Barbacan. She was no better off than was Francis when I came upon him on the field. I thought her death imminent, but then—"

"But then I kissed the bleeding palm," Dainsey interrupted, "and it was like all the angels o' heaven came down and burned the plague from me body."

"Francis is dead," the one-armed monk remarked. "You did not save him."

"He could not make the journey," Jilseponie replied. She turned and looked back to the hundreds at the tent city. "Nor will many of them," she admitted. "But many others will, and there they will find healing. And those who go though they have not yet been touched by the plague will find armor against it."

The monks didn't immediately respond, and when Jilseponie turned back, she found the Father Abbot stroking his chin pensively.

"You wished to speak with me, and so I assume that you believe that we have a role to play in this," he said. Again, the one-armed monk snorted.

"Preposterous," he muttered. "No doubt you wish us to come out on the field beside you, to work our sacred stone magic to help the peasants, that we might all die of the plague together."

"I wished to tell you of the miracle at Aida," Jilseponie explained to Agronguerre, again trying very hard to ignore the unpleasant one-armed monk. "You and all of your brethren must make the pilgrimage there, and with all speed, to enter the covenant. Only then can you truly begin to help the plague sufferers. Before you make such a journey, I would not even want you to try to tend the sufferers, for your brethren will prove vital in the long battle we must wage against the plague."

Agronguerre didn't immediately reply, but Jilseponie saw his emotions clearly. He didn't believe her, but how he wanted to!

"Take not my word for it," she said sharply, even as the one-armed monk started to jump in with another negative remark. "Go out with your soul stones. To Palmaris, where you will learn that the whole city is on the march to the north, Duke Tetrafel's soldiers and your brothers of St. Precious with them. Go out farther to the north, and see the lines of those living in the towns in and about the Timberlands, well on their way to that most holy of places."

She paused, just to see if the monks would try to interject anything, but she saw from their dumfounded expressions that she would not be interrupted.

"Go all the way to Mount Aida with your gemstones, Father Abbot," she finished. "See that holy place for yourself, if you must. Go and be convinced, and then send your brethren, all of your brethren, there in body that they might taste the blood of Avelyn's covenant and know the truth. Your aid will prove critical in healing the world."

"You ask much of us," Agronguerre remarked quietly.

"I tell you the truth and pray that you will choose correctly," Jilseponie replied.

"This is nonsense," claimed the one-armed brother. "Your friend survived the plague, but so have others. The ugly scarred woman on the field with the sick so survived. We did not cry miracle and send the whole world marching to the spot where she happened to be when her illness relinquished its grasp upon her!"

Jilseponie shrugged. "Believe what you will, or close your heart to the possibility of miracles and hide behind your walls," she said, and she gave a chuckle as the irony of her own words hit her. "I can do no more than tell you the truth and then pray that your faith is a real thing and not some mask for you to hide behind."

The one-armed monk scowled.

"For if you do not believe in the possibility of miracles, then wretched creatures you are indeed for hiding within abbey walls." And she turned and walked away. Dainsey, after a helpless chortle, followed.

"Those gemstones you carry!" the one-armed monk cried after her, and Jilseponie wheeled about.

"My gemstones," she said.

"They are the province of the Church," the monk corrected.

Jilseponie narrowed her eyes and glared at the man. "Come and take them," she challenged, and when he made no move toward her, she walked away.

She almost expected to take a crossbow quarrel in the back.

But nothing happened, and Jilseponie moved back to the line of patient sufferers again and went back to her duty, working tirelessly with the soul stone. Merry Cowsenfed directed the procession to Jilseponie and then to work gathering supplies.

They left in small groups, feeling better than they had in weeks, and moving with all speed for Palmaris, and for the north. If all went well, Jilseponie explained to them, they could expect to find soldiers guarding the road north and monks ready to give them more healing all along the way.

"At least we'll no longer need suffer the wails and the groans, and the stench," Fio Bou-raiy said to Glendenhook as they watched the spectacle of the thinning crowd. More sufferers continued to stream in, of course, but Jilseponie continued her work, and Merry sent them right on their way.

"Perhaps there is value to Jilseponie Wyndon after all," Glendenhook replied.

"Her words were correct," said Father Abbot Agronguerre, coming over to join the pair. His arrival made Bou-raiy and Glendenhook shuffle embarrassedly, given their previous callous remarks. "All of Palmaris, it seems, is on the road to the north."

Fio Bou-raiy threw up his hand in disgust.

"Suppose she is right?" Father Abbot Agronguerre asked. "Suppose there is a miracle to be found and we are too cynical even to look."

"And if she is wrong?" Bou-raiy came back. "Are we to send out all the brethren, as she bade us, only to have half of us die on the road and the other half return to St.-Mere-Abelle ridden with plague?"

"Her work with the gemstones seems nothing short of miraculous," Agronguerre remarked.

"She is not curing them, by her own admission," Bou-raiy reminded him.

Agronguerre turned and walked away.

Back in the abbey, the Father Abbot played all the possibilities about in his mind. Was he pragmatic or cowardly? What might be the cost of guessing wrong?

And what might be the cost of guessing right but not having the courage to act on that guess?

Inevitably, the Father Abbot kept coming back to the image of a brother dying on the field before the impenetrable walls of St.-Mere-Abelle, a brother whose courage surely humbled old Agronguerre.

"Ah, Francis," he muttered with a sigh. He remembered the night when Francis had gone out to the sick, the eve of the New Year. Not only had the man put himself in obvious physical jeopardy, but the action had brought him only snickers of derision from many of his so-called brothers.

That image haunted gentle Agronguerre as he walked slowly up to his private chambers, and it stayed with him all the way back down the circular stone stairwell.

Down, down, to the first floor of the abbey, he went, and then down again, until he stood before a little-used but extremely important doorway, ornately decorated—so much so that the great latch that secured it could hardly be noticed unless one looked at it carefully.

Agronguerre fumbled with the keys, wanting to get through the door and get done with this business before anyone could persuade him differently. For though his heart was strong now in his decision, bolstered by the image of poor dead Francis, his mind was filled with fear.

He turned open the lock, lifted the latch, and pulled the door open, but only an inch, for another, stronger hand came against the portal, pushing it closed.

Abbot Agronguerre stepped back and turned to see Master Bou-raiy, the man fixing him with a cold glare, a lock of eyes that would have gone on for a long while had not the two men heard the sound of footsteps descending the staircase back down the corridor.

"Live a long time, old man," Bou-raiy warned ominously. "For, if you do this thing, you must know that when you die, the Abellican Church will be thrown into turmoil beyond anything it has ever known."

"Is that what is honestly within your heart, Master Bou-raiy?"

"That is what I know to be true."

"Would you have me preside over a Church that turns its back on the agony of the common folk?" the Father Abbot asked.

"The plague will pass in time," said Bou-raiy, and he lowered his voice as Master Glendenhook, with Master Machuso right on his heels, appeared a short distance down the corridor. "The Church must be eternal."

Master Glendenhook walked over to stand equidistant from the two men, glancing curiously back and forth between them. "Pray, brethren," he asked, "what is it that so troubles you?"

Father Abbot Agronguerre turned a skeptical look on the man, then stepped back from Bou-raiy. "You know our viewpoints," he replied. "You have heard the tale of Jilseponie and thus have seen the drawing of the line. On which side of that line does Master Glendenhook stand?"

Glendenhook's shoulders sagged a bit at the blunt question, a reflection of the fact that he did not want to be so drawn into any open argument. He looked at Agronguerre sympathetically, then turned to Bou-raiy, who fixed him with an unyielding stare—one, it seemed to Agronguerre, that demanded the man take a definitive stand.

Glendenhook put out his hand to pat Agronguerre on the shoulder, but then stepped away from the Father Abbot, to Bou-raiy's side. He faced Agronguerre and bowed. "With all respect and honor, Father Abbot," he said, "I fear the plague and heed well the old words written about it— words penned from the bitter experiences of those who have suffered through it. I fear sending the brethren out from St.-Mere-Abelle, and I fear even more the release of the soul stones into hands untrained and undeserving."

"The brothers will carry the stones," Agronguerre replied, not understanding that second point.

"And what of the brothers who will surely die along the road?" Bou-raiy asked. "They will fall while carrying soul stones, and those stones will, inevitably, fall into the hands of the undeserving and untrained."

"Jilseponie will train them," Agronguerre argued, his tone sharp, for the way in which Bou-raiy had said the word "undeserving" had struck him as very wrong.

"And that, Father Abbot, I fear most of all," Master Glendenhook remarked.

The words hit Agronguerre as surely as if Glendenhook had just punched him across the face. The Father Abbot felt so old at that moment, so defeated, and he almost threw up his hands and walked away. But then he turned to see the face of Master Machuso, the kindly man who oversaw all the secular workers at St.-Mere-Abelle, the gentle man whom Agronguerre had caught on several occasions stuffing extra supplies into the loads sent out to the sickly masses.

"My young brethren spend too many days looking into old books," Machuso said, managing a smile, "and too many hours on their knees with their arms and eyes uplifted to the heavens."

"We are Abellican brothers!" Master Bou-raiy sharply reminded him.

"Who would learn more of the world if they spent more time looking into the eyes of suffering folk," Machuso was quick to reply. "Abellican brothers who are so wrapped up in their own rituals and own importance, who are so determined to elevate themselves above the flock they pretend to tend that they cannot see the truth of the opportunity presented to us this day."

"By a laywoman," Bou-raiy remarked.

"A false prophet," Glendenhook echoed.

"She who destroyed the dactyl with Brother Avelyn at Mount Aida!" Machuso shot back. "And who defeated the demon spirit within Father Abbot Markwart, by Markwart's own admission to Master Francis at the time of his death. And now she is showing us the way again, Father Abbot," the suddenly energetic Machuso went on, turning to aim his words directly at Agronguerre, "the way to Avelyn, in body and in spirit."

Agronguerre reached for the door again, and so did Bou-raiy, but then the Father Abbot fixed him with such a stare that he backed off.

"Do not do this," Fio Bou-raiy warned. "You are condemning us all."

"I am damning myself if I do not," Agronguerre answered firmly. "Send word throughout the abbey, Master Machuso," he went on. "This is a choice and not an edict. All who wish to join the pilgrimage should be ready to leave within the hour."

"The *hour*?" Glendenhook said, as if the mere thought that hundreds of brothers could be packed with wagons readied within that time was preposterous.

"It will be done," Machuso answered with a bow. "And I doubt that many will choose to remain."

"And if the hope is false?" Bou-raiy had to ask one last time.

"Then better to die trying," Father Abbot Agronguerre said, putting his face only an inch from Bou-raiy's.

He pulled open the door, the portal that led into the gemstone treasury of St.-Mere-Abelle, where more than a thousand soul stones waited.

❖ 43 ❖

Fulfilling Avelyn's Promise

When Jilseponie returned to the Barbacan near the end of summer, she found that her call to Vanguard had not gone unheeded. Led by Brother Dellman and Abbot Haney, the procession from the northernmost Honce-the-Bear province had nearly emptied the place.

The woman saw them up on the plateau, hundreds and hundreds milling about; and she went straightaway to find them, anxious to see Dellman again and Abbot Braumin, who had become the caretaker of the arm itself, the guide to any and all who came to enter Avelyn's covenant.

She found Dellman first and shared a great hug with him on the rim of the sacred plateau, then made her way through the crowd, toward the arm and Braumin. She was surprised, then, to find a pair of faces that she recognized.

"Andacanavar!" she cried. "Liam O'Blythe!"

The huge ranger wheeled, his face beaming with a great smile. To Jilseponie's surprise, though, another man off to the side, his hair bright red, his face covered in freckles, also turned to her, beaming.

"Do I know ye, beautiful lady?" the red-haired man remarked.

Jilseponie looked at him curiously as she made her way toward the ranger and the man she thought to be Liam. "I think you do not," Jilseponie answered politely.

"But ye're knowin' me name!" the man protested.

Jilseponie looked at him hard, then turned to see Andacanavar's companion, the man she had thought to be Liam, blushing.

"You are Liam O'Blythe?" Jilseponie asked the red-haired man.

"Anybody tellin' ye different?" he inquired back.

"Telling all the world different, and stealing your good name, I fear," Jilseponie said, staring hard at Andacanavar's companion.

"Then gettin' in trouble, not to doubt!" Liam O'Blythe roared, pointing his finger at his friend.

"I preferred to travel anonymously," the exposed liar explained. "To do otherwise might have invited trouble."

"A renowned thief, are you?" Jilseponie said, crossing her arms over her chest. "Or just a thief of people's names?"

"A prince, actually," Liam O'Blythe answered for Midalis. "Brother o' the King, he is, and Prince o' all Vanguard."

Jilseponie's jaw dropped open, her eyes going so wide that it seemed as if they might fall right out of their sockets. Now that the man's identity had been clarified, she could see the resemblance he bore to Danube, a younger and thinner version of the King.

"I would have expected you to tell her," Andacanavar said, looking past the woman, and Jilseponie took the cue and turned to see Bradwarden moving up beside her.

"Didn't think it was needed," the centaur said dryly. "Suren her head's big enough without her knowin' that she beat the Prince of Honce-the-Bear in a sword fight!"

"You knew?" Jilseponie asked.

"I told ye once, girl, there's not a thing in me forest that I'm not knowin'. When are ye to believe me?"

Jilseponie just shook her head helplessly.

"We are all in your debt," Prince Midalis remarked, moving up to her and taking her hand. He bowed low and kissed that hand.

"I was near death," Liam added. "I thought that'd be the end o' Liam O'Blythe! But for Avelyn's hand, it suren would've!"

"You saved the world, young ranger-in-training," Andacanavar said with a smile.

"That is Avelyn's deed," Jilseponie was quick to correct, motioning toward the upraised arm. "I was but a messenger."

"A fine one indeed," said Prince Midalis, and he had her hand clasped between both of his, then, and he stared admiringly into her dark blue eyes.

The sudden tension was broken almost immediately, as Abbot Braumin came bounding over, crying out for Jilseponie, then wrapping her in such a hug that he squeezed all the air out of her.

They spent the rest of the day together, and held a great celebration that night in the valley before the mountain. Jilseponie noted, then, that not many of Andacanavar's Alpinadoran people were in attendance.

"They fear the gemstone magic, and thus, the covenant," Midalis explained.

"I do not believe that conversion to the faith is a requirement for the healing," Jilseponie replied; and when she did, she noted that Abbot Braumin's eyebrows went up in surprise.

"This is a holy place for the Abellican Church," Braumin noted.

Jilseponie nodded, not beginning to disagree. "It is the place where the Abellican Church should understand that it stands for all the goodly people of all the world, whether Abellican or not," she remarked. "If this is the covenant of the Avelyn that I knew, then healing will be given to any who come to this place, without question of their beliefs."

Her tone became a bit more sharp as she ended, and that made all gazes settle on Abbot Braumin.

"I never refused Andacanavar's people," he explained, "nor would I begin to turn them away or demand anything of them should they taste of the blood. It is their own fears that keep them away, and not words from me or any others. Perhaps they fear that this is some ruse designed to convert them to a faith they have many times rejected."

"Or perhaps they fear to see the truth, fear that their old beliefs will become irrelevant," Dellman added, and Jilseponie did not miss the scowl that came over Andacanavar's face.

"That is as foolish as it is prideful," she said. "And neither are traits I would attribute to Avelyn Desbris." She turned to the ranger then, her face full of compassion. "Has the plague found your homeland?"

He nodded. "Not as bad as in your own, as yet," he explained. "But, yes, many have been stricken ill and many have died."

"Bring them," Jilseponie said. "Convince them. Tell them that this is as much a gift of your own God as it is of ours. Tell them whatever you must to bring them here."

"There are no conditions," Braumin Herde added, and Jilseponie was glad to see that he was seeing things her way.

"I intend to do just that," the ranger assured her. "Now that I have tasted the blood."

"And all the brothers of St. Belfour will go with you, if you desire," Dellman said, "to offer healing along the road, as the brothers of St. Precious are doing along the road south."

"We shall see," was all that Andacanavar would concede.

The procession from Vanguard left the next day. The next after that, to Jilseponie's absolute delight, the brethren of St.-Mere-Abelle began to show up. Nearly half the brothers of that greatest of abbeys arrived, some three hundred, led by Agronguerre himself. They went to the plateau and they learned the beautiful truth. And as they set out again for the south, that very night—for Agronguerre understood that any delay would mean more suffering to many people—the Father Abbot promised that the rest of the abbey would arrive within a couple of weeks.

Jilseponie slept well that night, knowing that her vision, the vision given to her by the spirits of Elbryan and Avelyn at Oracle, would indeed come to fruition.

A few weeks later, Jilseponie and Bradwarden watched from a distant mountainside the seemingly endless procession snaking along the road from the south, some heading for the mountainous ring and Mount Aida, others already rushing back to the southland in the hopes that some of the crop might be brought in before the onset of winter.

Now that the seven hundred monks from St.-Mere-Abelle had joined in the healing line, and soldiers from Ursal had come in support of Tetrafel's Palmaris garrison, the road was swift and secure.

"They're sayin' that King Danube's on his way," Bradwarden remarked.

Jilseponie nodded, for she had heard the same rumors, claims that his royal entourage, including a couple of sons, would arrive at the entrance to the Barbacan by nightfall.

"He's bringin' all o' his court," Bradwarden remarked, and he eyed her curiously as he finished. "Includin' a pair o' sons, by the tales I'm hearin'."

Jilseponie merely nodded, and did well to hide her smile. Bradwarden was testing her, she knew, trying to find out if she harbored some feelings for the King of Honce-the-Bear. In truth, it was nothing that Jilseponie had even thought about much before and nothing that she was in any hurry to examine more deeply.

They met with King Danube that very night, and it was obvious to all in attendance, particularly to Constance Pemblebury, that the years had done nothing to diminish the man's feelings for this heroic woman of the northland.

"My work is here," Jilseponie explained against his insistence that she reconsider accepting the position of baroness of Palmaris.

"It seems to me that the work here will continue with or without you," Danube argued.

Jilseponie conceded that fact—to a point. "The northern walls of the Barbacan teem with goblins and giants," she explained. "And thus I have become the self-appointed ranger of the Barbacan, for now at least."

"A title she should no' be wearin'," Bradwarden cut in with a chuckle. "But she's got meself to keep her out o' trouble!"

They all shared a good laugh at that.

"Palmaris awaits your change of mind," Danube said to her in all seriousness. "Whether today, tomorrow, or years hence, the city will be yours with but a word."

Jilseponie started to reply, but changed her mind. The man had just paid her such a great compliment that she could not deny it, whatever might then be in her heart. She bowed her head respectfully and let it go at that.

When she looked up, though, she didn't—couldn't—miss the look of jealousy that Constance Pemblebury had put over her, nor the narrow-eyed warning gaze of Duke Targon Bree Kalas.

Yes, indeed, she thought, the wonderful world of politics!

"He means to make her his next queen," Duke Kalas said to Constance as they trotted their horses along the road back to the south. "You know that, of course."

Constance didn't reply, but her silence spoke volumes to Kalas. Of course, she knew. How could she not? All Danube had spoken of in the five days since they had left the Barbacan was Jilseponie Wyndon, the savior of the world. He had promised her Palmaris, and sincerely; and Kalas knew that the invitation would be extended, at but a word from her, to include Castle Ursal and the city itself, to include all the kingdom.

Yes, Kalas knew it and so did Constance: King Danube was stricken with love for Jilseponie Wyndon. He had to bide his time for now, because she would not be moved from the Barbacan, but Danube was a patient man and one who knew how to get what he most desired.

"Queen Jilseponie," Kalas muttered quietly.

Constance Pemblebury fixed him with a perfectly awful stare.

They came in droves, the sick and the healthy, marching north from every corner of Honce-the-Bear, from Vanguard and from the Mantis Arm, from southern Yorkey, people living in the shadow of the Belt-and-Buckle mountain range, and from distant Entel.

Even from Behren, they came in small numbers, frightened people defying their yatol priests, daring to stow away on trading ships going around the mountain range's easternmost spurs, sailing up the coast all the way to the Gulf of Corona and to the mouth of the Masur Delaval, where they disembarked and began the land journey, desperate for healing.

The line of pilgrims thinned considerably, of course, with the onset of winter, but Jilseponie and Bradwarden and Braumin held their posts atop the plateau—an area sheltered by the magic of Avelyn from winter's coldest blows.

Few came as the year turned, and rumors filtered up the line to the sentinels of the covenant that many had died along the road, caught by storms or by exhaustion.

Jilseponie and the others held their faith, though. Yes, the plague would continue to claim victims, but hundreds and hundreds were now immune to its devastating bite.

And hundreds more would come to the Barbacan in the spring, they knew, for other rumors told of a great swelling of folk in the city of Palmaris, waiting for the word that the trails were clear.

One pleasant surprise came to them in the early part of the second month of the year, when a familiar form, bundled in layers of skins, scaled the rim of the plateau to stand towering above them.

Jilseponie's smile only widened and widened as more and more Alpinadorans followed Andacanavar up to that plateau.

"You did not believe that I could lead them here in the winter?" the ranger asked with a chuckle. "What feeble ranger do you take me for, woman-ranger-in-training?"

Jilseponie could only laugh and shake her head.

Andacanavar introduced them to Bruinhelde, then; and the man, to Jilse-ponie's eyes, didn't seem overthrilled to be there.

But, she noted, he was thick with plague.

A few tense moments followed, with Jilseponie and Andacanavar offer-ing their reassurances that partaking of Avelyn's blood would not be an admission of any change of faith, that the covenant would hold for them without any promises of that. "You can return to your homeland, safe from the plague, and go back to your ways and your God," Jilseponie said, but she was looking more to Braumin than to the Alpinadorans as she spoke.

"You know the Father Abbot of my Church, good Bruinhelde," Braumin said, surprising both Jilseponie and Bradwarden. But Braumin had spoken at length with Agronguerre about the possibility of this very meeting. "You know the value of the alliance that you entered into with him and with Prince Midalis. Well, consider this an extension of that alliance, a fur-thering of the bond of friendship between our peoples."

They all waited as Andacanavar translated the words into the Alpinadoran tongue, making certain that Bruinhelde understood not only the literal meaning of them but the manner in which they had been offered.

Bruinhelde then said something to the ranger, and Andacanavar turned to the trio. "He fears that his actions here will offend his gods," the ranger explained.

Jilseponie turned to her companions, then looked back to the Alpinado-rans. "Then you do it, alone," she said to Bruinhelde. "Act as vanguard for your people, the first to try."

Andacanavar cleared his throat.

"The second, then," Jilseponie corrected, for the ranger certainly had tasted the blood on his first visit to the Barbacan. "But the first of your people who was not raised and trained outside Alpinador. Go to the hand and accept the covenant, of free will. Then you will know better how to guide those who followed you here."

Andacanavar started to translate, but Bruinhelde held up his hand, motioning that he had understood the words well enough. He took a deep breath then, his massive chest swelling, and he strode past Jilseponie and the other two, right up to the upraised arm.

He dropped to one knee before the arm, studying it intently, even sniffing at the bloody palm.

Jilseponie came up beside him. "Kiss the palm and you will understand," she promised.

Bruinhelde looked up at her suspiciously.

"How can you properly guide your people if you do not know?" she asked innocently.

The barbarian stared at her long and hard, and then he bent low and, with but a single quick steadying breath, he dipped his head and tasted the blood.

His expression showed surprise, and then . . .

Elation.

He looked up at Jilseponie again.

"You are the same man, with the same God," she said quietly, "but now the plague cannot touch you."

And so it went, throughout the day, the barbarians of Alpinador finding salvation at the hand of a soon-to-be Abellican saint. They stayed in the Barbacan for some time, celebrating; and when they left, Bruinhelde promised Jilseponie that he would spread the word throughout his home-land, that other Alpinadorans would follow.

And she promised him that they would be greeted as friends.

As predicted, the swarm of pilgrims began again in the early spring, flowing endlessly out of Palmaris, filtering through the city from points all across Honce-the-Bear.

Jilseponie and Bradwarden watched them from their mountain perches, taking heart again that Avelyn's promise would be fulfilled, that the rosy plague would be washed from the land.

From the wooded trails far below the line of the Barbacan, another watched the procession, but with very different emotions.

For Marcalo De'Unnero, the flocking of all the world to Avelyn Desbris was like a dark mirror held up before his wretched eyes, a reminder of his own mistakes and failings.

He was a beast now as often as a man, consumed by the power of the tiger's paw gemstone that had somehow become a part of his very being. He understood it now to be a curse, and surely no blessing, for no longer could he control the urges of the hunting and hungry cat. He survived by killing, pure and simple. Deer, rabbits, and, when he could find no alterna-tive, feasting on the flesh and blood of humans.

He knew that he was sinking, that the creature was consuming him, mind and soul.

But not in body. Nay, it seemed as if another gemstone, the hematite ring he had taken from a merchant in Palmaris, had also found its way to De'Unnero's wretched being. He should have died from the wounds he had received on that day when he had been chased out of Palmaris, for sev-eral of the arrows had struck him in vital areas. He had spent days pulling out the arrowheads, the extraction on several occasions followed by a gush of blood that had left him weak and even unconscious.

But every time, he had reawakened, his wounds healed. The soul stone would not let him die!

And truly, at that time, all that Marcalo De'Unnero wanted was to die, to be released from the bonds of the weretiger, to be freed of this hellish prison his own body had become for him.

He had even considered going to the shrine of Avelyn. He didn't fear the plague—nay, he knew somehow that it could not affect him—but he wondered if this covenant he had been hearing repeated excitedly by every person going to or from the Barbacan, this gift of Avelyn, might extend to the curing of his present condition.

In fact, De'Unnero had even started toward the Barbacan on one occasion, but had become sidetracked, for a woman in the caravan on the road north of him had strayed out from the revealing light of the campfire one calm and quiet night.

After his gory feast, De'Unnero understood that he could not continue, that there would be no salvation for him from the likes of saintly Avelyn Desbris.

So he melted back into the forest, back to the west and the wilder lands, where deer were more plentiful and human flesh harder to find.

It went on through the seasons and the years, until the spring of God's Year 834. The previous spring had brought only thin lines of pilgrims—so few, in fact, that Abbot Braumin had returned to his duties at St. Precious and many of the monks along the northern road had been dismissed back to their respective abbeys—and by all the reports coming out of the southland, fewer still would make the journey this year.

The plague had been beaten, it seemed, and so, with mixed emotions, Jilseponie and Bradwarden left their post at Mount Aida and returned to the lands they knew so well, the Timberlands and Dundalis.

Jilseponie lingered a long time at Elbryan's cairn before going into the town. She went to Oracle there, and found that Elbryan's spirit was with her. For the first time in years, she was not Jilseponie but Pony. Just Pony: the girl who had grown up in the region beside Elbryan, who had taken such a strange and roundabout journey to get to this place in her life.

She stayed with the spirit of her lost husband for a long, long time, and it was late into the evening when she at last emerged. Bradwarden was nowhere about, but she could hear his piping distantly on the evening breeze.

So reminiscent of those long-ago days.

She found Dundalis larger than when she had left it, with many of the pilgrims deciding to remain there rather than march all the way back to their southern homes. The other towns of the region—and all along the south road to and including Palmaris—also boasted of many, many newcomers, so many, in fact, that Palmaris' population was now estimated as larger than it had been before the plague had begun to claim victims there.

Fellowship Way in Dundalis was a bustling place now, always full of patrons; and the cheers that greeted Pony when she walked through the door that spring night resounded as loudly as any she had heard at the previous Fellowship Way, one of Palmaris' busiest taverns.

She found Belster behind the bar along with Roger. Dainsey was working tables—whenever her toddler son was asleep enough for her to slip out to the front of the establishment and do some work.

"Can you take a break from the work?" Pony asked the trio after the greeting and tearful hugs.

Belster nodded to a couple of patrons, who quickly stepped into place serving the customers, and Pony led the three into the back room.

"Good to have ye back," Belster remarked.

"For a short while only," Pony replied, and she let her gaze drift from person to person. "I am going to Palmaris," she announced, "to accept King Danube's offer."

"Baroness Pony?" Dainsey said with a great and joyful laugh.

"Baroness Jilseponie," she corrected.

"What about yer Church friends?" Belster asked. "They're busy makin' Avelyn a saint now—should be done this very year—and are hopin' to open a new chapel in Caer Tinella. I'm thinkin' that Braumin's wantin' ye to head that chapel, girl, or at least to join with him in his Church."

Pony shook her head throughout the speech. "They will understand," she insisted. "I can do more good for the teachings of Avelyn as a secular leader than if I went into the Church, where I would have to fight every day for my survival in any position of power merely because I am a woman."

She looked to Roger mostly, for support, because he, above all others except for Bradwarden, knew her the best. And he was nodding and smiling.

This was the right course for her.

"I will have a place at Chasewind Manor for Belster," Pony promised, "and for Roger and Dainsey."

"And Bryan," Dainsey put in with an impish grin.

"Bryan?" Pony started to ask, and then, given the expressions worn by both Roger and Dainsey, she understood. Again came the hugs; and then Dainsey, leading Pony by the hand to the back room where little Bryan slept peacefully, detailed every moment of the child's birth and life thus far.

Jilseponie Wyndon left Dundalis a month later, after having sent word ahead to Palmaris requesting that King Danube honor his word and give the city to her as baroness. By the time she arrived in the city, Duke Tetrafel had long—and gladly—vacated Chasewind Manor.

Brynn Dharielle thought she had him beaten, a clever twist-thrust-disengage-and-thrust-again movement that seemed as if it had young Aydrian caught off balance.

But the disengage cut both ways, and as Brynn's slender blade knifed in for a low strike, Aydrian's slapped down atop it, driving the point to the ground. A twist of the wrist had the boy's sword tip at Brynn's throat.

"Finally," Aydrian said, for this was his first victory over the older ranger-in-training, a warrior the Touel'alfar regarded very highly.

"Remarkable progress," Lady Dasslerond said to Belli'mar Juraviel, the two of them standing in the brush off to the side, unseen by the combatants. "His work is even more promising than that of young Brynn."

Juraviel nodded, finding it hard to disagree, given what had just happened on the field before them. He didn't know much of Aydrian, hadn't spent time with the boy, but from what he had heard, the child was possessed of an enormous amount of pride, and more than a bit of a temper. Those factors seemed to bother Lady Dasslerond not at all, though, for whenever Juraviel had mentioned them to her, or anything at all negative about the youngest ranger, she had merely labeled it "passion," and had gone about her business.

"It is time to begin the other side of his training," Lady Dasslerond remarked then, catching Juraviel off his guard.

"The gemstones?" he asked hesitantly.

Dasslerond nodded. "With the inclusion of magical prowess, he will become the most complete warrior the world has ever known," she said. "Greater than his father, greater than the original Aydrian, and greater even than Terranen Dinoniel."

"He is still young," Juraviel dared to say, but what he really wanted to scream out at his lady was that this one needed more than training with weapons and gemstones. That he needed emotional training, as well, some measure of the balance within his own thoughts and, more important, within his heart.

He didn't say that, though, because he knew that she wouldn't hear his words.

He listened then to Aydrian, taunting Brynn Dharielle and begging her for another fight so that he could "beat her again."

Belli'mar Juraviel had a very bad feeling about all this.

Epilogue

She shrugged off her title, Baroness Jilseponie, as she descended the dungeon stairs in Chasewind Manor to a small and dark room she had taken as a private place for her meditations, becoming Pony, just Pony, once more.

And there, in the darkness, with all of the tumult of the politics and the public solidly put out of her mind, Pony stared into her mirror and sought the form of her lost love. She had found her place and her reason again, and when she spoke to Elbryan, with thoughts and not words, she did so with complete confidence.

I understand now, my love, and in that understanding comes a peace I feared I never would again know, a true contentment.

When I lost you, I came to fear that it had all been in vain, that we had really accomplished nothing by our sacrifice. I feared that it was the nature of man to continue with all that we fought against, that one battle only served to begin another, and that it could not end. I am still not convinced of the opposite, not convinced that paradise can be found in the kingdom of Mankind.

But now I understand that we must continue the fight, no matter the odds, no matter the outcome. We fight because, in doing so, we make a statement about who we want to be, about who we must become. We fight because the opposite is to surrender to a way of thinking that we know to be wrong. We fight to save ourselves, if not the world.

And we, all humanity, are better for the fight. The world is indeed a brighter place because of our battle against and victory over Markwart, because of our efforts and your sacrifice. The darkness will come again, I know; and I know, too, that there will be others to take up the mantle of battle, to cry out the name Nightbird, as many in our own struggle called out the name Dinoniel. You bettered the world, my love, physically by lifting the darkness from the highest level of the Church and spiritually by bringing inspiration to those of like mind who would take up the fight.

And so your death was not in vain, and though I miss you terribly, and always shall, and though my heart will never be whole again, I accept now the price of our victory. Yes, my love, the cost was worth the gain.

ABOUT THE AUTHOR

R. A. SALVATORE was born in Massachusetts in 1959. His first published novel was *The Crystal Shard*. He has since published more than two dozen novels, including *The Demon Awakens*, *The Demon Spirit*, *The Halfling's Gem*, *Sojourn*, *The Legacy*, *Starless Night*, and *Star Wars*®: *The New Jedi Order: Vector Prime*, the thrilling first book in an exciting new *Star Wars* series. He lives in Massachusetts with his wife, Diane, and their three children.

The Barbacan

Mount Aida

ALPINADOR

AndurBlough
Inninness
(The Valley of
Mist)

Weedy
Meadow

Dundalis

End 'o'
the World

Timberlands

The
Moorlands

the Wilderlands

Landsdown

Caer
Tinella

Palmaris

Masur Delaval

Amvoy

St.Mere-Abelle

Dusberry

All Saints Bay

Gul

Ursal

HONCE-THE-BEAR

Belt and Buckle

Youmaneff

BEHREN

Falidean
Bay

St.
Gwendoly
by the sea

Entel

Jacintha

Freeport

The Mantis Arm